6/18/14

People
of the
Morning Star

BY W. MICHAEL GEAR AND KATHLEEN O'NEAL GEAR
FROM TOM DOHERTY ASSOCIATES

NORTH AMERICA'S FORGOTTEN PAST SERIES

People of the Wolf

People of the Fire

People of the Earth

People of the River

People of the Sea

People of the Lakes

People of the Lightning

People of the Silence

People of the Mist

People of the Masks

People of the Owl

People of the Raven

People of the Moon

People of the Nightland

People of the Weeping Eye

People of the Thunder

People of the Longhouse

The Dawn Country: A People of the Longhouse Novel

The Broken Land: A People of the Longhouse Novel

People of the Black Sun: A People of the Longhouse Novel

People of the Morning Star

THE ANASAZI MYSTERY SERIES

The Visitant

The Summoning God

Bone Walker

BY KATHLEEN O'NEAL GEAR

Thin Moon and Cold Mist

Sand in the Wind

This Widowed Land

It Sleeps in Me

It Wakes in Me

It Dreams in Me

BY W. MICHAEL GEAR

Long Ride Home

Big Horn Legacy

Coyote Summer

The Athena Factor

The Morning River

OTHER TITLES BY KATHLEEN O'NEAL GEAR AND W. MICHAEL GEAR

The Betrayal

Dark Inheritance

Raising Abel

Children of the Dawnland

Coming of the Storm

Fire the Sky

A Searing Wind

www.Gear-Gear.com

People
of the
Morning Star

A NOVEL OF NORTH AMERICA'S
FORGOTTEN PAST

W. Michael Gear and
Kathleen O'Neal Gear

TOR®

A TOM DOHERTY ASSOCIATES BOOK · NEW YORK

PEOPLE OF THE MORNING STAR

Copyright © 2014 by W. Michael Gear and Kathleen O'Neal Gear

Maps and illustrations by Ellisa Mitchell

A Tor Book
Published by Tom Doherty Associates, LLC
175 Fifth Avenue
New York, NY 10010

www.tor-forge.com

Tor® is a registered trademark of Tom Doherty Associates, LLC.

Library of Congress Cataloging-in-Publication Data

Gear, W. Michael.
  People of the Morning Star / W. Michael Gear and Kathleen O'Neal Gear.—
First edition.
      p. cm.
  ISBN 978-0-7653-3724-5 (hardcover)
  ISBN 978-1-4668-3229-9 (e-book)
  1. Indians of North America—Fiction.   2. Mississippian culture—
Fiction.   I. Gear, Kathleen O'Neal.   II. Title.
  PS3557.E19P1936 2014
  813'.54—dc23

                                                            2013029675

Tor books may be purchased for educational, business, or promotional use.
For information on bulk purchases, please contact Macmillan Corporate
and Premium Sales Department at 1-800-221-7945, extension 5442,
or write specialmarkets@macmillan.com.

First Edition: May 2014

Printed in the United States of America

0 9 8 7 6 5 4 3 2 1

To Margaret Withey

For the gift of our best friend,

the Saratoga Tedi Bear,

and

your help when Michael needed it most

during those hard times in graduate school.

We haven't forgotten.

Acknowledgments

First we'd like to recognize our superb team at Tor/Forge books. Our publisher, Tom Doherty, has supported the First North Americans, or "People" series since the beginning. Tom has always believed in telling our nation's story as a means of perpetuating an understanding of what it truly means to be "an American." Especially when that story spins out of our Native American heritage.

Linda Quinton, Tor's associate publisher, has served as our guiding light for over twenty-five years. This is our chance to express our thanks for the times that she's listened patiently while we ranted, reassured us when we cried on her shoulder, and always given it to us straight. Bless you, Linda.

Our editor, Susan Chang, is the strong third leg of our Tor tripod. How can we ever thank you for your enthusiasm, critical eye, and endless support for our work? Susan, without you we'd be lost.

Special mention must go to Dr. Laura Scheiber for helping us to establish connections. To Dr. Tim Pauketat, we say thanks for your time at the Society for American Archaeology in Memphis; we didn't forget Old-Woman-Who-Never-Dies and the immense influence she had on Cahokia. When we mentioned the possibility of a new Cahokia book, an ebullient Dr. David Anderson grinned across his glass of beer and said, "Great! Go for it!" Thanks for your support over the years, David.

In writing *People of the Morning Star,* we have relied heavily on the research of many, but would like to specifically single out Tim Pauketat, James Brown, Robert L. Hall, F. Kent Reilly III, George Lankford, James F. Garber, John Kelly, William Iseminger, Thomas Emerson, George Holley, and so many others.

We were struggling over how to interpret Cahokia's political structure, when at the 2012 Society for American Archaeology meetings in Memphis, Dr. Gerardo Gutierrez, backed by Dr. Stephen Lekson, provided us with a viable hypothesis: something similar to the Altepetl system of political organization. From it we have postulated the Cahokian "Houses" used in the novel. To Dr. Gutierrez, and Steve Lekson (again), our most sincere thanks.

Finally we extend our thanks to the Cahokia Mounds Museum Society. Not only do they manage one of the greatest archaeological sites in North America, but the museum shop has carried our books and supported our work for more than twenty years now. We urge everyone to visit the Cahokia Mounds site and to tour the magnificent museum. You can contact them at www.cahokiamounds.org.

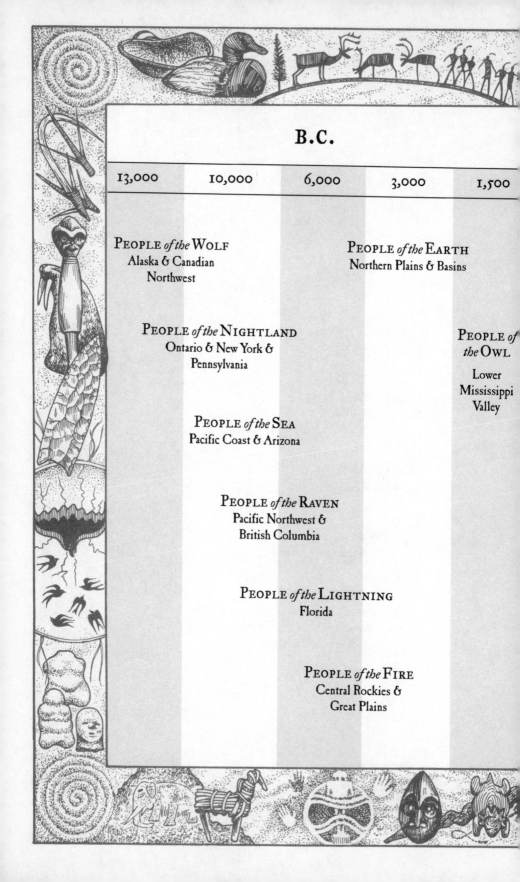

B.C.

13,000	10,000	6,000	3,000	1,500

PEOPLE *of the* **WOLF**
Alaska & Canadian
Northwest

PEOPLE *of the* **EARTH**
Northern Plains & Basins

PEOPLE *of the* **NIGHTLAND**
Ontario & New York &
Pennsylvania

PEOPLE *of*
the **OWL**

Lower
Mississippi
Valley

PEOPLE *of the* **SEA**
Pacific Coast & Arizona

PEOPLE *of the* **RAVEN**
Pacific Northwest &
British Columbia

PEOPLE *of the* **LIGHTNING**
Florida

PEOPLE *of the* **FIRE**
Central Rockies &
Great Plains

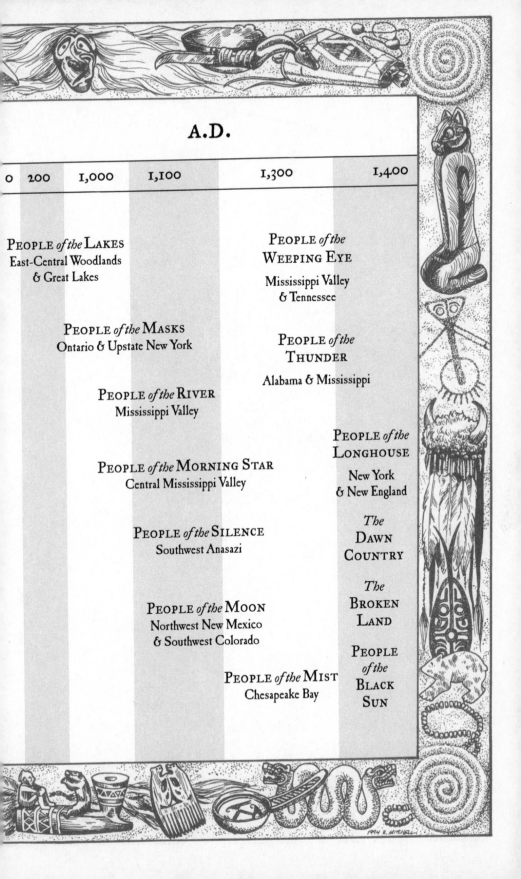

A.D.

| 0 | 200 | 1,000 | 1,100 | 1,300 | 1,400 |

PEOPLE *of the* LAKES
East-Central Woodlands
& Great Lakes

PEOPLE *of the*
WEEPING EYE

Mississippi Valley
& Tennessee

PEOPLE *of the* MASKS
Ontario & Upstate New York

PEOPLE *of the*
THUNDER

Alabama & Mississippi

PEOPLE *of the* RIVER
Mississippi Valley

PEOPLE *of the*
LONGHOUSE

New York
& New England

PEOPLE *of the* MORNING STAR
Central Mississippi Valley

The
DAWN
COUNTRY

PEOPLE *of the* SILENCE
Southwest Anasazi

The
BROKEN
LAND

PEOPLE *of the* MOON
Northwest New Mexico
& Southwest Colorado

PEOPLE
of the
BLACK
SUN

PEOPLE *of the* MIST
Chesapeake Bay

1994 E. MITCHELL

Serpent Woman Town

North

Marsh Elder Lake

CAHOKIA

Burned Farmstead

Right Hand Mound

Evening Star Town

Avenue of the Sun

Avenue of the Moon

River Mound City

Horned Serpent Town

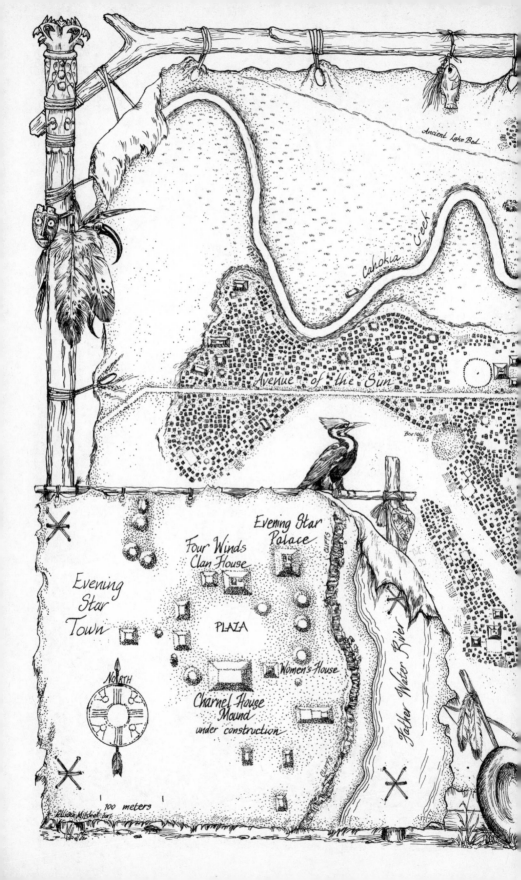

Ancient Lake Bed.

Cahokia Creek

Avenue of the Sun

Borrow Pits

Evening Star Palace

Four Winds Clan House

CLIFFS

Evening Star Town

PLAZA

Women's House

NORTH

Charnel House Mound
under construction

Father Water River

100 meters

1 Morning Star's Great Mound
2 Night Shadow Star's Palace
3 Tonka'tzi's Palace
4 Four Winds Clan Palace
5 Rides-the-Lightning's Temple
6 Record Keeper's Temple
7 Four Winds Burial Mound

Cahokia Creek

Avenue of the Sun

Avenue of the Moon

NORTH

CAHOKIA

Nonfiction Introduction

Archaeological research has revolutionized our understanding of the great site at Cahokia since we wrote *People of the River* in 1991. Today that novel still describes what researchers now call "Old Cahokia" at the end of the Edlehardt cultural phase, which ended at 1050 C.E.

At that time, we went out on a controversial limb and referred to Cahokia as a state because it made sense. Today researchers talk in terms of "imperial" Cahokia; as research has advanced, that, too, now makes sense.

A younger generation of archaeologists, such as Tim Pauketat, John Kelly, Kent Reilly, and others have beaten their way out of "processual" archaeology's straightjacket and taken a new look at Cahokia and its impact. In many ways, Cahokia was to North America as Rome was to Europe. Even today its stamp on Native American culture remains.

Cahokia, at its height, consisted of a series of mound centers built in strategic locations across the American Bottom on the eastern floodplain of the Mississippi and at St. Louis itself. Each appears to have been a semi-autonomous politico-religious center tied to its peers through a shared mythology.

At the beginning of the Lohmann phase at around 1050 C.E., something miraculous happened at Cahokia; what Dr. Tim Pauketat calls the "Big Bang." People, in the tens of thousands, from all over the American Midwest picked up and migrated to Cahokia. They brought their traditional designs, pottery, and household architecture, along, with their peculiar styles of clothing, kinship, and languages, and settled every bit of arable land in and around Cahokia.

Due to federal and Illinois cultural resource laws—which mandated archaeological survey prior to highway and in some cases, urban development—wherever archaeologists looked in the American Bottom and in the eastern uplands they found what we now call "urban sprawl." The mound centers around Cahokia weren't separate towns;

they were part of a megaplex. To date, more than two hundred mounds have been identified in association with the Cahokian phenomenon in the American Bottom and atop the upland bluffs in Illinois and Missouri. We know that then, as today, from the top of Monks Mound, the city expanded farther than the eye could see—perhaps thirty miles in every direction.

The amazing thing is that it happened, essentially, overnight. In 1050, Old Cahokia was razed, new Cahokia was planned, surveyed on a great scale as a cosmic representation of the heavens, and building began. More than five square miles of land was leveled and graded to create the great plazas around Monks Mound. Mounds were raised in precisely determined, astronomically important locations. Once completed, huge amounts of lumber were hauled in, and palaces and temples—some five stories tall—were constructed on their tops. To attempt this with modern earth-moving equipment would be a huge undertaking. What the Cahokians accomplished with sticks and strings, hoes and baskets, and bent backs, was nothing short of monumental!

But what force on earth would motivate a couple hundred thousand people to pick up, move hundreds of miles, and once plopped down amid a polyglot of strangers, to build an incredible city?

We think it was a religious miracle, perhaps inspired by the 1054 supernova, which spawned the Crab Nebula. Our best guess is that the Cahokians believed the nova, shining so brightly in the midday sky, to be the return of the mythological hero Morning Star. Then, in a dramatic ritual, the Cahokians somehow resurrected or "requickened" the divine hero in the flesh.

Messianic movements are common in anthropological literature, and we think eastern North America had a long tradition of prophesy and messianic movements with roots going back to the Woodland Archaic, that just such a movement explains the Hopewellian interaction sphere that we wrote about in *People of the Lakes*. It swept the woodlands two thousand years ago and may have laid the foundation for the religious phenomenon that reached its peak at Cahokia between 1050 and 1100.

Remove the question from the hypothetical: What if it were true? What if Jesus chose this moment to return to Jerusalem? Or if Mohammed miraculously reappeared in Mecca? What if tomorrow the Buddha stepped out of the sacred dimensions to sit and preach under the Bo tree? How many *hundreds of millions* of the faithful would trek to see or to revel in the mere presence of the miracle? Global chaos would ensue.

The notion that souls could be resurrected into other bodies was widespread across eastern North America when the Europeans arrived. If you have read our *People of the Longhouse*, *The Dawn Country*, *The Broken Land*, and *People of the Black Sun*, you are already familiar with the Iroquois "requickening" ceremony. For those seeking additional information, we refer readers to Dr. Robert L. Hall's *An Archaeology of the Soul*, University of Illinois Press, Urbana, 1997. For a discussion of Morning Star's presence at Cahokia see Dr. Timothy Pauketat's *Cahokia: Ancient America's Great City on the Mississippi*, Viking, New York, 2009.

Resurrected gods or not, Cahokia was an overnight sensation. Hundreds of thousands flocked there, and in doing so, they changed the face of North America. Cahokian colonies were established throughout the eastern woodlands, its traders and influence spread from the Atlantic to the Gulf Coast, to Oklahoma and the Dakotas. Reverberations from its messianic religion are still observed in renewal ceremonies like the modern Sun Dance. In a sense, we are all descendants—in one way or another—of Cahokia's majesty.

People
of the
Morning Star

Introduction

Listening to the St. Louis morning news on the car radio, John Wet Bear made a face. The entire world seemed to be crumbling, cracking, and coming apart at the seams. But then, he himself was emblematic of the problem. After all, if his source was correct, he was headed to Cahokia to kill a man.

Morning sun beat through the window as John's Toyota thump-thumped on the expansion joints as he headed east over the Mississippi on the I-55/70 bridge. Behind him, St. Louis gleamed in the morning sun, the silver arch looking pristine and magical where it stood before the backdrop of shining buildings.

Ahead of him, the Illinois shore waited, its appearance grubby after the chrome-and-glass opulence of downtown St. Louis. Below him, the great river flowed brown, roiled with spring runoff, the water welling, sucking, and swirling. Bits of foam and flotsam dotted the surface, and a barge was being shoved upstream, a frothing white wake rolling where a tug pushed it.

He stabbed the off button and silenced the oh-so-serious voice on the radio. Fingers tightening on the steering wheel, he took the exit ramp off Interstate 55/70. Slowing at the bottom, he followed the brown Cahokia Mounds signs to the old Collinsville Road and headed east.

John Wet Bear had just turned thirty, tall and muscular. His long black hair hung down his back in a braid. Uncle Max liked to remind

him that a braid was a historic Sioux style, while John's Osage ancestors wore their hair up. He had on a red-checked, long-sleeve shirt and
faded Levis that formed to his muscular legs. You name it, he'd done
it: stickball player as a kid living with his mother outside Tishomingo
City in the Chickasaw Nation, dropped out of high school, three stints
in the Marines serving downrange in the sandbox, tried and failed at
college, but thoroughly succeeded at substance abuse.

His Osage father's brother, Uncle Max, had saved him, reached out
and physically hauled John back from the edge of the abyss. Even the
memory of it hurt; John reached up and rubbed the top of his head.
He had been passed out between two urine-stained Dumpsters behind a downtown Kansas City bar. Uncle Max had found him somehow, knotted his callused fingers in John's thick hair and dragged him,
screaming and crying, through the filth to Max's battered old Chevy
pickup.

What followed would have been considered kidnap and torture by
the White world. After stripping John bare and shooting him down
with the garden hose and a spray washer, Uncle Max had chained
John to a post in his garage as if he were some sort of sideshow bear.
Food and water had been provided, and while John sweated out the
d.t.'s, Uncle Max had read to him from a whole pile of books about
Osage culture.

John had learned about *hunga ahuito,* the two-headed Creator eagle
who dwelt above the Rainbow realm in the sky, about the middle waters
of the earth, and the four realms of the Underworld clear down to where
First Woman lived in her cave beneath the roots of the world tree.

"This is who you are," Uncle Max had told him. "This is your father's blood and heritage as much as you are Chickasaw through your
mother. Chickasaws trace their ancestors through the mother, the Osage
trace heritage through the father. You are the descendant of two powerful cultures."

"Man, what the hell do I care? That world's dead, Unc. And who'd
want to live in it?"

Uncle Max had stared at him through the same hard and stony
black eyes that had once stared over M16 sights as he shot down Viet-
cong in Hue, Vietnam. "You'd rather starve and die in filth in Kansas
City? You'd rather pollute your souls with white man's whiskey, Co-
lumbian cocaine, and Afghan poppies? You don't know who you are.
Who you came from."

"Who's that? A bunch of conquered Indians?"

"Your ancestors built Cahokia. They changed the world. Descended from lords who ruled America, you would prefer to fade away in squalor until your corpse is rotting in a gutter?"

"Cahokia? Never heard of it."

Uncle Max had said nothing, only stood, walked out of the garage, and come back an hour later bearing another stack of books. The old army drill sergeant had seated himself in his plastic chair, propped his feet on his Snap-on toolbox, opened a book, and begun to read aloud. . . .

At first John thought it had sounded like a foreign language. Then, as he grasped the concepts, he had started to read the books himself. The archaeologists' terms had defied him in the beginning, but he'd begun to understand. And after a month of being chained like some wild animal, Uncle Max had unlocked the padlock, tossed John new clothes, and they'd made the drive to western Illinois to see Cahokia for themselves. That day walking among the mounds had changed John's life.

Now he was returning for what would probably be the last time.

When John Wet Bear's Toyota cleared the last of the buildings and drove out into the grassy flat, the effect was as mesmerizing as it had been that first time he'd seen Cahokia. Monks Mound immediately captured his eye where it dominated the horizon. Only when he peeled his gaze away did the other, smaller grassy mounds begin to imprint on his consciousness.

John bowed his head as he passed the reconstructed Woodhenge—one of the most sophisticated observatories in the prehistoric world. To the uninitiated it looked like nothing more than a circle of telephone poles about one hundred and fifty yards across. Or maybe some kind of framework for a circus tent, shy of its canvas. Instead Woodhenge functioned as a 365-day calendar, an 18.6-year lunar calendar, and who knew what else.

Like the rest of Cahokia, the sketchy remains merely hinted at the profound complexity of the Cahokian empire.

Wet Bear craned his neck to peer up the stairway leading to the top of Monks Mound as he drove past. That's where his quarry would be. And, like all pilgrims to Cahokia, he took a left into the parking lot.

Climbing out of the battered Toyota John shrugged on a Levi coat against the chill. He thrust the old Model 10 Smith & Wesson .38 in his belt at the small of his back. Perching his sunglasses on his nose, he locked the car and set off for the climb.

Once a warrior, always a warrior. But unlike Iraq and Afghanistan the battle he now fought had grown more convoluted, more insidious. He'd seen the announcement on the Internet, along with today's date. And from that moment on, he'd been in a rage.

John stopped at the bottom of the stairway and offered a prayer to his ancestors—many no doubt buried in this very mound—to give him courage and steady his hand at the last moment.

After reading the plaque at the bottom, he started up.

Archaeological research in the last twenty years—especially the FAI-270 highway project and proposed interchanges for the I-55/70 Interstate—had led to remarkable new research. And with it, a reinterpretation of Cahokia and its place in both the world of archaeology and its impact on America's Native people.

John was breathing hard by the time he stepped out onto the high top of Monks Mound. The breeze pulled at his coat and teased his long black braid. He could sense his ancestors, share the link across time as he stood where they had.

He turned, looking west to where the distant silver arch marked downtown St. Louis. In Cahokian times, that high bluff had been home to a thriving center of temples, palaces, and population.

A couple of miles away, between him and St. Louis, a new mound rose above the broad Mississippi floodplain. Maybe thirty stories high it dwarfed Monks Mound. But where the Cahokians had used mounds as foundations for sacred buildings, the modern mound encased St. Louis's discarded garbage. The irony wasn't lost on John Wet Bear.

"Leave it to a bunch of white guys," he muttered.

The Great Plaza with its extraordinary visitors' center lay just across the road, the Twin Mounds on the south. He could imagine his ancestors, bedecked in bright feathers, playing stickball and chunkey there. He could feel their passion burning as hotly as it had in his youth as he grasped the racquets and sprinted for all he was worth in pursuit of the ball.

Turning east he could see the irregular bluff behind Collinsville and the closer mounds that marked the Eastern Plaza. Someone sat at the eastern mound edge, a Pendleton blanket over his shoulders, a canvas hat pulled low over gray locks as he stared into the distance.

I'm sorry to disturb your meditation, mister. But you'll be witness to a day that changes lives forever.

As always, it took a moment to recover from the sense of awe, and only then did John locate the film crew on the northern end of the mound top. His heart slowed into an angry beat.

A camera rested on a tripod in what would have been the middle of the Cahokian's five-story mound-top structure. A skinny cameraman was fiddling with the focus; a burly man was folding out a chair and positioning it.

Aware of the pistol pressing against his sacrum, John stuck his hands in his pockets, strolling to where the overweight bearded man was cleaning his glasses. Wearing a white shirt and a big, blue tie under his tweed jacket, the big guy seated himself on a portable stool against the backdrop of the interstate and the old meander lakes. The cameraman, dressed in the requisite vest, stared into the viewfinder on the Sony digital. It looked like an expensive piece of equipment.

The cameraman called, "Sound check."

The big guy pushed his glasses on and positioned himself. "Testing, one, two, three, four—"

"We're good." The cameraman studied the LCD display and said, "Starting from the top, five, four, three, two, one."

"Hello," the big guy said heartily. "I'm Dr. Wig MacGuire. *Alien Quest* has traveled here, to Cahokia, Illinois, to the top of Monks Mound where we will attempt to unlock the secret behind the Alien construction of the most complex mound site in North America."

He stared intently into the camera, his brown eyes thoughtful. "What brought visitors from another planet here, to the Mississippi floodplain? Was it some deep deposit of rare minerals? Or perhaps the planetary coordinates that caused them to build such an intricate spaceport in the American Midwest?"

He smiled intimately into the camera. "Whatever the reason, they chose this place. We can wonder about the meaning of the mounds, and why the Aliens chose to build them, but—"

"I say you're a lying bastard!" John's hard voice carried.

"Cut!" The skinny cameraman spun around. "Who the hell are you?"

"I'm John Wet Bear, son of Billy Wet Bear and Mary Wet Bear. I'd tell you my clans, but being white guys it wouldn't mean anything. What I want to know is why?"

"Why what? We're filming here. I need you to leave."

John kicked at the gravel path with one of his worn Dan Post boots. He'd propped his thumbs in the back pockets of his Levis . . . inches from the revolver's grip. "You really believe that crap about Aliens? I mean, really"—he raised his hands, trembling them—"*ooooh!* Why'd they come *here*?"

The cameraman pulled out his cell phone. "You're leaving, or I'm calling the police, right now."

"They can't get here quick enough to save you." John squinted behind his sunglasses, looking across the distant oxbow lake toward where the North Group mounds had stood. "White people have already destroyed most of Cahokia. You two assholes aren't going to destroy the rest."

The cameraman hesitated, finally reading the threat in John's posture and expression. "Destroy the . . . We're, uh, not *destroying* anything."

"What were you smoking when you cooked up this 'Alien' crap, anyway?" He looked at the big guy who had stood from his chair, irritation in his eyes.

"I'm an archaeologist. We're just trying—"

"Yeah? Ph.D.?"

"That's right. Look, we've got a schedule to keep. And not a lot of budget. If you'd—"

"Where'd you study?" John asked mildly. "Who'd you study under? Tell me about your dissertation."

"That's none of your business."

"Yeah, yeah, I get it. If you'll tell me the Internet address, maybe I'll become an MD next week." He held up a hand. "No! Wait! It's coming to me: You're another con job all hot to run a load of fantasy lies for some cable channel to make a fast buck." He pointed. "Look out there. From St. Louis in the west, all the way past that bluff top on the east, for as far as you can see from the north, to way down past where you can see in the south, this was all city. At its greatest, Cahokia was bigger than contemporary London and Paris put together. My people did that."

"Then why did *your people* build the mounds?" the cameraman asked warily. "They got them from the Egyptians, right?"

"My people had been building mounds along the Mississippi for fifteen hundred years *before* the Egyptians first set one stone atop another to build their first pyramid." John shook his head. "God, you guys are pathetic."

"No offense," the fat guy said, "but Aliens sell."

"No offense? Bigoted racists like you always say 'no offense.'" John lowered his voice to a deadly sibilance. "Sorry, offense taken."

"Hey!" the cameraman jerked himself up straight. "I've never been a racist in my life."

"Yeah," John snorted. "Then what are you doing right now?"

Wig MacGuire stomped forward. "We're doing a show on Aliens building Cahokia. There's nothing racist about it, asshole."

John cocked his head, a thin smile on his lips. The fingers of his right hand caressed the Smith & Wesson's wooden grip where it stuck out past his belt. "Are you *that* stupid? My ancestors, the Dhegiha

Sioux built this city. By claiming Aliens built it, you're defaming me and my ancestors."

"That's bullshit!" MacGuire threw his arms wide. "We're not insulting anyone. We're *solving* the mystery of Cahokia."

John's smile thinned. "The assumption behind your film is that my ancestors were too stupid to build anything like Cahokia. First rule to dispossessing and marginalizing a people? Deny their heritage. You guys have tried the lost tribes of Israel, then the lost Welshmen, then the Vikings, the Phoenicians, the Mayans . . . and now its Aliens."

The cameraman growled, "How could a bunch of prehistoric people plan all this out? It's east-west, north-south. They didn't have compasses."

"Wrong again, asshole," John roared, feeling the anger build. "They had *expert* surveyors when they built new Cahokia during the Big Bang! Leveled the whole thing, sometimes with up to eight feet of fill. Laid it out with a graded slope and drop so it would drain. They had a standard unit of measurement, did the geometry with squares and arcs. And how did they know the directions? You can see the Woodhenge from here. That circle of posts? It's a big honking celestial observatory, you bigoted white fool!"

"An observatory? It's a *circle* of *posts*."

"Cahokians were plotting the movement of planets, the eighteen-point-six year cycle of the moon, and the seasons, when your white kings in England and France were wading through sewage in the streets and picking lice out of their beards."

"Where are the Indian cathedrals? Huh? Tell me that, smart guy."

"What the hell do you think you're standing on, bigot? If it was nine hundred years ago, we'd be inside a five-story-tall building."

"All I see is a big pile of dirt." MacGuire half-lidded his eyes. "Now Cochise, you've had your fun. Go away and leave us alone. We've got nothing against prehistoric Indians. Maybe they built this, and maybe they didn't. And frankly, outside of a few deluded radicals like you, who cares?"

John studied the man's head, seeing the spot in the center of his brow where he'd put the bullet. The slow rage that always got him in trouble was rising to full boil. "You're preaching the most insidious form of racism that there is: that my people weren't just culturally and intellectually inferior, but that the notion they built Cahokia is so absurd even the most outlandish alternate explanation, *Aliens,* is more believable."

The skinny camera guy, apparently reading John's reddening face, said, "Look, pal. No offense. Seventy percent of the American people are scientifically illiterate. Less than three percent have even heard of Cahokia, let alone what it might mean. They don't believe anything existed in America before the white guys came."

In a condescending voice, MacGuire said, "Me, I've got nothing against the Indians. Okay, your people got a raw deal, and I can't change that. People *do* believe in Aliens, and because they do, we're going to sell them Aliens. It's free speech."

"They got a term for what you're doing. They call it cultural genocide. Murdering a people's past as a way of marginalizing them."

"You're a lunatic. What happened? You forgot to take your Prozac this morning?" the camera guy said with a smirk.

"Before I send you on your way, take one last look." John tightened his right hand around the pistol grip. "The mounds were just the foundations for the buildings. They sent colonies as far as Georgia and the Carolinas, hundreds of thousands of people lived within a thirty-mile radius of this spot. My people built a stunning and remarkable civilization here. Saying it was Aliens is a moral crime. And since you know it's a lie, you're just a modern version of Custer."

"Hey, Mr. Red Man. Reality check. A lie? What's that? Everything's marketing, what you can sell. Just like in politics, truth is whatever you can get people to believe. So go on," MacGuire said with a wave of his hand. "Go away. Shoo!"

John took a breath. *Time.*

The cameraman was complaining to MacGuire, "Can you imagine that? That asshole called *us* racists? I voted for Obama."

John's vision fixed on MacGuire's face, at the point where he'd shoot. His heart was a slow and steady thumping beat, coursing blood through his body. He'd felt this way in combat—what he interpreted as the spirit of his warrior ancestors.

As the revolver slid out of his belt, a hard hand clamped on his wrist from behind, a voice near his ear saying, "Ah, yes. Thought you'd come here."

"Uncle Max?" John cried, stunned.

"So, you gonna kill them here, in the middle of the open?" Max asked as he wrenched the old Smith & Wesson from John's hand and stepped around.

Wig MacGuire and the cameraman both stared, wide-eyed, first at the gun, then at the older man with a Pendleton blanket hanging from his shoulders. Max's face was lined by his aging smile. VA benefits had paid for very nice false teeth that gave him a healthy grin.

"Wanted to make a statement, Unc," John told him. "You know, remind the world that we're tired of genocide. It's what you fought for in Kosovo with KFOR, remember? Genocide is pretty much the same if you use a camera or a gun."

Max nodded, his expression turning pensive. "Yeah, I suppose it is."

"Hang on here!" Wig MacGuire had finally found his voice, his wide eyes bugged behind his glasses as he stared at the worn revolver. His hands were up, his face ashen. "We're sorry. Okay. Do you want money?" He pawed desperately for his billfold. "You can have anything you want. We don't want any trouble."

"Shit!" John cried in disgust. "He thinks *we're* the thieves? He's the one stealing other people's lives and heritage."

Uncle Max thoughtfully opened the cylinder, inspecting the six cartridges. "Tell you what, MacGuire. My nephew here, he's got PTSD from Afghanistan, huh? Unstable veteran. Now, if I don't let him shoot you, you might grab that camera and run down the stairs and call the police."

Max gave the men a sidelong glance. "Me, I wouldn't blame you if you did. John here, he's always been a fighter for a cause. Ain't that right?"

"Yep. If you'd a let me shoot 'em, the publicity from my trial would stop this Alien shit right in its tracks. People would know it was our ancestors who built Cahokia. We could label these bigots for what they are. And, Unc, killing racists would be a crime of passion, I could plead it down to murder two, maybe even manslaughter or justifiable homicide."

"Probably could." Max nodded thoughtfully before clicking the cylinder back into the revolver. "So, here's the deal, MacGuire: Take your camera. Beat feet out of here. Call the cops if you want. They'll charge my nephew here with armed assault. My sister's girl, who's a tribal attorney, will file a shit-load of defamation, discrimination, civil rights violations, and a slew of other charges. You know, one of them class-action suits against you, the producers, the network, everybody involved. Something with big damages that will draw a lot of attention."

MacGuire shot a worried glance at the cameraman who was still fixated on the old, worn revolver. "We'll go. No cops."

"Too bad. Cops are necessary for a trial." Max was back to grinning again. "But then maybe you're not bigoted racists like my nephew thinks. Maybe you just hadn't thought through the implications behind your film. Maybe you don't mean to imply that Native peoples were too stupid to build a city like this. It'll be a win-win. We'll both go away thinking the other party turned out to be a whole lot smarter than we thought."

Even as MacGuire and his cameraman fled, a family of four had climbed onto the high flat.

"Think they'll call the cops anyway?"

"Nope." Max handed him the revolver. "You might want to stick that out of sight. You are in Illinois."

"How'd you know I'd come after them?"

"Spirits told me." Max stuffed his hands in his pockets as he looked eastward toward St. Louis. "You'd have really shot him?"

"At that last instant? I'll never know. But I'm tired of the lies. The assumption that if your ancestors were inferior, then so are you. Maybe that's what put me in that alley in the first place. They think it's harmless, a joke, to attribute places like this to Aliens or lost Vikings, but they're perpetuating evil."

"MacGuire probably never looked at it that way. He probably thinks he's a good man."

"Yeah, Unc." John started back for the stairs. "You think it was that way here? Think our ancestors had anyone like me? Ready to sacrifice himself in the battle against evil?"

Uncle Max paused at the head of the stairs, staring down at the grassy expanse of the great plaza as if he were seeing it through the Morning Star's eyes. "Of course they did."

"How do you know?"

"The same way I knew you'd be here today. The underwater panther told me."

"Yeah, sure, Unc."

But the old man just smiled in that enigmatic way of his.

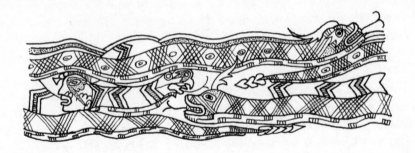

Prologue

*L*ike a knife blade, the Trade canoe's bow splits the sandy shore. Driven by
the vessel's weight and the speed at which my men drive it ashore, it cuts a
great gouge, piling furrows to either side of the polished hull. So quickly does
it finally stop that I am almost thrown from my feet.

I smile at that, and clambering over the raised cypress-wood bow, I leap
down and drop to my knees. For the moment I am oblivious of the hundreds
of curious observers who have watched our arrival at Cahokia's crowded
landing.

Heedless of the audience, my right knee planted, I reach down and rake my
fingers through the damp sand. Knotting a ball of it in my fist, I raise it to my
nose and draw deeply of its scent. The smell is of river, the musk of mud, and
the stale odor of decomposition. I press it to my breast, closing my eyes, savoring the moment. Then I rub the charcoal-flecked grit into my breastbone, over
my heart.

The voices, mostly quiet today, begin whispering, "Yes! Yes!"

Cahokia! I am home! By the Tie Snakes, I will drive a great bloody
wedge through your very soul!

Only when I finally stand does my crew hop out of the great canoe, and
together we begin wrestling the freight-packed vessel farther up on the beach.

From the crowd of onlookers come volunteers—some Traders, others simply
curious—to help drag the boat and its cargo up on the Saud.

"Where are you from?" a man asks as he glances speculatively at the *tarped packs snugged within the gunwales. He is in his midtwenties; his sun-browned skin is tattooed in designs I do not recognize. His hair is piled atop his head in a bun.*

"South," I reply. "Spent a couple of years with the Mos'kogee. Trade was good."

He glances at the packs again and starts to nod, only to hesitate as he takes in my companions. They are dressed as common fishermen or farmers and mostly naked but for the breechcloths and deerhide capes on their shoulders. Only now, noticing how they contrast to the locals do I realize that a cougar may dress like a dog, but the essence of his movements, the predatory glint in his eyes, cannot be disguised.

"Give them no mind," I say easily. "I have them on loan from the high minko himself. Part of the Trade I carry belongs to the chief. He was worried that someone might have tried to stop us on the river and take it."

"He shouldn't have," the local tells me, nodding warily at the closest of my picked Tula warriors. "If you travel under the Power of Trade, no one will bother you. And the Morning Star has even put a stop to the old practice of local chiefs insisting that a Trader stop and pay tribute before passing. The river is open like it has never been."

"He's Mos'kogee," I reply. "You can't expect ignorant southerners to accept everything."

Struggling—our feet digging into the sacred sand of Cahokia—we have dragged the great boat two thirds of the way up the bank. I smack my hands together and take stock. The crowd is growing around us. People in all styles of colorful dress are calling greetings and questions. The food sellers, of course, are pressing forward with spicy, roasted meats on skewers. Others offer Cahokian trinkets including clay chunkey stones, carved pendants of Morning Star, wooden plates engraved in the Four Winds Clan design, necklaces of wooden beads dyed red, black, and white.

In their native Caddo tongue, I order my Tula, "Don't just stand there looking dangerous. Smile. You're Traders. Act like it and Trade for something."

I watch the transition as their predatory souls struggle to behave like tame and friendly dogs instead of the vicious and wild wolves they are. It amuses me as little does in life.

To the nearest local—surely one of the agents scouting new prospects—I say, "I need to rent a storehouse for my Trade." I look up the bank at the rows of thatch- and cane-roofed buildings crowding the levee heights. Most are Trade houses or craft workshops.

The local studies me, seeing only an inoffensive muscular man in his twenties. I have my long black hair braided, and brown face paint obscures my telltale tattoos. Then he follows my gaze to the warehouses, saying, "Those are mostly taken. But there are others farther back from the river. For a token, I can take you to a man who has a nice warehouse, clean, with a tight roof."

Having anticipated this, I reach over the gunwale and remove a small bag of clamshell beads. As I hand it to the man, I ask, "Will this be sufficient to engage your services?"

He nods and smiles. The gift isn't exorbitant, nothing that would draw attention to me.

"This way," he calls. "I am Cord Knot, a man of the Bear Clan."

"Act smartly," I whisper to Half Bobcat. He has Traded some trifle for a roasted squirrel. As he sinks his teeth into the thick back meat, grease dribbles down his chin. He nods his understanding, but I can see awe and amazement in his dark eyes as he stares around at the impossibly crowded and busy canoe landing. My wild Tula have been told what to expect. But actually being here will challenge them down to their very bones.

Before I leave, I hire a guide for Bleeding Hawk. Then I place a textile-wrapped bundle in my willing Tula's hands. "You must deliver this to Right Hand. He is a chief of the Deer Clan. The guide will take you to his palace atop the eastern bluffs. Once you place this in his hand, return here immediately."

"Yes, my chief."

I turn then and follow the local; as I do I introduce myself: "I am White Finger, of the Deer Clan."

I glance around as we wind our way through the endless ranks of beached canoes, many inverted to keep the rain from pooling inside. Most are decorated with clan symbols and individual designs to mark ownership. Here the sand is almost black with charcoal from old fires. All up and down the landing, canoes are being unloaded or loaded. Firewood, matting, coils of rope, baskets of corn, squash, sunflowers, ceramic jars of goosefoot seed, bales of thatch, whole deer, turkeys, buffalo hides, and, well, you name it. I had forgotten the river of goods that constantly flow through, and maintain, Cahokia.

At the top of the rise, we enter the maze of warehouses and workshops. I smell smoke as we skirt a potter's workshop and see brownware ceramics firing in a pit. Green vessels are drying on racks in the sunlight; two women, both of them old, toothless, and gray-haired are splotched with clay as they dip their fingers in a bowl of river water and continue the endless chore of manufacturing pots, jars, and bowls.

We pass warehouses—clay-walled squares topped with thatch or split-cane roofs. They are marked with both clan images and the owner's personal designs. Paths between them are deeply rutted, and here and there we have to step across pools of vile-smelling water. I wave away the cloud of flies that rise in response. The odor from the latrines periodically burns my nose.

People, so many people! A pack of dogs waits just outside a tanner's workshop. The three men inside who are fleshing hides with long, bone scrapers periodically toss bits of dried meat and sinew to the snarling, snapping curs.

"You've been away long?" Cord Knot asks as we pass a wood carver's shop. Not only is the ground around the workshop littered with chips and the fine wood dust produced by sandstone abraders, but I can hear the tap-tap *of mallets on stone chisels.*

"Four years," I lie again. "It's good to be back."

"At least you didn't lose your accent. Sometimes that happens."

"I was lucky."

We wind our way past a clustered jumble of houses, each with a small garden. They are poorly kept, but just beyond is a peak-roofed, white-plastered building. I stop short when I see the Four Winds Clan design above the heavy-plank door. I do not recognize the spiral with a crosshatch image below it.

"This is the place I was thinking of," Cord Knot says. He points to the roof of a high palace just to the south. Most of the building is obscured by intervening houses. "It belongs to the River Mounds. War Duck is the high chief, but his sister, Round Pot, pretty much runs things. How long do you think you might need the building?"

"A moon, but I would be willing to pay for two just in case it proves necessary."

Cord Knot lifts the heavy door, swinging it on thick leather hinges, and I step inside. The only light comes from the gap where the roof overhangs the walls. The floor is packed clay, well swept. I can see only one place where water has dripped from a leak in the thatch.

I can hear the voices whispering among themselves, the words just below the threshold of my understanding. I can tell they are pleased.

"This will do. I have a bale of dried yaupon. Would that cover the rental?"

He watches as my hands form the dimension of the yaupon leaves. I can see the calculations behind his eyes. That much yaupon would brew enough black drink to last an elite household for a year.

"I'll throw in a shell columella for your effort if you can talk them into it."

He nods and touches his chin, a sign of respect, though a bit overdone given the nature of our bargain.

"Let me see," he tells me.

"I'll meet you back at the canoe." Stepping outside, I lift my hand to the sun, adding, "Perhaps in two-finger's time."

"If I'm just a little late," he says, "don't take another's offer."

"Not until a full hand of time passes," I reply, and watch him hurry off between the buildings.

As soon as he's out of sight, I grin. Then, calling upon old memories, I wind my way between the close-packed houses and back toward the canoe landing. Old-Woman-Who-Never-Dies, or First Woman, as she is often known, has a temple right where I remember it being. The mound upon which it sits has been added to, and the temple atop it is new. I resist the impulse to spit upon the guardian post before it: a carved rendition of Morning Star. The image looks nothing like the man I remember. A curious twisting, almost like the urge to vomit, stirs in my gut.

Then I am up the stairs; I pause on the flat before the temple. To the west I can look down on the landing, swarming with activity. The river is dotted with canoes, and Evening Star City dominates the high bluff across the river on the west bank.

Then I turn and look east. As I do, my heart leaps with sudden anxiety. The temple's elevation above the warehouse roofs, and its location at the highest point on the levee, allows me a faint glimpse of the high palace in the eastern distance.

The voices hiss with excitement. Images flicker in my memory: Love and desire swell in my breast as I lower myself onto her exquisite body. For that one sweet moment I am in bliss as my seed explodes. Broken memories of shouts . . . screams . . . hard hands clamping on my body from behind and jerking me off of her. His face as he orders me bound. A coarse-fabric wrapped around me. My body, bouncing in blackness . . . The sounds of water.

I tell the voices: "He is there. They all are."

So is she. The woman my flesh aches to possess. Love for her burns in my veins. Memories of her body, her smile, the lithesome way she moves, twine through me like a sweet liquid.

"Soon, my beloved. Soon."

They wouldn't expect me to return in the manner I have, nameless, without fanfare. The man they knew would come at the head of an army: proud, belligerent, and boastful.

"That man is dead," I whisper regretfully.

They, however, are still alive. And I have chosen a way to bring them down. Even him. The living god! And to do it, I will unleash Powers not even the Morning Star himself would dare to attempt.

"Hear me, Powers of the Sky, the Earth, and Underworld. The Wild One has come. And before I leave, the three worlds will be rent and broken as I unleash my passion!" I find a certain irony in announcing my challenge before Old-Woman-Who-Never-Dies' temple. Hopefully she is still slumbering *in her cave in the lowest depths of the Underworld. May she and her minions remain oblivious until it is too late.*

I am different now, hardened, and trained in a subtle manner of killing. They shall learn this lesson over the next couple of moons. Soon, all Cahokia shall feel my wrath. If the Powers of Sky, Earth, and Underworld permit, I shall tear sacred Cahokia right down the middle, and fill its avenues with blood.

The voices chortle in delight.

One

The acclaimed high chief of the Deer Clan, Right Hand, fingered his prominent and scarred chin as he looked westward across the sprawl of Cahokia. The Whisperer was coming. Right Hand had received word but two days past.

Plotting the murder of a living god is a dangerous business. We have no way of knowing how Power will react.

The thought sent a flutter of unease through him.

According to the latest of the Whisperer's messengers, the time to act had arrived. All Right Hand needed was the "token," the weapon with which to strike. If the Whisperer's messenger was correct, it would be delivered today or tomorrow at the latest.

Looking down at his mangled right hand, he wondered how the Whisperer had known. Memories of that day, the screams, the pain, returned as fresh as if it were yesterday. Chunkey Boy's brother Walking Smoke and a couple of Four Winds warriors had held him down as Chunkey Boy used Right Hand's own chunkey stone to crush the bones in his hand and fingers.

Chunkey Boy's vicious expression remained so clearly imprinted: his lips bared, his eyes slitted with rage. His arm rose and fell, hammering the stone down. Each impact made a wet smacking and snapping as blood spattered and bone crushed.

You took so much away from me that day, Chunkey Boy. But you couldn't take my birthright. And now I shall repay you with long smoldering rage.

Below his bluff-top vantage, the great city of Cahokia stretched across the floodplain in a confused pattern. Clusters of dwellings concentrated around mound-top temples and palaces, only to give way to interspersed fields before merging with the next batch of closely packed houses around their lofty temples and palaces. At night—as if thousands of stars had fallen to earth—even the distant Evening Star bluffs on the other side of the river were pinpricked with tiny dots of firelight.

Right Hand wore a high chief's white apron decorated with the image of two heavily antlered deer, their front legs raised. The bucks faced each other on either side of a pole decorated with severed human heads.

The high chief's broad shoulders narrowed to a slender waist, his body that of a longtime athlete. He wore his gray-streaked hair pulled back in a severe bun and held in place by two flaring copper pins. Though his right hand appeared mutilated, it functioned well enough to clutch a tall staff wrapped with strips of raccoon fur; Raccoon, Spirit messenger of the dead, had special meaning for Right Hand. Several of the characteristic ringed-tails dangled from the top.

So much humanity, he thought, wondering if the entire world's population had crowded together here. His tattooed face mimicked a raccoon's black eyes, lines down the cheeks like laid-back whiskers. For the moment it reflected extreme distaste.

As he expressed his displeasure, his sister—an older woman, and the Deer Clan Matron—stepped up beside him. "You worry about Power?" she asked. "You shouldn't. Since the Beginning Times, the Spirit creatures who dominate the Underworld have always fought in opposition to the Powers of the sky. Morning Star's soul was called down during the daytime, making him not only a creature of the sky, but of light as well."

She absently fingered the finely woven blue skirt that clung to her hips. A bright-pink spoonbill-feathered cape graced her shoulders. Her hair had been pulled back in a matron's bun, and polished shell columellas—imported from the distant gulf to the south—hung from her ears. The skin of her shoulders, back, and chest bore tattoos rendered in an intricate and endless knot of intertwined Tie Snakes—a tribute that marked her as a devotee of First Woman.

First Woman, the Old-Woman-Who-Never-Dies, the ruler of the Underworld, lived in her cave down below the World Tree's deepest roots. There she dreamed the patterns and Powers of the Underworld. Her realm was portrayed by the color red, indicative of fertility, creativity, war, and chaos. She had dominion over the waters and plants. The Spirit creatures of the Underworld including the Water Panther known as Piasa; the flying snake called Horned Serpent; Snapping Turtle, fish, and frogs answered to First Woman. So, too, did the Tie Snakes who guarded springs, lurked in the depths of the rivers, and invoked the rains; even though doing so infuriated the Thunderbirds, who unleashed lightning bolts in their constant battle with the Powers of the Underworld.

Right Hand narrowed his eyes as he studied the distant high mound. In a husky voice he said, "It is said in the old stories that at the Creation, First Being, *Hunga Ahuito,* took the form of a mottled, two-headed eagle. Capable of seeing in all directions at once with its four eyes, and being male and female, it orchestrated all things, ruling even the sun, rainbows, and thunderers. Now Morning Star claims *he* rules the sky."

"But is he a god?" Matron Corn Seed paused. "Really? Or has the lie been told so often that it now lives on its own?" She let her gaze fix on the distant pimple-like prominence; even through the haze of a thousand smoking fires, Morning Star's tall temple atop its great mound couldn't be missed. And that, from where she stood, was still a hard day's walk. Between her bluff-top vantage point and the Morning Star's palace, lived perhaps ten thousand people; their houses, temples, mounds, and fields spread like a poorly woven blanket across the wide floodplain with its curving lakes.

The chief extended his good left hand in a grand gesture to include the vast and irregular accumulation of humanity. "They believe it. All these simpletons who've flocked here to revel in the god's presence." He said it bitterly; a smile barely curled his thin lips. "And as long as they do, whatever we believe . . . the truth, if you will, is meaningless."

"It's not Power, or him, that I fear," the woman admitted softly. "Even if his Spirit really belongs to the hero god and is reincarnated in that young fool's body. It's the Four Winds Clan and that Keeper of theirs who troubles me. Old Blue Heron is like a spider with her bits of web spun everywhere. Make the slightest misstep and an unknown tendril will vibrate just enough to draw her attention."

"She's merely a woman."

"You fear Power. I've found people are so much more deadly." She gave him a sidelong appraisal. "Do not underestimate her. Others have. Hung in a square, people scream the voices right out of their throats when strips of skin are peeled slowly from their bodies."

"I don't intend on hanging from a Four Winds Clan square," he replied, referring to the vertical, open pole frame into which a man's naked body was tied for torture. "Myself, I've taken a lesson from the chickadee."

"Oh? Learned to chirp melodically, or just flit about in panicked terror when the sharp-shinned hawk comes diving?"

His expression soured at her caustic tone. "When a chickadee is hungry, it carefully plucks at a single strand of silk. Spiders can't help themselves. It's in their nature to dash out of their holes toward whatever creature is stuck in their web."

"You've given the problem some thought?"

He barely lifted a scarred eyebrow. The action shifted the beaded forelock that hung down over his forehead. "When the time comes, the Whisperer will draw the spider into striking distance . . . play her web like a child's string game. It's the Morning Star I'm worried about." He hesitated before adding, "And whatever agreements he has with the Sky World."

She glanced sidelong at him, suspicion in her eyes. "For all you know, our mysterious 'Whisperer' might just be the Morning Star himself! I don't trust him, whoever he is. Never have."

Right Hand fixed his eyes on the distant palace, now in shadow from one of the fluffy white clouds that drifted across the spring sky. "The token could come at any time. And when it does, it will be the signal to strike."

"My chief, no place on earth is more heavily guarded or monitored than Morning Star's high palace." She fingered her prominent nose, eyes on the distant palace where it rose above a thousand peaked roofs. "And that's a weakness all its own. I have a candidate in mind."

"One of ours?"

She smiled grimly. "Of course not. My agent has been in touch with a man from the Evening Star House, someone who is vulnerable to persuasion. And, well, he happens to have an incestuous relationship with his daughter. A fact he wouldn't like to have known lest his cousins sneak up and bash his brains out some fine day. He, in turn, has a nephew called Cut String, a proud and vain man who sincerely believed he had earned honors that were not bestowed."

"They can't be traced back to us?"

She chuckled hoarsely. "Do you think I'm an idiot? Of course not!

The nephew, along with being vain, has a brother in Spotted Wrist's squadron. He's been sent north to try, yet again, to bring Red Wing town and its heretics to heel. If the past is any guide to the future, that young war chief up there, Fire Cat Twelvekiller, he'll rip Spotted Wrist's squadrons to pieces. If the Four Winds Clan catches my assassin, it will look like vengeance and lead them down a false trail . . . right to the Evening Star House." Another pause. "Blue Heron and High Dance can tear themselves apart over it. And, who knows? High Dance has never had the subtlety to hide his aspirations. Maybe Blue Heron will find something smoldering there."

"You can get this assassin of yours into the palace?"

"If the Whisperer's messengers have told us the truth." She nodded absently, eyes half squinted as she stared at the Morning Star's distant palace. "Having made a careful study of the palace, I have just the place for Cut String to hide. He's already been given the instructions."

The high chief drew a deep breath. "The Whisperer is ready. We need but to receive the token, and we are free to strike. Once we kill the Morning Star, the Whisperer will slowly but surely pluck Blue Heron's web in a way that draws her into his reach."

"Be careful, brother. If this should go awry . . ." She laid a cautious hand on his shoulder.

"The believers would unleash a blood bath as they sought to snuff out even the faintest whiff of heresy." His smile bent the long scar on his chin. "The Whisperer is right. Everything must be traced back to the Four Winds Clan."

"If we do this thing—succeed in killing the Morning Star—we must act quickly. The Houses of the Four Winds Clan must be incited to turn on one another. If the dirt-farmers and immigrants panic and riot, chaos will be unleashed. Our world will consume itself. What will remain will be soot, ashes, rotting corpses, and ruin."

He nodded grimly. "Our duty is to ensure it never gets that far. But then, the Four Winds Clan has shown us all how to be gods. And . . . well, what's a little risk compared to those benefits?"

"Nothing that can't be bought by a little blood and suffering," she whispered. "Like the Whisperer, I just want the Four Winds Clan destroyed."

"Then, perhaps, we can resurrect the life-soul of Petaga, place it in a young man's body. Reunify the Earth Clans and place the worship of First Woman where it belongs. We can restore the heritage of the great priestess Lichen and the legendary Nightshade."

She pointed to a tall man who emerged from between the houses that crowded behind the base of the small, conical burial mound on which they stood. The runner bore a red-fabric-wrapped bundle in his arms. He slowed, chest rising and falling from his long journey. He looked around cautiously, and nodded as the high chief waved. Then he started up the grass-sided mound.

Reaching the top, he dropped to one knee, head down, asking in a thick and guttural accent, "For which hand?"

"The right," the high chief replied, glancing down at his maimed hand.

The runner, a foreign barbarian, fit-looking and in his mid-twenties, touched his chin in a sign of respect. Oddly, his face bore no tattoos to identify his nation or clan. Reverently, he offered up the red-cloth bundle. No sooner did the high chief lay hold of it than the man rose, spun, and trotted back down the mound. Within a matter of heartbeats, he'd disappeared back into the maze of houses.

"What man gains adulthood without tattoos?" Right Hand wondered. "Unless he's a slave."

"No slave has eyes that arrogant and proud. He was all warrior, that one." She gestured at the bundle. "That's it?"

Cradling the wrapping, his raccoon staff in the crook of his right arm, the high chief unwound the red cloth just enough to expose the tip of a long stone blade. Sunlight glistened in parallel rows of rippling flake scars. A master had carefully chipped the slim blade from a beautiful translucent brown chert; the edge sharp enough to split a hair.

"The Whisperer is as good as his word. Now all we have to do is get this to your assassin, Matron." He paused watching the light play on the deadly blade. "And hope it drinks deeply of the Morning Star's blood."

Two

But for the intrusion of a single dark knot, the inboard-side of the canoe's sanded and waxed hull exhibited straight and uniform wood grain. The reddish color, combined with the wood's faint pungent perfume, told Fire Cat Twelvekiller that the big war canoe had been hewn from a huge bald cypress—one felled far to the south. The workmanship was exquisite, the walls of the hull thin and light, its beam wide enough that parallel ranks of warriors manned the paddles.

That lovingly polished wood had become the boundary of War Chief Fire Cat's universe. Life, hope, Power—everything he'd ever dreamed of or aspired to—all had collapsed into what little space lay between his blurry vision and the wood's absolute reality.

A boundary beyond which he dared not contemplate.

He could have raised his head, looked beyond the gunwales to the broad river—its cool green surface swirling, welling, and sucking. Beyond the living water he would have seen the western bank as it ghosted past in a tree-lined glory of cottonwoods, elms, and willows.

Desolation made even that effort unworthy. What point would be served by watching the last of his world slip away? Misery and humiliation, pain, and ultimately ignominious death awaited him; and though he knew the river's Power bore him no malice, it seemed to be rushing him south to Cahokia.

Once there, after his hanging body endured the brutality, the thirst, the slicing and searing of his flesh, they'd chop him apart. His leg bones would be stripped of meat and sinew, cleaned, painted or engraved, and given away as gifts.

His arm bones would hang from some wall. His head would be carefully skinned, the skull polished to a sheen before being painted. Thereafter his gaping eye sockets would vacantly stare out at some Cahokian Men's House. Or perhaps it would grace the wall of the Morning Star himself.

Pustule of an imposter that he is!

Fire Cat winced and tried to shift his aching arms. They'd been bound behind him; the tight cord ate into his wrists. But what was that compared to the dull agony in his legs? Or the pain that burned through his wrenched back, shoulders, and arms. No sensation remained in his hands.

I was once the man known as Fire Cat Twelvekiller, high war chief of the Red Wing Nation. Now I am a dead man.

For whatever capricious reason, Power had abandoned him, his family, and his nation.

He dared not glance over his shoulder where what remained of his family crowded in the canoe bottom. He could feel his sister White Rain's body where it pressed against the back of his thighs. On White Rain's other side, his youngest sister, Soft Moon, huddled in misery, her head down. And, back to them all, Fire Cat's mother, Matron Red Wing, sat disconsolately, hands bound behind her. Her agonized stare remained fixed on the north as it vanished behind the river's forest-lined loops. Everything they had lived, dreamed, and hoped now receded as the current and the strong paddlers rushed them inevitably toward the south. Toward Cahokia . . . and death.

Fire Cat had only a foggy memory of the days since the Morning Star's warriors had taken them by complete surprise. Dazed by the impossible, his memory was a confusion of sunrises, shivering and endless nights, disconnected events, and half-remembered images.

He still wasn't sure how the Morning Star's warriors had accomplished the impossible feat of moving several thousand battle-hardened veterans upriver without raising an alarm. Or how—even more impossibly—the thousands had penetrated Red Wing town's palisades undetected that last fateful night.

Behind the soothing darkness of his closed eyelids, he relived that terrible moment. He'd been sound asleep. Where could a man feel more safe than in his own bedroom in the Red Wing palace atop its mound, his wife's warm body snuggled against him?

The impact of hard bodies as they slammed him down into the bedding had shocked him awake. His startled yelp rang in his ears. He'd frozen in that instant of confused disbelief. The screams of his second wife, False Dawn, tore at his memory as freshly as when she'd been dragged, clawing frantically at the blankets, from their bed.

Fire Cat had struggled for all he was worth, bellowing, trying to strike out as callused hands grasped his arms, legs, and head. Through the fog of his memory, the number of assailants remained a mystery. Five of them? Perhaps six or more? Who knew?

All he'd glimpsed in the darkness was shadowy arms, shoulders, and elbows as he was grabbed by the hair, his head pulled back. A leather wad was thrust into his mouth. Then a hide sack had been dropped over his head. They'd ripped the blanket away, wrenched his arms back, and bound them. The mass of their bodies proved too much to dislodge; his thrashing legs had been tied.

They'd borne him silently from his room. He'd heard False Dawn's pleading and whimpering as they'd carried him across the matting in the main room, out into the night, and down the wooden stairs.

No sound of his first wife, New Fall Moon, or their two infant children had come to his ears. All he'd heard was the elated murmurings of his captors. He'd felt only his body bouncing as they bore him away into the night.

Through it all, his souls had quaked with a panic and fear like nothing he'd ever known.

They had dropped him in this canoe, followed by the gritted order, "Do not resist. If you do, your family will be killed. Do you understand?"

Somehow, shaking with terror, he'd managed to nod. Only upon hearing the bitter weeping of his sisters did he begin to understand the extent of the tragedy.

"So," a man had said softly, "that's the great Red Wing Fire Cat? The one they call twelvekiller? The scourge of the north? Doesn't look like much, does he?"

"Not bound up like a puppy fit for a starving dirt-farmer's stewpot, he doesn't," another answered.

"Quiet, all of you," a commanding voice growled. "Anyone who could destroy War Chief Makes Three and the Morning Star's squadrons so effortlessly isn't to be taken lightly."

Someone cleared his throat and said, "It would be worth it to be there when the Lady Night Shadow Star gets her hands on him. When she heard Makes Three had been killed . . . Well, it's said she's been crazy with grief ever since."

"The lady Night Shadow Star deeply and truly loved her husband."

"Some people say she was unnaturally attached to him. Like an obsession. Devotion like that isn't healthy."

The commander growled, "Shut up. All of you. We're not out of this yet."

And then, moments later, the voice had announced, "Here come the others. They have the Matron."

Not ten heartbeats had passed before Fire Cat felt his mother's body dropped in beside him. Then the voice ordered, "Take them to the Morning Star."

The sick fear in Fire Cat's gut had left him nauseous. The Morning Star's forces had taken Red Wing town, and in doing so, had crushed the last bastion of Petaga's descendants.

Fire Cat's Red Wing Clan had its origins in Cahokia, but his ancestors had fled two generations ago after the defeat of High Chief Petaga's Moon Moiety in a terrible civil war.

Being followers of Petaga and the terrifying priestess Lichen, Fire Cat's ancestors had escaped northward up the river. Far beyond the reach of Cahokia, they had established Red Wing town, carved it out of virgin wilderness. Despite those first tenuous years of starvation, warfare with the local Oneota tribesmen, and brutal winters, they'd survived.

Then, everything had changed when the Morning Star had blazed for nearly a moon's time in the midday sky. Borne by Traders, the miraculous story filtered up the river. At Cahokia—it was said—the Four Winds clan had attempted, and achieved, the impossible: They had resurrected the souls of the Hero Twin, Morning Star, into the body of a living man! It had been accomplished at great cost. Calling a soul—especially one so exalted—from the Sky World required that something had to be sacrificed to maintain balance between the Sky World and earth. Grisly reports of the elaborate ritual told of tens of young women who had been clubbed, strangled, or bled to death before being deposited in a mass grave—all offerings to the Powers of the Sky World to atone for the "borrowing" of Morning Star's celestial presence.

All of Red Wing town had scoffed at the wild tales. People didn't just summon a hero's Spirit soul to fill a human body! Ridiculous! This was but one more trick perpetrated by the evil Four Winds Clan on the gullible people of Cahokia.

How—the Red Wing had asked—could a mortal body hope to contain the life-soul of a supernatural hero as Powerful as Morning Star?

It had to be fraud, a hoax perpetrated to concentrate and solidify the Four Winds' hold on volatile Cahokia with its fractious politics.

Over the years even more stories made their way upriver—tales of the massive leveling and rebuilding of the old town, of thousands upon thousands of pilgrims, all picking up pots, packs, and portables, and moving from distant lands to Cahokia to bask in the presence of the living god.

When Fire Cat had been a boy, the first sign of trouble came when River-Washed-Mountain—one of the upper river's landmarks a day's travel south of Red Wing town—was claimed by Cahokia as an outpost.

"A base from which the blasphemous dogs can launch attacks against us!" Fire Cat's uncle had cried. And forthwith, an assault was planned and launched, overwhelming the small party of Cahokians who'd begun clearing land on the craggy hill that jutted up from the river.

Blood forever calls for vengeance. Over the years, Red Wing town had beaten off various attacks. Sometimes years would pass before some slight would goad the so-called "Morning Star" to send his forces north again. Then had come word that the god's human body had died. All of Cahokia was said to be in mourning.

"At least that's over!" Uncle had proclaimed with relief.

Until the news burned its way upriver the following spring: The soul of Morning Star had been resurrected yet again. This time in Chunkey Boy. And, by so doing, the hero was now guaranteed immortality. His human bodies might age and die, but Four Winds Clan would always have another ready to act as host to the god's souls.

The night of his capture Fire Cat had heard the warriors clambering into the canoe, wooden oars clunking as they were picked up. Men chuckled among themselves, soft voices laden with the rich delight of victory.

Nothing could mistake the sensation of a canoe being pushed off, or the rocking as it shifted under the weight of warriors as the last of them leaped aboard, water trickling from their feet.

"Upon your lives," the voice had called from shore, "you'd better deliver all four of them to the Morning Star!"

Someone had called back from the canoe, "You think *we'd* disappoint the Morning Star? They shall be delivered alive, Spotted Wrist, upon our honor!"

Spotted Wrist! Fire Cat had longed to face the renowned Cahokian war chief, but in his fantasies it had been in battle. There, Fire Cat imagined they would fight, war club to war club, shield to shield, dodging, dancing, slashing, and circling. And in the end, Fire Cat had always known he'd strike the Morning Star's greatest war chief down. He'd place his foot on Spotted Wrist's neck, and cave in his skull with one, final, well-placed blow.

Fool!

When the end finally came, he'd never even cast eyes on his formidable adversary. Unless, of course, the war chief had been one among the jumble of elbows, shoulders, and hands in that mad melee atop his bed.

My fault. All my fault.

White Rain shifted in the cramped canoe and whimpered in pain. Her sudden movement jerked Fire Cat's bound wrists back, wrenching his arms. To keep from crying out, he ground his teeth and stared dully at the wood grain so close before him.

I am taken. Prisoner of the Morning Star.

He considered the nameless warrior's words: *"It would be worth it to be there when Lady Night Shadow Star gets her hands on him."*

She was the eldest of the Morning Star's sisters. Heir to the matronship of the Four Winds Clan. She was said to be a great beauty, a tempestuous young woman of remarkable abilities and passions.

"And I killed her husband," Fire Cat mouthed the words.

She and the Morning Star would be waiting.

The black bowl—known as a well pot—brimmed with water. The exterior had been polished until its deep luster reflected the world around it. The well pot sat cushioned on a black-panther hide atop a four-sided altar that rose from the floor. Night Shadow Star's altar stood in her personal quarters, a separate room in the rear of her palace.

She lowered herself before the well pot; her triangular face and naked body reflected disproportionately in the bowl's mirror-black surface. The intricately woven cattail mat she knelt upon ate into her unprotected knees. As she bowed her head above the bowl, raven waves of hair slipped from her bare back and slid across her arms like a silken veil that served to exclude the world.

"Sister Datura, I beseech you. Know the longing in my souls. Hear the echoes of love that resonate from my empty heart. Hollow. Feel the aching want in my womb, the longing in my sheath. All that makes me a woman is desolate. Look into my souls, Sister. See the shattered memories . . . the hope and warmth of my husband's smile torn away forever. Hear the words he once spoke to me, overflowing with love and concern. See his face, gone dead and cold. Feel the ghost of his touch slide across my skin. The warmth of his body next to mine is nothing more than the bitter cold of an endless and frozen winter.

"Hear me, Sister. Fill me with the essence of your Dance. I am blind. Allow me to see between the worlds of the living and dead. Enfold me in your arms, dear Sister. Hold me. Sway with me. Free my souls to journey to him, past or present, here or there."

She swallowed in her misery. "All is hollow and blackness."

The visions had grown worse since his death: flickers of movement at the corner of her eye; faint whispers that she alone heard. Voices of Power that spoke out of thin air. When she turned, she'd find no one there. She had stopped asking her house staff if they, too, had heard. Their wary glances in one another's directions had left her feeling foolish. Her people were already leery of her. More than once she'd lashed out at them in her grief.

Husband? You helped me, kept the voices in check. You never mocked me. I need you to help me understand.

She reached down, her slender fingers dipping paste from a small ceramic bowl that rested beside her right knee. Thick with crushed datura seeds, and the consistency of mud, the paste chilled her fingers. Slowly, carefully, she began massaging the mixture into her temples. As she did, she hummed a lilting melody, waiting for Sister Datura's Dance to slip around her like a protective cloak. Waiting for the freedom that would allow her to float away from this world and down through the well pot's portal into the Underworld. Down, until she could feel her husband's muscular arms around her. A place where she could once again look into his sparkling dark eyes. Where she could seek the endless reassurance of his smile. Soon now, he would speak to her again; his voice would be rich and melodious as he chastised her for such silliness.

She could love him again, and be loved.

The grief would evaporate; the pain would shimmer away into memory. Her souls would spring to life, wrapping and entwining themselves in his. And they would dance, laugh, and wind their bodies together for as long as Sister Datura allowed.

The voices and the flickers of people and things that appeared and disappeared at the edge of her vision would finally fade away.

The first tendrils of ecstasy began to filter through Night Shadow Star's nerves, soothing her anguished souls. Only then did she lean forward and stare down into the dark recesses of the well pot.

Well pots were crafted as symbolic re-creations of the world, the upper shoulder and rim representing the Sky World with its four winds. The opening above the rim exposed the contents as they would be viewed by *Hungo Ahuito,* the great two-headed eagle that saw all things as it looked in the four directions. The curve below the bowl's shoulders— now filled with water like its earthly counterpart—represented the Underworld, and it was through this portal that Sister Datura's Power carried her.

The reflection of her face on the still water wavered, and her gaze traveled down through the darkness, passing from this world into the eternal. . . .

Like a reflection, his face formed in the dark haze, the line of his chin growing firm. The familiar nose coalesced from nothingness, nostrils but dots of black. Flickers of light merged in the form of his eyes. Patterns of lines recreated the tattoos that had decorated his cheeks and forehead.

"Hello, my love," she whispered. "I have missed you so."

"You shouldn't do this," he told her softly. *"It only adds to your pain."*

"I can't help it. I need you."

"You have to be stronger than this."

"You are my strength, husband."

"I am dead, my beloved." His loving expression shifted to one of concern. *"Sending your souls into the Underworld is dangerous. He'll use me as a way to lure you—"*

"I have no reason to live without you, husband. And in Sister Datura's arms, I shall Dance to you so that we can be together. Nothing will ever part us again."

She mustered the smile she'd always resorted to when he chided her. "Come, husband. Reach out. Embrace me. I want you to pull me inside you, make you one with me."

"Do you understand the risks? Piasa may be closer than you know. He's tricky, calculating. To sink his fangs into a Four Winds Clan woman? You'd become his, Night Shadow Star, a pawn in his game of death."

"I *don't* care! Without you, I have nothing."

She saw him relent, as he always had. In all their life together, he'd never denied her.

"Is this your wish?"

"Oh, yes. Draw me to you, devour me, husband." Her voice broke. "I don't want to be *alone.*"

"Even at risk of the Piasa—"

She almost sobbed. "I can't *stand* the loneliness. . . . The grief and pain . . ."

Eyes closed, mouth open, her heart beginning to dance in her chest, she slipped her naked arms around the smooth sides of the bowl, and shuddered as his souls slipped around hers. In that instant, her body exploded with joy.

"Then you have nothing to lose," a strange voice boomed in her head.

Startled, she opened her eyes and stared into a nightmare. The yellow-eyed gaze of a great panther burned into hers. Black and empty it seemed to swell and suck at her. Each burning yellow eye was surrounded by the three-forked design of the Underworld. Furry round ears strained forward, and the beast's pink nose almost touched hers. Even as she gaped in horror, those bristly whiskers flared, and the mouth opened wide to expose gleaming white fangs.

Before she could fill her lungs for a scream, the terrible beast shot forward; the wide mouth snapped down on her head. Pain speared her as needle-sharp teeth pierced through scalp and bone. Like knives they drove into her brain, stabbed into her mouth and nose. Shrieking in agony and terror, she heard as well as felt her skull sheering between those terrible teeth.

And then came blackness, empty, impenetrable blackness . . .

Her limp body collapsed onto the well pot. The delicate and thin-walled bowl crushed under her weight. Then she slipped down the water-soaked panther hide and sprawled comatose on the floor.

Three

Riding atop her litter at the head of her small retinue of servants, Clan Keeper Blue Heron was carried across Cahokia's great plaza. From her swaying perch she squinted up at the spring sun. For the moment it burned hot enough to raise a sheen of perspiration beneath her armpits and where her white-and-red-striped feather cape hung over her shoulders.

She'd been advised to have the slaves bring her sun shade, an affair crafted from shaved buffalo-calf hide atop poles that could be extended to shelter her.

Probably should have listened, she thought bitterly. But her mind had been absorbed with the problem of her niece, the lady Night Shadow Star. With the exception of the occasional oddity when she'd respond to a voice that wasn't there, or suddenly glance off to the side and frown as if she'd seen a movement no one else did, the young woman had been progressing nicely—a logical successor to leadership should anything unexpected happen to her aunt, Matron Wind.

Until Makes Three was killed last fall.

It's not like she's the first woman to ever lose the man she loved.

Blue Heron made a face. Pus and blood! As if she'd know. For a time in her life she'd gone through husbands at the rate of one or more a year. A few had been able to stand her for less than a moon before they'd picked up their belongings and walked out of her house.

She squinted at the sun again as her litter swayed in time to the porters' gait. Enough fluffy patches of cloud soared over Cahokia to provide just a taste of relief before they marched on across the pale blue sky. Shadows moved lazily below them, slanting through the smoke-hazy air that forever cloaked the city. She raised her hand to block the blinding light, and estimated the angle. From long practice she guessed she had another five hands before it slipped behind the high bluffs west of the river. Time enough.

Blue Heron tapped her long brown fingers on the litter arms, scowling across the plaza in the direction of Night Shadow Star's tall wedge-roofed palace. What silliness possessed the woman? She'd been sent no less than three messengers and not a reply in return!

"So help me, Night Shadow Star," she threatened under her breath, "if you're moping around, feeling sorry for yourself, I'll give you some real grief."

She took a deep breath. The breeze came from the southwest, carrying the damp scents of wood smoke, cooking corn, and boiling meat. Spring grass, so recently crushed by the stickball games that had culminated the Planting Ceremony, gave off its characteristic odor.

Her porters avoided the carefully manicured chunkey courts where young boys sprinkled the clay with water. They carefully tamped down the old lance impacts with their bare feet before they rolled the surface smooth with a perfect cylinder of oak log. When finished they would either sift clean white or red sand over the surface depending on the court. This, too, would be carefully smoothed to eliminate the least imperfection.

These were the Morning Star's personal chunkey courts and the finest in the world. The gravity with which the boys worked was almost comical to her.

She cast a sidelong glance up at the Morning Star's palace where it rose skyward atop the great black mound. As usual, a crowd thronged at the base of the stairs leading up the south-facing ramp. The giant construction dominated the northern edge of the plaza. Behind the walls of the first terrace, the second rose against the northern horizon; its white-walled palisade was studded with intricately carved and painted guardian posts. Each depicted and concentrated the Power of one of the Spirit Animals from the Creation. Among them were Crawfish, Vulture, Eagle, Mother Spider, Horned Serpent, and the Piasa. There, too, were the Spirit creatures of war: Falcon, Snapping Turtle, Woodpecker, and Rattlesnake.

The great lightning-scarred World Tree pole—the highest point in

Cahokia—rose like a lance into the sky. Behind it, the roof of Morning Star's palace with its graying thatch cut the heavens like a great ax. Even as she watched, she could make out tiny figures of men suspended on ropes as they worked on the thatch. Given the immense height of the palace, its huge wedge of roof was constantly savaged by wind and storm.

On the stairways a steady stream of people, like brown dots, were coming and going. Here and there a speck of color denoted a noble or high-ranking individual. She grunted to herself at the similarity to an ant pile.

"Did you think of something, Elder?" Smooth Pebble, her aide asked. She was *berdache,* a woman born into a man's body. A distant cousin, Smooth Pebble had come to Blue Heron's attention more than two-tens of winters ago and had worked her way up to become Blue Heron's most valued advisor, administrator, and confidant. Now in her forties, Smooth Pebble wore her graying hair in a bun pinned at the back of her head with an ornate shell comb. A black skirt embroidered with chevrons, bits of mica, and shell hung from her too-narrow hips. An opossum cloak was thrown back on her broad shoulders out of respect for the warm temperatures.

"No," Blue Heron answered. "We've just enough time to fetch Night Shadow Star. May Horned Serpent take us if we're late to the Morning Star's reception. It's that new emissary from Yellow Star Mounds. Some war chief, what the Kadohadacho calls an *amayxoyo.* Frantic Lightning is his name."

"Assuming Night Shadow Star has remembered the reception," Notched Cane grumbled. He, too, was a cousin "appointed" to her by an errant relative who'd committed one too many infractions. Blue Heron had originally kept him as a hostage, but had come to rely on his skills at keeping her house in order. The man had a way with the slaves, somehow ensured that food—agreeable to her tastes and properly cooked—was on hand, swept the place clean, and managed to keep the bedding, matting, and roof in repair. Under his watchful eye, the fires always had an ample supply of wood, and the water pots were filled.

"Watch your tongue, old friend," she warned. Then she shot Clay Ball and Fire Temper, her two guards, a meaningful, slit-eyed glance. Both warriors responded with the slightest of nods. Over the years they'd learned to keep things to themselves. Especially *family* concerns. Like Night Shadow Star hearing and seeing things that weren't there.

Two Beads cleared his throat suggestively, nodding toward the tall, flat-topped pyramid that rose just to the northwest of the chunkey

courts and on the other side of the Avenue of the Sun, the thoroughfare that marked the great plaza's northern boundary. Atop it stood
the clay-plastered walls of Night Shadow Star's thatch-roofed palace.
It's supporting mound dominated the northwest corner of the great
plaza, while the Wind Clan House itself lay off to the west, in line with
the Great Mound and separated from Night Shadow Star's by the Western Plaza. The *Tonka'tzi's* imposing palace on its larger mound stood
midway down the western edge of the plaza. There, Blue Heron's elder brother, Red Warrior, resided in opulence. His front step provided
him with a perfect vantage to watch activities in the plaza.

Blue Heron remained painfully aware of Two Beads' dour expression. Also in his forties, toothless, and skinny, he served as her recorder. Among his duties he saw to the dispatch of messengers, read
and produced bead mats, and ensured that she was updated on events,
comings and goings, and generally informed.

"Blood and pus," Blue Heron muttered as she inspected Night
Shadow Star's palace. No doubt about it, her niece's entire household
was lounging on the veranda, shaded as it was by the sloping extension
of the roof. Some of Night Shadow Star's servants, like Blue Heron's,
were Four Winds Clan who had been volunteered or conscripted into
service. The others were slaves.

At Blue Heron's approach they began to rise, watching her with
worried eyes. The way they stood, shoulders slumped, hands fidgeting, feet shuffling, all suggested trouble.

Blue Heron gave a hand signal, and her porters lowered her carefully to the ground. She rose from the litter chair and climbed the
wooden steps leading up the ramp on the mound's eastern side; her
breath began to labor as she neared the top. She felt one of the squared
timbers rock underfoot.

"Watch that one." She pointed. Not good. The old Night Shadow
Star had never allowed *anything* to fall into disrepair.

As she cleared the top and stepped onto the flat before the palace,
Night Shadow Star's household staff looked everywhere but at her,
dusting off skirts and blankets as they coughed nervously and tried to
hide embarrassment.

To Smooth Pebble, she said, "Stay here."

"Yes, Clan Keeper."

She fixed on Field Green, Night Shadow Star's aide, and barked,
"That loose step needs fixed. See to it."

"Yes, Clan Keeper." The woman lowered her eyes. "Lady Night
Shadow Star asked me to inform you that she's indisposed to receive—"

"She'll see me now."

"But, Clan Keeper, I can't just—"

"Do you wish to pick a quarrel with me, Field Green?"

"I . . . I . . ." The woman's mouth opened and closed like that of a suffocating fish.

"Out of my way." Blue Heron marched past her, hardly noticing the woman's smudged black skirt or the panic in her eyes.

At sight of the two new guardian posts, Blue Heron stopped short; a cold fear sent a shiver down her spine. Carvings of Horned Serpent and Piasa stood just out from the veranda and to either side of the entrance. Each was immaculately sculpted and painted; both stared out through shell-inlaid eyes. The Underworld Spirits regarded Blue Heron with malevolence. Horned Serpent's sinuous body had been rendered in rainbow-colored scales, his head adorned with forked antlers painted scarlet.

Piasa's face mimicked that of a screaming cougar. The three-forked-eye design—indicative of his Underworld home—surrounded two fierce yellow eyes. A diamond-patterned snake's tail culminated in rattles and had been affixed to the creature's rump. Two raking arms were mounted on the front, ending in grasping, yellow-painted eagle's feet with curving black talons.

What possessed Night Shadow Star? These were *Underworld* beings! Four Winds Clan was affiliated with the Sky World. Unless Night Shadow Star had cleared this with the Morning Star, their presence acted like a slap in the face to the living god.

She turned again to Field Green. "When were Sky Eagle and Falcon removed and replaced with these?"

"Just yesterday, Clan Keeper. My mistress ordered it after seeing these carvings at the landing a couple of days past while on a journey back from Evening Star town."

Blue Heron gave the Piasa a glare of disapproval. The lord of the Underworld was a Spirit of darkness, water, and death. She stepped up on the porch matting, and several of Night Shadow Star's slaves scampered to open the wooden-plank door with its falcon—surrounded by the swirls of the four winds—artfully engraved in the wood. That, at least, hadn't been replaced, but the presence of sky Power in such close proximity to the Piasa and Horned Serpent jarred Blue Heron's sense of order.

As Blue Heron stepped into the main room, it took a moment for her eyes to adjust to the gloom. Second only to Morning Star's palace itself, this was the second most opulent structure in Cahokia—even outclassing *tonka'tzi* Red Warrior's palace, and the Four Winds' clan house where her sister Matron Wind held court. The cane matting that covered the floor was a one-piece weaving done in intricate patterns and design. Along the walls were benches that served both for seating and sleeping. Each was composed of hand-carved wooden frames topped with cattail-down-stuffed cushions covered with buffalo, panther, bear, and finely tanned deer and elk hides. The walls were hung with carved reliefs of Falcon, Eagle, and Morning Star. Clawing Panther designs were gilded in copper and inset with shell and dark wood. War trophies including bows, shields, human skulls, and other memorabilia hung between the carvings. A low fire burned in the central hearth, and behind it stood the raised clay platform topped with its detail-carved litter where Night Shadow Star conducted audiences. A lower rise of clay marked the one-time seat of Makes Three. The bear hides that covered it looked gray with dust.

He's been dead for over six moons now. Why hasn't she thrown them out?

Blue Heron strode across the room and passed through the single doorway that led into the back. Storerooms could be accessed by doors to the right and left, but what concerned her was the altar built just back from the rear wall. Several crushed sherds from the remains of a gleaming black well pot remained atop the panther-hide-covered pillar.

Night Shadow Star sprawled on the floor before it, her naked body unadorned by so much as a bracelet or gorget. Her hair spilled over the matting like a midnight wave. The little brown pot beside her had been rolled onto its side, a thick tongue of paste having leaked onto the matting.

Blue Heron paused as she took it all in, her analytical eyes missing nothing. Then she bent down, lifted the little brown pot, and sniffed.

"Fire and lightning, girl, what have you done?"

Blue Heron crouched and placed her hand over the young woman's mouth and nose, watching as the lungs began to starve and heave.

"At least you're alive."

Extending her callused hand, Blue Heron twisted a fistful of glistening black hair and lifted until Night Shadow Star's face was exposed. Blue Heron slapped her niece across the cheek. Then again, and again, until Night Shadow Star groaned and weakly extended one of her long brown legs.

Blue Heron sniffed, caught the acrid scent of urine, and—her eyes finally adjusting—identified the stain on the matting as vomit. She sighed. "Look at you. Pitiful."

"Husband?" Night Shadow Star mewed.

"Dead, you idiot. Come on. Wake up. The Morning Star specifically asked that you be at Council."

"Can't," she whispered. "Piasa . . . I've agreed . . ."

A cold shiver ran through Blue Heron. "The Water Panther is no Spirit to be playing with, girl. Not even for one such as you. Tell me your souls haven't done something foolish."

Even as Blue Heron said it, Night Shadow Star's body spasmed. The young woman jerked upright, eyes popping open. Blue Heron stepped back, a hand held up reflexively.

Night Shadow Star's head turned, her wide dark eyes gleaming in a feral, catlike manner. In a sibilant voice that wasn't Night Shadow Star's she said, "You're too late, old woman. The bargain is made."

Blue Heron could barely breathe. Finally she managed to croak, "Mud and slime! Niece? Was that really you?"

But beautiful Night Shadow Star had collapsed onto her back, hair spilled in an inky swirl. Her high breasts continued to rise and fall as if her lungs were starved for air. The dark triangle of her pubic hair vanished as she crossed her legs and writhed.

Blue Heron staggered back, stumbled through the main room and out into the reassuring light of day. To Smooth Pebble, she called, "Quick. Fetch Rides-the-Lightning. We need the earth clans' priest here now! *Run!*"

The Spider

*E*verything in Creation is related. I have spent years in careful study of the world around me. Some thought me mad as I crawled around the forest floor, my eyes even with the leaf mat. The fools had no idea what I was learning. Mostly I watched the spiders as they hunted each other.

Killing another spider, you see, is a most dangerous and deadly game. And some play it better than others. Will you eat, or be eaten?

The successful ones were those who blended with the background, becoming essentially invisible, patient, and cunning. A spider who looked like but another bit of forest duff would remain motionless, undetected as his prey passed heedless within a finger's breadth. Only when the hunted had passed, its fangs sheathed, and believing itself safe, did the hidden hunter pounce.

You see, the spider who hunts other spiders must strike from concealment. He must act when least expected, and attack from an unanticipated direction. His first bite must be lethal.

But the most important rule of all: the victim, just as agile and venomous, must never know it is being hunted.

I smile crookedly as I watch the Four Winds Clan Keeper's litter-chair approach. The ornate seat is borne upon the shoulders of strong young men. And following is Blue Heron's retinue: Old Smooth Pebble, Notched Cane, Two Beads, and her longtime guards, Clay Bell and Fire Temper.

For an instant, nothing seems to have changed. The intervening years *might not have passed, perhaps being nothing more than a bizarre dream or vision spun of my imagination.*

And then reality snaps back with the clarity and impact of a striking stone maul. I feel the rage. Injustice and pain flood back into me.

Careful. In this moment, at this place, you are hunting another spider—and perhaps the most dangerous of them all!

The crowd milling at the base of the Morning Star's black-sided mound parts for Keeper Blue Heron; people are touching their foreheads and respectfully bowing.

Once more the hunting spider that I am, I, too, act with humility. Carefully I force the hunger from my gaze, replacing it with worshipful respect lest her eyes accidently meet mine. I am becoming one with the forest litter, my true nature must freeze, still and invisible to my prey.

Blue Heron is lowered to the ground before the sloping ramp that leads up to the first walled terrace of the Morning Star's great pyramid. Her servants offer a hand and help the Keeper to her feet. Her two guards watch with bored eyes—a fact that makes me smile in anticipation.

The great Avenue of the Sun that runs east-west at the base of the mound is crowded, and I move through the dullards, drawing only the attention my disguise should warrant. The usual collection of Traders, food vendors, and trinket-barterers display their wares. A number of previously emptied litters have been placed out of the way. Their carriers are seated where the mound's sloping sides meet the avenue in a sharp angle. The black clay here has been smoothed to a perfect crease, and though the lounging porters squat on their heels, none would dare recline on the Morning Star's sacred slope.

To avoid drawing attention as I reach the bottom of the ramp staircase, I drop to one knee and fiddle with my sandal, as if having trouble with one of the bass-wood cord ties. Dressed as I am in a noble's wardrobe, my face is painted a most striking blue; a copper-falcon headpiece and scalp bundle are affixed to my tightly wrapped hair. I look like just another elegantly clad lord summoned to receive the embassy that has just arrived from the Yellow Star nation.

This fills me with delicious irony. I've never liked Frantic Lightning Mankiller, the Kadohadacho's, or Supreme Chief's, spoiled nephew. This cannot be serendipitous. Power is either teasing me or weaving some textile of its own that I cannot yet discern.

Blue Heron remains oblivious to my presence. The woman appears totally preoccupied as she resettles her cape and skirt. The expression on her face reflects a deep-seated worry.

She's hardly acting like the deadly shadow hunter I expected to stalk.

Which is worth considering. So far the vast throngs inhabiting Cahokia have allowed me complete anonymity and freedom to move and study my prey. A change of hairstyle, a different cloak, a dab of face paint, or any combination of the above, and I draw no more attention than any of the passersby. I have watched her from a distance for several days now.

The agitation the Clan Keeper barely hides has her off balance as she starts up the stairs. Normally she would glance around, catalog the faces and nod to those she knows. Her crafty eyes should be calculating and observant. This time her entire attention is focused on the stairway.

Whatever happened at Night Shadow Star's must have been important. But what? And how will it affect the fulfillment of my own aching love for the stunning Night Shadow Star?

I watched from the plaza when a runner was dispatched for the temple on the great plaza's southern end. In less than a finger's time, the renowned Earth People's priest Rides-the-Lightning had arrived on his litter. They'd carried him without ceremony up the stairs, and ushered him into Night Shadow Star's house.

Nor had the priest left before Blue Heron exited, wearily rubbed her face, and ordered herself carried to the Morning Star's great mound.

For the moment, I lose myself in concern over Night Shadow Star. She always was sensitive to things beyond this realm. Does she feel me? Does she whimper at the sucking emptiness of my devouring love?

With Blue Heron heading up the stairs, I've fiddled enough with my strap. Nodding to the guards at either side of the bottom step, I see that Blue Heron has disappeared through the first terrace gate.

Time enough. I start up the steps after my prey.

Passing into the tonka'tzi's *courtyard, I narrow my eyes and wonder just how close can I get.*

She is just up ahead of me, climbing slowly. Already I can see that she's breathing hard. And it's a long, long climb up into the Morning Star's sacred realm.

If she should misstep? Tumble and fall down the steep and unforgiving stairs . . . ?

Could it be that easy?

Four

Out of breath, Blue Heron almost staggered as she climbed the last of the steps that led to the highest level of the Great Mound. As Clan Keeper she could have been carried up in her litter. On the rare occasions when she'd given in to the "luxury" it had scared her half to death.

"Can I help you, Elder?" a voice, thick with Muskogee accent asked.

She placed a hand to her heaving chest and turned. The man, obviously a chief or some sort of high-ranking elite, was barely a step behind her; he had a hand out, as if to steady her should she totter. Even as she recoiled, the hand inoffensively withdrew.

A thick blue band had been painted like a mask over his nose and around his eyes. He was young, in his early twenties, with piercing dark eyes. A gray cape hung over his shoulders. While it looked nondescript from a distance, up close she could see it had been woven in an intricate geometric design. A copper falcon and scalp bundle were pinned in his long hair.

"I need to get out more often." She gestured absently at the remaining steps. "I used to sprint up this as a girl."

"Odd how the passing of winters changes things, isn't it?"

She almost frowned at the irony in his voice. "I don't believe that I know you."

"Tishu minko White Finger, Elder. Of the Raccoon Clan, of the

White Moiety. I come from Lightning Oak town, an emissary of my great uncle, Minko High Falcon, to pay his respects to the sacred Morning Star."

"Ah. I am Blue Heron, Keeper of the Four Winds Clan."

"I am both pleased and honored to make your acquaintance, Elder. Your reputation as a competent and capable leader is known far and wide."

He touched his forehead in deference and gestured her to precede him. She'd caught a whiff of the curious satisfaction he'd barely masked. Minko High Falcon had chosen his emissary well; the young man seemed almost too familiar in her presence.

Brushing him out of her mind, she bowed to the guardian posts at the top of the stairs. Her souls, however, remained knotted with worry over Night Shadow Star. That *had* been her niece, hadn't it? That booming and hollow voice was just the result of thirst, or perhaps the aftereffects of the datura loosening the young woman's throat and muscles?

Piss and blood in a pot! Only idiots fooled around with Sister Datura without supervision. If Night Shadow Star had been in search of a vision, why in *Hunga Ahuito*'s name hadn't she gone to Rides-the-Lightning and asked the old man to purify her, mix the potions, and lead her on a journey to the Underworlds? He, at least, had the training to do such things. But when the unwary and ignorant tried?

She shook her head, rasping out, "She's lucky to be alive."

Why didn't I let the porters carry me up?

She made a face as she glanced back at the long and steep stairs. She was too old to tumble down that. Others had, and all had broken bones. Some were crippled, others dead.

Breath back, she waited as the Muskogee tishu minko, White Finger, dropped to one knee and touched his forehead outside the gate.

Foreign he might be, but the young man has more reverence for our ways than we do. What does that say about the decline of Four Winds Clan?

After he'd risen and entered, she nodded to the tattooed guards standing to either side. Dressed in wooden armor, they held strung bows; quivers packed with arrows hung on their backs. The leather helmets encasing their heads were decorated with bright feathers. Their forelocks, sporting a single white bead in the middle, hung down almost to their noses.

Entering the gate, she found the courtyard crowded. Everyone had dressed in his or her best. The priests and conjurors were decked out in the symbols of their offices. Clan representatives wore white, red, and black tunics that denoted their affiliation, each sporting the clan totem to which they were subject. The matrons among them wore color-ful capes, beaded or quill-worked, furred, or feathered. These draped the women's shoulders, protection against the evening chill. Off to the side stood the engineers; each bore the symbolic stick-and-string, emblematic of their ability to survey.

In the center of the courtyard the giant, lightning-scarred, red-cedar pole jutted into the sky like a mighty lance. Blue Heron remembered the day it had been raised. A young woman—token of their respect for Old-Woman-Who-Never-Dies—had been sacrificed and buried at the base, a physical representation of First Woman who lived in her cave beneath the World Tree. The entire length of the pole bore carved images depicting scenes from Morning Star's storied life in the Beginning Times. At the bottom—facing east and carved in relief—was the figure of Old-Woman-Who-Never-Dies' daughter Corn Mother. She lay on her back, legs pulled up and spread as she gave birth to Morning Star. On the west was the depiction of her thoughtlessly tossing away her afterbirth. The Morning Star's twin brother, known as The Wild One, was depicted crawling out from the discarded tissue.

For some reason, White Finger stood before it, an amused smile on his blue-painted face.

Successive scenes depicting stories of the Hero Twins battling Spirit Creatures wound their way up the pole. In one they played chunkey against the giants who had killed their father, and won the giants' heads. At the very top had been carved Morning Star—fitted with eagle wings—as he looked toward the eastern sky. The sacred mace of office was clutched in his right hand, his father's severed head in the left. Burn scars from lightning only added to the pole's immense Power.

Behind it stood Morning Star's tall palace with its steeply pitched roof; it rose like a huge sky-splitting wedge. Atop the high center pole were affixed carved statues of Eagle looking to the east and west.

Nobles representing the various Houses of the Four Winds Clan crowded the small plaza. Representatives from the different nations were present, each dressed in the manner of his people. And there, too—at the Morning Star's invitation—were the clan leaders from the ever-influential Earth People clans.

She nodded to Matron Red Temple of the Fish Clan and endured the fawning smile from her brother, the obsequious Thin Otter. Like all of the Earth People clans, they remained matrilineal, all possessions being passed through the female line.

"You are looking well," a smooth voice announced from behind her, and she turned as Chief Right Hand, of the Deer Clan, touched his forehead respectfully. "A bit warm today, don't you think? The heat should germinate the seeds, and if we can just get a little rain . . . ?"

She shot him a smile, having never quite known what to do with Right Hand. Deer Clan had always been a supportive ally of the Four Winds Clan. Or perhaps "reliable" would be a better word to describe the handsome chief and his sister. Blue Heron looked around, asking, "And where is the Matron Corn Seed?"

"Slightly discomfited, Clan Keeper. A stomach ailment. Nothing that won't pass."

She studied his handsome face, oddly aware of his broad shoulders and narrow waist. The man had once been a crafty chunkey player, and no doubt remained faster on his feet than the strands of gray at his temples would indicate. Like so many, he, too, had once been interested in Night Shadow Star. "Please give the Matron my fondest wishes for a speedy recovery. If, however, she is not better in the next day, send word and I will have my personal healer attend to her."

The scar that marred his firm chin bent as he smiled. "I will communicate both your kind words and your generous offer, Clan Keeper."

She held his eyes for a moment longer, wondering how, after all the men she'd been through, she'd managed to miss at least a flirtation with Right Hand.

"Good to see you, Clan Keeper." Matron Soft Bread of the Hawk Clan stepped forward, touching her forehead. "Have you, by any chance, heard word of the attack on the heretics up north?"

"Not yet, good Matron. Let's see, your son commands a squadron under Spotted Wrist, doesn't he?"

"Yes, Clan Keeper. And given the history up there . . ." The white-haired woman barely stifled an uneasy smile. That she would tread so close to offending Blue Heron was but a sign of the tension that had run through the Earth People clans since the army left for the north. The move had been audacious, Spotted Wrist leaving a full moon before spring equinox in hopes of achieving surprise for his attack on Red Wing town.

"Remember, this is Spotted Wrist. As good as the other commanders have been, Spotted Wrist was under no illusions about the dangers."

Soft Bread glanced around, then leaned close, whispering, "Has the Morning Star had a vision? Some sign from the heavens? Power alerting him to the outcome?"

"Not to my knowledge." She tried to summon a faint resemblance to a conspiratorial smile. "You'll know as soon as I do, I promise."

"Thank you, Clan Keeper."

"And if you'll excuse me, I see Matron White Apron over there talking to Chief Flying Falcon. I need to discuss some business relating to Raccoon Clan with them."

Even as she escaped Soft Bread, Five Fists Mankiller, the Morning Star's palace chief, hurried forward. He was a big man, an old warrior with a face so intricately tattooed and faded it looked black. Years spent out in the weather had burned his scarred and grainy skin. The man's jaw hung crooked on his face, having been dislocated and broken so many times in stickball and war it had never properly healed. Decked in multicolored feathers from distant southern birds, he gave her a crooked grin.

"Clan Keeper? I was starting to panic."

Blue Heron ensured none of the Earth People were watching before she arched an eyebrow and replied, "Like camp dogs, the Earth People need occasional petting and special treats. Part of my job is to keep them sufficiently in their place, while dishing enough rewards to keep them enthusiastic and dedicated in their service to us."

"A task at which you are most adept, Clan Keeper." He lowered his voice, glancing around as if looking for someone. "And the Lady Night Shadow Star?"

"Indisposed," she rasped.

Five Fists' dark eyes narrowed the slightest bit. "That will displease the Morning Star."

She gave him a knowing look. "Old friend, I had her sent to Rides-the-Lightning. She's been in the datura. Keep that to yourself."

"Of course, Clan Keeper." He turned. "The Morning Star asked to see you. He's there, atop the observation post in the west palisade."

She glanced at the bastion, saw the lone figure atop it, and nodded. "Always more climbing, isn't there?"

"Only the most pure, chaste, and disciplined are borne to the Sky World on eagle's wings, Clan Keeper."

"Then any chance for me vanished before I reached the age of twelve."

Five Fists masked a chuckle and escorted her to the ladder that led up to the bastion. A group of soul fliers and sky priests—including Moon Gazer, the Morning Star's recorder—stood clustered at the ladder's base. These were the cherished servants and advisors to the living god. Each bowed respectfully to her.

Taking a deep breath, she grasped the uprights, placed a foot upon the first rung, and made her shaking legs lift her tired body to the high platform. She clambered through the hole in the floor, and sighed.

Morning Star didn't bother to reach down and offer a hand; he might have been oblivious. Instead he kept his gaze on the west, hands braced on the weathered tops of the palisade logs where they protruded through the plaster.

While his body had seen only twenty-six summers, he nevertheless looked older with his perfectly applied face paint. Of medium height, he had a muscular build, evidence of his prowess in chunkey and stick-ball.

This night he wore an immaculate white apron, its front rounded and narrowing to a point as it fell between his knees. A "soul bundle" had been attached to the fabric, and contained the life-souls of the dead men whose beaded forelocks decorated the bundle's outside. An eagle-feather cape, dyed a brilliant blue, hung from his shoulders. His hair was pulled tight in a bun at the back of his head. A small, copper-clad, wooden box containing a Spirit bundle had been tied atop his forehead. His ears were covered by triangular shell ornaments: long-nosed renditions of human faces representing the human heads Morning Star had worn for decoration in the Beginning Times.

While his face had been painted white, black forked-eye tattoos ran down his cheeks, and a black band, painted in charcoal grease paint, stretched from the angles of his jaw and across his mouth. His thoughtful eyes were pensive as he studied the far western horizon.

"She's not coming?" The words were clipped, barely containing the anger.

"No, my lord. And you don't want her here." Blue Heron hesitated, fear like little mice, scampered around in her gut. Very few individuals scared her like Morning Star did. "She's been in the Underworld, dancing with Sister Datura."

His mouth tightened. "I received a messenger today. Spotted Wrist has taken Red Wing town. He did it as he said he would. Bloodlessly. Matron Red Wing, her two daughters, and that wretched Fire Cat were taken alive. They should be delivered to me in the next couple of days. Perhaps she can work her grief out on their dying bodies."

"Perhaps." Blue Heron couldn't help but remember the possessed look Night Shadow Star had given her, or the blood-chilling words she'd issued in a stranger's voice.

"She is your concern, Clan Keeper. Her oddities grow worse by the moon. Bring her back in line before I am forced to take measures I would rather not."

She read the anger he worked so hard to subdue, and said nothing. The Morning Star had always shown a special preference for Night

Shadow Star. For reasons of his own he'd given her the magnificent palace at the Great Plaza's northwestern corner as a wedding gift in the first moon of his resurrection. No one, however, doubted that the god's patience had limits.

"Meanwhile, step up here." He waited while she climbed to her feet before he gave a slight gesture to the west and said, "What do you see?"

She declined to brace herself on the posts as he did, thinking that presumptuous. But stepping close, she peered over the high wall; the slope of the great pyramid dropped precipitously to the distant ground. The height was dizzying, and she fought the urge to step back. Then she followed his gaze to the west, past Night Shadow Star's palace-topped mound, past the Four Winds' clan house. Farther west, the circle of tall poles marking the great observatory cast long shadows as the sun hung low over the distant river. The setting sun shone in a swirl of reflected silver from the old oxbow lakes to the north and west.

In the yellowing twilight the air was smoke-hazed from the countless fires. Thousands of peak-roofed buildings stippled the floodplain—many perched atop the multitude of mounds that speckled their way toward the river—all silhouetted by the setting sun.

To the southwest, along the Avenue of the Sun that led to River Mounds City, an irregular string of temples and palaces pimpled the high ground along the margins of Marsh Elder Lake. The land around them was thickly dotted as if the thousands of buildings had been cast upon the land by the Sky Spirits themselves. Across the river, and tiny in the distance, rose the high mound-top palaces of Evening Star town.

"Do you see the three big clusters of tall mounds and palaces?" he asked.

"Of course." Each was governed by one of the subordinate Four Winds Clan "Houses"—a collection of lineages under the leadership of an appointed chief.

The dense concentration of taller palace-topped mounds on the eastern bank of the river called River Mounds City was ruled by Blue Heron's distant cousin War Duck. Many of the wealthiest families in Cahokia had built elegant palaces and temples in proximity to their warehouses there.

Across the water from River Mounds, the far-off bluff-top mound center that had once been known as Pretty Mounds rose in silhouetted black humps against the sunset sky. Morning Star had renamed it Evening Star town in reminder of his celestial victory over the "female" west. Evening Star town was ruled by yet another Four Winds

House, this one supposedly under the authority of Chief High Dance, though his much-more-capable sister Columella remained the real power. Blue Heron's marriage to High Dance had proved to be one of her more spectacular failures.

Turning her eyes on the hazy south, she could see the Avenue of the Moon, a raised causeway that ran straight south from the twin mounds at the base of the Great Plaza, to the distant Rattlesnake Mounds, before angling south-southeast. Through the smoke-filled and damp air Blue Heron could barely make out Horned Serpent City, the Avenue of the Moon's terminus. The lord there was called Green Chunkey; he'd married an even more distant cousin named Red Shawl Woman. The town had originally been known as Quill Dog, but Morning Star, seeing parallels in Cahokia's construction with the celestial world, had renamed it in honor of Horned Serpent's constellation in the southern summer night.

And in the interim were the closely packed settlements of the Earth People, the matrilineal clans of old Cahokia consisting of the more prominent Deer Clan, Hawk Clan, Panther Clan, Bear Clan, and Fish Clan. Sprinkled among them were a few lesser Clans, and around them, in even greater numbers were the tens of thousands of immigrants—the dirt farmers and foreigners who'd crowded into the city after the resurrection of the Morning Star.

Blue Heron cautiously asked, "Why, specifically, did you bring me up here?"

"I had a dream last night. One filled with terror, death, and suffering. In it a shapeless blackness stalked the night, walking through walls as if it were no more solid than smoke. The thing had only one very long, slim arm, and a narrow hand with but one finger. It was tipped not with a fingernail, but a thin and barely curved claw. I never saw the creature, only its shadow. As it passed over sleeping people, it seemed to trace that wicked-looking claw across their skin. The action was so delicate, the way a lover slips a fingertip across his mate's skin. But where it traced, black blood, pus, and corruption welled in its wake." He paused. "In the end, the earth ruptured, water blasting upward as fire spiraled down from the sky and bored into the earth. Great gouts of flame, lightning, and water like horrendous tornados ripped the world into pieces."

"A grim dream, great Lord."

Morning Star's face remained expressionless. "What is the greatest threat we face, Clan Keeper?"

Unsure of his motives, she asked, "The wild nations to the north?

Or perhaps those in the southeast? The Spirit Beings of the Underworld refusing to call the rains? A revolt among the immigrant dirt farmers? Most of the ignorant clods can't so much as speak a word of our language. Half of the Houses' time is spent keeping them from murdering each other."

"Refocus the eye of your soul to that which is nearer your heart."

"I don't understand."

"Seek the most destructive of human passions. That which consumes most of your energies as Clan Keeper."

"The factions within the Four Winds Clan?"

"Ah, and what drives those factions?"

"Ambition," she snorted irritably. "But they'd never act against you, great Lord."

"Directly? Of course not. But when they look across the magnificence of Cahokia, what do they see? We've unleashed a dangerous new Power, Keeper. I pray that we all do not find ourselves riding those burning whirlwinds in my dreams."

Blue Heron took a breath and shivered. "Have you heard something I have not?"

"You are most talented, Keeper." His voice was almost a whisper. "For the most part, you've been able to play one House against another. Often, just the suggestion of a threat is all you need to keep someone in line. Your kinsmen, however, are only human. I'm constantly surprised that your comprehensive network of informants provides just the right bit of salacious information to hold over a person's head. When it doesn't, exile to one of the colonies is employed. Other times simple bribery is effective. On the rare occasions when your intimidations fail, I'm aware that you have no qualms about assassination. You were chosen, after all, for the position of Keeper because of your devious mind."

Blue Heron fought to hide her building terror. "If I have committed some offense, great Lord, I swear, it was by accident. I've never purposely acted against your—"

"You misinterpret my concern," he said softly. "The astronomers at the great observatory have noted disturbing signs in the stars. You were but a child when Petaga was overthrown and I was first resurrected. Do you recall why Four Winds Clan attempted something so audacious?"

"To bring order," she answered automatically. "To stop the constant warfare between the major clans. Petaga only gained ascendance after he overthrew Tharon. Even with the great Dreamer Lichen's support, Petaga couldn't stop the petty bickering that erupted in the war where Four Winds Clan rose to prominence."

She gestured at the sprawling city. "And when your souls were resurrected in human form, Cahokia was reborn. Old Cahokia was leveled and rebuilt under your direction to become a suitable home for your earthly presence."

"An undertaking begun when I occupied my predecessor's body." He referred to his first resurrection—the remarkable ceremony that had reincarnated the god's life-soul into Black Tail's body. Black Tail's body, however, had died four years ago. Immediate action had been taken to ensure that Morning Star's essence was resurrected in this, her nephew Chunkey Boy's, body. She needed only to glance off to the west, to the great knife-ridged mound that held Grandfather Black Tail's body along with his kinsmen, servants, and five tens of sacrificed young women.

"Keeper, if your lineage could affect the miracle of placing me in a human body, why, then could not others?"

She swallowed hard. "You think that was the dream's portent?"

"Perhaps," he said absently, his eyes on the red glare of sunset. "That the specter passes through walls and stalks where it will worries me. That it is misshapen hints that it comes in a form we will not recognize, and may not know how to defeat. I called you up here to warn you. Something, some twisted power, has come to Cahokia and bears us ill. Death slips through the darkness, Keeper."

"I'll employ every effort to stop it, great Lord."

He smiled wistfully, the action disfiguring the black stripe painted across his mouth. "Of course you will. But beware the bitterest poison of betrayal, Keeper."

"Great Lord?"

But he had fixed his gaze on the west, gesturing her away with a flick of his fingers.

Five

Flat on his back in Spring Flower's bed, the big man known as Seven Skull Shield had fixed his gaze on the soot-caked poles supporting the small dwelling's roof. His attention, however, was most definitely occupied elsewhere. The pole bed creaked; the leather and rope straps supporting the woven-reed sleeping mat strained beneath the two bodies. From outside, the faint midday calls and sounds of people could be heard.

He tensed his muscular body and said, "That's it. Slow now. Arch your back and tighten those muscles, girl."

Where she straddled him, Spring Flower complied, her naked body flexing. Seven Skull Shield admired the view of her ripe breasts and pointed brown nipples. Her smooth skin glistened with a sheen of perspiration. The angles of her neck lay in shadow as she threw her head back and let waves of black hair tumble over her shoulders. He could just see her face at that magic moment when her breath caught and her expression pinched. He felt the vibrations of her tense body, and then cries erupted from deep in her throat as she strained up and down.

He needed no more encouragement. His own body trembled and burst in glorious delight. "Move, girl! Move!" he gasped.

Somehow she remembered what he'd told her, bouncing up and down like an animated rabbit.

Panting like a distance runner, she finally flopped onto his chest, and straightened her legs.

"I had no idea," she whispered between gulped breaths. "I've been married to Fivefish for nearly a year. In all that time I've just had to lay there for a brief bit until he was done. But what we just did? Morning Star take me! My body exploded in stars!"

Seven Skull Shield pawed through the tangle of her black hair and reached down to grip her full bottom in his strong fingers. "Now, did I lie?"

"I didn't believe you." She pushed up, staring down into his eyes in wonder. "Fivefish has never made me feel like that. He's . . . I mean . . . Is there something wrong with him? Maybe deformed? What he's got down there . . . ? Yours is so much more . . ."

"Not all men are equal," he told her with a grin. "Me? I was just born exceptional in all ways. Now there's a couple of more tricks we can explore—"

The voice from outside called, "Wife? Are you there? I could use some help with this wood."

He had to hand it to her, she was off him and grabbing for her skirt before he swung his feet to the floor.

Seven Skull Shield sighed. So much for a pleasant afternoon. Stepping into his breechcloth, he inspected the cane wall behind him. No way to make a hole there. Whatever else he could say about Fivefish, the man built a solid house. It would have to be the front door.

"You've got to distract him," he whispered to Spring Flower. "Just long enough for me to get out the door and out of sight around the house."

Panic filled her large dark eyes. "Distract him?"

"Anything. Tell him you want him to see the neighbor's ramada. Maybe there's a cute little boy next door. Drag him off to show him a pot you want."

"Wife?" Fivefish's voice demanded. "Are you coming or do I have to do it all myself?"

She frantically tossed a coarse-woven cape around her shoulders. "Coming!"

She started for the door, then swung back, fear mixing with longing. "You will come back? Maybe next time he's gone? I could learn so much more."

"Yes, yes!" Seven Skull Shield hissed. "Now, go!"

She hurried out. Seven Skull Shield made a face as he crept up to the door and glanced out. Fivefish was about what he'd expected: a normal-looking Panther Clan man, muscular, average height. He was a part-time farmer when he wasn't working for the clan on mound and temple constructions. He didn't look like any kind of trouble Seven Skull Shield couldn't handle.

Spring Flower was picking at the ropes that held together a bulky pack of firewood tied to the man's back. Even as Seven Skull Shield watched, she undid the knot that let the whole thing cascade to the ground in a clatter.

Come on, girl. Grab him by the post and drag him away, will you?

"There's a wonderful pot next door," she said with too much enthusiasm. "You've really got to see it."

Fivefish muttered, "I've better things to do than look at pots. Have we got any of those corncakes left? They're just inside, aren't they?"

"No!" She grabbed his hand, tugging. "Come look at Green Pollen's ramada. She's got a really cute little boy."

Fivefish stopped short, face screwing up. "Green Pollen has two daughters. What's the matter with you?"

Seven Skull Shield rolled his eyes. Spring Flower might have been young, frustrated, and voluptuous; where her husband was apparently "short" in one way, she was obviously severely lacking in another. Then again, he hadn't been charmed by her quick wit.

"You'll come now!" she insisted, stamping a foot.

"I'm hungry, and . . . Wait. Why are you looking so scared?"

The suspicious husband was faced away, hands on hips as he glared at his wife. It wasn't going to get any better. Seven Skull Shield slipped out the door and made a hard right for the side of the house.

Spring Flower's eyes flew wide and fixed on Seven Skull Shield the moment he emerged. Her mouth popped open, and she stiffened. Which meant that Fivefish immediately twisted his head around to see what she was staring at.

"What the . . . ? You! Stop! Who are you? What are doing in my house?"

Seven Skull Shield grinned, touched his forehead in a gesture of respect, and ran for all he was worth.

The man hesitated just long enough to pick up a piece of club-length firewood. "I'll get you, you foul worm!"

Seven Skull Shield had more than passing familiarity with this part of Horned Serpent town. He charged between the close-packed dwellings, zigging and zagging, hammering through freshly planted gardens and corn plots. People screamed, jumping to their feet, shaking fists, and generally getting in poor Fivefish's way as he pounded along in pursuit, waving his chunk of firewood.

Seven Skull Shield's muscular legs were warming. Now, this was life! First he'd lifted the statuettes, and while wandering through the . . .

The statuettes!

Five of them, remarkably rendered by one of the best stone-workers in River Mounds City. Carved from black siltstone, they'd been the center piece on the altar in First Woman's temple atop its high mound just off the Horned Serpent town plaza. The depiction of Old-Woman-Who-Never-Dies showed her seated, holding the infant Morning Star to her breast, a necklace around her throat, and her hair done up in a bun at the top of her head.

Traded to pilgrims at the canoe landing, or to Traders headed up or down river, they were worth a small fortune.

"And I just *left* them?" he cried incredulously between breaths. Pus and blood. Spring Flower had been distracting, but not *that* distracting.

He shot headlong through someone's ramada, leaping an old woman with a loom. At her scream, the dog at her feet leaped after him, growling and snapping.

Seven Skull Shield barely skipped away from the mongrel's snapping jaws, reached out, and toppled a latrine screen into the beast's path.

"Come back here!" Fivefish's bellow carried on the air.

In a glimpse over his shoulder, Seven Skull Shield saw the old woman throw her loom at Fivefish. Dodging it, he stumbled, slammed into the ramada post, and spun around. The whole wobbly structure collapsed with a clatter. The dog, ripping its way through the cattail matting, fixed on the reeling Fivefish, leaped, and sank its fangs in his thigh.

The last Seven Skull Shield saw, the old woman was swimming her way through the thatch of her ramada roof, Fivefish was wailing on the now shrieking dog with his firewood, and bellowing in pain and rage.

Charging through a gap between houses, Seven Skull Shield bulled headlong into a latrine screen, and remembering the dog, tore its flimsy poles out of the ground. Stopping just long enough, he grabbed a long wooden pestle for milling corn and propped it at an angle across the narrow gap between the houses.

At the side of a granary, he stopped, pulled the screen up to mask his position, and fought to fill his starved lungs.

Fivefish, running for all he was worth, rounded the corner, tripped over the pestle, and flipped face-first into the open latrine pit.

At the man's howl of rage, Seven Skull Shield slipped out of sight. Having caught his breath from everything but chuckling, he circled back toward Fivefish's house.

When he rounded the corner of her house, Spring Flower was pacing anxiously, her hands twisting in knots. She kept staring off in the direction Seven Skull Shield had fled, her face a panicked stew of anxiety.

Totally distracted, she didn't see him slip into her small dwelling. Crossing the clay floor, Seven Skull Shield found his fabric sack right where he'd left it. Undisturbed, it still held the five statuettes.

She started as he stepped out of her door, a hand flying to her mouth. "It's you?"

"Told you you'd see me again." With a tilt of the head, he indicated the interior. "Want to enjoy another quick romp? Those tricks I was telling you—"

"You have to *go*! Now! I mean . . . where's Fivefish?"

"Yes, yes, I'm leaving even as I speak." Seven Skull Shield gave her a confidential wink. "Oh, and Fivefish? Last I saw he'd stopped to use the latrine."

Six

Red Warrior Tenkiller, the *tonka'tzi,* or Great Sky, was responsible for the administration of Cahokia's business. He attended to his duties in the Council House on the Great Mound's palisaded southern terrace. No one—from foreign delegations to kinsmen from other lineages— could help but be impressed. Not only was the walled terrace a healthy climb from the plaza below, but as they entered through the gates, the immense height of Morning Star's palace rose still farther into the sky before them.

Every day *Tonka'tzi* Red Warrior was carried from his residence on the western side of the plaza. His ceremonial litter was borne up the ramp and through the gates. The Council House had been constructed on the western side of the enclosed terrace, and contiguous ramadas allowed him to conduct Cahokia's business outside when weather permitted.

This morning, as spring rain threatened, Red Warrior sat in his litter chair upon its raised dais at the rear of the Council House. He had dressed regally, wearing a brilliant red apron festooned with Four Winds Clan designs rendered in bits of mica, polished copper beads, and elaborate quill work. Eagle feather splays seemed to blossom behind each shoulder, and his face was painted in patterns of red and black.

To his right, in a smaller litter sat his sister Matron Wind. She wore a blue skirt, her chest covered by no less than twelve strings of gleaming white beads. Her gray-white hair had been carefully fixed in a beehive-shaped bun at the back of her head and pinned with copper. Though in her midfifties, her wits remained sharp, and fortune had left enough of her front teeth that she didn't suffer the speech impediments of the toothless.

Behind Red Warrior's dais, a rank of four recorders—their pots of beads and skeins of string before them—listened intently as the reports came in. Picking from their various sizes, shapes, and colors of beads, they strung them in patterns to document the proceedings. A line of aides waited along the left wall, including Dead Bird, the Morning Star's liaison to the *tonka-tzi*.

Two of Red Warrior Tenkiller's daughters, Lady Lace and Sun Wing, rested on litters. Lace's place was to their left and Lady Sun Wing on the right. The *tonka'tzi*'s wives had given him many children, but the most important were the ones his first wife, White Pot—a distant cousin from the Horned Serpent House—had borne him. His oldest son by that marriage had been Chunkey Boy, then the exiled Walking Smoke. After that she'd produced daughters beginning with Night Shadow Star, then Lace, and finally Sun Wing.

Cahokia's administration had barely kept up with its growth, and governance had evolved into a complex web of responsibilities. Most of its huge districts had been delegated to the different Houses, which managed a network of Earth People clans who in turn oversaw most of the immigrant areas. A few districts in Cahokia were governed by autonomous, but subordinate clans of the Earth People. Of these, Matron Corn Seed and the Deer Clan had become most prominent. The Bear, Snapping Turtle, Hawk, and Fish Clans respectively had been delegated ever more responsibility for governing the flood of "dirt farmer" immigrants who'd poured into Cahokia's outlying areas—especially atop the eastern bluffs.

Council Houses and temples had been built in each community. The Earth Clan sub-chief in charge there reported to his clan's district Council House, the districts to the clan lineage in a center such as Evening Star City. The lineage chief in turn reported to her House, and the House to the *tonka'tzi*. The system was ponderous, often clumsy, but given Cahokia's immense sprawl, nothing else had been found effective.

In addition to his domestic duties the *tonka'tzi* received the delegations and emissaries from the far-flung colonies Cahokia had established along the major rivers. Rolls of tanned buckskin maps recorded the location of each colony, and the associated beaded belts, blankets, and bead strings recorded the particulars.

Also within the *tonka'tzi*'s purvey were the diplomatic embassies from other nations including the Caddo in the southeast, Natchez, Tunica, and Mus'Kokee in the south, and the polyglot of nations that dotted the lower lengths of the Mississippi. Fortunately he could delegate many of these to the priests, since their interests were mostly religious.

He glanced at his daughters seated to either side and dressed in finery second only to his and the Matron Wind's. The Lady Lace, Night Shadow Star's younger sister, seemed to have the knack. Though she sat uncomfortably due to her pregnant belly, she paid close attention and had started to make constructive comments.

Red Warrior Tenkiller wasn't sure about Sun Wing. His youngest daughter had survived but sixteen summers; she seemed more taken with her new-found status than the needs of empire. Having just been made a woman at the equinox celebration, she'd been married to Hickory Lance, a young noble in the Horned Serpent House leadership. Since then her dreamy thoughts were obsessed either by her husband's penis and the novel delights she could conjure from it, or the flaunting of her so recently invested authority.

He cast a sidelong glance at Sun Wing, catching his daughter in the act of preening as she studied herself in a slab of mica she carried for the purpose.

"You're a lady in the Morning Star House," the *tonka'tzi* growled. "Be one."

Matron Wind noticed the object of his irritation and lit into the young woman, saying, "Stop acting like a piece of artwork, niece. Pay attention."

In another time and place the pouting look Sun Wing shot Matron Wind would have earned a slap followed by a tongue lashing. Lace, having caught the entire exchange, couldn't hide a mocking smile.

Matron Wind ground her teeth and fought to keep from fuming. Red Warrior could only agree. With Night Shadow Star lost in whatever world she'd plummeted to, one of these two would eventually inherit the mantle of clan matron.

Blessed Creator, for the Morning Star's sake, endow the Matron with long life. He gave Lace's child-swollen abdomen a speculative glance. *And let that child be both a male, and a survivor!*

The latest in the long line of individuals seeking audience was a Fox Clan man who'd arrived at River Mound City the night before. He'd appeared, looking exhausted, and bearing a pack full of map-hides as well as a beaded message belt. The map-hides had been carefully drawn of Reed Bottoms town, a colony of about six hundred persons that had been established last year at the bend of the Tenasee River far to the southeast.

Red Warrior returned his attention to one of the map-hides, studying the layout of the temple, the Council House, granaries, and the surrounding palisades that had been built at Reed Bottom town. While he did, the messenger fingered the beaded-shell belt he'd brought. Eyes half closed, he translated the pattern of the beads into words.

"We have twenty-three families planting fields this year," he said. "Of the one hundred and fifty-three warriors, only seven have been killed in fighting with the local tribes. Depredations have declined since War Chief Kicks Them burned three of their villages this winter and enslaved the head men and their families. A total of sixty were placed in the squares and tortured."

"And have there been conversions?" Matron Wind asked.

"Yes, High Matron. Most of the women and children captured as slaves are now taking part in the rituals."

She motioned with her finger, and one of the recorders stepped forward to take the beaded belt, squinting at the different-sized and colored beads. He nodded, then repaired to his place behind her, rolling it up.

"Anything else, *Tonka'tzi?*"

"No." He smiled at the messenger, and added, "I shall convey this report straight to the Morning Star."

Matron Wind added, "Please express our thanks to your chief and his clansmen." She gestured again, and one of the attendants stepped forward with a smoothly polished chunkey stone. Bowing, the attendant offered it to the messenger. The Fox Clan man received it, hands almost shaking, and promptly bowed his forehead to the matting in obeisance.

Matron Wind explained, "That is a token of the Morning Star's affection and appreciation for the hard work and deprivation your people are experiencing. It is a gift to your chief and clan, to be passed down from generation to generation." She gave him just enough time to absorb the enormity of the gift, then added, "May the Sky Beings protect you on your journey home."

Still shaking, the young man crawled backward, the chunkey stone pressed to his chest. Rising to his feet, he managed a wide-eyed, awe-filled last glance and hurried out past the guards.

Red Warrior handed the map to the recorder. "At least he didn't come weeping and asking for more warriors."

"The Tenasee isn't as dangerous as it was ten winters ago," the Matron replied. "The colony at Reed Bottom covers a strategic section of river. It's the eastern colonies that worry me. The ones beyond the great mountains. We've heard nothing for two years."

"And if we don't by summer solstice, we should send a party to discover their fate," Red Warrior said pensively. He'd thought the Morning Star half-mad when he ordered the massive expedition to colonize the far side of the eastern mountains. He'd known little about the country, other than it was said by Traders to be a fertile plain drained by great rivers that ran down to swampland and finally the eastern ocean.

"Next," he called.

The guard admitted a mud-spattered runner. The young man, wearing nothing more than a breechcloth and holding the painted rod of office that allowed him to pass, dropped respectfully on his belly, face down to the matting.

"Rise," Matron Wind ordered. "What news?"

He never raised his head. "Great Sky, the Red Wing Clan captives will land at River Mound City this afternoon. I am sent to ask what disposition to make of the prisoners."

Tonka'tzi Red Warrior fingered his chin and leaned forward in his litter. "They are to be bound to poles and carried here straightaway." Turning, he asked, "Dead Bird? Inform the Morning Star. See to the construction of squares." He turned back to the runner. "How many of them?"

"Four, *Tonka'tzi*. Three women including the matron and two of her daughters. One man. The war chief, Fire Cat."

Red Warrior grunted to himself. Red Wing town had been a constant thorn in his side: a reminder of the great wars before the resurrection of Morning Star. Worse, the place had been a weeping pustule of heresy. Not only had the leaders and people of Red Wing town scoffed at the resurrection, but they'd incited the wild northern tribes against Cahokia. Red Wing squadrons had even joined the forest tribes in the raiding of Cahokian colonies along the northern frontier.

"And the town itself?" Matron Wind asked.

"Completely ours, Matron. Spotted Wrist executed everyone he captured who belonged to Red Wing Clan. The bodies of the heretics were then cut into pieces and thrown into the river as an offering to the Spirit Beings of the Underworld. The war chief immediately burned the old temple to purify the taint. A new layer of earth will cover the old, and he will engage the surviving townspeople in the construction of a new temple to Morning Star. Those members of the Four Winds Clan who accompanied him have already been installed as rulers."

Red Warrior exhaled in relief and allowed himself to share a victorious glance with his sister. "Very well. Do you need anything else?"

"No, *Tonka'tzi*."

"Then take this vigorous young messenger, reward him with food and drink, and be about your duties."

"Yes, *Tonka'tzi*." Dead Bird stepped forward, touched his forehead in respect, and led the messenger out.

"Who's next?"

"A delegation from the High Sun Chief of the Yellow Star nation, *Tonka'tzi*. The Supreme Sun, the Kadohadacho of *Kadadokies* tribe, sends his sister's son, the *Amayxoya* Frantic Lightning Mankiller, bearing gifts and the good wishes of the Yellow Star nation. The official reception will be in the next quarter moon with all the appropriate ceremony and feasting. The noble Frantic Lightning has requested a more informal meeting *Tonka-tzi*. One without so many hungry ears."

"Has black drink been prepared?"

"Yes, *Tonka'tzi*."

"Well, send him in." He was always curious what the Caddo were cooking up down in the southwest. Whatever they wanted would fill in the hours until he could wander down and inflict a little misery on the Red Wing captives. Payback for what the heretics had dished out over the years. Would this Fire Cat be the terrible and resourceful warrior he'd been reputed to be?

By the Piasa, after what he did to Makes Three, I for one, will be glad to see him bleed.

And perhaps Night Shadow Star could balance her debilitating grief with the red Power of vengeance as she gutted the man. Anything to get back the once-clever woman who'd been so thoroughly destroyed by Makes Three's death.

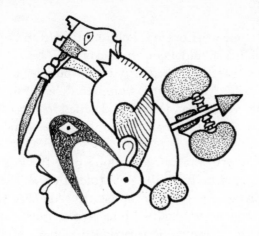

Seven

Be brave, my son," Fire Cat's mother called as they were lifted, gasping in pain, from the war canoe. The sleek craft had been pulled up on the sand among a thousand others. Across the roiling surface of the great Father Water, and atop the high bluffs, he could see a huge and magnificent city.

"That's Cahokia?" he wondered, puzzled that they were on the wrong side of the river.

His head rang as he was slapped hard by one of the Cahokian warriors. "Idiot, that's Evening Star town. You'll see Cahokia soon enough . . . but I don't think you're going to enjoy it."

His sisters wept as they were lashed to long poles cut from saplings. Then he, too, was dumped on his side in the filthy sand and bound to a slim carry pole.

"Not Mother, no." He winced as his mother, Matron Red Wing, was similarly bound; her disheveled gray hair hung loosely. The expression on her face spoke of abject misery.

"Power has abandoned you, you piece of sweating filth," one of the warrior remarked callously. "You're going to your death hung like deer. The squares are waiting. If you've got any guts left, perhaps you'd better suck them up."

Somehow, by marshalling all of his courage, Fire Cat kept from screaming as four warriors laid hold of his pole and lifted. His weight sought to pull his shoulders out of socket.

Both of his sisters shrieked like gutted puppies as they were lifted unceremoniously. Mother just whimpered, and the growing crowd who'd assembled laughed, jeered, and called insults.

Fire Cat barely caught a glimpse of their faces, his own agony taking precedence.

The journey to Cahokia took a long day; the burly warriors who bore his bouncing body on the pole traded off as they jogged along. The entire distance people ran up, spitting on Fire Cat, his mother, and sisters. They were pelted with feces, fish guts, garbage, and even had pots of urine dumped on them. Occasionally one of the warriors would roar, lashing out when someone grew careless with his aim.

"Heretics!" "Animals!" "Filthy foreign trash!" Insults were called as they passed. The escorting warriors did little to stop the abuse, only admonishing the crowd against the use of clubs or fishing spears.

Along that entire distance the broad trail never left sight of farmsteads, temples, palaces, and granaries. The sheer number of people they encountered, or who stopped to watch the last of the Red Wing Clan pass, shocked and amazed him.

Were all the people in the world in Cahokia?

Periodically he heard his sisters sobbing and pleading, but for the most part, he kept his jaws locked as filth trickled down his flesh. His throat was parched from thirst, his last drink having been the night before on the canoe. The agony of hanging, and the tight straps eating into his wrists and knees, left him delirious. If he managed to relax, his head bounced, almost popping his neck. The stench of the excrement dripping from his skin burned in his nose.

Can there be any pain worse than this?

And if there was, how could a living body stand it? But he'd seen it, inflicted it himself when he tied captives in the square.

And now it shall be my turn.

Somehow, he had to endure, had to grit his teeth and not scream as they burned his penis and testicles from his body. Not whimper as they cut bits of skin away and poured boiling hickory oil on the raw muscle beneath. Could he keep from shrieking as they pulled his eyes from his head? Could he die with the stoic courage a Red Wing war chief should?

Mercifully he passed out for part of the way, only waking groggily as his body slammed on the ground, the impact of his head on hard clay shooting lights behind his eyelids.

He blinked, asked, "Who? What?" as the warriors untied him. He laid there limp and dazed while his breechcloth was ripped away. Through blurred vision he caught vague images of tattooed warriors as they lifted his senseless body. He watched them extend his flaccid arm and bind his right wrist to the upper corner of the square. Then his left. Another warrior supported him around the waist as his legs were tied. Finally they stepped back, and his body sagged, pulling painfully down on his arms. He'd been tied to hang like a big X in the upright wooden-frame square.

"Give him water," a woman's voice ordered. "And a little food. If he and the women pass out completely, they could suffocate."

Fire Cat forced himself to pay attention, stiffening his legs to support himself. He shot glances to both sides, seeing the timbers and how his wrists were tied at the top corners, ankles at the bottom.

Leaning his head out, he could discern White Rain and Soft Moon, their faces obscured by their filthy hair, their bodies stripped bare. To his left he could just make out his mother, her square a little farther away. She'd shaken her gray hair back so she could study her captors through half-lidded eyes.

Fire Cat gasped as he struggled to keep his balance on the lower pole. Then he looked out at the crowd that continued to build. An older woman of perhaps fifty summers, her hair tied in a tight bun, stepped close. She studied him with thoughtful eyes. Her cheeks were tattooed with starbursts, and an elegant weasel-hide cape made from white winter hides hung from her shoulders. She carried a small copper-clad rod, and her red skirt was stunningly adorned with the swirling design of the Four Winds Clan. A brilliant splay of exotic scarlet feathers rose from her hair.

"So you're the great war chief who defeated Makes Three?" she asked.

He tried to swallow down his dry throat, and only gagged.

"Three times you defeated the Morning Star's armies and broke his squadrons, young fire brand. Did you think you could prevail forever?"

"Oh, hush," Mother rasped weakly from her square. "It's me you want, Blue Heron."

Fire Cat watched Blue Heron saunter over and extend an arm, lifting his mother's head to stare into her eyes. "It's been too many years, old rival. I'm almost sorry to see you here."

"Sorry, too," Mother whispered hoarsely.

Blue Heron stepped back. "Feed and water them like I said. No one touches them until Lady Night Shadow Star has inspected them."

Fire Cat heard the muttered assent of both the gathered warriors and the crowd.

But how long would it be? And how would he keep from shaming himself when the real torture started?

Pursing his lips, Seven Skull Shield leaned his head back and blew perfect smoke rings toward Wooden Doll's high roof. He was reclined, naked, one knee up, on her lavishly comfortable bed. Built into the dwelling's back wall, it was thick with wolf, buffalo, and fox hides.

In the light of the central fire, Wooden Doll bent over the woodpile by the doorway and plucked up another piece. Seven Skull Shield admired the view. Maybe thirty summers old, she had long legs, very round buttocks, and a delicious back. A tall woman given Cahokian standards, she turned, flipped her thick black hair over her shoulder and tossed the firewood into the flames as she sauntered back to the bed.

She'd made a practice of how to walk, giving just the right sway to her hips, placing one foot ahead of the other to achieve a graceful balance. Fully erect, head held high, her shoulders back and square to emphasize her high breasts, each stride proclaimed that she was all woman, and more than any man could handle.

"You're smiling," she told him as she seated herself on the edge of her bed and reached for the stone pipe he smoked. Taking it, she raised it to her full lips, and drew. Her eyes slitted in pleasure, her cheeks hollowed to accent her perfect facial bones and the triangular set of her delicate jaw.

She held the smoke and then, tilting her head back, blew it skyward before handing the pipe back.

Seven Skull Shield drew as the tobacco burned out and reveled in the tingling Power as Sister Tobacco's spirit ran through his body.

Wooden Doll had fixed her gaze on the little black statuette of Old-Woman-Who-Never-Dies. Her gaze was thoughtful, then she glanced back at him. "So, old friend. You offer a statue in Trade for my services, but what, exactly, are you expecting in return? Just to share my bed on occasion? A night here and there? Or are you looking for more?"

Seven Skull Shield fingered the pipe, a beautiful thing made from a red mudstone quarried a moon's journey to the southeast. The craftsman who carved it had fashioned the front into an eagle's head, the bird's folded wings were engraved along the sides.

"What if I told you I wanted more?" He accented that with a leer that he knew would bait her.

She took the pipe from his thick fingers and knocked it against the bed frame to free the dottle. "I'd say you were a fool."

"Living with me wouldn't be so bad, would it?" He emphasized his point with a forefinger. "We have a history. We helped to make each other. We're alike, you and I. We've known that from the very beginning."

Wooden Doll's lips bent in a crooked smile. "The very beginning? That day I first laid eyes on you? I saw you standing there, that basket over your shoulder, one leg forward. I knew right then that any man with that much insolent challenge behind his eyes would end badly."

"End badly? It's been how many years? And here I am, still filling your bed with bliss and entertainment. What would your life have been like married to old Stone Throw? I remember that first moment, all right. When I looked at you, you looked right back, practically tingling with excitement. No one, before or since, did the things to your body that I did. Still do."

"Don't brag." Her smile mocked him. "We taught each other in those early explorations. Tricks and talents have to be learned."

"And it worked out well in the end." He shook his head, remembering her excitement each time he'd sneak into her bed. And, oh yes, she'd definitely taught him a thing or two. When Stone Throw threw her out in disgrace, Seven Skull Shield had figured that she'd be his. But no. She'd struck out on her own, sensing correctly that a good life could be made in Cahokia trading her body and skills for wealth.

Still, on lonely nights, he often lost himself in dreams of what it would have been like to have lived a normal life with Wooden Doll. Dreams and other fantasies, unfortunately, had little to do with life's realities.

She placed a slim hand on his raised knee and squeezed. "You know I can read your souls, Skull. I wouldn't be your woman then, and I won't be now."

She was the only person who just called him Skull. "That's my entire point. We know each other inside and out. You're the only woman I've ever known who was a fit match for my many skills. We're a team, you and me. We have been ever since that first moment when you peeled my breechcloth off my hips and gasped in delight. I think I'm the only man you ever loved."

She studied him through half-lidded eyes. "I don't dare love you,

Skull. No woman with the sense Power gave a rock would. And the one thing I have is an abundance of sense."

"Would it be so bad? Compared to most of the chunkey players, petty chiefs, and Traders who exchange little trinkets for your services, I *know* you actually enjoy spending time with me. It must be nice not to playact when you're with a man."

"Those men come and go." She leaned forward to slide a long finger from his breastbone down to his navel. "You, Skull? You can't go on forever. Somewhere along the way, you're really going to offend Power. You're going to get crossways with some Cahokian lord. And yes, you've developed an eye for finding these young and foolish wives. But the day is coming when you're going to enrage the wrong husband. Steal the wrong statue or mask."

Wooden Doll leaned forward, her beautiful face a handsbreadth from his as she stared into his souls. He thought he could spend the rest of his life looking at that face.

In a precise and sad voice, she said, "When they finally hang you in a square, I will not go to see you, Skull. I couldn't stand it."

The intensity of her words, the certainty in her eyes, sent a shiver through him. "They haven't caught me yet."

A fleeting and wistful smile crossed her lips. "Yet."

She pushed back, flipping her hair over a smooth brown shoulder. "So, you've given me a statuette. Counting this evening, I'll give you another five nights."

"I'm Trading the others to Black Swallow for considerably more than five nights. That statue of yours? In a place like Split Sky City? You could buy an entire village."

"We're not in Split Sky City, or Pacaha, or Yellow Mounds. Six nights." She reached out, grabbing him by the shaft. An excitement built behind her smoky dark eyes. Her supple fingers, having long discovered his secrets, began to work their magic.

"Ten," he said through a gasp.

"We've all night to bargain," Wooden Doll told him as she pushed his knee to the side.

"You're not going to get the best of me," he insisted.

"You only think you're smart, Skull. I'll give you seven nights. But you're on your own during the day."

"I . . ." He'd forgotten his counteroffer.

Eight

*R*emember!" the sibilant voice ordered from the echoes of Night Shadow Star's fragmenting dreams. Through the brightening haze, she realized she was breathing, drawing warm air into her lungs. The comforting darkness seemed to recede.

Got to remember . . . Look him in the eyes . . .

"Ah, there you are." The voice sounded fragile, old.

She blinked, finding her vision cloudy and filmed. A gentle hand stroked first her left cheek, then her right. As she gasped, a warm damp cloth carefully sponged her eyes.

She managed to raise an arm and brush it away, then blinked to clear her vision. Overhead was a soot-thick roof of poles supporting a lattice of willow stems. Faint yellow light from a fire flickered, and she could smell the incense of boiled sagebrush.

Turning her head, she fixed her gaze on the old man smiling toothlessly at her. The lines in his face were deep, obscuring age-faded tattoos. His white hair had been pulled up in a severe bun to which a Spirit Bundle box had been tied, its copper inlays green with corrosion. The old man's nose looked more like a mushroom, but his sightless and grayed eyes seemed to see into her very soul.

"Rides-the-Lightning?" she croaked.

"You gave me a scare, Night Shadow Star. It is rare when one survives such an intimate dance with Sister Datura. She led me a merry chase in the search for your souls." His wrinkled expression pinched with worry. "That she took you so far into the Underworld is even more unsettling."

"I . . ." She swallowed dryly, fragments of memory now baffling and confusing. "Roots. There were roots. I was underwater, but didn't drown."

"Souls don't breathe like bodies do," he answered. "When I found you, you were in the presence of many Tie Snakes."

She nodded, remembering images of rainbow-skinned serpents, the spots on their sides so dark they might have been emptiness.

He reached to the side, lifting a large, yellow-striped water snake. The creature's black forked tongue flickered in her direction. "He led me to you."

She took a deep breath, her stomach tickling at the bottom of her throat. Knotting a clenched fist against her lips, she fought down the nausea. Then the room tried to spin, her stomach rising in that sick lurch of weightlessness.

Her entire body bucked as her stomach pumped painfully. Dry heave after dry heave left her breathless and panting. Her stomach ached as if she'd been buffalo kicked.

"What else did you see down there?" he asked mildly as he wiped her lips with the damp cloth.

"Piasa," she whispered, remembering the large yellow eyes with their midnight pupils. In that instant, she stiffened, memory and terror returning with a vengeance. "He bit . . ." She slapped hands to her head, frantically feeling her smooth cheeks and delicate ears. To her relief, the bone beneath was firm, whole, and unbroken.

She whispered in horror, "I remember his mouth opening . . . The teeth, so white and sharp, closing around my . . ."

The old man's sightless eyes widened, the toothless mouth opening in amazement to reveal pink gums and the rounded mound of his tongue.

"Bit you where?"

"Grabbed my . . . my head. C-Crushed my skull. I felt it." She whimpered against the terror. "*I felt my skull crack!*"

"So I see," he barely whispered, blind eyes narrowing.

Night Shadow Star shivered and forced herself to sit up. The water snake coiled itself around the old man's age-callused hands.

Think! It's not real. You're here . . . Somewhere. Alive!

But it *had* been real. The memories, the liquid fear in her veins, were all too fresh. She wanted to weep from the sheer relief of being alive.

Alive where?

She forced herself to look around and found herself on the mat floor beside the great fire. Her naked body was cushioned by a thick buffalo-wool blanket; the Four Winds Clan design depicted the curling spirals of the winds at each corner. The familiar interior of the Earth Moiety's great temple surrounded her with its intricately sculpted benches; the stunning relief-carved image of Morning Star dominated the back wall.

An arm's length away, the eternal fire burned brightly as it snapped flames and sparks toward the high roof.

Despite its radiant heat, a shiver ran through her as she noted the pots and carved boxes full of ritual items, bunches of dried medicine herbs hanging from twine, a line of masks representing Spirit Wolf, Bear, Falcon, Ivory-billed Woodpecker, Antlered Deer, and Buffalo. Hollow black eyes fixed on her as the painted masks glared down from the surrounding walls.

"What are you?" Rides-the-Lightning asked cautiously. "Who are you?"

"What?" She stared at him in confusion.

"*Who* are you?"

"I am Night Shadow Star!" she barked back, half frightened, and more than a little irritated at his sudden reserve.

"Are you sure?"

"Why wouldn't I be?" She crossed her arms defensively over her bare breasts and wondered where her clothes were. Struggling, she tried to remember. She'd been in her palace, at the altar in the rear. She'd been looking into the well pot, seeking Makes Three, desperate for his company.

The old man's sightless eyes seemed to peer into her very body, and her souls squirmed. His voice wavered as he said, "Because now that my vision clears, I don't see Night Shadow Star inside you."

She blinked, feeling woozy. "I am the *tonka'tzi*'s eldest daughter. Who else would I be?"

"Ah. That is the question, isn't it? Part of you is her, yes. But the rest . . . ?" His expression twisted with disbelief. "How can this be?"

She rubbed the back of her neck. "You're talking like a fool."

He pulled back, his age-callused hands carefully lowering the water snake to a burnished brown jar incised with the interlocked design of Tie Snakes. The creature glided through his fingers and into the pot's dark recesses.

"The Piasa, you claim? Let us see." Rides-the-Lightning turned his head toward one of the assistant priests who lingered in the background. The old man said something in a language she couldn't understand: the holy speech of the priests.

The assistant stepped to one of the sleeping benches and slid out an intricately carved box. He opened the lid and muttered a prayer before reaching inside and withdrawing what looked like a cape fashioned from cougar hide. As he lifted it out a long, tanned, rattlesnake skin dropped down from the back to sway suggestively. Spread eagle wings had been affixed to the pelt's shoulders.

She kept shooting worried looks at the thing as she rubbed her angular shins. Her normally smooth skin felt oddly cold, her stomach still on the verge of revolt.

"You say Piasa grabbed you by the head and crushed your skull?" Rides-the-Lightning asked absently as the assistant approached with the cape. "Describe him."

"He looked like Piasa," she snapped. "Cougar head, pink nose, bristly whiskers. Three-fork design around yellow eyes with empty black pupils. And then all I saw was the mouth. Big white teeth! Curling pink tongue." She frowned. "And down in his throat . . ."

"Yes?" he asked at her puzzled tone.

"A darkness like nothing I can . . ." Another shiver left her trembling. "His teeth punched through my head . . . the bone cracking and breaking. Pus and blood, I still *feel* it!" In desperation she pressed her hands against the sides of her head. "Why am I still alive, Elder?"

"I cannot tell you why, Lady Night Shadow Star. But let my assistant place the cloak upon your shoulders."

She gave the young man a wary glance as he approached. Her throat suddenly dry, she took a deep breath. As he finished unfolding the garment, she gasped as the thing's hood—made from a cougar's head— came into view.

Terror, cold as ice, settled in her bones. In her souls something whispered, *Yes!* She almost cried out as the man laid the cape over her shoulders, but at its touch a warm wave of energy tingled through bones, muscles, and nerves. Images of dark caverns, fish, turtles, and great serpents spun through her. She heard pitiful cries, as if they were born of the very air around her.

A presence stirred within her as the assistant fitted the hood over her head. It began to swell, flexing muscles, spreading great wings, as a tail that was hers—and at the same time wasn't—lashed behind her. The impulse to clench her hands caused her to glance down. Impossibly she saw yellow eagle's feet with polished talons curling in her vision, only to have the image fade back into her straining fingers as they curled.

Release the Power, a hollow voice echoed within her. *Now you are mine!*

"I am Night Shadow Star," she insisted doggedly.

The swelling presence laughed hollowly.

"Lady?" Rides-the-Lightning leaned close; His face intruded among the spinning bits of fantastic images. "Can you hear me?"

She gasped for air, blinking away fragments of incredible visions of wavering green moss, glinting fish, and rainbow-colored snakes as they swam past. Concentrating, she focused on Rides-the-Lightning, forcing his age-ravaged face to solidify.

A low whimper was torn from her throat as the cape was removed; she slumped, feeling exhausted. The booming laughter that battered her souls receded to a faint echo. Her hands were now her own, her body oddly empty and looted after the sensation of wings. The Power had drained away, a hollow sensation in its wake, as though all that remained of her was a gutted husk.

"What happened to me?" she whispered softly.

Rides-the-Lightning's blind eyes studied her thoughtfully. "You now belong to Piasa, Lady. His Power fills you, runs in your veins." He cocked his head. "When you Danced with Sister Datura, you didn't want to come back to this world, did you?"

She shook her head. "I went looking for my husband."

"You have my sympathy, Lady."

"Yes, everyone's sorry that he's dead."

"That's not what I meant."

She shot him an irritated glance.

As if he could read her expression through those opaque orbs, he added, "Those who go in search of the dead without making the proper preparations and taking the appropriate precautions must accept the consequences."

"What are you talking about?"

"You need to eat something, Night Shadow Star. Rest here for a while. I will send a runner to the Morning Star and tell him that your souls have returned to your body."

"I'll tell him myself," she retorted, unnerved by his wary manner. "He possesses my brother's body, after all."

"He's indeed your kind." The old man hesitated. "After a fashion."

She forced herself to stand, swayed, and almost lost her balance. Her stomach knotted, twisted in protest, but stilled when she pressed her hand to it.

"Thank you for your service, Venerated Elder."

He humbly replied, "It was my honor . . . great lord."

The way he said it left her unbalanced. Her vision wavered and turned runny, as if seeing the temple's interior from underwater. A peculiar elation filled her, and she blinked, trying to get her old self back. But her souls seemed to squirm around inside her, and faint echoes of visions—they had to be Sister Datura's fading embrace—flickered behind her eyes.

Remember . . . you don't have much time. The voice sounded so clear. Her gaze sought the source, finding only mute priests who watched her with wary eyes.

"Remember what?" She turned, searching the room. "Who spoke?"

Rides-the-Lightning's sightless eyes peered intently at her as he said, "No one spoke, Lady. You are hearing the Piasa's Spirit voice. You need to stay here and rest. It will take time to come to terms with this new—"

"I have to go."

"It is not wise."

She hesitantly walked to the great wooden door. Two young priests, staring at her with mouths agape, muscled the door aside. She stepped out into the night, thankful that a layer of clouds blocked the moon and a fine rain fell.

As she descended the polished wooden stairs of the temple mound, the hollow voice repeated, "*Remember what I showed you . . .*"

An image flashed between her souls, a man bending over a bed, bits of movement that ended in a gushing of blood.

As if of their own volition, her legs carried her forward, toward the great plaza.

"*Go. Look into his eyes, before it is too late.*"

Nine

The warrior known as Cut String Mankiller huddled in the claustrophobic darkness of the large wooden box. He made a face and wondered if he'd ever have feeling in his legs again. They'd gone to sleep several hands of time past, and now ached numbly. He forced himself to endure.

He was a blooded and honored warrior, after all. Since childhood he'd trained his body to ignore discomfort. As a boy he'd been forced to run for an entire day under the blazing midsummer sun. Only at sunset had he been allowed to spit out the full mouth of water he'd carried since morning despite a killing thirst. Had he given in to the temptation to swallow even a sip of the precious liquid, the punishment would have been merciless. Father had made him break ice in winter, and to crouch in the frigid water until, on the verge of losing consciousness, he was pulled out, and made to run barefoot across the snow.

As the bravest and most honored warrior in his lineage, this final duty had fallen to him.

"The fate of our clan lies in your hands," Uncle had said, some deep-seated worry hidden behind his hard brown gaze. The old man had cocked his head. *"You can do this thing? Succeed where others would fail, even though it will mean your life?"*

Of course he could. And should he succeed, the greatest glory would be heaped upon him by his noble lineage. No man except the one chosen as the home for Morning Star would have more prestige and status.

And I myself might be chosen for that greatest of all honors.

A possibility not without reason.

Assuming he somehow managed to survive.

The time to act had been thrust upon them. Word was that Morning Star had already decided that Cut String, and families of his lineage, would be chosen to lead and establish a new colony in the far north. Allegedly the Morning Sun had chosen him because of his war record, and the land in the north was now open after the defeat of Red Wing town and its dissidents.

As Cut String well knew from his battle walks in the north, establishment of a town, let alone a priesthood to convert the wild tribes, would be a hard-fought and chancy thing.

And, finally, he had no interest in spending the rest of his life in the bitter and cold north, waging constant war on wild men. Cahokia was more to his liking. Who'd trade an overgrown thicket of forest for the excitement, color, and energy of Cahokia?

The time had come.

He fought the ache of blood-starved muscles as he lifted the lid high enough to see out into the great room. The eternal fire burned brightly, two young men dozing before it. Their job was to ensure the fire never went out. Glancing this way and that, Cut String noted a few of the benches along the walls were occupied by sleepers.

Carefully, he maneuvered the heavy box lid to the side and rose from the cramped interior. Gritting his teeth against the pain, he straightened his back. Propping his arms on the box sides, he lifted himself, knives of agony shooting through his legs as circulation was reestablished.

He glanced down at the box in distaste. The thing had been a gift from some Southern chieftain, its sides and lid intricately carved in designs of Horned Serpent. Shell, precious stones, and copper had been inlaid into the relief.

Cut String endured while blood flowed into his deadened limbs. With the stoicism of decades, he waited out the cramps, and then—in case his legs failed him—stepped carefully from the box. Should he fail, and another need it in the future, he carefully replaced the blankets he'd stashed beneath the closest bench.

Closing the lid, he reached for his battered war club where it rested out of sight behind the box. Lastly, he retrieved the remarkable, finely flaked, chert knife Uncle had provided him. As long as his forearm, it resembled a giant claw, the concave interior edge so sharp it would shave hair.

On cat feet, he progressed across the intricately patterned mat floor. His heart began to pound. The faint gurgling of his empty stomach seemed like thunder in the quiet room. But no one stirred.

He could hear the wind as it whispered through the high thatch and whistled around the Spirit Guardians on the roof. Thankfully, the Powers that guarded this place would only notice another Four Winds Clansman. One who had passed this way many times before.

Reassured, he slipped to the Morning Star's doorway. Placing his weapons on the floor, he carefully lifted the door to the side, before retrieving them.

He couldn't help but smile as he studied the dim outline of the great wooden bed frame where it had been built into the wall. A wealth of buffalo and bear hides topped a thick goose-down mattress. The Morning Star lay on his side, the length of his body curled around a sleeping woman.

Poor thing. Her night with the god was about to end badly.

Perched on the balls of his feet, Cut String crept to the side of the bed. He flexed his muscles, toned by lifting and tossing stones. God though he might be, Morning Star would be no match. And not even gods woke from deep sleep with a clear mind.

Like rattlesnake, he struck, slamming his war club down on the sleeping woman's head. The pop-snap of impact accompanied the familiar caving of bone and brains under the blow. He turned loose of the war club, leaving its stone ax head still buried in the woman's skull.

As Morning Star jerked awake, Cut String was on him. Cupping his left hand under the man's chin, Cut String twisted as he lifted, pulling the head up against his chest; the angle clamped the mouth shut. Unable to scream, Morning Star thrashed, tangled in the fine blankets. Cut String placed the ceremonial knife's keenly curved blade around his victim's throat.

"I'll see you soon, Morning Star," he crooned, savoring this last moment before the god's rich red blood spurted over his blade and hands.

The impact was similar to someone slapping him on the back, and for an instant he didn't understand. Agony, like a spear of liquid fire, burned through his breast. Another impact, another slice of sharp pain. Then a third.

The knife slipped from his fingers, welling wetness rising hot in his throat. Stunned, he tasted blood. His strength vanished, and he toppled sideways onto the floor. Morning Star twisted away, crying out in fear.

Cut String's mouth filled with blood, and he coughed, blowing the spray over his arms and the bedding. He tried to crawl, but seemed pinned in place.

Shot! I am shot!

A hand reached out of the night, lifting his weak head. His last image was of Night Shadow Star's beautiful face, her dark eyes sucking the very souls out of his body, as she said, "Your souls will scream forever now. I give you to Piasa! He's waiting . . ."

Irritation mixed with fear as Blue Heron's litter bearers carefully worked their way up the slick stairs of the great mound. Not only did the rain continue to fall, but it made the climb treacherous. She swallowed hard as the litter lurched, and wrapped her blanket more tightly around her old body.

In the name of bloody pus, why didn't I insist on climbing on my own?

As to the purpose of the summons from the Morning Star? And at this time of night? Without so much as an explanation? That truly scared her half to death.

Nothing, absolutely nothing good would come of this.

Living in proximity to a god was fraught with enough danger—especially a god who'd participated in exploits as colorful as Morning Star's. In the Beginning Times, he'd killed his own father, then hung the dead man's hand in the sky to mark the path to the Land of the Dead. He'd played chunkey with the giants of the Underworld—and won their heads. Angering a being with a record like that wasn't conducive to a long or happy life.

Gods, tell me it's not Night Shadow Star.

She'd taken it on her own authority to send the woman to Rides-the-Lightning. If anyone could call her souls back and tie them to that young and vibrant body, he could.

But in doing so, had she usurped the god's authority? Was that what this was all about?

I'm the Clan Keeper, she declared to herself. Adding aloud, "He told me to deal with her. It was his order."

As if that would save her if something had gone wrong.

Tell me she's not dead . . . is she?

So what if in life—before the resurrection—the body the god now occupied had belonged to *Tonka'tzi* Red Warrior's firstborn male child? As a youth Chunkey Boy, his brother Walking Smoke, and Night Shadow Star had been close. Some said too close. They had shared games, jokes, and secrets. Nor had Chunkey Boy and Walking Smoke been averse to leading her astray. They'd committed enough mischief and downright evil deeds, in addition to teaching her the art of the bow, to play chunkey, how to fish, hunt, and trap.

For a terrible couple of years Matron Wind secretly made offerings to the Spirit World in the desperate hope that Night Shadow Star wouldn't end up a two-Spirit, a *berdache*—a woman who dedicated herself to the male arts, as was common when male souls had been born into a female body.

But several things had changed that. First, Chunkey Boy's grandfather—home to the god since the original resurrection—had died. Though barely twenty, Chunkey Boy had been chosen as the new host. In the elaborate ritual, he had been prepared and offered. Chunkey Boy's human souls had been consumed when the god accepted and inhabited his body.

Second, one of the first things the newly reincarnated Morning Star had ordered was the expulsion of Walking Smoke. To this day, despite her best efforts, Blue Heron hadn't been able to ferret out the details behind Walking Smoke's exile. A detachment of warriors had surrounded the young lord, escorted him to the canoe landing, and paddled off downriver. Neither they, nor Walking Smoke had ever returned, and Morning Star had forbidden discussion of the matter.

And what I'd give to know the reason behind that!

At the same time Night Shadow Star had had her first menstruation. She'd entered the women's house as the *tonka'tzi*'s wild daughter. When she emerged it was as a different woman in a changed world. In that short time, Walking Smoke had been banished. She had seemed more settled, withdrawn, and had taken her adult responsibilities to task. Even voluntarily joined her father and Matron Wind in the complexity of ruling Cahokia.

She had also asked to marry Makes Three. That Morning Star had immediately consented had been a blessing all the way around. Makes Three, though a Bear Clan man, had been a childhood friend of Chunkey Boy, Walking Smoke, and Night Shadow Star's. She had truly loved him, and they'd been good for each other. Makes Three had been a natural war leader and brilliant field commander. The only

worm in the acorn had been a lack of children. Discrete inquiries of
the household staff had assured both Matron Wind and Blue Heron
that Makes Three and Night Shadow Star maintained an active and
athletic relationship under the hides.

And now she's unhinged again.

Worry built as Blue Heron's porters climbed the last stairs into the
high courtyard. At this height, the wind blew stringers of rain past her
protective cover and spattered her with cold drops. Every time the litter swayed, her heart froze in her chest and her muscles tensed.

At the entrance to Morning Star's palace, she was thankfully lowered and helped to her feet. Only then did she notice the numbers of
people—palace slaves and advisors—crouched in the protective shadow
of the high walls.

Whatever this is, it's bad.

Gesturing her carriers to remain behind, she squared her shoulders, wiped the rain from her face, and stepped through the massive
door with its relief-carving of Morning Star.

Inside, the warmth hit her. Thankfully the eternal fire was crackling and burning, sending bright light through the great hall.

She shook out her hair, wet and loose, and walked forward. Matron
Wind—looking as disheveled as she, and also only wearing a wrap
about her body—stood to one side of the fire, a sour expression on her
face.

She noted Blue Heron's entry and jerked a curt nod. The tension on
her sister's face communicated everything: things were even worse than
Blue Heron had anticipated.

"What is it?"

"Assassination attempt."

Blue Heron almost staggered. "Attempt?"

"We're to wait here. Morning Star and the *tonka'tzi* will be out in a
moment."

Even as Matron Wind spoke, two warriors emerged from Morning
Star's quarters. The limp body of a naked young woman hung between them and swung with each step. One gripped her tied wrists,
the other her ankles. Like a vile paintbrush, the woman's bloody hair
dragged the floor and left zig-zag crimson streaks on the matting.

"Here!" Matron Wind cried. "Put her on a litter! By the Piasa's
balls, are you idiots?"

The warriors, already panicked, dropped the young woman as if
she were a sack of corncobs, and hurried out the door.

"He might have wanted his assassin's body to be carried out like a dead fish," Blue Heron muttered, worried for her sister's impetuous act.

"Then they can toss her down the side of the palace mound like the garbage she is." Matron Wind gestured to the pool of blood leaking from the young woman's crushed skull. "I was *trying* to keep ahead of the mess."

"Oh, and as you can see, you're succeeding marvelously," Blue Heron added dryly.

"She's Spotted Wrist's cousin, Evening Piper," Matron Wind noted as she squinted at what she could see of the face. "Bear Clan. I know the woman. She was delighted to be chosen for a night with the god. Not the sort to consider assassination. Proud, yes. Self-possessed. She had been monitoring her moons, hoping to catch a child. There's great prestige in that."

"Spotted Wrist? As trusted as he is, could this run deeper than—"

"She is not the assassin." Morning Star stepped out of his quarters, an apron around his hips, but otherwise naked. His hair hung down over his shoulders in a thick black mantle. Blood smears were visible on his hands and arms.

He was followed by Red Warrior Tenkiller. Her brother's ashen face reflected shock and horror. Normally attired in finery the *tonka'tzi* wore only a breechcloth and a cape.

"Who then?" Matron Wind asked, after touching her forehead respectfully.

"Cut String Mankiller."

"But he's Four Winds Clan." Blue Heron fingered the wattle of skin on her chin. "Is he still alive? Can we hang him in a square and ask some questions?"

"Unfortunately, he's bled out on my floor." Morning Star's expression pinched, and he seemed to stifle a shiver. "I am more interested in how he managed to evade the guards."

"The girl?" Matron Wind gestured to the corpse as the two warriors rushed in and, avoiding Morning Star's eyes, placed the woman carefully on a rain-wet litter. "Was she in on it?"

"Perhaps. He killed her with the first blow."

"You must have moved fast to have avoided the second," Blue Heron said thoughtfully, still leery of a trap.

"He didn't wish to kill this body with a club," Morning Star said as he walked over and extended his hands to the fire's warmth. "It was to be accomplished ritually."

The warriors lifted their litter, bearing the dead woman from the room.

"Huh?" Blue Heron scowled at the blood pooled on the matting. "How?"

Night Shadow Star's voice took her by surprise as she emerged from the door, and said, "With this."

Blue Heron gaped at the sight: Night Shadow Star stood naked, her hair rain-soaked and hanging in strands that trickled water down her smooth brown skin. Outside of her taut nipples, she seemed oblivious to the cold. The wicked-looking knife she held before her glistened in the firelight. A master craftsman had knapped it from a single long piece of semitranslucent brown chert.

"Thank the Creator you're not dead," Matron Wind blurted.

Blue Heron felt cold wind blow through her souls. Night Shadow Star's eyes possessed an eerie look, large and glistening. The effect was as if they were oddly inhuman. Her face, so perfectly formed, remained expressionless. The woman's wet hair seemed to be touched by a breeze the way the long black locks moved. And more unsettling, why was she naked? Last Blue Heron knew she'd been in Rides-the-Lightning's care as he fought to recall her souls. Now, here she stood in the light of the fire, her athletic body bronzed by flickers that glinted gold in her thick mat of pubic hair.

Night Shadow Star held the knife out like an offering. The viciously hooked blade at one end glinted in the light.

"Does anyone recognize that knife?" Red Warrior asked.

"No." Blue Heron studied it. It wasn't the sort of thing a person could forget. "Sister? Do you?"

Matron Wind shook her head. "Never seen it before. If it was Four Wind Clan's I'd know it."

"So," Red Warrior pondered, "what could possibly entice Cut String Mankiller to act against the Morning Star?"

"He's from Evening Star town, isn't he?" Blue Heron studied the knife. "And he's Four Winds Clan by birth?"

"I think so." Matron Wind glanced at Morning Star. "Did he say anything? Give you a reason?"

Morning Star had been standing to one side, positioned where he could watch their faces. Now, in an emotionless voice, he announced, "He said only that he'd see me soon."

Night Shadow Star's voice had a peculiar resonance, the sort that might have mimicked speaking down a long cane tube as she said,

"You see only the reflection. Like the surface of a still pond. You must go deeper . . . into the very darkness."

Matron Wind frowned. "Niece, I don't understand."

"No . . . you don't." Night Shadow Star cocked her head, as if hearing a distant voice. "I have to go now. Any longer, and he'll be dead."

She turned, fixing her eerie gaze on Morning Star. "Do we have an accord? You agree to the terms?"

He nodded, something unsettled in his expression. "As you wish."

"I'll take Five Fists." And with that, Night Shadow Star tossed the brown-chert knife to her father; Red Warrior barely reacted in time to snatch it from the air. She turned in a whirl of damp black hair and strode purposefully for the door.

The *tonka'tzi*'s expression looked shocked and confused. Five Fists nodded when Morning Star gestured he follow Night Shadow Star.

"Accord?" Matron Wind asked. "What terms?"

"Patience, Matron. Even the most ancient of enemies can make alliances when they face a mutual threat." Morning Star might have been staring into an eternity only he could see.

"An alliance!" Blue Heron sputtered. "With whom?"

"What threat?" Red Warrior demanded. "What was Night Shadow Star doing here? And without so much as a skirt? I don't understand—"

Morning Star cut him off with a slash of his hand.

"She saved my life," he said simply. He turned his preoccupied gaze on Blue Heron, and she recoiled at the turmoil reflected there. "We shall need your assistance, Clan Keeper. No one knows the patterns of intrigue as well as you."

And at that moment, two more warriors emerged from the Morning Star's room. These bore the body of Cut String. Blue Heron gaped at the three arrows, neatly driven through the dead assassin's back.

The fletching, she noticed immediately, was Five Fists'. But how had he allowed anyone, even a trusted man like Cut String to get so close?

"Night Shadow Star did that?" The woman had been wet, obviously from the rain. Which meant she'd come straight here from Rides-the-Lightning's? She'd known?

"Yes," the Morning Star whispered softly, as if reading her thoughts. "Chaos is shifting like an evil smoke. And we are caught in its eddies and swirls. Something terrible is brewing, and unless you find it and stop it, Clan Keeper, Sky, Earth, and Underworld will be burst open like a dropped pot."

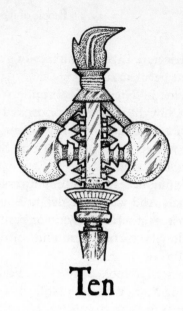

Ten

The faintest graying of dawn barely penetrated Fire Cat's stumbling mind. Some distant part of him recognized the event, but the rest of him had gone numb; the breath in his weakening lungs was barely enough to keep him awake. And when that failed, he'd go limp, the stretching of his arms pulling his chest tight. Lack of air would send a panicked signal through his souls, and he'd jerk upright, gasping.

Just die, he told himself. As it was, he could no longer feel his hands or upper arms. The terrible pain that was his body had been deadened by the cold rain that soaked his skin and leeched the last warmth from his claylike flesh.

Hands of time had passed since he'd last called to his sisters. Even then he'd received no answers.

Mother, however, somehow had managed to rasp back, "Save your breath, son. They'll be coming with torches and knives in the morning."

Why haven't they already?

Throughout the day, the guards had remained vigilant, keeping the throngs of passersby from doing any more than looking, pointing, or shouting insults.

They're waiting for something. Someone.

He blinked, trying to clear the droplets of water that ran down his forehead.

Some presence made its way through the numb ache, and with what little energy remained in his sodden flesh, he raised his head.

I'm dying now. First Woman has come for me.

She was inspecting him with eyes from another world, large and dark, almost luminous with Power. Mist lay thick in her long hair, graying it in years beyond the perfect triangle of her face. She had a full-lipped mouth, her nose straight and balanced between delicate cheekbones. The woman's broad shoulders and muscular arms reminded him of a swimmer's. Cold-hardened nipples seemed to strain from high, round breasts, and her waist narrowed before flaring in a perfect curve of hips. The woman's long legs were slim and muscular, adding to the illusion of otherworldliness.

"Take me," he croaked. "I'm ready."

Her expression sharpened, her eyes still boring into his. "Do you give yourself to me fully, Fire Cat?"

"Take me."

How would she do it? Suck his souls from his tormented body? Reach out with her Spirit hands and tear his heart from his chest? He'd once heard that the souls could be drawn out of the body the way a spindle whorl spun thread.

"You are not afraid?" she asked.

He managed the faintest shake of his head. "Ready . . . to die."

She cocked her head the slightest, eyes narrowing. "I have paid a terrible price for you. Don't make me regret it."

He blinked, confused by the anger in her words, the bitter hatred in her dark eyes. "Price?" He could barely mouth the word.

Just stop *the pain!*

"If you give yourself to me, your life becomes mine. Do you swear to follow my orders, no matter the consequences?" The words seemed to thunder in his head.

"Yes," he croaked. "I swear on the graves of my ancestors." If a Spirit like First Woman pulled the souls out of a body, were they ever allowed to make the journey west in search of the Land of the Dead?

"Done," she whispered as if disappointed. Then she turned, saying, "Cut them down." She pointed at Fire Cat. "Take this one to my palace and attend to him."

She indicated the other squares. "Five Fists you will bear the Red Wing women to the Morning Star's palace. The Morning Star will give you instructions there."

"Yes, Lady."

The words didn't make sense in Fire Cat's reeling and confused thoughts. He struggled to lift his head. First Woman should just reach out and rip his souls away. He should die there in the square, leaving nothing but his senseless corpse for the Cahokians to savage.

Instead, the Spirit of First Woman stepped back and warriors closed in.

He was piteously crying, "No . . . no . . ." as they severed the thongs holding him to the square. This time they didn't catch him. He toppled face-first into the slippery clay. The impact blasted lights through his vision.

He had vague images of other warriors cutting his mother and sisters down. Limp as sacks, they were carried off to the east toward the great palace-topped mound that jutted into the very sky.

In a gray haze he felt himself being carried, and before him, like a forbidden dream, First Woman walked with the sultry stride of a seductress.

His last thought was, *How can a Spirit be that beautiful?*

A steaming cup of rich yaupon tea—"black drink" imported from the south—warmed Blue Heron's chilled hands. Matron Wind and her daughter Sun Wing cradled their own cups. At the Morning Star's orders they'd remained at the palace, and been completely surprised when the Red Wing women had been carried in and dropped on the floor at the rear of the room.

Blue Heron sipped the thick, bitter brew, and glanced sidelong at the miserable women. They huddled, naked, exhausted, and shivering on the floor in the rear. Their filthy bodies jarred with the room's perfect splendor.

There sits the last despicable remnants of the Red Wing lineage of the Moon Clan.

Which begged the question: Why were they still alive?

Matron Red Wing and her two daughters, exposed, bruised, and broken were all that remained of old Cahokia. Remnants of the terrible religious wars that had ended with the sacrifice of Petaga to achieve the first resurrection of Morning Star.

In those first years Cahokia had begun its remarkable transition. As authority shifted, old clans had been replaced with new. Governance of the various villages that were being devoured by greater Cahokia had been awarded to different lineages among the victorious Four Winds Clan and the "Houses" had been established. As people from all over the known world flocked to Cahokia to live in the shadow of the re-born god, Cahokia itself had been leveled, resurveyed, and rebuilt as an earthly representation of the cosmos. A new magnificent city rose where once the chiefs Keran, Gizis, Tharon, and Petaga had walked. The detailed planning, surveying, leveling and grading, remodeling and construction, already had taken an entire generation, and still the earthworks continued to rise. Logs by the thousands were floated down the Father Water and its upper tributaries from forests far up-stream as the expanding need outstripped the logging of the uplands.

And into those freshly cleared uplands—as well as any vacant ground in the broad floodplain—hordes of pilgrims and immigrants had con-gregated. Every plot of tillable soil was now under cultivation. Villages of foreign "dirt farmers" had sprung up like mushrooms after a rain.

And the people, speaking tens of different languages, bowed their backs to work for the greater good of the living god. Families contrib-uted their corn, their labor, and their meager wealth for the glory of the Morning Star. In ritual reenactment, they played chunkey in the god's honor, mimicking his fine rolling stones with shoddy replicas made of fired clay.

But not all had accepted the resurrected Morning Star. Some, like the Red Wings, defeated in war, had fled rather than submit. And year by year, the dissident towns had been brought to heel. Either they had been brutally conquered and the leadership executed, or they'd slowly been converted to the truth of the Morning Star's human existence.

For some, the stunning reality of Cahokia itself had been sufficient. How, after all, could the Cahokian miracle be based on a falsehood?

A few, like Red Wing town, far from the majesty and might, had managed to resist. Preaching heresy, they'd tried to spread their poi-son. Red Wing town had been the most successful. Not only had the town flourished, but they'd constantly goaded the wild forest tribes to raid the frontiers as Cahokia established colonies farther up the Fa-ther Water and its eastern tributaries.

Three times the Red Wings had defeated Cahokian armies. Then, as the Morning Star had predicted, the sacred fourth attempt had suc-ceeded. Spotted Wrist had done by guile and stealth that which could not be accomplished by brute force.

"They are the last," Blue Heron whispered as she took another sip and felt the tea's Power slip through her body.

"Look at them." Sun Wing almost giggled. "Those pitiful wretches dared stand against us?"

Matron Wind shot her niece a narrow-eyed look. "There's a lesson there, girl. Misguided she might have been, but Matron Red Wing was a cunning and worthy adversary. Even the greatest among us can fall if Power favors another."

"Morning Star would never let that happen," Sun Wing asserted primly, and lifted her head to look down her nose at the huddled captives. About her shoulders she clutched a priceless cloak made from painted bunting feathers. A skirt crafted from prime winter martin hung at an insolent angle from her hips.

"Nothing is forever, niece," Blue Heron added in a sibilant whisper. "As we almost learned last night. But for Night Shadow Star's peculiar timing and fast reflexes, not even a god is safe."

Sun Wing's expression conveyed her irritation. "Of course my sister got here in time. Power protects the Morning Star."

Blue Heron jabbed a hard finger into the young woman's breastbone. "Power is just Power, simple idiot. It goes where it's called. Nothing, no one, not even a spoiled little sheath like you should forget it!"

"Sister," Matron Wind warned. "Don't be so hard on the girl."

Blue Heron willed all the threat she could into her expression, refusing to back down. "Pay attention, *Lady* Sun Wing. Your father may be the *tonka'tzi* and may run Cahokia, but I know its passions and secrets. It has fallen to me to read the deep and dark currents. You think the Morning Star protects us, but you've a whole world full of cousins in the other Houses who bow to you and smile while their hearts burn with envy and desire. Why, simple girl, do you think the colonies are so pus-dripping important to us?"

"They're a symbol of Morning Star's Power," she asserted positively. "With them we spread the miracle of the resurrection. By means of their warriors and temples, all the world will come to him." But Blue Heron could see the building uncertainty behind the young woman's eyes.

"You've never listened to a single important thing your entire life, niece," Matron Wind groused. "But I'll try one more time. Yes, the colonies are a symbol of Cahokia's authority. They're also a vent, like a hole left in a newly made clay figurine, so that when it's fired, the steam has somewhere to escape without exploding the sculpture."

Blue Heron gave her niece a wicked grin. "The ambitious ones want to rule? Well and good, we've been able to use that to our advantage. They get to govern their own towns, build their own legacies, and do it without tearing Cahokia apart."

"For the time being." Matron Wind rubbed her nose as if it itched. "But we've missed something. No one has ever gotten this close before."

"And that is exactly why we need to talk," Morning Star announced as he entered through the door behind them. White paint covered his face; the starkly contrasting forked-eye designs had been painted in midnight black. He wore an iridescent cape made of spoonbill feathers. His spotless white apron sported tassels of black-tipped winter-weasel tails. He carried two copper-clad chunkey lances in one hand, his polished red-granite stone in the other.

Blue Heron, Matron Wind, and Sun Wing all touched their foreheads respectfully. From the corner of her eye, she watched Matron Red Wing. The woman had her head down, but her eyes were slitted like a hunting wolf's.

Morning Star walked around the fire, heedless of the bloodstained matting, and laid his chunkey equipment to the side as he mounted the raised clay dais behind the central fire. Like a young panther, he settled himself on the cougar hides that covered his chair. Finally composed, he cocked his head, eyes lost in thought.

"What service might we render?" Matron Wind asked.

He fixed his eyes on Blue Heron. "You have informants throughout the Four Winds Clan?"

"I do." Why was he asking what he already knew?

"You once told me that, like a living body, a clan had a pulse and life of its own."

She nodded, a tingle of unease growing in her breast.

"You stated that emotions ran through a clan like blood, that you only needed to keep your finger on the various parts to know where discontent might be brewing. In your words, by your sensitive feel, you could tell which parts were festering."

Blue Heron swallowed hard and nodded.

"Tell me, Clan Keeper, did your extraordinary touch give you any warning that someone would try to kill me last night?"

"No, great Lord."

Pus and blood, the look he was giving her cut right to the bone.

After a long silence, he said, "I see."

"See what, my Lord?"

"I see that whoever is plotting against me is either not of the Four Winds Clan, or he is so close to us as to be well-versed in our secrets and clever enough to avoid your nimble fingers."

Blue Heron cautiously replied, "If the latter, it narrows the number of suspects considerably."

"Someone among the Earth clans?" he asked mildly.

Blue Heron shrugged. "While nothing's impossible, it would take incredible courage or foolishness for any of the Earth clans to attempt an assassination like last night's. Great Lord, since you have come back to live with us, the Earth clans have enjoyed peace, prosperity, and riches like they've never known. But to unleash chaos? They have too much to lose, and whichever clan acted so rashly, the others would retaliate just to protect their investment in the system."

Matron Wind touched her forehead, and asked, "What about them?" She jerked a head toward the huddled Red Wing Clan women. "Is it coincidence that Red Wing town is taken by Spotted Wrist, they are delivered here, and Spotted Wrist's niece is murdered in your bed?"

He tilted his head the way a predatory bird might as it inspected prey. "I turn the question back on you, Matron. Is it?"

Blue Heron watched her sister squirm, then ask, "If it is, why are they still alive?"

A flicker of anger crossed his face then vanished. "Because Lady Night Shadow Star requested that they live for the moment."

"Night Shadow Star?" Blue Heron blurted. "But . . . why?"

Morning Star once again fixed his unsettling eyes on her. "When I took this body, Chunkey Boy's memories remained. That being the case, I've been kindly disposed to the lady Night Shadow Star. But only last night did I learn how completely we've all misjudged her."

He took a breath, waving down any interruption. "Clan Keeper, you will accompany Lady Night Shadow Star and assist her in her current undertaking. In doing so, you will respect her ultimate authority . . . no matter what your predisposition or experience might suggest."

"Defer? To my niece?" Blue Heron tried to keep from growling.

He gave her a godly, thin smile. "A reverse of the old line of authority. Reconciliation of opposites. Most suiting. But sometimes, when we turn the world upside down, the most interesting things come tumbling out of dark places."

She ground the few teeth she had left, and said, "Yes, my Lord. Just what undertaking are we embarking upon?"

His face had closed into an expressionless mask. "I have ordered Five Fists to keep last night's attack to himself. His trusted warriors have disposed of the bodies. Until I decide, no one else will know what happened here last night. Perhaps our lack of response will bewilder the plotters into revealing themselves. They may even feel emboldened to try again.

"Meanwhile, you will ferret out this plot, Clan Keeper. Discover who is behind it, and expose them to my wrath." He paused for effect.

"Know this: what stirs isn't just the passions of men, but the workings of Power."

"By whom?" Matron Wind almost snapped.

"Whoever it is who seeks my death is clever, skilled in his conjuring. He has powerful and frightening allies." He gave them a slight smile. "But so does Lady Night Shadow Star.

"Clan Keeper, I ask that you communicate your findings to either the Matron, or Sun Wing, here. And after both have been apprised of the situation, they shall communicate them to me."

Sun Wing? Blue Heron struggled to keep surprise and dismay from her expression, but she nodded. One didn't argue with the Morning Star's direct order. At least, not more than once.

She locked eyes with Matron Wind's, seeing confusion and surprise reflected there.

"Yes, great Lord," Blue Heron made herself say.

"Then you had better be about it, Clan Matron."

Blue Heron drank down the last of her black drink with a feeling of unreality. As she started for the door, Morning Star called, "Oh, and Clan Keeper, I would be very careful if I were you. Anyone desperate enough to make an attempt on my life surely wouldn't hesitate to murder a woman such as yourself, no matter how venerated."

Eleven

Someone touching his body brought Fire Cat awake. His first impulse to jerk away died as his muscles and nerves jolted him with pain.

"Hold still," a raspy voice told him.

Fire Cat blinked, memories flooding into his souls. He'd been following the Spirit form of First Woman, as if through a dream. The men carrying him had climbed a high set of stairs and lowered his body onto a veranda as she vanished into an ornate palace with painted walls and a magnificently carved door.

They'd fed him a meal of cooked venison and allowed him to drink all he could hold. He'd barely been conscious, and delighted enough to fall into a deep repose when they brought him a warm blanket.

Horrible dreams had tormented his sleep, and now? Well, just where, exactly, was he?

He lay on a soft pallet, beside a warm fire, and in the center of a most incredible palace. The high ceiling was smoke-filled. Images of Morning Star, Horned Serpent, Falcon, and Rattlesnake decorated the walls. In the back, to either side of a single door, large wooden disks carved with the four swirling curls of the Four Winds Clan had been hung. Weapons interspersed with trophy skulls, articulated arm and leg bones, as well as shields, war clubs, and quivers of arrows decorated the walls. Each of the benches that had been built out from the walls was intricately ornamented in spiraling twists, or as twining snakes.

The uprights extended a man's height above the benches, the tops of the poles exquisitely sculpted into heads with lifelike faces. Others were topped with spirit images of Eagle, Snapping turtle, Ivory-billed woodpecker, or Hummingbird, all fitted with inlaid shell eyes. The blankets were among the finest he'd ever seen, tightly woven of fine hemp fiber, buffalo wool, or spun human hair.

Also remarkable were the beautifully burnished jars and pots visible beneath the benches. They rested between fantastically detailed wooden boxes inlaid with shell, mica, and copper.

Then he turned his attention to the old man who crouched over him and attended his wounded wrists. The elder wore only a plain brown shirt that hung down in a crumpled fold. The face was positively ancient—a mass of wrinkles that obscured the meaning of long-faded tattoos. His excuse of a nose could be likened to a round knob of flesh; the old man's eyes were grayed with blindness.

"The salve will heal the skin on your wrists," he said gently. "I've already attended to your ankles. The pain in your shoulders and joints should diminish over the coming days, but in the meantime, you're to drink willow-bark tea. The lady has enough in supply to last you a half moon."

"Who are you?"

"Humans call me Rides-the-Lightning. I am known by other names among the dead and the Spirits."

Fire Cat swallowed hard. "The great Earth Clan healer of Cahokia?"

Then it hit him: *I'm alive!*

"Fortunately," the old man was saying, "you're both young and strong. I can tell that your souls are firmly anchored in your body, so there should be no long-term effects."

"Elder?" A melodious voice asked, "May we proceed?"

The old healer looked up, and Fire Cat followed his gaze to the woman who emerged from the single doorway in the back. The sight of her shook him: the woman he'd thought to be First Woman, and a Spirit. Now she was dressed in a vivid blue skirt, a bright yellow cape over her shoulders. Her midnight-black hair was up and secured with a long copper pin that flared into the form of the sacred turkey-tail mace. The sort of thing only worn by a distinguished ruler.

"Who are you?" He tried to think, to make sense of it.

"Your master," she replied coldly, and narrowed her eyes. "Do you remember your vow, given upon the graves of your ancestors? If not, and your memory is as faulty as the rest of you, you may go back to the square."

His oath? Of course. But he thought he'd been talking to a Spirit woman. "My memory is fine. Where are my mother and sisters?"

"They belong to the Morning Star and serve the lord's wishes."

"He's not a lord," Fire Cat forced himself to say. "He's a man, playing at being a god."

Her full lips formed into a deadly smile. "He told me you'd say that."

"Well, he's right. Whoever he is."

"Lady?" Rides-the-Lightning couldn't hide the fear in his voice. "Are you sure you want this one? His mouth is most foul."

"As is the rest of him, old friend." Her expression hardened. "He is a means to an end, a tool to be used, and nothing more. Let's see if this *thing* is what I was told to expect, or if it's a distraction."

Thing? "Lady, if that's how I address you—"

"It is."

"Then know that I am Fire Cat Twelvekiller, of the Red Wing Clan, of the Moon Moiety, and whatever vow and promise I made, my word is my life. My memory is impeccable. You took me from the square, and having given my word, I'll serve you to the best of my ability."

She stepped closer, saying, "The beast speaks brave words, doesn't he?" Then she added, "Very well, beast, you will hold still. You will not cry out or resist in any way."

"What are you doing?"

"Determining if you, and what's left of your clan lineage, will live or die."

He was looking into her eyes, reading her hatred and loathing. *What have I bound myself to?* "I will follow orders."

"Then do so," she said coldly as she knelt beside him.

With a belly-twisting fear, he watched as Rides-the-Lightning handed the woman a small blade of stone: obsidian. Its glassy surface glittered in the firelight.

"Keep your arms out," Rides-the-Lightning suggested. "This will sting, but nothing like what you've been through."

"What are you doing?"

She positioned the thin sliver of obsidian in her long fingers, a slight frown of concentration lining her forehead. "How much?"

"Just a small piece from the crucial areas. Top of the head first."

She shifted, and Fire Cat's heart began to pound. "If you're—"

"Be *silent*! If you're this much of a coward, I'm better served to slit your throat and be done with it." Then to herself, she added, "On your souls, husband, I am sorely tempted."

At the disgust in her voice, Fire Cat stiffened his body, clenching his teeth. No woman called him a coward.

She fingered through his hair at the top of his head, and began softly singing. The words made no sense, but at her touch a tingle ran through his head, as if Power sparked from her long fingers. A spear of panic shot through him. *Ancestors, she's going to scalp me!*

Muscles rigid, expression like a mask, his guts twisted as the sharp sting at the top of his head announced her cut.

"That's good," Rides-the-Lightning said.

Fire Cat tried to swallow past the fear in his throat, but she had only taken a bit of scalp smaller than a fingernail. Still singing, she studied it and the attached hair, and handed it to Rides-the-Lightning.

From a little pouch the priest removed what Fire Cat recognized as a rattlesnake fang. Singing in the same incomprehensible voice, the old man pierced the bit of scalp with the fang and dropped it into a small black ceramic pot. The vessel's sides had been engraved with the sinuous forms of Tie Snakes.

"What are you *doing?*"

She ignored him while her deft fingers sliced a pinch of skin from each of his shoulders. As she continued to sing, she handed them to Rides-the-Lightning, who pierced each one with a rattlesnake fang before dropping it into the pot.

Fire Cat's terror built, and he felt trickles of blood leaking from the small wounds. Rigid as a board, he battled the growing horror. The words of her incomprehensible song hit him like blows to his souls.

Horrified, he channeled all of his courage into the struggle to keep from flinching each time she touched him, took a pinch of skin, and sliced it away. She cut a tiny bit from the inside of his elbows, a bit from the palm of his hand. Pinching each breast above the nipples, she sliced more bits of him away. Then from his belly, thighs, and feet.

The old man continued to pull snake fangs from his pouch, carefully pressing each through the piece of skin she handed him.

Fire Cat watched with wide eyes as she reached for his penis. He trembled as she grasped and pulled his foreskin taut. With a deft and stinging slice, she removed yet another tiny bit.

He couldn't control the whimper in his voice as he asked, "What are you *doing?*"

The woman leaned back, her large eyes glistening. His blood stained her fingertips as she placed her hands on her knees, and lifted her face toward the ceiling.

The old man's singing stopped. Holding the black rattlesnake pot so that the opening faced Fire Cat's mouth, he said, "Blow into it."

"No!"

"I told you he was a coward," the woman said disdainfully. "A coward and a liar."

"I *don't* understand!"

She fixed him with dark, eternal eyes that only added to his fear. "You are *mine*. Do as the elder orders you."

Summoning his courage, Fire Cat blew into the pot.

"Now spit," the old man ordered.

Mouth dry as sunbaked leather, Fire Cat managed a dry attempt at spitting into the pot, and as he did, he couldn't help but look inside. To his dismay, only an impossible black infinity met his gaze, as if there were no bottom to the little vessel.

The old man raised the pot high, offered it to the four cardinal directions, and finally touched it to the floor. With careful fingers, the old shaman withdrew a snakeskin sack from his pouch. He pulled the sack around the little black pot and tied off the open end.

Fire Cat could see the fear in the old man's eyes as he struggled to his feet, saying, "I will attend to it as you ordered, Lady."

She exhaled, as if from tension, and nodded. "I thank you, old friend."

Some curious communication passed between them, and to Fire Cat's eyes, while she'd called him an "old friend" Rides-the-Lightning just didn't look like he wanted to be anywhere close to her.

The priest gave Fire Cat one last dismissive stare, his blind gray eyes narrowing. "I hope he is worth it."

"We all do," she whispered, and rose to her feet.

"What have you done?" Fire Cat cried, suddenly dizzy as he gasped for air. It felt as if some part of him was draining away. He fought to keep the room from spinning.

She turned those dark and eerie eyes on his. "Your oath may be sufficient for what's coming, but I had to be sure. Now, I have claimed both your souls and your body as mine."

And with that she turned on her heel and followed the old man outside.

"I am taken by a witch," he managed through gritted teeth, tears leaking from the corners of his eyes.

He reached up, the movement agonizing to his arms, and scrubbed at the tears, hardly aware as a man padded in on bare feet and knelt beside him. With a damp cloth, the man scrubbed at Fire Cat's little wounds, wiping away the blood.

"Forgive me if this hurts."

"I . . . I'm a warrior."

"Not anymore. You are whatever the lady says you are."

"Who *is* she?"

The man gave him a solicitous look. "She's the lady Night Shadow Star, first daughter of the *tonka'tzi,* of the Four Winds Clan. The woman whose husband you killed." He paused, no sympathy in his expression. "I have no idea why you are still alive given the grief she's suffered on account of you. Whatever you do, I wouldn't disappoint her. Not if you value what little life you have left."

Twelve

A warm spring sun burned down on the plaza; wisps of mist rose from the trampled grass on the stickball field. As the sun burned away the last traces of the rain, Blue Heron delighted in the warmth. She reclined on her litter, her attendants clustered around her. She'd come to think, to watch the stickball practice—and to get an informal word with Night Shadow Star.

She glanced around at the crowd that lined the field, mostly older people with spare time on their hands. Here and there, pots, shell, pieces of copper, blankets, sacks of corn, and other goods had been wagered on the two teams' practice scrimmage. Odds were on the team wearing flaring black skirts.

To the north, Morning Star's soaring temple seemed to pierce the sky where it dominated the great mound's heights. A throng of people congregated at the bottom of the ramp that led up to the first, walled terrace. There, in the Council House, *Tonka'tzi* Red Warrior was already holding audiences with the endless line of chiefs, councilors, Traders, and messengers.

Better him than me. Blue Heron had always preferred the deeper, more intricate games of deception, move and countermove, and the subtle intrigue that went with them.

But I missed Cut String's attack on the Morning Star.

How? Nothing she had heard had sent so much as a prickle of premonition through her.

Who could have planned it?

Matron Columella? Cut String was one of the Evening Star House matron's cousins several times removed, and the wily Columella was more than capable of plotting such a strike. But had Columella done so, she would have prepositioned herself to take advantage of a successful assassination. Something that in retrospect would have given her away.

The same for Matron Round Pot at River Mounds City. Next to Columella, Matron Round Pot would have had the most to gain. But again, Blue Heron was aware of no machinations that would hint at the woman's readiness to take advantage of the ensuing chaos. The signs would have been evident: accumulations of warriors; actions that would have raised her profile; feasts to increase her prestige among the other lineages, or feelers for support.

A yell went up. Blue Heron resettled herself on her litter and returned her attention to the stickball practice. Around her, her attendants shouted support and applauded with glee.

In the middle of the field fifty-some women battled ferociously. Naked to the waist, only short skirts clung to their hips. Night Shadow Star's team wore red, the opposition black. A melee developed as the two teams struggled for control of the ball. Racquets clattered, long black hair flew as women collided. The hollow thumps of blows carried across the morning grass. Someone bellowed in pain.

The few rules were simple: An opponent couldn't be struck with a racquet or hand; and a player couldn't use her hands to so much as touch the ball, let alone catch or throw it. Anything else, including head-butts, body blocks, tripping, kicking, and elbowing, were legal. Black eyes, bloody noses, dislocated joints, sprains, and broken bones were normal. On occasion a dead player was carried straight to his clan's charnel house when Power completely abandoned him.

The object was even simpler: toss the ball between the two tall goal posts at the end of the opposing side's field.

Someone screamed in triumph; the crush of women broke apart. Breasts bouncing, feet hammering the ground, the red team charged forward. Sunlight glistened on muscular brown legs as the women sprinted. Night Shadow Star, the ball in the pocket of her right-hand racquet, sought to circle to the side, seeking an open player.

The blacks responded with shouts as they surged her way. Night Shadow Star's arm went back, and twisting her body, she flung the ball. Blue Heron watched it arc through the air, bounce. A red-clad woman who had slipped around the mass on the east snared it with her racquet and sprinted south toward the goal that stood below the Four Winds Clan charnel house and burial mound.

Yes, that was Pretty Corn, a Snapping Turtle Clan woman from a farmstead over by Petaga's tomb. She excelled at stickball, lived for it, and played almost as well as Night Shadow Star.

"It's good to see the lady playing again," Smooth Pebble noted. "If you ask me, she hasn't lost her keen edge."

"Given her close brush with the Spirit world, it's a miracle," Blue Heron agreed as she watched Pretty Corn's flying heels, the horde of women racing in her wake.

From the angle, Blue Heron couldn't see how it ended, but a shout went up from the reds, racquets clacking in celebration. The blacks bellowed in dismay.

"That's the final score," Smooth Pebble cried. "I win!" And promptly she trotted a couple of steps to claim the long-necked pitcher she'd wagered for with an Eagle Clan man.

The women broke into clumps, slapping one another on the backs, banging their racquets together.

Moments later, Night Shadow Star emerged from the mass and came trotting across the flattened grass, her two racquets glinting in the sun.

Blue Heron watched her approach. The muscles in her niece's tight belly tensed with each stride. Long legs ate away the distance. Her black hair caught the wind, flipping behind her like a raven's wing.

"Aunt," she greeted, panting. She stopped before Blue Heron to brace her hands on her knees, lungs heaving as she caught her breath.

"Good game. You won by how many?"

"Two. It was only a practice." She straightened and tossed her hair back. Filling her lungs with air, she exhaled and wiped at the sweat that beaded on her face. "That Pretty Corn, I'd like another ten of her kind."

Blue Heron glanced at Smooth Pebble who'd returned with her pitcher, a beautifully burnished brownware piece of southern manufacture. "If you would be so kind, the lady and I need to talk."

Smooth Pebble touched her forehead, and with a few gestures of her hands, formed the rest of Blue Heron's servants and carriers into a loose ring just out of hearing. Even as they did, well-wishers, many bearing the fruits of their wagers, were waved away.

"You have seen the Morning Star." Night Shadow Star lowered her racquets and seated herself on the grass beside Blue Heron's litter. Flipping her hair back, she hugged her knees and cast a knowing look toward the great palace atop its steep-sided black mound. ". . . And now you are confused."

"You've tickled my curiosity, niece. I'm to defer to you. And how is it that one minute you're flat on your back in the healer's temple, your souls flown away with Sister Datura? The next thing, you're shooting Five Fists' arrows into an assassin's back in the Morning Star's bedroom?"

She whispered, voice distant, "He didn't leave me much time."

"He? Who? Cut String?"

She shook her head, eyes locked on some painful distance. "Piasa."

"We're talking about the Spirit Beast?"

She nodded, eyes tightening. "He warned me you'd be skeptical, and that I was to tell you he enjoyed the Red Wing feast. Does that mean anything to you?"

"No, it . . . Wait. You mean the ones we threw in the river?" Blue Heron shifted uneasily on her litter. "It was my suggestion to the Morning Star that, but for the Matron, her daughters, and that miserable war chief, the rest were to be executed, dismembered, and tossed into the river. Not only did it make a potent symbol of our Power, but there'd be no bodies for any survivors to mourn over."

She watched Night Shadow Star for a reaction as she added, "But you could have heard that from anyone."

Night Shadow Star's eyes seemed to expand, a darkness filling them. She cocked her head, as if listening to someone, and nodded. "He says that for the moment, your belief isn't necessary."

"Oh, I believe." But, just what, exactly, she wasn't about to tell her niece. "So, the Water Panther himself told you Cut String was going to kill the Morning Star? Did he say why?"

"No. Only that if he succeeded, the resulting struggle would tear the world apart." Her voice sounded hollow. "We dance with death, Aunt. A wondrous Power has filled Cahokia, but what frightens the Piasa is that it might burn out of control, unpredictable, and dangerous. Not just to us, but to the Spirit World as well."

"And Piasa specifically chose you to deal with this?"

"Chose?" Bitter laughter exploded from her lips. "I was lucky to escape with what little I did. It cost me to come back, cost me . . . everything." Her voice faded, expression falling.

"You're not talking sense." Blue Heron waved up toward the palace. "And why are those accursed Red Wings still alive up there? Because their kin were tasty?"

"When you dance in blood, Aunt, the ground gets slippery. You can no longer leap in exaltation, because when you do, your feet fly right out from under you. When you fall, you land in gore."

"You've gone from talking nonsense to riddles."

"They are alive because they have to be." Night Shadow Star studied her with eyes possessed of an unearthly gleam. "Piasa demanded your involvement. Only you can weave the pattern. He has orders for you: find the thief known as Seven Skull Shield."

"Find a thief called Seven Skull Shield? I can find anyone. But if you're talking about the two-legged scum I think you are, I'd rather run a couple of hot copper needles through that slippery weasel's eyes than—"

"And . . . And then . . ." Night Shadow Star's eyes had lost focus as she struggled over the words.

"Then . . . what?"

"And then there's the Red Wing war chief."

"Bah! I'm going to Rides-the-Lightning. Your souls are still loose, flying around like some—"

"Enough!" Night Shadow Star half crouched, eyes slitted like some dangerous panther's. "And you *will* listen to me, Clan Keeper. A whirlwind is gathering. Before this is over, you'll cry tears of blood. And the souls of all you love will be forfeit."

At the tone of her voice, alien, empty, Blue Heron felt a cold premonition run through her. "Who *are* you?"

"I'm the sacrifice, Clan Keeper. The one who has lost everything I once had . . . and everything I might be. Look at me, and you see a dead woman."

Blue Heron barely deigned a glance at her niece's lithe body, bursting as it was with vitality. "You're a lot healthier, and certainly a lot less 'dead' than I am. And you still serve the Morning Star."

Her weird other-worldly eyes seemed to enlarge. "Not anymore, Clan Keeper."

"I wouldn't tell Morning Star that."

The twist of her lips was faint, amused. "I've already told him."

"And he let you live?"

"He can't kill a body that's already dead."

"You're scaring me, Niece."

The stranger's eyes living in Night Shadow Star's face reflected slivers of sunlight. "Good. Because you'll be living true terror soon enough."

The Fly

*F*lies are drawn to corruption and rot. Which is why, I suppose, I am drawn to the Four Winds Clan. Flies are creatures of the air and sky, as are the four swirls of the Four Wind Clan's favorite design.

Flies are also innocuous, they go where they will, buzzing here and there, and no one notices. The same with me. I stand now, arms crossed, one leg thrust forward as I chatter aimlessly with Smooth Pebble. The berdache sees nothing but a fly, a harmless being, buzzing just enough to irritate him as he clutches the ceramic pitcher I wagered him over the outcome of the stickball game. It's a Casqui piece I picked up for almost nothing.

Like a fly, I was able to stand within hearing distance of Blue Heron, and stare my eyeballs out as I watched every move my beautiful Night Shadow Star made. I could revel in the sight of her, fantasize about that spring-taut body. As she raced past, I could smile gleefully at her gleaming black hair, watch the muscles in her thighs and calves. In my imagination my hands were full of her breasts, fingers sinking into the softness as her nipples hardened against my palms.

One day, my love, I will look down into your marvelous dark eyes, watch your pupils expand as my shaft drives into your warm depths. At that moment, I'll feel every muscle in your marvelous body tense, hear the breath straining in your lungs, and my love for you will explode like a thousand stars into a coal-black sky.

Soon, my love. Soon.

*Meanwhile—and the reason that brought me here in the first place—
something has gone wrong. That was readily apparent when I arrived at
dawn toting a couple of Casqui pitchers in a sack to give the allusion I was
but another Trader. I'd come to enjoy and revel in the spectacle. I couldn't
wait to see the panicked faces, hear the screams of dismay, and delight in the
mass hysteria as the ignorant wretches tore their hair and clothing. Instead
of news of the Morning Star's heinous murder, only silence rolled down the
long stairway to the plaza.*

*Glancing past Smooth Pebble, I can see and barely hear Blue Heron and
Night Shadow Star as they talk. Tense, yes, and obviously plotting, but I'm
not quite close enough to catch more than an occasional word.*

*My agents assured me that Cut String would act last night. I have assur-
ances that the warrior was seen climbing the stairs to the high palace, and
that he carried the ritual knife.*

. . . And nothing!

*The day proceeds as if Cut String never existed. The Morning Star plays
chunkey, unconcerned, and my beloved Night Shadow Star wins at stickball.*

*This actually excites me. To have succeeded too easily would have been
boring. A tingle, not unlike the sexual anticipation I have for Night Shadow
Star, runs along my bones. Instead of simple victory, I must now apply all of
my brilliance. Winning will boil down to who can keep whom off balance,
plot and act the quickest, and seize unexpected advantages.*

*Either it is the incompetence of my allies, or Power has taken a hand in
the game.*

Which means I must now employ other weapons and strategies.

Beware, Blue Heron. I am about to raise the stakes!

*I have preparations to make. It no longer seems that I can trust either the
locals, or Power. I must take a more active role. I pack the last of my pitchers, take leave of Smooth Pebble, and saunter off into the crowd.*

*Wild Cat has been watching, now I catch his eye and nod. In an instant
I have made the transition from a harmless fly to a stalking lion. Wild Cat
is off to dangle a baited hook.*

*Me? I am off to challenge Power in a way that will shake the depths of the
Underworld.*

Thirteen

The damp clay sank with each step Matron Columella took. She'd come to inspect the progress of the new mound her Evening Star House lineage was raising on the river's high western bluff. The heights overlooked both the broad expanse of the Father Water and the endless sprawl of Cahokia where it stretched across the floodplain to the east. Given the elevation to which the new mound had already risen, Columella was exposed to the breeze blowing in from the west; it tugged playfully at her bright yellow skirt, heavy as it was with its decorative shell and copper beads. They glinted in the sunlight and had been sewn to the fabric in an Evening Star pattern. She had thrown her cloak back out of respect for the warm morning sun. Her hair was fixed in a bun and secured with an ornately carved eagle-bone pin.

Columella's brother High Dance Mankiller, high chief of the Evening Star House, gave her a sidelong glance, refusing to betray his distaste for the short caricature of man who struggled to keep pace beside her. The dwarf called Flat Stone Pipe waddled precariously over piles of soft clay where they'd been dumped by the endless line of laborers. To do so, he had to windmill his arms for balance, his short legs almost flailing.

High Dance bit off an irritated curse. He was a handsome man entering his forties, tall, muscular, immaculately dressed in a yellow-and-black apron. He was everything that the dwarf was not.

"Building a mound," the dwarf said, "is like creating an empire." He turned his attention to the long line of laborers as they climbed the ramp, panting. Sweat streamed down dirty chests and shoulders. The closest man gave them a wary glance, slowed, and shifted his burden basket to touch his forehead respectfully.

Columella gave him a faint nod of acknowledgment and watched the man plod wearily forward and dump his basketful of damp black clay atop the thick layer of white sand. So far the struggling line of humanity had managed to cover half of the new mound top with a knee-deep layer of silty clay.

Immediately behind them, another twenty or so men tamped the black clay, using flat-bottomed logs like giant pestles to ram the basketloads into a compact and flat surface.

The construction of a stable mound was an art, and it was here that Flat Stone Pipe, a noted engineer, excelled. Plain dirt piled into a pyramid would last only as long as it took the Tie Snakes in the Underworld to call a heavy rain. As soon as the soil became saturated, the sides of the mound would slump down into a gooey mess. Instead, a complex layering of loam, topped with clay, topped with sand, topped with loam, topped with clay was used. Loam provided most of the fill. Clay of just the right consistency was used to create a mostly waterproof cap. Sand acted to absorb any water that infiltrated past the overlying clay caps and let moisture slowly dissipate.

Where they stood atop the growing charnel mound, Columella could just make out the lumpy texture of distant forest to the west. Between that far tree line and the main Evening Star complex's twenty-five mounds, palaces, and temples, lay a sea of houses. They'd begun as tens of independent small villages that had grown into one another to create chaos. Each "center" boasted a cluster of Council Houses, temples with their tall poles, and granaries. Around them what had been farmsteads were surrounded by a patchwork confusion of garden plots.

We should have planned better. But who could have foreseen the constant and massive influx of entire peoples?

The air carried the redolent scent of a thousand fires as morning breakfasts were cooked, charcoal was burned, and potters fired their ceramics.

Evening Star City's great plaza stretched immediately to the north, with Columella's pitch-roofed palace atop its steep-sided earthen pyramid at the south end. To the east, just below the bluff, she could see the river's wide expanse, its silt-laden waters catching sparkles of sunlight. Men bent their backs, driving pointed paddles into the water as they propelled an endless procession of canoes back and forth. From her vantage point, the east-bank landing thronged with activity, the distant shore littered by the parallel ranks of beached canoes. Even as she watched a raft of logs was being towed to shore just up from River Mounds City. Floated down from somewhere in the north by enterprising Traders, the logs would be muscled up on the bank. Then one by one or as a group they'd be dickered for. Cahokia was constantly in need of timber for construction, carving, firewood, roofing, house walls, and a hundred other needs.

Behind the landing, River Mound City's tall buildings jutted from their palisade-topped mounds. Surrounding them were the Council Houses, warehouses, and the cluttered sprawl of the city's great port. A smoky morning haze hid the normally visible heights of distant Cahokia where Morning Star's palace jutted from the broad floodplain.

"Mounds are not just piles of dirt, old friend," she told Flat Stone Pipe. "They are a re-creation of the world itself, Mother Earth reaching toward Father Sky. Each serves as a portal and a platform, a means of transporting between all three worlds. A gateway, if you will."

Flat Stone Pipe nodded, his attention fixed on the disappearing layer of white sand as another of the long line of laborers dumped his basket of black clay beside its predecessor. Immediately a swarm of women began stamping the clay flat with their feet. Behind them the men followed with their logs to tamp the clay into a compact layer.

He said, "Clay to seal, sand to drain. And from my practiced eye, the thickness of the layers is perfect."

"Why did you call us here?" High Dance asked. He'd never really cared for either the dwarf or the influence the little man had with Columella. And she hesitated to elicit her brother's certain reaction by a reminder that Flat Stone Pipe had sired her firstborn son, Panther Call. The only thing she shared with that vile Blue Heron was a long list of husbands. For whatever reason, she always ended up with the dwarf in her bed.

"Power stirs," the little man told them, his tiny hand shading his eyes as he looked off toward mist-hidden Cahokia. "The Ancestors were shooting streaks of fire across the night sky like flaming arrows in a battle. And this morning at dawn, an owl flew out of the rising sun."

"Underworld Power aligned with the Sky World," High Dance mused.

Columella pursed her lips, her attention, too, turning toward Cahokia. "Word is that Red Wing town fell without a fight. Morning Star has the last of the Red Wing Clan's ruling lineage hanging in squares. The others, I've heard, were killed in the town plaza and the remains dismembered and thrown into the river as an offering to the Underworld."

Flat Stone Pipe chuckled at some inner thought. "Old news, Matron. I've learned that as of this morning the squares are empty. My source tells me the Red Wing heretics were cut down alive and carried off. But to what fate, no one is saying."

"Did you get that from Blue Heron?" High Dance tried to ask casually.

Flat Stone Pipe humored the stumbling attempt. "The Clan Keeper allows little to slip unless it serves a deeper purpose. I heard it from a passing Trader."

That's a pus-dripping lie. But she knew from long experience that Flat Stone Pipe considered it a matter of honor to offer a suitable lie rather than the truth any time he found himself in High Dance's presence.

Flat Stone Pipe, like Mother Spider herself, had a web of informants throughout Cahokia and its vassal towns. Nor did it bother Columella to substantially fund his activities. Since she had, the numbers of her relatives "honored" by the opportunity to found a distant colony had subsided to a trickle—and those were the ones she was only too glad to be rid of. The moment one of her kinsmen began to figure both prominently and unfavorably in Four Winds Clan politics, Columella was now able, for the most part, to maneuver the offender back into the *tonka'tzi*'s good graces.

That she had to do so, however, left a burning sting worthy of cactus thorns. Four Winds Clan was more than just the *tonka'tzi*, Matron Wind, Blue Heron, and, of course, the Morning Star. That so much authority had been concentrated in Morning Star House frustrated her to the bone.

High Dance shrugged as he accepted Flat Stone Pipe's lie, the expression on his tattooed face smug. "Good riddance to them. The last of the heretics is gone."

"There are others, good chief," Flat Stone Pipe said evenly. "The heresy will never be completely dead. The Morning Star may have finally overcome one obstacle. But Power, like all things, must have an opposite. It is the nature of Creation."

"But where does this new opposition to the Morning Star come from?" Columella asked.

"That, Matron, is the question." He was watching her with knowing dark eyes. "Conjuring Power carries great dangers. It would have to be done with extreme care."

"And why are you telling me this?" A constriction seemed to tighten in her chest.

"Because you, my lady, are the strongest and most capable lineage leader. Were Blue Heron given an incentive to look for rivals to *Tonka'tzi* Red Warrior's rule, she would look here first."

Columella stiffened, heart beginning to pound. Lightning blast him, the little man was reading her rising panic. "And what makes you think I might give her any incentive?"

His triumphant smile seemed to split his face; those eyes that knew her so well gleamed. "Why, never you, great Matron." Then he shifted his slitted gaze to High Dance, saying, "Because as smart as the Matron is, not all of her relatives have the delicate finesse necessary to engage the Clan Keeper in a game of wits."

High Dance just gave the dwarf a hard and distasteful glare. "I don't know where you're going with that."

"Wherever it is, High Chief, let's hope it doesn't entail a square measured to fit your sister's body."

Columella, long familiar with her brother's mannerisms, noted his shock. *What are you into, brother?*

Fourteen

Seven Skull Shield leaned his head back, singing at the top of his lungs. *"Five days she laid with me, riding my shaft as if it were a tree!"* The split-cane roof overhead provided relief from the midday sun, and the shell workers often allowed him to loiter in their open-sided workshop. They were Deer Clan men, most of them third-generation bead cutters and shell carvers.

"Her sheath so slick and tight, sucked in my shaft, giving pure delight." He added facial expressions as he bellowed out his song, hands pantomiming the action.

The men working around him shook their heads and grinned as they continued their shell cutting. The sour-onion smell of roasting shell permeated the air where the discard was darkening in the fire. The rasping sound of the cane drills rose and fell like hoarse cicadas accompanying the high-pitched screeching of chert microdrills as they bored tiny holes.

"Upon my shaft she rose so high, drove herself down, nearly broke my thigh."

"Blood and thunder, man," Elder Crawfish declared, "you have a voice like . . . like . . ."

"Cracking rocks?" Meander asked as he removed his drill from the piece of clamshell and wet the end of the cane in a pot of water by his knee. Next he rotated the damp end in fine quartz sand until it was coated. This he fitted back in his bow-drill and resumed cutting yet another perfectly round bead from the piece of shell.

"More like wounded and dying dogs," Right Fist muttered. "And with songs like that, it's no wonder he can't keep a woman."

"I keep them just fine," Seven Skull Shield replied, overemphasizing his words. "And I don't have to sing to do it."

"That's absolutely obvious."

"It's your refined sense of manners," Meander offered flippantly as he fitted a fine-pointed chert drill tip in his hardwood dowel. With long practice he centered it on the bit of conch he was perforating.

"Surely not his fine looks." Right Fist screwed his expression into distaste. "With a face like that, not even one of them corn-worshiping dirt women would look twice."

"Gods, and you *know* what sort *they'll* spread for," Two Fish said with a gesture as he poured shell scraps into a carry sack.

Seven Skull Shield bellowed a laugh and shook his head. "Looks have got nothing to do with it, you needle-headed clods of mud. You're overthinking this whole woman thing." He slapped a hand to his muscle-packed thigh. "Oh, I know. I heard the same old hot blow from my old matron's mouth. 'You've got to be steady, respectful. Show her family that you're solid, worthy to sire her clan's next generation. Convince them you're going to be a man of status, looked up to in the community.' And that's all night shit!"

"Night shit?" Meander looked up as his drill ate away the last of the shell and the new bead dropped free. "Then why am I working so hard trying to make a good impression on my wife's clan?"

" 'Cause you have to," Seven Skull Shield told him.

"And you don't?" Meander gave him a skeptical squint. "Like I said, men who sing about women do so because they sleep alone at night." He shook his cane drill in emphasis. "And nothing you've said here leads any of us to think otherwise."

Seven Skull Shield scowled as he squinted at his thumbnail. "I forget the kind of men I'm dealing with sometimes."

"Yeah," Bent Cane said with a smile as he carried a fresh sack of shells into the building. "Unlike you, they're *married* men. They enjoy warm beds every night."

"Captured men," he replied with a yawn. "Me I'm free, and too encumbered with women as it is."

"Liar." Meander shot him a sidelong look as he began sawing on his bow drill.

"Liar? Me? These lips have never uttered a falsehood. Your problem is that you don't know the secret to beguiling women."

"And you do?"

"Of course." He dearly enjoyed the skeptical look they were giving him.

Meander suggested, "Are you going to tell us that to beguile a woman you have to be homeless, footloose, clanless, for the most part despised, as well as completely untrustworthy? Like yourself? Why would any woman you didn't have to *pay* want anything to do with the likes of you?"

Seven Skull Shield drew a deep sigh, stood, and said wistfully, "You'll never be satisfied with yourselves as men again. Sorry to do this to you." With a flourish, he whipped off his breechcloth, thrusting his hips forward. "There's the secret! Give her a choice of completely filling herself with a tree trunk like that, or one of your thin little saplings? A woman wants to know that a man's in her! Compared to the pathetic things you've got hanging down over your scrawny balls? You'd better be sure and tell her when you drive it in so she doesn't miss it!"

Seven Skull Shield gave them a knowing smile and rocked his hips to swing his oversized member. He delighted in their wide-eyed and disbelieving . . .

"Seven Skull Shield?" A hard voice asked behind him.

"At your will and pleasure," he boomed, turning around and thrusting his hips at . . . a woman? And an older one at that. Well, sometimes Power just gave a man the right audience, the sort that . . . Four large warriors slipped into the shell cutter's workhouse. The big one, a tough-looking tattooed man with a crooked jaw, cocked his head as he inspected Seven Skull Shield's dangling glory, then narrowed an eye in disgust.

The woman, however, arched a skeptical eyebrow, lips pursed as she studied his penis. "So, he'll be useful after all."

"How is that, Clan Keeper?" the broke-jawed warrior asked skeptically.

Clan Keeper? Was this old . . .

"If we ever stick a canoe in the mud, we'll have a tow rope." And with that she turned, calling over her shoulders. "Bring him."

Seven Skull Shield barely had time to stuff himself back in his breechcloth before the four warriors had grabbed him by the shoulders and were hustling him out of the bead works.

Do I dare make a break for it?

He gave the men that boxed him a furtive inspection. Each warrior was alert; they gripped their war clubs as if the weapons were old friends. Watchful as the warriors were of the passing throng of people bearing firewood, sacks of corn and sunflower seeds, jars of water, and bales of thatch, they each made eye contact when they looked his way, as if daring him to try.

Nope. Don't risk it. He gave them his best "I'm a charming and good guy" smile. No change of expression crossed their faces. Whoever the Clan Keeper was, she'd hired very competent men.

Which left him with his next problem: who was she? He watched in surprise as she seated herself upon an imposing litter, and eight strapping young men lifted her high. People had stopped to watch. Seven Skull Shield shot a glance over his shoulder. The bead cutters clustered in the doorway of their workshop, eyes wide.

This was a busy part of town. If he could just get a head start, there were enough people to screen him, and he knew the cluttered huts, warehouses, and workshops of the riverfront like the lines in his palm.

If you're going, it had better be now. The best bet would be to break for the river. It lay no more than six bow-shots to the west. As soon as they lost sight of him, he'd duck to the right behind the Deer Clan's cane warehouse. That would put him in the workshops where they packed in tight atop the levee. The thick cluster of craftsmen depended on the river-Trade supply of shell, copper, cane, firewood, raw stone, mica, hides, horn, bow wood, and other raw materials.

He faked a cough, bending, ready to leap when a war club was laid over his shoulder. "The Keeper just said bring you," the cock-jawed warrior reminded firmly. "She didn't specifically say you needed to be conscious or have all your bones unbroken."

"Why, I'm happy to accompany you," Seven Skull Shield told him with a disarming smile. "Wouldn't miss it." He paused. "Um, this isn't about Spring Flower, is it? I never touched the girl. Fact is, I was as surprised as any when she drew me into that room. It was all just ruse on her part, you know. She'd been seeing that other man. What's his name? Short Wing something? She only lured me in to take the blame if she was . . ."

"Who?" the cock-jawed warrior asked.

"Not Spring Flower?" He gave the man another of his disarming grins. "Um, you wouldn't mind if we stepped up closer to the litter? Just to ask a few questions?"

"If she wants talk, she'll tell you. If not, you'll follow along politely and quietly."

For a sense of humor as limited as yours, she must have had to pay extra.
Seven Skull Shield kept his wide smile in place and hurried forward,
noting that each of the guards mimicked his movements perfectly.

"Um, Matron? Excuse me."

She glanced down from the litter, head cocking again in that bird-
like manner of curiosity. "What?"

"Well, I . . . um, Matron, is there something I could explain to you?
Surely you've confused me with someone else. Whatever your granddaughter may have told you, I—"

"I have no granddaughter, so perhaps you're the one confused?"

"Ah," he touched his forehead, bowing slightly. "Perhaps you're concerned about the blessed statuettes from First Woman's temple? I might
have information on their whereabouts. If you would be kind enough
to allow me a couple of hands of time, I believe I could manage to have
them back on the altar before—"

"First Woman can take care of herself," the woman replied sharply.

"Then, great Matron, surely there is some special service that you
have in mind?"

"Actually, there is not. Nor am I a Matron." She was riding faced
forward, eyes on the bustle of traffic, refusing even to waste a further
glance on him.

"Then, um, Keeper? Clan Keeper?" That's what cocked-jaw had
called her. "Am I to understand you want to hire me for a special project? Perhaps something that a woman of status such as yourself might
shy from doing? Perhaps a bothersome relative? Some rival that might
need a . . . shall we call it, a change of perspective?" That *had* to be it.
"I assure you, I can be most discrete. And, subject to your instructions, not even the Morning Star himself could ever pry—"

"I deal with my own rivals," she stated flatly. "And I certainly don't
need the likes of you to cover my tracks."

The surety with which she said it left no room for doubt.

"I um . . . well, what could you possibly need me for?"

"That," she answered caustically, "is the single question currently
dominating all of my thoughts."

At the wave of her hand—and the immediate gesture of cocked-
jaw's war club—he backed away, as puzzled as he'd ever been.

"Who *is* she?" Seven Skull Shield hissed out the side of his mouth.

"The clan keeper," cocked-jaw growled.

"What clan keeper? Which clan? One of the immigrant ones?"

"Are you always this stupid?"

Seven Skull Shield gave the man an irritated glance of his own.

"Actually, no. For the life of me I can't figure out what I might have . . . I mean, seriously. She's a clan keeper? Which clan? Who does she serve?"

Cocked-jaw gave him the look he'd give an insect. "She's the clan keeper of the Four Winds Clan, and she serves the Morning Star. *Personally.*"

Seven Skull Shield stumbled, panic settling in his chest as he looked past the warriors at the woman perched so regally atop her litter. "She's . . . You mean, *the* Clan Keeper? And she wants *me?*"

"Apparently so, but I am completely baffled as to why."

Fifteen

With his distinctive clan tattoos covered in tawny face paint, and dressed as he was in a plain tan hunting shirt, High Dance Mankiller should have appeared anonymous. Instead he felt as conspicuous as a coral snake in a brownware bowl. He'd always been a noble. His lineage house had been in charge of Evening Star town since Petaga was overthrown and the town renamed. From the time he was a boy, he'd been trained to step into his father's position as high chief of the Evening Star House. The position carried a great deal of authority by itself, but his father had always fumed under the yoke of the *tonka'tzi*'s rule and the unbridled authority of the Morning Star. That the latter had been reincarnated in the *tonka'tzi*'s lineage, Father had claimed, was but a matter of luck.

And now there is a way to change that.

He strolled idly along the row of vendors who had laid out blankets and erected temporary ramadas along the western edge of the great plaza. As he inspected brightly colored fabrics, stacks of brownware pottery, piles of tanned deer, rabbit, elk, and bison hides, he wondered if his walk gave him away, if his hairstyle—the thick black locks wrapped around a wooden ball and tied—looked appropriately common.

Casting sidelong gazes at the milling people who chatted, perused the offered wares, and nodded pleasantly at the vendors, he could see no one sparing him more than a dismissive glance.

Is it really this easy to become faceless? The notion stunned him.

A cheer sounded behind him, and he turned, barely able to make out the Morning Star through the cluster of spectators watching his chunkey game. They came every day when the weather was nice. Nor did the Morning Star disappoint them, dressed in all his regalia, he descended the stairs from his palace on high. Trotting with the vigor of a yearling elk, his copper-clad lances and gorgeous white marble stones in hand, he'd meet whoever had won the honor of competing against him that morning. The bets would be wagered, and the game commenced.

No one ever beat the Morning Star. He would take his starting position, keen eyes on the chunkey court. For breathless heartbeats, he would stand, balanced, concentrating. In an instant he'd launch himself. As he sprinted forward, his right arm would extend behind him, the stone cupped in his palm. As he swept it forward and released, the stone would just kiss the smooth clay, shooting ahead like a shot. In the next pace, Morning Star would transfer his gleaming copper lance from left to right hand. Shoulder rolling back, he'd extend, and with a supple twist of his body, cast the lance after the fleeing stone.

High Dance had watched the living god's skill in amazement, often when he—no mean chunkey player himself—had challenged the Morning Star. Invariably, Morning Star's lance, like a thing alive would seek out the stone and impact within a hand's distance of where it stopped.

The game was played to twenty. As points accrued ten "point" sticks were first twisted into the ground by the observing priest, and then removed until twenty points had been scored. The first player to have the last of his sticks taken down, won.

Morning Star always won. As was the tradition, the loser dropped to one knee, bowed low to expose the back of his neck, and offered the living god his head. Morning Star would raise his face to the heavens, arms held high, and grant the loser his life. As the crowd cheered his clemency, Morning Star would turn toward them and donate his winnings. At that point priests went through the anxious and milling crowd, handing out feathered wands to those they thought worthy. The wands, in turn, would be exchanged for one of the wagered items which generally included fine bowls, beautiful capes, decorative blankets, and the like.

"Does he ever lose?" an accented voice asked at High Dance's shoulder.

Startled, he almost reacted like High Dance Mankiller instead of a common farmer. But, catching himself in time, he made a dismissive gesture with his hand. "He is the Morning Star. How could the god lose?"

The man who'd stopped beside him was young, muscular, his face darkened with ash to obscure his tattoos. As tall as High Dance, he had the characteristic look of a noble. Instead of wearing his hair up, a single thick braid on the left side of his head hung down over his left breast. Now the man crossed his arms, one foot forward, and said, "Thank you for meeting me."

"Do you have a name?" High Dance asked, keeping his voice low as he glanced around at the other spectators. They might have been but two casual strangers meeting amid the slowly moving throng inspecting the Trade goods the merchants had brought in.

"You can call me Bead."

"Just Bead?"

"For the time being."

"And what did you wish to speak to me about?" A tingling of unease began at the bottom of his spine. This could be a terrible trap, some machination of Blue Heron's. She'd been known to attempt such things in the past.

"Someone tried to kill the Morning Star the other night." Bead said it emotionlessly. "The attempt was audacious. From what I've *finally* been able to ferret out, it would have succeeded but for the unlikely arrival of Lady Night Shadow Star."

A band of fear tightened around High Dance's chest. "I've heard nothing of this."

"No. I suppose you haven't." Bead's voice hinted of indifference. "They're keeping it quiet."

"And the assassin?" Though he struggled to maintain an appearance of calm, he could feel fear sweat tingling in his skin.

"Dead." Bead kept his eyes on the crowd watching the chunkey game. "The corpse was sunk in the river as an offering to Piasa."

"Who would attempt such a thing?"

"Anyone who wished to upset this sham of a living god," Bead replied, not taking the bait. "But in this case a man named Cut String. I believe you know him since he's from one of the Evening Star lineages. Which is why I thought having this little discussion might be worthwhile."

"I don't know what you mean." Tickles of terror began to stroke his very bones. *Cut String . . . ? Why?*

"No, you do not, Chief High Dance. That doesn't mean that Blue Heron isn't going to find herself incredibly interested in Evening Star

House. Fortunately, she will find nothing, which will turn her in other directions."

"Why are you telling me this?"

"So that you will be warned." Bead cocked his head as he watched the Morning Star bowl his stone. "But I also know a great deal about Evening Star House . . . and its ambitions. In the near future I will have need of a strong House to step in and maintain authority."

"Are you a madman? Or simply insane?"

"Within the next couple of days, I will give you a demonstration of my abilities. Once we have both made our positions clear, we can talk again."

High Dance, on the verge of panic, swallowed hard. "What makes you think I won't go straight to the Clan Keeper and report you?"

Bead chuckled. "It would be tempting. A way to distance yourself from Cut String's failed attempt. But what would you tell them? Some man named Bead talked of the assassination attempt and vanished into the crowd?"

"What do you want from me?"

"For the moment? Nothing, High Chief. I think, however, that in the next couple of days, everything will be different."

"Different how?"

"You'll know. And your greatest fear, Blue Heron, will no longer leave you uneasy in your bed when sleep is difficult."

"You mean to eliminate her?"

"Her and some others. Let's call it smoothing the way."

"And how will I know if you have succeeded?"

"Someone will bring you a plain wooden bead. When you receive it, the messenger will tell you when and where to take it."

With that, Bead turned and walked casually away, vanishing into the crowd that milled around the stands filled with various goods, sacks of corn, and other Trade the vendors had brought in.

On the chunkey court, the Morning Star had scored his final point, and the crowd roared as another defeated opponent dropped on one knee to offer his head to the living god.

Sixteen

In his youth, the old man had had many names; each was replaced with a new one as he passed through the four ranked societies of Sky Priests. Until he had been chosen as the Sky Flier, the head of his society, he'd been known as Wild Lightning Lance. Now approaching his eightieth year, his grasp of the heavens and their secrets was unparalleled by any of his subordinate colleagues.

His hair had gone white and thin; barely enough remained to pin together into a sort of bun, pathetic though it might be. His face had shriveled into a map of wrinkles more intricate than the night sky itself. Not a single tooth remained in his mouth. Sky Flier's fingers now ached and burned, the knuckles swollen; his joints were a fiery collection of assorted pains. These days his urine only flowed in dribbles and fits.

Nevertheless, he only needed to close his faded brown eyes and run fingers across the record beads to recall celestial events as long gone as his boyhood. He'd survived the overthrow of Petaga, helped orchestrate the first resurrection of Morning Star, and marveled at Cahokia's transformation.

He lived in a humble trench-wall house just north of the Avenue of the Sun, behind the Sky Priest temple atop its low mound. The temple—storehouse for the society's records, sacred measuring strings and pegs, and sighting tubes—itself stood a stone's toss east of the great circular observatory.

Three times during Sky Flier's life, he'd seen the observatory expanded from twenty-four, to thirty-six, and finally—under his supervision—to forty-eight posts. Each time the Sky Priests had been able to refine their observations of the living heavens. Now they marked the rising and setting of Father Sun, the eighteen-and-a-half year cycles of the moon, and the movements of the constellations. Slowly, surely, the secrets of the Sky World were being unraveled, and with them, an understanding of the miracles of Power.

Sky Flier was surprised therefore, when one of the young initiates appeared at his door around midday, bowing, and announcing, "Forgive me, great Sky Flier. Lady Night Shadow Star has arrived. She requests an audience at the temple."

"Right now?" he demanded, rising painfully from his pole bed. "I'm taking a nap!"

"I'll tell her you are indisposed, Sky Flier."

"You'll tell her no such thing," he said with a sigh. "She's Morning Star House, boy. Young, yes, but steeped in Power and authority."

In their younger days, she—and her wild siblings—had been no end of trouble for Sky Flier. That Night Shadow Star came to him? And after rumors of her soul-flying in the Underworlds?

That had portents even the stars would have trembled to contemplate.

He struggled to his feet, reaching out with a thin arm to brace himself on the bed as he tottered for balance. From a storage box, he retrieved his simple black tunic with its dots of stars portrayed by shell beads; they'd been sewn onto the fabric in the pattern of constellations.

To the initiate, he said, "Find the venerable Day Keeper. Have him pull down the Morning Star House box from the temple shelf where it rests. Tell him I need the record string for Night Shadow Star's birth."

"Yes, Sky Flier. Do you need your litter?"

"No. I'll walk." He belted his tunic about the waist, irritated by his forever-full bladder. He dared to take enough time to relieve a bit of the pressure.

Two young men of the Day Society, finely dressed in their capes and feathers, waited to take his arms and assist him as he toddled around the mound to find Night Shadow Star. She waited, tall and stately in a brilliant blue skirt, a raven-feather cloak about her shoulders.

Even through his blurry vision, she looked magnificent.

"Greetings, Lady."

"Greetings, Sky Flier."

She offered something to one of the Day Priests who waited on one side. The man bowed and touched his forehead, indicating that whatever Trade it had been, it would be more than satisfactory compensation for whatever Night Shadow Star wanted.

"And what can I do for you?" Sky Flier fought to control his balance.

She stepped close. "I would speak to you in confidence."

"Ah, that, then."

"You already know?"

He indicated the great circle of the observatory, its forty-eight finely carved posts rising to create a ring; the midday shadow's shortening length marked the progression of spring. "Through the observatory, I learn many things." He gave her a wide, toothless grin. "But everything else I learn through listening, thinking, and drawing simple conclusions."

The Day Keeper exited the temple, descended the short stairs, and bowed as he handed a beaded record string to Sky Flier.

"All of you, leave us, please."

Touching their foreheads, the others departed.

Sky Flier glanced at Night Shadow Star. "Could we sit on the step? These old bones, not to mention the rest of me, could collapse at any moment."

She took his arm, steadying him as he sat, then lowered herself beside him. "I shouldn't have bothered you."

He bent his rickety neck as he fingered the patterns in the beads, refreshing his memory. "Perhaps you should have indeed. I can hear the worry in your voice, feel it tensing your body." He snorted. "Odd, isn't it, that in all of Cahokia, you can only come to me?"

She stared at the ring of tall, carved, effigy posts that made up the observatory. Elbows between her knees she rubbed her hands together in nervous agitation. "We caused you a lot of trouble. I'm sorry for that."

"Your brothers may have been more at fault than you." He raised a finger. "Though you joined in with wild abandon. Took us nearly a quarter moon to reconstruct the measuring cords, get the knots right." He shook his head. "That Chunkey Boy, he was a bad one. So many of the things he and his brother got away with were nothing less than evil. And what he did to that poor Fish Clan girl and her family . . . ?"

Night Shadow Star exhaled through her nostrils, head dropping. "They've had their comeuppance: one consumed by Morning Star, the other dead somewhere in the south. That leaves me. Power has seen fit to exact pain for pain."

His fingers traced out the patterns in the beads again. "Word travels that you have become intimate with Piasa and the Powers of the Underworld."

"Word is correct." She chuckled. "Reconciliation of opposites, Sky Flier? My clan is aligned with the Powers of the Sky World. But my dream soul has been devoured by Piasa, one of the Underworld's greatest Spirits. Now he whispers to me at odd hours of the day. I catch glimpses of him in the corner of my eye." She gestured toward the record strings with their patterns of beads. "Was that foretold at my birth?"

He held up the record strings. "I had forgotten the signs on the night of your birth. Twenty years you've been alive, Lady. All that was prophesied from the constellations. I myself counted the falling stars that night. Twenty."

"Am I to die soon?"

"That, I cannot tell." He laid a fragile hand on her arm. "Nor can I tell if those twenty years referred to the length of time you had before your wandering soul was devoured by Piasa in the Underworld. If so, you now manifest yourself only as an element of his Power. Night Shadow Star is gone. Piasa's creature remains. Think of Piasa's presence inside you like a shadow cast from afar. And drawing from its Power, you might live for decades more. It could also be that from the moment you fell under the spell of Underworld Power, your auspices could no longer be read among the stars."

Her laughter was bitter and self-mocking. "For the greatest Sky Flier to have ever lived, your ability to prophesy seems to consist of picking and choosing possibilities."

He laughed in return, making a tsking with his lips. "I am sorry to disappoint you, Lady. Nevertheless, since Power now surrounds you like a cloak, I will share a secret with you. After a lifetime of dedicated study, I can tell you that the more I learn, the more I am disheartened to discover that even more mysteries lie beyond the horizon of my comprehension. Some prophesy is easy. Some, like yours, impossible to scry." He paused. "You are at the center of a whirlwind, Night Shadow Star. One I cannot see through."

She took a deep breath. "When I danced with Sister Datura and sent myself into the Underworld, it was with the intention of joining my husband's life-soul. I was tired of the pain, of the heartbreak. I can't even sleep without nightmares. . . . They fill my souls, so explicit, disgusting. They shame me." She rubbed her face. "No wonder Piasa devoured my soul."

"I hear you have taken the Red Wing war chief."

"Pus and blood! Why did the Water Panther demand that of me? Saving the Morning Star, allying with the living god against the assassin, yes. But the Red Wing?" Her fists knotted. "He *killed* my husband. The very sight of him sickens me. Having him close? It's torture. All I want to do is drive a stake through his heart and burn his corpse." Her voice broke. "Were my misdeeds as a youth so atrocious that I should suffer so, Sky Flier? Is that the meaning of your prophecy?"

"I do not mean to dissemble, Lady. But what we read in the sky the night of your birth is an enigma. Power obscures any prophesy beyond twenty years."

"I am so weary and confused, Sky Flier. And yes, I'm afraid. No matter what disguise I adopt, down deep, my bones are trembling with fear. Sometimes I'm so scared I want to throw up."

She sniffed. "I don't want to be Night Shadow Star. I just want to stop hurting all the time. Is that too much to ask?"

"Power wouldn't have called upon you if it didn't think you possessed the necessary strength. Whatever the evils you and your brothers committed before you became a woman, and in spite of the grief you bear for your husband's death, you are born of Morning Star House, of the Four Winds Clan."

"Brave words Sky Flier. Why is it that all I want to do is flee?" She wiggled her fingers in a running gesture. "Escape. Run away."

"The greatest among us live in constant fear. You won't flee."

"You know that?"

"I know that you'll reach down inside yourself and pull up whatever strength you need for the situation at hand." He smiled in the midday sun. "I think Piasa knows that, too. And this darkness descending upon us? I think you had better beware."

Seventeen

Columella's body ceased to pulse with the explosions of ecstasy. She lay on her back, fingers knotted in the buffalo-hide pillow above her head. Panting for breath she waited as the flush faded from her breasts and the tingling delight in her pelvis became a warm sensation of contentment.

She rotated her hips and straightened her legs as Flat Stone Pipe crawled up her torso. The dwarf slipped down into the hollow of her arm as she laid it along his back. A shiver ran through her as he reached out with his small hand to finger her nipple.

"What is it about you?" she asked. "All these years, and it's as if my very bones explode."

"Caught your breath yet?" he asked.

"Mostly."

"Good." He shifted enough to study her. "We need to talk."

She raised her head just enough to pull the buffalo pillow down behind her. "What have you heard?"

"Did you attempt to have the Morning Star murdered? Something that, given your busy schedule, you might have forgotten to mention to me in passing?"

She craned her neck to see him more clearly. "If I did, I forgot to mention it to myself as well. No. Not that the idea doesn't have a certain appeal. Why?"

"You know Cut String Mankiller?"

"He's made quite a name for himself as War Second. Chances are good that he'll be given command of one of the squadrons. Don't tell me . . ."

"Oh, yes." Flat Stone Pipe had forgotten her nipple, his thoughtful eyes on hers. "Apparently he hid somewhere in the palace. Then, in the middle of the night, he managed to sneak into the living god's quarters. He bashed the brains out of one of Spotted Wrist's female cousins, and was about to slit the Morning Star's throat when Lady Night Shadow Star appeared out of the night, naked and dripping wet, and drove three arrows into Cut String's chest at the last possible instant."

Columella frowned. "I'd like to think this is some crazy story someone heard after smoking too many hemp leaves."

"Unfortunately, I have a source. He tells me it happened just that way."

"Why hasn't the Morning Star turned the whole city upside down? You'd think he'd be furious."

Flat Stone Pipe shifted, gently massaging her breast. "Blue Heron is using the subsequent silence to set her trap. Morning Star himself wants her to quietly find the plotters so he can deal with them." He paused. "Which is why I thought perhaps . . . ?"

Columella frowned as she settled her hand on his hip and cupped her fingers around his rump. "No. Not that I wouldn't have tried it given half a chance for success. Do they suspect us?"

"They suspect everyone. My worry, beloved, is that something might link Cut String to you."

She shook her head absently. "No. There are rumors, however, about Cut String's uncle and his daughter. Or is it his niece?"

"Not just rumors," Flat Stone Pipe told her. "My first thought was to dispatch him over the pollution of incest. After Tharon's transgressions no one would so much as cock an eyebrow. And I would have, had you been involved."

"No." She rubbed her chin over the top of his head. "He might have more value alive for the time being."

"I've someone watching him. Should whoever goaded Cut String to act try and contact the uncle again, we'll grab them for a little chat."

"What would I do without you?"

"Suffer dissatisfaction under the clumsy fumblings of awkward lovers with no idea of how to coax your body into a frenzy?"

She slapped his round bottom playfully. "I wasn't thinking about that."

"Then perhaps you were wondering about your brother?"

"Why, in the name of the Sky Eagle, would I think of him?"

"Because he's up to something."

"Oh, really? What now? Some new woman? An angle on Trade?"

"Political, I think."

"He'd have told me."

"Then why did he sneak out before dawn, dress like a common Trader, blank his tattoos in brown paint, and skulk through the crowds at the Great Plaza this past midday?"

She shifted to stare into his hard dark eyes. "He did that?"

"He did." Flat Stone Pipe took a breath. "Do you think it had anything to do with the attempt on the Morning Star? Something he's pursuing without your knowledge?"

"He'd never dare!"

But he would, and she knew it. She frowned, saying, "He's never been clever about these things."

Flat Stone Pipe gave her a reassuring pat. "I'll keep an eye on him." He hesitated. "And if he's managed to get himself into trouble?"

She massaged her forehead with her free hand. "Then I'll have to deal with him. One way . . . or another."

"He's your brother."

"It's *my* life! The lives of *our* children!"

His eyes fixed on hers as he nodded. "We'll do what we have to do."

"No matter what it costs," she agreed, images of High Dance's laughing eyes playing between her souls.

You stupid fool! Please don't make me kill you.

Fingers of unease stroked his souls; Fire Cat came awake with a start. The fire had burned low, leaving the great room poorly lit. But in the glow he could make out the furnishings of Night Shadow Star's palace. The carved likenesses of snakes and raptors along the wall benches had fixed their intent gazes on him. Their shell-inset eyes gleamed red and seemed to have a malicious intensity. Growing anxiety flitted about between Fire Cat's souls as if on bat wings.

What is it? What's wrong?

His heart began to pound; he listened to the silence. From the corner of the room he could hear the faint rhythmic gnawing of a mouse.

Still, that feeling of threat hovering over him might have been a grim mist.

He blinked, slowly taking a breath, smelling the musty blanket on which he slept, drawing in the faint scent of smoke. And something else. He sniffed again, catching a hint of musk.

Someone was close. Too close.

Turning his head, he froze. Eyes wide, his gaze fixed on the stone knife poised over his heart. The blade was as long as a man's forearm, and two slender brown hands gripped it at the top. He followed those athletic female arms back to Night Shadow Star.

She knelt beside him, knees together in the manner of a well-bred woman. A finely woven hemp skirt patterned in black and white diagonal lines conformed to her hips. Her long black hair hung loosely over her shoulders like a midnight mantle. The expression on her fine triangular face bespoke tortured indecision.

"Go ahead," he whispered. "You've taken everything else from me."

Her nod was faint, as if she heard from a great distance. The knife poised over his heart didn't so much as waver.

"Piasa," she whispered, as if talking to herself, "you ask too much!"

"Piasa?" Fire Cat studied the knife, shifting ever so slightly. If he could get his right arm clear of the blanket, move quickly enough, he could thrust up, grab her hands, and pull that long chert blade straight down into his body.

Am I that ready to die?

A weary smile curled his lips. What an easy escape from his pledge to serve this vile woman.

"Do you know what it's like?" Her voice sounded hollow. "How do you expect me to sleep in peace, knowing he's here? In my house, eating my food, drinking my water? Breathing my air?"

"I could be elsewhere," he suggested softly. "Just release me from my vow."

Her eyes tightened the slightest bit, accenting the faint shake of her head. "It would be so easy. Just like tonight. He sleeps soundly. A simple thrust. The blood would flow, rich, red, pulsing with each dying beat of his heart." She closed her eyes, tipping her head back, as if relishing the dream. "Would it wash away this endless feeling of despair and pain?"

"Try it and see," Fire Cat suggested. "I don't wish to be bound to you any more than you want me polluting your house with my eating, drinking, and breathing."

Her brow lined in pain; she glanced down at him, and seemed to see him for the first time. "You *killed* him. And doing so, you killed me."

"That is the red nature of war, Lady." Fire Cat shrugged. "And had he won that day? Had Power favored him and his squadrons? Would I have fared any differently? Your brother sent him to destroy us. We defended ourselves. Nothing more. Nothing less."

"You could have reached into my body and torn my heart out. It wouldn't have hurt any less."

He narrowed an eye, wondering at the muscle control that allowed her to hold the knife without even a faint quiver. "I think I'm catching a glimmer of what this is all about. Your pain is an obsession with you. You've been raised to be the exalted and overindulged sister of the Morning Star, daughter of *Tonka'tzi* Red Warrior Tenkiller, niece to the Matron Wind. You've never been denied anything, have you? Never had life, Power, or fate slap you hard in the face. Now it has, and the spoiled child inside you can't stand it. You poor, pampered little sheath, my souls just *ache* for you." He sniffed in disdain. "Now, will you act like a *competent* woman for once in your life and end this sham?"

For the first time, the knife quivered slightly; her muscles tensed. She held his gaze, loathing and hatred in her large dark eyes. Her mouth worked, jaws clamping hard as she ground her teeth.

Then she abruptly tucked the knife into her lap, a defeated emptiness in a gaze gone vacant. "I would love nothing more, you Red Wing maggot. Every nerve in my body cries out to kill you."

"Just do it. Spare us both the discomfort."

She shook her head. "You're part of the bargain. When a Spirit Beast tells you to do something . . ."

"Stop it! Your brother is just a man. Even in Red Wing town we heard about Chunkey Boy and the way he abused people. You were all Four Winds, spawn of the *tonka'tzi* and above punishment. No matter how heinous the crime. Nothing's changed. He panders to you. A smile, a shrug on your part, and he'll forgive you. Tell him I goaded you, insulted your virtue, called you names."

For an instant she seemed confused. "Morning Star could care less."

"Then who? You're *Lady* Night Shadow Star. Who could possibly give you orders?"

Her expression went distant again. "I do as my master tells me." And with that she rose elegantly to her feet, and head down, walked wearily back to her private quarters.

Rot and stink take me, I've promised on my honor to . . . serve the insane?

The Serpent

What I am about to attempt has taken years of planning. They never would have thought me capable. Certainly I shouldn't have accomplished all that I have, been to all those places, done the things I have. Call it the culmination of a family's love. That's what families do, don't they? Provide incentive to exceed expectations?

I certainly wouldn't have dedicated myself to such intense study of the chaotic Powers of the Underworld. It is there—and to a lesser extent from the Powers of the Middle World—where true guile and stealth are learned.

I've watched bobcats, weasels, foxes, and wolves, but the stealthiest hunters of all are the snakes. And they are the true Power of the Underworld. No one stalks as silently, as carefully, or with the invisibility of the serpent. Watch them approach. Not a blade of grass quivers as they close with their prey. Nor do they hurry, but stop, wait, and sense, totally attuned to their surroundings.

Oh yes, I have studied. Now the moment has come to return my love in full measure. The Four Winds Clan is dedicated to the Sky World. But, in all things, there can only be harmony with equilibrium. The Underworld is about to cast the balance, and I am its warrior.

I move with the night, ascending the steps to the palace. I know this place, can imagine the rooms and where my victims await. My feet barely caress the wood as I climb. Sky Beings are creatures of the day, and the guardian posts of Eagle and Falcon do not see me, cloaked as I am in Serpent Power.

My body is painted black, the color of death and invisibility. I wear the night like a cloak, hidden within its darkness. I slick a finger through my black grease-paint and smear a slithered black serpent over the shell eyes of the guardian posts. Come dawn's light, they will find themselves blinded.

Grasping my war club, I ease my way across the porch with a snake's silence and stop, listening, breathing slowly in the same manner a snake does.

In contrast to the war club in my right hand, the long and deadly chert knife in my left has a light heft, like the deadly serpent's fang that it is.

Confident that no one watches, I ease the door open and slip inside. There, like a stalking serpent, I wait, allowing my eyes to adjust. I make out sleepers along the wall benches. The fire has burned down to a glowing pit of coals in the center of the room. One by one I study the sleeping forms. Even those closest to me do not stir, but continue to breathe deeply.

Like a serpent through a nest of rodents, I start across the floor, passing the fire pit, veering around the tall clay altar in the rear where the lordly ruler normally sits atop his ornate litter.

Again I pause when I reach the doorway to the sleeping quarters. Looking back, nothing moves, though the shadows seem deeper behind the altar.

Carefully I lower the war club, then insert the thin chert blade to feel for a thong latch. Finding none, I lift the door and ease myself inside.

Again I wait, letting my eyes adjust to the deeper darkness as I catalog the room's contents. The sleeping bench is against the back wall, and there I see my quarry.

On silent feet I cross to stand above the recumbent form.

The stories of the Beginning Time are told for a reason. What the Morning Star can do, so too, can the Wild One. I must prove myself worthy, capable of following in the god's footsteps. I expected to feel remorse, some hesitation. Instead, to my surprise, a building anticipation rushes through my veins.

Yes, this night I am the god!

I lean down, setting my war club on the floor. Positioning myself just so, I lower the beautiful stone knife, its carefully sharpened edge keen enough to cut hair. I orient it so that with a single slash, I will sever that beloved throat.

Eighteen

Seven Skull Shield blinked awake. He'd always had that particular skill, as if his souls kept track of the passing night, and alerted him when it was time. If asked, he'd never be able to describe how it worked; it just happened. In this case, he'd ordered himself to awaken halfway between midnight and dawn. Thereafter he'd slept deeply, his belly happily digesting an outstanding meal of roast deer haunch, maygrass cakes, baked persimmons, and acorn mash all washed down with sweetened sassafras tea. If he could say nothing else about the Clan Keeper, her people definitely ate well!

But the time had come to extricate himself from this mess.

He carefully raised his head from the sleeping mat. That intimidating cock-jawed warrior, Five Fists, had given it to him and ordered him to sleep on the floor, just inside the door. A place generally reserved for the dogs.

What had been meant as an insult couldn't have served Seven Skull Shield better. He'd struggled to keep from grinning in anticipation as he'd accepted the mat.

You poor pathetic fool, Five Fists!

His plans aside, it hadn't been the sort of slight that would have offended Seven Skull Shield in the first place. For the excellent meal alone he would have been willing to sit on his haunches and bark.

Now fully awake, he grinned to himself and eased the blanket off his shoulder. The blanket he would keep. He'd never owned such a regal piece of the weaver's art. Woven out of the fine undercoat curried from winter bison hair, the thing was heavy, soft, and uncomfortably warm despite the cold draft circulating around the door.

He'd had ample opportunity to inspect the great room, memorize the locations of the most valuable carvings, ceramics, a fantastic scarlet-feathered cape the likes of which he'd never seen before, and a couple of small red siltstone statuettes that would bring a fortune among the river Traders. All he needed to do was retrieve them without a sound, wrap them carefully in the buffalo blanket, and slip out the door. By morning he'd be hidden in some nondesript warehouse. By tomorrow night he'd be signed onto some Trader's canoe. Within two weeks he'd be bartering his goods for a fortune in some Pacaha town far downriver.

He started to rise when the barest whisper of a moccasin-clad foot rasped on the matting outside. Dropping flat, he clamped his eyes into slits, emulating the deep breathing of a man asleep.

The door shifted, allowing more of the night breeze to waft over Seven Skull Shield's face. Then it swung open just enough that a man was able to slip inside. Carefully, the intruder replaced the door just so. Then he waited, standing silently, letting his eyes adjust to the darkness.

So, who's this? A household member who'd slipped out for an illicit rendezvous with a married man's wife?

Seven Skull Shield opened his eyes wider in the gloom, casting a sidelong glance up at the dark form.

If he were a household member, he'd know the layout. He'd have already begun sneaking his way toward his bed.

No, this was a stranger. Seven Skull Shield could sense it. The man was doing exactly what Seven Skull Shield did when he sneaked into someplace where he wasn't supposed to be. Like this intruder, he took his time, let his eyes adjust, studied the layout of the place.

Not only that, the intruder was too dark, and Seven Skull Shield caught the faintest odor of grease. *He's painted himself black!*

The man turned his attention to Seven Skull Shield, cocked his head, and listened. Seven Skull Shield maintained the easy deep breathing, catering to the illusion.

On cat feet, the intruder eased forward. As he passed the glowing coals in the puddled-clay central hearth, Seven Skull Shield caught the reflected gleam from a long, flaked chert blade. A ceremonial knife! Nothing else had that kind of rippled surface. A long-handled war club hung from the man's other hand.

Seven Skull Shield shifted, eased his blanket off, and considered. First option was to slip out the partially cracked door with his blanket— but no additional loot—and vanish into the night as originally planned. But that might lead to embarrassing questions if the intruder were up to as much malfeasance as Seven Skull Shield suspected.

Second, he could call an alarm, grab as much as he could in the ensuing confusion, and beat-feet for the landing. But that, too, en- tailed way too many potentials for disaster.

Meanwhile, a sense of indignation began to chafe against his irri- tated souls. Never before had he been *invited* into such a wealthy and influential person's house, one literally bursting with rare items, any one of which could be Traded for a year's worth of lodging, food, and will- ing nubile young women. Even more aggravating, he'd awakened just in time to help himself to the largess, and what happens? This pus-sucking interloper slips in to spoil the whole thing.

"Maggot," Seven Skull Shield mouthed silently as he rose to his feet and ghosted after the intruder.

You think you're going to cost me the greatest opportunity for loot that life and fortune has ever thrown my way?

Creeping silently was a skill Seven Skull Shield had perfected over the years. Tiptoeing had kept him alive in more situations than one. An amorous lover just didn't live long if he couldn't quietly escape another man's wife's bed. So, too, had he learned to blend into the shadows, slip thongs off door latches, pry apart thatch and matting, and numerous other methods of entry necessary to the unique art of sneaking around strange houses in the night.

The black-painted intruder went straight for the Clan Keeper's room in the rear. From the way he moved, the fellow was no ordinary farmer or craftsperson, but a trained warrior. His movements were spare, no effort wasted, totally balanced and poised.

He's going to pause at the door. Seven Skull Shield side-stepped and crouched in the shadow of the Clan Keeper's raised dais in the rear of the palace. And, as expected, the intruder paused, glancing back to make sure the room's occupants remained undisturbed.

Is the light good enough that he'll notice my blanket's empty by the door?

Apparently not. The intruder lowered his war club to the floor, and using both hands, slipped the long chert knife through the crack and lifted, obviously severing any thong on the inside. Then he carefully swiveled the door to one side, picked up his club, and vanished into the blackness.

Seven Skull Shield made a face, battled the sudden urge to just grab a couple of the better pieces of copper and pottery and run for it, and shook his head as he tiptoed to the Clan Keeper's doorway.

As he'd anticipated, the intruder was just inside, again demonstrating his skill as he let his eyes adjust further to the gloom.

Seven Skull Shield closed his eyes, willing himself to be one with the darkness. He sensed the intruder's movement, and slipped in after him.

The hunt had grown serious now. No way out. Seven Skull Shield's heart began to pound, a tickle of energy spiking in his muscles. Opening his eyes to the darkness he ghosted after the intruder.

To Seven Skull Shield's surprise, the man stopped before the Clan Keeper's bed and carefully lowered the war club to the floor. Like a hawk over a sleeping rabbit, he positioned himself. Then, in an instant, he clapped a hand over the sleeping woman's mouth and pressed the long stone knife to her neck. In a thickly accented voice, as though repeating from memory, he said, "Greetings from the one you threw away!"

Seven Skull Shield's fingers closed on the man's war club. Pivoting on one foot, he swung the vicious club up, and drove it smack into the base of the intruder's neck where it rose from the shoulders. Vertebra cracked and snapped under the impact. The black-painted man dropped the way a heavy wet stone slipped through greased fingers . . . full onto the Clan Keeper's breast.

Seven Skull Shield reached down and muscled the twitching corpse off of where it pinned old Blue Heron to her blankets. A scream of terror ripped from the old woman's throat, and outside the door, the palace erupted in shouts and confusion.

Nineteen

The ordeal was excruciating. Blue Heron wasn't sure which was worse, the pain from Rides-the-Lightning's ministrations, or reliving the terror of her near execution.

She sat on her raised dais, her blankets wadded into a knot behind her. The crackling fire illuminated her ornate walls, the sleeping benches, boxes, fine baskets, and highly polished brownware jars.

"Don't flinch," Rides-the-Lightning muttered. His gray-blind eyes stared emptily as he sewed her up by feel. "It just makes it more difficult."

She grimaced as he slipped another cactus spine through the bloody cut that transected her throat. When the assassin had jerked under the death blow, the incredibly sharp blade had sliced her skin.

"You try having your throat cut in the middle of the night, you old . . ." No, she couldn't say it. No matter how angry and frightened she might be.

"Any deeper," Rides-the-Lightning reminded yet again, "and it would have severed your windpipe. You're a very lucky woman."

She made a fist, and shot a sidelong glance at where Seven Skull Shield was standing off to the side, a calculating animation behind his dark eyes.

Fire and vomit! Now I'm indebted to the likes of him?

She needed but close her eyes, however, and the terror flashed like white light behind her eyes. The hand clapping to her mouth, the sharp edge of the knife pressing into her throat, and that soft voice, *"Greetings from the one you threw away!"* sent a shiver through her.

"Stop moving!" Rides-the-Lightning insisted again as he wound thread around the cactus spines to pull her severed skin together.

How could a blind man sew with such perfection?

"It burns!"

"Of course it does! They're cactus spines. Pain enhances healing. Just be glad—"

"Yes, yes." She winced as he pushed her chin up again.

With a sidelong glance she could see Clay Bell and Fire Temper, her supposed guards, standing by the door. Both gripped their war clubs and looked sheepish. They'd been asleep in their beds to either side of her door, of course.

Smooth Pebble emerged from Blue Heron's sleeping quarters, a torch in her hands. The *berdache* stepped over, shaking her head. "I've never seen him before. His entire body is painted in black. Rubbing the paint off his face, I was surprised to discover he has no tattoos."

"All men have tattoos," Blue Heron growled. "They get them when they are made men. All civilized people mark their men that way. How else do you know to whom you are speaking?"

"Not this one." Smooth Pebble frowned.

"Um . . ." Seven Skull Shield glanced back and forth at the guards and the rest of the household staff.

"Yes, what?" Blue Heron barked. "I suppose you've got the answer to the mystery?"

"Well, good Matron, I—"

"I'm *not* a matron!"

He gave her one of his ingratiating smiles, touched his forehead, and started side-stepping toward the door.

"Oh, blood and snot! Out with it! What were you about to say?"

She tried to read his canny expression as he said, "Great Lady, there are men without tattoos. Slaves taken as children from among the wild western tribes, for example."

"And you think this assassin was a grown slave?"

"No, Great—"

"Stop that gushing and insipid fawning. Call me Keeper, if you can't quite find it in you to use my name. Now, give it to me without the obsequious mish mash."

"He was anything but a slave." Seven Skull Shield's eyes had narrowed, a knowing glint behind his guarded expression. "It was the way he moved, nothing wasted. And, Keeper, he's done this before. Call it practiced. Whoever this man was, he knew exactly what he was about."

She kept her eyes on his as Rides-the-Lightning pulled the last of his threads tight and used a cloth to blot up the blood. To the rest of the room, she said, "Leave us. I need to speak candidly with the thief. Smooth Pebble, find Five Fists, have him inform the Morning Star that I've got another dead assassin here. He doesn't have to alert the *tonka'tzi*, Matron Wind, or Lady Night Shadow Star until morning."

She watched as the others left, stepping out into the darkness of the veranda. Rides-the-Lightning lifted an inquiring eyebrow, but she dismissed him with a word. His assistant took his arm; together they turned and headed for the door.

She focused on Seven Skull Shield. The man looked like a trapped woodrat in a grain bowl.

After the last person was safely outside, she said, "It seems that I underestimated you."

"How is that, Great . . . uh, Keeper?"

"I figured I'd awaken in the morning to find you gone along with a selection of my possessions. I've already arranged to have several of my agents circulating along the riverfront at dawn offering the most remarkable Trade for Four Winds Clan items, and buffalo blankets in particular."

To his credit, he didn't pale, or so much as bat an eye. "Why would the Keeper think that I, of all people—"

"Is it even possible for you to carry on a conversation without a lie passing your lips? I know exactly who and what you are. You've a reputation for beguiling and seducing married women, brawling, and you're a thief. Even my people—and they're the best—can't discover what your birth clan was, or where you came from. And incidentally, we've recovered all but one of those statuettes you stole. It will take a couple of months for your 'friend's' fingers to heal, but I doubt he'll feel inclined to deal in the Trade of stolen statues again."

At that, she detected the slightest tremor in Seven Skull Shield's expression. Then he said, "Why am I, of all people, here?"

She gestured both frustration and futility. "I haven't the foggiest notion. I don't understand it, and I understand everything. I was *ordered* to find you by Lady Night Shadow Star. Something about a deal she brokered with Piasa when her souls were captured in the Underworld and . . . And why am *I* telling *you* anything?"

His eyes narrowed even more. "Keeper, if Power were everything it's made out to be by the priests and chiefs, I'd have been blasted dead years ago for the things I've done."

She grunted in affirmation. "So now that we're talking honestly, why did you save me tonight?"

Taking his time to calculate, he finally said, "His untimely arrival interrupted what would have been a glorious increase in my Trade worth. Would it make sense if I told you that his arrival was like having someone stick a finger in your eye just when you get the first glimpse of extreme beauty? How *dare* he?"

She erupted in laughter. It made the skin pull and sting on her wounded throat. He didn't share her mirth, but a feral gleam grew in his eyes.

Gaining control of herself, she added, "But I already told you, my agents would be looking for . . ."

He was shaking his head. "Not down in Pacaha, they wouldn't. A smart man doesn't lift the personal possessions of the Four Winds Clan Keeper—and then Trade them in Cahokia. Not without hanging in a square for a most painful quarter moon before pieces of his body become fertilizer for some dirt farmer."

She said nothing as she studied him, feeling the rightness of his presence, and finally beginning to understand his value. For long moments he just returned her inspection, expression completely neutral. Confident bit of bird shit, wasn't he?

"What do you want, thief? Call it your ultimate goal in life?"

He shrugged. "I like fine food, good clothes, willing women in a warm bed, and having it all at someone else's expense."

"Bah! If I supplied you with your desires, within a half moon, you'd be as frantic as a squirrel without a nut. You like the challenge and thrive on the game. Knowing that you got away with it? That allows you to really savor your success. Therein lies the true sweetness of the food, the added thrill of driving your peg into some woman's sheath, or the delight in trading off some forbidden trinket. And there's your weakness, the one that will eventually bring you down."

"You do me an injustice, Great Lady. If there were any other way for a clanless man like me to survive, be assured that I'd immediately—"

"Now you're lying again."

He started to protest, then gave her a sly smile. "Well, perhaps I like a little bit of a challenge." It broke into a grin. "You're pretty good yourself, Keeper. Only one other woman has ever picked her way down to my souls the way you have."

She grunted, then noted, "You may not believe in Power, but I do. Tonight isn't the first time in recent days that an attempt has been made on someone's life. Someone very important."

"I've heard nothing, and believe me, I would have."

"I wouldn't be the cunning Clan Keeper I am if you had," she retorted. "But let's just say that I have a proposition for you." She paused. "If you're up for the challenge."

He crossed his heavily muscled arms, the smile widening. "Working for you comes with considerable risk, Clan Keeper. I'd be tainted, never trusted again. I have a reputation among certain kinds of people. One that serves me just fine, thank you."

"As do I."

"I know. You're known for eliminating individuals once they have fulfilled your purpose and might become a liability."

"Then perhaps I'm wrong about you." She reached up to finger her chin, remembered the stitches, and winced in irritation. "I thought you had a better opinion of yourself and your abilities."

"Oh, I do. That I'm still alive speaks for itself." He narrowed an eye in what might have been a wink. "At the same time, a man who underestimates his adversaries suffers a short life. And you, Keeper, are one of the most capable and dangerous people in Cahokia."

She gestured toward her sleeping quarters where the dead assassin still lay. "Apparently not everyone shares your sentiment."

"Actually, they do," he countered. "But for my chance presence, you'd no longer be a threat to them."

She met his eyes and nodded. "You weren't here by chance, thief. No matter what you think of Power. Nor are you a tool of the Four Winds Clan. You serve Power."

He shrugged dismissively.

"Believe what you will. The recent attack on the Morning Star, and here tonight, have taken me by complete surprise. The fact that I had no warning from any of my sources tells me that this is something new, and very dangerous. That Sky Power and Underworld Power are aligned, tells me the threat is greater than just politics. Therefore, I'm giving you a choice. Help me find the assassins. Doing so will require all of your cunning and guile, and may very well get you killed. I'd call it the greatest challenge of your life. Or, if you're not up to it, help yourself to whatever you can carry away, vanish down to Pacaha, or sell them on the riverfront for all I care."

Oh, yes. She had him. No way he could turn his back on the challenge. Not now.

"I don't take orders well." He inclined his head to make the point.

"How could I have missed that?" she asked dryly. "If we can't work together, that offer to take what you want and leave remains open."

She glanced back at her sleeping quarters where the assassin lay dead on her floor. "But you might want to consider the stakes, thief. Whatever this is about, apparently they have no hesitation about killing people who get in their way."

He gave her an irritating grin. "I think I like you, Keeper."

"By the Piasa's balls, don't tell anybody. I couldn't stand the shame."

At that moment, Smooth Pebble burst in the door, crying, "Keeper! A runner just arrived from the Matron Wind. Your brother, the *Tonka'tzi*, he's *murdered*!"

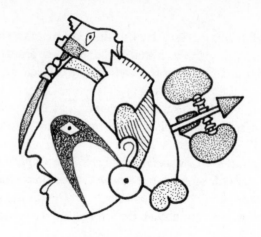

Twenty

Night Shadow Star cast a disdainful glance behind her as she hurried along in the pre-morning twilight. Smooth Pebble had arrived at her palace, rudely shoving the door aside, and calling, "Lady? The Clan Keeper and Matron need to see you now!"

Piasa's voice had hissed sibilantly within her: *Take the Red Wing!*

As she hurried forward she clasped a cloak made of split feathers to her shoulders and glanced uneasily about the misty landscape. Dew sprinkled the grass where it stubbornly grew despite the pounding of thousands of feet, and slicked the mud where even the most hardy of grasses couldn't withstand the traffic.

Behind her, Fire Cat followed along, his muscular body still not recovered from the abuse of the square. *Why him?* The fact that she hadn't plunged her long ceremonial knife into his body still chafed.

Piasa, if it were anyone, anything, but you, his corpse would already be chopped up and the pieces sunk to the bottom of the river. You want him? You could put the pieces back together and have him!

In answer, disembodied and eerie laughter wound between her souls.

She shivered as Piasa's shadow filtered through her. Inexplicably, her thoughts centered on that last instant before the beast had crushed her head between those terrible jaws: the bristly whiskers were spread wide, the great teeth shining and sharp; she almost choked as the stink of the monster's breath filled her.

If she could only go back and undo any mistake she'd ever made, it would be that day she'd mixed the datura, rubbed it into her temples, and stared down into the well pot in search of Makes Three's soul.

You cannot go back, Lady. And now I dance within you.

"Go dance somewhere else," she muttered. "I was happy enough without you."

Of course you were . . . so hollow with grief that ripples of it rolled through the Underworld. Had you not been so empty, I could never have filled as much of you as I have.

"Not much of a bargain, was it?"

You'll never be lonely again.

"Loneliness has somehow become more appealing."

If I can't be with you all the time, the Red Wing can.

"I'd rather share my company with a hungry weasel."

She glanced back again, loathing the man who followed so obediently behind her. Couldn't he just slip away some night and vanish? Did both word and honor *have* to be so sacred to the piece of filth?

That's why I chose him for you.

"How about letting me do my own choosing, beast?"

If your "choosing" had been so laudable, woman, how did you end up as mine?

When she glanced back, the filthy Red Wing was giving her the sort of disgusted look he'd give a babbling fool. What? Did he think she'd lost her souls to madness?

"About time," Five Fists called from the top of the Four Winds Clan House stairs. His figure was silhouetted before the steep-roofed clan house with its Four Winds effigy poles rising from the thatched roof. Night Shadow Star glanced up the ramp and took the wet stairs with care. She didn't deign to look back at the Red Wing, but demanded, "Why am I here?"

Five Fists gave her a sober look, his crooked jaw even more askew. "We'll discuss it inside. But first, note the guardians."

She followed him toward the effigy posts of Sky Eagle and Falcon that guarded either side of the approach. She didn't need Five Fists' gesture to see the black sinuous lines that had been painted over the Spirit Beasts' eyes.

"Snakes, we think." Five Fists studied them uneasily. "Perhaps to blind them to the assassin's presence?"

"Assassin?" she asked, a sudden shiver running down her spine.

Then she was past him, sprinting for the partially open door. "Blessed Spirits, no!"

She burst into the palace great room at a dead run. The horrified looks on her father's attendants barely registered; they huddled on the sleeping platforms against the south wall. Matron Wind waited by the door in the rear, putting out an arm and ordering, "Stop, niece. Blue Heron's not ready for your . . ."

Night Shadow Star batted her aunt's arm out of the way. She burst through the doorway and stopped cold. For the moment she could only gasp for breath, aware of the coppery stench of the blood. So much blood . . .

Blue Heron stood over the bed, head cocked, her right hand held protectively at her throat. A stranger, a rough-looking man dressed as a commoner, lurked at one side of the room. He glanced her way and fixed his gaze on her as if he'd never seen a woman before.

"Lot of blood isn't it?" Blue Heron remarked almost casually as she straightened from Red Warrior Tenkiller's body. A second corpse lay beside him, slightly curled against the back wall: Yellow Aster, his third wife.

Night Shadow Star stared in horror at her father's gaping throat wound. The wide cut exposed the tube of his windpipe and the severed bundles of muscles and tendons. An impossible amount of darkening blood gleamed on his chest and soaked the bedding. Even as she watched, it continued to drip onto the floor. Yellow Aster's throat, too, had been slashed. Her sightless eyes had already gone gray behind dilated pupils.

Night Shadow Star tried to catch her breath, and despite gasping, remained oddly starved for air.

"Whoever it was, no one heard a thing," Blue Heron continued, eyes narrowed to slits. "And he was definitely different from the one who tried to kill me earlier tonight. Had to be two of them. My killer would have had blood under his fingernails if he'd done this before he came for me."

"You . . . Your killer?" Night Shadow Star's voice sounded weak as her reeling souls struggled to comprehend, much less accept the notion that the crimson-drenched corpses on the bed belonged to her father and his wife.

"There were two," Blue Heron gestured at an ugly stitched wound in her throat before pointing at the gory corpses. "This one succeeded. Look at the wall."

Night Shadow Star turned, her shock deepening as she took in the image someone had drawn in blood on the cane wall: a snake, long and sinuous, the head triangular, the tail ending in a blotched representation of rattles.

"Like the black snakes on the guardians' eyes?" she mumbled, trying to find herself in the stunned horror. Then she returned her stumbling gaze to the caricature of her father's corpse. "Who . . . Who'd do . . . ?"

"This?" Blue Heron rubbed her hands, expression bitter. "The snake indicates Underworld Power was invoked by the killings. Piasa is your Spirit, Niece. He's one of the masters of the Underworld. Four Winds Clan and the *tonka'tzi* are allied with the Sky World." She shot Night Shadow Star a hard look. "Is there anything you want to tell me, Niece? Any . . . *revelations* from your dreams?"

Night Shadow Star could only stare at her father's remains. Memories of him came flooding back: his laughter when she'd been a little girl; the times he'd spoiled her with trinkets; his strong arms as he'd held her after she'd fallen down the palace steps; the relief in his eyes at her wedding feast; and the pain he'd felt at her grief over Makes Three's death.

Gone.

All gone.

"Night Shadow Star?" Blue Heron demanded attention, her eyes like black stones in her implacable face.

"He was your brother," she whispered. "Are you so unmoved by his murder?" She felt her heart tearing in her breast.

"I'll grieve when I have time. For the moment, all of our lives are in danger. I must know. Where were you this night?"

"In my palace." The words were choked in Night Shadow Star's throat.

"Which of your attendants could swear to that?"

The absurdity of the question shook Night Shadow Star out of her disbelief. "What . . . What are you asking?"

"You've tied yourself to the Underworld. You whisper of Piasa himself. And the murderer here, as well as the one who tried to murder me tonight, are aligning themselves with the serpents." She pointed to the bloody snake painted on the wall.

"You think I . . ." She knotted her fists, hot tears of rage and grief silvering her vision. "He was *my father!*"

"She was with me," a subdued voice said from behind.

Night Shadow Star turned, dismayed to discover Fire Cat's muscular body filling the doorway. Before she could find her voice, Blue Heron asked, "Doing what, Red Wing?"

His gaze didn't waver as he met Blue Heron's. "Struggling, Clan Keeper. Battling with her souls over whether to drive a chert knife into my heart."

Blue Heron fingered her chin thoughtfully, then winced, obviously having pulled the wound at her throat. She glanced disdainfully at her fingers, fixing on her dead brother's drying blood. For a long moment, she said nothing. Then: "Tell me, Red Wing, do you have agents in Cahokia? Men who'd be capable of treachery like this?"

Still reeling, Night Shadow Star physically stepped back at the look of hatred in Fire Cat's narrowing eyes. "If I did, Keeper, they wouldn't be painting snakes with your blood. The design on that wall would be a great red wing, and we'd have started with your nephew up on his private mountain."

"You speak blasphemy!"

He shrugged and countered, "Blasphemy is where you find it. I think its living atop the great mound."

Blue Heron's eyes glittered, her expression tightening into an enraged mask. "Five Fists, take this *thing* out and tie him in a square. I want him to die slowly, over a moon if you can—"

"You'll do no such thing," Night Shadow Star finally found her voice. "He's mine."

"Blood and spit, why?"

"Piasa has a twisted sense of humor to go along with his cruel streak."

"I need to hear more about that."

She felt the beast curl inside her chest, prodding her to look again at the bodies.

"We both do. So far, however, Piasa hasn't bothered to inform me just what his reasons are for saving this bit of filth." Night Shadow Star's grief-laden thoughts began to coalesce. "We're distracting ourselves." She pointed at the corpses. "Who did this? Why now?"

Blue Heron took a deep breath, raising her hands in agreement. "Yes, yes. But I have one last question." She looked at Fire Cat. "What is your purpose in this, Red Wing?"

Again his eyes never wavered as he said, "While hanging in the square, I pledged my life, honor, and souls to serve Lady Night Shadow Star. I am the son of Matron Red Wing, maybe the last of my clan. My vow is inviolate, and once bound, I do *not* go back on my word."

"Even though you hate us?"

"Even so, Clan Keeper."

"And you are not part of a plot to commit these . . . atrocities?"

He smiled humorlessly. "Unfortunately, I am not."

Night Shadow Star snapped, "Since you *claim* to serve me, whatever your blasphemous opinions concerning the Morning Star, you will *keep them* to yourself. That is my will. Do you understand?"

He nodded. "I understand."

If nothing else, at least she could respect his honor.

She asked, "If you were going to act against us in this fashion, Red Wing, who would you contact in Cahokia? How would you proceed?"

He glanced at the bloody corpses, rubbed his jaw, and said, "I'd look for someone in the Four Winds Clan. Each of these 'houses' you've established to run a part of this giant city is still composed of greedy and ambitious lineages. Your"—he made a face—"Morning Star may have brought peace to the warring factions, but it is nothing more than a fragile patch over deep and festering resentments."

"A name?" Blue Heron prodded.

He gave that odd, one-shouldered shrug. "Which houses have you humiliated the most?"

Blue Heron said nothing.

That could be any of them, Night Shadow Star thought as she glanced again at her father's dead body, fought back the ache of grief, and rubbed the new welling of tears from her eyes. "For the moment, aunt, we've a bigger problem: the *tonka'tzi* is dead. The people have to be told something. If we admit assassination, the entire city might explode."

"Dead in his bed," Blue Heron agreed. "That's all they need to know. And in the interim, Matron Wind can assume his place as *tonka'tzi*."

For the first time the man standing in the rear of the room spoke. "Then you'd better act quickly. I counted seven of the *tonka'tzi*'s personal attendants out there. As soon as they walk out of that room, their jaws are going to be flapping. If there are any you can't trust to keep their guzzle-traps shut, you need to remove them immediately. Otherwise, someone's going to wag his tongue."

"And it will spread like a wind-driven prairie fire," Blue Heron agreed.

Night Shadow Star tightened a fist on her grief and forced herself to study the stranger. He was big, muscular, perhaps in his early thirties, with an oddly blocky face and strong jaw. He wore only a nondescript, smudged, and grease-stained shirt that hung to mid-thigh. His hair was pulled up in a simple bun and held in place by two wooden pins.

"Who are you?" she asked.

Blue Heron arched an eyebrow. "You ordered me to find him. I thought you wanted me to locate him for a reason."

She frowned, trying to make sense. "I did?"

The man gave her a lecherous grin accompanied by an insolent wink. "I'm known as Seven Skull Shield." He touched his forehead with just enough brevity to leave her unsure if it had been a measure of respect, or an insult.

Seven Skull Shield? He's this despicable person?

"It was just words," she whispered.

"What words?" Blue Heron asked. "Heard where?"

"Piasa told me. I was talking to you at the stickball grounds."

"He *speaks* to you?"

Images of pain and terror spun around her memory like a whirlwind. She felt Piasa's shadow stir within her. In that instant, she was back in the Underworld, living it again. The horror, the pain and terror . . .

"Seek the same blood!" The words boomed inside her skull and her vision shimmered into a silvery gray.

Dazed, she came to, the room spinning out of fragments of the vision. The choking odor of Piasa's hot breath surrendered to the scent of blood and death.

To her surprise, it was Fire Cat who steadied her, supporting her weight where she leaned weakly against him.

"Piasa," she murmured hoarsely.

"What just happened, Niece?" Blue Heron demanded as she stepped forward, hands clasping Night Shadow Star's shoulders as if to stabilize her.

"I was there again . . . being eaten alive."

"What? In the Underworld?"

She blinked, scrubbed at her eyes, trying desperately to understand. Piasa stirred somewhere deep in her souls. "Seek the same blood, that's what he said."

Blue Heron turned her attention to the crimson gore covering the corpses and bedding. "He took some of their blood? Is that what it means?"

Seven Skull Shield pointed at the serpent on the wall. "Perhaps he did and then painted another of those someplace in the city."

Night Shadow Star took one last glance at her father's body. His horrified eyes were wide, dry, and gray in death. His mouth, blood-filled, hung open. The lips were pulled back to expose teeth stained crimson. Trickles of blood had run from his nostrils and left trails across his tattooed cheeks.

"I have to leave," she almost cried. "Now. Take me home. I'm going to be ill."

"I've got her," Fire Cat insisted, supporting her weight as she struggled to walk. Grief and horror, mixed with the flickers of visions of the Underworld, left her so weak she couldn't even protest help from the man she hated.

Who is doing this? Will I be next? The questions kept echoing in her head.

Now you begin to understand, Piasa's voice reverberated hollowly inside her.

Twenty-one

Climbing the long flight of wooden steps to the high mound top on which Night Shadow Star's palace stood, Seven Skull Shield looked back at the crowd. People ebbed and flowed in the Great Plaza as they watched the *tonka'tzi*'s palace burn. A line of warriors kept them back; Traders and vendors, always alert for advantage, were working the fringes, offering food, trinkets, and keepsakes.

A somber disbelief lay over the crowd—that sense of shared awe at being in that place, at that time, to see the last earthly remains of the Great Sky Red Warrior's presence go up in thick black wreaths of smoke.

Walking among them had been Seven Skull Shield's idea, and the conversations he'd overheard had tickled something in his souls. He'd always been one of the mob—as eager as the next person to catch a hint of gossip about the doings of the high and mighty. That he was on the inside—and knew the truth—while the poor clods around him had no clue titillated him something fierce.

From under his cloak, he produced the small loaf of goosefoot bread he'd stolen. The Hawk Clan woman who'd baked it had laid a whole selection of breads out on a blue-and-white blanket. She'd focused her entire attention on the Snapping Turtle Clan woman who hawked pottery in the spot next her, saying, "If you ask me, the *tonka'tzi*'s sudden death is nothing more than the divine justice of the Sky World for his transgressions."

The Snapping Turtle Clan woman had shrugged and said, "It's a lesson. Death comes to us all."

"But to go so quickly?" The Hawk Clan bread Trader snapped her fingers. "That's Power taking its retribution, I tell you. There's something dark about the Four Winds people making the changes they have. I miss the old days under Petaga. And the *tonka'tzi*, he was as crafty as they come. I heard that he *prefers* to share his bed with other men!"

"Why would anyone care if he's *berdache?*" the potter asked.

"Mark my words. It'll come out. The *tonka'tzi* had indiscretions. These kind of deaths, they're drawn to indiscretions, I tell you!"

So the tonka'tzi *had indiscretions? What normal man didn't?* Though he'd never met the Great Sky in life, Seven Skull Shield had taken umbrage. The man he'd seen had been murdered sleeping with one of his wives! And besides, Seven Skull Shield more or less worked for the Four Winds Clan now. Stealing a loaf of the old woman's bread was no more than retribution for her slight, not to mention a chance to keep his fast hands in practice.

After leaving the crowd, he'd retreated to the veranda fronting Night Shadow Star's palace. The Avenue of the Sun ran along the southern edge of her mound where it stood at the northwest corner of the Great Plaza. The Morning Star's palace atop its towering mound dominated the view to the east. Looking south across the Avenue of the Sun, he had a clear view of the roaring yellow fire as it consumed the *tonka'tzi*'s palace. A billow of black smoke rose in a slanted column from the crackling timbers.

People stood in a wide ring, held back from the base of the mound by a cordon of red-dressed warriors. The mood in the crowd remained somber.

Even from his elevated perch, Seven Skull Shield could sense the people's uncertainty, could read it in their shifting bodies, the way they leaned their heads close to whisper their suspicions.

"What do you think?" Fire Cat asked as he stepped out onto the veranda.

"They're unsure. Apprehensive." Seven Skull Shield gestured at the crowd. "Look close and you'll see it, like a faint ripple running through a pond."

"And you know this? How?"

"I'm one of them, Red Wing."

"What does that mean, one of them?"

"For a dead man, you ask a lot of questions."

Fire Cat shot him a measuring sidelong look. "Blue Heron says you're a common thief."

"Bah! Common? Red Wing, I could have lifted one of your wives right out of your bed while you slept in her arms. And there's *nothing* common about talent like that."

"My wives have been taken as slaves, thief. I am told their labor and bodies now serve Four Winds masters."

Seeing the man's pain, he said, "Power must not favor you, Red Wing."

"Obviously it does not. And as much as I'd like to choke that smug expression off your ugly face, my lady requires your presence."

Seven Skull Shield hesitated just long enough to give the Red Wing his most offensive smile. "Don't start what you can't finish alive and well, Red Wing. I've heard all about your precious honor. I grew up in a different world. Where I come from, I learned to do whatever it takes to stay alive."

He glanced at the Piasa and Horned Serpent guardian posts. The things looked so lifelike they sent a shiver through him. Then he brushed past the fuming Red Wing and entered the main palace. The great room had taken his breath away when he'd first stepped through the door. Nothing had changed. The opulence remained every bit as stunning.

Just a couple of these pieces Traded down south would set me up for life!

Behind the fire pit with its glowing embers, and seated on their litters, were Blue Heron, Matron Wind, Lady Sun Wing, and Night Shadow Star. Off to the right a man named Dead Bird, who served the Morning Star, waited with a frowning face. Blue Heron's *berdache* assistant, Smooth Pebble, and Night Shadow Star's head of household, Field Green, stood behind their respective ladies. He wasn't sure who the other people present belonged to.

"How is the crowd?" Blue Heron asked as he walked closer and stopped just back of the fire.

"Tense, Keeper. Unsure." He bit another bite off the small loaf. Good. The woman had sprinkled some walnuts into the dough.

"You heard no rumors?"

"Oh, plenty. Mostly idle speculation about divine justice from the Sky World. A couple of the ignorant two-legged turds came up with the notion the Morning Star blasted the *tonka'tzi* over some slight, or found him unworthy, or some such. About what you'd expect. The important thing is that no one is mentioning assassination. By moving as fast as you did, you've taken the opposition by surprise."

"How is that?" young Sun Wing asked, an arrogance in her voice.

He took another bite of bread, chewing as he studied her. She looked like an overdressed child atop her litter. No one that young and stuffed so full of self-important goose excrement should be given her kind of authority. "Lady, if the assassins wanted to create panic they'd have picked people working the crowd to whisper rumors. No one's doing that, not at the tinder points."

"What's a tinder point?" Her too-pretty face tightened in disdain.

"The places people like me gravitate to. Concentrations of the curious, the lunatics, and the slightly addled who can't wait for a disaster and want to be the first to see it happen. They are the ones anticipating that first spark, anxious to blow it into a bonfire that will flare out of control."

Night Shadow Star, her poise recovered from earlier, asked, "If they had the opportunity to sow discord, why didn't they?"

Seven Skull Shield ripped another bite of bread from the loaf, talking through a full mouth. "They thought you'd panic."

"We almost did," Blue Heron muttered under her breath, gaze unfocused as she considered what he'd said. She glanced up as Five Fists' burly form darkened the door.

The broke-jawed warrior gestured his respect and dropped to one knee, saying, "I escorted the *tonka'tzi*'s household staff to the Trader this one suggested." He indicated Seven Skull Shield with the barest tilt of his head. "I think they believe our story that we're removing them from Cahokia for their own safety. The Trader has enough muscular young men to ensure they will be delivered to the supreme chief of the Kadadokies at the Yellow Star City."

Blue Heron granted Seven Skull Shield a thin smile. Her first inclination had been to sacrifice them in order that their souls accompany the *tonka'tzi* to the afterlife. She figured that once dead, their souls could chatter all they wanted about assassination.

The Keeper doesn't cringe when it comes to getting a bit of blood on her hands. A good fact to remember.

Seven Skull Shield's counterargument had been that such an action might play into the killer's hands. With assassins prowling around in the night, prudent potential victims wouldn't be well served by making their households nervous about their future prospects.

"Then we've contained the situation?" Matron Wind asked.

To Seven Skull Shield's mind, the Matron looked exhausted, stricken, and uncertain. Given her expression, elevation to the *tonka'tzi* didn't exactly fill her with joy. Still . . . she'd definitely benefited by her brother's murder.

Might pay to keep an eye on the good Matron.

But what would she gain by killing the Keeper at the same time? Elimination of the one person who might ferret out her involvement?

Blue Heron fingered the stitches under her chin as she said, "The bodies have been carried to the charnel house. Rides-the-Lightning has already begun stripping meat from the bones. By midday the *tonka'tzi*'s flesh will be feeding the crows and eagles. A fitting tribute to the Sky World."

"We'll need to begin clearing the charred rubble of his palace away as soon as the ashes cool," Matron Wind remarked, a dazed look on her face. "I want the mound recovered with a layer of white clay to signify peace before a new palace is built."

"What did the Morning Star say?" Night Shadow Star glanced at Sun Wing.

Seven Skull Shield munched on his bread, hawklike eyes fixed on Lady Sun Wing as she absently stroked loving fingers down her cardinal-feathered cloak. No woman should be that taken with herself. His imagination pictured her being plopped down as a dirt farmer's wife to make due on a freshly cleared farmstead. Laboring day in and out, with nothing but brown burlap to wear, and dirt under her fingernails. It would do her good.

"The Morning Star is terribly distressed." She put too much emphasis on the words. "He urges Lady Night Shadow Star to hurry her investigation into these mindless and chaotic attacks."

The rest waited, attention on Sun Wing.

"And?" Blue Heron finally asked. "That's it?"

"The Morning Star has complete faith in you," Sun Wing added. "He urges you to give full attention to your duties."

"As if we wouldn't when strangers are sneaking into our bedrooms to *slit our throats?*" Matron Wind cried.

"Beware of the tone you use when addressing the Morning Star," Sun Wing warned coldly, and to Seven Skull Shield's amazement, Matron Wind paled.

By the Piasa's balls, Matron Wind is aunt to both the Morning Star and this little tight-sheath, and the girl uses that kind of tone?

Night Shadow Star, however, gave her little sister a scathing look. "Have a care with your tongue yourself, Sister. You can wind up atop a burning pyre as quickly as the rest of us."

That referred to the act of burning a person alive to send their souls posthaste to the Sky World. The underlying belief was that their freshly freed souls would ride the column of thick black smoke up to the Thunderers' realm among the clouds.

Sun Wing barely narrowed a brown eye. "Your Underworld master may trust you, *Sister*, but Morning Star knows you for who you really are."

Seven Skull Shield watched Night Shadow Star's beautiful face darken, a flat coldness behind her eyes. For just an instant he might have seen the reflection of a hunting cougar in her eyes. The sudden sensation of chill air, of threat and danger, however, felt incredibly real.

"Stop it!" Blue Heron snapped. "Fighting among ourselves isn't going to solve the problem."

"Correct." Matron Wind rubbed her face, then looked around with worried eyes. "Who will be next among us? They've tried for the Morning Star, and now in one night they have murdered Red Warrior and would have had Blue Heron but for the work of Power."

Her quick and nervous glance Seven Skull Shield's way was met with his bland smile. Let her believe he was Power's instrument. There might be profit in it down the road.

Five Fists spoke, "In addition to whatever you decide, we're moving a squad of warriors around each of the palaces."

"Which will do what?" Seven Skull Shield asked mildly as he slapped the crumbs from his hands.

The astonished look Five Fists gave him was almost better than the outburst: "Why . . . it will keep our people *safe*, thief!"

"Of course. Silly of me not to have figured that out." Seven Skull Shield inclined his head in mock salute. "But then I'm just as dumb as that crowd out there. I'll never make a connection between full squadrons of warriors surrounding the ever-so-exalted Four Winds palaces and the *tonka'tzi*'s burning palace over yonder. Let alone the bodies being de-fleshed up in that charnel house. And I certainly would never begin to spin lurid tales about why Cahokia's lords were suddenly surrounded by armed ranks of warriors. Or for what purpose the Morning Star ordered it."

Sun Wing cried, "He is *the Morning Star*! Who cares what the ignorant crowds think? He exists above us all."

"It's a wonder they haven't stormed the great mound and pulled you all down," Seven Skull Shield muttered, ignoring Sun Wing's fury. He couldn't help it, her attitude just *begged* to have someone slap her down.

"Watch your mouth," Blue Heron warned. Evidently her memory of why she was still alive and breathing had grown foggy.

Seven Skull Shield noticed Fire Cat watching from beside the door, his arms crossed, head cocked in amusement. Ignoring him, Seven Skull Shield calmly said, "I don't understand you people. Moments ago you were all relieved that you'd fooled the crowd—that they didn't have a clue that the *tonka'tzi* had been murdered. Now you're dismissing that crowd out there as insignificant? Going to throw away what advantage you've gained by posting squadrons of warriors? And remember, Morning Star exists for them, they don't exist for him. You do understand that part, don't you?"

Matron Wind and Sun Wing were giving him a look that communicated a promise of immediate flaying. Night Shadow Star, however, was watching him with large, predatory eyes.

"Why are we listening to this . . . this putrid *thing*?" Matron Wind slapped her hands on her legs. "I say we hang him in a square, and let him learn a little respect for his betters."

Sun Wing's voice strained with anger as she said, "Just because he saved the Clan Keeper's life he thinks he's one of us? As good as us? Hang him!"

Seven Skull Shield experienced that familiar warning tickle down in his gizzard. Instinctively he considered his way out. He'd have to kick broken-jaw before the old warrior could grab him. Fire Cat was at the door, and a couple of other warriors could block the exit if he wasn't fast enough. But once he was outside, and assuming he could keep his feet sprinting down the side of the steep mound—and not break a leg at the bottom—that huge crowd would swallow him like . . .

"Enough!" Night Shadow Star clapped her hands with a bang. "Power chose him. And I begin to see why."

"To insult us?" Sun Wing cried. "It's like being pawed at by a dirt farmer!"

"Quiet!" Night Shadow Star thundered. Rising from her litter chair she crouched eye-to-eye with her little sister. "Learn this, young *lady*!" The voice, oddly, didn't sound like Night Shadow Star's, but had deepened, almost hollow. "Our world is about to be torn apart. This isn't about your pride, or our status. Someone out there wants to destroy us. If they do, you are going to be among the dead. And Cahokia, with all of its magic and wonder, will be a burned and gutted corpse upon which your pitiful fleshly remains will fall unnoticed and unmourned. Humanity will be despised and discarded. The Powers will be unleashed. The Morning Star will flee back to the Sky World in despair."

Sun Wing swallowed hard, face pale. "Why are you doing that to your voice?"

"Do you begin to understand, young *lady?* Fingers of chaos and blood are reaching out for us. And if they manage to grasp hold, they will crush us all in misery and death."

Five Fists took a deep breath, saying into the ensuing silence. "A small squad of picked warriors will be placed on guard. *Inside.* And out of sight." He glanced at Seven Skull Shield. "Nothing that will alarm the people."

"Now you're thinking," Seven Skull Shield told him. A cold understanding began to flow through his souls. "I think . . . think . . ."

"What?" Blue Heron barked.

He chewed at his lips for a moment, letting his souls gnaw on the revelation he'd just had. When she opened her mouth to demand more of him, he raised a hand, saying only, "Let me check on some things, Keeper. Just a hunch."

"Go," she told him.

"Wait!" Sun Wing stared at Blue Heron in disbelief. "You mean you *trust* him? Once he's out that door, your precious thief is going to vanish like summer mist."

At that Seven Skull Shield made a face, but turned, heading for the doorway, muttering under his breath, "Nasty little sheath, that one. But if I'm right, it's more than Four Winds Clan they're after."

They mean to destroy the whole of Cahokia.

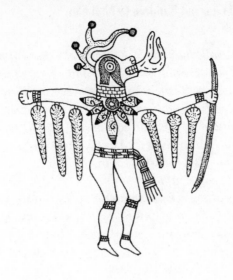

The Resurrection

*T*he farmstead sits in Deer Clan territory atop the high eastern bluff. Looking west from the front door I have a remarkable view of Cahokia's floodplain sprawl. The distant river and Evening Star town on the other side are
invisible in the smoky haze. But from here, I can still discern the dot of
Morning Star's palace atop its great mound.

I smile to myself. By now terror has grabbed them by the throat. First
came the attempt on the Morning Star himself. How propitious? I could almost have believed Power was with me—but for Night Shadow Star's odd
appearance. How did she arrive out of the rain just in time to revive her
youthful skills as an archer?

Granted, I never expected everything to unfold perfectly. Creation, by its
very nature, is a mixture of order and chaos. What my Mos'kogee friends
call the white and red Powers. The tonka'tzi is dead. The Keeper is not. In
victory I feasted on the blood of my victim. In defeat, one of my wolves has
been chopped into pieces, his bones and flesh sunk into the river to be devoured by the Spirits of the Underworld.

What do the Tie Snakes, Water Panther, and the turtles make of my human wolf's souls and flesh? Just like fishing, the right kind of bait must be
dangled on the hook.

Do they have the slightest hint of my ultimate goal? Are they insulted?
Horrified? Confused?

I laugh at the thought and turn to inspect my farmstead. The house is *average sized with walls built of clay plaster over vertical poles. The roof is thickly thatched. Two storehouses and a ramada border the small yard with its log mortar and wooden pestle. Outside of the grand view of Cahokia, the most important thing is its bluff-top isolation. The nearest neighbor is five bow-shots to the east. And tonight that farmer and his family are away at the local temple and Council House. Most of the locals are making offerings to Old-Woman-Who-Never-Dies, praying for a successful growing season, asking for rain and good weather.*

Perfect! The only people who will overhear are my wolves. They will prowl around throughout the night to ensure my privacy. One can't be too careful when it comes to resurrecting the souls of the dead. Tonight I shall attempt to wield my awesome Power. If I can repeat tonight what I have done twice before in the south, I will shake the world.

I cast one last knowing glance at the Morning Star's distant mound-top home. "Sleep in blissful ignorance, you fool. If I am successful, you will awaken to a different world come dawn."

Then I step inside.

The central fire crackles and burns brightly as it illuminates the farmhouse interior. Bench-beds line the walls. The frames are covered with shoddy, coarsely woven blankets. In the space beneath I can see a mismatched collection of jars and pots, many cracked and held together with thongs. The styles are mindful of a half dozen of the immigrant groups who've flooded Cahokia.

I turn my attention to the six people on the back platform bed. My wolves have securely bound each of the captives; wads of ragged cloth fill their mouths. Five are crowded closely together for whatever comfort they can derive: a father, a mother, two daughters, and a young son. The family members stare at me with horror-filled eyes as I throw a couple of pieces of firewood on the blaze.

The sixth captive is a young woman who made the mistake of stepping out to use her latrine in the middle of the night. She swallows hard as my gaze falls upon her.

"I know you can't understand me," I explain. Their language is something incomprehensible from over east. "But you've been chosen for a great honor."

I point at the young woman. "The Clan Keeper killed one of my wolves. Tonight we will see if, together, we can resurrect his soul in this young woman's body."

I experience a rush of excitement as I undress and begin the process of purification. After washing my body with water, I cup handfuls of smoke and ritually rub it on my arms, legs, chest, buttocks, genitals, and face. As I do I watch the young woman with anticipation.

Opening my box of paints, I apply them in exactly the order I did last time, feeling my skin tingle as the Power of the colors and designs begins to pulse.

When the lengthy ritual is complete, I step over and lift the struggling young woman from the bench.

The farmers cringe away from me, terror bright in their eyes as I remove a sharp chert blade and begin to cut the young woman's clothing from her body. Bound as she is, I have no other way to strip her. What I did not anticipate is the delight I take in revealing her smooth brown skin. With some regret, I can't help but stroke her young breasts.

I remind myself that purity is of the highest essence, and sigh as I begin washing her healthy brown body. This is sacred work and I try to ignore the tingling in my loins as I sponge the length of her slim legs and feel tense muscles slide beneath that so-smooth skin. I re-wet my cloth and move to her neck, then follow the contours of her shoulders. The way her arms are bound behind her makes washing them difficult. I start on her chest, and perhaps linger too long on her breasts as I roll them under the cloth. When I am done her dark nipples have hardened, and so have I.

I need to finish, to battle both my impure thoughts and my traitorous genitals. Both she and I will have to be absolutely cleansed for this to work. Nevertheless, my heart begins to pound as I carefully smooth my damp cloth over the slight swell of her abdomen and allow my finger to dip into her navel. She is shivering and crying against the gag in her mouth as I wind the cloth back and forth to the dark-matted prominence of her pubis. Somewhere between my souls, I am saddened that such a marvelous pelvis will never cradle new life within its warm, liquid depths.

"Discipline!" I whisper harshly. After all, if I am successful, and Bobcat's soul is actually called back, he's going to be angry enough awakening in a female body, let alone one I've just ejaculated into.

I set the cloth aside and begin the ritual of painting her for the ceremony. Oddly I do not find this nearly as stimulating to my male nature, and thankfully, my body begins to relax. I am unsure of which colors go where on her. But the colors are right: red for life and blood, yellow for renewal and first dawn, blue for the sky, and black for night, death, and the Underworld.

Finally I am done. I throw more wood on the fire and stand above it, letting the heat and smoke carry the last of my carnal thoughts to the high smoke hole and out into the night. I sing softly as smoke bathes my body, and I inhale the acrid scent, letting it burn through my nose and throat.

From where I left it beside the door, I retrieve the beautiful brown-chert knife with its razor-sharp curved blade. I am sorry for the terror dancing brightly behind the girl's eyes. The farmer, his wife, and children are screaming into the gags, twisting against the binding ropes. The little boy has wet himself, and tears are streaking down the little girls' faces.

In that moment I realize I, too, am terrified of what I am about to attempt.

Then, purifying the thin stone blade in smoke, I turn to begin the ritual. . . .

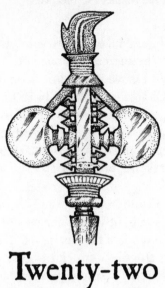

Twenty-two

Passing himself off as a Hawk Clan man was as easy as painting his face brown to cover his Four Winds Clan tattoos, and repainting the Hawk Clan designs on his cheeks. But High Dance's stomach had tied itself into a worry-tight knot. The few Hawk Clan people he'd passed had just nodded and smiled. What unnerved High Dance was the chance that he might have to stop and talk to one, at which time his sham would be instantly discovered.

And what would they do? Shout, "He's an imposter!"

What then? Just run? And what if the Hawk Clansman pursued? Kept shouting and pointing?

High Dance's stomach pulled its uncomfortable knot tighter as he hurried across the clay-packed causeway. On either side lay boggy marsh. The rains had left standing water in the low spots and turned the rich black mud to goo beneath the new green shoots of swamp grass.

High Dance nodded at a stone Trader and stepped as far to the side as the arched surface of the causeway would allow. The man was older, perhaps in his mid-thirties, short, with a knob of nose, deeply lined face, and stringy black hair. The heavy leather sack over his shoulder bulged with flat slabs of sandstone quarried from the distant bluffs.

"Quite a load," High Dance said as the man plodded past, his muscular calves knotting like gnarled pine roots with each step.

"Yes, yes. Good stone. Make Trade, yes?" the man panted, voice accented, then added something else in one of the immigrant languages.

After he passed, High Dance stepped back on the trail and continued on his way. Most of Cahokia had been built on silt-laden floodplain. Sandstone, limestone, and cherts were locally available in the distant bluffs and uplands, but every bit of stone used for tool making, abrading, sculpting, ballast, cooking fires, axes, adzes, hammers, hoes, woodwork, net sinkers, burnishing pottery, bolas . . . you name it, had to be imported.

He immediately had to give way again as a woman came plodding down the causeway, back bent under sheaves of bound grass for roof thatching. High Dance made a face as he tried to step aside, his right foot sliding down into the black muck beside the causeway's sloping side. The woman muttered, "Pardon, pardon," as she passed with her load, head down, her voice strained.

High Dance almost toppled into the ooze as he tried to extricate his foot. The mud sucked the deerhide moccasin off his foot.

Cursing, he finally managed to reach down and pull it from the gooey mess.

"If they knew who I really was . . ." He smiled wickedly as he beat his moccasin on the packed clay surface, glaring at the people who passed on their business. Then, seeing no more large loads headed his way, he hurried as fast as he could on the irregular rounded surface.

"If this was my territory, this thing would be fifteen hands wide, and paved with gravel," he growled as he raced to make the higher ground before two men bearing a litter filled with peeled saplings could block his way.

High Dance managed a smile as the men nodded at him. From their dress and manner, they must have been Illini. Each, however, had a crude image of the Morning Star sketched on the front of his sweat-stained work shirt.

High Dance kicked at the mud still clinging to his moccasin and followed the entrenched path. It ran off to the northwest between a cluster of cane-roofed houses with their gardens, ramadas, and storage pits. He could just see the temple roof on the far side of the houses where it overlooked Marsh Elder Lake to the south.

To his relief, none of the women tending their little plots of corn, beans, sunflowers, goosefoot, and squash gave him so much as a second look. Instead they kept on with their weeding, corn milling, and weaving. Around the houses, little naked children ran, screamed, and played, often accompanied by hollow-ribbed, tick-infested dogs with slashing tails.

Cutting off from the main path, High Dance made a face as he passed wide of an overflowing latrine and stepped carefully around piles of excrement and broken pottery. High Dance fought the urge to hold his nose and waved away columns of flies. Like so much of Cahokia, the houses were packed close here because the soil was marginal. Clay didn't grow good corn. Unproductive ground generally ended up crowded with immigrant housing.

He nodded uncomfortably as a young woman stepped out from one of the latrines and resettled her skirt. Given a good wash and a combing she would have been attractive. At his hawkish glance she lowered her large dark eyes and hurried around to the front of her house where an infant was screaming.

Wearing an expression of distaste he hurried toward the temple atop its low mound. Four tall men, obviously warriors, stood in an arc before the building. Each held a war club and nodded at him as he approached.

Tough men, he decided, trying to place their thick-boned and wedge-shaped features in comparison with any of the peoples he was familiar with. They had a curiously foreign look to them, and he was surprised to note that none exhibited the characteristic facial tattoos that proclaimed a man's people and clan.

He almost gasped in relief as the breeze blowing in from the lake carried fresh air to his abused nostrils. He climbed the five steps to the mound top and walked to the temple door. There a bone-rack of an old man sat, eyes white and sightless, his mouth gaping in a toothless smile. He seemed heedless of the flies crawling over his wrinkled skin. A weathered and cracked wooden bowl was clutched in his filthy hands—empty of even the slightest offering from passersby.

Stepping into the dark interior, High Dance found the floor to be packed clay. Daylight cast slivers of light where cracks in the walls hadn't been repaired. A central hearth looked cold, the ash having blown out over the floor in a black shadow.

In the rear, perched on a scaffold made of old cedar branches, sat a wood-and-straw statue of Old-Woman-Who-Never-Dies. She crouched on a split-cane mat, the top of her face painted white, the bottom black. Her eyes were charcoal dots, and her mouth was a half-open gape in the round head. A squash vine had been wrapped around one shoulder, and the burden basket on her back contained ears of corn, most of the kernels chewed away by mice.

"They come here to share the miracle of the Morning Star," a voice stated from the left. "But their hearts forever belong to First Woman."

"It's only natural." High Dance glanced at the man who stepped out of the shadows. "The Morning Star can dazzle them with the ritual displays, with stickball games, colorful chunkey tournaments, and all the elaborate pageants and feasting. They see him, so grand and mighty, a living god among them. But in the end, everything depends on the harvest. Old-Woman-Who-Never-Dies exhales her fertility into the seeds, goads the Tie Snakes to call the rains, and balances the powers of the Underworld with those of the earth and sky. From her cave deep in the earth she encourages the Tree of Life to flourish."

The man grunted. "They find no conflict in that. The dirt people admire and fawn over Corn Woman's resurrected son in its frail human body at the same time they worship and implore his Spirit Being grandmother to save them. How . . . typical."

High Dance watched Bead step out into light. He looked exhausted as he stared absently at the shrine in the back of the temple; his face appeared oddly blotched from smeared paints. He wore a simple hemp-thread shirt that hung just below the crotch. Sandals were on his feet. His hair was tied behind his head and hung loose down his back. The faintest slump of his shoulders implied disappointment.

The man arched his brows, took a deep breath, and asked, "You received my token?"

High Dance reached into his belt pouch and displayed the broken half of a wooden bead between his thumb and forefinger. "I was a little surprised by the directions your runner gave me. Here? At the edge of the swamps?"

"Among all these unwashed and uncaring dirt farmers." The man nodded. "People who'd never remember the likes of us, and of whom no one would ever think to ask questions."

"And the old man outside the door?"

"Blind and deaf. Removing him might have drawn attention I'd rather avoid."

"You only sent *half* of a bead."

Bead pursed his lips and stared at the packed clay of the temple floor. "For reasons I don't understand, Power has taken a hand in our mutual undertaking."

"Mutual?" High Dance slipped the bead half into his pouch.

"At the last instant your clansman Cut String was killed by Lady Night Shadow Star. Up until a moment before Cut String acted, she'd been lying naked and groggy on the Earth Priest's floor. Apparently she was writhing in the delirious grip of Sister Datura. Though wracked by the dry heaves, she nevertheless got to her feet, wandered out into the rain, and arrived just in time to use Five Fists' bow and arrows to kill your relative."

"You seem very well-informed."

"Let's say that Power whispers to me on occasion."

"Then maybe you'd better rethink your 'Power.' If what you say about Cut String is true, he's not 'my man.' I don't know what you're talking about."

Bead's forehead lined. "What if you had the ability to—"

High Dance barked, "I *don't* appreciate whispered accusations about Evening Star House having *anything* to do with attempts on the Morning Star's life!"

Bead frowned, his forehead lining. The smudges of color mottled his brow. "You do know that they will be coming, don't you? Sniffing around for clues, their agents asking discrete questions."

"They'll find we had nothing to do with this."

"Curious . . . and double curious." Bead's cunning eyes fixed on High Dance. "Yet here you are, meeting with me, a willing conspirator in the overthrow of the Morning Star?"

"Let's say I had no love for the *tonka'tzi* or his spawn. Morning Star House has cost us too much over the years." High Dance flashed his hand in a dismissive gesture. "That someone used a kinsman in an attempt to assassinate the Morning Star is worth knowing. But you, Bead, claimed that I would know the actions of your hand. What, exactly was I supposed to have seen?"

"The *tonka'tzi* is dead."

"In his sleep we are told."

Bead's face twisted in a distasteful grimace. "What *is it* about those people? Can't they do *anything* right? I left that arrogant Red Warrior and his sulky little wife with their throats gaping wider than an idiot grins! The whole of Cahokia should be torn and shaking in horror!"

"*You* killed the *tonka'tzi*? We heard the Great Sky died in his sleep, that when his wife awakened beside his lifeless body, she took her own life to accompany his souls to the Sky Path and the Land of the Ancestors."

Bead rubbed the back of his neck, pacing irritably. "I've dreamed this. . . . Dreamed it for years. Each step, taken so carefully. The order of their deaths just so. And then as the waves of fear and terror flow across Cahokia, then . . . Yes, that's the moment Power shakes and trembles. The moment when the grand sacrifice will splinter the

Underworld and sunder the Sky!" His eyes were blazing like fire rocks, his fist knotted and raised, muscles standing out on his sweat-damp skin.

High Dance stiffened at the passion. "You almost sound as if you knew the *tonka'tzi*. That it's personal between you."

"The great Red Warrior Tenkiller! Whose fire ignited when the re-incarnated Morning Star's hot semen first shot into Magic Woman's fertile loins! And what did he in turn sire? Nothing but descending orders of ash and charcoal."

"It's not wise to use the name of the dead. Doing so not only at-tracts the attention of the life-soul as it struggles to begin the journey to the Realm of the Ancestors. Naming the dead draws bad luck."

"Bad luck?" Bead chuckled to himself, his ferocity draining as a confused expression spread over his features. "Luck has nothing to do with it. It's them! I should have had panic. I *needed* panic. Expected it in fact for the ceremony." He gave High Dance a conspiratorial glance. "That was Blue Heron's work, no doubt. My assassin got close enough to leave a gash in her throat."

His brow knit further. "Just not a deep enough one. The old camp bitch was saved by some commoner Night Shadow Star prompted her to find. A ruffian and thief."

"I don't understand."

"Neither do I, but Power is aware of what we're about, High Chief. It has taken an interest in our struggle. But which Powers favor which side? That remains uncertain. My source has heard that Piasa favors Night Shadow Star, but is unsure if the claims aren't just the lingering visions of Sister Datura." He paused again, raising his hand to rub the side of his head.

High Dance noted dark outlines around the man's nails. Blood?

"Why would Underworld Power care what we do to Morning Star? He's of the Sky World."

Bead's lips twitched; he shot High Dance an evaluative glance, read-ing the thoughts in his head as if they were written in the beads. "Ah, yes, you're imagining the opportunities, aren't you? You see what I'm about. Look beyond the chaos you suddenly hope to exploit after the Morning Star's murder. Myself, I have no problem with your House ascending the heights of authority and prestige. Supplant Matron Wind's lineage for all I care.

"But for the Clan Keeper's quick wits, half of Cahokia should be abuzz with the *tonka'tzi*'s assassination. Each of the Houses should be accusing the other . . . everyone looking up at the Morning Star's palace, wondering why the reincarnated god remains impotent to anticipate, let alone stop, the murders."

Bead smacked his hard fist into his palm. "But instead of chaos, what do I get? A simple funeral, a soft, sad mourning for a suddenly dead *tonka'tzi* instead of a boiling turmoil . . . or a stewing accusation that would take but one more good kick to spill into riots!"

"There will be other chances," High Dance replied evenly as the pieces began to fit together in his head.

Bead seemed to tremble, then took a deep breath, nodding. "Yes, other chances. I gambled on their arrogance, on their belief that they were untouchable. They are alerted now. As good as my wolves are, our enemies will take precautions with their security."

High Dance watched the interplay of expressions, the quick eyes, as the man's agitation built. He was whispering softly to himself, head slightly cocked, as if searching for distant voices.

"Your . . . wolves?"

Bead's train of thought seemed to snap, and he glanced suspiciously at High Dance. "It's all about living gods, isn't it? The miraculous ability of the Four Winds Clan to call souls back from the Land of the Dead? It's supposed to be in the blood! Something unique to the Four Winds Clan's ancestry . . . perhaps going back to the Creation? Perhaps being descended from Morning Star himself? The Power of resurrection is key, High Chief. You understand that, don't you?"

High Dance frowned. "The Morning Star's life-soul has been rekindled in two different men now. Had Cut String's assassination attempt—"

"Exactly!" Bead frowned again, raising a hand to stop the conversation. For a moment longer he scowled at the floor. "It was such a simple thing. Bobcat's life-soul hadn't been separated from his body for more than a day. What could have possibly gone wrong? The cleansing? The painting? Or was it the lust. It's not like I gave in to the temptation . . ."

"What are you talking about?"

Bead snorted and began picking at his fingers. The dark matter in his cuticles was definitely dried blood.

"High Chief?" Bead's sidelong glance fixed on High Dance. "You understand that you are inextricably involved now, don't you?"

High Dance felt a chill hand tighten around his heart. "My goals remain unchanged, Bead. Or whatever your name is. But remember, *you* contacted *me*. Beyond that, you really don't want to challenge either me or Evening Star House." He bent his lips into a frigid smile, and added, "Doing so wouldn't be conducive to either long life or attaining whatever goal it is that you've set yourself with all your blood and barely rubbed-off paint."

Bead's expression flickered, his lips twitching. He gave a slight nod. "We understand each other." A pause. "When you return later this evening, you will find your eldest son Fast Thrower still worried. He's a handsome young man. You must be extraordinarily proud. The black granite chunkey stone he went to sleep with two nights ago remains missing. You will find it in a jar of corn meal. The jar's a burnished brownware. Under the third bench from the right, I believe."

"That's Brown Bear's sleeping bench," High Dance barely whispered. "He's responsible for my family's—"

"Their safety, yes. I know. You might want to replace him. Old Brown Bear Fivekiller sleeps too soundly these days. It's terrifying enough that Fast Thrower might just 'misplace' his chunkey stone. At least he *awakened* the next morning to find it missing."

High Dance swallowed hard, a runny sensation of unease deep in his guts. *He took the chunkey stone out of Fast Thrower's bed! This man walked into my palace and stood over my son's sleeping body?*

Bead's triumphant black eyes had fixed on him, reading every thought while a knowing smile began to curl his lips. In the shaft of light spilling through the door, High Dance could see that the man's face bore a thick layer of brown, as if to obscure the broad planes of his face.

"Ah, yes, High Chief. You're not as thick-witted as your sister thinks you are. And just between the two of us, I really don't care if Evening Star House ends up running Cahokia, or if you ascend the *tonka'tzi's* chair."

"Who *are* you?" High Dance's souls were awash with a sudden and cold fear.

With an icy smile, Bead added, "There, now. Doesn't matter. We've managed to put the mutual threats behind us so we can get on to the real problem: killing the Morning Star. It is going to be so much harder and dangerous than either of us thought. Let's put our heads together and really think this through. Blue Heron has to go, that we already know. But now, this Piasa thing? It starts to make sense. My dead assassin Bobcat was chopped up and thrown in the river. Last night when I tried to call him back, his life-soul didn't appear where it was supposed to. I *know the ritual.* I've done it twice before in the south, called dead souls into new bodies. It's not that hard, mostly a matter of purity, blood, and sacrifice."

Bead stopped short, his expression going slack, as if he were listening to something.

"Oh, yes." Bead glanced at High Dance, revelation in his suddenly pained eyes. "They tell me Piasa wouldn't free Bobcat's soul. That somehow Lady Night Shadow Star . . . ?"

He cocked his head again, struggling to hear something. After a slight nod, he looked as bereft as a man kicked in the gut. "But of course. I understand. Nothing comes free. She's the ultimate sacrifice, the price I have to pay. But how can I stand the pain? I lost her once before, and it nearly . . ."

His face contorted. "Can I do that? Stand that?"

An instant later, his animation returned. "But it won't be forever. I can call her souls back from the dead! Find her another beautiful body, and it will be just like it was."

The chill in High Dance's souls deepened. "Your warrior's life-soul? You tried to call it? But, I mean . . . call it where?"

Bead gave a slight shrug. "Into a young woman's body. Bobcat was only a Tula, mind you. But maybe the failure was due to my trying to call a male soul into a female body? But . . . No, no, no! It shouldn't matter. I've done it before. The ritual should have worked! You *should* be able to call a dead soul to any place, and into any body you want to!"

High Dance tried to control his incredulous expression. "So . . . what happened?"

Bead sighed and rubbed the back of his neck, sandaled toe scuffing the packed clay. "I did everything correctly. Bathed her entire body in the blood of the farmer and his family. Sang with the appropriate vigor. When dawn came, Bobcat's soul should have taken over her body. When I pulled the gag out of her mouth, all she did was sob and scream like a maniac. She couldn't understand or speak a single word of Tula . . . Couldn't tell me any of the things Bobcat's souls would have known."

"And the girl?" High Dance asked, his skin crawling as he slowly backed toward the door.

"I was so enraged . . . that sense of absolute frustration! You understand that, don't you, High Chief? By the time I stopped hacking and slicing, well, there just wasn't enough left to satiate that lust I felt while I was washing her."

Then a slow smile spread across his lips. "Well, that's for another day. Now, what are we going to do about Blue Heron?"

"I think it would be best if we each went our separate ways, Bead."

The man's knowing smile cut through High Dance's souls like a winter gale. "Oh, no, High Chief. You have other children. Fast Throw's younger brother White Stem and his sister Two Leaf are just as vulnerable. And then there's Columella's children. But for this silly rule the Morning Star instituted concerning the Four Winds Houses, they are the true heirs of Evening Star House. It'd be a terrible shame if anything happened to even one of those children, don't you think?"

High Dance tried to swallow. It took two tries to get past the tightening knot in his throat. He took another step back, ready to . . .

"That's far enough." Bead extended his arm, palm out. "Besides, even if you ran, you'd have to get past my wolves outside. You'll go when I tell you, and not a moment before."

"What do you want from me?"

Bead gave him a wary smile, his eyes gleaming like angry obsidian. "Just your cooperation. Oh, and you might place the Earth Clan squadrons under your control on high alert. When I *finally* kick Cahokia into a panic, I'll need them to maintain order while you take over."

Twenty-three

In her palace great room, Columella hunched as she sat on in her litter chair atop the clay dais. Through half-lidded eyes, she stared uneasily at her solitary "guest." Her palace, high atop its mound in Evening Star City, should have been her safe haven. Instead the now-empty great room left her feeling vulnerable and curiously impotent. The fire attendants, her servants and slaves, everyone having excused themselves at the Keeper's request.

The great room with its familiar war trophies, the brightly painted red, white, and black walls decorated with shields, bows, and the giant effigy carving of Birdman behind her, radiated an inexplicable chill. The sleeping benches displayed rumpled hides and an abandoned pile of weaving that Cricket had been working on. Here and there bowls had been left behind, dropped at her command.

Clan Keeper Blue Heron—the focus of Columella's unease—sat just to the right of the fire where her porters had placed her litter on the intricately woven, mat-covered floor. Blue Heron's pensive eyes were fixed on the large and detailed carving of Birdman where it hung on the woven-cane wall behind the dais. The piece was an older design that many now said presaged the resurrection of the Morning Star. The depiction invoked the memory of when Morning Star had changed into an eagle and flown up into the sky world in the Beginning Times.

Columella had waited long enough. The silence had stretched her nerves to the breaking point. "Very well, Cousin, we can't get more alone unless you rout the mice from their holes in the walls." Columella accented her words with a suggestive eyebrow as she propped her chin in what she hoped looked like apparent unconcern.

Blue Heron took just enough time to flaunt her authority before asking, "Do you think there are more sparkflies this spring?"

"Excuse me?"

"I haven't seen as many." Blue Heron continued to stare at the great carving behind Columella's elevated perch. "I can't decide if it's because of the weather. Warmer this year. Or is it the number of children we have running around and catching them? Used to be deer closer than a couple of days' walk, if you'll remember. Now hunters won't even try to bring in fresh meat in the summer time. It takes so long to get it here that the meat sours. Too many people, too much hunting. Is it the same with the sparkflies?"

"I haven't a clue, Clan Keeper. Somehow, I just can't fathom you spending the time to journey to River Mounds City, be loaded onto a canoe and ferried to my side of the river, then brought up to Evening Star City, to empty my great room and ask about sparkflies."

"Doesn't seem logical, does it?" Blue Heron agreed. "But sometimes logic fails us, cousin." Blue Heron's gaze shifted, her keen eyes boring into Columella's. "For example, it seems entirely illogical that the *tonka'tzi* would just die in the night."

"I don't understand. What does illogic have to do with his death? You're not making sense." She paused, putting the pieces together. "Unless the facts of the *tonka'tzi*'s death are not what we've been told."

Blue Heron was watching her with the same intensity her namesake watched a little fish as it surfaced in a still pond.

"That's it, isn't it?" Columella felt an icy tingle run through her guts. "And if you're here . . . Ah, I begin to understand. You're looking for the responsible person. And that leads me to assume this was no crime of passion, no spontaneous fit of jealousy. What was it? Poison? Someone sneaking up from behind with a club?"

Blue Heron lifted her chin so that Columella could see the dark line of stitches. "More like a ritual sacrifice."

Columella's heart skipped, and she swallowed hard. "I don't understand, Clan Keeper."

"The *tonka'tzi*'s throat was slit. The same was done to his wife. A second assassin was in the process of cutting my throat when a fortuitous interruption left me alive . . . and him dead." She pointed a gnarled finger at the long wound. "But he came this close."

Columella's souls froze. For long heartbeats, she and Blue Heron sat with locked eyes.

Blue Heron broke the silence, her words measured, toneless. "The *tonka'tzi* was my brother. That's enough reason to stir me to rage. That the assassins came this close to sending my souls to our ancestors, that makes it even more personal."

Distracted by the queasy sensation in her bowels, Columella fought to clear her wits. Massaging her temples with the tips of her fingers was probably a mistake, but she needed the ability to order her frantic and tumbling thoughts.

She says nothing about the attempt on the Morning Star. But who is behind the tonka'tzi's *murder and the attempt on the Keeper?*

Or was that a ploy, a careful trick to mislead her? It wouldn't be the first time a supposed "victim" faked her own attack as a means of pointing the finger of guilt in a different direction.

Columella forced herself to take a deep breath. "Upon the graves of our ancestors, Keeper, I know nothing about any attempts on either your life, or the *tonka'tzi's*. The House of Evening Star is *not* involved in any way in these despicable actions. I give you my word on that."

"And your brother's?"

Columella nodded. "The High Chief knows nothing of these things."

"High Dance has told you so?"

Columella avoided the trap, snapping, "No! If he didn't know the *tonka'tzi* was assassinated, how could he tell me he wasn't involved? Stop playing your tricky little games. If he'd been involved, I would know!" She let the anger run through her, then added in a more reasonable voice. "Not to mention the fact that coming here, to us, first, is even *more* insulting."

Blue Heron's fixed stare hadn't so much as wavered. "Actually, you should feel flattered. It's a measure of your competence and innate ability, Matron. You, of all people, have the cunning, initiative, and courage to attempt something like this."

Columella chuckled dryly, the first fingers of relief stroking through her. "And the Morning Star would just sit mildly atop his high perch and let his family be murdered and displaced?"

"Do not make the mistake of thinking the Morning Star carries any allegiance to our House just because Chunkey Boy's host body was ours once." Blue Heron gave her a grim smile. "From my experience, Morning Star is ultimately pragmatic."

"As you wish." Columella sniffed, thinning her nostrils in the process. "But in the meantime have you given any thought to the possibility that whoever assassinated the *tonka'tzi* hoped that you would come here, make your accusations, and drive a wedge between us that could not be repaired?"

Blue Heron's dark gaze sharpened. "Indeed I have. But if our antagonist is that calculating, perhaps you, good Matron, and the High Chief—capable as you are—might be his next victims. If he's eliminating potential threats, you'd be next."

Columella tried to keep her lips from twitching as she considered that. "That leaves another House as the perpetrator."

"I've known for years that you collect information on the other Houses." Blue Heron pressed the palms of her hands together suggestively. "Is it possible that some bit of information . . . perhaps something you might have heard from one of your sources, didn't make sense until now?"

Columella arched an eyebrow. "Would it be a crushing revelation for you to learn that you are neither loved, nor cherished, by *any* of the other Houses of Four Winds Clan?"

"Neither crushing . . . nor a revelation," she muttered dryly.

"Then I have heard nothing that would lead me to suspect any of the other Houses of this particularly heinous act."

"I'll take your word for that." Blue Heron pursed her lips, frowned, and then cautiously said, "Meanwhile, I want you to consider this: the attempt to assassinate both the *tonka'tzi* and me was not the first attempt to upset our world. An attempt was made on the Morning Star several days ago."

Columella stiffened, struggling to maintain an appearance of appropriate shock.

Blue Heron added, "Have you heard anything about that? Statements of frustration? Worries about upset plans? Pointless rumors?"

"No. Nothing . . . well, outside of the ordinary grumblings, envy, and resentment."

"What if I told you the assassin was Cut String?"

Columella slowly narrowed her right eye into a knowing squint. "You're saying that one of my cousins tried to kill the Morning Star?" She paused, meeting glare for glare. "And I only hear of it now?"

"We purposefully kept the information quiet, hoping that the silence would lure anyone involved to betray themselves."

"Sorry to disappoint you," Columella growled. "Ah, now I see yet another reason why you are here. And, no! Don't even ask. Cut String never confided his plans to either me or the High Chief. Had he, we would have dealt with it quietly. As your presence here indicates, we don't need *that* kind of trouble."

Columella let herself fume appropriately, then added, "It makes a certain kind of sense that it would be Cut String. The man's uncle . . . let's say he's vulnerable to 'persuasion' since he has an unhealthy attraction." She waved it away. "If Cut String shows up we'll—"

"He's been taken care of."

Columella nodded. "Then we'll immediately have the unlamented Cut String's uncle, Pond Water, rounded up and dealt with. We've let him go for too long as it is."

Blue Heron's gaze hardened. "No. We want the uncle delivered to us. Alive. We'd like to hear the story from his own lips."

"You'll have him as soon as my people can run him down." Columella slowly shook her head. "The Morning Star? You and the *tonka'tzi*? Whoever is doing this is playing with fire, Clan Keeper."

Blue Heron nodded soberly. "They're so anxious to burn the Morning Star's temple down, that it looks to me like they're willing to burn it from the outside in. Even if it means they'll be trapped and consumed in the process."

Columella frowned. *I'm missing too many of the pieces. Who else is moving against Morning Star's House?* Aloud she said, "If they succeed?"

"Cahokia will tear itself apart. Riots, chaos, old clan feuds burning out of control, the immigrants turning on their neighbors."

Columella nodded sagaciously. "In these dangerous times, Clan Keeper, I will be more than willing to send you any information that comes to my ears."

Blue Heron watched her through predatory eyes. "I would expect no less of you, Matron. Please give my regards to the High Chief. Let him know how sorry I was to miss him. You don't happen to know his whereabouts, do you?"

Columella shrugged her ignorance, saying, "Had we been notified in advance of your arrival, we both could have welcomed you appropriately, and you could have had our combined counsel."

"I suppose." Blue Heron cocked her head, one eye glinting. "But we wouldn't have had such a spontaneous conversation had we been burdened by all that formality." A pause. "Now, if you will excuse me, I must be getting back."

Only after the Clan Keeper had been ceremoniously carried from the room did Columella once again wave her attendants out, demanding they leave her in peace.

She waited until the last of them had filed out the main door and pulled it closed.

In the silence, she asked, "Well?"

She felt as well as heard the wooden door being opened in the dais beneath her seat. The dwarf, Flat Stone Pipe, crawled out from the hollow, made a face, and stretched his small body. His skin had taken on the impression of the matting upon which he'd been lying. His hair had been mussed by the cramped ceiling of the small hole.

He rubbed his back in irritation as he said, "I am taken as much by surprise as you are, Matron. *Two* assassins striking the *tonka'tzi*'s House at the same time? And we haven't heard of them? Both following so closely on the botched attempt on the Morning Star?"

"But who?" she wondered. "We've ears in High Chief War Duck's palace, in Green Chunkey's House down in Horned Serpent Town, as well as every other House. Something would have warned us." She paused. "What about Cut String's uncle?"

"Old Pond Water is ignorant. A simple tool that we knew would fall into Blue Heron's hands. I'll send Red Thigh to help Blue Heron's people with the interrogation. Since Red Thigh knows nothing about the plot, he'll be as horrified as anyone, and just as eager to expose the plotters. Blue Heron's people will be satisfied with his zeal on the way to ultimately discovering a dead end."

"But who organized the assassination of the *tonka'tzi*?"

Flat Stone Pipe gave a shrug of his small shoulders. "Since we don't know, Matron, perhaps we should pay attention to Blue Heron's warning: you and the High Chief could be next."

"Don't be silly."

"Matron, anyone capable of murdering the *tonka'tzi* and nicking the Clan Keeper's throat without tipping his hand to either her or me is someone we most assuredly do not want to underestimate."

Twenty-four

Seven Skull Shield propped his elbows on his knees as he watched the chunkey game. The bark sun hat on his head not only shaded his face, but he'd used a charcoal-laced grease to darken his features. Up close it didn't do much good. Anyone who knew him would recognize him. From a distance, however, it granted him a degree of obscurity. Just why he'd thought a disguise was a good idea, he wasn't sure. Something, some itch of nervousness, had urged him to take the precaution.

If a person were looking for information, River Mounds City was the place to get it. And if anyone knew anything, it would be the man perched on the platform beside him. He was called Crazy Frog. In whatever family he'd been born to, he'd probably been known by some common name like Corn Boy, or Brown Stem, or Jumping Rabbit; but that had been so long ago even Crazy Frog probably had forgotten. Assuming he even still remembered which clan he'd really been born into. With so many tens of thousands of people living in Cahokia, like Seven Skull Shield, Crazy Frog switched clans the way most people changed shirts. In the new Cahokia, for those willing to employ the ruse, one's clan affiliation depended upon necessity, circumstance, and potential opportunity.

Crazy Frog was a common-looking man of perhaps forty, medium of frame, average of features. His nose was neither too wide nor too thin; his face was shaped about like everyone else's. If he had any distinguishing characteristic, it might have been his tattoos: they'd been reworked sometime in the past to create a design that was completely unrecognizable. When he laughed, most of his teeth were missing—not uncommon in Cahokia, for a man of his age. The Healers said tooth loss was higher among the poor who ate a higher percentage of corn. But what choice did they have?

Crazy Frog had his finger in just about everything that was happening in River Mounds City, but his passion was chunkey. To better watch the games Crazy Frog had built himself a portable platform that his men carried around to the various matches. Elevated as he was above the heads of the crowd, he could see every moment of a match. After watching a player's first few casts, Crazy Frog could evaluate his chances of winning with uncanny accuracy. Calling down bets to his runners, he'd maintain his own markers on a flat piece of engraved red cedar by means of a complicated pattern of beads.

Seven Skull Shield now perched beside his old friend on the raised pole platform with its plank floor. The wobbling framework didn't inspire confidence. Nevertheless, Crazy Frog had been using the thing for years, and it hadn't collapsed yet.

The matches were being played on the River City Mounds grand plaza, dominated as it was by High Chief War Duck's mound-top palace. River City Mounds formed a semicircle instead of a square or diamond. Here topography dictated form. The high ground atop the levee formed by the river and its confluence with Cahokia Creek had been packed with mounds and buildings. The curving community ended in a cluster that included the large River House palace with its high roof, towering red cedar pole, and guardian effigies. The temple and charnel mounds were close beside it. The site overlooked the bustling canoe landing as well as the marshy bottoms of Cahokia Creek to the west. Across the river Evening Star City stood atop its smugly dry bluff.

Cahokia thrived on chunkey. In the grand plaza beneath the Morning Star's mound, chunkey was played as a ritualized reenactment of the hero's battle against the giants in the Beginning Times. Among the dirt farmers and immigrants it was played as a form of prayer, the outcome of the games being interpreted as an expression of divine will. At River City Mounds, however, the game had grown into something else: a true sport upon which piles of Trade were wagered. Most of the better players who made their living playing chunkey had adopted striking names like "Rolls His Head," "The Lightning Lance," and "Skull Pinner." They wore flashy costumes of brilliantly dyed feathers and literally jangled as they walked, so bedecked were they in shell and copper jewelry.

They were in the right place. As the gateway to Cahokia, not only did most of the Trade land at the River Mounds, but so, too, did the emissaries, foreign chiefs, and warriors with their wealth. Many arrived with reputations as chunkey players among their own people, and at River City they had their first chance to prove their skill against the best in the world.

While Cahokia's prestige and influence had drawn foreign chunkey players and their wealth, it had also created something absolutely unique: a city of strangers.

Among strangers the old rules of behavior no longer applied. Never before had such opportunities for greed, wealth, and nefarious indulgence existed. A man no longer had disapproving kin looking over his shoulder; he could act reprehensibly and disappear into the crowds without fear of censure. In a town of two or three thousand, if a thief took another person's possessions, someone was bound to know. Any immoral behavior was immediately reported by rival clans.

In contrast, a sack full of corn stolen in River Mounds could be Traded a day later in the Horned Serpent community with impunity. A distinctive shell necklace lifted from an Earth Clan chief in Evening Star City could be Traded for a copper effigy in the eastern uplands without fear of discovery.

It wasn't even a difficult undertaking. Newcomers who had lived all their lives in communities where everyone knew and trusted everyone else, couldn't conceive that the smiling local who greeted them at the canoe landing didn't have the same scruples they had. Even after half their Trade had disappeared, many of the simpletons approached the local high chief with the absolute conviction that somehow a misunderstanding had occurred, and surely the missing goods would be returned as soon as the absconding party was made aware of the mistake. For many of those, even after it was explained to them, the concept of blatant theft remained utterly unfathomable. How could anyone behave in such a soulless manner? And especially in the Morning Star's Cahokia?

In the city, with its teeming throngs, a man's ambition was only limited by his lack of imagination or cunning. Crazy Frog was full of both.

On the chunkey court a dazzlingly bedecked player crouched slightly, his polished red-granite stone in his right hand, waxed wooden lance in his left. The breeze batted playfully at the bright blue feathers sticking out of his headdress. He'd painted his face white, with two large black forked-eye designs. Giant copper ear spools gleamed in the sunlight, and his muscular body tensed.

"Badger Cape will make the point if he doesn't release too high," Crazy Frog noted. "If he'd ever get that right, just letting the stone kiss the ground instead of dropping it, he'd be a master."

"He looks the part. He must win enough to afford the copper and paint." Seven Skull Shield propped his chin, having never developed Crazy Frog's eye for evaluating a player.

"The important word is 'enough.' What he needs to do is win 'more.'"

Badger Cape stepped off on his left foot, taking four paces before his arm went back. His body bowed, chest dropping as he bowled the stone down the court in one fluid motion. The stone left his hand at least two finger-widths above the smooth clay.

"Too high," Crazy Frog said. "Did you see that bounce?"

"I did."

Badger Cape straightened and shifted his lance to his right hand in one poetic movement, ran four more paces and whipped his arm back. He cast, using his body as a spring to fling the lance forward. Then, muscles knotting in his strong legs, he slowed to a stop just shy of the penalty line. All eyes followed Badger Cape's spinning lance as it arced against the hazy sky. The red stone was slowing, curving to the right as the lance dropped toward it. At the last moment the stone's curve increased, carrying it away from the lance's path. The lance impacted the clay a heartbeat before the stone flopped onto its side a good body length to the right.

A groan went up from the crowd.

"It always veers like that when he lets it bounce," Crazy Frog muttered, bending down to his plank and moving one of the colored beads.

The next player was dressed in yellow and black, his face painted in diagonal lines. He wore his hair in a bun, to the front of which was tied a stuffed oriole, its wings spread wide. Tattoos of interlinked diamonds ran down his bare arms and legs.

"Sun Bird can't lose now." Crazy Frog rubbed his chin. "Should have bet a second pot of shell beads on this game."

"All because Badger Cape bounced his stone?"

"Losing by that much on his first cast?" Crazy Frog gestured futility. "When he starts well, he ends well. Now he thinks Power isn't with him on this game. It would be a miracle if he recovered, and Badger Cape isn't in the habit of making miracles."

Seven Skull Shield watched Sun Bird start his run with a little hop. On the fourth pace he bent, whipped his arm back, and smoothly bowled a white marble stone down the court. Straightening, he sprinted forward, switched his lance, and launched it in a perfect overhand throw. He came to a stop, bouncing on his toes as he watched the lance speed after the fleet stone.

"Good cast," Crazy Frog admitted as he moved his counter bead even before seeing the lance impact no more than two hand's distance from the stone as it slowed and toppled onto its side.

"I'm curious about something," Seven Skull Shield said softly. "When I get curious, I think about who might have the answers to my questions."

"Is that why you gave me that nicely polished whelk shell and asked to sit with me?"

"You're a remarkably bright man, old friend. And not just about the ins and outs of chunkey. I need information."

Badger Cape and Sun Bird went to retrieve their gaming pieces and the judge raised an ornate stick at the side of the chunkey court to mark Sun Bird's point.

The crowd along the court was busy calling encouragement to their favorite player, or haggling over bets.

Crazy Frog gave him a sidelong glance. "A big shell like that earns you not only my wisdom on chunkey and a seat on my platform, but more than just a little information. What is it this time? You need an introduction to some unlucky young woman?"

"What do you mean, 'unlucky'?"

Crazy Frog shrugged, his nondescript face expressionless. "If I were a pretty young woman, and I woke up to find you in my bed, I'd feel unlucky."

"Good thing you're not a young woman. And if I were *ever* to wake up and find *you* sharing my bed? I'd slice my own throat open before I'd live with the memory."

Crazy Frog laughed and slapped his knee.

Seven Skull Shield concentrated on his friend's expression as he added, "That would take a special knife, of course. Something ceremonial, perhaps made of translucent brown chert and chipped out by a master flint-knapper. You heard of any such knives being Traded around?"

Crazy Frog's eyes narrowed as he thought. "Nope. But I could put the word out. What do you need it for?"

"Maybe I'm worried about waking up with you in my bed?"

"Not a chance. And you didn't bribe me with that shell just to get a line on an expensive ceremonial knife."

Seven Skull Shield watched Badger Cape take his position, all of his concentration on the course. Spectators shouted advice and support from the sidelines. The player sprinted forward with a passion, tucked, and bowled his stone. Shifting the lance was smoothly done, and he cast before pulling to a stop just shy of the penalty line.

"He's throwing long," Crazy Frog muttered, moving his counter.

Seven Skull Shield watched the lance impact a good six hands beyond where the stone stopped. "I don't think I want you watching when I play."

"You're not too bad. With practice and someone who knows the game to tell you what you're doing wrong, you'd be pretty good."

"But not great?"

"Not to the point that I'd play the Morning Star for my head if I were you."

"He usually grants the loser his head back."

"You assume he'll be in a good mood when he plays you."

"What do you hear about the Morning Star? Myself, I've heard that some parties aren't very pleased with him these days."

Crazy Frog watched Sun Bird take his position, study the court, and then charge forward to bowl his stone and cast his lance. He moved another bead in Sun Bird's favor even before the lance had made it midway through its flight. "Being 'displeased' with the Morning Star and clapping one's jaws about it doesn't sound like the best path to a long and happy life."

"Apparently someone has done just that. Anything you might have heard that actually proves worthwhile might earn you considerably more than a whelk shell or two."

Crazy Frog gave him a careful inspection from the corner of his eye. "Tell me that you're not thinking about challenging the Morning Star. I always thought you were smarter than to desire a slow death in a square. And, if that's where you're headed, I want nothing to do with you."

"Me? Challenge the Morning Star? Not in this or any other lifetime."

"So far you're not making much sense, old friend." He arched an eyebrow. "Say, this doesn't have anything to do with that rumor that the Four Winds Clan Keeper ran you down in old Meander's shell-carving workshop? I figured it was some exaggerated story." He chuckled. "Did she really call that third leg of yours a tow rope?"

"It was just a misunderstanding about some Old-Woman-Who-Never-Dies statuettes."

"Oh, yeah, and I heard they broke every finger in Black Swallow's hands for stealing them."

Seven Skull Shield made a face. "We're getting away from the point. Tell me something: Do you like the way things are? Enjoying wealth, fine food, gambling on chunkey, living like a high chief, running your own little squadron of hired men?"

Crazy Frog's eyes were flat and emotionless. "What do you think?"

"I think you want everything to stay just as it is. I think you really like living the way you do. Me, myself? I want things to stay as they are. I think Cahokia's perfectly fine just as it is." He paused. "Someone doesn't share our way of thinking."

"Who?"

"That's what I need to find out." Seven Skull Shield met Crazy Frog's intent stare. "Not much goes on around the River Mounds or down on the canoe landing that you don't hear about. And if you *had* heard something, you might not have realized just how much of a threat it might be to your continued and future enjoyment of chunkey."

"What's this all about?" For the first time, Crazy Frog was no longer paying attention to chunkey. His flat brown eyes were now fixed on Seven Skull Shield.

"Someone is trying to overthrow the Morning Star and destroy the Four Winds Clan. You and I might not think that was our problem, and that the elite can rotted-well take care of themselves. Then if we think a little further we realize that if the plotters succeed in assassinating the Morning Star and brewing a civil war . . . ?"

"I won't be watching much chunkey." Crazy Frog's expression tightened the slightest bit. He didn't even notice when Badger Cape took his position, bowled, and cast. "The *tonka'tzi?*"

"The Four Winds Clan has managed, so far, to keep the pot from boiling over. Your people are in a position to hear things. If anyone mentions the *tonka'tzi*'s throat being slit with a big ceremonial knife? That, I'd want to know about immediately. And if you could nab the source of the rumors? You might end up having a chunkey match held in your honor."

After thinking for a while, Crazy Frog said, "I'll put my people on it. How do I contact you?"

"Send someone you can trust to the Four Winds Clan Keeper's palace. Have them"—he watched Sun Bird take his position—"deliver a chunkey stone. A red one if it's critical and needs immediate attention, white if you just think it's important."

"The Clan Keeper's?" For the first time Crazy Frog's face reflected astonishment. "So, that's really true?"

He gave Crazy Frog a narrow-eyed squint. "Which is why you're going to keep this in the strictest confidence, my friend. I've watched the old woman work, and believe me when I say your life will be both longer, and more profitable, with her as an ally."

"And to think," Crazy Frog mused, "I always thought you were something of a buffoon when you weren't playing slick to seduce some woman."

"I like being a buffoon. People who don't take me seriously don't watch their wealth or their wives. It's just that I have trouble keeping up appearances when people are dying right and left, and assassins are sneaking in at night."

"Then I guess I'll have to rethink my opinion of you . . . *Tow Rope!*"

Twenty-five

The stench was overwhelming, worse even than the charnel houses where bodies were allowed to rot before the bones were picked clean. The difference, Blue Heron thought, was that in charnel houses the entrails were removed first and respectfully disposed of. Here they lay in smelly, fly-and-maggot-crawling piles where they'd been tossed into corners on the blood-soaked floor.

She batted at the buzzing flies and slowly cataloged the dim farmhouse's interior. Body parts from five dismembered corpses were laid out in a large circle that arced from wall to wall. The pieces of a man, woman, two girls, and a small boy had been laid out artistically; the woman's torso at the top, nearest the door, the man's back by the benches. All were naked and had symbols painted in red, black, yellow, and blue. The throats were neatly severed under the angle of the jaw. So precise was the cut on each victim, and so wide the wound, that she could look down onto blood-caked vocal cords in their severed voice boxes.

Each torso had been opened from sternum to pubis. Their hearts and livers had been removed and placed in a smaller ring on the lip of the fire pit; the charred organs, having cooked through and desiccated, were easily identifiable. The intestines, however, had just been dropped and kicked to the corners. Each of the empty gut cavities now held a brownware pot filled with ash.

Blue Heron suffered a shiver, as if each person's body-soul—the one that remained in a person's bones at the time of death—was screaming at her through those now-gaping throats.

But it was to the corpse lying in the middle of the clay floor by the fire pit that her eyes kept returning. There—in a pool of coagulated blood and crawling with flies—sprawled the remains of a young woman. Her breasts had been cruelly hacked from her rib cage; packets of fly larvae rimmed her dried, gray, and shrunken eyes. Crisscrosses had been incised so deeply in her forehead they cut into the bone. The fleshy part of her nose along with her cheeks and mouth had been cut away from ear to ear to expose blood-caked teeth and her jaw bone. The tendons inside her thighs had been severed and her legs inhumanly spread wide. Long slices had been taken down the inside of her thighs. The wreckage that had been made of her pubis and mutilated vulva sent a shiver through Blue Heron's bones.

Instinctively Blue Heron made a warding sign against the haunting souls of the outraged dead. She jumped, unsure if the tickle on her skin came from grasping Spirit fingers, or scores of fly feet.

"I'm here to help you," she implored the dead, and forced her heart to beat normally as she shielded her lips to keep from sucking any of the vile flies into her mouth or lungs.

Once more she glanced back and forth between the victims. The ones laid out in pieces in the circle had been carefully sacrificed, each cut made with precision and for an apparent purpose. She could almost think they'd been treated with reverence. The woman on the floor, however, had been hacked at, the viciousness of the attack readily apparent.

Why the difference? What had the young woman done to incite his anger?

She sucked a breath, two flies racketing around her mouth. Her gag reflex spasmed as she spit the little beasts out.

Come on, concentrate.

She glanced again at the interior walls. Intricate images had been painted carefully, first in blue, yellow, black, and red. Then the artist apparently went back and savagely splashed bloody designs over them, as if to deface the bright images.

"Keeper?" Five Fists asked from where he stood just inside the door.

She turned, glancing at him from the corner of her eye as she batted away the buzzing flies. "I've never seen anything like it. But something . . . There's a similarity here. As if . . ."

He pointed. "The blood on the wall, like with the *tonka'tzi?*"

She glanced at the smears and crisscrosses on the plaster. The colorful images beneath had once been butterflies, cocoons, tadpoles, frogs, mudpuppies and salamanders, seeds, and corn stalks. All images of transformation.

"No snakes," she murmured.

"What do you want done with this place?" he asked softly. "The crowd outside is waiting, as are High Chief Right Hand and the Matron Corn Seed. People are worried, Keeper. The talk of witchcraft is spreading."

She sighed, making another warding by twining her fingers together then flinging them apart to disperse both evil and the angry ghosts of the dead. "Burn it."

She turned as Five Fists stepped out the door, admitting a shaft of light that illuminated the woman's wounded crotch. Something glinted in the mutilated flesh. Blue Heron slashed impotently at the column of flies that rose as she crouched, careful to keep light on the gleam.

She reached out, grasping a thin bit of cold stone between her thumb and forefinger. The sliver had been jammed into the midline where the two bones joined above the sheath; it had apparently stuck in the cartilage before being snapped off. Patiently she worked the fragment loose, holding it up in the slanting light.

I know this stone. She'd seen the like of it before: brown semitranslucent chert, finely chipped to a razor edge. A knife of similar stone had been held by Cut String before Night Shadow Star had driven arrows through this chest. Another had been wielded by a nameless assassin as he came within a whisker of cutting Blue Heron's own throat.

"And now here," she mused, cocking her head as she studied the body pieces laid out so carefully on the floor, their throats gaping wide. "Ritually sacrificed," she murmured. "To appease what Power? Which Spirit world?"

None of which explained the savage brutality inflicted on the slashed remains of the young woman. "What went wrong?"

And what does it mean?

She stepped outside, away from the flies, maggots, stench, and horror, and into the clean afternoon sunlight. Nevertheless the feeling of pollution and filth stuck to her, as if a clinging film. The crowd went silent as she glanced around the bluff-top farmstead with its shabby ramada, worn log mortar and pestle.

Right Hand, High Chief of the Deer Clan, under whose jurisdiction this part of the bluffs fell, stood uncertainly with his sister Matron Corn Seed. She was the titular ruler of the Deer Clan, which remained traditionally matrilineal. The Matron stepped forward, touching her forehead respectfully, and asked, "What happened here, Keeper? Have you seen anything like this before?"

Blue Heron considered, eyes thinning as she weighed her options. Corn Seed looked uncharacteristically nervous. Generally the woman was a rock; now her eyes had a frantic quality. The set of her mouth was almost that of guilt. Power alone knew why? She couldn't oversee every single dirt farmer on the bluffs. As to being upset, all it took was a glimpse inside that accursed farmhouse, and anyone would have been shaken.

"Witchcraft," Blue Heron declared in a voice loud enough to carry to the crowd. But for a handful of younger individuals, the rest just stared at her with uncomprehending eyes. Then the few who understood began translating. The word, in several languages, ran through the crowd like ripples from a cast stone.

Making a cut sign for patience, Blue Heron added, "You all listen to me!" She watched the translators as they repeated her words. "Inside are drawings indicating that the witch changed shape and flew away. I want this house and the corpses inside burned immediately. You will bring wood, pile it around the house, and keep a roaring fire burning atop it for four days. Do you understand?"

The crowd nodded as did Corn Seed and Right Hand.

"Then you will scoop up the dirt for a stone's throw in every direction around the ashes and cover the remains," she told them. "When you have folded the evil in upon itself, you will bring ashes from the sacred fire in your temples, and cover the mound with a purified ash layer. Only then will you bring in white clay to seal the entire mound. After that, no one shall live within an arrow's flight of this place."

People were nodding, eyes wide as they glanced between her and the horrible farmstead.

"Be about it!" Blue Heron ordered, clapping her hands as she spoke.

She watched the people turn away, muttering among themselves and shaking their heads. To Corn Seed she asked, "Who found this, Matron?"

"One of the neighbors. He hadn't seen the family around for a couple of days and got curious."

Blue Heron studied Corn Seed as she talked. "Was there any talk about witchcraft? Tensions in the community? Anything that would have led you to believe that something like this could happen?"

Corn Seed spread her arms helplessly. "What could we know, Clan Keeper? These people, this whole community, they're dirt farmers from somewhere a moon's travel off to the east. They're barbarians. Ignorant farmers come to share the glory of Cahokia. This could be some silly ritual of theirs for all we know. Or a personal vendetta. Keeper, we have people packed together here who have been at war with each other since the Beginning Times. Mostly we relocate traditional enemies as far from each other as we can. Half of my time is spent keeping the peace. Honestly, if it weren't for their belief that chunkey can settle just about every dispute, we'd have a constant war up here."

"Yes, I know." Blue Heron rubbed her tired face. Not a hand of time after her return from Evening Star town she'd been called here by a frantic messenger from Corn Seed. All she wanted to do was climb back into her litter and sleep while her porters carried her back to her palace.

Instead she turned, looking out from the bluff to the endless city that filled the floodplain. The curls and swirls of meander lakes and marshes contrasted to the patterns of dense settlement. The higher the ground, the more buildings packed it—refuge against the periodic floods that overwhelmed the bottomland every couple of decades.

"What happened to those people in there," Right Hand interrupted her thoughts, "that wasn't just witchcraft, Keeper. That was something else."

"Your dirt farmers don't need to know that." She cocked her head to study the Deer Clan chief. "It almost reminded me of an attempt to recall a soul from the Underworld, the way the corpses were laid out in a circle. But what was done to the young woman in there? The slashing and hacking and mutilation? That's not part of any ritual I'm familiar with, but I'll ask around. Perhaps Rides-the-Lightning has heard of this."

"Don't forget the blood on the walls," Five Fists reminded.

Blue Heron nodded her agreement. "The first drawings, butterflies from cocoons, frogs from tadpoles, salamanders from mudpuppies, all speak of transformation."

"And all were ruined with spattered and smeared blood," Right Hand reminded.

"Almost as if a soul recall were being purposefully profaned." Her brow furrowed, cold fear running through her. "But what sort of insane *fool* would offend Power this way? This is like slapping the Morning Star across the mouth, throwing feces into the very face of the sun, and pissing on the Powers of the Underworld, all in one!"

Right Hand nodded, lips thinning above the scar that ran down his knobby chin. "It would unleash the winds. No one would be safe."

She gave him a wistful smile. "How right you are, old friend. But hopefully whoever did this is already dead, struck down by Power for blasphemy and pollution. If we're lucky, it will be considered an isolated act of witchcraft and buried under a mound. Your people up here will be owl-eyed for the next moon or so. Let me know if you need anything. I can have a Four Winds squadron up here within a couple of hands' time to help you keep order."

"Thank you, Clan Keeper." Corn Seed touched her forehead again, her expression pinched, as if she were biting her tongue.

Blue Heron took a step toward her litter before turning back and producing the bit of flaked stone that had been wedged in the dead woman's crotch. "Out of curiosity, have either of you seen stone like this? Perhaps a large chert knife?"

Corn Seed took it, holding it up to the light, and squinting. "Looks like a bit of . . ." She hesitated, face oddly pale. "Where did you find this, Keeper?"

"Whoever did that"—she jerked her head toward the farmhouse—"broke it off his knife while in the process of coring her sheath out of her hips."

Corn Seed seemed to tremble, swallowed hard, and offered it back. "I don't know the stone," she said softly, eyes distant.

"I didn't mean to startle you," Blue Heron told her gently as she plucked the knife fragment from Corn Seed's unresisting fingers. "And, unlike these dirt farmers, at least you've got the protection of your clan."

Corn Seed nodded, cast an almost desperate glance at her brother, and turned away.

"Enough of terror and death," Blue Heron muttered as she waved to Five Fists. "Take me home."

Her words might have been brave, but when she was safely on her litter, she looked back. The farmstead seemed so ordinary, one of thousands. Nothing on the outside hinted at the terror within its now-polluted walls and the screaming souls they contained. To one side, Right Hand and Corn Seed stood, their retainers huddling just out of earshot. She could see Right Hand waving his maimed hand, apparently in anger or frustration. Corn Seed had her head down, no doubt still shaken by the horror she'd seen in the farmhouse.

If you only knew the extent of terror being loosed on us, Matron, you'd never sleep restfully again.

Twenty-six

The heavy chunkey stone slapped into Fire Cat's hand as he deftly caught it. Then, with a swing of his arm, and a roll of the shoulders, he tossed it high again. The beautiful black stone shot up, just shy of the high ceiling rafters, and plummeted. It dropped into his hand with a solid slap.

Whoever had crafted the stone had been a master. The diameter fit perfectly into the palm of Fire Cat's hand. Both sides had been ground equally concave and polished until he could see his distorted reflection inside. That the piece had been used often was apparent by the dull scuffing on the rim.

When Field Green had seen him pick up the stone, she'd almost cried in horror. For whatever reason, he'd responded with a hard squint that in his old life would have promised mayhem and murder.

By the Piasa's balls, anything was better than this endless waiting. Field Green had immediately charged off toward Night Shadow Star's private rooms in the rear, ducked through the heavy hanging, and frozen. Then she'd slowly backed out, ashen-faced, and swallowing hard. She'd given Fire Cat the kind of look that should have shriveled his souls. For whatever reason, the woman had gathered the household staff, ordering them to clean everything, restack the pottery, dust the statuary, carry in firewood and water, carry out the ashes sifted from the burning coals, and straighten the bedding.

Through it all, Fire Cat played with the stone, tossing it high, and catching it. He was beginning to feel the burn in his muscles, the skin on his palm red and sore.

But the control was still there.

Wonder if I'll ever play again? He'd been good, one of the best in Red Wing town. As if he'd had any choice, being his uncle's heir and the only son of the Red Wing Matron. He'd barely been able to walk when Uncle first put a little clay chunkey stone in his tiny hand.

Around him the room suddenly went quiet, the slaves and servants freezing where they worked. All eyes had gone toward the rear of the room.

The falling stone smacked into his hand.

Night Shadow Star stood in the rear doorway that led back to her private bed and the shrine. She held the door hanging with one hand, the other propped on the door frame. Her hair was down, falling over her shoulders in a tangled wave that seemed to accent her enlarged eyes and almost slack face. She stood watching him—a hardness reflected in her clamped jaw and the way her full lips pinched, as if in pain.

Has there ever been a more beautiful woman? he wondered as he took in her full body, long legs, and wide shoulders. And how could such a gorgeous woman be wrapped around such a tortured soul? He could see it in her eyes, in the way she stood: *dancing with the Datura again.*

The servants were staring anxiously between Fire Cat and Night Shadow Star, expressions horrified. She just pinned him with those hollow and shining eyes, head tilting slightly as if hearing some distant voice in the room's complete silence.

"Leave us," she ordered, voice barely more than a rasp.

Forest finches didn't scatter any quicker when a sharp-shinned hawk flew over.

Fire Cat took a deep breath and held the stone up propped on his thumb and forefinger. "Whoever made this knew his business."

No expression crossed her face, her almost vacant gaze sucking at him. Then she stepped forward, each step balanced and languid as she strode up to him.

Stopping no more than a pace away, a tear broke free and coursed down her left cheek as she reached out and gently lifted the stone from his hand. Then she slapped him hard across the cheeks.

Fire Cat turned his face with the blow, lessening the impact. Shaking it off, he gave her a wry smile. "I apologize for upsetting you." He gestured at the stone. "A piece like that should be held, used, not left on a shelf like statuary."

"I should kill you for even laying a finger on this." She cradled the stone between her breasts.

He inclined his head slightly. "I won't touch it again. Hard as that will be for me. It has an allure, perfect balance."

Her slim fingers slipped across the polished stone in a caress worthy of a lover. He started to step away when, voice catching, she asked, "How did he die?"

"In war, Lady."

"How did you defeat him?"

"Are you sure you want to hear this?"

Her head tilted to expose the soft angle of her cheek. "He says I must."

"Who says? Morning Star?"

"Piasa," she whispered, her eyes growling larger, lips parting, as if the beast had just stepped into the room.

Fire Cat glanced uncertainly around and swore a cold draft had just blown through.

She'd fixed her dark gaze on his, waiting, fingers lightly stroking the stone.

He took a breath, oddly hesitant to inflict yet another hurt upon her. "We'd been warned that they were coming. Word came up the river when they passed River-Washed-Mountain. Our scouts were in place when the Morning Star's squadrons landed two-day's march downriver. My orders were that no one was to alert them, that they believe they'd caught us by surprise."

She nodded, as if seeing it in her head.

"It was last fall, just before harvest. They were coming up the main trail from the south where the forest gives way to the corn, bean, and squash fields south of town. The corn was head-high on either side, and the trail drops off a low terrace that gives a good view of Red Wing town maybe ten bow-shots in the distance.

"I let the Morning Star's commanders see just what they wanted to in the distance: Red Wing town's squadrons pulled up in formation around the town walls. It was the logical way to fight a defensive action. Right there on the flat before the walls so that if Red Wing were to be outfought, we could retreat behind the fortifications and carry on the defense."

She'd shifted her attention from the chunkey stone to him, listening intently.

Fire Cat spread his hands sympathetically. "Emerging from the trail that way, they were clustered in a thick column and streaming along between the cornfields. They were perfectly massed, trotting six deep, shields to the fore. They didn't even have their bows strung. At sight of the squadrons before the town, they began singing, clacking their bow staves against their shields.

"That's when I ordered the pot drum to beat the attack. At that first boom my squadrons rose from the corn and a first volley was on the way. We caught them from both sides, pouring arrows into them like a dense hail. And through it all, the squadrons advancing from the rear just kept coming, spilling out into the confusion, screams, dying men, and raining arrows."

"And my husband?" she asked softly, another tear trickling down her cheek.

"Three times he almost managed to get them organized, though to do so he literally had to clamber over the bodies of the dead and dying." He narrowed an eye. "I couldn't let him do that. You do understand. He was much too talented."

She gave him a slight nod, and he continued, "I signaled the drum again, and we charged forward to overwhelm them. He was calling orders to his seconds, and they to their thirds. He was desperately trying to establish a shield line to allow his men to reform. I waited until he raised his arm. When he did I had a clear shot and drove an arrow under his armpit where it wasn't protected."

Her expression began to crumble, her swallow loud.

"The squadrons he'd seen before the town? They were a ruse, far enough away that he couldn't tell they were composed of women and children, old men, anyone capable of holding a piece of matting that would look like a shield, or a stick or hammer that might be mistaken for bows or war clubs over the distance."

"Did he die well?"

"Yes, Lady," he lied, wondering why he'd spare her. "He died well."

For long moments she stared down at the chunkey stone. Then, stroking it reverently, she turned away, walking toward her private quarters. She hesitated, back toward him, and said, "I need you to go to the Morning Star. Tell him that I must see him tonight, after dark. You can do that?"

"I can, Lady. Assuming they'll let me past the gate."

"They'll pass you, Red Wing. They know you are mine."

"What a charming fate," he muttered under his breath.

She must have heard because her sibilant whisper carried, ghostlike on the still air: "Piasa tells me that Power condemned both of us to this before we were even born."

Twenty-seven

In her room, Night Shadow Star dropped the hanging back in place and collapsed onto her bed with its soft hides. In the eye of her souls, she struggled to replay her husband's last moments, imagining him as he marched out at the head of his squadrons. His eyes would have been bright with anticipation as he emerged from the oak-and-maple forest to find cornfields spread before him. In the distance, the waiting Red Wing squadrons would have been crowded before the town walls, right where he'd hoped they'd be.

Women, children, and old men?

She could see his smile, wide and assured, as he ordered his ranks of warriors forward and down the path between the cornfields.

War Chief Makes Three's image filled her souls with a remarkable clarity as he led them forward, his wooden battle armor jerking with every pace. In her imagination he headed down the slope from the terrace, heedless of the head-high rows of corn to either side. That familiar grim smile curled his lips. The glint of conquest had been alight in his eyes, for he'd always enjoyed a challenge. His men would have shouted their encouragement.

And then the boom of the drum.

"No, Husband. Please. Step back. Order them to retreat."

But he wouldn't.

He hadn't.

In pain, she clutched the smooth chunkey stone to her breast, aware of its odd warmth against her skin. A knot of grief hardened under her tongue; her heart went hollow. A sob caught in her throat, and then another. Unstemmed the flood of hot tears burst from her eyes. Throwing herself on the bed, she cradled the chunkey stone and wept.

A deep-seated worry crawled around in Blue Heron's gut like some sort of multilegged insect. She fingered the scabbed wound on her throat where Rides-the-Lightning had removed his stitches less than a hand of time before she'd been summoned to the Morning Star's high palace. This time, she'd happily abandoned her litter at the foot of the ramp. Better to wheeze her way to the top than ride up the long stairs in the abject terror that one of her porters would slip in the darkness.

The ornate palace great room was illuminated by a leaping fire, its sparks flickering out long before the rising smoke vanished into the soaring heights of the towering ceiling.

Five people sat in a semicircle before the fire: herself and Five Fists, Night Shadow Star and her new Red Wing slave, and finally Seven Skull Shield who'd returned from his peregrinations.

Across from them and behind the fire, Sun Wing reclined on her litter where it had been placed to the right and slightly forward of the Morning Star's raised dais. Morning Star had seated himself on a black panther hide, and now leaned forward, elbow propped on one knee, chin resting in his palm as he listened.

His eyes took them in one by one as firelight shone in the copper headdress attached to his tightly coifed hair. A wolf-hide cape was thrown back over his shoulders; a white apron clung to his narrow hips. Like always, his face was immaculately painted, the forked-eye design prominent on a light blue background. The two familiar white-shell face maskettes covered his ears.

"I've ordered the farmstead and bodies burned," Blue Heron continued with her report. "Corn Seed and Chief Right Hand are ensuring that the dirt farmers are following through. You can see the fire from the bastions outside when you look off to the east and slightly north on the bluff."

Sun Wing fiddled with the thick shell necklaces hanging at her throat; she'd been riveted as Blue Heron gave her report. Her gleaming eyes had taken on a hawkish intensity as Blue Heron described the wounds and disfigurement of the dead.

"Some sort of ritual?" Morning Star asked in an absent voice, his eyes fixed on the distance. The shell maskettes covering his ears had taken on an orange hue in the firelight.

The Red Wing slave, Fire Cat, kept his head bowed, but Blue Heron noted the man's absolute hatred, radiating like a white-hot stone from behind those narrow-lidded eyes.

"It looked like someone tried to recall a soul from the realm of the dead," Blue Heron finished. She glanced to the side, aware that Night Shadow Star had paled, a tension in the set of her mouth. For some odd reason her niece had brought her dead husband's chunkey stone with her. The black stone disk was clutched tightly, Night Shadow Star's long fingers wrapped around the curve.

She had applied no makeup or face paint, and wore a simple muskrathide cape that hung down past the unadorned fabric skirt she wore. With her thick hair worn loose, she appeared more feminine and attractive than usual.

"Does that mean anything to you, Niece?" Blue Heron asked.

Night Shadow Star's mobile lips curled, her eyes wistful. "Only if it had worked to recall someone from the dead," she replied.

"Apparently it didn't," Blue Heron growled, irritated by the desperation Night Shadow Star hid so poorly. "The way the woman lying on the floor had been brutally butchered had nothing to do with any recall ceremony I'm familiar with. The family on the bed were obviously offerings. That poor young woman's life-soul was driven out of that tormented body by rage."

"What purpose was served?" Morning Star wondered.

"A message." Night Shadow Star fixed the living god with her dark gaze. "The Powers of the Underworld are disturbed. Not only by the attempt to summon a dead soul for uncertain purposes, but by the strength of the frustration and rage that ensued."

Blue Heron added, "Not to mention that somewhere in the city, that dead woman's life-soul is loose in the night. Enraged as it is, it will find a home in some newborn, or chase the loose souls away from someone who's sick and possess his body."

Sun Wing made a warding against the evil, her face echoing a sudden fear.

"Nor is the ritual pollution conjured up on the bluff just an isolated incident of witchcraft." Blue Heron reached into her pouch and pulled out the bit of brown chert, holding it high. Her eyes fixed on the Morning Star. "He was jamming his knife into her sheath with such violence that this bit wedged between the bones. It snapped off." She paused.

"It's the same kind of stone as the knife that almost took your life, Lord. And mine." She saw his eyes narrow as she added, "I would imagine that if we had the knife that slashed the *tonka'tzi*'s throat, we'd find it, too, was the same translucent brown chert. Perhaps the very blade from which this snapped." She wiggled the fragment suggestively.

Sun Wing half rose, staring at the bit of chipped stone with rabid intensity. "He was *cutting out* her sheath?"

"More like shredding it."

"And you made a determination of witchcraft," Morning Star mused, his eyes distant again.

She was acutely aware of Fire Cat's balled fists, the clamped muscles knotting in his jaws. The man's hatred for Morning Star radiated like smoldering coals. *Why did Night Shadow Star bring him here?*

Blue Heron shrugged it off. "What else could I do? Too many people had seen the victims. Matron Corn Seed and Chief Right Hand have to keep order up there. I made a point of saying the witch had flown away into the sky. The last thing we need is for the ignorant dirt farmers to start murdering each other if an owl hoots outside their house some night. You know how a witch scare works. People turn on their neighbors first."

"What of the Deer Clan?" Night Shadow Star narrowed her eyes. "Could Right Hand and Corn Seed be involved in this in any way?"

"I doubt it." Blue Heron shook her head. "Why would they have sent a runner to me? Why not just torch the place before it could implicate them?"

Sun Wing declared, "Deer Clan is one of our strongest allies among the Earth Clans. I've heard the stories. Chief Right Hand once boasted he was going to marry Night Shadow Star when she came of age. I heard he used to tease her, bounce her on his knee when she was little."

"You only heard *half* the story. His arrogance also cost him his hand." Blue Heron cast a sidelong glance at the Morning Star. Not so long ago that body had belonged to the jealous Chunkey Boy. Losing his souls to the god hadn't been a complete tragedy for the Four Winds Clan.

She glanced again at Fire Cat, trying to assess his place in all this, and why Night Shadow Star had cut him down from the square instead of simply slicing him up.

"They still bear watching," Night Shadow Star insisted as she monitored Morning Star's response. Whatever she was looking for, he remained oblivious.

"You should have seen the horror in Matron Corn Seed's eyes when she saw this bit of the knife." Blue Heron studied the finely flaked fragment, aware that even now the edge remained sharp enough to cut. "It might have been a rattlesnake poised to strike."

"Do she and Right Hand know of the other knives?" Night Shadow Star asked.

Blue Heron arched an eyebrow. "With the exception of the assassin himself, or assassins as the case may be, only the people in this room and Matron Wind know. If we hear anyone else mention the blades . . . Well, it will prove to be a most interesting interrogation when we find out *how* they know."

Morning Star now watched Sun Wing from the corner of his eye, as though intrigued that she stared so raptly at the bit of broken knife.

On impulse, Blue Heron tossed it to her, saying, "You find the magnificent stone knife that is missing that piece, and whoever is carrying it will turn out to be our assassin."

Sun Wing caught it with a snapping twist of her hand, and lifted it, a rapt look on her face as she inspected the keen edge.

Blue Heron added, "Cut String's uncle, Pond Water, has been hung in a square. He's crying, pleading, insisting that it's all his fault. He says some stone Trader gave him the knife, told him that if he couldn't talk Cut String into the assassination attempt, he'd disclose Pond Water's incest. My belief is that he's telling the truth. Someone, very cleverly, used him as a tool."

"What of the thief?" Night Shadow Star asked as she tried to hide the distaste at her sister's fascination with the knife. "What does he add to our understanding?"

Blue Heron saw Seven Skull Shield cast an uneasy glance at the Morning Star; then the man touched his forehead respectfully. Even in the presence of the living god, he gave Night Shadow Star a lascivious grin. "I've been seeing to things, Lady. Whoever is behind carving, or trying to carve, Four Winds Clan throats, he's a canny one."

"And you know this how, thief?" Sun Wing couldn't keep the disgust from her voice.

Seven Skull Shield was good. The only hint he gave of his irritation was the slightest tightening at the corners of his eyes. "I know it, Great Lady, because no one else knows it."

"Why is this idiot here, Night Shadow Star? You're the one who had the Clan Keeper find him. To what purpose?"

Seven Skull Shield, to his credit, spread his hands wide and inclined his head respectfully as he continued in a reasonable voice. "Great Lady"—he kept the sarcasm to a faint inflection—"there are people in Cahokia who make it their business to know everything that's going on. Who is dealing with whom. Which embassies are arriving, and what Trade they bring. They know who has committed crimes, and what it is worth to either find, or hide, those people. Sometimes just knowing is worth a great—"

"Who?" Sun Wing demanded hotly. "Who *dares* infringe on the right and authority of the Four Winds Clan in this manner?"

"Half the city," Blue Heron blurted dryly. "Which you'd know if you *ever* got out *among* the people."

"No," Seven Skull Shield countered matter-of-factly, "she wouldn't, Clan Keeper. She's who she is, and she wears that identity like face paint. Even you, Clan Keeper, as talented as you are, and knowing what you do, have no idea of the true identities of those people."

"And you do?" Sun Wing bit off the words.

"Yes."

"You will tell me. Right this moment."

He glanced uneasily at the Morning Star, then at Blue Heron, and said, "I will not."

"Enough!" Morning Star broke his silence, gesturing Sun Wing back into her litter seat as she started to rise, her face burning, eyes enraged.

"But, my Lord—"

"The thief has his place." Morning Star waved her down, but his suddenly intense eyes were locked with Night Shadow Star's. They might have been waging some unspoken wrestling match.

To Seven Skull Shield, Sun Wing added, "I could have you hung in a square, torture the names out of you."

Seven Skull Shield kept his wary eyes on the Morning Star as he said, "You could do that. But I'd never live long enough to give you the names. As soon as word traveled that I was in a square, and that you wanted names, I'd be found dead within a couple of hands' time. They'd see to it. One way, or another."

"How?" Morning Star asked, turning his thoughtful eyes on Seven Skull Shield.

This time there was no insolence in his deep bow as he touched his forehead, and voice low, answered, "They control the homeless, the lost individuals, those with no hope. They hold sway over others as well. Even chiefs and matrons have gambling debts, owe favors, or are otherwise beholden to such persons. Their influence and authority comes not from birth, but from who and what they control."

"Why have I never heard of this?" Sun Wing demanded, stamping her foot.

"Because you live above it," Blue Heron replied, keeping a wary eye on the Morning Star. His gaze had gone vacant again, as if his souls were digesting this new information. To Seven Skull Shield, she added, "You were making a point?"

"Yes, Keeper." He, too, was keeping a wary eye on the Morning Star. Smart man, this Seven Skull Shield. He instinctively knew where the danger lay. "If one of the Houses, or one of the Earth Clans, was behind the plot, one of my sources would know. A slave or servant would have overheard something. In return for news this big, a trinket would have been exchanged for the information, and it would have passed along."

"They monitor the houses and Earth Clans that closely?" Night Shadow Star asked in surprise.

"Of course, Lady," Seven Skull Shield gave her a knowing grin. "Information, like a good whelk-shell cup, can be sold for as many sacks of corn as the market will bear. Think about it. By knowing the very night a marriage is brokered between Hawk Clan and Bear Clan, a clever man can move a supply of face paints, lotus-root bread, smoked cuts of deer haunch, dried fish, corn, and hickory oil to the aforementioned clan's plaza. The next morning when the matrons walk out to obtain those very things with brimming pots of Trade, who will maximize his profits?"

"And what does this have to do with assassins?" Sun Wing demanded coldly.

Fire Cat fought a sneer of disgust, turning his loathing glare from Morning Star to the younger woman.

Seven Skull Shield gave Sun Wing a slit-eyed stare of his own. "I just told you. If the clans or one of the houses were involved, someone would say something. Too much profit is at stake. One of my people would have heard something. To my surprise, they didn't even know the *tonka'tzi* had been murdered. That's how efficient the assassins are, and a measure of your own success."

Blue Heron added, "Much of which we owe to you, thief, for your quick response."

She could see that he was conscious of every change of the Morning Star's expression, keeping track at the corner of his vision as he made a dismissive gesture. "You don't think in the same terms I do, Clan Keeper."

"Thank the stars for that," Sun Wing muttered naively.

"Yes," Night Shadow Star's thoughtful expression turned on Seven Skull Shield, as if she saw him for the first time. "But if our sources know nothing of the assassins, and yours don't, someone must."

Blue Heron admitted, "I thought it might have been Evening Star House. Columella is the canniest of the House Matrons, and that cunning little dwarf of hers has a network almost as good as mine when it comes to information. While she was hiding something, she was clearly shocked at the extent of the plot."

Morning Star leaned his head back, watching curls of blue smoke rise from the leaping tongues of flame. "*Hunga Ahuito?* Do you throw your heads back, laughing from both of your mouths?"

Blue Heron almost winced, wondering why the Morning Star would implore the great Sky Eagle now, in the middle of the night. It hinted, oddly, of sacrilege.

"Lord," she asked cautiously, "do you have anything for us? Perhaps some intuition from the Sky World?"

He lowered his head, eyes narrowed in thought. Moments later he smiled, first at her, and then at Sun Wing. Then his gaze met Night Shadow Star's. For moments they stared at each other, the sensation like cold rain upon the souls. Finally he said, "Like the worlds themselves, layers of treachery are laid one upon the other."

Then Morning Star stood, at which time Blue Heron and the others bowed their heads. She reached out with a questing right arm, wound it into the clueless Seven Skull Shield's hair, and dragged his head down toward the mat. From the corner of her eye she saw that Fire Cat had barely bowed. Given his expression, he might have had something more sour than a green chokecherry in his gut.

They all waited until Morning Star walked silently back to his personal quarters.

"Sorry," the thief muttered as she let him up. "Didn't know which steps to take in the dance."

"So, what have we learned?" Night Shadow Star asked.

Blue Heron glanced at where Sun Wing sat thoughtfully, her eyes fixed on the doorway through which the Morning Star had left. Under her breath, Blue Heron whispered, "We're in deeper waters than we thought. Let's just hope your Piasa doesn't drag us all down into the depths."

Twenty-eight

Clouds had moved in to cover the night sky. Fire Cat followed Night Shadow Star's finger as she stopped on the steps just below the Morning Star's high palisade gate and pointed. "Look. Blue Heron's witches are burning."

He inspected the faint flickering light on the distant bluff. "Do you think Blue Heron's crazy notion that those people were sacrificed in an effort to recall a soul is correct?"

"It sounds like the ritual I saw when Morning Star was recalled to fill my brother's body. Although smaller, with fewer people sacrificed. But the savaging of the woman's genitals and face the way the Clan Keeper described it smacks of sacrilege. No wonder Piasa is stirring within me like a wounded snake."

"Maybe the assassin perverted the ritual?"

She shrugged, continuing down the steep and dark steps. Fire Cat curled his fingers, arms half lifted. All it would take would be the slightest shove. From this height, in the cloud-blackened darkness, with the wind sawing at them in irregular gusts, no one would expect treachery.

He smiled crookedly at her dark shape as turbulent air whipped strands of her hair back to slap at him. He made a face and let her get another step ahead, having no desire to share even that little contact with her.

"So you watched your brother become the god? What was that like, seeing him try to change himself into another person?"

"My brother's souls were devoured when Morning Star took possession of his body."

"Of course." He rolled his eyes as he felt his way down the squared wooden steps.

"Why do you find this so hard to believe?"

"Lady, do you mean to tell me that after they conducted that perverted ceremony, killed all those women and men, and buried their bodies in the mound, that after that divine moment, your brother never slipped? He never gave you that old familiar wink? He didn't move the same way? Use a secret phrase that only the two of you shared? Maybe give you that special smile a brother gives to his sister?"

"He became the god," she said flatly. "Just like our grandfather before him."

"Just like? No variations?"

She vented an irritated sigh as they reached the flat on the first terrace. "Red Wing, are you so jaded that you simply cannot find it inside yourself to accept a miracle? Is that why you and your kind were driven into exile? Because you had all the imagination of frozen winter stones?"

"Maybe we found the company of the overly gullible too oppressive to bear."

They passed the guard at the lower palisade gate and started down the stairs that led to the plaza. She asked, "Do you think all Power is a sham? Or just the Morning Star?"

"After what your people did to mine? I'm beginning to wonder myself."

She stopped short as they reached the foot of the stairs, her attendants coming forward with her litter. Field Green ordered it placed on the ground for her to mount. Four warriors took positions around the porters, wary eyes on the other parties waiting at the foot of the stairs.

Facing Fire Cat in the darkness, she slowly shook her head as she said, "I wish, for once, that I didn't know the truth. How lucky you are, Red Wing, not to have Piasa's shadow sharing your souls. I could almost wish I were you."

"You wouldn't like being me, Lady. You'd find yourself an angry knot of rage and fury. Your thoughts would be about your wives, the women you loved, now little more than bed-slaves to strange and uncaring men. You'd know that your children were murdered, and beloved relatives are dead and unmourned."

She huffed softly, saying, "Then we are much the same, you and I. We've each murdered the other's happiness."

With that, she stepped onto her litter and seated herself. A gust of wind whipped out of the night, carrying the mixed scents of water, smoke, and the sour taint of human waste. Her gesture was but charcoal in the darkness as she waved to her porters. "Take me home."

Maybe I do believe in Power, Lady. Only a divine presence could find humor in the fact that you and I are bound together in such a manner.

He chuckled softly as the wind batted him with bits of grass and debris. Then he took his place beside the litter as it was lifted and the party began feeling their way west along the dark avenue toward Night Shadow Star's high palace.

"The value of a man's word is only as good as the man who gives it." The saying had been Uncle's. He had most emphatically impressed it upon Fire Cat's souls from the time he'd been a boy. And it meant what, exactly, in this new and worrisome circumstance?

Thinking back to the Morning Star's palace, he wondered. How had he been able to kneel there, just back from the fire, while his absolute hatred pooled and boiled? All the while he'd watched the Morning Star where he sat on his raised dais, looking ever so thoughtful, eyes half-lidded, face so perfectly painted. The human-faced maskettes that covered his ears had given the man's head a grotesque shape.

Granted, Morning Star played the part of a god well. But Chunkey Boy would have had his entire life to study, watching every move his grandfather made, perhaps mimicking them to learn the art of posture, gesture, and affectation. Then, when the day came, all Chunkey Boy had needed to do was adopt the persona.

But do they all believe it?

That was the question. No doubt about it, even Blue Heron—tough old nut that she was—feared the Morning Star. Nor did she betray by so much as a flicker any indication that she was talking to anyone less than the god himself. Surely she and Night Shadow Star of all people would know the truth.

Unless they've all played the role for so long it's just their nature.

Was that it? The hoax had been in place for so long, the act so well practiced, they couldn't step back from the trickery?

And now I am bound to the very people who destroyed my life, my family, and world. He tried not to think of his wives, of the guilt and horror. Late at night when he awakened—and needed to torture himself—he freed his souls to imagine what they were enduring. In extreme cases the wives of captured chiefs were passed off to the warriors for their amusement.

In the darkness of the coming storm, he could almost hear the tortured souls of the dead from Red Wing town. They'd been clubbed, shot, or strangled in Spotted Wrist's vicious attempt to forever break the Spirit of Red Wing town. Now, like that ruined young woman up on the bluff, their souls roamed the empty forests around Red Wing town, wailing in their lonesome and aggrieved misery.

My fault. All my fault.

"There. There's the stairs," Field Green called from the front where she'd been leading the way. "Set the lady down. And be careful!"

Fire Cat watched the litter being carefully lowered as another gust of wind blasted out of the night. Night Shadow Star's steeply pitched mound and the dark palace above were but looming blots. Given the gusts, not even pine-knot torches would have stayed lit.

"Here's my hand, Lady," Field Green said, reaching down to help Night Shadow Star to her feet.

In the gloom, it would be so easy. The thought returned as if it clung to Fire Cat's souls like spider silk. *I could get halfway to the top, reach out, and grasp her by the head. Pulling and twisting, it would break her neck as her body weight fell. Then all I'd have to do is let loose, and she'll tumble right to the bottom.*

He'd be free. The woman he'd given his word to would be dead.

And what sort of man would you be then?

It would seem an accident, an unlucky misstep in the night.

The value of a man's word . . .

Fire Cat heard the hiss and hollow thump of impact—even the twang of the bowstring—so close in the night. From the battlefield he instinctively knew Field Green's choked grunt and startled jerk: an arrow hard in the chest.

Fire Cat hesitated—understanding, with complete clarity, that instant of opportunity. Then, with a curse, he grasped Night Shadow Star and yanked her backward off the litter. As he did, three more arrows whistled in; two slapped flesh and evoked whimpering cries among the porters and guardian warriors.

"Run!" he bellowed as he wheeled and tossed the stunned Night Shadow Star over his shoulder. *"Ambush!"*

Then, despite her savagely thrashing body, he pounded off into the darkness. Dodging and weaving, he kept hearing the vicious hiss of arrows as they cut the air too close to his panicked body.

Three paces. Jump left. Three paces. Jump right. Three paces . . .

"Put me *down!*" Night Shadow Star's panicked cry was accompanied by her fists beating his back. Her strength, and the firmness of her supple body surprised him. Keeping a grip on her muscular torso took all of his effort.

"Quiet!" he hissed. "Pus and blood, woman, they're trying to *kill* you!"

Maybe it was his tone. She ceased her kicking and clawing and let him run for the deeper safety of the darkness. Getting the balance right he dedicated himself to sheer speed. He was on the stickball field where the grass was beaten level. Perfect footing for running flat out.

Behind him, he heard a shrieking wail as someone, perhaps one of the guards, succumbed to the pain and terror of an arrow through the guts.

Running for all he was worth, he began curving to the right and slowed. Panting, he lowered Night Shadow Star to her feet. In the process he pressed his lips against her hair, whispering, "Quiet. They'll be hunting us."

Pulling her down with him, he dropped to one knee, keeping his right hand on her elbow.

"Who?" she whispered back, voice tinged with rage and fear.

"Shhh." He cocked his head, hearing screams and shouts from where they'd fled the litter.

"Lady Night Shadow Star?" a voice called in the night. "Are you all right?"

Fire Cat tightened his grip on her elbow as he softly repeated, "Quiet."

"Lady Night Shadow Star?" the voice called. "Please. Answer! This is your guard. We have wounded here."

"I know his voice. It's commander Talon." To her credit, she barely mouthed the words.

Keeping his lips next to her ear, he added, "Doesn't matter who's calling if we give ourselves away." A pause. "Trust me."

He felt her nod.

Easing to his feet, he took her hand in his and headed away into the night and wind. The chaos of shouts and cries at Night Shadow Star's stairway served as a beacon.

"When can we go back?"

"When it's safe." He barely breathed the answer, ears attentive, eyes searching the darkness. Behind them in the distant west, white flashes of lightning sent just enough flicker across the stickball field that he caught a glimpse of the World Tree pole.

Someone screamed in surprise and pain back at Night Shadow Star's. "There!" Talon's distant voice cried. "He's running!"

"After him!" someone else shouted.

"This is madness," Night Shadow Star whispered to herself.

Off to his right, Fire Cat heard the muffled pounding of bare feet, then a wary call in some tongue he couldn't understand.

Heart skipping, he pulled Night Shadow Star down.

Blessed ancestors, please! No lightning. All we have is the darkness. Then he thought: *They're armed, unafraid, continuing the attack even though Night Shadow Star's guard is alerted.*

He frowned as two voices hissed in the night, each tense and questioning. The language was nothing he'd ever heard. Dark shadows in the night, they were no more than twenty paces away. A distant flash of lightning illuminated them trotting back toward the west.

A torch was being carried down from Night Shadow Star's palace. Fire Cat could make out a ring of guards, bows drawn as they stared anxiously out at the night. In the torchlight, a knot of people were clustered around the litter.

"Come," Fire Cat whispered. Which way? Back? Or would the attackers be waiting, needing only to get a clear shot? Lightning flashed again, illuminating the cloud-thick western sky.

"Where are we going?"

"Anywhere they don't expect us to go." He turned east, tugging her along. Heading deeper into the safe darkness cloaking the great plaza.

The Lizard

*I*n many ways I have become a creature of darkness. Like the lizards I have seen in the south, I can change my colors to better mingle in any company or background. As I did that day when I followed Blue Heron up the stairs to the Morning Star's palace, I can act as noble as the rest of them. Or I can become a humble dirt farmer, as common and simple as I was the day that immigrant family invited me into their little farm for a meal of boiled corn and walnut bread. While I can walk in anonymity in the daylight, I nevertheless feel more at home in the darkness.

Most of that, I realize, is because of the shadows in which my souls are now forced to eternally dwell. They did that to me. Taught me to hate. Hatred, you see, is a blackness all its own. Deeper, darker, as impenetrable to illumination as wet charcoal. It coats the souls, leaves them gasping and desperate for the feeblest flicker. While the body basks in a relentless and blinding midday sun, my souls smother in a midnight longing for so much as the shine of a distant spark.

Another gust comes whimpering out of the darkness and pushes at my body as I loiter to one side and caress the arrow nocked in my bowstring.

I had watched and waited patiently as Blue Heron's people remained with her litter. So, too, did Sun Wing's. They barely recognized my presence. Many people lingered in the plaza before the great mound. To them I was but another messenger, an emissary, or perhaps just a curious pilgrim basking in the Power of the Morning Star's mighty palace.

And then she came, descending the stairs. I recognized her voice, tight with tension, and speaking slowly to the Red Wing she's taken into her household. I couldn't make out the words, but savored the bitterness with which they were expressed.

Perhaps because I love her with all of my heart, I'm not the least bothered that hers isn't a happy life.

Little more than a dark shadow, she led the way to her litter. With but a few more words, she was seated, lifted, and they started off to the west. Even as her porters were feeling their way, I was moving, keeping downwind. As I hurried ahead of them, I unrolled the reed-fiber matting and freed my bow and quiver. Ghosting along on silent feet, harried by the wind but buoyed by the anticipation of how I would send yet another shock through the Four Winds Clan, I found my wolves waiting. They were hunkered down in the inky shadows along the slope of Night Shadow Star's clay-sided mound.

I slapped White Hawk on the shoulder, and told him, "They're coming."

Memories of who she once was remain ever sharp in the eye of my souls. Her eyes back then were dark and daring, literally dancing with delight. I can still see her bright white teeth flash behind soft lips. Her hair, in swirls of blue-black, flows around her as she glances at me over a brown and impossibly smooth shoulder.

I tremble from the love that I feel. Such a terrible love. The kind that crushes a man like a cocoon of drying leather. It tightens, presses, and finally squeezes my beating heart and frantic lungs into a strangled silence.

The voices have spoken.

Tonight I must sacrifice the woman I love. It became so clear during my talk with High Dance. I have to kill my Night Shadow Star, abandon everything I desire, to purify the Power. Only when my grief is overwhelming will I be cleansed. I must endure the pain, so much pain, but perhaps when I stand over her bleeding corpse, I will once again be able to breathe, to feel the blood racing in my veins like it did so long ago.

And more, I pray the keen stone point tipping my arrow will pierce the swelling darkness and allow the faintest shaft of light to penetrate the eternal midnight of my souls.

Earlier, while appearing as a salt Trader, I'd taken time to study the mound and its angles, to gauge the distance to our killing zone. My wolves are located where they can shoot from either mound corner without danger of hitting each other.

While I'd hoped for better light, I waited until just the right moment when she'd be rising from her litter. Dark forms clustered around her. My first release was perfect; I heard the arrow hit solidly. At the sound, the rest of my wolves released. We should have killed them all.

At the cry, "Run! Ambush!" At least one figure broke for the plaza. I heard him run heavily, as if perhaps wounded? Then the screams intensified as the rest were shot down.

I hurried forward, just close enough to tell she wasn't among the shrieking victims!

So now I search the night, remembering the blurred form that fled into the dark plaza. Behind me, Night Shadow Star's foolish guards have brought torches to the foot of the stairs and are exclaiming their shock and disbelief to one another as they survey the carnage. Night Shadow Star is not among the dying.

Out here in the plaza my wolves and I scour the night, glancing about with each white flash of the approaching lightning.

I hear something. The soft scuffing of a foot? The rasp of cloth against cloth? I tighten my grip on the arrow, holding its notch to the bowstring with old familiarity.

Where are you, Night Shadow Star?

Let me dance in the light of your smile just one more time.

Twenty-nine

"I think we should go back now." Night Shadow Star shot a sidelong glance at Fire Cat as he tripped over a burden basket someone had left beside a farmstead ramada post.

She could sense the disquiet in Piasa's presence, as if the Spirit Beast's essence were unsure. From the corner of her eye, she kept catching glimpses of the Water Panther as he stalked through the storm-black night.

At the sound of Fire Cat's curse and her words, a dog began barking inside the house they were skirting. The owner would be irritated enough when he found their footprints in his newly planted garden the next morning.

Fire Cat growled to himself, gestured her forward, and hurried beyond the household. Lightning flashed to light their way as they stepped onto the broad east-west Avenue of the Sun that transected Cahokia. He was panting and wet to the knees, but so was she. After crossing the great plaza, their flight had become a terrifying comedy of indecision, backtracks, and stumbles—especially when they couldn't find their way out of the marshy land that lay just beyond the society houses and temples immediately to the east.

Someone in the house behind them shouted "Quiet!" followed by a thump and a canine yelp.

"Going back isn't smart." Fire Cat was but another shadow in the darkness.

"Why not?"

"Because we're still alive."

"And by now, Red Wing, half of Cahokia is out searching for us. My people need me."

He turned ploddingly down the avenue, still heading east. "Lady, here's my call: it's pitch-black back there. Oh, sure, there's lightning and a couple of torches flickering, but how good are they going to be in the wind and rain?"

"They'll have my palace surrounded."

"Your people? Or theirs?" He paused. "If Field Green had been a half step to the left, that first arrow would have taken you right through the upper chest. Either the archer was accursedly lucky, or he knew just where you'd be, darkness or no."

"I'm worried to death about her."

"Lady, guilt is a weapon they can, and will, use to kill you. Organizing an attack like this? At least three, probably four bowmen, firing from two sides of your mound? These people are deadly serious, and equally competent. If it were me, I'd have my shooters waiting around, just out of sight in the darkness. They know you're going to be back sooner or later."

"By now the alert has been sounded. My palace is probably surrounded by an entire squadron."

"A squadron in darkness," he reminded her simply. "A bunch of warriors called in from here and there. Mostly strangers. And a couple of assassin archers added to mix in with theirs. To be ready for your return. And as soon as one of the commanders lifts a torch to identify you . . . *thwip!*" He mimed an arrow being released.

"How do you know all this?"

"Because if I were trying to kill you, that's how I'd do it."

That left her with an empty feeling in her breast.

"Do you think these are the same people who tried to kill the Morning Star, slashed my father's throat, and tried to kill my aunt?"

"Probably. And, Lady, I wouldn't take any comfort in the fact that they're using different tactics. If so much as a patch of stars had been out, they'd have had enough light to have killed us all."

Lightning flashed, catching him in the act of rubbing his neck, a most worried gesture.

"If you hadn't grabbed me back there, I'd be dead now, wouldn't I?"

"Most likely."

Thunder rumbled across the city.

She plodded along, feeling the Piasa's presence where it stalked the darkness beside her. The terrible beast seemed to be smiling.

"Why?" she asked.

"Why what? Attack you? I assume the culprit is some poor and desperate fool like I'd be but for that accursed oath. Someone who's sworn to pay you and your kind back for ruining his life, destroying his clan, murdering his relatives."

"No," she told him coldly. "Why did you save me?"

"I've been asking myself that same question over and over."

"Any answers, Red Wing?"

"I can only conclude that you're alive because my uncle once took time to impress something on a very young boy."

"What was that?"

"I owe you my loyalty and obedience, Lady. Not the intricacies of my souls."

She smiled wryly. "If the attackers are fleeing to the east, you know they're going to come right down this road."

"Are we past that big marsh?"

"Pretty much." She waved around. "From here to the bluffs the country is dry. But pick any other direction and you're going to end up in marsh or an old oxbow lake if you go far enough. And as dark as it is, we'll get turned around among the houses."

Patters of rain streaked down from the sky.

"Looks like we'll get wet one way or another." He was looking around when lightning illuminated the rising bulk of a building atop a mound. "What's that?"

"Fish Clan charnel house. Matron Red Temple's lineage processes their dead here."

"Come on," he said, reaching for her hand. "It's someplace no assassins are going to check. The combination of being safe and dry outweighs the stench of decomposing corpses."

"And you won't fall into anyone's latrine in the darkness."

"Thank you for reminding me."

"I did let you walk into the marsh to get the stink off."

He couldn't see her carnivorous smile as she savored the memory. But his feet really had stunk. It wasn't her fault that they'd gotten turned around and floundered this way and that trying to find their way back to dry land. In the end a strong gust carrying the scent of other latrines and smoke had given them the direction.

As they climbed the stairway to the top of the Fish Clan mound, he hesitated. They were high enough to clear the roof lines of the buildings to the east. "What's that?" He pointed to a flickering yellow light on the bluff top.

"Blue Heron's witches," she replied wearily. "They'll be burning for another three days."

She paused as he passed the guardian posts, nodded respectfully, and opened the door. She followed him into the stygian interior. The cloying odor of rotting human beings thickened in the back of her nose. Down inside her gut, she felt the tendrils of Piasa's presence stir at the proximity of the dead. Fish Clan had Spiritual ties to the Underworld. Perhaps the Spirit Beast felt the body-souls, perhaps it even called to them. She grunted, placing a hand to her stomach.

"You all right?" Fire Cat asked.

"Piasa is stirring."

"Of course." He sounded bored. "Your brother's a god and you've got a Spirit panther in your belly."

"A fact for which you should be glad."

"Oh, really?"

"It was at Piasa's insistence that I had to forego the pleasure of holding a torch between your legs for as long as it took to cook your penis and testicles into charcoal. I wanted to hear you scream as I burned them from your body." A pause. "Instead he told me to cut you down."

"Charming."

The sound of heavy rain beating on the roof preceded the musical patter of runoff as it sluiced from the thatch. Thunder banged just overhead.

She heard him shuffling around before he said, "Here's a bench. We might as well sit. There's no sense for us to be stumbling about in here and bothering the dead more than we have to."

She felt the plank-top and seated herself, testing it. It seemed solid enough. Then she took a weary breath, a spear of grief lancing her heart. "Did you happen to see how badly Field Green was wounded?"

"No. But from the sound, it was a chest shot."

"You can tell?"

"Having heard enough arrows strike home? Yes. Anything going into the lungs makes a hollow thump. Muscle gives off a meaty slap, and striking bone makes a snapping sound."

"The reality is just sinking in, Red Wing."

"And that is?"

"Uncertainty is the worst part, isn't it?"

She could feel his gaze through the darkness. "They want you terri-fied, Lady."

"From here on I'll never know, will I? The only warning I'll get is the whistle of an arrow before it spears my heart. I'll be afraid to sleep knowing he could be creeping over my bed. I won't feel anything be-fore the sting of the knife. Then I'll be choking on my blood, blowing it out in a hot red spray from my severed windpipe."

"You must have some clue about who's doing this?"

She rubbed her face as hard rain hammered down onto the roof. Thunder banged and boomed, rolling away in the storm. The smell of the dead seemed more acute in the damp air.

"When you're Four Winds Clan and as influential as we are? The list of potential enemies is endless." She paused. "Why don't they want us to know? Why not give us at least a clue?"

"Because it adds to the terror. If he succeeds you'll die without even knowing who did this to you." He paused, then muttered to himself. "Oh, I see . . ."

"See what?"

He chuckled humorlessly. "Just putting it into perspective is all. I have no love for the Four Winds Clan myself. I'd love nothing better than to be in the position to destroy you all. Like I said at the *tonka'tzi*'s that night. There would be a big red wing on that wall so you knew I was taking my revenge. I'd want you feeling helpless in the face of Red Wing retribution. You know, so you'd have time to regret your de-struction of my clan."

"I should have driven my knife into your heart that night."

She felt, rather than saw his answering shrug.

"I wish you had. I'd have been free of my oath, and my souls would have gleefully watched Piasa suck yours down into whatever finality the Water Panther inflicts on those he owns. Because, Lady, but for me, they'd have killed you tonight. And the terror would have grown. That's what I was getting at. This isn't just vengeance. More than wanting you and your family dead, they want you terrified."

She shivered in the deadly darkness.

Thirty

Crouched against the wall on Blue Heron's veranda, Seven Skull Shield watched morning begin to brighten the stormy skies. The pink-gray light was finally bringing an end to what had been a sleepless night. Through it all, a constant string of messengers had been coming and going as communications were carried back and forth from the Morning Star, Matron Wind, and Sun Wing.

After the meeting Seven Skull Shield had been lost in thought. It wasn't just every day that a thief and rascal like Seven Skull Shield participated in a conversation with the Morning Star. Let alone addressed him in his palace!

In a sort of daze, he had followed Blue Heron down the long stairs from the Morning Star's palace. He'd paced beside her litter as they made their way west through the dark toward the Clan Keeper's palace. Only to stop short as screams and chaos had erupted at the foot of Night Shadow Star's palace stairs.

Thinking about it afterward, it had been dumb to just rush into the line of fire where, but moments before, Field Green, the guards, and porters had been shot full of arrows. The realization had slowly sunken in that he and Blue Heron had made excellent targets in the flickering light of wind-batted torches brought down from Night Shadow Star's palace. Fortunately, enough of the guardian warriors had charged off into the surroundings to rout the attackers. So complete had the confusion been that two of Night Shadow Star's guards had spent a couple tens of heartbeats shooting at each other. Only sheepishly did they discover the mistake as they cursed each other vehemently—and recognized each other's voices.

Seven Skull Shield actually admired the way Blue Heron had taken control, ordered the wounded and dying to be carried up to the palace, and set about alerting not only the Morning Star and his guard, but Matron Wind. Runners had been sent to warn the other Houses; Healers had been summoned to attend to the wounded and dying.

Another runner had been dispatched to the Four Winds Men's House, and an alarm had been raised that called out the local squadron by means of a thumping drum. By the time the warriors had been assembled and trotted to Night Shadow Star's the attackers were long gone.

All that, and in a pouring rain to boot! Seven Skull Shield arched an eyebrow in tribute to the Clan Keeper as dawn burned pink behind thin patches in the somber gray overcast. Twisted tufts of cloud continued to scud across the sky to the east.

But as impressive as Blue Heron's organization had been—and despite the crisscrossing messengers and squads of warriors who'd been splashing around in the lightning-riven night—several things remained problematic: Two porters, three guards, and Field Green were dead; two other porters were dying, and two were seriously wounded; no one had any idea of who the attackers were; and most terrifying, Night Shadow Star and the Red Wing were nowhere to be found—alive or dead.

Seven Skull Shield hunched and pulled his cape more tightly around his shoulders. He'd braced his back on the plaster wall, knees pulled up to support his elbows. When he sniffed the damp, smoke-filled air, the scent of wet earth, trodden grass, and the sullen taint of too much humanity filled his nostrils. The comings and goings of warriors had tracked a slick coating of mud up the stairs, past the guardian posts, and onto the matting as though some huge slug had left its glistening trail.

"Tell the Morning Star that we can only assume they have been taken," Blue Heron was saying to the latest messenger, one of Dead Bird's slaves. "It is light now, and we have enough warriors scouring every nook and cranny around the palaces, temples, and shrines, that someone would have found the bodies."

"Yes, Clan Keeper." The man dropped to one knee, first lowering his forehead to the ground, then following it up with a touch of fingers to the smudge the muddy mat left above his eyes. With that he was on his feet, pounding away.

Not for a hand's time had Blue Heron had so much as a moment to herself. Now she sighed, massaged her face with tired fingers, and turned her attention to one of the attacker's arrows they'd collected.

"No markings." Seven Skull Shield forestalled her remark. "I've looked them over to exhaustion. They are too perfect. The shafts are absolutely identical; the stone war points are as similar as twins and chipped out of bluff-milky chert. It's that stuff that comes from the gully quarries in the bluffs a hard day's run to the south. Even the turkey-feather fletching is cut just so. My guess, Keeper, is that they're from one of the arrow maker's workshops in River Mound City."

She arched her eyebrows, sighed, and nodded. "Could you find the maker?"

"I can." He gave her a humorless grin. "But as good as the attackers have been up until now, I suspect they weren't clumsy enough to introduce themselves and ask, 'Will these arrows be right for shooting down the lady Night Shadow Star's people?'"

Blue Heron gave him a shadowy smile. "No, I suppose not. But wait a moment." She turned, calling back through the doorway, "Smooth Pebble? Is breakfast ready? If so have Notched Cane bring a plate to Seven Skull Shield."

"Coming, my lady."

Blue Heron rolled her neck as if it were cramped, her face drawn into a grimace. She added, "You might as well go on a full stomach. Save you stealing breakfast from some poor innocent soul who's struggling to get by."

Seven Skull Shield spread his hands defenselessly. "Keeper, I swear, I never steal from the innocent." He accented the gesture with a wolfish grin. "It's the arrogant, crafty, and rudely overbearing ones I can't pass by."

She actually laughed at that as yet another runner came pounding his way down the sloppy avenue from the Four Winds Clan House. The young man leaped his way up the stairs, bowed deeply before the guardian posts, and dropped to his knees just beyond the veranda.

"Come," Blue Heron called, nodding acknowledgment as the youth touched his forehead. "What news?"

"*Tonka'tzi* Matron Wind wishes to inform you that by the time the sun is two hands high we should have three squadrons called up for the search for Lady Night Shadow Star." He withdrew a folded section of hide from his breechcloth, handing it to Blue Heron. "Those are the respective areas Matron Wind has detailed each squadron to search."

Smooth Pebble stepped out the door, a fine brownware bowl steaming in her cloth-wrapped hands. She lifted a questioning eyebrow, unmistakable disapproval in her dark eyes, as she told Seven Skull Shield, "It's hot. Don't burn yourself."

Seven Skull Shield nodded, carefully easing the bowl from the *berdache*'s hands, smelling turkey, persimmons, and walnut, all thickened with ground lotus root.

"Thank you, Smooth Pebble." He jerked his head toward the Keeper. "She hasn't had so much as a morsel. And if you'll recall, she'd barely sat down to her supper when the summons from the Morning Star came last night. Even as good as this smells, she's not going to take the time to eat a stew. But if you poked a hole into one of those fingers of bread from last night and stuffed it with mashed up turkey, it would be just practical enough that she could take bites and chew as they talked."

Smooth Pebble's brow arched higher, as if he'd taken too free a liberty. Then the growing irritation eased as she shot a measuring look at where Blue Heron bent over the deerhide map with the runner. "Actually, thief, that's a pretty sharp observation. I've spent half my life trying to get her to eat."

"And you could pour some of the stew into her tea cup. The one with the handle. It's got to be cool enough that she can chug it. If it were me, I'd walk up during a break, hand it to her, and say, 'Drink that so I can clean the cup.' As soon as she takes it, cross your arms and glare at her in that 'I'm in a hurry' fashion of yours."

"Why would I risk angering her that way?"

"Because she'll drink it down. All these years and you haven't noticed?"

The *berdache* now was studying him thoughtfully, lips slightly pursed. "You think that would work? First Woman knows I've tried to my wits' end to keep her fed when she's in a hurry." She poked a hard finger at him. "But if she lashes out at me for doing it, I'll make you wish you were hanging in a square!"

"She won't. Just don't be too obvious about it." He lifted the bowl, blowing to cool it. Carefully he slurped at the hot liquid. Too hot. Having nothing else to do, he added, "She'd take a chunk out of you if she thought you were doing it for her. But just the hint that she's keeping you from attending to your duties? She simply can't abide the notion that she's inconveniencing you."

Smooth Pebble's frown etched her forehead as she watched the Keeper. "How do you know so much about her, thief? You've only been here a couple of days."

"People are my business, *berdache*. If I don't judge them right the first time, my life gets short and very uncomfortable." He gestured. "She's got a right to worry this morning. Whoever this assassin is, he's cussed clever."

The *berdache* nodded, crossing her arms. "I've never seen her this way. She's scared, thief. Right down to the root of her souls."

"If my neck had come that close to being cut, I'd be shivering, and like *Hunga Ahuito,* trying to grow eyes in all four sides of my head."

"And never closing them, even for a moment's sleep."

He sipped at the soup. "She and Night Shadow Star seem close."

"The daughter she never had. She told me about what happened to those dirt farmers up on the bluff. She hasn't said it, but she's terrified the assassins have taken Night Shadow Star. That they'll try the same ritual, but this time with a Four Winds Clan woman."

He rocked his jaw as he considered it. "Maybe. Me, I'm missing something here. These attacks, they're not just political."

"Meaning?"

"Assassination might be a fundamental part of the plan, but whoever's behind this has thought it through . . . obsessed on the details for years. Using Pond Water to control Cut String. The brown-chert knives, the manner of the *tonka'tzi*'s execution and the attempt on the Keeper, the ritual sacrifices up on the bluff, all this is a carefully planned performance. No local chief or House leader that I know of is behind it, either. This is someone . . . some*thing* different."

"Different how?"

"Dark and malicious. And not just witchery. If I had to use a term, I'd call it brilliant evil."

"You're scaring me, thief."

He nodded absently as he lifted the bowl and blew. "We'd all be a heap better off staying scared, too."

Another runner came pelting across the wet grass of the plaza, his bare feet slapping. In flying leaps he took the stairs, barely hesitated at the guardian posts, and slipped and slid to a precarious stop. He slapped at his forehead to gesture his respect as he shouted, "She's alive! Lady Night Shadow Star and the Red Wing are on the way! They got away from the assassins in the dark. I'm to tell everyone!"

He turned on his heels and slipped in his haste, barely catching himself, before he streaked like a panicked fox down the stairs.

"But . . . *Wait!* Rot take you, come back here!" Blue Heron demanded angrily as the youth raced away. For a couple of tens of heartbeats she fumed, then sagged. "She's alive!"

Smooth Pebble exhaled in weary relief. "I'd better be about getting some food into her."

"And I'd better be about finding the source of these arrows."

"Will it really help?" Smooth Pebble asked.

"Probably not." He shrugged. "But you never know what might turn up."

"Let's hope it's not what you said," she muttered darkly, expression wary. "Brilliant evil? You watch yourself, thief."

"You, too, *berdache*. You're too good a sort to go the way of Field Green." He said it with levity, but nothing cut the fear in her eyes.

Thirty-one

"We had no warning. I was just rising from my litter when the arrows shot out of the darkness." Night Shadow Star looked bedraggled and filthy, her hair stringy, the muskrat cape having lost some of its fluff. Her toned legs were mud-caked from the calves down to her feet. Somewhere she'd lost her sandals. The brown dress looked like something a dirt farmer would wear in from the field. But worst of all, the set of her eyes expressed a deep-seated fright.

Blue Heron turned her attention to the Red Wing. He looked equally unkempt, his hair matted, mud splotched everywhere. The normally disagreeable set of his jaw had softened. So, too, had his continual expression of loathing. Now his tattooed face with its lines and patterns had grown introspective. Like Night Shadow Star, he, too, reeked of a charnel house's cloying odor.

"No shouts of warning?" Blue Heron asked. "No reason for the attack?"

"It would have been easier to bear if someone had cried out, 'Die, you foul camp bitch.' Instead they attacked in complete silence." Night Shadow Star paused. "But for the gusting wind and hissing arrows."

"We heard from your guard and the surviving porters that someone yelled, 'Run' and 'Ambush.'"

"I did," Fire Cat told them. "That's when I grabbed the lady and jerked her backward off the litter." His gaze went half-lidded as he added, "She wasn't particularly pleased with the gentle and dignified manner of my assistance. Especially when I threw her kicking and screaming over my shoulder and ran for it."

"At least I didn't charge headlong into an open latrine, Red Wing," Night Shadow Star shot back.

He gave her a diffident look. "You might at least warn the people living next to that marsh not to drink the water."

Blue Heron heard the tension behind the words. The reason why Night Shadow Star had saved the Red Wing still eluded her, but her current concerns lay elsewhere. "How many of them were there?"

Night Shadow Star shrugged, but the Red Wing met her gaze, his own confident as he said, "My guess, after thinking about it, is that there had to be at least four, maybe six, total. They were lying in wait on either side of the mound base when we got there. Given the way the palace ramp and staircase extend, they had us in a cross fire, as if we were the center of the X. Pinpoint accuracy wasn't necessary, just shoot at the screaming shadows with as many arrows as possible."

"It worked. Field Green, three guards, and most of the porters are dead."

"I would have been, too." Night Shadow Star frowned into a distance only she could see. "I heard the arrow hit Field Green in the chest."

"In the dark like that," Fire Cat told her, "someone had to take the first hit. It was simple chance."

"But you managed to keep my niece safe," Blue Heron interjected, a cold thought creeping between her souls. *Just as that culprit Seven Skull Shield saved my life. And both—if we can believe Night Shadow Star—were around to do so at the insistence of Piasa.*

For long moments she studied the younger woman, her memory dredging through her niece's tumultuous childhood, her unsettled and rebellious adolescence. No girl could grow up normally in the midst of the Four Winds Clan's fractious politics. Let alone in the Morning Star's presence. Her grandfather, and then her brother had sacrificed their lives, souls, and bodies to provide a temporary abode for the god's resurrected Spirit. The girl had had a special bond with both Chunkey Boy and Walking Smoke. Why shouldn't she? No other children in the world grew up in that rarified environment that had them literally playing at the feet of a miracle.

Night Shadow Star had been a target all of her life. The Four Winds Houses—and half of the Earth Clans—had plotted, wheedled, or cajoled to elevate their status by marrying one of their young men to her. Nor had Matron Wind; *Tonka'tzi* Red Warrior; his wife, White Pot; or even the Morning Star hesitated to dangle her future as a potential prize in the political gamesmanship that was Cahokian politics.

They'd forced her into the company of her troublesome brothers— the only "safe" males she'd been allowed to associate with. And in the process, the boys had turned her into something of a feral young woman with their archery, stickball, chunkey, and club-fights.

At least until the Morning Star had been reincarnated in Chunkey Boy's body. And then something had happened. Something more than just the sacrifice of Chunkey Boy's souls. That, after all, had been inevitable; Chunkey Boy had willingly stepped forward, his entire life having prepared him for the moment he would surrender his body to the god.

Whatever had happened in the aftermath, Night Shadow Star's relationship with her brothers had exploded the way a wet ball of clay blew up in a too-hot fire. Chunkey Boy, of course, was gone, his disregard for others and his dark moods consumed by the god. To Night Shadow Star it had to have been like a death; except her brother's familiar body remained alive, visible every day as the god wore it around like a suit of clothing.

The night after the ritual that resurrected Morning Star's body into Chunkey Boy had been completed, and the god had retired to his palace to rest, Night Shadow Star had presented herself at the Four Winds Clan's Women's House to undergo her transition from girl to womanhood. Through the four-day period, she'd been quiet, self-absorbed, as if possessed of a Spirit not her own.

Looking at her now, Blue Heron wondered what, if anything, had changed to cause that first menstruation. Her niece had been peculiar, withdrawn, and distracted, as if her souls entertained more than just themselves within that lithe and healthy young body.

It's a miracle any of us can still function as human beings.

"Niece," she said aloud, "why did you risk offending the Morning Star and take it upon yourself to cut down the Red Wing? You ordered me to find that miscreant, Seven Skull Shield. What specifically did Piasa tell you?"

Night Shadow Star's eyes seemed to enlarge, and she smiled slightly as she gave her aunt a careful inspection. "Piasa doesn't confide in me. I am only his tool."

"You're the *tonka'tzi*'s daughter! Perhaps even the future Matron of the Four Winds Clan."

"And Piasa is the undisputed lord of the Underworld."

Blue Heron glared into Night Shadow Star's eerie eyes, reading the insistence there. In a low voice she said, "I wonder how First Woman takes such statements? Discovering that Piasa is the 'undisputed lord' of her realm must be disconcerting."

Night Shadow Star tilted her head as she laughed. "Who do you think carries First Woman's orders about the Underworld and enforces her will? They are entwined. Part of the same creative and destructive Power. First Woman sits in her cave at the bottom of the world, dreaming her dreams. And through them flow Piasa, the Horned Serpent, the Tie Snakes, fish, and turtles. The life-souls of the dead bow and offer their respect as they seek the ancestors who have preceded them. And through it all, Power beats like a great heart, all subject to First Woman's will."

"You speak like a priest," Blue Heron muttered.

"Only because you ask questions for which there are no answers." Night Shadow Star cocked her head suggestively. "When I was Dancing in the Underworld, Piasa seized my souls, crushed them out of my body . . . and swallowed them."

"Like Bird Man is said to have done to the great priestess Lichen?"

Night Shadow Star shrugged. "Only Lichen herself could have answered that. I am Piasa's creature."

"If that's the case, he's not taking very good care of you. You'd think Piasa would have given you some warning before that attack last night."

"I felt a sudden chill. Nothing more." She raised a hand. "Aunt, you have to understand. We're at the center of a struggle for more than just our lives. This is a battle over Power and its uses. The resurrection of the Morning Star came as a shock to the foundations of our world. Cahokia, by the miracle of its existence, has changed everything. The tremors continue to shake the Underworld. Unease breathes its way through the Sky World, unsettling Thunder Beasts, upsetting Grandfather Sun's path through the sky, and Moon Woman's soft glow."

Blue Heron was peripherally aware of Fire Cat's expression, tightening like an overstretched mask. Her own skepticism had to have slipped past her control, because Night Shadow Star's eyes flashed anger. Her fiery gaze intensified as she thrust her face into Blue Heron's. For a moment, the Clan Keeper felt herself grow dizzy as she peered into the endless depths of those pool-like eyes. As if seeing into a shadowed eternity.

As Night Shadow Star spoke, the words echoed off Blue Heron's souls. "When the Four Winds Clan called the Morning Star's Spirit out of the Sky World, we upset the balance. Human beings should not have been capable of concentrating that kind of Power. We stunned the Spirit

Worlds, both above and below. Since the miracle, Cahokia has become like a great whirlpool, sucking people and Power from all corners of the earth. And it's spewing it right back out, spitting colonies in every direction. We've imposed a new order . . . and with it a new chaos."

A shiver worked down Blue Heron's spine as she realized Night Shadow Star's eyes were changing, yellowing around the edges, as if a mirage shimmered there. Voice cracking, heart pounding, she asked, "What's changed? It's been over sixty summers since Petaga and his clan leaders were sacrificed to reincarnate the god."

The voice that answered wasn't Night Shadow Star's but a deeper, almost hollow, echo. "What if someone didn't want to stop at just recalling the Morning Star?"

"I don't know what you mean?"

"Think, Clan Keeper." The hollow voice seemed to vibrate her very bones. "Four Winds Clan created the ritual, manipulated the Power, and recalled the Morning Star. In the aftermath, you rebuilt Cahokia, drew people from every direction. They came, carrying their own Power bundles and sacred objects. Never before has so much Power been concentrated in one place. Cahokia literally breathes, the air throbs, the earth and water swell and pulse."

For an instant Blue Heron would have sworn she was staring into a great panther's predatory eyes.

The beast lifted its lips in a snarl as it said, "But what if you'd captured the very lightning, and its Power was in your fingers? What could you touch without bursting it asunder? What would you caress without scorching its surface to blackness?"

"We're not talking about lightning," Blue Heron rasped.

"No. We're talking about breaching the boundaries between the three worlds. Flood, pestilence, fire, and war, as the Spirit Beings clash and destroy each other. Death . . . so much . . ." Night Shadow Star's odd eyes rolled back in her head, her body weaving.

Fire Cat leaped forward, catching Night Shadow Star's body as she fainted dead away.

Thirty-two

Tapping one of the arrows on his left palm, Seven Skull Shield made his way down the busy path—more of a transportation artery actually—that wound through the dense cluster of houses, temples, workshops, storehouses, and ramadas that made up the thriving strip of River City Mounds where it dominated the river's eastern bank.

The long walk from the Clan Keeper's had been sobering, and he'd looked at Cahokia with new eyes. He'd always viewed the problem from the other side: How do you stay hidden in Cahokia?

Now, the converse surprised him: How do you find someone who is hiding in Cahokia?

Having left just after his breakfast, and before the dawn had fully broken, he'd been walking through solid city where the mound-studded avenue skirted the southern bank of Marsh Elder Lake. It had taken five hands of time just to reach the main congestion of River Mounds City where the four or five arrow makers maintained their workshops. In the process, he'd been in the constant company of people. An endless stream of on-comers had been headed toward the Great Plaza, most with packs of food, blankets, colorful textiles, bundles of firewood, pack frames heavy with pottery, teams of men carrying bundles of peeled poles. He'd encountered people literally obscured with bales of thatch, occasional nobles atop their shouldered litters, men with haunches of venison or braces of turkeys, young men with loads of dried fish, or whatever the mind could conjure. Sometimes he had to duck to the side as teams of sweating, panting men, stumbled along under the weight of immense logs bound from some major construction. Other times it was to allow for the passage of loads of stone borne inland on litters by muscular two-man teams.

Once again the incredible and ravenous immensity of Cahokia, and the amount of food, material, and fuel it demanded left him amazed. The fact that the city could actually function, that it could meet the needs of tens of thousands, reeked of an impossible miracle.

He just made it to the first workshop when a conch horn sounded, and people scampered out of the way as a squadron of warriors appeared. Duck Clan designs decorated their aprons and shields. They came trotting down the center of the thoroughfare, equipment clattering, feet beating out a rhythmic cadence in the damp sandy swale that served for a road. Their Squadron First was a scarred and burly man, whose entire hide had fallen victim to the copper tattoo needles in his clan's men's house.

In the wake of their passage Seven Skull Shield watched men, women, children, and the occasional dog emerge from gaps between buildings, doorways, and wherever they could step aside. Then he slipped into the arrow maker's.

The workshop was little more than a peaked, thatch roof held up by eight heavy support posts. Mat walls draped a third of the way down from the roof and were tied off on the upright posts. Around the walls, large bundles of green shafts rested on wooden racks to season. Ignorant as he was of the craft, Seven Skull Shield could identify at least six different woods as well as lengths of cane. Another bench was covered with differently sized sandstone abraders and shaft straighteners. Boxes of different assorted bone, antler, stone, and wooden points rested below the work benches. Loosely woven burlap sacks of feathers hung along the far wall ready for cutting and fletching. Coils of buffalo, deer, and elk sinew as well as spools of thin cordage filled additional pots.

While none of the eleven men working at the benches so much as raised their heads, the old man in the back rose to his feet, calling, "Welcome. May the blessings of the Morning Star be upon you."

"Greetings, yourself, elder," Seven Skull Shield replied, touching his chin respectfully. "I've an arrow for you to look at."

The old man limped his way to the front, taking the arrow from

Seven Skull Shield's hands. Stepping into better light, he held the shaft at arms' length, narrowed his eyes into a thoughtful squint, and rolled the shaft in his fingers.

"I can make you as many like this as you need."

"Is it yours?"

"Hmm? Oh, no. One of the others. I'd say Gray Mouse's family given the double-knotted sinew hafting on the point. The stone point was made down south by Wild Eye. He ships baskets of them up here. The shaft's hickory, from a third season sapling. Green-cut but well seasoned."

"Gray Mouse? His workshop is around here?"

"Just up from the main canoe landing. Only arrow maker north of the River House palace, just at the edge of the storage houses above the landing."

"Thank you, elder." Seven Skull Shield reached into his belt pouch and produced a clam shell in payment. "May the Morning Star bless you with health and old age."

"I need no Trade for identifying an arrow," the old man told him. "But thank you."

"Gray Mouse," Seven Skull Shield mused as he worked his way through the maze of buildings until he could see the top of High Chief War Duck's palace and its towering World Tree pole. In River Mounds, everything was oriented from that one soaring landmark.

Three fingers of time later, after wandering through a confusion of structures, he found the arrow maker's. Apparently they liked the same kind of architecture: open-sided, thatch-roofed, with mat walls, and the interior filled with benches. Here, too, men were bent over their work, some peeling shafts, others sanding, one carefully notching a tip, yet another winding sinew around a freshly fitted, chipped-stone point.

"Gray Mouse?" Seven Skull Shield asked, only to have a smiling, toothless, white-haired man rise from where he carefully spun a completed arrow in his ancient hands.

Walking over, Gray Mouse gave his shaft another spin, saying, "Bless you, this fine day, warrior." His gaping smile exposed pink and toothless gums; his brown, deeply wrinkled face rearranged itself into a serene mask. "Got to spin them when they're done. If there's a flaw, I can feel it."

"Did you make this one, elder?" He handed Gray Mouse the shaft.

Gray Mouse laid his arrow down, took the shaft and raised it to a hand's length from his nose as he inspected the point, shaft, and fletching. Then he spun it. "It's been shot," he muttered. "Probably hit the ground at an angle. Lucky you didn't snap the point off."

"You can tell that? That it's been shot?"

"It's in the balance." The old man grinned and winked conspiratorially. "Been doing this awhile. That's why I'm the best there is. Yes, that one was shot. But don't shy away from using it again. It'll fly truer than most men can shoot."

"And you made it?"

"Oh, yes. And not so long ago. Probably one of that lot that we Traded out of here a couple of days ago. Hickory shaft, third season. Green-cut. I know that wood. Traded it up from the Tenasee River. Seasoned it myself. That's why we don't have walls here. Wood changes with the temperature, and whether the air's wet or dry." He spun the arrow again on his fingers, asking, "You make your own arrows?"

"No."

"Ah, good. You can't make them as well as we can. Most warriors and hunters, they think they got to breathe their own Spirit Power into the arrow. Put part of themselves in the work. Here, we've got even more of the right Power. Comes from what we know."

"Do you know who Traded for that arrow that was shot only once?"

"Young man. Noble born, if you ask me. Not a veteran warrior, didn't have the way about him. But the two warriors with him? They were blooded, I'll tell you. Tula, if you ask me."

"Tula? Is that some rank? A society?"

"A people. Wild tribe from out in the southern plains west of the Granite Heart mountains." He seemed to be enjoying himself. "There are so many different peoples come to Cahokia now. Who would have thought the world had so many nations and languages, eh?"

"How could you tell these were Tula? I've never even heard of them."

He grinned again, exposing his pink gums. "By the bows! And they didn't speak a word of Cahokian tongue. Now, that's not saying they's Tula themselves, but their bows were of Tula make. Made of flats of Osage-orange-wood. Laminated with some thin sections of horn. Recurved . . . and very potent. That's why that arrow is so long." He pointed to the tall baskets bristling with finished arrows. "See. We sell different lengths, made to match a bow's pull. That's why that last basket is empty. They bought every last war arrow we had in that length."

"If they didn't speak Cahokian, how'd you know what they wanted? Signs?"

"No, no, no. The younger man, the noble, he spoke Cahokian. Had his face painted in a light gray to cover his tattoos. Like the Tula, his hair was wound into a twist and pinned with bone pins. He wore a buffalo calf-hide cloak, fabric breechcloth, bare feet."

"You said young?"

The old man shrugged. "To me, anybody looks young anymore. Maybe he was in his midtwenties? Medium-sized."

"Do you know where I can find him?"

The old man spun the arrow again. "I have no idea. The canoe landing is right over there. For all I know he's on the river and headed back to Tula. Or he could be renting a house within an arrow-shot of this place. It's like a big bustling ant hive here."

"How many arrows in total did he obtain from you?"

"Seven tens, and three."

And we recovered three tens and six from around Night Shadow Star's palace.

"What did they Trade, elder Gray Mouse?"

The old man pointed to a shelf filled with shell, wooden carvings, bowls and jars, several quivers, a copper relief of Morning Star, and on the end, two effigy bowls that represented Piasa. It was to the Piasa bowls that the old man pointed. "Those," he said.

Seven Skull Shield stepped over, lifted one of the bowls off the wood plank, and cocked his head as he inspected it.

The round body of the bowl was slipped in red on top, black on the bottom. Punctations indented the flaring flat rim. Piasa's rattlesnake-hatched tail had been artistically rendered as a looplike handle on one side, the diamonds painted in red-and-black patterns. Piasa's neck had been sculpted from the other. The prominent head extended high and alert, the tooth-studded jaws agape, nose curled in a snarl. Mica-inset eyes glittered in the light, surrounded by a black three-fork design.

Seven Skull Shield arched an eyebrow. "From one of the great nations in the southern valley. Maybe Casqui? Perhaps Pacaha? Or could be one of the Keegwaltam clans?"

"You know that style?" Gray Mouse asked.

"They like this design." *But why Piasa?* He frowned uneasily. Just because that voluptuous Night Shadow Star was supposedly possessed by the Spirit Beast didn't mean the Water Panther was behind everything. After all, it was the value of the effigy bowls that mattered, not the design.

"Elder Gray Mouse, these bowls are worth a fortune. *Two* piasa effigy bowls for seven-tens and three of your long war arrows?"

Gray Mouse's grin grew even bigger and rearranged the man's wrinkled face into a mass of bent lines. "Noticed that, eh? He and his two warriors had pulled out samples of the arrows, looked them over, and were talking and nodding. The young noble reached into a sack, withdrew those two effigy bowls, and asked if we had a Trade."

"Just like that?"

"Just like that," Gray Mouse agreed. "Who was I to say no?"

Seven Skull Shield sucked his lip as he inspected the Piasa bowl. The Spirit creature's mica eyes stared back malignantly in the subdued light. "What happened next, elder?"

"I had the arrows carefully tied into a bundle to protect the fletching and points, and they left."

"These Tula, what do they look like?"

"Tall, muscular. They don't cut their hair after any particular fashion and don't shave their scalps. Most notable of all, they don't have tattoos."

"None?"

"Not that I saw. But there were only two of them. If they were really Tula."

No tattoos. Just like the assassin whose brains I knocked out as he was trying to kill Blue Heron.

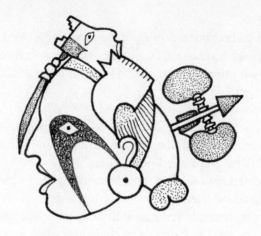

Thirty-three

The palace was oddly silent. Some presence brought Fire Cat awake where he lay on the sleeping bench. In the dim light, he looked up to see Night Shadow Star's dark form looming over him.

"Not the knife over my heart again, I hope," he managed as he fought back a yawn and stretched his tired muscles.

He heard her stifle a bitter laugh. "No, Red Wing. I have been struggling with myself. Field Green has been with me for years. Looking back, I never treated her the way I should. Or told her the things she should have heard. Her body has been carried to her clan's charnel house. The priests are seeing to her. I have asked that she be buried in her clan's mound with honors at the summer solstice. I will be at her interment and tell her ghosts the things I should have said during her life."

He studied her through a narrowed eye. "She'd appreciate that." *Why are you telling me?*

Night Shadow Star shifted, and he could see her rubbing the back of her neck, as if perplexed.

Finally she took a deep breath, and he tried not to notice how it accented her breasts.

"Your quick reflexes last night . . . But for them I would have been dead."

"It was a well-laid-out ambush."

"I wanted to let you know . . . I'm not blind to what you did. Nor ungrateful. Were it up to me, I'd release you from your bond. Not that it would do you much good since Morning Star would probably have you back in a square again, and the clans and families of the warriors you killed have their own vendettas."

"I would take my chances."

She chuckled in dry amusement. "I suppose you would." A pause. "I do not understand this, but perhaps for those very reasons, Piasa insists you and I will both die if I release you from your oath. He's given me visions of death, of great blasts of water bursting into the sky to mix with lightning lancing down from torn clouds. Tornados race across Cahokia, and in the flying debris, thousands of people murder each other."

"Charming."

He could see her dark eyes as they fixed on his. "Piasa's insistence that I hold you confused me in the beginning. I think that now, for whatever reason, and no matter how great the pain and hatred between us, our world and everything we cherish, hangs in the balance."

"What are you getting at?"

She seemed to struggle for words, gesturing her impotence. "I think . . . the pain and anger that separates us is too great to bridge or forgive . . . but that somehow we're connected. Essential. Power's grand joke in the struggle to come."

"Did your brother tell you this? Or the Water Panther in your souls?" He tried to keep the sarcasm out of his voice.

"That's just it," she told him coolly as she stood. "Last night, I learned that no matter what my heart desires, I need to respect you. Perhaps, Red Wing, you could do the same for me?"

And with that, she turned, striding purposefully for her quarters.

Fire Cat, suddenly ashamed, rubbed his brow with thumb and forefingers. "You could have put me in my place with a war club, Lady. But it wouldn't have smacked me down with the same weight your words just did."

Sitting up, he pushed the blanket back, and stared thoughtfully at her doorway.

So, what are you going to do about it, Fire Cat?

Matron Columella swept into the Evening Star palace great room, ordering, "Leave us!"

The people in the room turned, reading her expression through startled eyes, then looked back at High Chief High Dance where he sat on his litter atop the dais. He had draped his left arm over a pulled-up knee, his muscular right leg straight. Since this was a formal session, he'd painted his face in blue with striking white diagonal lines down his cheeks. A polished copper headpiece rose above a scalp bundle pinned at the crown of his severely pulled-back and greased hair.

With a languid gesture of his left hand, he waved the various dignitaries, recorders, supplicants, and messengers out. As they filed past, Columella saw them trying to read her expression through sidelong glances. High Dance sat as if frozen, his dark and knowing eyes meeting her burning gaze. Only when the door was lifted shut to seal them from prying eyes did she stalk forward past the fire, climb the dais, and bend over to glare into his slitted eyes.

"Who is he?"

"Who?" He cocked his head as he met gaze for gaze.

"You've never been smart, brother. Tricky, yes. But smart? Never. Who is this man you've been meeting?"

"Why would you think I'm meeting some man?" He had adopted that bland and totally emotionless look—the one that had betrayed his lies since they were children. That he refused to so much as change his posture further infuriated her.

"Fine. Let's say you're not sneaking out, painting your face dull brown, donning a commoner's clothing, and strolling off to immigrant neighborhoods to meet some mysterious man at trading bazaars, or seeking out dirt-farmer temples dedicated to First Woman. Who, then, could this man be who looks just like my brother, sleeps in my brother's bed, and copulates with his wives before these forays? Because this man who isn't you has also quietly insisted that Brown Bear Fivekiller have at least two warriors remain awake through the entire night while others, in pairs, patrol the palace grounds. I'm sure you'll have an idea of this mysterious stranger's identity."

"You sound distressed, sister. Are you not sleeping well yourself?"

"You're playing with fire, High Dance. Blue Heron is sniffing around us like a hunger-thin dog around a rabbit den. Attempts have been made on the Morning Star and the Clan Keeper. The *tonka'tzi* has been murdered in his bed. To cap the pot, so to speak, I've just learned that someone came within a whisker of skewering Lady Night Shadow Star last night in an ambush. Her household head, Field Green, some guards, and most of her porters died under a hail of arrows shot from the darkness. She barely got away with her life."

She sighed, sank down at the foot of the dais, and stared at him from under a raised eyebrow. "What have you done?"

"Nothing that you or your little shrunken bed-toy need to concern yourselves with. I've had communications with someone whose interests may be aligned with ours. That's all."

"Communications. With 'someone.' After which you've had runners dispatched to the Earth Clan chiefs all up and down the west side of the river. I hear that you've asked about the readiness of their squadrons . . . should they need to be called up." In a tart voice, she asked, "Planning for a little war, are you?"

"Not in the slightest, *Sister*. But should any social unrest break out, it wouldn't be prudent for Evening Star House to be caught by surprise. I simply asked how long it would take the Earth Clans to assemble their squadrons. Nothing more."

"Stop it, High Dance. Right now. Whoever this stranger is, he's poking at the living god himself. Jostling that wasps' nest will bring ruin to us all."

"I thought you didn't like the *tonka'tzi*? Thought you'd do anything to knock his lineage off the Great Mound so you could move Evening Star House into the high palace. My understanding was that you detested Matron Wind, and that copperhead of a Clan Keeper of theirs."

She spread her arms, disbelief in her wide eyes. "Is *that* the total of your comprehension? All right, the *tonka'tzi* has been assassinated. One down. Now, supposing your shadowy assassin kills the Morning Star, Matron Wind, Blue Heron, and entire family in one sweeping attack. What then? Tell me, brother, how do you see this unfolding?"

"Cahokia will be shocked and leaderless." He touched the tips of his fingers together and flexed them. "Before the others can react, we move the squadrons under our command to control the great plaza, occupy Morning Star's palace and the Council House. Our squadrons are ready to defend the Four Winds Clan House the moment we install our lineage heads into them.

"At the same time we have runners crisscrossing Cahokia, informing the other Houses of our dedicated effort to maintain order. We plead with them to call up enough of their own squadrons to ensure that the Earth Clans—and especially the immigrant settlements—don't panic. If we're lucky, by the time they manage to get their squadrons assembled, enough rioting will have broken out that they have to stomp out their own little fires. Meanwhile we're effectively installed at the center."

"And you think the Morning Star squadrons won't resent our people marching in?" She gestured impatience. "Let alone how the other Houses will react."

He shrugged. "By the time they can finally catch their breath, we'll already have begun the ritual to reincarnate the Morning Star into one of our own young men. Once that is done, the sacrifices will have been made. The dirt farmers will be employed building the new ridge mound. We'll have made our offerings to the Underworld and Sky World to celebrate the successful return of the Morning Star. Once that's done, Cahokia will be ours."

She blinked hard, as if by the very effort, she could drive the insanity of what she'd just heard from her head. "How many people are in on this plan of yours, brother?"

"Currently? Just the two of us."

She squeezed the bridge of her nose, knowing full well what the flattening of his gaze meant. He was digging in his heels, his old way-too-familiar obstinate streak asserting itself.

"Don't," she whispered, raising a hand to forestall what she knew was coming next. "Don't say it."

"I *am* high chief," he insisted, despite her attempt.

"Step back, brother. Pause and think. This time, if you're making a mistake, it's not a matter of inconvenience or embarrassment. We're talking about potential disaster for our House, lineage, and families."

"I thought you didn't mind taking a little risk? That you were ready to act yourself?"

She let her gaze burn into his. "I am, *you fool*! But on our terms. And I'm still not sure that Night Shadow Star and that simpering Sun Wing aren't the fatal links in the Morning Star House. Matron Wind has been elevated to *tonka'tzi*. That's bad for us because she's so much smarter than her brother ever—"

"She might 'die in her sleep' some night, too."

Columella's heart skipped. "Tell me you had nothing to do with the *tonka'tzi*'s assassination."

He set his stubborn jaw, lifting his chin defiantly. "What if I did, Sister?"

"Then more than just the two of us know about it." But she read his posture for what it was. "He did it, didn't he?"

"Who?"

"This mysterious person you're meeting. Bead. I think that's what you call him."

A center hit! His pupils briefly dilated in time with that telltale twitch of the lips.

"How do you know that?" he asked softly, a deadly fear now filling his eyes.

"Flat Stone Pipe has his sources, Brother. Even supposedly blind and deaf ones like that old blind man outside the temple." She rubbed the back of her neck. "By Horned Serpent's dripping poison, be thankful that old beggar wasn't one of Blue Heron's, or our entire family would be decorating squares in the Great Plaza."

She had him now, watching his eyes flicker with uncertainty. "The old beggar couldn't hear everything you and Bead said, just bits and pieces about how everything wasn't working the way you'd planned. That you and Bead argued. And that Bead, as I was told, 'put you in your place' through some sort of threat."

High Dance took a deep breath, finally wilting in partial surrender. "If you know all this, why are you asking me?"

"Because I just *heard*! Because like water down rivers, information has to flow through Flat Stone Pipe's sources. Because a great many things are happening just now. Like this attack on Night Shadow Star. Which, if you didn't do it, perhaps Bead did?"

"I don't know."

"But I'm sure you know how he 'put you in your place?' "

High Dance glared at her. "He, or one of his wolves, took Fast Throw's chunkey stone out of my sleeping son's blanket and hid it in a meal jar under Brown Bear's bed. He was *in here*! He could have slit my boy's throat . . . *any* of our throats, for that matter."

"Tell me," she managed through a strained whisper, "everything he said to you, everything you've committed to. And brother, since our lives are now threatened from *two* directions, by the Piasa's balls, *don't* leave anything out."

Thirty-four

What is happening to me? Night Shadow Star clamped her eyes tight, fists knotting, as Piasa's voice whispered at the edge of her hearing. Tensing her muscles, she managed to drive the Spirit Beast's presence back. Then, trying to take a casual breath, she opened her eyes and glanced around the Council House interior, desperate to see if anyone had noticed.

"I've barely heard the name," *Tonka'tzi* Matron Wind remarked as one of the recorders produced a series of rolled deer hides and laid them out on the floor before the raised daises. Around them the Council House was silent, but a handful of the most trusted recorders sat in the back, and several runners waited along the ornate room's walls.

Blue Heron and Seven Skull Shield crowded forward as the recorder began unrolling and arranging maps across the floor. Each was covered with a series of black lines, inverted Vs, and other squiggles.

"We really need to do something about these maps. They are all drawn to different scales," Blue Heron muttered as she cocked her head.

"No, we don't," White Brow, the recorder, replied. White Brow and his fellows maintained maps in their society house several bow-shots to the east. "The details of each region are more important than making everything fit. Otherwise we'd fill the entire room."

"You'd think you were an engineer," Matron Wind responded. As the new *tonka'tzi* she didn't look at all at ease wearing her dead brother's stunning jewelry, or his ornate trappings of office.

The recorder gave her a patient and suffering look as he explained, "All you need to do, *Tonka'tzi,* is keep track of the relationships between the maps. Look. You start here at Cahokia and follow the river south, past the chains, past the confluence with the Serpent Water where it comes in from the east. This next map takes you south to the Pacaha nation. And just below that is the confluence of the great western river. Following it west, its course runs past all these nations, strung like beads on a string just south of the Granite Heart Mountains.

"Then you move to this map of the Yellow Star Mounds and the Caddo towns it controls. But here, go north, into the grassy plains. And that's where you'll find the Tula."

Blue Heron was fingering her chin as she followed the logic of the maps. "About as wild a bunch of men as exist, I suppose. What do we know about them?"

Matron Wind lifted an inquiring eyebrow at another of the recorders. Sky Shoulders stepped forward bearing a heavy stack of beaded belts. With the help of one of his assistants, Sky Shoulders lifted several off the top and produced six beaded record belts from the middle of the pile. These he lay to one side and began going through them. He carefully lifted the top three layers away and ran his fingers over the patterns of beads.

"They are an exiled Caddo people who Trade mostly in bison," he said as he deciphered the patterns and colors. "They don't grow corn or other food plants. They move with the land, seasons, and herds." He set that record to the side lifting the next, before continuing. "They raid Yellow Star Nation as well as Trade. Relations are undependable. Punitive raids from Yellow Star sometimes get lucky and take a few slaves. Tula are very fierce warriors."

Sky Shoulders lifted the third. "Ah, here. Once they fought Yellow Star for dominance in war. Upon their defeat they fled into the grassland prairie to avoid complete destruction."

"That's it?" Blue Heron asked.

The recorder touched his forehead in reply, indicating that he had read everything in the bead mats.

"Yellow Star Mounds." Matron Wind said after considering. "They have an embassy here." She turned and beckoned to one of the runners standing along the back wall. "Go find that emissary the supreme chief of the Kadadokies nation sent. What was his name?"

"Frantic Lightning, or as close as it translates to our tongue from the Caddo," one of the recorders replied from the back.

"Yes, well, politely ask if Frantic Lightning would be so kind as to come and tell us about the Tula."

Night Shadow Star watched the messenger leave before she stepped forward, saying, "I'm sure I've heard of the Tula before, but I can't remember when. Why would they wish me ill, let alone attempt my murder in such a fashion? They are a distant people, and if they had succeeded, and my death were tied to them, the Morning Star would send an entire army to destroy them."

"Assuming we could ever catch them out in the buffalo lands," Blue Heron grunted. "They might be like night mist on a hot morning and simply evaporate every time we got close. If Yellow Star can't destroy them, what makes us sure we could?"

From the back of the room, Seven Skull Shield added, "Keep in mind that Gray Mouse, the arrow maker, told me they were carrying Tula bows. While he recognized the weapons, he wasn't sure if the men holding them were really Tula."

"No tattoos?" Matron Wind asked. "What people have we ever heard of who do not tattoo their men, for recognition if nothing else?"

"Wild barbarians have their own ways," Blue Heron noted.

You miss the essence of the question. Piasa's voice insisted from the depths of Night Shadow Star's souls.

"The essence of the question?" She was aware of eyes turning her way.

Why? Piasa's sibilant hiss sounded from within her.

"Of course," she whispered to herself. "What would motivate Tula warriors to come all this way to attack us? Not just Cahokia, but the Morning Star and Four Winds leadership?"

The growl of Piasa's satisfaction vibrated down between her souls.

"The Yellow Star?" Matron Wind mused. "Could they have perhaps hired these Tula? Paid them to come here and attack us?"

"For what reason?" Blue Heron countered. "Seriously, Yellow Star is four to five moons' distant by land, and perhaps four by river. We have no interest in their politics, nor do we meddle in their affairs. They not only share our reverence of the Morning Star, but we Trade priests back and forth."

"They might want to free the Morning Star from his current body and resurrect him in a body of their own," Sun Wing pointed out. "Those people are uncivilized."

Tonka'tzi Wind gave her niece an irritated look. "Is everything so simple for you?"

"It doesn't make sense," Blue Heron decided after considering it. "If they attempted a resurrection, they know that we'd hear about it and take offense. All of Cahokia would be incensed. The Houses and Earth Clans would unite to produce an army such as the world has never seen to march on Yellow Star Mounds. The colonies would send squadrons, and no matter the distance, tens of tens of thousands of vengeance-minded warriors would descend on them. When the wrath of Cahokia had finally exhausted itself, their city would be nothing more than a barren flat devoid of even grass."

"What of this 'young noble' as Gray Mouse called him?" Seven Skull Shield asked. "The arrow maker said he spoke our language. He guessed him to be in his midtwenties."

"We're supposed to take his word?" Night Shadow Star asked. "He knows a noble when he sees one, this arrow maker of yours?"

Seven Skull Shield shrugged, then reached into a sack that sat next to him. "Maybe. The man in question Traded two of these for the arrows that were shot into your party, Lady."

Night Shadow Star watched him remove a ceramic bowl, and felt her souls jolt at the sight of the Piasa image molded into the ceramic. The glinting mica eyes seemed to drill right into her. Piasa's shadow flexed within her breast.

"It's southern workmanship." Seven Skull Shield rotated the bowl in his hand. "After I lifted this one from the arrow maker, I had a friend of mine look at it. He specializes in exotic pottery. Said it was made by a renowned potter in a town in southern Pacaha on the Western River."

Night Shadow Star fought for breath, hearing Piasa whispering, *He mocks me. Even now. He knows I will see this.*

"Mocks you how," Night Shadow Star asked, almost shivering as Piasa's rage built.

He thinks himself invincible.

"No man is invincible." She closed her eyes, struggling for control, desperate to damp the rage bursting through her. "He's just a man."

A very, very dangerous man. If he succeeds . . .

"Succeeds in what?"

A chaos beyond repair.

"Night Shadow Star!" The sharp voice, coupled with a loud clap of the hands, brought her back to the Council Room. She blinked, slightly off balance. Slowly the room swam into focus. Blue Heron laid hands on her shoulders to steady her, and was looking her hard in the eyes.

"What's *wrong* with you?"

"Piasa," she mumbled, the beast's words still vibrating within her. "The bowl. It's a message to the Piasa. An affront."

Heart pounding, she glanced around, aware that everyone was watching her with wide eyes. Her legs weak, she sank slowly to the floor, then glanced at Seven Skull Shield. With a wave of the hand, she added, "Go on. About the bowl. What makes you think it was a noble?"

"He Traded two of these bowls," Seven Skull Shield said unsurely. "Never even bargained when one would have been more than enough."

Sun Wing asked, "Why is that important?"

Seven Skull Shield seemed to shake himself as he managed to shift his gaze from Night Shadow Star to Sun Wing. "Lady, no one who's been in the Trade, or had anything to do with moving goods, would offer *two* such bowls for a bundle of arrows, no matter how good they were. The Power of Trade is served by haggling to find fair value. Don't you barter for things you want?"

"I have servants for that," she told him sharply.

"So he is a noble?" Blue Heron mused. "But he could be from anywhere. Even Pacaha."

"With respect, Clan Keeper," Seven Skull Shield added, "I don't think so." He glanced at Fire Cat who'd stood silently at the back of the room. "Red Wing, would anyone in your family, no matter how highly ranked, have paid out two bowls of such value for a bundle of arrows?"

Fire Cat crossed his arms, shaking his head. "We survive on Trade. Being wise in the ways of it, establishing fair value, is how we maintained ties not only with the wild forest tribes, but the established Traders as well. Perhaps we don't . . . *didn't* show the same passion for it as some of the better Traders, but we weren't held up to ridicule, either."

"The south might be different," Sun Wing pointed out. "That's where those bowls came from."

Seven Skull Shield looked distinctly uncomfortable when he said, "I've spent more than my share of time on the canoe landing. The southern chiefs are the subject of considerable discussion among the Traders. While some have better reputations than others when it comes to Trade, none are, as the Red Wing would say, 'held up to ridicule.'"

Sun Wing glared daggers at Seven Skull Shield. "Correct me again, thief, and I'll—"

"Enough," the *Tonka'tzi* ordered, shooting her niece a warning look. "I think it's pretty clear that we are dealing with an anomaly here. The assassin was obviously raised without an understanding of Trade. Determining where that place might have been will lead us to the assassin's origin."

"Um . . ." Seven Skull Shield had his eyes firmly fixed on the floor.

"Here." Night Shadow Star announced with finality. She was vaguely aware of the thief's look of relief. "In all the world, Cahokia is the ultimate recipient of Trade. It all comes here eventually."

"But Cahokia is awash in Trade!" Sun Wing cried. "The Earth Clans, the immigrants, the Traders, the colonies, everyone is Trading."

"Except the Four Winds Clan." *Tonka'tzi* Wind looked thoughtful. "We expect, and receive, anything we want as gifts. Nor do we "Trade" as such with the embassies who come here. They bring the most remarkable offerings to us. We "gift" them in return, offering like for like. But it isn't like real Trade where we compare values and haggle."

"So," Blue Heron mused, "it's one of us?"

Very good! Night Shadow Star heard Piasa murmur from the depths of her souls.

"But who?" she asked.

Someone close.

Night Shadow Star felt a tremor run though her. Involuntarily her glance went to the people in the room. "Surely," she whispered under her breath, "it *can't* be one of us!"

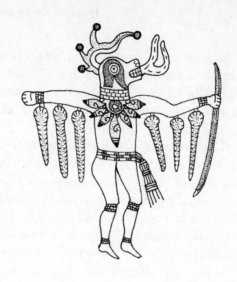

Where Tie Snakes Lurk

I am curious. And, to be honest, a bit frustrated. I cannot escape the notion that some aspect of Power is working against me. Not that I blame it. By now even Piasa is aware of the threat I pose. I doubt, however, that the cunning Spirit Beast has the slightest notion of just how dangerous I really am. Someday soon he, and all the Spirits of the Underworld, will have an awakening.

The attempt to call back my dead warrior's souls from the lower realms will have alerted them. Granted, the ritual didn't work as anticipated. Nevertheless, they would have felt the pull on my dead warrior's souls. That anyone would have the temerity to attempt such a thing must have upset the Tie Snakes, Piasa, and perhaps even Old-Woman-Who-Never-Dies. Normally First Woman remains in her cave where it winds around through the roots of the World Tree. There, undisturbed, she dreams fertility into the soils, plants, and forests.

I grew up on stories about Lichen, the great priestess who actually sent her soul to First Woman's cave, and pleaded with her to restore the rains. Compared to what I'm about to attempt, Lichen comes across as a bumbling novice.

I laugh, and the Mos'kogee man beside me gives me an uncertain appraisal.

For the moment I mingle with the crowd that has gathered at the base of

Morning Star's great earthen pyramid with its palisaded Council House, and even loftier palace. I am desperate for news, hungry for any tidbit. Everyone is talking about the attack on Night Shadow Star; they wonder who could possibly be behind it. Many speculate that it's the Red Wings, while others remind them that a Red Wing now serves the lady. Others speak of a Powerful witch loose who might have possessed a band of hunters with madness. Still others whisper that it is incipient warfare between the Houses, and tie it to the tonka'tzi's *mysterious death. I am amused. None of them, however, appear to have any information that will benefit me.*

People hardly look twice at me, figuring I'm just another of the endless stream of pilgrims who pass through Cahokia. They think the large roll of matting I carry contains my bedding. One of the miraculous things I've learned about people is that they generally dismiss what they see as what they expect.

If they thought about it, would any pilgrim wear my current expression of wary contemplation? I am obsessed by what went wrong last night. And delightfully relieved.

How did Night Shadow Star extricate herself from my attack? I'm irked that I killed so many of her worthless servants, and somehow she escaped without so much as a nicked finger.

Power saved her for me.

I hear the voices whispering agreement.

It only makes sense. The rains are called by the Tie Snakes; their Power is with water. The mighty beasts inhabit dripping caves, lurk in the depths of springs, and lounge in the silt-laden depths where the great rivers twist back on their courses. Somehow they knew I would act last night; they called the storm into which she disappeared.

But for their interference, my wolves and I would have at least had starlight, perhaps a sliver of the new moon to pick our targets. Instead, given the inky blackness beneath the storm, we had to shoot blindly.

But in doing so, I demonstrated the lengths to which I would go, the depth of the sacrifice I am willing to make. Only the exceptional are willing to murder that which they love the most.

I now know that Power has saved her for me. So great is my certainty that my dreams last night were filled with Night Shadow Star. Like the young woman at the farmstead, she was bound, naked, and I was washing her body in preparation for the ritual. As I stared into her eyes, she spread her muscular legs, opening herself to me. The moment I drove myself into her the explosion of my loins had been so vivid I jerked awake, panting.

"I understand, my love," I whisper to myself. "When I released that arrow, it was proof that I was finally worthy to possess you."

I look up at the great mound's first terrace. The edge is bordered by its stout palisade, and behind it I can just see the Council House roof. Night Star Shadow, Blue Heron, and the rest are up there. What I would give to listen in on that worried meeting, to hear what measures they plan to take.

Around me, people continue to whisper about the attack on Night Shadow Star. At least I have made them wary, anxious, and uncertain. I must feed that fear, grow it. I will need their panic when my plans finally come to fruition.

It takes all of my concentration to keep my painted face from smiling. Here, in the crowd, I am just another foreigner, come to share in the glory and excitement. In the throng, I am faceless.

"Look!" a fish Trader cries, pointing. "It's a runner from the Council House."

I glance at the young man with his painted staff of office as he trots down the stairs from the palisade gate and work my way closer to the ring of warriors who guard the bottom of the stairs. They look fierce in their bright paint and plumage. Instead of the two ceremonial guards, today three tens surround the base of the stairs. They ensure that no unauthorized person passes their line. I can read their barely masked rage, see the anger in their eyes in the aftermath of the attack on Night Shadow Star.

I am close enough that I can hear the runner as he approaches the squadron leader and says, "The tonka'tzi requests the presence of Amayxoya Frantic Lightning, of the Yellow Star embassy. Please prepare an escort for us upon my return."

That startles me. I have purposely avoided any direct contact with the Yellow Star embassy. Not that I fear that Frantic Lightning, or any of his people, might recognize me. I not only passed the war chief on the avenue several days back, but attended his reception atop the Morning Star's mound with impunity. Dressed as I was he never gave me a second glance, but he, or one of his assistants, might comment on my Tula wolves should they catch sight of one. The last thing I need is anyone asking questions about the Tula—or why they might be in Cahokia.

The runner hesitates, then, looking puzzled, asks the squadron leader, "Have you ever heard of a people called Tula?"

Hot anger and the cold chill of fear both coil inside me. Did the fool just hear my thoughts? And if not, how else did they make this leap?

My gaze narrows to a slit as I watch the runner pass the line of warriors. His staff of office held high, he calls, "Make way! I am on an errand for Tonka'tzi Wind!"

I dare not sprint after him. But then, I know where the Yellow Star embassy is quartered. They have been given a large house, courtesy of the Morning Star. It lies a short run off to the west, just back the main avenue, on a terrace overlooking Cahokia Creek's marshy bottoms.

I must hurry.

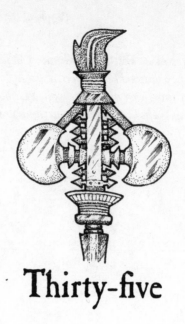

Thirty-five

He had earned the name Frantic Lightning Mankiller for his exploits in a battle against the Tanico Nation. Located on the Great Western River, several days' travel downstream from Yellow Star Mounds, the Tanico had been subordinate and paid tribute to the Yellow Star's Kadadokies tribe for nearly a generation. Then the great Kadohadacho, or "Supreme Chief" of the Yellow Star Nation had died. Two of Frantic Lightning's cousins had made a play for the high chair. Civil war was narrowly averted at the last instant when a stickball game was played between the two brothers to settle the succession.

The Tanico *Caddi*, or high chief, meanwhile, took the opportunity to revolt. Mistakenly, he and his people had assumed that Yellow Star mounds would consume itself in the struggle. Instead the newly installed Kadohadacho had dispatched a small army to march on Tanico. In the subsequent fighting, Frantic Lightning had distinguished himself by charging back and forth between hard-pressed squadrons as they battled through swampy bottomlands along the river. No sooner had he snatched victory from defeat by his heroic actions on one front, than he raced off to another. Afterward the warriors reported that he acted like a frantic lightning bolt, striking first in one place before being called to strike at another. The name had been formalized and bestowed upon him at the ceremony that marked him as an *amayxoya*, or squadron commander and war chief. Subsequent responsibilities had cemented his reputation and led to his nomination to head the most recent embassy to Cahokia.

The fact that, on this particular day, the *tonka'tzi*'s messenger found him in the luxurious dwelling the Morning Star had offered for his use was somewhat fortuitous. Since his arrival in the city, Frantic Lightning had availed himself of Cahokia's phenomenal entertainments. Not only did the food stands, Trader's booths, lapidary, and ceramic workshops, coppersmiths, and exotic Traders constantly amaze, but endless games of chunkey could be had. And Frantic Lightning was a player of no mean skill.

He had just returned from a morning of chunkey in River City Mounds, having won an embossed copper falcon from an Illini opponent. Halfway through the process of sponging sweat from his neck and shoulders, his squadron second—a renowned war leader named Takes Horn FiveKiller—entered the room and touched his chin. The man was in his mid-forties, his weathered face and faded tattoos bent by a wry grin as he announced, "*Amayxoya*, a messenger has just arrived from the *tonka'tzi*. Somehow they've come to the conclusion that some Tula were involved in the attack on the Lady Night Shadow Star. The *tonka'tzi* has sent a request that you attend her and hopefully provide some information on the Tula."

Frantic Lightning stopped short, half bent to his bath. Water dripped from the rag he held and trickled down the ripples of his muscular body. He gave his second a flat stare. "I am to believe this? Tula? Here? In Cahokia? And shooting at Lady Night Shadow Star? How ludicrous is that?"

"Nevertheless, *Amayxoya*, you are summoned to the Council House. They want to know about the Tula."

"As if anyone *knows* about the Tula! What do I tell them?" He touched his forehead in mock submission. "Great *Tonka'tzi*, being an expert on the Tula I can tell you that they're just human versions of the short-grass coyote. Forever howling, they like sneaking close in the night and snapping up whatever is left unattended. They drink the blood from their kills while it's still hot and steaming and paint their faces and bodies with it. Their women are made of sinew and muscle, and as terrifying as it is to be captured by the men, it's the women who take the greatest joy in slowly murdering a prisoner. They slit his belly just wide enough to reach in with a hooked stick and pull out a knuckle's length of intestine. The next day, they pull yet another knuckle's length, and so on. Unless they're aroused, in which case they let the camp dogs pull out and consume the man's innards as he screams himself to death. It's said a Tula woman will snap a man's neck if he leaves her disappointed with the arts of his shaft. And so, great *tonka'tzi,* if you think you've got Tula sneaking around in Cahokia, just listen for the shrieking of women and children. Your Tula will be close by."

He reached for a second cloth and dried himself. "Are they serious, second? What would entice a Tula to come here? Since their exile, they've become completely wild. Acting more four-legged than human."

Takes Horn spread his arms wide. "It's probably nothing, some rumor spinning out of last night's attack. Perhaps someone desperate for an explanation heard the word Tula in passing." He grinned. "Besides, with all the other concerns they have to worry about, maybe hearing your stories about the Tula will provide some diversion."

"Diversion? Nightmares, you mean." He pointed to his paint palette and dress finery. "If you'd be so kind, second. I can't go looking like this."

"Of course, *Amayxoya.* What colors would you prefer for this meeting?"

"Yellow and blue. Something as comic as the notion of a Tula war party attempting to kill Lady Night Shadow Star."

In less than a finger's time, *Amayxoya* Frantic Lightning was carefully painted, his hair twisted tightly into a bun, pinned, and a copper headpiece attached. He wrapped a grizzly-hide cloak over his shoulders, and let it hang down the rear past his sky-blue apron.

"You look magnificent, *Amayxoya.*" Takes Horn FiveKiller gave him a gnarly grin that exposed the gaps in his teeth. "Worthy of the Kadohadacho himself."

"Let's go amuse the *tonka'tzi* with stories of half-human Tula."

He strode through the front room where most of his retinue had been scurrying back and forth to prepare. At his entrance, they flocked to the front doorway, making ranks to either side as he emerged into the shade of the veranda. The breeze from the north carried the musky scent of the marsh along Cahokia Creek. No more than a bowshot to the south, and beyond the cluster of houses, he could see the busy Avenue of the Sun where it passed on the other side of a conical burial mound. A constant stream of people almost clogged the avenue.

Frantic Lightning settled himself in the litter and braced his hands on the polished wood of the chair arms. He took a deep breath as his warriors lifted him high, a familiar Caddoan work song breaking out on their lips. Frantic Lightning smiled at that, delighted to have a reminder of home. He waited a couple of beats, and joined in, knowing it just strengthened his bond with his warriors in this remarkable and alien place.

His carriers started forward in their swinging gait. War Second, Takes Horn FiveKiller trotted along in front, the Cahokian messenger leading with his staff of office held high to clear the way. Frantic Lightning checked to the side, making sure his two translators were there. The Cahokians provided a translator, but having two of his own guaranteed that nothing was missed. And behind them came the recorder, his pack filled with strings and beads.

Frantic Lightning let the song roll through him, singing, "As I labor, the sun warms my skin. I feel the breeze and join my kin." His hands were patting the chair arms in time. "The soil smells rich as I raise my hoe."

Of course—the sudden notion came to him as he sang—there was one possible connection between a Cahokian lord and the Tula. And it made a curious kind of sense. The image of a young man's face flashed in his memory, as if teased out by the song. Yes, the knot-headed Cahokian had gone out to find and study the Tula—not that he'd ever exhibited much sense so far as Frantic Lightning had ever seen. At the time, he'd thought that a black sickness of the soul, like a twisting knot of intestinal worms, had been slowly consuming the young Cahokian. Blood and thunder, surely he hadn't—

The impact felt as if he had been hit in the middle of the back with a hard-thrown, fist-sized stone. The sound, surprise, and sensation were indistinguishable.

What the . . . The words in the song were forgotten, even as he stared down at the sun-bright crimson coating the arrow point that protruded from his breastbone. Fire lanced through his chest.

The warriors bearing his litter had ceased to sing, having felt and heard the arrow's impact. Now they swiveled their heads, staring in disbelief as *Amayxoya* Frantic Lightning struggled to take a breath. He kicked out in panic and coughed, blowing a fine crimson spray like a misty cloud to speckle the faces of his horrified warriors.

He tried to mouth the words through the blood. "The young Walk . . ." The rest vanished as the high sun turned dim, then gray, leaving a fading glare in the memory of his vision. . . .

Thirty-six

Old Blue Heron pulled at her chin as she stared down at the Yellow Star war chief where he had been placed on the floor in the embassy main room. Frantic Lightning looked anything but what his name implied. His body lay sprawled in his litter, limbs akimbo. The man's head was flung back, exposing his throat, jaws agape. The slanting afternoon sun shining through the doorway illuminated his wide brown eyes as they dried in the muggy air. Clotted blood outlined his tongue and teeth, and packed the back of his throat. An expression of disbelief lingered on his painted face, the bands of blue and yellow now speckled in a browning spray of dried blood.

Several of his warriors hunched beside him, shooing the flies from his sightless eyes. She immediately recognized the blood-caked arrow they'd withdrawn from the leaking puncture in the Frantic Lightning's chest. Oh yes, familiar indeed!

"He's always a step ahead of us," Blue Heron growled. "Murdering piece of filth!"

One of the translators said, "The Yellow Star squadron second, this man, Takes Horn FiveKiller, says he demands you hand the killer over to him."

She glanced sidelong at the older, weathered, squadron leader who rattled on in Caddo, his arms swinging as he added emphasis to his words.

Blue Heron met his angry eyes with her own burning gaze. She jabbed a finger at the man, words pinched, as she said, "You and me, Second. We're going to have a race. Whoever catches the murdering weasel first gets to cook the testicles off his body."

As her words were translated, the Second's tattooed face reflected a bitter satisfaction. Following his barked question, the translator said, "Who did this? Why?"

"I think it's the same filth who tried to kill Lady Night Shadow Star. It's the same kind of arrow. We want him as badly as you do." Blue Heron took a deep breath, glancing around. The "guest" house, looked oddly forlorn. She stepped out onto the veranda, and took in the environs. Behind the house the marshy bottoms of Cahokia Creek lay like a green swamp just above its confluence with Marsh Elder Lake. Toward the avenue to the south, the conical burial mound thrust up like a green cone. A crowd, held back by a line of warriors, had gathered around the warehouses, workshops, and dwellings belonging to various craft specialists from the Earth Clans.

"The shot came from there." The second had followed her out and was pointing back toward the marsh as the translator continued. "We were headed toward the avenue, attending to your summons. As you can see, he was shot from behind. The distance is a good sixty paces. Not an impossible shot, but one requiring a skilled archer."

"And you and your warriors didn't see the shooter?" she asked.

As this was translated the second slowly shook his head. "We were too surprised. Then we were concerned with the *Amayxoya*. By the time I thought to send anyone to find the assassin, there was no one. Just bruised grass where he'd stood behind the corner of the house. There's a trail back there running through the grass. My best tracker followed the smudges of a running man west for a couple of bow shots. The fugitive cut back to the main avenue on the west side of that temple mound over there to the west."

"Where he would have disappeared into the crowd." Blue Heron followed the pointing finger to a Turtle Clan charnel house where it topped a low mound in the distance. She could just see its peaked roof.

Angrily she rubbed the back of her neck, announcing, "All of Cahokia is at your service, second. The great Kadohadacho and the Yellow Star Nation are beloved and valued allies. Cahokia shares your outrage and grief over the vile assassination of a brave and respected *amayxoya*. Anything we can do to help you prepare the body for transport back to your home will be freely granted. You no doubt need to conduct special rituals to ease the transition of his life-soul into the afterworld. We intend to show him every honor."

"Thank you." He touched his chin forcefully, his angry gaze barely ameliorated.

"But first," Blue Heron said as she raised her hand, "what were you discussing just before he was killed?"

"The Tula," the Second growled. "The *Amayxoya* was bemused by the notion of a summons to discuss the wild barbarians."

"Amused? Why?" She listened as the translator turned her words into Caddo.

"Great Clan Keeper, the Tula were once a part of the Yellow Star Nation. They rose in rebellion against Kadadokies' rule and attempted to seize the leadership. In the end they were defeated in war. Rather than surrender, they exiled themselves to the prairie country to the west. In protest, they ceased to tattoo themselves, to cut their hair, or adopt the ornamentation of civilized men. Instead they concentrated on war and the hunt, believing such a way of life would harden them to battle. Not being a numerous people, they one day hope to regain their place as leaders of the Yellow Star nation and dominate the Kadadokies tribe through exceptional skill, valor, and proficiency of arms. They favor the bow and are renowned for making their own. It is a terrible weapon, and if they ever managed to breed enough warriors, they might pose a threat."

"But you don't seem to take them very seriously."

He smiled at her, a knowing glint in his eyes as the translator repeated his answer.

"Great Clan Keeper, one out of every two of their boys dies during their arduous process of training and deprivation. They must exhibit superb discipline and suffer extreme privation as youths. Any who falter in the slightest, or are considered weak or somehow flawed, are eliminated. Tula end up as remarkably tough warriors, superior archers, and physically formidable. What they are not is smart, adaptable, or resilient when it comes to combat." He made a "cut-off" gesture with his right hand before cocking his head and demanding through the translator. "Why are we talking about Tula? What makes you want to know about them?"

She dabbed mindlessly at her healing throat wound. "They gave up all form of ornamentation? Even tattoos?"

"It was a renunciation of Yellow Star's affluence, Clan Keeper. They wanted to breed 'pure and focused' warriors, men undistracted by vainglory and frivolous ostentation."

She took a deep breath, staring at the doorway behind which the dead *Amayxoya* lie. "What would it take to recruit a party of them?"

"A leader who could inspire either fear or discipline, and being ignorant as they are, they are susceptible to those who claim to have special Power, such as magicians and conjurors." The second gave her a humorless smile. "And they would relish any opportunity to test their courage and hone their skills while they learn new ways to kill enemies and prove their superiority."

She absently rubbed the red slash on her neck where the scab had peeled away. "I think, noble second, that someone has done just that. I think a small group of Tula warriors has been brought to Cahokia. And given what happened here, the *Amayxoya* might have known the man's identity." She frowned. "Or the assassin feared that possibility."

The second swallowed hard, glancing furtively at the guest house. "He might have slipped up from the marsh, listened at the back of the house. I didn't post guards. Here? In Cahokia?"

She chewed at her lip as she thought about it. "Phlegm and excrement! He might have been standing in the crowd at the base of the mound. Watching, waiting to see what we'd do in the aftermath of his attempt on Night Shadow Star. If he overheard the messenger talking about the Tula, or summoning the *Amayxoya,* he'd have known we were on to him."

Takes Horn FiveKiller threw a speculative glance at the crowd that had grown behind Blue Heron's line of warriors. "Look. There are hundreds of eyes upon us. He may be out there even as we speak, Clan Keeper. Watching to see what you will do next. Planning who he will kill next."

Thirty-seven

The soft whimpers brought Fire Cat awake. He blinked, battling nightmares in which he could only watch impotently as his sisters were run down by sweat-reeking men. The sound of fabric had ripped right through his souls as it was torn from their bodies. He'd been hanging in some monstrous square as his sisters screamed for his protection.

Arms and legs spread and aching, he'd only been able to watch in horror as his sisters were thrown to the ground, their bodies bouncing. White Rain's eyes had fixed on his, her fright and disbelief unmistakable as her arms were wrenched over her head to expose her breasts. Then she screamed as her ankles were pulled apart. The men howled as they pointed and clapped at the sight of her. He'd shot a frantic glance at Soft Moon, seeing her brown young body spread and pinned on the ground as the first man threw himself upon her. She'd screamed as the man's buttocks rose high and jerked down . . .

My fault. All my fault.

Fire Cat sat up, relieved to find himself in the dark confines of Night Shadow Star's Palace. With a shaking hand he rubbed his perspiring face; his heart hammered raggedly at his breastbone. A tingle of adrenaline charged his muscles as he reached out and carefully pulled his blanket back.

A bad dream. Horrors spit up from the depths between my souls.

Swinging his feet down from the bed he took a moment to scan the palace great room. In the central hearth, the fire had burned down to a red bed of coals accented by an occasional flame. Each time it flickered, the polished copper ornaments on the walls gleamed a gaudy crimson.

The two guards stood at weary attention, war clubs in hand, one on either side of the closed and latched door. Here and there a bed was occupied by one of Night Shadow Star's decimated staff, but all seemed to be sleeping soundly. The number of empty beds proved a grim reminder of the midnight attack. In one of the corners, a rodent was scratching impotently at one of the large ceramic seed jars.

A gasp, as if from panic, carried faintly to Fire Cat, and he remembered what had awakened him in the first place.

He willed himself to rise and pad on silent feet to the door of Night Shadow Star's personal quarters. He lifted the heavy plank and slipped it soundlessly to the side.

In the darkness, he could just make out her form as it tossed on the bed behind the altar. A miserable sob escaped her throat, and she shifted, kicking the blanket from her long muscular leg.

"No," she whispered. "Please, don't hurt me." Something choked in her throat. "You're . . . Chunkey Boy . . ."

We both have our nightmares, he thought woodenly.

The suffering sound she made deep in her throat was half strangled, as though she choked on disgust.

He started to turn, willing to let her suffer her own miseries. Then he stopped short, took a deep breath as she whimpered again, and crossed to her bed.

"Lady," he said gently. "Night Shadow Star? Wake up."

"Please . . . don't . . ." she whispered hollowly.

He reached out with a foot and prodded her toes, saying, "It's a nightmare, Lady."

At his touch, she jerked, sucking a gasp. Coming awake she pawed the hair out of her face. Blinking, she sat up.

"Night Shadow Star," he told her calmly, "it's a bad dream."

"What are . . ." She frowned up at him in the blackness. "Why are you here, Red Wing?"

"It's only a dream, Lady. Cast it out of your mind, and go back to sleep."

"A dream?" She shook her head. "There are no limits to my ability to disgust myself."

"You're safe tonight. Well-guarded. And with nightmares of my own to keep me awake, I'll be sure to spot any Tula before they get to you."

She ran slim fingers through the black fall of her hair, shaking her head. "Tula are the least of my nightmares, Red Wing. Now get out of my room. Blood and pus, if I thought the Tula could end this I'd help them slit my throat."

Patience was often the key to opportunity. Those who took their time, concentrated on the world around them, and didn't allow themselves to be distracted could discover the most interesting things. This morning Seven Skull Shield had dedicated himself to discovering facts about Frantic Lightning's death that the Keeper, despite all her resources, could not. Blood and spit, the old gal had been too right about him. He just couldn't turn down the challenges. The greatest, of course, was finding the accursed assassin. The pus-sucking maggot just couldn't be that good at hiding his tracks.

The second—which would prove absolutely delightful—would be to watch the Clan Keeper's expression as Seven Skull Shield laid out the information he'd come by.

But first there was the matter of breakfast. Prowling slowly past the farmsteads between Cahokia and River Mounds, he acted true to form: patiently watching for an opportunity.

It came in the form of two little boys, maybe three and five, tossing dirt clods at each other, laughing and giggling. Their mother crouched at the fire just outside the door of her farmstead. She was using a long stick to poke and rearrange the coals. Above them, slowly roasting pieces of turkey projected over the heat on willow-stem spits.

As soon as the screaming and laughing boys ran behind the woman's house, Seven Skull Shield ambled over, and absently stated, "Um, just thought I'd let you know you've got two little boys climbing the latrine screen out back. Not to mention that one or both might end up in the pit, but they're sure to tear the thing down."

Her head had jerked up, her suddenly panicked gaze shooting toward the rear of the house. Even as Seven Skull Shield had taken a step in the other direction, she was sprinting for the rear.

He whirled, plucked the spit that propped one of the legs over the fire, and vanished between the houses before she could herd her troublesome little males back into view. Then, proceeding down the Avenue of the Sun, he let the meat cool.

At the conical burial mound, he took the beaten path north between the buildings, and past the residence where Frantic Lightning
had been ambushed. Six Yellow Star warriors squatted on the veranda, talking softly, smoking, and gesturing. No doubt they were re-
hashing yesterday's events, wondering about the future, and wishing
they could get their hands on the culprit.

Seven Skull Shield could almost sympathize. To be foreigners so far
from home, to have their war chief assassinated, the whole thing had
to be unnerving.

As they fixed their hostile gazes on him, he circled wide and found
the path where it skirted Cahokia Creek's confluence with the lake.
There he stopped and looked around. No one would have looked
twice at a man trotting along with a bow. It was spring, after all, wa-
terfowl were migrating. Huge Vs of ducks, geese, herons, and cranes
were following the river flyway north. Out on breeze-rippled Marsh
Elder Lake, several large flocks could be seen safely out from shore.

Turning, he studied the approaches from the east where the assassin would have come after hearing that Frantic Lightning was being
summoned. The killer would have hurried to within sight of Frantic
Lightning's residence, then slowed, walked casually to avoid drawing
attention to himself. He might have even slashed at the grass with his
bow stave in a display of boredom as he eased up to the corner of the
house.

Skulking along the back, he would have done the same thing Seven
Skull Shield now did: listened to the occupants through the gap between the thatch and wall. Assuming he understood Caddo, he'd have
known when Frantic Lightning was ready to leave.

But after the shot, where did he go?

West. Seven Skull Shield stepped back, looking at the lines of tracks
through the spring grass. Too many people had walked here since.
Back at the path, he followed it west along the lake shore. To feed Cahokia's immense need, the cattails, willows, and reeds had been har-
vested long ago for building materials, matting, and baskets. Despite
the size of the lake, he could probably count on one hand the number
of fish that had avoided the nets, traps, and trotlines. Only the tiniest
of minnows darted among the shallows. Even the killifish had been
seined out of existence, destined as filler for the city's stewpots.

Returning his attention to the task at hand, he took another bite
from the turkey leg and tucked the spine back to free up more meat.
The first fork in the trail led south past one of the charnel houses that
served some group of immigrants. Seven Skull Shield took it, finding

a mish-mash of tracks in the soft soil. To his right, and not surprisingly upwind, a wizened old man of forty summers sat in the doorway of a small hut with a split-cane roof. No doubt the priest who served the charnel house, he wore a simple smock. His hands cradled a gourd tea cup, and he smiled into the morning sun.

"Greetings, Elder. A fine morning."

"In First Woman's name, yes, it is," the man spoke through an atrocious accent.

"Do you always enjoy the morning with your tea?"

"For the most part. As the winters go by, they've started to make my bones ache. I'm ready for the warmer weather."

"Must have been exciting when the Yellow Star war chief was killed yesterday."

"Who would have thought?" the old man shook his head. "Can't tell about these foreigners."

Seven Skull Shield let the irony pass. "I'll bet the archer ran right past you with his bow."

The old man shook his head, his gaze following a young woman who stepped out of the nearest house. "No. I was sitting right here. No one passed. Would have been good to see him, though. Would have been a bit of excitement." He paused. "Care for a cup of tea?"

"Some other time. First Woman's blessings upon you, Elder."

Seven Skull Shield gnawed the last of the meat from his turkey bone as he backtracked to the lakeside trail. He hadn't hoped to get lucky enough on the first try.

Resigned to a long day, he tossed the bone into the lake and took the next branch that led up from the lake shore.

At the third house he stopped. A toothless old grandmother proved to be his loadstone. She kept reaching up absently with a misshapen right hand, pulling at the few remaining patches of white hair left on her nearly bald scalp. Large brown age spots freckled her lined face.

"Ah, just before the excitement? Yes. A man passed. Walked right there on the trail where you're standing, but he carried no bow. He had a sleeping mat rolled up. A really clean one. Looked new. Odd, don't you think? No one around here makes them. Not for Trade. Too hard to get the material. Mostly around here we farm. My grandson, he hunts ducks out in the lake. Ties stones around his waist and breathes through a hollow tube as he sneaks up from below and drags them down by the feet. He can only do that when the water's clear."

"A man with a clean sleeping mat?"

"Oh, if he'd been sleeping down by the lake, the mat would have been stained with grass or that dark silt. Like I said, it was a new mat."

"And what did he look like? Tall, short, young, old, what kind of tattoos?"

"Maybe twenty-five summers?" she guessed. "Tall and muscular. You've seen those stickball players? The kind who can run all day? Had his face painted funny, mostly brown. Very pleasant."

"He spoke to you?"

"Oh, yes. Just like you. Asked how my day was. Then people started shouting about the commotion over east, and he said he'd go see what that was all about."

"Odd that he'd paint his face brown. How was he dressed?"

"Just a sleeveless hemp-fiber shirt belted at the waist with a rope. His hair was in a bun pinned with a wooden skewer. Looked just about like everyone else." She frowned slightly. "He's a noble."

"And how would you know that, Grandmother?"

"They have that way about them. Like they own the world. Arrogant, haughty, superior . . . even when they're trying to make believe they're just like you. I know this. I was brought here as a girl . . . slave to serve the Moon Chief, Jenos. He was the ruler at River Mounds back then. I was there the day the mighty war chief Badgertail brought Tharon's demand for tribute and the return of Priestess Nightshade." She chuckled. "I hid in a big seed pot as Tharon's warriors looted and killed the Starborn warriors. So, yes, I know nobles." Shading her eyes with a gnarled hand, she studied him, as if to see if he believed her.

"Could you recognize the man with the mat again, Grandmother?"

She shrugged. "Probably. It was his eyes. Excited, dangerous, and deadly. I was of less importance to him than something unpleasant he'd have to scrape off his feet. So, why then, did he want to stop and talk to me? Why did he seek to convince someone as unimportant as me that he was something other than he was?"

Before Seven Skull Shield could speak, she added, "And why are you, yet another nondescript man, so interested?"

He laughed at that. "Very good, Grandmother. Yes, I'm hunting him. And I'd really like to find him before he kills someone else."

"Beware, hunter." She tugged impulsively at one of the remaining locks of brittle white hair. "I knew Badgertail, Tharon, and the great Nightshade. Powerful and dangerous people, they were. But this one? Hunting for him will be like reaching your hand into dark places in search of a scorpion. You will not like it when you finally find him."

As if to finish, she pointed. "He went right between those two corn granaries and turned east, mingling with the traffic on the road."

Like a scorpion in the dark. The phrase stayed with Seven Skull Shield as he touched his chin respectfully, and walked out to the Avenue of the Sun.

The scorpion had turned east? Obviously to watch the results of his handiwork from the crowd, to assess his success, and monitor Blue Heron's response. He could have gone anywhere after that. Seven Skull Shield turned his feet toward River Mounds, thinking, *It's just a hunch. That tingle at the base of the spine, but I've got that feeling . . .*

The Falcon

The lesson surprised me. I'd been in a clearing in the deep forest, the old growth. There the black oaks, the various hickory trees, maple, sycamores, and chestnuts grow to giant heights. Towering beech and mighty sweet gum fill the low spots. Walking through deep forest is a journey down from the shadows with only an occasional shaft of sunlight filtering through the green heaven high above. The leaf mat beneath one's feet is a soft and spongy layer of hollows transected by circuitous patterns of giant roots. Vines of all sizes, the largest as thick as a man's thigh suspend themselves like ropes from the branches above.

Instead of what should be haunting silence, the noise almost hurts the ears as the endless chirring of insects, the musical songs of birds, and the chatter of squirrels create a cacophony.

That day I'd been occupying myself by stalking a huge flock of passenger pigeons where they fluttered and chuckled through the high canopy. As they plucked apart seeds, bits of detritus rained down like a perverted snow. I clutched my long cane blowgun with its slender dart, and stared up at the heights in despair.

The chances that any of the birds would drop down to my distant earthly level were slight.

And then I broke out into the clearing. Here a tornado had blasted a narrow path through the forest giants, snapping branches, toppling trees this way and that, splintering the mighty trunks and littering the landscape with broken forest.

I stopped short after I climbed onto a broken arch of branch and squinted in the bright sunlight. Awed by the devastation, my attention was nonetheless drawn to the thousands of passenger pigeons as they swarmed out of the surrounding trees to hunt the recently made clearing.

Still half blinded by the dazzling sunlight, I fumbled in my pack for more darts, and tried to pick a target from the fluttering columns of descending birds. I'd no more than target one, than two or five or twenty would fly between me and my prey. I stood paralyzed, the blowgun to my lips, lungs filled with the breath that would propel my dart, and I could do nothing.

The surprise was complete. I'd just come to the conclusion that I needed to wait, to shoot one on the ground, when the streak flashed down from the sky.

The pigeon never knew what hit it. One moment the bird was following its fellows, intent only on the feast below. The next it had been smacked senseless from above and behind, feathers trailing in its wake.

I stared in stunned amazement as the falcon's wings rasped in the air, braking its descent. Feathers still trailed from the hammered pigeon where it dangled from the falcon's taloned feet.

Time seemed to stop for an instant. A heartbeat later, the vast flock of passenger pigeons exploded in a roar of fluttering wings. In mad confusion thousands of birds thundered into the safety of the forest, some fouling others in the process.

My own response was to duck, tossing away my blowgun to wrap my vulnerable head in my arms.

As quick as a snap of a twig, it was over. I peered through my fingers to see the clearing empty but for a sprinkling of falling feathers.

And high in the sky, the falcon was climbing, the dangling body of his pigeon firmly clasped in his talons.

And what might the lesson be? It was that the most dangerous of predators strike from nowhere, when least expected.

Today, I am the falcon. My sky is the crowd of vendors carrying packs of dried corn, ceramic bowls, skeins of cord, and other necessities. On my back is a large bundle of firewood.

I have taken a station at Lady Lace's palace, for I know that soon someone will step out and come down the stairway.

As I wait, I glance off to the west. If I am going to succeed I can take nothing for granted. I've had too many setbacks as it is. They are my fault. I was overconfident, arrogant. I underestimated the talents and Power of the opposition.

The game has grown more complicated, and I must adapt. Traps must now be laid within traps. The threat posed by that fool Frantic Lightning has been eliminated. What began in panic has now become an opportunity. If I am correct, I may be able to use Frantic Lightning's murder to eliminate yet an even greater threat. Assuming, that is, that anyone is smart enough to follow in my tracks. If nothing happens by tomorrow, I will be relieved, but slightly disappointed that Blue Heron isn't as smart as I'd come to believe.

I am interrupted by the arrival of a runner, a young man of maybe fifteen summers. He wears a buckskin breechcloth, his brown skin sleek with sweat. Panting as he trots, he carries a black-and-yellow painted staff of office that identifies him as a messenger.

I can see the change in his expression as he glances up at Lace's palace, a slight smile of relief on his lips. He slows to that loose-jointed walk of a runner crossing the finish line. I step away from my firewood stack, and offer him my water bottle.

"You look like you could use a drink," I tell him. "How far did they send you today?"

"From up north," he tells me, taking the water bottle. "Heavy Cane has finished his business. They'll need to make preparations."

"I heard that he's been gone for a half moon's time."

The runner nodded and slugged down water from my gourd bottle. "He's heard the stories."

"I've brought wood, but no one has so much as stepped out of the house. If the Lady's husband is returning, they'll want to make a feast."

The runner wiped his lips. "The Lady Lace should be in council." He glanced at the wood. "Come on. I'll tell Fine Silt the news, and that you've brought the wood."

I touch my chin respectfully, pick up my bundle of firewood, and follow the runner up the forbidden steps to the palace veranda.

The falcon taught me well.

Thirty-eight

Bleeding Hawk had taken his warrior's name after his Spirit quest and trial of the flesh. That was the Tula ceremony that marked a boy's passage into manhood. The rock-studded hilltop on which he'd fasted and prayed for five days had been hit by lightning, and in the stunned aftermath, he'd seen a giant black hawk descending from the sky. The terrible bird had been ripped and torn, feathers peeling away as drops of blood were whipped free by the wind.

Not everyone received such a powerful vision, and Bleeding Hawk had known from that moment that he was special.

In war, he'd been blessed by the Sun, and once managed to steal three women from the Grass-Lodge People who lived in the open plains to the north. Bleeding Hawk understood the two realities of existence: war and Power. When the Sorcerer had arrived in his village, speaking of magical worlds and the chance to gain great honor, Bleeding Hawk had immediately fallen under his spell.

And yet again, the Sorcerer has seen the future. The thought filled his head as he watched the Cahokian from his hiding place. The man was talking to the old woman where she sat in the sun, shielding her eyes.

"Secret yourself in the corn granary, Bleeding Hawk. I spoke to the old woman specifically to see who, if anyone, hunts for me. If, by the time a day passes, no one has come, you may return to the warehouse. Should, how-

ever, anyone search out the old woman and question her? Ah, then he or she is yours to hunt and kill."

Bleeding Hawk shifted, his souls growing calm and sure. Through the slats of the granary wall, he watched the big man pass, recognizing him as the slovenly thief who attended the Clan Keeper.

The one who killed Bobcat!

The Sorcerer had overheard one of the Keeper's household slaves remark how the "rootless thief" had fortuitously sneaked up behind Bobcat and brained him.

Coward! But then, two could play at that game.

Bleeding Hawk had dedicated himself to the stalk. While his skills had been learned in the wilds surrounding Tula, the principles were the same here in this magical and revolting city.

He waited until the thief had stepped out onto the Avenue of the Sun. He watched as the man hesitated, and then headed west.

Bleeding Hawk shouldered his hide-cased bow and quiver, then unlatched the granary door. On agile feet he clambered down the notched pole that led to the ground, made his way to the great avenue, and joined the flow of other pedestrians on their way west.

Like a good hunter, Bleeding Hawk kept enough distance that he could occasionally glimpse his prey. The man remained heedless as he passed the Traders' stands, houses, workshops, and garden plots.

A bare hint of smile bent Bleeding Hawk's lips as he witnessed the big man deftly steal an ear of boiled corn from one of the roadside vendors. Unconcerned, the thief mindlessly gnawed kernels from the cob before pitching it to one of the begging dogs who'd been drawn to follow him. The pesky beasts followed anyone with food.

His quarry turned off at the outskirts of the River Mounds, and here the hunt grew more difficult. Had the city been built in any kind of order, the stalk would have been easier. Bleeding Hawk could have anticipated his prey's direction. Instead, Bleeding Hawk had to proceed in leaps, waiting until the thief had walked behind a building or latrine screen before he could hurry forward and sneak a peek.

Adding to the problem, the thief seemed to know everyone, stopping to chat at workshops and stalls, calling people by name, laughing and joking. At one he'd pick up a piece of pottery, holding it up to the light as the maker pointed out decorations. At the next he'd be handed a piece of fabric by some weaver who winked at him and was in turn slapped on the back.

Through it all, Bleeding Hawk had to circle, portraying to the other locals as if he were not stalking someone, but was simply lost, or bemused. Often, when he'd try to circle around a building for another vantage point to watch his prey, he'd find the way blocked and have to hurry back. More than once he barely caught a glimpse of his vanishing target as the thief's broad back disappeared down some narrow way.

Then the process would begin again as some passerby called out a greeting and stopped the thief for a brief chat. There would be more laughing, stories or jokes, and then a drawn out parting with some kind of incomprehensible promises called back and forth.

Bleeding Hawk didn't need to speak the language to understand the gist of the conversations. But how did a thief amass so many obvious friends? Among the Tula, the moment a man's dishonesty was discovered, he would be staked out in the sun naked, a slit cut in his belly, and a length of intestine pulled out for the camp dogs to fight over. Here, among these people, the miscreant appeared to be celebrated!

A convenient section of woven matting provided cover, yet allowed Bleeding Hawk to stare through the lattice as the thief Traded a bit of shell to obtain a leaf of tobacco from yet another of his endless associates. More laughing and joking ensued before the thief bit off a section of leaf and walked off chewing it.

After what seemed an eternity of delays, that moment of glee began to grow in Bleeding Hawk's breast. Better and better! The thief was making his way straight for the tightly packed warehouses above the canoe landing. And somewhere in that random and chaotic warren of buildings, away from the workshops and Trader's stalls, the unconcerned fool would be entirely alone and vulnerable.

Stepping behind a latrine screen, Bleeding Hawk paused just long enough to pull his beloved bow from the tanned-hide case that hung from his back. Bracing it with his foot, he used his hip to bend and string it. Then he pulled the rawhide quiver from the case and slung it over his shoulder.

As he passed the last of the workshops, he nodded and smiled at the workers who looked up from their grinding, sanding, cutting, and carving. All the while, he kept his distance, comparing what he knew of this district to the direction the thief seemed to pursue.

Blessed be Power, I know this place.

He needed to close the distance now. The warehouses, granaries, and storage facilities were packed tight here. This was the highest elevation on the levee, the least susceptible to floods.

All Bleeding Hawk required was a narrow passage, time enough to whip an arrow from his quiver, and a momentary glimpse of the thief's broad and unprotected back.

The next passage would fulfill all those requirements. To his absolute delight, the warehouse where they stayed was but a couple of buildings over. If the thief went right where the next plaster-walled building blocked the way, it would lead to a dead end, but surely, the . . .

No, to Bleeding Hawk's amazement, the man took the one-way turn into the dead end. Why? The explanation leaped into Bleeding Hawk's brain: a man had to empty his water somewhere. It had been all morning that he'd been following the fool.

Bleeding Hawk drew his arrow, nocked it, and sprinted around the curving wall of the warehouse. Even as the narrow alleyway appeared, he was drawing, taking his bead on the long Cahokian war arrow. . . .

Bobcat, old friend, I send you this foul maggot's soul!

Thirty-nine

Seven Skull Shield would have grinned if his mouth hadn't been full of tobacco juice. He continued rolling and crushing the quid between his molars, filling his mouth with the rich tang. Sister tobacco's magic fingers were stroking his muscles, bones, and blood with her enchanting tingle.

Anyone who didn't know the doorway was there would have thought someone entering the dead-end passage had just up and disappeared. Through the crack, he could see the man's dark shadow as it passed. His stalker walked on cat feet, so quiet was he.

After he'd passed, Seven Skull Shield eased the doorway aside on its silent leather hinges, and stepped out behind the warrior.

I can just back away and . . .

How silly that he could even think it? Too much was just plain too much. He stepped forward, taking the stalker's measure: tall, muscular, wearing a hunting shirt from which dangled a half-full quiver of very familiar arrows. Folded over his shoulder was an empty bow case. The stalker moved like a wary lion, his bow up and drawn, the long braid forward. And that unusual bow? It had been made of dark hardwood laminated with layers of horn, both ends of the staves having an odd double curve.

A Tula bow?

As the stalker cleared the last of the wall's curvature, he stopped, frozen, the bow held so steady he might have been stone. The dank smell of feces and human urine hung in the air, the sounds of the city distant. The man grunted an exclamation of surprise.

Seven Skull Shield juiced his tobacco for the last time and spit just as the Tula began his turn. The stream of tobacco-laced saliva took the man full in the face.

And then Seven Skull Shield was on him, bellowing, *"You foul piece of walking shit!"* He piled headlong into the warrior, barely aware of the arrow as it released and dug a groove out of the plaster wall to the left.

"I'm gonna break you!" Seven Skull Shield bellowed. "Gonna *stomp* you!" He head-butted the Tula in the face. His knee rose like a hardwood stump; the Tula's body shuddered as it slammed into his crotch. "You *rat-choking* maggot meat!"

Grabbing the stunned Tula by the throat and dragging his face into each blow, Seven Skull Shield continued to head-butt him. He delighted in the pain and flash behind his eyes as he felt and heard the bones breaking in the man's nose and cheeks. Blood and tobacco juice splattered his forehead as he drove it into the Tula's face.

"Think you can hunt me? Shoot *me* in the back! In my own city? *Worthless dog shit! I'm gonna kill you!"*

He felt the man's grip slacken on the bow, heard it clatter to one side. The Tula was pawing at something on his rope belt. From instinct, Seven Skull Shield shifted, knowing the move from old.

He tightened his hold on the Tula's throat, screaming, "No you don't! Foreign bit of trash! Come here? To *my* Cahokia? Think you're gonna stick me!" Seven Skull Shield's left hand caught the Tula's wrist, stopping the bone stiletto before it could be driven into his side.

Pus and vomit! The Tula was as strong as bull buffalo!

Screaming like a war eagle, Seven Skull Shield stared into the Tula's half-dazed eyes, dripping as they were and half blinded with blood and tobacco juice. As the Tula tried to squirm out of Seven Skull Shield's grip, he levered the man off his feet. Together they crashed onto the smelly filth that filled the blind passage.

As they hit the ground, Seven Skull Shield had brought his knee up, landing so his weight drove it down like a ram onto the man's genitals. The Tula shrieked, twisting away like a writhing rattler. The man had obviously wrestled, was going to break loose. Just a matter of time . . .

"You pus-weeping infected sheath! Back-shooting, worm-eating maggot!" He spit the tobacco quid fully into the Tula's gory face then opened his mouth wide and bit. He sank his teeth into the Tula's cheek and lower lip as the man tried to turn his face away.

Unable to shout, Seven Skull Shield could only growl and squeal his rage as he chewed, ripped, and jerked at the resisting flesh.

The Tula was kicking, bucking, and doing no little squealing of his own. Unlike Seven Skull Shield's enraged vocalizations, the Tula's sounded like sheer terror.

The man was clawing futilely at Seven Skull Shield's hair, winding his fingers in and pulling desperately. His trapped right hand flexed and strained as he tried to drive the deer-bone stiletto into Seven Skull Shield's side.

Which was when Seven Skull Shield let out a particularly wild shriek through his nose and mouth and let loose with his right hand. Before the Tula could react, he'd driven a hard thumb as deeply as he could into the man's left eye. He felt the orb tear loose, then pop wetly.

The Tula's scream might have come from a dying animal; his legs kicked in spasms. Then whimpering sounds broke from his throat as Seven Skull Shield did his level best to rip the tissue in his teeth from the man's head.

"I think that's enough," a somber voice called.

Seven Skull Shield let his rage slowly drain, turned loose of the bloody remains of Tula lip. He spit blood-soaked saliva into the half-conscious Tula's ruined face.

When the Tula wouldn't release the stiletto, Seven Skull Shield braced himself, levered the man's arm up, and broke the elbow over his knee.

Only when he had the weapon in his hand, did he rise, panting and drained. The Tula, gasping and choking, curled into a fetal ball around his broken arm, his one good eye clamped in agony.

"Who is he?" Black Swallow asked where he stood blocking the narrow alleyway.

"Tula assassin," Seven Skull Shield said through panting breaths. The adrenaline of battle still surged through him. "One of many."

In the narrow confines behind Black Swallow a collection of men were taking turns peering past one another. Most were grinning at the wreckage.

"Remind me never to make you mad," one muttered.

Another whispered, "Blood and pus, Seven Skull Shield, from the sound of it I thought someone was torturing a pack of dogs back here."

"And what's with all the head-butting?" Black Swallow asked. "Looked to me like you were doing a better job of beating yourself up than he was."

"Yeah, well, my head's the closest thing I've got to a big rock." He realized blood was trickling down his face. Probably from repeatedly smashing his forehead into the Tula's broken and bleeding nose. He dragged his sleeve over it.

"What do you want done with him?" Black Swallow asked. "When you dropped by my Trade stall, you said I'd get paid back for my broken fingers. How does that work?"

Seven Skull Shield wiped more of the Tula's gore from his lips and chin. "I need all of you to help me. We need to get this pus-licking maggot to the Four Winds Clan Keeper. I think the wealth you'll carry home will more than make up for those fingers." Seven Skull Shield reached out and laid a hand on Black Swallow's shoulder. "I didn't handle that business with the statuettes very well. Time to make amends."

"After the way I was treated, why should I?"

"The best reason of all: wealth."

Black Swallow glanced at the writhing remains of the Tula. "Yeah, well, I was going to take a splitting maul to your head, but after seeing what you did to him, I've reconsidered any such foolish flights of fantasy. No matter how tempting they may be."

Seven Skull Shield chuckled and gave him a bloody grin. "Me? I'm harmless as a suckling puppy." He glanced at each of the men, aware they didn't get the humor. "Come on. Let's get him to Blue Heron. And we've got to do it smart and quick. We don't want this guy's friends to recognize him. Cause if they do, they're gonna do their best to kill us and him before we can get him there."

One of the other men cocked his head skeptically as he studied the Tula. "Seems to me you didn't leave much left to recognize."

Forty

With her father's death, and her aunt's elevation to become the new *tonka'tzi*, Lace's position in the Council House had changed. Now her litter rested on the elevated clay platform beside her aunt's. She occupied the spot normally reserved for the clan matron. Nor was she unaware of the implications. The expectation had been that Night Shadow Star would have been elevated to the dais should anything have happened to either Red Warrior or Matron Wind.

But Night Shadow Star's souls had broken at the news of Make's Three's death. Instead of a gradual recovery from her grief—if Rides-the-Lightning could be believed—her souls were now possessed by Piasa.

The same killer who had apparently tried to murder the Morning Star and the Keeper, and who had successfully slit her father's throat in his own bedroom, was now stalking them and committing mayhem throughout Cahokia.

Nor could the leaders of the Four Winds Clan be in any way assured that the other Houses weren't involved. Plotting was the normal state of affairs between the Houses, but now, after the assassination attempt on Night Shadow Star, anything was possible.

And onto this stage, Lace had been thrust, having lived barely eighteen summers, pregnant with her first child, and feeling completely terrified and unprepared.

Nevertheless, she listened as Blue Heron and the Yellow Star war second gave their report to the *tonka'tzi*. The attendants all stood in their places along the walls. She could hear the recorders in the rear; their fingers rattled among the beads in various jars as they dug for whichever color and size they needed.

From the corner of her eye, she could see Sun Wing where she idly twisted a loop of her long black hair around a finger and studied the Yellow Star war second, Takes Horn, from half-lidded eyes. The pout on her lips told Lace that her sister considered the man nothing more than a worthless barbarian.

You've been my favorite for years, little sister. But eventually you're going to have to grow up. Given the terrible events of the last seven days, it may be sooner than later. I won't be able to help you then. These black waters in which we swim will be too deep.

She felt the growing child in her womb shift, pressing on her bladder for a moment. She took a deep breath, irritated that the life within her didn't have the decorum to pick a less auspicious time. She shifted to ease her discomfort.

"The inescapable conclusion," Blue Heron exclaimed, "is that whoever is taunting us has a tie with Yellow Star mounds. We could have discounted the arrow maker's identification of the Tula bows. After all, what's an arrow maker's judgment worth? But when we send for the *amayxoya*, and he's immediately killed to prevent us from learning anything about the Tula? I may be simple, but that is pretty convincing to me."

"I'm still having trouble with this." *Tonka'tzi* Wind touched the tips of her fingers together. "Why these Tula? What have we ever done to them? A people I've never even heard of? Yes, I could understand if it were some barbarian tribe on the eastern coastal plain, or in the southern or northern forests, who had been displaced by one of our colonies. But we have not, and will not, infringe on the territorial rights of our allies. And Yellow Star is an ally."

Takes Horn Fivekiller had been listening as his translators whispered in his ear. Now he spoke, the translators saying, "Perhaps this is a means of breaking that alliance?"

Blue Heron, fingering her healing throat, shook her head. "I think not, my good friend. Though I almost wish that were the case. If it were, we could foil the plotters with a simple reaffirmation of our alliance and good will. Strengthen it, in fact." She touched her chin respectfully to augment her words.

That's a good trick, one I need to remember.

Lace, to show her agreement, nodded and touched her own chin.

"No," Blue Heron continued, still speaking to the Yellow Star emissary. "The strike is aimed at us, and only at us. The *amayxoya*'s death, through tragic, was incidental. Your good friend and leader, unfortunately, either knew, or may have known, something that would have damaged the assassin and his plans."

"But what?" the translators asked as they repeated Takes Horn's question. "His last words were 'The young walk.' Of course the young walk. They also swim and run. He was trying, through the blood, to tell me something. I have struggled, laid awake, and tortured myself, but cannot imagine what it might be."

"Perhaps it will come to you," the *Tonka'tzi* said wistfully. "Or perhaps we may yet uncover the plot on our own. Surely the assassin will make a mistake." She glanced up at the darkening smoke hole overhead. "For tonight I think we've done enough. Tell those who are waiting at the bottom of the steps that we shall take up their claims and requests in the morning."

With that she raised her head and arms, calling out the blessing of the Morning Star upon all who were present.

Lace gestured, signaling White Squash, her household chief to collect her porters. Then she waited as the people present prostrated themselves, bowed, or lowered their heads depending upon class and status.

Only after the *Tonka'tzi* had been carried out did her porters lift her litter and bear it from the room and out into the dusk. From the look of the clouds, it would be another rainy night.

She pursed her lips, considering the recent events, as the litter was born through the massive wooden gate. Her bearers started down the ramp. The great plaza, in evening shadow, still hosted a couple of stickball teams as they raced back and forth, apparently having more fun than success, since they could barely see the ball when it was pitched.

At the foot of the stairs, the crowd made way for the *Tonka'tzi*, a squad of warriors marching out in formation as they bore her aunt toward the Four Winds Clan house. By the time Lace was carried to the bottom, most of the crowd was filtering away into the darkness. The Traders were packing up their wares, the pilgrims singing their chants and leaving offerings at the base of the Morning Star's great earthen pyramid.

Her own warrior escort fanned out. The outermost scouts took position no more distant than an arrow could be shot.

"Lady?" White Squash began where she walked beside the litter. "I have news. Your husband has returned from his clan business up north. He arrived with a couple of friends this afternoon and sent a runner. I didn't have the time to inform you, as busy as your schedule was."

She smiled at that. "Thank you." As desperate and confused as things had become, sleeping next to him would be reassuring. She'd been so frightened since the attacks began that she'd actually allowed two armed Four Winds warriors, kinsmen, to stand just inside her door for the last couple of nights.

"I've had a special supper prepared. Fresh venison tenderloins are being slow roasted with beeweed seasoning, some of those peppers Traded up from the south, and fermented corn. Sassafras and raspberry tea will be served with cattail bread and cranberry syrup sweetened with honeysuckle nectar."

"I notice a couple of his favorites there."

White Squash glanced sidelong at her as they passed Night Shadow Star's palace. "I thought a celebration might be in order, my Lady. There's been more than enough fretting and danger to go around. Nor do we know when the terror is going to end."

"When we catch the plotter and kill all of his Tula assassins," she replied shortly, and rubbed her forehead. "Forgive me. Maybe it's being pregnant, but I feel so helpless. Everything has me worrying to the point I've chewed my lip raw." She chuckled hollowly. "Maybe I should be more like Sun Wing. She's either fascinated or horrified. She doesn't seem to feel this sense of growing fear."

"That why you're not sleeping?"

Lace placed her palms on her swollen abdomen. "Do pregnant women ever sleep? I just want this to go away. I imagine eyes in the night, watching me as I sleep. I dream that my guards are murdered, their throats slit where they stand by some unseen attacker. This menace, he exists as a shadow . . . a darkness that fills every corner of the room. But when I raise an oil lamp, he flits from one to another, darker, corner."

White Squash looked up skeptically. "You haven't been listening to your sister, have you? That's how Night Shadow Star describes Piasa."

"No." Lace shook her head. "This isn't Piasa. It's him." She hesitated. "I can almost see his face. I know him, White Squash. I swear. It's just at the edge of my souls, like a shadow mist. And each time I spin around and stare, the figure dissipates into smoke." She stopped, feeling her souls shift with certainty.

"Lady?"

"No. It's nothing." But it wasn't. She almost had it. Just awhile more, she closed her eyes, willing the sense of . . .

"Lady? We're here."

The image that almost formed evaporated as her litter was placed on the ground before her palace. The structure was nothing like Night Shadow Star's huge and opulent palace. Nor did that bother Lace. Overbalanced by her belly, she walked up the ten paltry steps to the top of her mound, touched her chin respectfully as she passed the guardian posts, and was thankful for the sacrificed dog that had been buried beneath the top of the stairs. The canine's Spirit was there to guard against intruders.

At the same time she watched her warriors marching out to surround her low mound, two taking position by her door, and one each positioning himself at the corners of her palace.

Her two living dogs greeted her at the door, tails wagging.

"Were the two of you good today? You didn't cause Fine Silt any trouble? Didn't raid the venison or bread as it cooked?"

Apparently not, for neither dog betrayed even the slightest hint of guilt. They rubbed enthusiastically against her legs, panted, and waited to be scratched.

Entering she smelled the food, and started forward, wondering where Fine Silt might have been.

Lace passed the fire, seeing it was burning brightly. Meanwhile White Squash went about checking the cooking pots where they bubbled and filled the air with tantalizing odors.

Lace removed her cape as she stepped into her sleeping quarters and stopped short. In the dim light she could barely make out the line of people prostrate on her floor. Her husband, Heavy Cane, stood awkwardly just to the right. And behind him, a shadowy second figure.

"Husband? What is—"

"Call White Squash in here." His voice sounded horrible and strained. And, as her eyes adjusted, she gasped. The odd shape at his neck was a long, thin, chipped blade—the kind of ritual knife they had all become too familiar with.

From behind Heavy Cane, a familiar voice, in a most reasonable tone, said, "Please, if you like your husband alive, make no alarm. If you scream, you both die. Now, call the delightful White Squash in here. And if you don't behave, I'll cut that darling little child right out of your womb."

"It's . . . you," she choked, the mists around her souls parting with a terrible certainty.

Forty-one

The hollow terror in Blue Heron's stomach knotted and twisted like a physical pain. With a flickering torch in her hand, she stared in abject horror at the room's contents. Her instinct was to call for a squadron of warriors and, once surrounded by them to run, flee, as fast as possible from Cahokia. When she made it—if she made it—to the canoe landing, her impulse was to take the first worthy craft she could find, and launch it into the river. Only after a moon's travel, born wherever the river carried her, would she land, hopefully to disappear into the forest where no one would ever find her again.

But even then, will I ever be safe?

Would any of them?

She stared at the line of bodies in Lace's sleeping quarters. White Squash, Fine Silt, Bread Woman, Blue Flower, and the rest were laid out like an offering, their blood pooled and drying into black on the intricately woven mat floor.

And then there was the gruesome display pinned to the wall above the bed. The way the torch flickered, a trick of the light seemed to make it move and wiggle like a thing alive.

That . . . That . . . Words failed her.

The urge to shiver, to break down and weep, weakened Blue Heron's spine. Tried to turn her knees into water.

Can't. Got to be strong.

Never had she resented and hated the fact that so many looked up to her than at that moment. The entire world expected her to be the central supporting pillar of Four Winds strength, and all she wanted to do was run screaming from the memories.

"Aunt, I just got your messa . . ." Night Shadow Star's voice trailed off as she stepped into the room. Her gasp of disbelief was followed by a dry swallow.

"I was on the verge of retiring for the night." Blue Heron's voice came out strangled. "A terrified warrior came charging out of the night. Said he'd gone to deliver a message from the *Tonka-tzi* to the Lady Lace. The warriors were standing at each corner of the palace as prescribed, but the two who were supposed to be monitoring the door were missing."

"Those are the two just inside the door with their throats cut," Night Shadow Star observed unsteadily.

"It's raining, black as charred pitch out there," Blue Heron noted, her eyes still locked in horror at the thing hanging from the wall above the bed.

"Where is Lace?"

"I don't know. But that thing above the bed? I'm pretty sure it's Heavy Cane. It's almost hard to tell, but he would be about that size. Even with what's been . . . uh, sliced away, you can tell it was male."

Night Shadow Star staggered sideways to prop herself against the door frame. The Red Wing had appeared out of nowhere, one hand bracing her. He was staring at the wreckage in the room with dark, narrowed eyes, a hardness in the set of his mouth.

"Niece? Are you going to be all right?"

Night Shadow Star barely managed a faint nod, and kept swallowing as if to forestall the urge to throw up.

Blue Heron didn't blame her. The smell itself would have gagged even the bravest warrior.

"Has . . . Has Mother been told?" Night Shadow Star ran the back of her hand across her lips. "Or the Morning Star?"

"Not yet." Blue Heron blinked against the misery. "I'll attend to it as soon as we decide what to do here." She hesitated; her soul-sick gaze fixed on Heavy Cane's corpse with its oddly flayed skin and the weirdly severed muscles that hung from the bones like perverted, and too-fat, fringe. Pegs had been driven through the wrist bones to pin them to the wall like outspread wings. From a single remaining patch of scalp, the long, blood-soaked hair had been tied to yet another peg to keep the skinned head from lolling.

"This is evil, Aunt."

"What does Piasa say? He's still whispering to your souls, isn't he?"

"Cold terror, Aunt. That's all I feel." She turned half-frantic eyes toward Blue Heron. "All the Powers in the Underworld are shaken." Her delicate brow lined. "Do you understand what that means? Do you understand what kind of evil is loose among us when it's scaring Piasa, Horned Serpent, and the Tie Snakes? Even the souls of the dead are shivering and cringing." She fought tears. "Who can do that, Aunt? Who has that kind of Power?"

The Red Wing, his expression grim, said, "Someone possessed of a terrible hate."

"You, Red Wing?" Blue Heron asked, a desperate hope welling in her breast.

He shook his head, a flicker of pity there as he studied what had been done to Heavy Cane. "My hatred for the Four Winds Clan was born fully formed and true. Whoever did this? His hatred was born malformed, demented, and twisted with soul disease. As much as he hates you, he hates himself, and all of existence even more."

"I suppose you'd be an expert on that," Blue Heron scoffed.

"Keeper, only someone who once loved with all his heart could come to hate you this poisonously."

Blue Heron took a deep breath, unable to stop the shiver that ran through her. The Red Wing's words might have cut her like a lash, but to Night Shadow Star they came as a physical blow. She would have collapsed had not the Red Wing caught her.

"Call for oil," Night Shadow Star's voice had changed, gone hollow and coarse, as it did when she was possessed by the Piasa. "Burn this place. Burn it now."

"We should inform the Morning Star before we—"

"I said, *burn it!*"

Then, in a weaker voice, she whispered, "Not Lace. Tell me he doesn't have Lace."

"Well, she's not here. Perhaps she escaped. Like you did the night they attacked you. She's just as smart—"

"Her terror whispers on the night wind, Aunt. I can feel him, ecstatic, joyous, and earth and sky tremble." Night Shadow Star looked sick. "Red Wing? I need to leave here. Take me home." And to Blue Heron's surprise, she added, "Please."

★ ★ ★

Fire Cat stepped in out of the rain and found Night Shadow Star's diminished household staff huddled on blankets, eyes downcast. They looked any direction but toward him as he stopped long enough to pick up a piece of firewood and toss it on the dying flames in the central hearth.

Since the night he'd been captured, it seemed that there was no end to the spiraling madness. Not even the stories the barbarians told around northern winter fires of the Windigo could have prepared him for the impossibility of his current situation.

He straightened and walked back to Night Shadow Star's sleeping quarters. He paused at the half-open door, calling, "Lady?"

"What is happening?" she demanded, a flat tone of defeat in her voice.

He stepped into her room, glancing at the small hickory oil lamp, its wick supporting a single wavering flame. She sat on her bed, legs drawn up to support her chin, her arms wound around her shins. The way her long black hair had fluffed out in the damp air seemed to frame her face. Her eyes appeared larger, darker, like bottomless pools that overshadowed her delicate chin, pursed full lips, and straight nose.

The sight of her stopped him short, stirring conflicting emotions within his breast. The image she conjured was of vulnerable beauty and femininity. Had he not known her, the impulse would have been to pull her close as he placed protective arms around her.

A response totally at odds with good sense given the influence of the Underworld creature that he knew hovered near her souls. Or the fact that she was a participating member of her pit-viper's nest of family, drowning as it was, in blasphemy. If only someone else could have been inside that magnificent, charming, and sensual body.

"Lace's palace is burning like a torch. Middle of the night like this, raining like it is, no alarm has been raised. The Keeper should be most of the way up the stairs to the Morning Star's palace. Assuming she hasn't slipped on the slick wood and tumbled . . ." He winced, immediately regretting the words.

"I suspect she's more sure of foot than you give her credit for, Red Wing." Night Shadow Star narrowed an eye as she shot him a hard look.

"The *Tonka'tzi* has already made the climb. She'll be made aware of your sister's disappearance—and what has happened—as soon as the Keeper can tell her."

Night Shadow Star's full lips twitched as if unspoken words lay behind them. Once again, her eyes fixed on the distance, visualizing something beyond the limits of this time and place. "For a lying Red Wing, you have a way of speaking truth."

"It might have only been wishful thinking that the Keeper had slipped on the stairs."

"I was referring to what you said in Lace's room. To hate someone that much, and that violently, you once had to have loved them."

"Something like that." He paused. "Who loved the Four Winds that much? Unless you're Four Winds, most people seem to bear a distinct dislike."

He saw the barest reflection of pain in the set of her mouth, her gaze growing even more distant.

For long moments he stood there, silent, leaving her to roam the visions and memories in her head.

Finally she took a deep breath, a decision behind her eyes. "I need you to stand watch for me, Red Wing."

"Stand watch? You think the monster is coming for you next?"

She nodded absently. "If I'm right, he has to. But it won't be tonight. No, I need to dance with Sister Datura, I need her to help me see."

"See what?"

"If I am right."

"About?"

"About who the monster is." She extended her long legs and stood from the bed, her hair falling over her shoulders like a mantle. "I need you to ensure that no one enters to slit my throat, and to call for Rides-the-Lightning if I lose my way back to my body."

Standing face-to-face, he gave her a crooked grin. "You're entrusting your life to me? Talk about a twisted and knotted understanding of the way things are."

She gave him a conspiratorial smile, one filled with a sad irony only he could comprehend. "Maybe you'll discover that you're not the kind of man you think you are, Red Wing. You can cut my throat yourself, knowing when my body's found he'll get the blame. It will be easy to vanish into the night never to be heard from again. Maybe you'll give in to your brutish male needs and rape me while I'm helpless? You'll have ample opportunity to determine the best way to avenge yourself and redeem Red Wing honor."

Her eyebrow raised in challenge.

Fire Cat took a deep breath and shook his head. "How do I tell if you can't get your souls back from the Underworld? I'm not a priest."

"If I stop breathing? Well, that's usually a big clue. Assuming you're not occupied stroking your rod to relieve your unfulfilled fantasies, or sound asleep when it happens."

"Hadn't thought of the former. But then, I haven't seen a woman whose charms are worthy of a real man's fantasies since I was taken from Red Wing town. In the end, I guess if your souls are lost in the Underworld for more than a day or two, you'll eventually figure out I let you down."

He could see the anger stirring behind her eyes, and said, "Good. Keep that rage. Hold on to it and use it like a weapon. I don't know much about soul-flying Spirit journeys, but you've got a lot better chance of getting back when you're mad than afraid."

A flicker of a smile crossed her lips. She glanced away, then stepped over to one of the immaculately carved wooden boxes. Lifting the lid she reached in and removed a small brownware jar.

Setting it on the floor before the altar, she shook her hair back and undid the clasps at her shoulder. Her dress slipped down her athletic body.

Despite his taunts to the contrary, he wondered: How could a woman that perfect, sensuous, and gorgeous be home to such tortured and angry souls? And what was it in a man's make-up that he could desire her so desperately at the same time he'd have liked nothing better than to drive a stiletto into her heart?

Reconciliation of opposites? Wasn't that what the priests called it? And wasn't that what he and Night Shadow Star were all about? Some curious mix, thrown together by Power in a misguided attempt at saving the world?

He watched her drop to her knees before the altar with its mirror-black well pot. She bowed her head, her fluffy black hair gleaming in the lamplight as it cascaded down her back to the twin globes of her rump. Almost reluctantly she extended her long fingers into the brownware pot and dipped out the greasy contents. She was praying under her breath as she rubbed the compound into her temples.

Taking a deep breath, she bowed her head over the well pot to stare down into its depths. Fire Cat slipped out of the doorway, and walked across the main room to the corner. There he knew a box of Makes Three's old weapons were stored.

Dragging it out into the firelight, he opened the lid. One by one, he removed the contents. When he'd made his selection he returned the box to its place, settled the slightly-too-large armor on his shoulders, clapped the leather helmet to his head, and strung the heavy war bow. The quiver full of arrows, he set beside her door along with a leather-bound wicker shield he took down from the wall. When he checked, she was still singing softly to herself, staring intently into the well pot.

"All right, Lady," he muttered to himself, "when you come back to your body, let's see who's more disgusted that I'm still here. You? Or me?"

Hate her, he might, but after what he'd seen in Lace's sleeping quarters? The monster might indeed try to get Night Shadow Star. Pray he wouldn't be coming tonight.

Forty-two

The way Smooth Pebble was looking at Seven Skull Shield, he wasn't sure if it was outright hatred, or just simple loathing. The *berdache* had suggestively placed a war club just inside the door, but whether it was to intimidate him, or Black Swallow and his crew, he just couldn't be sure.

Or maybe it was the song they were singing that upset her. To occupy themselves as they waited on the Keeper's veranda they'd been singing the song called "Woman with a Cactus-Lined Sheath." An old Trader's song about . . . Well, the title actually did a pretty good job of describing the lyrics.

Why would Smooth Pebble care? She was *berdache*, and didn't have a sheath, let alone one lined with cactus spines. And, well, it was just a song, right?

"Is that her?" Mud Foot asked. He pointed beyond the veranda's drip line.

The song died away as they all climbed to their feet and stared at the warriors surrounding Blue Heron's litter. The Keeper was born through the gray morning drizzle. A rain shield consisting of a square of matting on extended poles was being held over her by slaves following along behind.

"That's her," Seven Skull Shield agreed. He stepped out into the mist, bowed at the two guardian posts depicting fierce-looking birds, then made his way down the steps to where the canoe lay at the foot of the stairs. The craft was a pretty thing, thin-walled and light, and capable of seating four. He wondered if its owner had discovered it was missing yet.

Black Swallow and the others descended to stand behind him as the squadron second marched up and gave Seven Skull Shield and his companions a suspicious squint.

"Greetings, War Claw," Seven Skull Shield touched his chin. "Yes, yes. I know. But this riff-raff is with me. We've got something for the Keeper."

War Claw glanced around, gestured for his men to scatter and search the premises. Seven Skull Shield was surprised to see four grim-faced warriors trot up the stairs and into the palace, war clubs in hand, shields forward, as if expecting an ambush. Perhaps Smooth Pebble was more dangerous with a stew kettle than he'd thought?

"Don't know how you scored such a win, thief. Weaseling your way in here," War Claw muttered. "You know, the Keeper trusts you. I'd be very unhappy if I discovered that trust was misplaced."

Black Swallow, who never took threats well, was giving the squadron second a predatory look as the man walked off. Seven Skull Shield gave him a "be patient" gesture. He looked back in time to see a couple of warriors rush out of the palace, bending their heads to discuss something with War Claw.

Meanwhile, Blue Heron's litter was brought up and lowered by her wet and shivering porters. Seven Skull Shield stepped forward and took her hand, helping her to her feet. The look she gave him sent a spear through his breast. Instead of her normal plotting, composure, the woman looked exhausted, frightened, and defeated.

"What happened?" he asked.

"They got my niece, Lace, last night." She swallowed hard, fighting for control. "*Right under our noses!* Murdered most of her household . . . and what they did to her husband? An abomination of death and disrespect! I had it burned, all of it. Didn't you see the fire?"

"We only arrived a hand of time ago, Keeper." He glanced toward Lace's palace, hidden as it was in the misty gray predawn. "She dead?"

"Worse. Missing." She gestured futility as War Claw came hurrying down the stairs. "We've organized search parties. Warriors are scouring in all directions."

"Keeper?" War Claw called, still shooting suspicious glances at Black Swallow and his muddy henchmen. "There's a man just inside the door on your floor, tied and gagged."

She glanced at Seven Skull Shield, her haggard eyes lacking the sharp inquisitiveness. "Is it him?"

"Sorry, Keeper," Seven Skull Shield told her. "Just a Tula. But before you go see him, I need you to look at this canoe. Tell me what a wonderful thing it is, inspect it carefully. Then I need you to have Smooth Pebble bring down some very valuable Trade for Black Swallow and his men, here."

For a moment she fixed her bloodshot and fragile eyes on his. "And why am I wasting my time looking at some pus-rotted canoe?"

"If you're carrying a captured bound-and-gagged Tula from River Mounds to the Keeper's palace, and you know that the scorpion is watching, can you think of a better way to transport him here in secret than hidden inside a canoe?"

"A Tula, you say?" She seemed numb.

"He's in the house. I admit, he's a little worse for wear. I think he can still talk. But he only speaks Caddo. I need good old War Claw, here, to slip off and let that Yellow Star war second know that we need him to *carefully* and *unobtrusively* make his way here on some pretext that won't get him killed."

"Do it," she ordered War Claw. "And after I look at this canoe—"

"And ooh and ah over it."

"And ooh and ah over it." She hesitated, glancing at Black Swallow and his ruffians. "Why am I giving valuable Trade to Black Swallow and . . . Isn't he the one who's fingers I—"

"We're referring to that as an unfortunate misunderstanding," Seven Skull Shield told her pointedly. "One that we all wish to, um, make amends for."

She narrowed a hard eye at him, worked her jaws, and hissed some curse under her breath. "He and his dark-shadow stranglers had better be worth it."

Seven Skull Shield gave her a flat-lipped smile, then said, "Lady, had it been anybody but me"—he jerked a thumb at Black Swallow and the rest—"and without them, our scorpion would have covered his tracks completely, stymied you again, and denied us even this advantage."

"But you got one?" she asked, finally realizing what it might mean.

"I got one. But I learned something in the process."

"What?"

"I learned just how smart and cunning your scorpion beast is."

"I think we've been underestimating him all along," she agreed sadly. "Tell me? Do you think we can win?"

"After yesterday? I don't know, Keeper. I really don't know."

Forty-three

As Night Shadow Star stared into the depths of the well pot, she could feel Sister Datura's first gentle caress as it flitted lightly around her souls.

Beneath the reflective surface, the black water shimmered and stirred. Invisible threads of Power undulated in the depths. Fragments of images formed then turned liquid and faded. Any perception of time dwindled into the eternal now. Subtle currents drew her down, wafting her first this way and then the other.

Sister Datura's embracing arms tightened as she swayed in time with Night Shadow Star's souls. Twirling slowly, they began the dance, bobbing and dipping, rising and whirling in the perpetual descent into iridescent midnight. Matching each beat of her heart, the darkness pulsed. With the drawing of a breath, it seemed to expand, to fill the universe, only to contract as she exhaled. The endless depths had become a living presence that surrounded and flowed through her.

The fragments of images, sights, faces, visions of the past, snatches of conversation, broken laughter, shattered weeping, spun themselves from nothingness, only to vanish without coherence. . . .

She felt herself settle, rocking slightly on some soft surface resembling sandy mud. Though in darkness, she had vague impressions of being at a junction.

Whichever direction she looked, it was to see yet another shadowy cave vanishing into obscurity.

Something moved to her right, and an impossibly huge snapping turtle rose from the mud. As it lifted its bulk, streamers of sand flowed from the beast's shell to ripple and flow in patterns. Moss and silt clung to the arching carapace. The thing's plated head, with its hard angles, extended to fix her with questioning eyes, the round pupils expanding in black interest.

"He'll be coming." As it spoke the turtle's sharp jaws barely moved. The great head drifted toward her, moss waving on the beast's blocky shell. She shivered in fear as the two nostrils at the point of its snout took her scent.

"You're still alive," Snapping Turtle noted, slightly surprised.

Night Shadow Star tried to swallow, only to choke. Sister Datura's arms tightened around her, squeezing with each terrified beat of her heart.

"Ah." Snapping Turtle's head cocked slightly. "You dance with Power. But it does not calm your fears. Were you summoned here?"

"No."

Snapping Turtle lifted his head slightly, turning it to stare closely at her with one eye. "Courageous . . . to come on your own. Walk unprotected into *his* domain." A pause. "Tell me, Lady of Cahokia, did the Water Panther choose well? Are you the one we need? You? Barely more than a spoiled child, weeping and heartbroken over a too-soon-dead husband? Courageous, yes, but drowning in self-pity, grief, and undirected rage. Why are you even here? Why not simply walk out of your splendid palace and surrender yourself to the inevitable? An abomination hunts you, and he will get you in the end."

Snapping Turtle's jaws gaped like a sick grin. "Capture would be excruciating, but the pain would be over in a day or two. The woman you are now—possessed by Spirits, hearing voices, afraid, and insecure—might live what? Another fifty or sixty summers? And all of it in slow pain and mindless terror, forever convinced that those around you are plotting, seeking to destroy you. As the years pass, you'll fall deeper and deeper into despair and self-inflicted misery. The voices will grow louder, and you'll beg for Piasa to end it once and for all."

He snapped his jaws like shears. "But by then, you'll be so pathetic he'll turn away, unwilling to lower himself even to the point of sullying his talons with the stroke it would take to end your pathetic life."

Night Shadow Star whimpered, curling in on herself as Sister Datura's arms wound around her like vines of light.

The voice came from behind her. "Snapping Turtle always expects the worst."

Night Shadow Star turned, heart hammering; a giant coiling serpent filled the cave behind her. How could such an enormous creature have crept up so soundlessly? She'd felt not a tremor, nor so much as a whisper of its presence. The snake—its body thick as a canoe and as long as a chunkey court—had a head the size of a small boulder. Glassy scarlet antlers rose from the beast's shimmering head; wings, graced with barred-and-spotted feathers, sprouted from the center of its back. The scales gleamed metallically, glowing with every color of the rainbow. Between the diamond-hatched patterns running down its body, the black circles on its sides seemed to be depthless, as if they were portals into eternity. Rattles the size of pumpkins tipped the mighty beast's tail. But most terrifying of all were the crystalline eyes that fixed on her. She flinched when the forked tongue flicked in and out.

Night Shadow Star gasped, backing away until she felt Snapping Turtle's wedge of a nose against her back. The great turtle hissed in irritation.

"Horned Serpent," she whispered, a coldness settling in her bones.

In the pantheon of the Underworld, Piasa, the Water Panther, and Horned Serpent, the winged snake, were adversaries. Governed only by First Woman, who dreamed the world from her cave beneath the World Tree's roots, the two Spirit beasts constantly vied with each other for dominance.

"You carry Piasa's stink, woman." Horned Serpent inspected her with crystal eyes the size of plates, each surrounded by the three-forked design of the underworld. "Four Winds Clan. What's left of the Sky Moiety, victors in the great civil wars fought for control of Cahokia. And you've brought us to this."

"I smell ignorance inside her." Snapping Turtle spoke from just behind Night Shadow Star's head. "She truly doesn't know."

"Know what?" Night Shadow Star whimpered as Sister Datura's grasp tightened in time to her fear.

Horned Serpent replied, "That you have done this to our world. Your Four Winds Clan. And your family in particular. You have meddled in what you should never have contemplated. You have dared to attempt, and succeeded in a thing that should have horrified you. You have rent the world asunder and changed everything."

"I don't understand," she whispered, fear running bright through her.

Horned Serpent hissed the words. "Spirit possession runs in the Four Winds Clan. But most particularly in your lineage. The mad evil of Tharon? That perversion came of drinking galena tea. But you and your family? The madness lies in the blood, passed from one generation to the next. It infects the male seed and lurks in the wombs of the women. The brilliance that allowed Black Tail to overthrow Petaga and defeat the Dreamer Lichen? It was driven by the Spirit voices that whispered between his souls. They drove him to attempt the impossible and recall the Morning Star's souls from the Sky World.

"The voices skipped your father's generation, leaving Red Warrior, your aunts and uncle only the cunning brilliance. But it was reborn in you and your brothers with a vengeance. You hear voices from a world not your own, and it incites you to madness."

"And Lace and Sun Wing?"

Horned Serpent's crystalline eyes glowed from within. "Your sisters do not concern us."

She saw a flicker from the corner of her eye, felt Piasa's presence as what seemed a blur materialized into the Water Panther. His wings spread wide and radiated a bluish light. Hard yellow eyes fixed on hers, the whiskers quivering as he flexed his eagle-taloned feet. The snake's tail lashed back and forth in either irritation or threat. A cerulean ripple ran across the Spirit beast's fur as he bared white curving fangs in a feline snarl.

"We've done her no harm," Snapping Turtle said. "Yet."

Piasa arched his back, head cocked. "Then you understand her value?"

"If she's the one." Horned Serpent's head remained motionless while his body slipped sideways as if in preparation to strike.

"She's broken," Snapping Turtle insisted. "A whimpering, grieving shell. She couldn't even endure her husband's death without sending her souls into our realm in search of him. How do you expect her to find enough courage to defeat the abomination?"

Horned Serpent had fixed his crystalline eyes on Piasa; his tongue flicked out like a forked black whip, before he said, "She reeks of pity and privilege. Her Spirit possession will lead her to self-inflicted misery in the end. She knows this . . . knows she's different. Nor can she bear the fact that she shattered like a dropped pot, ran to the women's house, and afterward, married the only man she knew would never question the voices, or the events of that day. Look into her soul, Piasa. She's hidden the memory of what they did to her, covered it over as if it were a mold-ridden seed cache that could be sealed away with a layer of hard-packed clay."

Piasa stepped close, his terrible yellow eyes burning into Night Shadow Star's. "You know who the abomination is, don't you? I can see the cracks in your souls. Tendrils of memory from that day are filtering through you. It's been bubbling up in your dreams. Appearing as nightmares that you refuse to believe to be real."

She bowed her head, wrapping her arms over her breasts. "I . . . I . . ."

The images came reeling up, memories, the physical sensation of hands on her body, of his eyes. That was the worst. His eyes seemed to expand, filling the entire world as hungry hands slipped along her skin. Then came the feel of soft fur beneath her back. His weight slammed down, his knee like a wedge between her legs.

His eyes became the universe. His black pupils burned into her, violating, piercing, penetrating her shivering souls. . . .

She opened her mouth, but no scream came from her paralyzed lungs.

Forty-four

Blue Heron yawned and tried to collect her sleep-muddled thoughts. Her dreams had been nightmares, and in them she kept discovering Lace's mutilated body pinned to the wall of a filthy hut, swarming with flies and crawling with maggots. She pinched her eyes shut in an attempt to force the details from her souls.

She sat in her bed, a blanket around her hips. The cup of black drink Blue Heron cradled in her hands sent warmth through her stiff fingers. Her cup was a traditional Cahokian design, the handle sticking out from the side like a yearling buffalo bull's horn. An image of the sun decorated the outside.

She sipped, thankful for the bitter richness of the black drink. Smooth Pebble had brewed it strong, boiling the yaupon leaves into a foam before allowing it to steep.

"Feeling better?" Smooth Pebble asked as Blue Heron tossed her blanket aside and lowered her feet to the floor.

She yawned again, blinked, and took another sip of the hot tea before she said, "I needed the nap. Any news on Lace?"

"No. They are turning Cahokia upside down, but there is so much to search."

"What about the Caddo? Is the Yellow Star sub-chief here?"

"He made it safely, Lady. He and the thief have been adding to the

Tula's unease. The captive knows that they're biding their time, that whatever comes, it won't be pleasant."

Long association and familiarity told Blue Heron that Smooth Pebble was hiding something. She narrowed her eyes. "How long did I sleep? Tell me the truth. You know I'll find out."

"It's afternoon, Keeper." Smooth Pebble averted her eyes. "Do not rage at me. You'd hardly have the wits, or ability, to outthink Lace's captor if you were stumbling around, sleep-stupid, and with your eyes swollen half-shut from fatigue."

"You take chances, *berdache*." Blue Heron tried to force all the threat she could muster into her voice, knowing all the while that Smooth Pebble was probably correct. Not that it eased her guilt.

Please, Niece, be safe. We're coming.

She drank down the last of the hot tea, used her chamber pot, and tried to pull the wrinkles out of her woven-hemp skirt. For the sake of propriety, she draped a blue bird-feathered cape over her shoulders, and allowed Smooth Pebble to fix her hair into a copper-pinned bun. Squaring her shoulders, she nodded, and Smooth Pebble opened her door.

Blue Heron retrieved the cloth-wound bundle where it rested atop one of her boxes, and walked out into the main room. The warm air was heavy with the smells of roast venison and baking squash. Her household slaves went about their usual tasks, clearly curious about her entrance, and what it meant for the captive where he lay trussed beside the door.

Seven Skull Shield stood over the bound Tula, arms crossed, his hunting shirt bloodstained and filthy. His forehead was swollen and black with bruise. Takes Horn Fivekiller rose, bowed, and touched his chin as she walked up. The Yellow Star war second had stuck a couple of eagle feathers in the tightly wound bun atop his head. Several shell necklaces hung down on his muscular brown chest, and he wore an apron decorated with embroidery of the Hero Twins dancing around the World Tree.

"Forgive me," she said irritably. "Smooth Pebble takes too many liberties with my schedule."

Seven Skull Shield, lout that he was, grinned insolently. "Keeper, trust me, you needed the sleep. The way you dragged in just before dawn? You looked like the kind of refuse desperate dogs might have scratched out of a trash midden."

She narrowed an eye, hissing, "And you take too many liberties with your guileless tongue, thief."

His grin just widened. "Of course, I do. But down deep, a part of you enjoys the fact that at least someone is willing to talk to you like a friend."

"The last thing I need is a common thief for a friend."

Seven Skull Shield screwed his expression into feigned complacency and said, "If I were a common thief, I'd be lying dead in a blind passage in River Mound City with one of old Gray Mouse's arrows sticking through my heart. And trust me, Keeper, the trap the scorpion laid was a good one. Layers within layers, carefully baited. Had it worked, it was designed to not only take out any opponent clever enough to sniff out his escape route, but to keep you off balance when yet another of the few people you can depend on was eliminated."

She glanced at Takes Horn Fivekiller, who stood with arms crossed, his tattooed face impassive. To the side, one of his translators was whispering her and Seven Skull Shield's words to him in Caddo.

To Seven Skull Shield, she said, "But you spotted the trap?"

He spread his hands as if in mock surrender. "I've been hunted by the best, Keeper. Angry husbands, jealous Traders, offended rivals, incompetent fools I just couldn't help but cheat. I am so misunderstood . . . and by so many."

"Get to the point," she snapped.

"The Tula was good. He'd have fooled anyone who was half blind, from out of town, or just plain dumb."

"So you set him up?" She stared down at the Tula, wrapped up in rope as if he were a fish. "What happened to his lip?" Blue Heron's expression soured. What remained of the man's face was a mess. Pale red fluids drained from the wreckage of his eye socket. The nose was swollen, misshapen, and turning black. But that lip? It sent a shiver through her.

"Um, I think it was bitten."

"Can he even talk?" the translator asked for Takes Horn.

"Ask him."

Takes Horn bent down, staring into the Tula's pain-slitted eye. With great deliberation he began speaking.

The translator said, "He asks if the Tula can understand him. It's a misleading question since Tula speak perfect Caddo."

The Tula nodded.

"Can you talk?"

The Tula's voice slurred, and he winced at the movement of his savagely torn and swollen lip and cheek.

The translator said, "The Tula says he thinks so."

Takes Horn continued, the translator repeating, "Who do you work for?" A pause as the Tula answered. "He says he serves the sorcerer." Another pause as Takes Horn questioned. "The Tula says the sorcerer is here to unleash great magic. He will uproot Cahokia the way a tornado does a giant oak. And the Tula says he does not fear death, for the sorcerer will recall his life-souls from the land of the dead and install them into other peoples' bodies. He says he's seen the sorcerer do this. This makes him happy, because the body he now has is damaged, but he will be resurrected in a new body after his death."

Takes Horn asked something else.

The translator took up the Tula's words. "He says he will say no more. He asks that you kill him now."

Blue Heron unwound the cloth from the beautifully chipped blade the assassin had tried to use on her throat. The Tula's eye widened, and he gasped, then winced at the pain it caused him.

"Ask him where this came from," she told the translator.

"He says he will speak no more. Use the blade and kill him."

Takes Horn glanced up at Blue Heron. "I know a way to make him talk. Do you have a drill? The kind a wood or shell worker would use? And I'll need a spindle whorl. The common kind for spinning buffalo wool or yarn."

"And what would a drill and whorl gain us that a sharp knife would not?" she asked.

"Your sorcerer has convinced Bleeding Hawk, here, that once he dies, his souls will be resurrected into a new body." Takes Horn shot a sidelong glance at the thief. "Since Seven Skull Shield has made rather a mess of this one, that new body is now rather appealing. But he's a Tula, Lady. Torture will not work. The more you hurt him, the more he'll laugh because it proves his courage and endurance. Tula, however, are superstitious and do have fears that will unnerve them. They can be manipulated by playing on those fears, just as this 'sorcerer' has discovered."

"Find a drill," Blue Heron told Smooth Pebble. The *berdache* slung a cape around her broad shoulders and was out the door.

"And just what are you going to do with the drill and spindle whorl?" Seven Skull Shield asked, sidling over to extract a boiled ear of corn from a cooling pot. Obviously he'd been waiting for Smooth Pebble to leave. Before Blue Heron could say anything, he'd sank his teeth into the kernels.

To Blue Heron's amazement, Smooth Pebble was back—just that quick—a lapidary's drill clutched in her hands. Takes Horn accepted it with a smile. Smooth Pebble noticed the corn, gave Seven Skull Shield a reprehensible scowl, then went to one of the storage boxes under Mica's sleeping bench. She opened it and retrieved a spindle whorl.

The Tula was watching through his single pain-crazed eye.

"Seven Skull Shield, I will need you to hold his head." Takes Horn said, then glanced at Smooth Pebble. "Keep the spindle whorl at hand where he can see it."

Seven Skull Shield had laid his dripping corn on the closest bench and now hunkered down, his knees on either side of the Tula's head. The man tried to flop, but the rope windings made it futile.

Smooth Pebble prominently displayed the spindle whorl: little more than a ceramic disk on a pointed stick as long as her forearm.

"What does this gain us?" Blue Heron asked.

Nodding to the translator, Takes Horn bent down over the squirming Tula and spoke in Caddo, the translator repeating, "We're going to drill a hole in his head. And with the spindle whorl, we're going to use ancient Cahokian magic to draw his life and body souls out of his head the way a root is pulled out of moist dirt. Then we're going to place his terrified souls in an enchanted well pot, and bury it beneath the corpses of four decapitated snakes. Locked away, imprisoned so, the souls will wail in terror and blackness forever."

The Tula's eye was flicking back and forth, a panicked whimper tore from his throat. Seven Skull Shield clamped the man's head between his knees. Takes Horn leaned forward and placed the drill tip against the Tula's forehead. The captive tried to swallow, but choked on his fear. He coughed, blowing clots of coagulated blood from his nose and tearing part of his lip loose. The howl in his throat sounded like a wounded dog's.

"You can stop this," Takes Horn said reasonably. "Who is the sorcerer? What is his name?"

The Tula gasped for breath. The translator filled in when Bleeding Hawk finally spoke. "He is called the Two-Footed Smoke. He came to us demonstrating great Power."

"Came from where?"

The Tula narrowed his eye. "He is Cahokian, but lived among the Yellow Star for a time."

"And that's why he had you kill the *amayxoya*? Because the war chief knew him?"

The Tula tried to sneer, but it pulled at his bleeding and ruined lip. "My master's arrow killed the Yellow Star pollution. So great is his

Power he walks among you like a winter mist. But you do not see him. He hears your words, though you do not speak to him. Your hearts are like fresh tracks in the forest to him. Laughing, he will destroy you all."

"Tell me about this knife." Blue Heron held the slim and delicate blade before the Tula's eye. He averted his gaze, tried to clench his jaws, despite the pain.

Takes Horn pressed against the drill and began to turn.

"It was Bobcat's!" came the translation.

"And do you have a blade like this?"

He nodded, glanced at the spindle whorl, closed his eye in defeat. "I gave it to the Deer Chief."

"What Deer Chief?"

"The one up on the bluffs. The one with the wounded hand. Two-Footed Smoke, the great sorcerer, owns that one's souls. What the Deer Chief did with my blade, I do not know."

Blue Heron felt her heart skip. "The wounded hand? It is his right? And he has a scar here, on his chin?" She pointed.

"That is him."

"Was a woman with him? Older, with snakes tattooed on her back, arms, and chest?"

"Yes." The translator gave her a sidelong glance.

Blue Heron sank to the bench beside Seven Skull Shield's half-chewed ear of corn. She should have suspected, but over the years Right Hand had never given so much as a hint of his resentment.

"What's this about?" Seven Skull Shield asked, reading her shock and dismay.

"Nothing that concerns you." She gestured. "Go ahead, Takes Horn. Keep him talking. Ask him where they've taken Lace."

Takes Horn lifted the drill to the Tula's head again, preparing to spin it. As he did he asked something in Caddo.

"I do not know where the Two-Footed Smoke has taken your woman!" the Tula cried. "This I swear upon my umbilical cord! And my father's umbilical cord! We only serve! And then only at his orders!"

"Umbilical cords?" Seven Skull Shield asked.

"Tula believe it is the most Powerful talisman," Takes Horn told him. "They think it controls the length and quality of their lives. Each warrior takes his cord and hides it in a secret place, knowing that as long as it remains hidden, his souls are safe."

"Until you drill a hole in his head and draw them out with a spindle whorl?" Blue Heron countered, still stunned at the Tula's revelation.

Right Hand? I never would have guessed.

"Ask him if he has any idea why Lace was taken."

The answer translated as, "The sorcerer needs her for the ceremony. Like the one he conducted in the Deer Chief's land on the bluff. The final ceremony. The one where he unleashes the greatest of Powers. That will be the day he brings devastation to Cahokia. He has told us that even First Woman will tremble at his feet."

"Bah!" Seven Skull Shield growled, "As if anyone could conjure *that*!"

"Where are the rest of the Tula?" Takes Horn asked.

"You do not want to find them. They will kill you, Yellow Star."

The drill was placed to the Tula's forehead, and this time, Takes Horn actually had to begin grinding it into bone before the Tula wailed, "The warehouse! Just west of where the thief caught me. Some chief owns it!"

"War Duck?" she asked, and the name was translated.

"The fool sells us his warehouse even as we work toward his destruction!" The Tula's frantic eye darted back and forth. "But you are too late! Two-Footed Smoke is drawing in the strands of Power that will trap you all! There is nothing for you, only death from which you will never be resurrected!"

Forty-five

A half-throttled shriek brought Fire Cat fully awake. He'd dropped down to sit propped in Night Shadow Star's doorway, a position where no one could pass. That he had fallen asleep was a sign of how weary he'd become.

Now he winced as he raised himself, seeing slanting daylight from a high sun through the gaps in the door. The household staff was huddled in a far corner, doing something on the matting. Gambling with gaming pieces, he realized. And probably hoping all the while that their lady had fallen into an endless slumber and would never come back to order them around.

A croaking sound reminded him of what had brought him awake. He winced and stood as his cramped and stiff muscles complained. The armor had bitten into his flesh, and now prickled where blood flowed.

He stepped into her room, peering down in the gloom. She lay curled on the floor before the altar. He'd thrown a blanket over her in the night, but it lay twisted into a knot at one side.

The choking sound was barely audible now. Her mouth was open, lungs sucking desperately for air she couldn't find.

Bending down he lifted her limp head, seeing her eyes rolled back behind slitted lids. Her frantic mouth struggled for air.

"Lady? Wake up. You're not breathing."

Her lungs continued to heave. He pulled her long hair back, ensuring that nothing was tied around her throat.

"Night Shadow Star! Wake up." He shifted her onto his lap, patting the soft curve of her cheek. Her entire body now jerked in the battle for breath. But what on earth was restricting her airway?

"I said, *wake up!*" He slapped her hard enough to send a tremor through her.

At the sound of voices behind him, he turned, seeing the wide-eyed household staff.

"Green Stick! Go! Fetch Rides-the-Lightning. Get him here! But by the souls in your body, do it with discretion. I don't want half the city running here to gawk and gossip. Do you understand me?"

The man nodded, stopped short, and cocked his head. "Who are *you* to order me around? You're nothing but a slave yourself."

Like a striking copperhead, Fire Cat shifted Night Shadow Star from his lap, leaped, and clamped a hard hand around Green Stick's throat. As the man clawed to get free, Fire Cat lifted him until he perched on tiptoes. Glaring into the slave's frightened eyes, Fire Cat said through gritted teeth, "When I give you an order, you piece of two-legged shit, you obey. Now, get your limp and dragging self to Rides-the-Lightning, and get him here without alerting half the town. If she dies in the meantime, I'll cut you apart to feed the crows!"

With that he turned the man loose, and bent back to Night Shadow Star. The woman's gasping attempts to breathe were weakening; her eyes quivered in panic behind twitching lids. The way her mouth opened and closed reminded him of a dying fish.

"What are you going to do?" one of the slave women asked.

"Save her . . . I hope." But how?

He hesitated, uneasy at laying hands on her naked body, then placed both of his palms on her breast bone and pushed down.

A gurgling came from deep in her throat, but nothing seemed to dislodge. He could feel the frantic beat of her heart as it hammered her rib cage.

"Come on, Lady. If you die on me, who will I have to hate?"

Growing frantic, he gave up pressing on her chest, shifted, and dragged her by the head onto his lap. Supporting the back of her neck with one hand, he pinched her nose shut, made a face, and took a deep breath.

Covering her mouth with his, he exhaled with all his might.

Something gave, her chest expanding. He pulled his head back, feeling her purling breath as she slowly exhaled and coughed. Her next breath was shallow, and rasped in her throat, but she was breathing.

Sighing relief, he laid her back on the floor, crouching so he could press down on her breastbone each time she exhaled. If he could just get the old air out of her, keep her breathing, at least she'd have a body for her souls to return to.

The frantic beat of her heart began to slow from a panicked race to normal.

"Well, at least now I know you've got a heart, black and wicked though it might be." He gave her a relieved smile.

He turned, ordering, "Someone, bring me water. A bottle-necked gourd will do."

Moments later young Winter Leaf cautiously stepped in to hand him a gourd. "You didn't mean that, did you? What you said to Green Stick?"

He glanced at her, at the rest of them, watching him like half-panicked field mice. "I meant it. When I give an order, you jump."

"I'm the Lady's cousin," the man called Clay String remarked haughtily. "I'm Four Winds Clan, slave. You try and order me around, and I'll have you in a square."

Fire Cat made a final check of Night Shadow Star, satisfied that she was still breathing normally. Then he rose and advanced on Clay String, who backed away unsteadily.

"You know what I think of the Four Winds Clan, you worthless excuse for a man?"

Clay String shook his head, still backing away, trying to keep his expression stern and commanding.

"I think they're trash, you gutless fish. And you can tell them so, because I've got nothing left to live for. That being the case, I will not grovel before you, *free* man. Or before any other Four Winds maggot." He thrust a hard finger toward Night Shadow Star's room. "But I gave my word to serve the Lady. So, serve her I will, and to the best of my ability. If it means breaking a couple of your worthless heads in the process, then by the bleeding stars, I will do so. And you, you wiggling little maggot, will accept it and like it."

Clay String's feigned resistance collapsed like a punctured bladder. His hands rose defensively. "Don't hurt me. I was just . . . I was . . ."

Fire Cat looked around at the rest. "Since Field Green was murdered, this place has started to look more like a weasel's den than the Lady's palace. Within the next hand of time, I want it straightened up, the bedding folded, the ashes taken out, the matting swept, and the dishes cleaned. I can smell that brimming chamber pot clear across the room.

"Meanwhile, I want a feast ready for when the Lady returns from her Spirit journey. Not that half-burned corn gruel you've got on the coals, but real food. And a pot will be kept boiling for black drink when she comes to." He paused, smiling grimly. "You've got a hand of time, get to it."

Then he walked back to ensure that Night Shadow Star hadn't relapsed. Behind him the room was bustling with activity.

Kneeling, he placed a finger on her smooth neck, feeling her pulse, weak, but there.

In a gentle voice he told her, "So there it is, *Lady.* I probably created a miserable mess for myself with your household staff, but they really need to be slapped into shape. If you want to save me any more such trouble, you'd better get back here so you can keep me in line, or I'll have half the Four Winds Clan trying to cut my throat." He paused, studying her vulnerable and slack face. "You wouldn't want that, now would you? You did want to save that privilege for yourself, didn't you?"

No change of expression darkened her smooth brow, so he sighed, patted her on the cheek, and lifted her naked body onto the bed where he should have put her in the first place. Then he settled himself beside her and studied the alluring charms of her round breasts. Her brown nipples seemed to tease him with their demand for attention. The swell of her hips and flat abdomen accented the dark shadow of her navel. He struggled to ignore the promise of what lay hidden beneath the thick black triangle of pubic hair.

"Power mocks me, Lady. I'd worship that body if it belonged to anyone but you." He shook his head to rid it of unwanted images and desires, and then carefully arranged a blanket to cover her. He gently tucked her in. Drawing his bow across his lap he fitted an arrow into place.

In addition to the assassin, he wouldn't put it past Green Stick or Clay String to sneak up behind him and bash his brains out.

"Good thing we dislike each other so much, Lady. I'd never put up with this nonsense if you were just someone I only mildly despised."

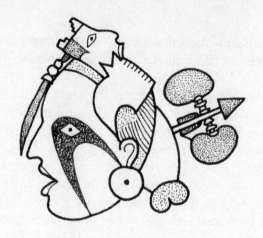

Forty-six

Seven Skull Shield entered through the Council House door and looked around. Stepping to the side, he crossed his arms and placed his back to the wall. He dabbed at his sore forehead, discolored from the bruises it had suffered while banging the Tula's face into pulp, and he'd strained a couple of muscles during the fight, but nothing that wouldn't heal.

Blue Heron sat on the raised dais beside *Tonka'tzi* Wind. The spoiled niece, Sun Wing, looked sullen where she sat on her floor-level litter to the right. Perhaps she appeared so petulant because—though another rival for the *Tonka'tzi*'s chair had conveniently vanished—the Keeper now occupied the spot she might have claimed for the first time in her short life.

Four Winds warriors, resplendent in waxed wooden armor, their shields at rest before them and war clubs at hand, lined the walls. The usual messengers and recorders were missing.

Tension, like a gut-string pulled too tight, vibrated in the room.

"Thief?" Blue Heron called as she looked up and recognized him. "Come forward."

He glanced sidelong at the warriors who were staring at him with hard eyes. Approaching the dais, he dropped to his knees and bowed his head just short of the matting. He did, after all, have a bruise to coddle. "You've really got to find a better way to address me at these things."

"And I suppose you'd have me call a fish a bird?" she asked caustically. "You are what you are."

He supposed it could be worse. She could have called him "tow rope," which he'd be hearing for the rest of his life.

She asked, "Why didn't you fetch Lady Night Shadow Star as I requested?"

Seven Skull Shield lifted his head, staring up at first the Keeper and then the *Tonka'tzi*. In a voice barely above a whisper, he said, "I was able, at least, to get in to see her. The Red Wing guards her well; he kept an arrow nocked the entire time I was there. Also present is the Earth Clans healer, Rides-the-Lightning." He could see them both pale as he added, "She's Spirit flying, sent her souls into the Underworld, according to the Red Wing."

Tonka'tzi Wind closed her eyes, looking both anxious and defeated at the same time.

"She doesn't know about her sister, then?" Blue Heron asked.

"Not from any source in this world. Though I did, however, shoo away the slaves and staff and inform the Red Wing."

"What possessed you to disclose information like that to a slave?" the *Tonka'tzi* asked.

He met her now glowering eyes. "With all respect, *Tonka'tzi*, half the city is abuzz. Armed squadrons now guard all the Four Winds palaces around the Grand Plaza. Lace's palace is the second Four Winds palace to burn in days. And warriors are searching the surroundings like ants through a garden. No one gets up or down the steps on the Morning Star's mound. Nor has the Morning Star been playing chunkey for the last few days . . . and the excuse that he's 'praying for the people' is about as thin as last week's rabbit stew. Maybe the Tula was right and this Two-Footed Smoke sorcerer can walk through walls, but the Red Wing, no matter what his other faults, has kept your daughter alive so far. And, it appears, he's rotted well determined to do it again. Maybe Piasa really did tell her to keep him close. Maybe it was one of her voices speaking from some bent need down in her souls. The girl's not quite right, we've all figured that out, yes? But the Red Wing's not going to let harm come to your niece."

"Watch your mouth, thief," the *Tonka'tzi* said coldly.

"It's all right," Blue Heron murmured. "To my discomfort and dismay I've actually come to appreciate someone who tells it straight."

Sun Wing whispered hotly, "And how will the Red Wing tell her about Lace when she finally comes back to her body? This is her sister, after all. Done incorrectly, it might shock her into some unwise action."

"No trace of where she vanished to, huh?" Seven Skull Shield asked.

"Not through the usual sources." Blue Heron narrowed an eye at him. "What did you hear from that weasel, Black Swallow?"

"That he received the shell carving you sent. I can repeat the fawning drivel he spewed to express his appreciation if you really want to hear it. But he's got the word out. And with the right parties."

"You've entrusted this to thieves and human garbage?" the *Tonka'tzi* gritted through her teeth, dismayed eyes on her sister.

Again Blue Heron lifted her hand, stilling the outburst.

Seven Skull Shield interjected, "If she's in the city, great *Tonka'tzi*, my 'thieves and human garbage' will find her within the next two days." He lightly touched his forehead, bowed his bruised forehead to the cane matting, and then backed away.

He could see the simmering anger in Sun Wing's eyes, and wondered what had kept her from using the opportunity to let her mouth overload any balance of spoiled sense she might have. The look she was giving him would have melted a siltstone ax head.

Squadron second War Claw picked that moment to march through the door, and behind him—followed by another six warriors—came two prisoners. From their clothing, they both appeared to be Deer Clan, and high ranking.

Right Hand and his sister Corn Seed.

"Oh, my," Seven Skull Shield murmured to himself. "We got two more before Two-Whatever-Smoke could silence them. The question, however, is if the scorpion is slipping? Are we finally ahead of him? Or were we supposed to capture these two and hear their confessions? Has he played them as well as he's played everything else to this point?"

Forty-seven

"I should have known when I pulled the broken knife edge from that poor woman's ruined sheath that day." Blue Heron watched the building terror in Corn Seed's face. "But, like everything else when it came to the two of you, I misread that entire event."

She lifted the knife they'd taken from Cut String, and raised it, seeing shock and defeat in Corn Seed's eyes. "Look familiar, does it?"

The Deer Clan matron dropped to her knees, then fell forward on her face, crying, "Clan Keeper, we had no idea! We thought he was just a Trader."

"Who?" *Tonka'tzi* Wind demanded. "What is his name? Where do we find him? Hidden in your territory? Butchering more poor immigrants as he tries to resurrect his dead Tula warriors?"

"We don't know. We called him the Whisperer," Right Hand declared, straightening. "We were as shocked as you when we saw what happened in that farmstead." He glanced down at his groveling sister. "It's my doing, *Tonka'tzi*. I dragged my sister into this. Our kinsmen, children, and the rest of Deer Clan have no knowledge of what I did. They remain loyal to the Morning Star and the Four Winds Clan. In fact, given the shame I've brought upon them, they would be harder on me than you will."

"Why?" Blue Heron asked, feeling sick. "What have we ever done to you?"

He looked around the room, lips curling at the irony, and said, "Keeper, I've always respected you and the *Tonka'tzi*. Because of that respect, I ask that you order the warriors out. Unless, of course, you want every gossip monger in the city wagging his tongue and repeating what I have to tell you. War Claw can stay, of course, and perhaps a handful of very, very trusted kin."

Blue Heron, heart like a stone in her chest, gestured it to be done; she watched the warriors file out, curiosity in their eyes. To her amusement, the notion of leaving hadn't even crossed Seven Skull Shield's mind. A look of animated anticipation filled the thief's face. On a hunch, she allowed him to stay.

"Speak," she ordered.

Right Hand, in the manner of a man with nothing to lose, studied her thoughtfully. Then he raised his maimed hand. "You remember how I got this?"

"Some fight with Chunkey Boy. I heard you made up afterward."

"Some . . . *fight*?" He wiggled his maimed hand. "I told him I would marry Night Shadow Star when she came of age. Corn Seed was first in line to become Clan Matron. I was going to be Deer Clan's high chief! A man worthy of Night Shadow Star's bed when she came of age. Nor was she opposed. You know. You were there. You supervised the negotiations between our clans. Your brother, the *Tonka'tzi*, communicated his approval of the marriage."

"Then, why did you back out?" *Tonka'tzi* Wind asked in fury.

"In private Chunkey Boy told me that I'd never marry his sister. He refused." Right Hand made a fist with his good left hand, shaking it in anger. "So I challenged him to chunkey. A match in which Power would decide. If I won, I would marry Night Shadow Star when she became a woman. And win that match I *did*!" he thundered.

His face lit at the memory. "Can you imagine my delight? The woman of my dreams would be mine. Power had reaffirmed it in a sacred chunkey match. And, you can imagine Chunkey Boy's frustrated reaction as he stalked off the court, shoulders bent by a rage as black as thunder.

"The two of them caught me on the way home. Had ten of your loyal Wind Clan warriors throw me down and hold me." The Deer Clan chief raised his mangled hand and inspected it. "He used my own chunkey stone to do this. Had my hand placed on the hard clay, and then he hammered it, and hammered it, and hammered it until it was bloody pulp."

The room was silent.

"Looking into my eyes, Chunkey Boy said, 'I demand a rematch.' I refused to answer. As long as I held my silence, I'd won." Right Hand pointed at the disfiguring scar in his chin. "This he did with a sharp chert flake he picked up from the dirt. He told me, 'You can have a rematch, or you can marry my sister without lips, a tongue, or nose. And when I'm done with you, I'll make your lovely sister's looks match yours.'"

Blue Heron closed her eyes, imagining it just the way Right Hand claimed.

Right Hand said reasonably, "This is Chunkey Boy we're talking about. He'd have done it, sliced Corn Seed's face off if I'd refused. You *know* how he was when he lost! How acid burned in his souls when he sulked. Him, his fawning and worshipping brother, and Night Shadow Star, nothing about that threesome was right!"

Blue Heron made a face, pinching her nose. "What about now? When did the sorcerer contact you?"

"Midwinter. A messenger from the Whisperer arrived and asked an audience of me. He sent an offering of Trade, and told me that I would finally have my revenge on Chunkey Boy."

"Chunkey Boy is dead!" *Tonka'tzi* Wind thundered.

"Maybe. So people believe. And he plays the part well." Right Hand shrugged. "But every time I see the Morning Star, I see Chunkey Boy. And every time he looks at me, he grins, knowing full well what he did to me."

"So, you received the knife from Bleeding Hawk. How did you get it to Cut String?"

"Through a stone Trader who knew about the incest in Cut String's family. And Cut String had his own trouble with Chunkey Boy when he was little." He barked a bitter laugh. "What *normal* boy didn't?"

"Where do we find this stone Trader?"

"You don't." Right Hand glanced sadly at his maimed hand. "I gave him a wealth of Trade, two comely young immigrant women for wives, and told him that he was implicated in an attack on the Morning Star. He's fully aware that if he ever comes back, he'll bleed the last of his life out on the square."

Right Hand gave her a triumphant smile. "It was the only way to . . ." His stomach seemed to cramp.

"To what?" *Tonka'tzi* Wind asked.

Right Hand made a face, as if in pain. "To ensure that you'd never get him to talk."

"And how did you get Evening Star House to cooperate?" Blue Heron asked. Right Hand was looking sick, the confidence gone. And well he should, given the . . .

Right Hand jerked, stomach rising as if in a dry heave. He swallowed hard, what looked like foam at the corner of his mouth.

"That, you'll have to find out for yourself." His entire body spasmed, and he collapsed next to his sister. Seven Skull Shield dropped to a knee beside the man as War Claw rushed forward. Together they rolled the convulsing Right Hand onto his back.

Blue Heron and Sun Wing had both risen.

Right Hand's gut heaved, spewing vomit.

"What is it, Aunt?" Sun Wing asked.

"Water hemlock." Blue Heron sighed and dropped back onto the dais in defeat. Then Corn Seed gagged, twitched, and threw up. "Somehow they've managed to poison themselves."

Blue Heron leaped down to stare into Right Hand's dark and fearful eyes, demanding, "Where's Lace? Where did they take her? Tell me, and I'll cut short the suffering."

Right Hand's tongue pushed out another gob of foam, his muscles twisting and jerking, his feet kicking at the matting.

"Don't know . . . Nothing . . . Where's Lace . . ." His eyes rolled back in his head. With a violent contraction he threw up yellow slime and foam.

Seven Skull Shield stood, backing away, and shook his head. "Now, Keeper, the question remains: How much of what they said is true? And how much is lies concocted in accord with the scorpion to mislead us?"

Do you believe that Piasa's souls are actually inside her?" Fire Cat asked Rides-the-Lightning as he squeezed a rag and trickled water into Night Shadow Star's mouth. He sat beside her on her bed. Her room was illuminated by a circle of hickory-oil lamps that cast a warm yellow glow over the walls, bed, altar, and storage boxes.

Where he sat on a large box, Rides-the-Lightning lifted a shaggy white eyebrow. His opaque eyes stared into emptiness. "I had trouble with the notion at first. How can such a Powerful Underworld Spirit as Piasa project such a strong reflection of his Power into a young woman? Even one as gifted as Night Shadow Star? And then I realized, old and slow as I am, that her brother is home to the living god."

The old shaman smacked his toothless gums. "Power runs through the Four Winds Clan like a deep-water current."

Fire Cat rewet the cloth in a bowl of water. "I've watched your supposed 'living' god. He does play the part, acts like he is the Morning Star. Night Shadow Star, however, acts like she's trying to be herself."

Rides-the-Lightning sighed, resettling himself on the box. "I cannot change your heresy through any argument or proof. Belief is a choice we all make as individuals. Worship, however, can be, and often is, an enforced behavior. But whether or not you believe in the Morning Star? Any time we waste in debate over it is a distraction."

"It doesn't seem like a distraction to me, Soul Flier."

"Oh, I don't argue that your heresy isn't in some way crucial to our current circumstances." The old man pointed a cautionary finger. "Power is shifting, Red Wing. Something terrible has come to Cahokia. The entire Underworld is shaken clear down to First Woman's cave. Power has brought you here, reeking of heresy, and placed you with Night Shadow Star for a purpose. But what purpose? I cannot say."

"The only thing we have for each other is burning hatred," Fire Cat murmured. "I killed her husband, she killed my world."

"Yes. It has become so very apparent." The old man's lips quivered, as if he were hiding something. "This most special hatred you and the lady share, along with your obligation to serve her, is somehow vital."

"You'd think Power would have picked two people that didn't despise each other when it went looking for such, in your words, *vital* allies."

"Yes." Rides-the-Lightning's lips quivered again. "You would, wouldn't you?" He seemed to be on the verge of some revelation, then he chuckled to himself.

"What?" Fire Cat watched Night Shadow Star swallow the last of the water he'd trickled into her mouth.

"I was wondering, musing absently about the ways we can delude ourselves. That is all. How long would you stay and continue attending to Lady Night Shadow Star if her souls don't return? Sometimes bodies can live for years as soulless husks."

"As long as her heart beats, and I can keep breath in her lungs, Soul Flier." Fire Cat used a square of cloth to wipe away a bit of spittle that leaked from the corner of her mouth. "I gave my word."

"And that is important to you?"

"I'm the last Red Wing. My honor is the only thing which remains mine."

"That . . . and the part Power has chosen for you to play in this final confrontation." The old man's lips bent in a wry smile. "Yes, I see."

"See what?"

"You heard Blue Heron's thief when he came to summon Night Shadow Star to the Council House: Lady Lace is taken by the abomination." He raised a withered and gnarly finger. "That is the term they are using in the Spirit world for this mad sorcerer. Abomination."

Seeing Night Shadow Star swallow, Fire Cat began trickling water again. "Abomination? That's the term we use . . . excuse me, the term we *used* when we talked about the Morning Star."

Fire Cat pursed his lips, glanced at the blind soul flier, then asked, "Is this appropriate . . . or even right? This spreading practice of calling the souls of the dead back into the living? Doesn't it reek of an arrogance to wrench the Morning Star out of the Sky World and insert him into a human body? Especially one as sordid and mean as Chunkey Boy was storied to be?"

"Sordid and mean? Strong words, Red Wing."

"Rumors have long legs, elder. And on those legs they traveled often to Red Wing town. Once there, people spoke without fear of Four Winds Clan retaliation."

"And perhaps without fear of bending the truth, as well?"

Fire Cat shook his head. "There were too many stories, for too long a time, clear up until Black Tail died and Chunkey Boy stepped into his place." He paused, considering. "Although people did stop talking about Chunkey Boy's abuses after that."

"Perhaps a glimmering of the truth that Chunkey Boy's souls were consumed? Hmm?" Rides-the-Lightning suggested mildly.

"Or that being known as a 'living god' no one ever denied him anything he wanted. He even exiled and murdered his brother as one of his first actions. They were such good friends, weren't they? We heard the stories way up in our frozen north of how they went everywhere together, played chunkey and stickball, committed pranks and high jinks. The boys and Night Shadow Star were in one another's constant company, no matter the improprieties of a high-born girl acting in such an unseemly manner. The jokes where that Chunkey Boy would have her installed in the men's house, that she'd pass her monthly cycle there instead of in the women's house." He arched an eyebrow, only to realize that Rides-the-Lightning couldn't see it, and added, "And the more vicious among the rumor mongers crowed that, as a 'warrior' the only blood a pampered high-born bitch like her would ever see would be on her menstrual rags."

Rides-the-Lightning nodded, as if this was nothing new. "Those same fools might wish to clip their tongues. The three arrows she shot into Cut String's back would have fit into the size of a cottonwood leaf."

"Why did Chunkey Boy have his brother exiled and murdered? They were best friends, weren't they? Inseparable, boon companions?"

"It was the *Morning Star* who ordered the exile. Not Chunkey Boy." Rides-the-Lightning rubbed a callused hand over his face, rearranging the faded black patterns of tattoos where they hid among the wrinkles. "The living god is under no obligation to explain his orders. Warriors took the younger brother by surprise, escorted him to the canoe landing, and bore him downriver."

"You do not speak his name. Which tells me the rumors are true, that he really was murdered somewhere in the Nations down south."

Rides-the-Lightning grunted, knowing full well the Red Wing had tricked him. "We don't know that he was murdered. The story was that he drowned in a canoe mishap."

"How convenient."

"These things happen, Red Wing."

"Yes. Of course." He dribbled another couple of drops into Night Shadow Star's mouth. "Such an unlucky family. The old *Tonka'tzi* murdered, attempts on the Keeper and Night Shadow Star, and now Lace is abducted. But only after her husband was flayed like a butchered turkey and tied to the wall with his severed muscles hanging like obscene feathers. Makes you wonder why the abomination is hunting them so hard."

Fire Cat raised a forestalling hand. "But wait! Perhaps, like me, he has a hatred for the Four Winds Clan."

"There is another explanation: he seeks to destroy them because they control the Power. Whoever controls the Power, controls Cahokia. And whoever controls Cahokia, controls the world." Rides-the-Lightning smiled, displaying sunken and toothless pink gums. "And Night Shadow Star controls you, Red Wing. You and this 'hate' you are so fond of. I would be afraid, because Power is depending on the way you feel about the lady. For whatever purpose it chose you? I think it is going to be very unpleasant."

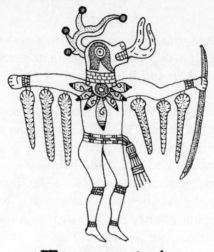

Forty-eight

The flimsy ramada stood just up from the beached canoes that packed the river landing. Across the Father Water, high atop the bluff, Evening Star town could be seen, the high palace jutting from its mound. Sunlight sparkled on the broad river, bobbing as it was with canoes. A float of firewood was being hauled ashore just below where High Dance's canoe had landed. The laborers called in unison as they struggled with the wet wood.

The ramada consisted of four slim poles, saplings really, that supported a lattice roof covered with old reed matting gone gray with mold. Bead sat in its shade on a gorgeous red-white-and-black-striped blanket, his feet pulled up, knees clasped in his arms. He had his hair up in a bun, pinned with a turkey-bone skewer, and wore only a stained buckskin apron suspended from a plain belt. The muscles in his arms flexed and relaxed, as if in time to his thoughts.

He glanced up as High Dance walked up from the canoe he'd hired to bring him across the busy river crossing. Like Bead, he had dressed like a commoner, pulling his hair into a twist the way some of the western dirt farmers did.

High Dance stepped into the shade, nodded to Bead, and then at the two warriors, or wolves as Bead called them. They stood out in the sun, bronzed skin shining from perspiration, their young, tattoo-free faces indeed reminding High Dance of the hunting prairie beasts.

"I am so glad to see you," Bead said easily, a lazy smile on his lips. He'd painted his face a pale gray with two light blue streaks down the cheeks, a pattern with which High Dance was unfamiliar. "And even better, it's good to see that you've come alone."

He gestured at the tens of men and youths loading and unloading canoe contents around them. Older women, dressed in bright colors, offered cooked and raw food from the shade of nearby ramadas, or paraded past with bowls of victuals. Skinny boys lurked in the crowd, each offering a carving, or other memento of Cahokia in return for a shell.

"As though one could actually tell in this confusion," Bead amended.

"I came alone." High Dance squinted at the two guards who watched him through suspicious eyes.

"So glad!" Bead popped to his feet, smacking his hands as if to free them of clinging sand. "I hoped that your sister hadn't completely frightened you away. I really should make some time to have a visit with her. She seems . . . I don't know, serious? Wouldn't you say? You're her brother. You'd know why she acts like such a nervous and close-minded old forest hen."

"My sister is none of your concern."

Bead glanced at him, an eyebrow lifting. "I've got it! Could it be? Tell me she isn't still letting that ugly little dwarf crawl under her blanket. For the life of me, I just can't get my imagination around a full-grown and handsome woman like your sister finding any kind of satisfaction from that tiny and misshapen little man."

"You had better restrict your comments to things that are your business." High Dance felt a cold fury blow through him. That Columella allowed that cunning little imp into her bed was bad enough, but to have the slippery Bead throw it in his face? Absolutely unacceptable!

Bead seemed nonplussed. "Oh, but it is my business, as you shall see. Come on. I've got something that will excite you to no end. Hah, I'll bet you'll be so overjoyed you even forgive me for that last deplorable comment about your sister."

Bead started walking upslope toward the warehouses, and placed his fingers thoughtfully on his cheek. "Perhaps, when they're eye to eye, the dwarf employs some remarkable dexterity with those tiny little toes?" He shook his head. "Doesn't seem possible, given that they're but nubbins. Ah, but when you go back to the original question about why your sister comes off as such a shriveled and dried persimmon, that would make perfect sense."

"I told you to stop it." High Dance fumed, but when Bead shot him a sudden, dangerous look, his anger was quickly smothered by a cool resurgence of worry.

They reached the warehouse area where it stood at the highest part of the levee north of the River Mounds. Glimpses of War Duck's high palace were periodically visible between the rooftops as they wound between the buildings.

Bead stopped at one of the warehouses, shot High Dance a smile, and said, "Come on in. Let me show you what you have only dreamed about for . . . oh, all of your life."

With that he opened the split-plank door and gestured High Dance to enter.

The very act of ducking into the dark interior took all of High Dance's courage. For all he knew, a couple of Bead's wolves were waiting in the gloomy interior, bows drawn, or war clubs lifted. If they struck him down there would be no witnesses. No one would have the slightest clue about what might have happened to him, or where or when he disappeared.

Just this once, could that meddling little pest of a dwarf have one of his spies following me?

But no blow fell. Instead, Bead's two guards slipped in and off to one side while Bead refastened the door, deepening the gloom. The only light filtered indirectly through the gap between the roof and walls, blunted by the overhanging eaves.

It took a moment for the room's contents to come into focus as High Dance's eyes adjusted. Boxes and packs of what looked like Trade goods were stacked to either side of the door, as if ready to be moved at a moment's notice. The back of the room appeared vacant but for a . . . ?

He squinted, at first unsure of what he was seeing.

"Go ahead!" Bead almost chortled, clasping his hands in expectation. "Go look up close."

A sense of foreboding rising in his breast, High Dance warily crossed the packed-clay floor, realizing that what he saw was a litter chair atop raised poles, and upon it was a reclining figure.

His eyes were adjusting now, and as the gloom gave way, he stopped short at the sight of a pregnant young woman, naked, artfully tied to the litter. She stared at him through terrified wide eyes, her hair disheveled, a cloth gag in her mouth. He made her to be in her late teens, the ropes passing just under her enlarged breasts and over her hips. The young woman's arms were tied down on either side of the litter, as were her ankles. The sight of her distended navel, popping up like an acorn on her swollen abdomen, struck him as incongruous.

"I don't understand," High Dance said as Bead walked up beside him.

"Ah, perhaps you don't. One of my wolves, Bleeding Hawk, is missing. Which may mean a complication. We need a new warehouse, and well, your Evening Star town is a bit more secure. As I proved today at the canoe landing, you can see who's coming and going on the river. Here? In this warren of buildings? Why, they could come from any direction, at any time."

He had no more than said that when the door opened, and one of the wolves entered, his eyes narrowed to slits, as if to pre-adjust his vision to the gloom. He closed the door and crossed on quick feet to communicate something urgent in his guttural tongue.

Bead snorted an amused laugh, then glanced knowingly at High Dance. "Poor Bleeding Hawk has indeed run into trouble. A half squad of Four Wind warriors just raided the first warehouse we rented when we got here." He looked around unhappily. "We'll be needing that new location sooner rather than later, I'm thinking."

"And you just expect me to give you an Evening Star warehouse to hide this woman?"

"I'm sure you will. And you disappoint me, calling her 'this woman.' I thought you'd be bouncing from toe to toe, delighted in victory."

"I don't understand, Bead."

"Look close, oh noble chief." The words were laced with scorn.

High Dance did, discounting how her tear-stained cheeks were puffed out by the gag, how her eyes were swollen from weeping, and grief. Something about the lines of her face, the high brow . . .

"Pus and blood! Lady? Lace, is that you?"

But she just stared back at him, a bright and half-mad terror burning behind her eyes.

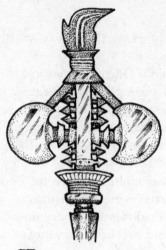

Forty-nine

From a great distance, Night Shadow Star slowly returned to herself, as if to find a stranger's body and soul in place of her own. It might have been an instant that she'd been gone, or a lifetime. Like fading echoes, images from her memories slowly evaporated from her souls.

This time she couldn't forget, couldn't wall it away and pretend that day had never happened. His burning eyes, her screams and pleading, the pain and tears, remained stark and plain. Her humiliation and violation lived, raw and exposed, like a quivering muscle stripped of its protective skin.

Both of them. Why both of them?

She found herself crouched on a sandy mud, aware of the weight of water pressing down. Aware she was still in the Underworld, safe within the dark warrens, protected by the depths. And she finally understood why some souls sought refuge here both before and after death. They could return to the womb, away from trouble and violence, safe from abuse and betrayal.

Piasa, Horned Serpent, and Snapping Turtle were regarding her with otherworldly gazes. They knew, had relived the memory with her, felt the disbelief, confusion, and shock.

Piasa's hollow voice reverberated inside her. "You know why he wants you. You can feel his hunger. The dispossessed voices that whisper to and stroke his twisted souls have convinced him that he must have anything forbidden." He paused. "As you were forbidden, Lady of Cahokia. He has had his taste, fleeting and self-destructive as it was. He convinced himself that, despite his love, he could sacrifice you for a greater gain. But your escape has only increased his desire to possess you no matter the cost."

"Don't send me back," she whispered, squeezing tears from between her tightly pressed eyelids. "Let my souls stay here in the darkness. Let them drift with the currents. I won't be any trouble."

Horned Serpent hissed in frustration. "Do you know *why* we care? It's not about *you,* or what they did to you. Your exalted Four Winds souls have no value here. Are you so completely preoccupied with yourself that you fail to understand the real threat? What this abomination intends to attempt? The Morning Star's latest resurrection only *whetted* his appetite and obsession. Do you understand the ramifications if he should *succeed*?"

She blinked, shaking her head, unable to . . .

Piasa reached out, his taloned feet catching her by the throat. Panic-stricken, terrified, she looked into black pupils surrounded by a sea of burning yellow. Her gaze was drawn down into an endless midnight. And there, in the stygian darkness, she finally saw.

The scream was trapped in her throat by Piasa's crushing grip.

"Now do you understand?" Piasa's voice boomed through her.

As she writhed in his crushing grip, she nodded, her head exploding with pain.

"Then you know what you must do." Piasa released his hold, letting her drop to the soft mud. "I know what this will cost you, Lady of Cahokia. By possessing me, he will completely own you. Either you will save yourself, and our world, or he will destroy you in ways too horrible to contemplate."

"How do I defeat him?"

"By surrendering yourself to him."

"I can't." She placed a hand to her wounded throat, glancing up at Horned Serpent, and then Snapping Turtle, knowing they didn't believe she had either the courage or will. When she shot a frightened glance at Piasa, she could see the beast's own growing skepticism.

Like voices inside her, she could hear their thoughts: *Weak. Pampered. Despicable. Spoiled. Pitiful.*

What was it the Red Wing had said? Anger was a better weapon in the Underworld than fear?

"I am Night Shadow Star," she gritted through her teeth. "Of the Four Winds Clan, daughter of the *Tonka'tzi.* I have unfinished business."

"Then finish it!" Piasa's whiskers trembled, and his ear flicked. "I will help you when and if I can. There is a way. . . ."

After the Keeper's household finished supper, Seven Skull Shield sidled up to Smooth Pebble. The *berdache* had her hair up in a gray bun, the muscles in her arms flexing as she scraped one of the boiling pots and threw food remains into the fire as an offering to the Spirits. Dogs were licking the plates, cleaning up scraps. The fire crackled and spit sparks toward the palace great-room ceiling.

"Where did the Keeper disappear to?"

"She wants time to herself. Leave her alone." Then Smooth Pebble relented, her lined face tensing. "I'm worried. I've never seen her like this. What happened up there in the Council House?"

"It takes something out of a person to realize they've been betrayed by friends they trusted. Though why she'd put any faith in that Deer Clan chief after what Chunkey Boy did to him?" He shrugged. "I thought she was supposed to be so smart about these things."

"She thought Chunkey Boy had made amends before he became the Morning Star. Even if he hadn't, when the Morning Star took his body, Chunkey Boy ceased to be. Nothing was left to hate. Since then, they'd worked to earn her trust."

"Chunkey Boy and this brother of his seem to have left quite a wake of destruction in their passage. Does the Keeper think she has to accept responsibility for all of it?"

Smooth Pebble studied him for a moment. "You like her, don't you?"

He gave her a sheepish grin. "In spite of all my better sense, I . . ." He scowled at her. "And what if I do? I've been around, *berdache*. It takes a special kind of woman to pry any kind of respect out of me."

Smooth Pebble's knowing smirk communicated a shared understanding. "She's out back, southwest corner, leaned against the wall. Just don't add to her distress, thief."

"Why'd you tell me that?"

"Because, may the lost Spirits of the dead help her, and for reasons I'm barely able to understand, she's come to respect you. You're something different for her. Maybe even a . . . Well, never mind. But if you let me down? Make her feel worse? Poisoning by hemlock—like you've just seen—would be mercy compared to what I'll do to you."

"You are indeed dangerous with a stewpot."

"What?"

"Nothing."

He stepped out into the cool spring evening. Sparkflies were dancing in the dying light, rising from the new grass in blinking columns. Palely illuminated clouds marched up from the south, and between them he could see the early stars casting patterns across the black.

The smells of Cahokia's great city were carried on the damp evening breeze.

He saw the red glow of her pipe on the southwest corner and walked along the mound edge to where she sat. She was staring off to the west, the smell of burning tobacco sweetening the night.

Seven Skull Shield dropped down beside her and propped his arms on his knees, hands dangling.

Cautiously he said, "I think I'd open an artery before I chose hemlock. Dying that way? It's nothing pretty."

She nodded, sucking on her tubular stone pipe. "If you're picked up by a squad of warriors, and you don't know the reason for your summons, what do you do? For all they knew, I wanted to talk about how much corn the dirt farmers were growing. It's not always easy to slice an artery when you learn the terrible truth. And even if you could get to a blade, your captors might be able to plug the bleeding with a finger long enough to get it sewed up. After that, you're dying on the square for days. Being slowly skinned alive. And having your dangling parts burned off while you scream your voice out."

"I'm sorry it turned out that way, is all."

She drew on her pipe, held the smoke, then exhaled. "I've always considered myself the strong one in this family. The one who can do whatever's required to get the job done. For the first time since I was a little girl, I'm not sure I'm up to it."

"You're up to it."

"Oh? You learned this down on the canoe landing, or perhaps in some cuckolded man's bed while his wife flopped around beneath you?"

"The value placed in the knowing of something is in the knowing of it, not the where or how it was obtained."

She chuckled hollowly.

"Keeper, you've never had the game changed on you like this, that's all. You and the other Houses, you play by certain subtle rules. This scorpion, he's attacking you head on, and throwing it right in your face to keep you off guard."

"To achieve what? That's what baffles me."

He stared out at the darkness. Dogs were barking in the distance.

People were singing somewhere. A woman was calling for her children to come in.

Finally he said, "The difference this time is that he's not trying to just topple your House in order to supplant it with his own. He's trying to destroy Cahokia and, as the Tula said, 'pull it up by the roots.' That's a different kind of antagonist. He doesn't care what he breaks in the process, because he's not interested in fixing it later."

"I still should have anticipated Right Hand and Corn Seed's treachery." She paused, took another drag on her pipe, and exhaled. "Did you believe him when he said Chunkey Boy beat his hand to a pulp?"

"That part, to my ears, was no lie. I've been thinking about this all evening, and if you'll let me have a puff off that pipe of yours, I'll tell you my thoughts."

"Just who do you think you . . . ?" She paused, considered, then chuckled at herself as she handed the pipe over. "No one has ever *dared* ask that of me before."

"You need a better quality of friends." He drew deeply of the tobacco, held it, and exhaled through his nostrils. "I'll be taken and whipped, that's smooth and strong, Keeper." He quickly drew again and handed the pipe back.

"If I so much as hear a peep that anyone knows I shared my pipe with a thief?"

"Your secret is safe. My threshold for honor may be lower than catfish crap, but what little I've got is sacrosanct. Mostly. Depending upon the price."

She knocked what was left of the ash and ember out into a small dish, fumbled a thick pinch of tobacco from the pouch at her side, and rapidly tamped it into the bowl. Using a twig, she coaxed the few red coals on the dish into the pipe, then drew to light it.

Almost absently she noted, "You saw War Claw when he stepped in and whispered to me just before supper?"

"I did."

"The raid on that warehouse of War Duck's netted us nothing." She extended her lips, blowing out smoke. "Nothing but a big red snake painted on the back wall. Just like the one in Red Warrior's sleeping quarters and on Lace's wall. He's mocking us."

"Not unexpected, but discouraging nonetheless."

"Not a single indication that Lace had been there. The people around, they'd just seen men coming and going. Young men who looked like warriors but dressed like slaves. In River City? Who'd notice?"

He took the pipe when she offered it. Rot take him, that was the best smoke he'd ever enjoyed. "I need to know about Chunkey Boy and Night Shadow Star. And this other brother. The banished one that no one speaks of. Are the rumors true? Did the Morning Star have him murdered out of jealousy and fear?"

Even in the darkness he knew she was giving him that "don't go there" hard-eyed look. "My pipe is one thing. I wouldn't discuss such family matters with a Four Winds kinsman, let alone you, thief."

"Like I said, I do have some standards when it comes to discretion. I've made a stock and trade of family secrets, but those have been artfully stolen through guile and craft. Earned the hard way, if you will. But information given willingly in confidence from a friend?" He handed her pipe back. "That, like the names of my confederates—if you'll recall—cannot be tortured out of me on the square."

"What in the Sky Worlds and down below makes you think I'd believe you?"

He was considering his answer when she unexpectedly sighed and said, "They likened themselves to being the living incarnation of the Creation story: Chunkey Boy was Morning Star, Walking . . . the younger brother, played 'Thrown Away' the wild one, and Night Shadow Star fashioned herself as Corn Woman. Looking back, I'm sure they almost came to believe it, what with Morning Star's souls living in their grandfather's body.

"The brothers acted as brothers do, squabbling to the death in one heartbeat, best friends the next, and ready to stand shoulder to shoulder in defense of each other at the toss of a rock. Night Shadow Star, however, provided the special glue. She was game for anything, trying to outdo both of her brothers, and pretty much succeeding until the change came. The boys' muscles hardened, their voices deepened, and they grew into men. Meanwhile her breasts budded and her hips widened, but she never stopped competing. She might not have been able to throw a chunkey lance farther, so she threw it straighter. The same with her archery, what she lacked in strength, she made up for with skill and accuracy."

"People still talk about her out there," he gestured. "Some say she was becoming *berdache*."

"We wondered." Blue Heron puffed on her pipe. "But that last year they spent together, there were strains. Tensions none of us understood. Some, like you heard tonight, came from the constant stream of suitors vying for Night Shadow Star's hand. And then, like a breaking branch, everything came crashing down. The Morning Star's human body was dead.

"Chunkey Boy's body was the first choice. He'd been groomed for the honor all of his life. But until that moment it hadn't been real for any of them. Chunkey Boy hardly had time to dwell on it as he was prepared, cleansed, purged, smoked, and sweated."

"The other two had to watch the ceremony from the sidelines, realizing they were losing their brother. That nothing would be the same again. How did they take it?"

She nodded, handing him the pipe. "Walk . . . I mean the younger brother—"

"Why was he killed?"

"I heard he drowned."

At his silence, she shot him a glance. "I mean it. No one knows why Morning Star exiled him. Night Shadow Star refuses to even discuss it."

When he handed her the pipe, Blue Heron used it to gesture toward Morning Star's palace. "He knows. It was his order. One of the first he issued when he finally recovered from the ordeal and walked again among men."

"One rumor says it was jealousy. Another is that Morning Star finally had his fill of the boy's unseemly behavior."

"So I've heard." The pipe bowl glowed red in the darkness. "What I know is that I woke up one morning and was informed that warriors had escorted my nephew to the canoe landing, and that he was going downriver to a new life. No sooner had that shock soaked in, than I was told that Night Shadow Star had entered the women's house for her first menstruation." She paused. "In one stroke, Chunkey Boy's, my nephew's, and Night Shadow Star's lives were transformed."

"Keeper, people whisper behind their hands that Chunkey Boy and your nephew were, how do I say, in trouble a lot? That but for who they were, they might have been, um . . ."

"Severely disciplined?" She blew smoke through her nostrils. "More than once we paid out to Earth Clan families to compensate for the boys' indiscretions and unfortunate choices. On occasion we had to resort to other measures. What could we do? They were the *Tonka'tzi*'s sons and daughter. And young."

"Which, of course, absolves them of any kind of punishment and places them above the sanctions mandated for lesser beings?"

"I don't like your tone."

"If you think my tone is unsettling, you haven't been paying attention to the lengths someone is going to in an attempt to destroy your family. And Cahokia with it."

"I suppose." She rubbed her face anxiously. "Lace has always been the good one of the bunch. Why is it that she's the one they've taken? Where's the justice in that?"

"The justice? It's everywhere. She's Four Winds Clan, the *Tonka'tzi*'s daughter. And young. I'd say someone Chunkey Boy, Night Shadow Star, and your maybe-or-maybe-not-dead nephew really hurt now wants revenge. Some significant person? A family? An entire House? Perhaps someone denied justice and unfairly exiled, sent off to found one of your colonies? They've been waiting, biding their time. They've chosen now to strike."

He paused, glancing sidelong at her. "Who might that be, Keeper? Where in the abuses of the past do we find explanations for the actions of today?"

"There are so many, thief. I wouldn't know where to begin." She bowed her head, the tobacco having gone cold in her pipe.

The Web

*I*n the darkness, I can see the Keeper's pipe. She sits at the southwest corner of her palace, her feet at the edge where the mound surface slopes away; her back is against the wall. Someone is with her, though in the darkness, I do not know who. Some old lover, perhaps? I can't think of anyone else she'd share a pipe with.

The person's identity is inconsequential. My joy comes from the fact that she's out here at all. I've known her to spend entire nights perched there in solitude, her brooding eyes fixed on the Avenue of the Sun as it heads west-southwest through the cluttered city. I've always wondered if, deep in her souls, she'd like to follow the road, just head out and vanish to someplace quiet and small. Perhaps some woods-surrounded farmstead with a creek and fertile fields where no one would demand anything of her.

She only escapes to the seclusion of her mound edge like this when events have taken a turn for the worse, when she's dispirited, confused, and feeling defeated. To see her so, delights me. I have her completely off balance, reeling.

I now know two things. Bleeding Hawk is dead. And while his capture was unforeseen, I'd nevertheless planned for that eventuality. I'll probably never know the details of what went wrong; nor do they matter. Any damage is forestalled; the Keeper will be preoccupied trying to work out the details of Right Hand's treachery, desperately hoping to find the clue that will lead her to me.

"Search, Keeper. Search hard and diligently. Keep your eyes on the east, send your agents to scour the uplands and poke among the dirt farmers for my hiding place."

The moment I learned that they had raided War Duck's warehouse, found the red serpent I painted on the back wall, I rid myself of that fool High Dance and hurried here. The Keeper's agents will be quizzing old War Duck, sniffing around his household, seeking any hint that he's involved.

"Sniff hard, you little camp dogs. Dig up his garden, piss on his pots. I wish you all the luck as you infuriate War Duck and sting his pride."

I am reassured. If she had any inkling of my plans, the last place she would be is outside her palace smoking. Tomorrow I will take them all by surprise. My web is now spun. I have my sticky tendrils everywhere I need them. All I have to do is draw in my mired prey.

Well, except for Night Shadow Star.

I expect Power to bring her to me before the end.

I turn in the darkness, my pack-load of smoked fish sending enchanting odors to tease my empty stomach. Even as I pull one of the oily fish from the pack and sink my teeth into it. I stare worriedly at Night Shadow Star's palace. I can see it just off to the east across the western plaza.

Where are you? What are you doing, my forbidden love?

Is she even in there? I have heard nothing, seen nothing. She should have been at the Council House when Right Hand and Corn Seed were interrogated. She should have been rushing to and fro, her anxiety goaded to a fever pitch by Lace's abduction. Of them all, I have counted on her quick brilliance and impetuous emotions to goad the confusion, to incite violent efforts to find me.

We have unfinished business between us, love of my life.

Without her, what I am planning simply will not work. Any chance of success hinges on having them all—each and every one of Red Warrior's daughters. A sacrifice of such importance it will be worthy of the greatest resurrection ever. Before I can achieve the impossible, First Woman must be placated, convinced of my sincerity. The blood poured on her earth must be rich enough to compensate for the disruption I am bringing to her realm.

And there can be no higher sacrifice than the most influential women of the Four Winds Clan.

Time to see what helpless creatures I have stuck in my web. You see, like this fish I now chew, terror can also feed an appetite.

Fifty

As she came swimming up through dreams, the first physical sensation Night Shadow Star was conscious of was hunger.

She stretched—only to find a blanket tucked tightly under her chin. Flopping onto her side, her eyes flashed open as her full bladder demanded attention.

She lay on her bed. The blanket—a wedding gift she'd shared with Makes Three—half strangled her. The remains of a blinding headache lay partially dormant behind her eyes as she sat up and flipped the blanket to one side.

"Rides-the-Lightning said you were coming back," a weary voice intruded from behind. She gasped and turned.

Fire Cat watched her through knowing eyes. He clutched one of Makes Three's bows; ill-fitting armor and a helmet on his head completed his dress. A wicked-looking war club her husband had once used lay beside him.

"What are you doing in my room? Why are you wearing my husband's armor?" She felt the anger rising hard and bitter.

"I'm following your orders to the limit, Lady," he replied without inflection. "And, since you've awakened alive, with a beating heart, unraped and unabducted, perhaps I was successful."

She reached up, rubbing her gummy eyes, recalling her last order to him. "And the weapons?"

"If anyone decided they'd take you, I planned on making it as interesting for them as I could."

"You said Rides-the-Lightning was here?"

"Runners have been coming for him for the last half day. Some emergency with a clansman. He left perhaps a hand of time ago. He said he could feel your souls coming back, that the danger had passed." Fire Cat's eyebrow arched up under the rim of the leather-and-wood helmet. "Your Spirit journey was apparently filled with fears and terrors. You only really panicked me once, but there were a couple of other instances when things got frantic enough that I grew hopeful."

"Hopeful?"

"That you wouldn't be coming back. That my honor would be satisfied."

Visions spun through her like wind-tossed matting: Piasa, Horned Serpent, Snapping Turtle in the Underworld. The unleashed memories of that day when the Morning Star first summoned her after the resurrection. Piasa's voice hissed in her head as she relived the horror and disbelief, almost feeling the physical violation.

She clamped her eyes, fighting back tears, shaking her head in an attempt to clear her sight.

"Here," he said softly. "Take this."

To her surprise, when she opened her eyes, he offered her a cup of still-steaming black drink. Anxiously she drank it down; the bitter brew refreshed as it hit her empty stomach.

He stood, pointed at the chamber pot, and said, "I'll be back in a bit. Food should be ready. If it's not, I'll have to bruise a couple of Clay String's bones just on principle."

"He's Four Winds, a cousin," she murmured.

"So he reminds me periodically. As soon as they catch you alone, the whole lot of them are going to demand you put me back in a square so they can pay me back for the last couple of days."

"Couple of days?" She rubbed her face, trying to massage away the wooden feeling. "That's how long I was in the Underworld?"

He nodded, hesitated. "The scorpion—that's what they're calling the assassin—he's abducted your sister, Lace. The Keeper's been turning the whole city upside down looking for her."

"Lace?" She shuddered. "Of course. He's going to want us all. Sun Wing, mother, even the Keeper if he can get her."

"Do you know where he's taken Lace? What he's after?"

She nodded. "Now go. Grant me a moment of privacy, and bring me back whatever we have to eat. Piasa knows what kind of corn gruel they've kept burning, but I'm past complaining."

And to her surprise, he shot her a crooked grin. "I'll see what we've got."

Then he was gone.

Wearily, stiffly, she climbed down and squatted over the chamber pot. Past her door she could hear Fire Cat snapping out orders, heard the quick assent of her slaves and servants. Not even Field Green, on her best day, had commanded that kind of respect.

When she had finished she set the pot outside, and peered around the door post. The place smelled of roast venison, cattail bread, baked squash, and steeping black drink. The great room appeared neat, blankets folded, the matting swept, everything in order as if for a visit from the Morning Star himself.

Her servants were glancing sidelong at her, a plea in their eyes, before they shot worried looks at the Red Wing where he crouched in his battle armor and filled a wooden plate with steaming food.

Retreating back into her room, she opened a box, withdrew a black dress with white lightning zig-zags down the sides, and hesitated. Counting the time she'd been in the Underworld, nearly four days had passed since she'd bathed, but her body was clean and smelled of yucca—a luxury imported from the western Plains.

Rides-the-Lightning, of course. He would have insisted. She slipped the dress over her shoulders and belted it with a leather strap. She then took a moment to refold the blanket and lay it on the bed.

Then the Red Wing was back, his eyes fatigued. Makes Three's old helmet was pushed back on his head at an insolent cant. She seated herself. Famished, she dove into the food, almost burning her fingers on the hot venison. He stood, back braced against the door frame, muscular arms crossed on the armor breastplate.

"What else did I miss?"

"Your aunt's pet thief caught one of the Tula. Apparently one of the men who tried to kill you that night." He grinned. "The thief once told me he didn't fight clean. I hear he spit tobacco in the Tula's eyes, then mauled him like a mad bear. Bit the man's lip off. Then smuggled him to your aunt's palace in a canoe."

"And what did the Tula tell them?"

"The word I got is that the scorpion had something on a Deer Clan chief named Right Hand. Used him and his sister to put pressure on Cut String to try and kill the Morning Star. Right Hand and this Corn Seed managed to swallow enough water hemlock to . . . Well, you know."

She glanced down at the squash, nodded, and fingered it into her mouth. "The scorpion? Not inappropriate I suppose. He would have known Right Hand had never forgiven Chunkey Boy. He was probably part of the maiming."

"Not the nicest of people, this brother of yours."

She felt a dead emptiness inside, a hollowing that no amount of food would ever fill.

"No," she whispered. "Not nice at all." Memories, unvarnished, rose behind her eyes. Piasa whispered, causing her to glance to the side, as if she'd see him in the corner of the room. The flicker of his movement kept vanishing at the edge of her vision.

She ordered her thoughts and said, "The world would have been a better place if Mother had taken us one by one as we were born, and drowned us in the river."

"That's a bit extreme."

She swallowed hard, took a big bite of succulent venison, and shook her head as she chewed. Swallowing, she washed it down with black drink, and told him, "We were doomed from the moment we took our first breaths. And along the way, so many others were going to have to suffer, bleed, and die because of us. If I hadn't been allowed to live, Right Hand would be alive now, unmaimed, and probably a happy man. Perhaps my brother wouldn't be crazed with Spirit voices as he seeks to destroy us all and become an even greater monster than he is."

"What's this? An admission of the truth about your beloved Chunkey Boy?"

She glanced at him, eyes fixing on his. "Chunkey Boy? He was the mild one. Your scorpion? I learned his identity in the Underworld. His name is Walking Smoke. My *other* brother. He's the one driven insane with jealousy and rage, the one the voices are telling to destroy Cahokia, and sacrifice us all."

"I thought he was dead."

She felt the quiver of fear around her heart. "No. And, cunning and twisted as he is, it's up to me to find a way to kill him before he can do more harm."

The sick feeling in High Dance's stomach had nothing to do with bad food. In fact he'd barely touched his breakfast that morning. As he strolled across the Evening Star town plaza, he tried to look relaxed, but the broken half of a bead in his palm felt as poisonous as unprocessed coontie root.

As he passed the charnel house mound, one of the Tula seemed to detach himself from the eagle guardian post. The man fell in behind him; sunlight glistened from a chert-studded war club in his right hand.

High Dance fought the impulse to say something. As if it would do any good; the accursed Tula couldn't speak a word of civilized tongue.

As he passed behind the engineers' mound and society house, yet another Tula stepped out and followed.

"Yes, yes," High Dance muttered. "I'm coming."

The broken bead might have been a hot pebble, burning against his skin.

At the warehouse, two more Tula nodded to his "escort," as if giving their assent that he might enter.

"I'm a high chief of the Four Winds Clan, you barbarian pond scum." A spear of anger warmed his breast. Then he glanced at the war clubs dangling from their hands. As quickly, any desire to protest drained away.

The warehouse door was painted with Four Winds design, marking it as his clan's property. But the door was opened by yet another Tula who gestured him inside.

To his surprise, the Tula warriors within were clustered around the door, all in the process of checking weapons, inspecting arrows, some swinging war clubs as if to loosen their shoulders.

"You're probably asking how you've come to this," Bead told him as he emerged from behind a knot of warriors. He had a paint palette in one hand and was just putting on the finishing touches—radiating lines of blue—on a Tula's face. To the side, a nervous-looking messenger held a copper-clad staff that looked suspiciously like those carried by the Morning Star's messengers.

Bead had painted his own face to resemble Piasa's. Both eyes were surrounded by yellow circles similar to the Water Panther's; black, three-forked patterns surrounded them to designate the Underworld. Black lines on his cheeks evoked whiskers, and his nose, like a cougar's, was pinkish brown. The black line drawn around his mouth mimicked the big cat's, and was accented by a touch of white on his chin.

It came to High Dance that he'd never seen Bead's face without some sort of paint on it.

"What do you want this time?" He glanced over to see Lace, still atop her platform, eyes closed as she breathed in and out in obvious agony.

He'd never cared for the Morning Star's House, thought them all stuffed with shit and over-full of themselves. Nevertheless, watching young Lace's misery touched something inside him. She was kin. And she, personally, had never done anything to offend him.

He pointed. "You might want to change her bonds. Seated like that can't be good for her. She could end up crippled, perhaps lose that baby."

Bead frowned and cocked his head as he considered her. "Yes," he remarked thoughtfully. "She could."

"Well?"

Bead, as if interrupted in mid-thought, asked, "Well, what?"

"Are you going to do something about lady Lace's bonds?"

After more consideration, Bead told him a flat, "No."

He turned back to the Tula he was painting and carefully finished the last blue line on the man's left cheek.

"Why am I here?" High Dance demanded.

After a long enough pause to be irritating, Bead asked, "Have you seen your sons today? Fast Thrower and White Stem? I believe those are their names. Oh, and that cousin of theirs, Panther Call. He's your irritating sister's oldest boy, isn't he? I've heard she rather fancies him."

Cool premonition blew through High Dance. "No. I haven't seen the boys today. Brown Bear Fivekiller, my war chief, is looking after them. He's . . ."

High Dance stopped short as, at a gesture from Bead, one of the Tula reached behind a basket and rolled something round, heavy, and irregular across the packed clay. Loose hair flew in every direction, the spongy flesh giving. The stub of neck brought the thing to a halt at High Dance's feet. Blood and fluid dripped from severed tissues.

Even though the angle wasn't right, and the thing lay canted, High Dance could see half-lidded and sightless gray eyes; the lips were drawn back to expose blood-caked teeth. Familiar tattoos could be discerned beneath the wildly loose hair.

High Dance's stomach clenched and knotted, his heart dropping like a rock in his chest. His knees went weak, and it was all he could do to keep from collapsing.

"You'll recall my advice concerning him," Bead said absently. He reached out, fingers under the Tula's chin as he inspected his handi- work. The messenger with the copper staff stared owl-eyed at the sev- ered head.

"My boys?" High Dance's voice sounded like gravel rubbed on a board.

"Oh, they're quite fine. A little nervous, but having an adventure the likes of which they'll be able to talk about for years to come." He turned loose of the Tula and went about securing his paints and re- turning them to a small carry box. "Or, well, *maybe* they'll be talking about it for years to come. That's the thing about a grand adventure, isn't it? I mean, if you know you're going to survive, that sense of ur- gency really isn't there. Nor does that rush of relief run through you when you realize you've made it. You've felt it, haven't you? That sense of euphoria that you only experience when you've beaten the odds? Breathing is fresher, the blood racing in your veins warmer. Food tastes better . . . and driving your shaft into a woman?" He waggled his finger at High Dance, a knowing glint in his eyes. "That, my friend, becomes the ultimate reaffirmation of existence. A cry to the earth and skies of, 'Here I am! Unstopped! Shooting my seed into the future!'"

High Dance reached out, imploring. "I'd like for the boys to have that moment."

Bead glanced sidelong at him as he closed his paint box. "Good. It would make my life easier and simplify things if I could bring them home to you as soon as possible. Is that satisfactory?"

High Dance swallowed hard. "It is."

"Excellent." Bead clapped his hands in delight, a grin spreading across his face. He glanced at the messenger and the painted Tula. "Go. Be about it."

As the two left, he walked up to High Dance, his dark brown eyes agleam with excitement. "Let's see, we were . . . Yes, yes, bringing the boys home. Perhaps within the next hand of time? Would that be con- venient?"

His gut churning like a whirlpool, High Dance said, "It would."

"Good." Bead rubbed his hands together in satisfaction. "I'm sorry I'm not thinking quicker, but I was up most of the night. I get so irri- table when I don't get enough sleep. How about you?"

High Dance nodded, unsure where this was going.

"So, yes, I'd like to nap." He gestured around. "But not here. Too many people know where it is. And, as you'll see, there's much to do this afternoon. Oh, and I'd appreciate it if you would stand down the guard. The boys will be right behind us." He raised his finger. "Less chance of misunderstandings that way. I wouldn't want them to accidently lose that future chance to relate the adventure of their kidnapping."

High Dance, the sick feeling growing in his gut, shook his head. "No," he whispered, "you wouldn't."

"See? You're a very responsible father, concerned with the fate of his boys. I like that, I really do. My father?" He waved it away. "You really don't want to know."

"So, you're bringing the boys? With us? Right now?" He shook his head. "I could just take them with me. Leave you to your—"

Bead's clever eyes narrowed. "You do understand, Great Chief High Dance, that the boys will follow along behind, at the rear of my column of wolves. I will be with you, listening as you stand down the guard, and then order the entire household staff into the palace with us."

"But why?"

Bead reached up, patting him reassuringly on the cheek. "Because I want to deliver a message to your sister, High Chief. It's not that I don't trust you. I do, I swear. But I certainly don't trust her! Or that nasty little dwarf of hers." He paused. "He will be there, won't he?"

"It's hard to say." High Dance's mouth had gone dry. "If it's just a message, I could—"

"Some things, High Chief, must be delivered in person. This is one." He shrugged. "Relax. She can say yes or no. And then I will be on about my business."

"Then why take the boys hostage? Why do all this?"

"Did they really make you High Chief on purpose? Are you this slow? I told you, I don't trust her! I have sixteen Tula to accompany me. Doing it my way, I deliver my message. It doesn't end in a fight, people don't die." He extended a toe to rock Brown Bear FiveKiller's head. "Well, but for him. Trust me, you truly, truly needed to replace him."

"That's it? Just deliver a message to my sister?"

"That's it." Bead smiled, as if in victory. "I just want to get in and out without any misunderstandings, betrayals, or complications."

High Dance took a deep breath, wondering why it seemed as if he were suffocating. "Very well, I'll ensure that you can deliver your accursed message, but this is the last time, Bead. Then, I'm done with you."

The man narrowed his eyes, a ghost of a smile on his lips. "As you wish, High Chief."

Fifty-one

To Sun Wing's absolute delight, Hickory Lance's body tensed, muscles knotting under his damp skin. He drove deep, a stifled cry in his throat. His shaft pulsed, seed jetting inside her. She cried out as yet another burst of tingling waves rolled through her pelvis, up her back, and down her legs.

His reassuring weight settled on her, trickles of his sweat mingling with hers to slip down her ribs.

"Blessed stars," he whispered when he finally rolled off and smiled up at the soot-stained roof.

She reached for a cloth and propped herself on an elbow as she studied her husband's muscular body. His skin seemed to glisten in the subdued light. She hadn't thought marriage would be like this. The stories she'd heard had prepared her for the occasional satisfaction, but tended to emphasize more of a duty and obligation rather than the kind of insatiable explorations she and Hickory Lance experimented with. To his surprise, she was willing to try anything, and to hers, he was a master at coaxing and massaging until she was quivering like a plucked bowstring.

Best of all, the more they played, the quicker his seed would plant a child in her womb and secure her position as a true woman in the family.

"You caught your breath yet?" he asked with a grin. "I wasn't sure you'd sing out like that with all these warriors standing guard around the palace."

"They know to keep their distance."

"But given what happened to Lace, you must surely be worried."

If you only knew, Husband.

Hickory Lance was Green Chunkey and Round Pot's oldest son, heir to the chieftainship at Horned Serpent town. And although she held nothing back when it came to her body, her thoughts, plans, and plots were inviolately her own.

To reassure him she said, "We must all be cautious, but you're not Heavy Cane." She patted his muscular chest to reassure him and play on his masculinity. "You're a blooded warrior, honored at the Men's House. I think he'll leave you alone."

And he would, of course. She'd demand it.

A slow smile crossed her lips, one that she was sure Hickory Lance would attribute to a much more physical satisfaction.

"Lady?" came a cautious call from beyond the door of her personal quarters.

"What?" she snapped, rolling her eyes. Pus and blood, was even this slight relaxation to be cut short?

"A messenger, Lady. He bears the Morning Star's staff and would speak to you."

"Coming." She sat up, feeling the cooling sweat trickle down from where it had pooled between her breasts. She glanced at her husband, meeting his knowing eyes. "You'll be here when I get back?" With a forefinger she tapped his flaccid shaft. "Maybe work this some more?"

"I might need a little help." He grinned.

"You'll get it."

She quickly washed using damp cloths, and from her engraved boxes, chose a bright red skirt decorated with frog motifs. Frog being one of First Woman's symbols of fertility, she hoped it would settle Hickory Lance's fresh seed. Over her shoulders she draped a shawl crafted from the skins of over two hundred painted buntings. Her hair she quickly twisted into a knot before she pinned it with no less than three polished copper turkey tails.

"How do I look?"

"From top to toe, a proper and dignified lady."

She giggled at that, given what they'd just been doing.

Her household staff was appropriately clustered outside the door on the veranda. She'd have to give that some thought. She didn't want them in the next room, listening. On the other hand, every time they clustered on the porch, it was a symbol to the whole rotted city that she and Hickory Lance were "active."

Stepping out she noticed with satisfaction that the warriors stood their posts in a solid square around her low mound with its thatch-roofed palace. Not that she had to worry, but to have refused them would have drawn the wrong kind of attention and questions.

At the bottom of her short stairway, two men knelt. One carried a copper-clad staff the length of his arm that bore a wooden sun symbol at the top: the Morning Star's messenger.

The second man was taller, muscular, his face painted white with blue lines radiating from his eyes. His long black hair was braided and hung down over his left breast. Dark and predatory eyes fixed on hers.

"Come forward," she ordered, and waved her household staff away. As they scattered, the messenger and his companion climbed the seven steps.

One day soon, they shall have to climb a great many more steps, and they'll grovel when they reach the top.

"Lady," the messenger greeted in a low voice, glancing around uneasily. "This man comes bearing a message."

She glanced closely at the copper-clad staff. Someone had quickly wrapped copper sheeting around a dowel—not the Morning Star's high standard at all.

"What message?" she asked, a slow smile coming to her lips.

The braided warrior spoke softly, his voice rising and falling in Caddo. As he spoke, the messenger nervously translated, "Your brother, Walking Smoke, sends greetings to his beloved sister. He says to tell you that we have the pieces in place. By the time you are hearing this, The Evening Star House will have discovered the importance of their role. Your presence is requested, and with it, all of Cahokia shall be yours within two days. He asks if you need help eluding your current guard."

She nodded and stifled a chuckle. "Tell Walking Smoke I am coming, and he need not concern himself. I have everything here in hand. Slipping away will be no trouble at all."

As her words were translated, the Tula bowed and touched his forehead. As he and the messenger rose and left, she watched the tall barbarian descend the steps.

Turning, she hesitated, glancing east toward the Morning Star's great black mound with its high-walled palace. Someone stood in the soaring southwestern bastion. Sunlight glinted on a polished copper hair piece, the sort of thing only worn by a high-born chief or lord. The Morning Star? Had he been watching her meeting with the Tula?

Surely the distant figure couldn't be the Morning Star. He had more important things to do than watch her palace from afar. Most likely, some lord paying tribute had been invited to enjoy the view.

If an important chief was expected, I should have been informed.

She forced it from her thoughts. Not her problem.

"Let's hope you're recovered, Husband. This is the last chance we will get to enjoy each other's bodies for a while. And next time, we'll be playing with each other in a much nicer palace."

Fifty-two

Lady Columella had taken her midday meal in her personal quarters, away from prying eyes. She sat on her sleeping bench, a wooden trencher on her lap. Beside her, Flat Stone Pipe, his hair up in a bun, balanced his own dish.

Columella sank her teeth into the succulent white meat. She absolutely loved paddlefish. The curious fish grew to huge sizes, often weighing as much as two men, and was netted from the river's deep waters. There, down in the depths, they used their long, spoonlike noses to stir the mud for food.

The steak she now ate was cut from the sweet-tasting white meat; not the red, inner meat that tasted like mud. Hers had been basted in walnut oil, sprinkled with onion leaves, and finished with a pinch of salt.

"How's yours?" Flat Stone Pipe asked. His own plate sat propped on his diminutive lap. He'd requested his to be flame-seared and seasoned with bison gall.

She shot him a ribald wink. "Excellent. I don't know how you can ruin yours with those gall drippings."

"Keeps me virile and potent in bed . . . as you well know. Foods have Spirit and qualities they impart to the body. Gall, roasted testicles from bison and deer, falcon breast meat, wolf hearts, these are foods that enhance a man's ability to satisfy a woman." He licked his stubby fingers and studied her from the corner of his eye. "Or would you rather limit yourself to your husband's hearty ministrations?"

"Considering that I haven't seen him in two moons?" She tossed her head back, exposing her throat. "I think I'll let you eat all the gall, buffalo testicles, and onions you'd like."

"Perhaps this evening?"

"That would be nice." A flicker of a smile played at her lips. "You should probably know . . . I've missed my moon. At my age, and given the stresses, I rather doubt that you have planted a child. I've missed before, sometimes twice in a row, so it's nothing for certain."

"No morning upsets?"

She shook her head, staring around her private room with its boxes, carved bed posts, and wall hangings. Across from her, the woven cane wall rose nearly to the roof. She loved that wall, had caught herself staring at the intricate pattern for hands of time. To her knowledge it was the largest, most intricate in all the world. "I don't feel pregnant. Usually there's that queasiness, that need to alternately shout or cry. Instead I feel remarkably focused, much too preoccupied with what's going on over at the Morning Star House, and almost desperate for your company. So eat more gall drippings. Drink it if you have to. If it wasn't for you, I'd have no relief at all."

He grinned to himself. "You do sleep better after I've worked my magic."

"That's only half of your magical qualities. For the moment I need your other talents. What word about Lady Lace?"

"Still missing." He ripped off a piece of fish and popped it in his mouth. "I don't understand," he murmured as he chewed. "The Keeper and the *Tonka'tzi* are tight-mouthed. Something terrible happened that night in Lace's palace. They wouldn't have immediately burned it otherwise. And raining like it was? They ordered a lot of oil to be poured on the flames to ensure it burned to the ground. That was a cleansing, my love. An act to counter some terrible pollution like the old *Tonka'tzi* getting his throat cut."

"So, do you think Lace is dead?"

"If they'd burned her remains along with her palace, they wouldn't be searching so hard for a young pregnant woman. Warriors are everywhere poking around. And even more interesting, word is out among the less desirable elements. In this case, Crazy Frog, Black Swallow, and their kind. A man can become wealthy, no questions asked, if he provides the Four Winds Clan with information on Lace's whereabouts."

He smiled. "Clever, clever. That had to be the thief's work. The

Keeper, aloof as she is, would never have thought of it. No, Lace was definitely taken. Spirited away in the darkness and rain. But whether she remains alive or dead? That, I can't say."

"What about Night Shadow Star? Could she be behind this? Conveniently soul-flying while her agents commit havoc?"

Flat Stone Pipe wiped his greasy hands on his apron, then went about meticulously cleaning his fingers. "The presence of Rides-the-Lightning in her palace for so long, and his refusal to leave her side when one of his own kinsmen was sick, argues against that. I'd say she's really soul-flying. I have heard that the Red Wing is guarding her." He chuckled. "The fool has her whole household turned upside down and hating him. Clay String is livid. Apparently the Red Wing threatened him with violence if he didn't straighten up and do his job."

Columella finished her fish, washed it down with sassafras tea, and nodded. "That's a good thing to keep in memory. The day may come when we can use Clay String against her."

Flat Stone Pipe gave her a flinty squint. "I'm hearing stories. That thief the Keeper has taken up with? Apparently he ambushed a foreign warrior in some dead-end passage in River Mounds City. Few details accompany the story, but he captured the man alive and somehow got him to the Keeper's."

"And?"

Flat Stone Pipe shrugged his small shoulders and laid his empty plate to the side. "All I know is that the upland Deer Clan chief and matron—the ones called Right Hand and Corn Seed—were escorted by warriors to the Council House last night. My sources were ordered out of the building along with the other messengers and recorders, so I don't know what was said. I do know, however, that Right Hand and Corn Seed's bodies were carried out by some of Five Fists' trusted warriors. Secretly, and long after everyone else had left."

Columella leaned back on her bedding, eyes tracing the patterns on her beautiful cane wall, trying to fit the new pieces together.

"Lady?" a voice called from beyond her door. "The High Chief asks that you attend him. He has a visitor who needs to speak with you."

She sighed, set her plate to the side, and stood. "Stay put. Depending upon what stupidity my brother has stirred up now, by the time I've dealt with it, I may need to call a recess, send the entire household out on errands, and have you 'relieve' my stress with your magic."

He gave her a mock bow, touching his forehead with his small fingers.

She draped her cardinal-feathered cape over her shoulders, felt to ensure that her hair was fixed appropriately, and swept out into the palace great room with its decorations, smoking central fire, and wall hangings.

The first thing she noticed were the warriors, a solid line of them in the rear. Dressed in battle armor, they clutched weapons; their faces were without tattoos, their posture insolent.

Absolutely unacceptable, brother. What madness—let alone stupidity— convinced you to allow an armed force inside my palace?

Her household servants and slaves were seated uncomfortably on the wall benches to the right. And in the rear were High Dance's boys, Fast Thrower and White Stem, and his daughter, Two Leaf. Her own son, Panther Call, his brother, Night Wolf, and her daughter, Onion Flower. The children clustered in a huddled knot. From their terrified expressions, they were anything but happy.

Terrified? But why? By whom?

Her anxiety built as she climbed up on her dais and settled into her litter chair. High Dance, rigid as a log, stood just this side of the fire, a tall and muscular man beside him. She thought the man's face had been painted to resemble Water Panther's with its yellow circles around his eyes surrounded by a three-forked design in black. What seemed to be whiskers streaked his cheeks, pale red on his nose.

The design unsettled her even more. Humans didn't meddle with or mock Piasa. The Underworld Lord was a dangerous and Powerful Spirit Creature. Anything that hinted at calling, or representing, his Power could bring disaster.

She met the newcomer's eyes, shocked to find them filled with amusement, almost insolent in their challenge. He looked to be in his mid-twenties with a spare body that suggested he might be a warrior, stickball player, or runner. Something about his face harkened to the familiar, as if, but for the Piasa face paint, she should know him. Then, a flickering finger of fear tickled her heart as she glanced back at the warriors in the rear.

His warriors. But . . . is this the enigmatic Bead?

"Very well, High Dance." She forced her voice to sharpen. "Perhaps you can start by explaining why I have strange warriors in my palace?"

Her brother looked ashen, his hands almost trembling. A spear of panic shot through her as she stiffened on the litter.

"My friend, here, has asked to deliver a message to you."

She forced herself to relax, to control her rising panic as she met the man's gleaming, almost triumphant eyes. "Let me guess, you're the one who calls himself Bead."

"Among other things, great Matron." He tapped his fingers insolently off his forehead, a mockery of the gesture. "Recently I've called myself White Finger." He made a face. "But I really didn't like that. White Finger?" He seemed to be rolling the words over his tongue. "It doesn't have . . . how would you say, fire? Spirit? Energy? Is that the word I'm looking for?"

"You said you had a message? Could you, perhaps, find the fire, Spirit, or energy, to finally deliver it so that I could be rid of you?"

He chuckled as if to himself as he placed a foot on the bottom step of the dais.

"That is far enough!" she snapped, extending an arm. "One step closer and I shall call for warriors to remove you!"

His lips flickered, which made that cat-painted mouth seem to sharpen in anticipation. Then he pursed them, as if to stop the smirk from forming. After elaborately and obviously composing himself, he said, "You at least have the presence and character to be a matron. Yes, indeed! You are Four Winds."

He jerked a thumb over his shoulder at High Dance. "I've begun to worry about him. He's more like, oh, let me think . . . soggy clay? The kind you can push and poke and then squeeze through your fingers?"

"Get out of my palace now!" A desperate fire began to rise in her breast.

He grinned and stared into her eyes, meeting her anger with amusement. "Don't you want to hear my message first?"

"No!"

"That stings me, Matron Columella. Cuts my very souls."

"Your souls are the *least* of my concerns."

He made a tsking with his lips, then sighed and straightened as he backed away, raised his hands, and gestured.

Four warriors leaped forward as Columella rose to her feet, crying, "What is the meaning of this?"

High Dance looked panicked, his arms out as he cried, "Bead? What are you *doing*?"

As the warriors raced up and grabbed her by the arms, the man called Bead laughed like a cackling grouse.

"*Let me go!*" Columella shouted as the warriors easily lifted her and carried her, kicking and screaming, to the wall benches on the palace's side.

"Go!" Bead ordered the rest of his warriors. "Check the rooms in back. See if that nasty little dwarf is here."

They just stared at him. He made a deprecating wave of the hand. "I'm getting ahead of myself, silly me." Then he barked out a series of commands in the guttural tongue that Columella recognized as Caddo. The warriors sprang like foxes, searching the rear. Meanwhile her hands were tied behind her, and she was seated on the bench with her ankles bound to one of the support posts.

High Dance stood impotently, his hands hanging. Disbelief and amazement filled his face as two warriors escorted him over and shoved him down beside her.

Enraged and terrified, she watched Bead climb lazily onto her litter and seat himself insolently, one leg dangling off the side.

She just glared, sputtering, until she could say, "Tell me that there are no more of them. That the warriors I see here are all of his company."

"All but one that I've seen," High Dance croaked.

"Good. Then it's just a matter of time before Brown Bear or one of his seconds checks on us."

"Brown Bear's dead." He swallowed hard. "I . . . I . . ."

She felt her gut heave. "Rot take you, *say it!*"

"I dismissed the warriors."

She closed her eyes, a terrible emptiness hollowing her gut.

Bead's warriors were filing out of her bedroom, shaking their heads as they reported.

"Who *are* you?" she demanded of Bead, determined to be the Matron no matter what.

Bead gestured for a piece of cloth, and began scrubbing at his face. Brown, yellow, and black smeared on the fabric. Even before the familiar patterns were revealed, she gasped. "They said you were dead."

Walking Smoke shot her a dismissive glance. "They've said a lot of things about me, cousin. Most of them, sad to say, are unfortunately true."

She had almost formed a response when a litter was carried in the front door, across the mat floor, and placed in the rear of the room behind the dais.

As it passed, Columella blinked, recognizing Lace's naked body where it lay lashed to the top. The woman looked as if she were in shock, her face pain-laced.

"But she's . . . she's *your sister!*"

Walking Smoke gave Lace a sleepy glance as he stood and stepped down from Columella's dais. "Yes. More's the pity." He walked over and stared down at Columella, a blankness behind his eyes. "You . . . and she . . . can chew on that unpleasant fact while I go take a nap. It's been a beast's own night getting here, getting set up. Been awake for most of two days. I'm assuming your bed is comfortable enough for a good sleep?"

When she didn't answer, he just chuckled, called an order to the Caddo warriors, and sauntered back through her door.

"What's this about, High Dance?" she whispered miserably.

"I don't know, sister. I really don't." He swallowed hard. "I'm sorry. I'm so sorry."

Fifty-three

In the back of the Morning Star's palace great room, Seven Skull Shield stood respectfully before one of the ornately carved benches. The poles had been artfully rendered as serpents by using the natural bends of the wood. Interlaced strips of hide had been woven across the frame and supported richly woven blankets and perfectly tanned hides. These either served to cushion someone's seat, or covered a sleeper.

He wondered how many people were allowed to sleep in the Morning Star's palace. He could see the slaves—including Fire Cat's mother and two sisters—where they huddled on rugs in one corner. He suspected they weren't allowed on the fancy bedding.

Fire Cat, standing beside him, glanced thankfully in their direction, obviously relieved to see them healthy and washed, and apparently not outwardly abused.

Must be agonizing to know that your once-exalted family is now some-one's property. He glanced at the Red Wing, seeing the effort the man put into keeping his expression neutral.

Better to live like me.

He grinned to himself. The only responsibility he had was to keep his belly full, elude whatever pursuit was behind him, and avoid, at all costs, hanging in some lord's square while his fellow rabble sliced and burned his body.

The Keeper, sitting to the left of the fire, had a hand to her breast as she slowly got her wind back. She'd insisted on making the climb herself. Not that Seven Skull Shield blamed her, he couldn't imagine letting the porters carry *him* up that frightening stairway on some precariously bobbing litter.

Tonka'tzi Wind also had seated herself on the west side of the great crackling fire in the center of the room. She had a huge copper headpiece tied into her gray hair and wore a rich-purple dress dotted with elk ivories. He figured that he could just about Trade that dress for an entire town in the southeast.

Night Shadow Star, in contrast, stood beside her aunt, arms crossed. A tan apron was suspended from a wide leather belt. Woven from the finest hemp, the piece hung below her knees in front and back. The sheer fabric swayed delicately as it caught the draft. She had thrown a cape of colorful parakeet feathers back over her shoulders, and her arms were crossed under her perfectly proportioned breasts. Instead of a head piece, she wore her hair loose, spilling down over the feathered cape to just above her belt. Her expression seemed distant, worried.

Seven Skull Shield let his gaze trace up and down her muscular legs, around the curve of her butt, and across her flat belly. He could imagine nuzzling between the full swell of her breasts . . .

"Did anyone ever tell you you're nothing more than a rude, snuffling dog?" Fire Cat almost spat from the side of his mouth.

"You talking to me?"

"Keep some respect in your eyes when looking at Night Shadow Star, or I'll pop them out of your head like hazelnuts from the shell. I won't have a drooling wretch like you stripping her clothes off, even if it is only in your imagination."

Seven Skull Shield chuckled. "And you'll do this how?"

"When I deal with you, it won't be in a shit-filled, dead-end passage."

"Now I'm shivering with fear." He bent his head closer. "What did they do? Slice open your sack and take your balls while you were hanging out there in the rain? I swear that woman might be any man's Spirit Dream, to have been put together like that."

He paused, seeing the anger flashing behind Fire Cat's eyes. "Ah, but wait. You'd know all about her charms, wouldn't you? Sitting there day by day, 'guarding' her from assassins and who knows what else."

"That's it," Fire Cat hissed with finality. "You're a dead man."

Seven Skull Shield grinned, returning to his prior stance. "Thought you hated her."

"Who, or how, I hate, is none of your concern, thief. From what I hear, though, I shouldn't be surprised. The rumor is that you'd be satisfied to stick that tow rope of yours into anything moving, and if not, the closest charnel house will provide something equally satisfactory."

He felt a cold chill run through him, eyes slitting. "You and me, Red Wing. Just as soon as opportunity permits."

"Wouldn't miss it. And in the meantime, keep your shit-slathered eyes off my lady."

His lady?

At that moment the Morning Star walked out from his room in the back. As usual, he was resplendent. An immaculate white apron was hanging down between his knees. On it, embroidery depicted the Cahokian sun symbol in black thread. A falcon-feather cape hung from his shoulders. The magnificent headdress depicted *Hunga Ahuito,* with his two heads, perched on high.

With a gesture of his hand, Morning Star excused the recorders and advisors, waiting until they had filed out of the room, taking the servants and slaves with them.

Only when they were finally alone, the moaning of the wind in the thatch and the crackling of the fire the only sounds, did he mount his dais and seat himself in the high chair. His head remained fixed, eyes staring into the distance.

So, is he Chunkey Boy playing at being a god? Or is he really the Morning Star?

Seven Skull Shield cocked his head, studying the young man in the dazzling costume. He tried to see the jealous Chunkey Boy, his face twisted in rage as he beat a rival's hand to pulp. Somehow that image didn't conjure when compared to the ostentatious figure before him.

"What have you come to report?" Morning Star asked.

"The Piasa sends his greetings, Lord," Night Shadow Star stated coldly as she stepped forward. "My souls have just returned from the Underworld. Piasa, Horned Serpent, and Snapping Turtle wish you to know that they are aligned with you against the threat that now seeks to destroy Cahokia and unhinge our world."

"Why would they send me this message?" He barely flicked his eyes in Night Shadow Star's direction.

"Because they do not wish the conflict between the Sky World and the Underworld to burn free among humans. In the Beginning Times, *Hunga Ahuito* separated the Powers of the three worlds for a reason. Should the barriers between the worlds be broken, Power from one called into the other, chaos would result. While the lords of the Underworld distrust you and the Powers of the Sky World, we face a mutual threat."

"Have you determined the nature of this threat? Identified the individuals behind it?"

"I have," she said crisply. "The one you banished, Lord Walking Smoke, has returned to Cahokia."

Seven Skull Shield and Fire Cat both straightened, as did the rest of the room. *Tonka'tzi* Wind gasped. The Keeper bit off a curse.

The Morning Star, however, just seemed to smile, as if it were no news at all. A glint seemed to harden behind his narrowing eyes. "You say he's back? Stirring mayhem, brewing trouble? But to what end?"

Night Shadow Star, her arms still crossed, brazenly walked into the sacred space between him and the fire, and stood hip-shot before him. The pose was defiant, and to Seven Skull Shield's mind, incredibly provocative.

Her voice rang out. "He comes to destroy you, among other things. Not that that comes as any surprise after the assassinations. He comes to avenge himself on the Four Winds Clan."

"He *is* Four Winds Clan," *Tonka'tzi* Wind cried. "He's my nephew!"

"He *killed* his father, your brother, and has tried to kill the rest of us." Night Shadow Star barely shifted, only turning her head far enough to glance at her aunt. "He believes himself to be the Wild One. The reincarnation of Thrown Away Boy, the discarded twin who crawled out of Corn Woman's afterbirth and, adventuring with his brother, went to war with his father and family."

Blue Heron cried, "But that's crazy! Walking Smoke? You're telling me he's the one who conspired with Right Hand to *kill* the Morning Star? By Horned Serpent's shining scales, why? Surely not because Chunkey Boy surrendered his body to Morning Star. It was done willingly. And what would poor Lace have to do with the story? Why butcher her husband that way? Why abduct her? Why would he try to kill you, Night Shadow Star? You're *his sister*!"

Night Shadow Star raised a muscular brown arm, hand out to stop her aunt. "Clan Keeper, a foul and black wind blows through his souls. He sees this world with different eyes than the rest us. Disembodied Spirit voices whisper and guide him, and he listens to them as declarations of truth. Under their sway, he remakes the world as the poisoned voices would have it." She paused. "Do you understand? He is convinced he *is* the Wild One, the chaotic twin. He truly believes that the Wild One's Power is his. And he is about to unleash it."

"Unleash it how?" *Tonka'tzi* Wind asked. "We're *hunting* him! It's only a matter of time before we find him, run him down, and kill him for the diseased beast he is!"

"Where is Sun Wing?" Night Shadow Star asked softly, as if changing the conversation.

"She was sent a summons to be here like the rest of us," *Tonka'tzi* Wind replied, looking around. "How should I know? Perhaps she's distracted by her husband again?"

"She's gone to her brother," the Morning Star interjected, eyes fixed on the distance.

"Gone to him?" Blue Heron asked, cocking her head. "To Walking Smoke? Why?"

"Because he has offered her all of Cahokia if she will serve him."

"That's insane!"

"It is all insane," Night Shadow Star said in a low voice. "The twisting of senses and thoughts by the winds and storms of perverted Power. Black and deceiving voices from other worlds whisper among our souls like stroking fingers. We are warped and bent, molded into the tools of a dark and destructive Power. Then we are made to serve. All the while our lost and frightened selves wish for nothing more than peace. To be left alone to nurse our fear and hide from the prying eyes of those who do not understand . . . and cannot conceive."

At her words, a shiver ran down Seven Skull Shield's back. Pus and blood, the woman sounded absolutely possessed.

"And you think Lord Walking Smoke is deceived by this evil Power that blows through him?" *Tonka'tzi* asked.

"I know it, aunt." Night Shadow Star's haunted gaze seemed to bore right through the *Tonka'tzi*.

"How?" Blue Heron barked. "Did he tell you? Have you seen him? Heard from him?"

She shook her head absently. "I know because, but for Piasa's Power filling me, whispering to me, I would be the same lost and wretched being my brother has become."

Spooked as he was, Seven Skull Shield caught the stiffening of Morning Star's shoulders, the slight narrowing of his eyes as he watched Night Shadow Star. He certainly believed it.

Blue Heron seemed to shake herself. "Getting back to the problem, Walking Smoke has violated the Morning Star's banishment. He has returned with Tula warriors to murder his own family, and has been playing us for fools." She snapped her fingers, expressing irritation. "No wonder he's been so successful. He knows us, knows Cahokia.

He could have walked among us at will, his face painted, wearing rags. He could blend in with the crowd, hidden right before our eyes, and we'd never have known."

"But why?" *Tonka'tzi* Wind demanded. "What did we ever do to him except treat him as the heir to the Four Winds Clan? We covered for that boy, cleaned up after his crimes, gave him everything he ever wanted."

"Like his brother before him, he discovered he wanted even more than you, or anyone, could give," Night Shadow Star snapped, a harsh anger in her tone. She was looking hard at the Morning Star. "Chunkey Boy and Walking Smoke? My brothers shared everything. What one had, the other couldn't stand to be without. They were Four Winds, of the Morning Star House, sons of the *Tonka'tzi* and the legendary Black Tail. They lived above the laws of Power and men."

She sniffed derisively, her hot glare on Morning Star. "It *could not* have happened! Not to me. The images were spun of something whispered by malignant voices—a fantasy nightmare promoting discord. A nightmare that repeated itself over and over. It woke me shivering from the deepest sleep. I blamed myself, felt ashamed that such vile and sordid images could inhabit my dream soul. I had convinced myself that I was somehow perverted, that my souls bore some pollution that led me to even dream such a disgusting and revolting event. I might have even continued to keep it at bay, but for my brother's return. It provided the opening Piasa and Horned Serpent needed to pull back the midnight I'd draped around my souls and memory."

Her fists knotted. "It was real! That happened to me."

The Morning Star now gave her a cold smile in return. He said in level tones. "I am *not* your brother. But he is."

A grim set to her perfect mouth, she snapped bitterly, "And I will deal with him. You will *not* interfere."

Seven Skull Shield heard both *Tonka'tzi* and the Keeper gasp at the order. Apparently one didn't use that tone of voice with the Morning Star.

The living god gave her the faintest of nods. "He is yours . . . and your master's. Presuming you can deliver him."

"You and I, however—"

"*That* will be for a different day." His eyes, too, narrowed, boring into hers. "Let us accept, *Lady,* that we serve different worlds, and leave the actions of humans behind us for the moment."

The very air seemed to vibrate with tension. Both the Keeper and *Tonka'tzi* were cringing, expecting some explosion.

"Agreed," Night Shadow Star told him through gritted teeth, her rage apparent. Then she relented, a bitter smile bending her lips. "Despite what lies between us, Morning Star, a greater danger must be addressed." She paused. "You know what he's going to attempt? Why he's taken Lace and summoned Sun Wing?"

Morning Star's nod made the two-headed eagle headdress bob. "And I finally understand Piasa's interest in you." He paused, shifting his glance to the cowed Keeper and *Tonka'tzi*. To them he said, "The one called Walking Smoke is attempting to conduct a resurrection. If Lady Night Shadow Star is correct—and he truly believes himself to be the Wild One—he must surpass the achievement of his brother, Chunkey Boy."

"How?" Blue Heron demanded. "Chunkey Boy's souls were replaced by your own. How can he surpass his brother's sacrifice of willingly surrendering his body to you?"

Night Shadow Star's brittle laughter crackled in the still air. "Aunt, don't you see? He's going to sacrifice Sun Wing and Lace and her unborn child in the attempt to resurrect another Spirit being inside his own body. One greater than Morning Star."

"The Wild One, the real Thrown Away Boy, wasn't greater than Morning Star," the *Tonka'tzi* growled.

"No," Morning Star told her evenly. He glanced sidelong at Night Shadow Star as he spoke. "We were equal, but opposites. But if Lord Walking Smoke could resurrect Piasa's Spirit to occupy his body? What sort of triumph would that be for the once-banished and disgraced brother of Chunkey Boy?"

"But that's impossible!" Blue Heron cried.

"Is it?" Night Shadow Star demanded, spinning around. "But for a couple of mistakes he came close to resurrecting a dead Tula into a woman's body up in that farmstead on the bluff. Close enough that the Powers of the Underworld fear he might succeed. And then what happens to our world?"

"Vomit and blood," Seven Skull Shield whispered to himself. "It would be like the Beginning Times, monsters and mayhem everywhere."

"For once, thief," Fire Cat muttered through gritted teeth, "you and I agree."

Fifty-four

Possessed of a sense of disbelief and shock, Blue Heron descended the long stairway. The late-afternoon sun slanted in the northwest, filtering through the low-hanging orange-brown haze created by Cahokia's thousands of fires. It glistened on the ox-bow lakes that curled around the wide floodplain like lazy shining serpents.

The vista that normally amazed her, and the miracle it represented, paled against the revelations she'd just heard. And could almost refuse to believe.

She glanced sidelong at Seven Skull Shield who descended the steps beside her in an ambling gait. "Well, thief?"

"I'd give a Tunica pot to know what the terrible secret is."

"The terrible secret?"

"The one between the Morning Star, this Walking Smoke, and Night Shadow Star. Whatever it is, it's a snap and crack."

"A snap and crack?"

"Yes. You know. Like you have to do to get at the best and juiciest meat hidden inside a nutshell?"

"You have a peculiar way of talking."

"You have a peculiar family. Makes me glad that all my children are being raised by men who think that they're the fathers."

"I really ought to hang you in a square," she muttered. "What I *want* to know is how preposterous this claim really is. Can Walking Smoke actually resurrect the Piasa's souls into his body?"

"Keeper, I'm not the one to ask. For me, most of this business of Power is just that. Business. A way to be on the take. Oh, sure, there's storms and seasons and floods, and life and sickness and death. And ghosts, I do believe in ghosts, and forest and river Spirits. But praying and making offerings, and priests and temples and great festivals to keep the sky and earth in line? That's a way for people like you and the priests to safely separate the dirt farmers from their harvest."

"Such a skeptic, are you?"

He gave her a half-lidded thoughtful look. "If half of what the priests and people believe was really true, I'd have been blasted by lightning or swallowed by the earth years ago. The easiest place to rob is a temple. No one guards the shell or copper, figuring any thief would be charred to ash just touching the sacred holies."

"So you think this is all a sham on Walking Smoke's part?"

"Sham? No." He screwed his face up as he thought it through. "He's killing people, Keeper. And no matter what I think, Lady Night Shadow Star and Morning Star, they think he can do it."

"Now you're an expert on my niece and the living god?"

"I'm pretty good at spotting liars, Keeper. Being not such a bad one myself, if I do say so."

"Apparently you do."

He gave her a measuring glance, his normally deceitful eyes unveiled. "She believes it. And so does Morning Star. He's good that one. He just gives off the faintest of tells, the quiver at the corner of his lips, the slight narrowing of his eyes. Sometimes it's just the barest change in his posture, or the squaring of his shoulders. He likes playing the living god."

"Maybe because he *is* the living god?" She tried to keep the bitterness out of her tone.

"Not my decision to make," Seven Skull Shield admitted as he lowered his moccasin-clad feet from step to step. "But for those of you who do believe in such things, your charming Walking Smoke is going to cut Lace's throat and then Sun Wing's, just like he did with those dirt farmers. And if he makes his ritual work this time, he's going to call one really mad Piasa to inhabit his body."

"But what does that *mean*?" she demanded. "For all we know, if Walking Smoke actually succeeds, Piasa might just tear the body into bloody chunks, strew the meat and bones around, and dive back into the Underworld."

"And there's another concern. I'm hazy on it, but you might want to ask that Lightning Rider—"

"Rides-the-Lightning."

"That's him. Now, if an element of Piasa's Spirit is already whispering to Night Shadow Star—an element we'll assume is some sort of dream-soul, a projection of Power, or whatever it is—what happens when the whole Water Panther's Spirit takes complete possession of Walking Smoke? Does he then control Night Shadow Star? Or does it jerk Piasa right out of her like ripping out a piece of her souls?"

She gave him a horrified look. "I have no idea. It's . . . It's . . ."

"Breaking all the rules that govern Power?" He spread his arms wide.

"Or it might break those barriers Night Shadow Star was so concerned about. Create an imbalance between the Spirit Worlds that empowers witchcraft, disease, upsets in the weather, spawns tornadoes, makes things fall from the sky . . . who knows?"

He led the way down onto the Council House terrace. "In the Creation story *Hunga Ahuito* separated the Powers of the three worlds, making them balance. Morning Star was a terrestrial being once, he and his brother. Only after he ascended to the Sky World on eagle wings, did that status change. So, calling him back into a human body isn't an abomination."

He raised a cautionary finger. "Messing around, bringing Piasa's Spirit fully into this world? Putting the Spirit Beast's souls in a human body? What kind of abomination is that? Such a deed could lead to complete chaos." He winced. "If you believe in these things."

She nodded at the guards as they left the Council House palisade gate and started down the last flight of stairs to where her litter waited on the broad roadway. She could see her porters where they lingered in the crowd. Pilgrims were watching her descent, pointing, talking back and forth, amazed that right before their eyes, here came the Four Winds Clan Keeper.

"I've never cared for all this," she muttered to herself. Then louder, added, "Thief, we really have to find Lace. And Sun Wing if he's got her, too. You understand the hurry now, don't you?"

He nodded, leading the way down to the Avenue of the Sun, waving away the crowd as they sidled closer. "She can't be far. And knowing the kind of man your Walking Smoke is—"

"Seven Skull Shield!" A thickly muscled man, his forearms scarred, pushed forward, calling, "By the droop-balled Spirits, you look like a man who could play chunkey." He grinned, mouth wide in his round face. Three peglike teeth remained standing in his jaws. "A good friend sends you this. Says with it, you can change your winnings."

Blue Heron was on the verge of calling her guards to have them deal with the ruffian, but Seven Skull Shield raised a restraining hand as the man offered a beautifully crafted red-granite chunkey stone.

Seven Skull Shield took it, glanced at Blue Heron, and said, "Give my good friend, here, a nice piece of Trade, Keeper. I think I'm off to try my skill. If this stone changes my luck, I may have something for you." He actually winked at her in a most conspiratorial manner. Then he was off, almost pounding his way through the crowd as he headed west on the Avenue of the Sun.

The arm-scarred brute was looking at her as if he'd never seen a noble in his entire life. Maybe he hadn't. She gestured as Smooth Pebble and War Claw appeared at either side. "Give the good fellow a piece of copper, will you? And thank him for his service."

"But, I . . ." Smooth Pebble touched her chin, adding, "Yes, Keeper. But I've received a message. A runner, almost spent, arrived as you were coming down the stairs. Lady Columella requests your presence in Evening Star town. She informs you that she's discovered some very unsettling information, unsettling enough that she will only disclose it to you in person."

"How soon does she want me there?"

"Her messenger said immediately." Smooth Pebble's brow lined with worry. "Keeper? With everything else that's going on, do you dare leave?"

Blue Heron frowned, all the while searching the crowd around her. She had a face and name to put on the threat now. He'd disguise himself, of course, paint his tattoos with a thick layer of paint. But now that she knew to look for his eyes, she would recognize him, wouldn't she? He couldn't have changed that much in the few years he'd been gone.

"Curse it!" She glanced around. "Now that I really need him, he's gone!"

"Who? The thief?"

"Oh, very well." She glanced up at the sun. "But I'm not going tonight. We'll leave first thing, before dawn. That should get me there by just after midday tomorrow. But send a runner to River Mounds. Have War Duck pre-position porters at the midway to relieve mine when they become winded. I don't want to be gone a moment longer than I need to."

"Yes, Keeper."

"What's the matter?" She squinted at Smooth Pebble. "You've got that look on your face."

"I just don't like it is all, Keeper. The scorpion has been ahead of us all along. What if he's somehow staged this to get you away from Morning Star House, away from the *Tonka'tzi* and Night Shadow Star?"

"We've got a name now," she said, lowering her voice. "It's Lord Walking Smoke. He's back, and he's behind all of this."

"Don't go to Evening Star town," Smooth Pebble warned. "You'll be vulnerable the entire way."

"Maybe that's what he's planning on," she mused. "But if I go fast, leave even earlier, I can be there at first light before he expects. Once I'm inside Columella's palace, I'll be untouchable."

Fifty-five

At dusk the smoke always thickened in the air as endless fires were stoked or fanned into life for evening meals, or perhaps to provide enough light as a family gathered after a hard day's labor in the fields.

As Seven Skull Shield hurried down the Avenue of the Sun, he watched the great city succumb to night. The hawkers and Traders had closed up their packs and rolled their blankets, or taken down their small wicker stands. Packs of dogs grew more active, knowing that bones, scraps, and occasional untended plates might now be found in greater abundance.

Parents called for their children, who, desperate for another game with their friends, argued for "just awhile longer."

The rank smells of latrines and the cloying stench from charnel houses drifted on the long fingers of the evening breeze to mix with the tang of rot and the acrid stink of unwashed humanity.

No sooner would the stench become nearly unbearable than a fresh eddy would replace it, and tease the nose with the mouth-watering scent of baking nut bread, or pit-roasted meat. Sometimes the odors of roasting corn would almost overpower, to be followed by the tantalizing fragrance of a boiling rabbit or fish stew. The drifting scent of sassafras tea, a trace of mint, or berry juice just added spice when mixed with turkey or rosehips.

He passed a constant stream of men and occasional women, hurrying along to beat the darkness and return home. Sometimes they bore packs, other times their arms were full, or baskets hung from tumplines.

Laughter could be heard from around the crackling fires he passed. At other times voices were raised in acrimony. Babies periodically screamed and cried, and singing rose as worshippers melodically thanked the now-set sun for the gift of the day. Dogs barked, and the occasional howl mixed with flute and drum music.

The sky darkened, and stars by the thousands emerged from the deepening blue. The high roofs, palaces, and temples loomed like darker silhouettes, while beneath them, internally lit buildings cast yellow light from doorways, and along cracks in the walls.

Teaming Cahokia was a noisy place at this time of night, with wooden dishes being knocked together and ceramic pots clinking. The conversations around fires and evening meals made a constant, rising and falling cadence as he passed in the deepening gloom.

All this could vanish, torn apart by Walking Smoke and his perversion of the Spirit World.

But a half moon past, the notion would have seemed ludicrous. Cahokia had projected itself as eternal, invincible, and immortal due to its very size, and the sheer momentum of its existence. Like a giant rolling boulder, how could·it be stopped? Any obstacle, Spiritual or physical, would be overwhelmed, inundated and smothered by the mass of the population and the flow of goods and energy.

Can Walking Smoke really resurrect Piasa's souls inside his body?

The notion was a perversion of everything Seven Skull Shield considered to be right. Even seeing the Morning Star—if indeed that was the reincarnated god—didn't contradict the inherent wrongness of Walking Smoke's plan. Morning Star had been born human, or at least human shaped. But the Water Panther? Part lion, part snake, part bird? How did you stuff and entire Underworld Spirit creature like Piasa into a mortal human body?

It smacked of perversion unlike anything Seven Skull Shield had ever known. And, well, he'd known of a lot.

As he passed the guardian posts that marked the boundary of River Mounds City, he touched his forehead with a new-found reverence.

Despite the darkness, he turned off the Avenue of the Sun. He knew by heart the way through the mad warren of dwellings, society houses, granaries, and workshops. His only worry was tripping over something in the darkest shadows. He cut behind the Snapping Turtle Clan charnel house and surprised a pack of dogs that growled over some kind of carcass. They ran at his shouts and clapping hands, dragging their prize away.

Winding among houses and cramped gardens, he rounded River House's hickory oil warehouses and ducked under their elevated corn granaries. A thousand mice—all right, maybe a hundred—skittered away in the darkness.

He called greetings and waved as he made his way around small evening fires that flickered beneath ramadas attached to craftsmen's houses, and sidestepped the latrine screens out back. Cutting past a firewood warehouse, he stepped out onto the winding main trail that wound along the levee crest. Enough people passed here, coupled with light from the occasional fire, to allow a quicker progress.

A crackling fire burned outside Crazy Frog's large, three-room, two-story house. Before it, on one side, in ranks according to status, sat Crazy Frog's four wives, seven sons, and eight daughters. Across from them reclined no less than six tattooed, athletic-looking men. Oiled skin reflected in the light, expensive aprons on their waists, and their hair was coifed and pinned with shell, copper, and colorful feathers.

These were the lucky chunkey players who had been fortunate enough to be invited to Crazy Frog's nightly feast. Just behind them, kneeling in the shadows, sat a line of well-dressed and—though Seven Skull Shield couldn't make out their features—undoubtedly beautiful women. Such attractive and ornamental young females swarmed around successful chunkey players like moths around a blaze. Some could almost be classed as professionals, the others just opportunistic.

"Greetings, all," Seven Skull Shield called, stepping into the firelight. "The best of the evening and Morning Star keep you." He produced the chunkey stone. "I have some business with Crazy Frog."

The oldest of the wives, Mother Otter, a tall woman wearing a white-fox cape Traded down from the far north, rose, studied him thoughtfully, and tilted her head toward the dark passage leading behind the house.

"My husband is in the back. Announce yourself at the storehouse door. You know the way, Seven Skull Shield."

He touched his chin respectfully, giving her a private wink. For years he'd tried unsuccessfully to wiggle his way into her bed; she'd never given him anything more encouraging than a mocking smile.

Entering into the darkness between the buildings, he cocked his shoulders to clear the narrow walls, and stepped into the back where a small triangular space was bounded by Crazy Frog's house on one side, his storehouse on another, and the rear of a stone carver's workshop on the third. The storehouse looked dark, a mere shadow in the night.

Seven Skull Shield walked up to the door, and softly called out his name. Moments later, the door was lifted aside, and a shadowy figure told him, "Step in."

Seven Skull Shield—his skin prickling with unease—slipped through the door, encountering a thick fabric hanging on all sides while the person who let him in reset the door.

"Here, to your right. You'll have to slip through the folds of the curtain."

Almost being led, Seven Skull Shield pushed his way past hanging blankets and into the main room. The walls here were covered with shelving and boxes—essentially the treasure house filled with Crazy Frog's winnings. As obscure as the building looked from the outside, it had been built like a fortress with two layers of vertically set, thickly plastered, white-ash logs, a stone floor, and solid timber roof overhead. At least two burly warriors were known to guard it at any given moment.

Several hickory lamps burned brightly, adding their sweet odor to the warm air and casting the room in a yellow glow. Crazy Frog sat on a tripod chair, his legs out before him, arms resting on large, intricately carved wooden boxes to either side. Stepping in behind Seven Skull Shield was one of the guards; the other—the man who'd let him in—took up position on his right.

Crazy Frog cocked his head and narrowed an eye as Seven Skull Shield lifted the chunkey stone, and said, "Thanks for sending this. I could use a little luck about now."

"You may not like what I have to tell you, old friend."

Seven Skull Shield grinned humorlessly as he hefted the stone disk. "If what I already know is the way of things, there's not much good news to go around."

Crazy Frog, his dark eyes shining in the light, smiled warily. "Have you identified this assassin?"

"Word came straight from the Underworld. Or so I'm to believe. If my source is right, the assassin is Lord Walking Smoke himself. The old *tonka'tzi*'s son. The brother to Chunkey Boy and Night Shadow Star."

"What's he here to do?" Crazy Frog played his fingers like dancing spider legs across the chest's carved wood. He had his hair up in a bun, pinned with polished copper that caught the light. His lips were pursed.

"He's here to destroy the Four Winds Clan, old friend. If we can trust one of his Tula warriors, he wants to rip Cahokia up by the roots and cast it away. Apparently his ultimate goal is to resurrect the Piasa's souls inside his human body. Some mad scheme about unhinging the Spirit worlds and plunging Cahokia into a massive chaos."

Crazy Frog stiffened; his normally blank face and placid demeanor tensed. "That's heresy and . . . That's . . . That's . . ."

"About as crazy and insane as a man might be?" Seven Skull Shield tossed the beautiful red stone up and let it smack into his hand. The thing had perfect balance. "Normally, I'd agree with you, say let him try, and see what it gets him."

"But you don't think that's such a good idea?"

Seven Skull Shield shook his head. "Some people—who know a whole lot more than I do—actually think he might pull it off."

Crazy Frog's spiderlike fingers flipped over in a questioning gesture. "It might bring even more players to Cahokia, more people to try their skill on our courts. The games might be even more challenging than they are now."

"Assuming you avoid the riots, vengeance killings, and open religious warfare Walking Smoke is hoping for, you've still got one major problem with that, old friend."

"And what is that? A lack of faith?"

"No." Seven Skull Shield tossed the stone up and caught it, his eyebrow lifted. "Piasa would kill Morning Star and break the Four Winds Clan . . . all of it. Destroyed. To do that he needs that civil war, turning sky clans against the earth clans, rekindling old feuds among the dirt farmers, and unleashing Underworld Power. But let's say he succeeds without a bloody and devastating war that depopulates half of Cahokia. Now, old friend, your worst fears come true. You see: Piasa, being all snarly and Underworldly, *doesn't play chunkey*."

Crazy Frog leaned forward, rubbing his hands thoughtfully together. His expression was pained. "When, my friend, have you cultivated such a persuasive eloquence?"

"I assume you sent me this stone for some other reason than just to chat about the Piasa?"

Crazy Frog chewed at his lips for a moment, eyes narrowed. "What if I'd located the Lady Lace and knew where you could find this Walking Smoke? What would that be worth to the Keeper and the Morning Star?"

"You could probably name your reward. Maybe your own private tower to watch the matches on the Grand Plaza? I'd be tempted to suggest the Morning Star would throw a couple of games for you. Let the other guy win so that you'd collect on the odds. But I'm not sure he's that grounded in the subtler strategies of gambling for profit."

At that Crazy Frog chuckled. "No, I imagine not. Do I have your word that this Keeper of theirs will remember me fondly when this is all over?"

"My word may not be what you should be depending on when it comes to Four Winds politics and decisions, but my growing understanding of the Keeper is that yes, she'll be most generous with her gratitude. Assuming, that is, that this whole thing can be brought to a satisfactory conclusion. Our charming Lord Walking Smoke has managed to turn Morning Star House upside down, and the Keeper would like to put it back up right before clans are turned against clans, and there's rioting, burning, looting, and other unpleasant mayhem."

Crazy Frog shook his head, sighing. "Of all the people in the world, who would have thought *you* would turn out to be a hero?"

"Heroes usually have to suffer terrible hardships and sacrifices before they die in most unpleasant ways." He made a pained face. "So let's agree I'm no one's hero, all right?"

Crazy Frog chuckled dryly. "I hold your Keeper to your promise." Then he glanced off to the side, saying, "What do you think?"

Seven Skull Shield cocked his head as a dwarf stepped out from the shadows behind a large seed pot. The little man was dressed in expensive fabrics. An iridescent raven-feather cloak hung over his narrow shoulders; his hair coiled in a tight bun atop his head, pinned with a conch-shell columella.

"So this is the thief we've all been hearing about," the dwarf said, his voice wary and high-pitched. "My old adversary, the Keeper, has taken a peculiar twist in the selection of her agents."

"But then," Crazy Frog told him dryly, "so have you." He paused, then gestured grandly. "Seven Skull Shield, I give you Flat Stone Pipe the dwarf. A small man of large—"

"Yes, yes," Seven Skull Shield waved it away. "The Evening Star matron's famous little spy and bed toy. But, tell me, spy, what are you doing here?"

"Apparently, the same as you, thief. Trying to stop Walking Smoke and save people who are important to me."

"It may not be easy explaining your involvement in this to the Keeper, little man."

Flat Stone Pipe absently fingered the extraordinary reliefs of cosmic spider carved into the side of the storage chest beside him. "Oh, I doubt that. Your Lord Walking Smoke captured Evening Star House this morning. His Tula warriors control the palace. He has lady Columella, that dolt High Dance, the lady Lace, and all the Four Winds children captive inside. He's sent a messenger summoning Lady Sun Wing, and I imagine he's laid additional traps and snares around the city to trip up any potential adversaries."

Seven Skull Shield narrowed his eyes as he thought this through.

Crazy Frog noted, "He has what? Less than twenty Tula warriors? He won't be able to hold out if the Four Winds squadrons are called up to assault the palace."

Flat Stone Pipe's expression pinched. "So far, no one knows he controls the palace outside of those held captive inside, and those of us here. I'm hoping Walking Smoke will keep quiet long enough for us to act."

The dwarf glanced up at Seven Skull Shield. "I said that because as soon as Walking Smoke thinks he's running out of time, he's going to start cutting the throats of every man, woman, and child he's holding in there. And as he pours out their blood in sacrifice, he's going to begin the ritual to call Piasa into his body."

"Assuming it actually works," Crazy Frog mused, eyes distant.

"Whether it works or not"—Flat Stone Pipe pointed a stubby finger—"it makes no difference if you're one of the hostages having your throat sliced open. Either way people I care for are going to end up dead."

Fifty-six

This can't be happening to me . . . to us.

The thought kept running around and around Columella's souls like some sort of worried rabbit. She sat on the eastern bench, fingering the rattlesnake's head carved in the upright post that supported the cross pieces in the frame. She had watched, stunned, as the barbaric Tula ripped down wood carvings of the Morning Star, Bird Man, and the curled Four Winds Clan insignia. They stripped off the copper, tossing it into a growing pile. They didn't bother with the shell inlay, giving up after shattering most of the pieces they tried to pry out of the inset. The immaculately carved reliefs and sculpture were broken up and thrown into the central fire. The trophy weapons and shields had come down to burn; the skulls and long bones of Evening Star House's long-conquered foes had been tossed into the flames where they splintered, whitened, and cracked.

Even the stone carvings of Morning Star, Snapping Turtle, Eagle, and Falcon had been consigned to the fire, and now lay, white hot, among the glowing coals and calcined fragments of human bone. Surely any Spirit Power they once contained had been purged from the sacred stone.

A physical pain pierced her heart as the symbols of her world were consumed.

Of her beautiful palace, only the woven-cane wall behind the dais still stood, the intricate design reflecting pale shadows where once-stunning reliefs had hung. She'd waited for most of a year while the craftsmen wove the complicated patterns. For all she knew, Walking Smoke left it standing because it was too cumbersome to tear down.

And perhaps, like her, he placed too much value on keeping his privacy in her personal quarters behind them.

Just this side of the fire a low dome had been lashed together out of cane and blankets before hides were laid over the whole. To her practiced eye, it looked like a sweat lodge.

Even as she pondered it, Walking Smoke emerged from her sleeping quarters, rubbing his eyes and yawning. He wore only a breechcloth, the Four Winds tattoos on his muscular young body stood out vibrantly on his light brown skin. The Morning Star House pattern with its forked-eye design, to her amazement, had been altered. Now a third point, creating the three-forked design of the Underworld had been added to the tattoo.

Walking Smoke yawned again and absently scratched as he studied the plaster walls.

"What's he doing?" High Dance asked.

"He didn't tell you?" she shot back. "All those clandestine meetings? All the careful plotting and sneaking you did? Even after you learned he was dangerous you couldn't let go, could you, brother?"

"Stop!" he said through gritted teeth. "As if you did any better with your shifty dwarf." He shot her a sidelong glance. "But then he's a smart one, isn't he? Haven't seen him around since Walking Smoke trapped us in here."

"Be patient." She narrowed her eyes as Walking Smoke called out orders in Caddo, and two of the Tula, using antlers, began fishing the stone statuary from the coals.

"What's this? He's really going to sweat? Here! In the middle of our palace? Using our burned statues for heat?" High Dance wondered.

"Why not?" she asked dryly. "Or did you figure he'd walk out in the plaza like everyone else?"

"Now what?" High Dance tensed as two more Tula dragged a tall boiling jar from under one of the sleeping benches and placed it on the floor just back from the sweat lodge's entrance.

Another Tula had rounded up one of the water jars. Flipping back the blankets on the sweat lodge, he placed it inside, then walked over to where the slaves huddled against the back wall. He joined three of his companions who stood guard.

Walking Smoke sauntered around the room before stopping to size up the children, one by one. None would meet his eyes. He shook his head, as if in self-argumentation, and turned his attention on the slaves.

He pointed at Cold Water, a longtime slave who had served her for years. She'd obtained him as a young man, and valued his big body, though a wound to the head at the time of his capture had always left him a little slow.

Now the Tula made whistling and hooting sounds as they rushed forward and grabbed Cold Water, who kicked and fought as they dragged him over the matting to the middle of the room.

A war club lashed out, the wet smack loud in the silence.

Columella tensed, half rising. But High Dance, despite his tied hands, managed to drag her down. "Don't get in the middle of this, Sister. Don't call attention to us."

"But Cold Water—"

"Is already stunned and quivering," High Dance gritted.

She watched in horror as the slave's head was lifted by his hair; his eyes rolled back and fluttered in his head. The Tula positioned him over the corrugated cooking jar.

A long brown-chert blade appeared in one of the Tula's hands. Columella gasped as it was drawn quickly across Cold Water's stretched throat.

She heard her children cry out and glanced down the bench to see them cringing, hiding their eyes, crying in horror. They'd loved Cold Water. He'd always taken care of the children, his big dumb heart delighted to look after them.

Now his blood jetted red through the wide slit under his chin. She could hear it splashing and trickling into the corrugated jar. So deep and clean was the severing cut, and so skillfully did the Tula catch the flow, that no blood bubbled up from Cold Water's nose or mouth.

Then, to Columella's horror, she watched the Tula hoist Cold Water's feet ever higher until they held him almost vertically above the pot to drain every last bit of blood from his body.

Walking Smoke smiled lazily and walked over to the sweat lodge. Slipping his breechcloth over his hips, he let it slide down his legs and stepped out of it, naked.

For some reason, he glanced at her, gave her a wink, and shook his head. "Sorry, Matron," he called. "You'll have to remain in frustrated denial. It's all about purity, you see."

She bit off a hot retort, forced her gaze away from his, and realized her mouth had gone dry. By clenching her fists she was able, for the moment, to still the shivers and terror that ran along her bones.

Where the Tula still struggled to elevate Cold Water's body, the flow from his gaping neck was now down to a threadlike stream. One of the Tula thumped Cold Water's chest over the heart, and a couple of breaths later, another gush of blood drained from the severed arteries.

"Why?" High Dance rasped. "In *Hunga Ahuito*'s name, why?"

To her relief Walking Smoke had ducked into the sweat lodge and sealed the interior. She could hear the explosion of steam as he poured water onto the white-hot statuary stones and began his sweat. He was singing to himself, some sort of Power song.

She whispered, "It's just . . . barbaric."

That's when the Tula finally dropped Cold Water's body to flop loose-limbed on the floor, his dead eyes seeming to lock on hers with a pleading she couldn't stand.

Every eye in the room was on the Tula as two of them lifted the pot and walked over to the south wall. Dipping their fingers in the hot blood they began drawing on the naked plaster. Crude though the work was, dripping and poorly rendered, she nevertheless recognized images of tadpoles, caterpillars, mudpuppies, frogs, butterflies, salamanders, and long red snake images.

Sun Wing's litter was born up the trail from the canoe landing by eight strong men. Calling on the authority of the Morning Star House, Feather Wand, her head of household, had simply ordered canoes to be made ready. Sun Wing, her litter, and porters, had been ferried to the great river's western shore.

The sun had set by the time they started up the steep bluff trail; she glanced up at the mottled clouds that darkened the sky. Two slaves bore smoky, resin-ball torches to light the way as she was carried past the two-headed eagle guardian posts and into Evening Star town proper.

Passing through the temples, society houses, and around the charnel mound, her porters trotted across the dark plaza. As she was carried past the World Tree pole Sun Wing touched her forehead in respect. Her porters bore her to the base of the stairway ramp in front of Evening Star House palace where High Dance and Columella held sway.

Two heavily armed warriors and a single man holding a staff of office stood by the guardian posts at the foot of the stairs leading up to the palace.

Sun Wing's porters lowered her litter to the hard-packed clay. Feather Wand helped her to her feet before he turned, lifted his staff of office, and announced, "The Lady Sun Wing, of the Morning Star House, of the Four Winds Clan, of the Sky Moiety demands audience."

The two warriors, both young Tula, tightened their grip on their war clubs while the third man stepped forward and raised his own staff, saying, "High Chief High Dance and Matron Columella are involved in ceremonies and purification, and will not be disturbed until mid-sun, two days from now. That is the order of the Evening Star House."

Sun Wing stepped forward, motioning Feather Wand back. The two Tula warriors gave her a slit-eyed inspection that unsettled her—the kind of look wolves gave a whitetail deer fawn. To the man who carried the Evening Star House staff, she said in a low voice, "Go inside and tell my brother that Lady Sun Wing, his sister, is here."

"By order of the Evening Star House—"

"Do you know who I am?" she snapped. "Go tell him Sun Wing is here. Do it!"

The man hesitated, clearly afraid.

"I know you were hired for this. Tell Walking Smoke, or White Finger, or whatever he's calling himself, that his sister is here, or he'll have you skinned alive."

The man murmured something to the Tula, then turned, almost running up the steps.

Not even twenty breaths later, he was back, crying, "He'll see you, Lady. But you alone."

She turned to Feather Wand. "Stay here. I'll call you when I need you. It may be awhile so don't worry."

"Yes, Lady."

Taking a moment to ensure her hair was pinned properly, and to arrange her skirt and cape, she then climbed the stairs, back straight, moving with all the regal grace expected of a Morning Star House lady.

Two more warriors were waiting at either side of the closed door, bows and quivers of arrows at hand, war clubs slung. They, too, watched her with those same predatory eyes. She forced herself to ignore them as if they were nothing more than bugs.

With a gesture, she indicated they should open the door for her. She could read their disdain as they did so.

"Time will tell," she told them in a voice dripping venom. She would remember, and when she ascended to rule Cahokia these two would regret their actions, thoughts, and expressions.

Stepping inside she stopped short, staring around. The walls had been stripped. Where ornaments, carvings, and trophies had once hung, the plaster was painted in drying blood. She recognized the images as depicting transformation motifs and magical signs. Even the high, woven-cane walls in the rear that separated the personal quarters from the great room sported bloody drawings. She had always admired the artistry and skill that had gone into the wall's creation. The old woman who'd supervised its intricate weaving was long dead. From the amount of blood spattered on the tightly packed cane, the wall would never be the same.

Ah, the sacrifices we have to make.

Her sister, Lace, lay bound and naked on a litter behind the dais. Nothing about the way they'd tied her to the chair looked comfortable. She had to be in excruciating pain.

So sorry, dear sister, but nothing worthwhile comes without sacrifice, blood, and death.

Behind Lace's litter a terrified batch of slaves crouched on the floor as if trying to make themselves small. High Dance and Columella's six children, cowering and naked, were crowded onto the benches to her left. Each had been artfully tied to the bench frame. Half way down the room, and guarded by a Tula, sat Columella and High Dance. Sun Wing almost chuckled at the desperate hope that lay behind her cousins' eyes as they recognized her.

"Sorry, you self-inflated fools," she murmured to herself. "But I never liked you even in the best of times."

She recognized Walking Smoke, his body naked and painted where he knelt in prayer before what was obviously a sweat lodge. At the fire a ceramic pot filled with black drink cast fingers of steam into the air. To one side in the rear lay a dead man, his throat slit wide.

She walked forward onto the matting and stopped. "Hello, brother."

For a moment he remained, eyes closed, lips moving in a sub-vocal prayer. Then he gazed up at her and smiled.

"It is good to see you again, little sister. You've grown into a young woman. Better yet that you've come to share in the miracle I'm about to perform."

"Was the information I provided useful?"

"Very much so." He spread his arms wide. "As you can see, Morning Star had no idea what I was about. They still have no clue as to who I am. Or do they?"

"No," she told him craftily. "The Keeper is stumped. Aunt *Tonka'tzi* Wind is stunned and reeling. The Morning Star, who depends upon them, has no idea you've returned, let alone why you are here. He's too taken with playing his role of the living god."

"And Night Shadow Star?" Did she detect a wistfulness behind his voice?

"She's soul-flying. Whatever the goal of your attack the other night, she's so lost in the Spirit world you will have been in charge of Cahokia for a half moon before she realizes any differently."

His vision seemed to fix on eternity. "I had hoped I could lure her here, be able to share, as you will, the glory of Piasa's incarnation in my body." He sighed. "I have always loved her. So much that my souls ache."

"I thought you loved me?" she asked, irritated by the longing in his eyes. She stamped her foot. "I was the one you contacted. Not her. You came to me."

Coming back to himself, he smiled slyly. "Yes, I did. And I have no regrets. You've become an outstanding woman, fulfilling all of my wildest expectations. I saw it in you as a little girl: the petty tantrums, the pouting, the way you looked at Lace with such longing when she got all the attention for being good."

"Are you trying to make me angry?"

He gave her a dismissive glance. "Make you angry? I could care less. You see, now that you're here, telling me what you've just told me, only one use remains for you."

"I don't understand."

His lazy smile was followed by a rapid staccato of orders, the cadence of which led her to believe was in the Caddo language. And, for the first time in her life, she began to wish she'd studied it like her mother had suggested.

As two of the Tula walked up behind her, she asked, "What did you just tell them?"

His mild eyes fixed on hers. "I'll need you to be naked for the ceremony."

"Oh, *of course,* brother. I'll surely do *that* for you while surrounded by these barbarian men. What? You think I want them ogling and dreaming about what they'll never have? Discussing my charms and what they'd like to do with them? I'm a lady of the Morning Star House." She jerked a thumb back where Lace moaned on her litter. "I gave her to you. Told you how to gain entry to her palace. In doing so I've fulfilled my obligation. After you resurrect Piasa, I will be the Matron. Ruler of Cahokia."

"Of course you will." He gestured submissively. "It's easier if you cooperate. Less chance of tearing those beautiful fabrics or breaking the laces on your cloak."

She stiffened, glaring at him. "You're serious? Why?"

He pointed at Lace. "As in all things, you will have to follow your sister."

"I *gave* her to you! Told you when her husband would be returning . . . how to gain entry—"

"You did indeed." His simple smile widened. "And now you have given yourself to me as well. I really do thank you for that. Hopefully the Keeper and the *tonka'tzi* will also offer themselves."

"You said that if I helped you, I'd receive the greatest honor in Cahokia!"

"And you will!" he exclaimed. "You, Lace, the Keeper, Matron Columella, good old High Dance, and all the children over there. Can you think of a higher honor than resurrecting the Water Panther's souls into my body? Think, Sun Wing! What nobler offering is there in all of Cahokia than you?"

She gaped at him. "What are you talking about?"

"Once Lace has been through it, your part in all this will come perfectly clear. You have a choice: you can strip yourself, or my wolves will do it. You see, I have to tie you up now. Otherwise you might decide that you're . . . well, unworthy of the honor and try to escape."

Fifty-seven

"$G_{et\ up.\ You\ need\ to\ go.}$" Piasa's voice sounded so clear, as if he were whispering from right beside Night Shadow Star's head.

"Walking Smoke's going to kill me, isn't he?"

"*Most likely.*" A pause. "*Does that frighten you?*"

"Yes."

But then Sky Flier had only seen a span of twenty years written in the stars of her birth.

In the blackness of night, Night Shadow Star opened her eyes to her dark room. She eased her blanket aside and rose silently from her bed. She could feel Piasa's close presence, caught his shadow at the corner of her eye as he flickered from one side of the room to the other.

She stepped over to the storage box where she'd laid her carefully folded black fabric dress the night before. Slipping it over her shoulders, she snugged it at the waist with a rope belt. With a toss of the head she shook her hair back; her practiced fingers quickly braided it.

Pulling tall war moccasins over her feet, Night Shadow Star tied the laces at the top. She loved those moccasins. Makes Three had given them to her as a gift, and they fit perfectly. Wearing them, she could run like the proverbial wind.

From the corner she took her bow and the quiver of arrows. Just the feel of the wood sent a shiver through her. Walking Smoke had given it to her summers ago, a slim stave of Osage-orange wood, springy and resilient. With it, she'd outshot him and Chunkey Boy at marks. They, of course, could drive a war arrow farther, but she'd been a better shot at measured distances.

Now, if Power willed it, she would use that selfsame bow to kill him.

Those had been better days. Before the resurrection. Before that terrible night.

Perhaps the world died that night, and I died right along with it.

Her war club came next. The arm-long ash-wood club was lighter than a man's, and instead of a knob at the end, hers was fixed with two sharpened copper blades, the edges finely honed.

She took a deep breath as she slipped the war club's handle under her belt. "It all comes down to me."

"*Yes,*" came the whisper from Piasa's dark shadow. "*If you are good enough . . . clever enough.*"

"I am afraid," she whispered, and ran loving fingers over the bed she'd once shared with Makes Three. Perhaps the only time in her life when she'd been safe, cherished, and unselfishly loved.

The memories she'd hidden in the midnight of her souls had been freed. Never again could she seal them into the darkness to be forgotten. What had happened that night hadn't been her fault, wasn't a perverted creation of her twisted imagination.

"*Existence is fear, Lady. Death is but the constant shadow of the living.*"

She nodded, steeled herself, and eased to the door. The Red Wing slept uncomfortably, his back against the door frame. Fire Cat's head was down, kinking his throat, causing his breath to rasp in his throat. In the faint light cast by the great-room fire, she could see that he'd placed the helmet to one side, but still wore the poorly fitting armor. The war club had slipped from his sleep-lax fingers; the handle now leaned against his leg.

"*He guards you well. Good thing the long vigil has him exhausted.*"

Carefully she stepped over him, easing her feet down.

Then she crept through her neat palace, thankful the Red Wing had ordered everything cleaned.

At the door, she hesitated, then moved the heavy planks to one side. As she stepped out, a voice asked, "Who's there?"

"The lady Night Shadow Star," she told the warrior who stood guard. "You need to ensure that my palace remains secure. Walking Smoke could try to sneak in at any moment. Just like he did at Lace's."

"Yes, Lady." The warrior bowed and touched his forehead. "Let me call you an escort. Summon your porters and the litter to—"

"No." She tapped the war club at her side. "I need to do this alone."

"But I—"

"Alone!"

"Yes, Lady."

She smiled grimly as she hurried forward, patted Piasa's guardian post with quick fingers, and almost skipped down the dark stairs.

Passing the last of the warriors guarding the approaches to her palace, she turned onto the Avenue of the Sun, faced west, and forced herself into a warrior's distance-eating trot.

As she passed the Great Observatory with its monitoring priests, she touched her forehead in respect, whispering, "I understand now, Sky Flier. Your prophecy was correct. Twenty years was all the time I was allotted."

The inevitability filled her with a curious serenity.

A low mist clung to the ground; it turned silver on those occasions when the three-quarter moon broke through the patchy clouds. At other times, she ran in almost total darkness.

Breathing easily, she felt her legs warming, catching their stride in time to the rhythmic working of her lungs. She'd always loved running, but tonight, she felt a different exaltation as she kept catching glimpses of Piasa where the Water Panther's Spirit image loped along behind her. She could feel his presence and hear the occasional patter of his taloned feet on the packed surface of the roadway.

I go to kill my brother.

A sense of destiny filled her, pulsing in time to her quickened heartbeat, rushing with the blood that pumped through her running legs.

"You've been chosen as the champion of Power." Piasa's voice seemed to entwine with the damp night air.

"I find no honor in that."

"Honor? Hardly." Piasa's voice hardened. *"For those touched by Power, let alone those who would pervert it, there is only suffering and misery. Nothing comes free, Lady. Not even your birthright."*

"Where will I die?"

"If you are successful—and very, very lucky—his fingers will be locked around your throat as you drown in darkness and terror." He paused. *"You do understand, don't you?"*

"I understand," she answered, seeing it in the eye of her souls. His fingers might already be around her neck given the tightness under her tongue.

★ ★ ★

Lace blinked, startled into awareness as the unwelcome sensation of hands on her body finally registered in her numb and pain-wracked brain. For long moments she couldn't place herself. She squinted her eyes, trying to make sense of the young men who now flipped lengths of rope from her arms, legs, and torso.

Who are they? What are they doing?

Groggy and filled with agony, a fluffiness like cottonwood-down filled her thoughts.

She struggled to understand.

"Mother?" she whispered hoarsely. "Who's there?"

Then one of the men lifted her right arm into view. How odd that she couldn't feel it, that it flopped down senseless and dead when he let loose of it.

Her other arm was lifted, and she could see where tight ropes had purpled her skin, the imprint of the fibers visible. Next they removed the ropes from her completely numb legs. As two of the men worked their arms under her back, however, spears of pain shot through her; she screamed as they lifted.

They carried her through a palace of some sort, but the walls— bathed in flickering yellow light—had the oddest decorations: crimson snakes, tadpoles, frogs, caterpillars and butterflies, mudpuppies and salamanders, oddly proportioned Spirit beings, all painted on the plaster in rusty red-brown tones.

Her back spasmed again as the four men who held her stopped and turned her. In the process, she screamed again as they bent her backward and her head dangled. She could just see her long black hair where it trailed across intricately woven matting. The first tingles of agony began to be felt in her arms and legs. Her baby squirmed in her womb, as if it too were now afraid.

From her upside-down vantage point, she could see a line of children seated on the benches along one wall. And there was Chief High Dance and Matron Columella. Glancing to the other side she was surprised to see Sun Wing, naked, her body painted and tied securely to one of the wall benches. Her younger sister's hair was down, a cloth gag in her mouth. Even as Lace watched, Sun Wing was tugging at the ropes binding her. A desperate fear glittered behind her eyes.

"Hello, Sister," a soft voice cooed, and she fixed her upside-down gaze on the young man who approached.

"Help me," she whispered hoarsely. "I'm Lace. Lady Lace, of the Morning Star House. Call them. Call the Morning Star . . . he'll . . ."

He smiled warmly, his face so familiar, yet odd. His naked body had been painted in the sacred colors, red, white, black, blue, and yellow. His face was painted like a panther's ropy muscles slid under smooth skin as he cocked his head and studied her. Burning brown eyes stared into hers, and he smiled slightly.

Pus and blood! Walking Smoke!

Horrible memories came flooding back. Heavy Cane had screamed against the gag in his mouth as Walking Smoke had cut him apart. Of all the terrifying images, she remembered her husband's throat, the sinews bulging, veins popped from the taught, muscle-tight skin. His eyes had strained as though trying to burst from his head while sweat beaded and ran from his forehead.

Walking Smoke just kept cutting, laughing in delight as he did, and now he has me!

"Morning Star's not coming, Sister. He doesn't even know where you are. More's the pity. Imagine the gift if I could offer *him* to the Underworld."

"Gift?" she rasped, trying to swallow. Her thoughts were reeling, half dazed by the pain spearing through her body. Memories of what Walking Smoke had done to her husband, the brutal torture, kept whirling through her souls like a foul wind.

One of the other warriors was approaching with a large corrugated cooking pot. Pushing her hair out of the way, he positioned the pot just so on the matting below her head.

"Please, Walking Smoke," she whispered hoarsely. "You're hurting me."

"It will stop soon," he told her with a smile. "I'll fix it, I promise."

She glanced to the side again, at the children who stared at her with horrified eyes. High Dance looked sick, and Matron Columella gaped in disbelief.

"My baby, Walking Smoke. You've got to help me keep him safe." She turned her gaze back to his, trying to remember something that pain and fear kept hiding. Each time her thoughts reached for it, the revelation jetted away like a trout from a grasping swimmer.

"Your baby is among my greatest concerns," he told her seriously. "I can't tell you how important the first heir to Morning Star House is to me. To everyone in the Spirit World."

Her heart was hammering, the tingling pain in her arms and legs almost unbearable. Thirsty as she was, tears silvered her vision. "Please, Brother. Put me down. It hurts! I'm afraid!"

"Pus and blood!" she heard Lady Columella cry. "*She's your sister!*"

Walking Smoke had turned toward her and pointed. "Be quiet, camp bitch! Or your boys will be next."

Lace screamed as the men holding her shifted her position, raising her hips, arching her back further. Yellow lances of pain burned up and down her spine, her head now dangled, blood pulsing in her brain with each panicked beat of her heart.

She could feel her child as it kicked frantically inside her.

"Help me." She tried to swallow. Almost choked on fear. "Help me," she whispered. "I don't understand."

Walking Smoke was singing now, some kind of ritual song.

She shivered, fighting the pain, as someone began bathing her cold skin with a damp cloth. Even upside down as she was, she caught glimpses of men with palettes as they began painting designs on her skin. She felt their fingers tracing patterns on her breasts, and the extended girth of her belly.

"Please, Brother. *Please*. What are you *doing*?" Her voice caught in her throat. They were painting her arms and legs now. Breathing had grown so difficult due to the angle at which she was held.

This is some terrible game he's playing.

Her last memory of Heavy Cane banished that hope as a lie.

Her stomach knotted, heaved, and spewed burning fluid into her throat and mouth. She coughed, blowing the bile into the back of her nose.

A hoarse scream was torn from her throat.

Walking Smoke's eerie song sent terror through her trembling bones.

"Are you ready, Sister?" The words seemed to come from across a huge distance.

"Please," she whispered weakly. "Stop it."

Half-blinded, choking and coughing, she felt her hips lifted even higher. Craning her neck, she glanced past her hanging breasts, painted now in red spirals, and saw Walking Smoke looming over her. His eyes were slitted as if in rapturous delight, his arms out. She fixed on his blue-painted penis now fully erect and just above her; a tension filled his voice.

"No!" she tried to cry, but coughed on the bile.

She saw one of the warriors offer him a long, chipped-stone blade. It's glassy surface rippled in the firelight.

"*Let me down!*"

Sheer panic burned through her in waves.

Twisting her head, her eyes fixed on the blade as Walking Smoke bent down. Then she looked into his gleaming and excited eyes.

"Got to do this just right, Sister. The timing has to be perfect."

She tried to jerk, to kick away. Her weak limbs hardly moving.

Hard hands grabbed her hair, yanked her head down and back. Someone was holding the corrugated pot so that she stared down into its dark depths.

From the corner of her eye, she saw Walking Smoke crouch, the song rising on his lips. Her heart was hammering, blood pulsing in her head. She felt the sharp blade as it was placed against her stretched throat.

He waited until she'd screamed her lungs empty.

The sting surprised her as it burned through her neck from front to back.

She had the momentary glimpse of her head being pulled back even farther, felt the rush of air into her lungs despite her closed mouth. Heard her blood as it splashed into the jar. She could see the man now who tugged on her hair.

The last horrifying sensation was of a stinging line of fire as her belly was sliced open from breast bone to pubis. But that, too, vanished in an encompassing darkness. . . .

Chrysalis

*P*ure blood, Powerful blood.

This is the blood of my family. The life force of the Four Winds Clan, taken in the most beautiful and pure way. I have drawn it from my sister, and even better, from the unborn son who would have one day become tonka'tzi. Or, should the Morning Star have worn out Chunkey Boy's body, the son whose souls would have been sacrificed to resurrect the living god yet again.

Such is the Power and purity of the blood I have offered to the four corners of the Earth that I don't need to break my concentration to look at the places where my Tula have torn the matting up and dug sacrificial pits into the mound top. I can still see the dark holes through the eye of my souls, see the blood I poured pooling in the bottoms. Like a well pot in the very soul of the earth, I looked down and saw my reflection in that still surface. The same image Old-Woman-Who-Never-Dies was seeing as she looked up from the other side: me, staring down into her world with reverence and respect. Meeting her, eye-to-eye, and assuring her that I, Walking Smoke, alone of all men was worthy of the great task that I am attempting.

The voices tell me that Old-Woman-Who-Never-Dies knows I have no choice, that when I call her servant forth, the Water Panther will have a worthy host for his dark and violent souls.

In return I have offered her the noblest blood in the world.

I open my eyes to a slit and glance sidelong at Sun Wing. She sits tied to a bench post in such a way as to restrict the circulation in her legs and arms. Her face is tear-streaked, eyes swollen and panicked. The gag in her mouth distorts her lips. She understands the incredible honor I'm bestowing on her. I realize that the immensity of it has momentarily overwhelmed her.

"Lace was but the first offering, First Woman. Just as you begin to revel in it, I will offer yet more. And when you think there can be no greater sacrifice, I shall double it!"

For the moment, I am but a caterpillar, tempting Old-Woman-Who-Never-Dies. Through Lace's offering she knows my heart. Knows that I will offer her my entire family, the very might of Cahokia, in return for Piasa's souls.

I am shaken and awed. Is there no end to my love?

The voices whisper no.

For what greater sacrifice can a man make in the name of love than to offer up his family in the attempt to change the world?

I cannot take too much time, or gloat. I must focus as I dismember Lace's body. Each cut has to be made just so. Both with her and the infant. The Underworld is watching and judging the perfection of my performance.

Unlike my last fumbling attempt in the farmstead, I cannot make a mistake.

With a glorious sense of rapture flowing through me, I fill my lungs and begin to sing!

From a caterpillar, I shall now become a chrysalis.

Fifty-eight

Columella's stomach churned, and she dared not close her eyes lest it all replay behind her eyelids. Instead, she hunched forward, arms clenched over her now empty and growling stomach.

"It's a dream. A twisted fantasy. I'm going to wake up soon, and it will be morning. None of this will have actually happened." If she repeated it over and over, insisted with enough passion, believed hard enough . . .

She needed only to cast her gaze to the right where Lace's corpse lay to disabuse herself of any such fantasy.

My children . . . ?

Just down the bench from her, the heirs of Evening Star House—product of her own womb—huddled against the wall, feet up, curled against one another for reassurance. She could hear their weeping, feel their terror. Her heart ran cold. This day's terror would scar them.

Assuming they survived. Assuming they didn't end up like Lace, their throats slit, their blood offered to the Powers of the Underworld.

Across from her the once-proud Sun Wing stared through fear-dazed eyes into a distance of nothing. Her shoulders periodically shook as she wept. Her young body had been painted in the transformation symbols before she'd been tied to the bench post. From the angle of her binding, the circulation had to be cut off. How cunning of Walking Smoke. His victims couldn't struggle effectively with their limbs gone numb and useless.

In an attempt to stem her failing courage, Columella let her eyes play over the walls of her once-beautiful palace. But everywhere she looked *his* presence and malignant Power was manifest. Every surface was covered by the hideous drawings. The brilliant crimson of fresh blood had darkened, browned, and was now edging into red-black.

Whatever the symbols meant, they were some part of Walking Smoke's polluted magic.

By the Creator, please, get me out of here.

She purposely kept her eyes away from where her soul-twisted cousin now sat cross-legged before his sweat lodge, arms up, hands out as they held a steaming cup of black drink. The drying blood had turned them dark red, and his singsong chant filled the air.

The Tula warriors watched him with a mixture of awe and wonder. Nor did they lower their guard in the least when it came to her, her family, and the remaining slaves.

She steadfastly refused to look at the limp remains of Lace or her bluish-pale and lifeless male fetus. For the moment, Walking Smoke had placed the tiny corpse on Lace's chest, the infant's slack mouth pressed to her left nipple in a mockery.

Columella fought to purge the images from her memory. But she kept hearing the echoes of Lace's scream, seeing the flash of the long chert knife. Even while Lace's and the infant's dying bodies were being bled out, Walking Smoke had performed some peculiar ritual with a spindle whorl, twirling it above their nostrils and repeating some incomprehensible singsong chant.

The Tula had watched, awe-struck, each whispering softly to himself and making warding signs with their fingers; so it had to be some barbarian trick Walking Smoke had adopted from the south.

Where he shifted uneasily beside her, High Dance rubbed his face as if to peel it from his very skull.

Just wait, Walking Smoke will do it for you.

"Someone will come," he whispered under his breath. "It's just a matter of time."

"It's been most of a day," she answered. "I don't know how, but he's taken steps. Some sort of spokesman outside giving orders in our name that we're not to be disturbed."

"Where's your dwarf when we need him?"

"If he's got the sense Power gave a pollywog, he's running like a winter hare from a red wolf." Flat Stone Pipe had obviously seen enough to know when to slip out his hidey hole and flee. In spite of her brave words to High Dance, she fervently wished that even now Flat Stone Pipe was being carried at the head of War Duck's massed squadrons as they crossed the river to storm her palace.

Please tell me that's the case. Please, blessed Father Sun, get me out of this, and I'll prostrate myself before you for the rest of my life.

Down from her, her children whimpered and squealed in terror as Walking Smoke opened his eyes and shot a radiant smile in their direction.

"Soon," he promised them. "I'll be ready for you soon!"

Tilting the cup, he raised it to his lips, throat working as he chugged the strong and bitter tea to the last drop. One of the Tula stepped forward and handed him a short stub of rattlesnake master root, bowed, and retreated.

Walking Smoke tilted his head back, chewed, and stiffened. Leaning forward on his knees, his stomach pumped. Vomit spewed out to splatter on the bloody matting.

Having purged, he climbed to his feet, carefully washed the long chert knife in a jar of water, and began cutting Lace's dead infant apart.

Columella's stomach knotted as he carefully laid the dismembered little limbs on the matting, placing them just so, as if to create some abominable pattern.

With each rhythmic stride, Fire Cat's moccasined feet hit the hardpacked surface of the Avenue of the Sun. For once he could actually bless the Morning Star for his administrative prowess in keeping the avenue graded, flat, and free of holes and dips. For a runner, in the middle of the night, Fire Cat was making extraordinary time.

Occasionally the three-quarter moon would peek through the clouds illuminating the avenue. But even when obscured by the moon-silvered fog the route was easily followed, having been surfaced in white sand.

Pus and blood! How far is it?

The last time he'd been this way, he'd been carried like a dressed-out deer, half-conscious, soaked in pain.

This time, even in the middle of the night, the immensity of Cahokia awed him to the bones. For the hand of time he'd been running, he'd never been clear of buildings. Sometimes they were more widely spaced, other times he ran through densely packed clusters of houses, temples, granaries, and mound-top palaces. Nor was his nose used to the endless medley of the city's odors. Mostly, he decided, when this many humans lived in such teaming proximity, they stank.

His weapons knocked hollowly against his armor as he pushed his distance-eating gait. Assuming he managed to survive this, he was going to insist on fitted armor. Makes Three's oversized wooden breastplate was rubbing his chest raw, the straps eating into his shoulders as the front and back bounced. The bow, however, was a quality piece of workmanship—as if Night Shadow Star's husband would own a lesser weapon. The same with the war club.

"West, she turned west," he muttered to himself as he ran.

Rounding a slight bend to the southwest, he caught the flicker of lights ahead of him. He picked up his pace, and within a finger's time had closed on a litter-bearing party trotting along in flickering torchlight.

"Who comes?" a warrior in the rear called as Fire Cat's heel strikes could be heard.

"I am Fire Cat, in service to Lady Night Shadow Star, of the Morning Star House, Four Winds Clan."

He made a face, having no sooner said it, than feeling an ill resentment at both the words and the arrogance with which he'd uttered them. He quickly added, "Myself, I am Red Wing, right down to the root of my souls."

"Fire Cat?" the dark figure on the litter called back to him. "What are you doing out here in the night? Where's Night Shadow Star? Pus and blood, tell me she's not soul-flying again."

He trotted up to just behind the litter. "Good evening, Keeper. Surprising to find you out here. I'm in pursuit of your niece."

"Do want to explain that?"

"She slipped out while I was asleep. Her bow, quiver, and war club are missing along with her trail moccasins."

"You seem quite familiar with her things, Red Wing."

"I spent a lot of mindless and unproductive time in her room during her last soul flight, Keeper. When I wasn't dribbling water between her lips, I had nothing to do but stare at her possessions."

"Did she receive a summons from Evening Star House?"

"If a messenger had come from Chief High Dance, I'd have known. Whatever she's about, she's decided upon it on her own."

"And what's your purpose out here?" He heard the skepticism in her voice.

"That she took a war club? Bow and quiver? Trail moccasins? Even to a clod like me these things suggest her purpose isn't a social call. My guess? She knows where Walking Smoke is, and she's going to confront him."

"I see." The Keeper's shadowy form turned back toward the front, her figure outlined in the torchlight.

"You asked about a summons from Evening Star House?" He shrugged his armor back straight, wincing where it had chafed. "I assume you received one."

"I did."

"And why travel in the middle of the night, Keeper?"

"In case it's a trap, Red Wing. If Walking Smoke is behind it, he might have an ambush set along the road. If Columella has discovered something about his activities, and where to find him, I want to know what, and how. My nieces are at stake." A pause. "Apparently all three of them."

"Where's the thief?"

"Off on some errand of his own."

"Clever of him. This way he can pop up when it's all over and claim to have discovered something fascinating."

She was silent for a bit. "You don't like him, do you?"

"Lady, only in Cahokia could a squalid sort like Seven Skull Shield thrive. Anyplace else, his relatives, for the sake of social propriety, would have been forced to knock his brains out years ago."

"Only in Cahokia," she agreed.

"I should probably run ahead," he told her, having pretty much caught his breath. Her porters were making good time, but he could almost double it.

"You think you can catch her?" the Keeper asked.

"May Falcon Above help me if I can't."

She laughed. "With those long legs of hers? I don't know if she's half elk, or, given the way she swims, part fish. How much lead does she have on you?"

"According to the warriors guarding her palace, about a hand's worth of time."

"You'll never catch her."

"She's a woman."

"Despite those hips of hers, she's as fleet as any man. Besides, she knows two things you don't."

"What would those be, Keeper?"

"She knows this road, and . . . *where* she's going."

He shrugged, not that she could see him in the darkness.

"I have a suspicion, Red Wing. I think she's gone to Evening Star House. Several of my sources reported that Lady Sun Wing passed this way late yesterday. I think we're going to discover that Walking Smoke has formed an alliance with Evening Star House. That he's convinced High Dance and Columella that he can actually accomplish this resurrection—call the Water Panther into his body. And when he does, he can defeat the Morning Star."

"You think Lace and Sun Wing are now hostages?"

"I do." She grunted to herself. "And, may the Horned Serpent help us, it will be a miracle if he doesn't take Night Shadow Star as well."

"Then, you dare not cross the river, Keeper. He'll have you as well."

"Not if I cross with a couple of squadrons of warriors. He's been ahead of me from the start, Red Wing. That stops now. I've already sent a runner on to War Duck asking that he have two squadrons meet me at the canoe landing, and that canoes be collected to ferry us across."

"All the more reason for me to run ahead."

"Stay, Red Wing." Her voice tightened. "Please. I may have need of you. Especially if, as you say, you serve my niece."

"What use would that be, Keeper?"

"As an intermediary to bargain for her life."

"My oath is not to you."

"No, it isn't." She bitterly added, "But if you do this, help keep my nieces alive, I'd be willing to offer your mother and sisters a deal: restricted freedom in my household. That may not be the best of worlds, but it certainly is not the worst. They would have some control of their lives and bodies. Your sisters could marry if they desired. They'd at least have a future beyond the Morning Star's next whim. The uncertainty would be over."

He frowned. "How about if—"

"No bargains!" she snapped. "Take it, or leave it."

He chuckled hollowly. "I'll take it." A sense of relief blew through him. "Though I have to ask why you'd make the offer."

She was silent for a time. "Your mother and I were young together once. A long, long time ago. It was a different world. Back before the fall of Petaga, before the resurrection."

"You know we hate you."

"Hate all you want, Red Wing. As long as oath and honor carry weight in your souls. I can already see that your hatred of my niece has caused you great discomfort. It's kept you from a relaxing night's sleep as you charge off through the darkness. Maybe I can make your mother suffer so in my service."

And then she laughed hollowly.

"I still have to keep Night Shadow Star and the others alive once we get to Evening Star town."

"Yes," the Keeper agreed from the top of her swaying litter. "There's always that. Let's just hope things aren't too messy when we get there."

In the distant west lightning flickered, a sign that the Thunderbirds were again at war with the Underworld.

Oh, they'll be messy, Keeper. As far ahead of us as he's been all along, he's anticipated anything you might try.

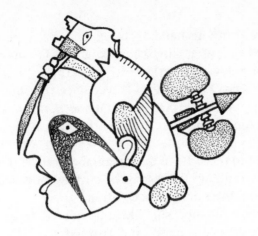

Fifty-nine

What have I done? The words seemed to echo hollowly between Sun Wing's souls. *Please, please, don't let this happen to me.*

Sun Wing had watched in disbelief as Walking Smoke dismembered their sister and the tiny infant. Her brother's motions had been smooth, practiced, and he wielded the long, brown-chert blade with an uncommon dexterity.

Terrified to the point of trembling, she needed only to look down to see the paintings her brother had so carefully drawn on her shivering skin. Spirals on her breasts, tadpoles, mudpuppies, and caterpillars.

I am nothing more to him than an offering. Why?

She must have cried out when she wondered, *What did I ever do to you?* because he answered, "Nothing, little sister. You were too small, too helpless to do anything to me. Not at all like my brother, or your sister Night Shadow Star. They betrayed me, betrayed the whole world."

"What . . ." She swallowed, trying to wet her mouth. "What are you doing with those body parts?"

Yes, keep him talking, distract him.

He glanced at her where he worked so carefully to reposition one of Lace's severed legs. Even from where she sat, she could see that he was fashioning an arc out of the body parts. Laying them out on the floor in a pattern. Head at the top, torso, the arms and legs out to either side like drooping wings.

He gestured with his hands as he explained, "When I'm finished, it will surround the sweat lodge, don't you see? I'm making a vulva, the opening from the womb of the earth. A path for Piasa's soul to follow when I offer Old-Woman-Who-Never-Dies the final sacrifice. Lace and her baby, of course, had to go at the bottom, which is where I started. The top will be there, on the other side of the sweat lodge next to the fire."

He pointed to the sides of his imaginary circle. "Your pieces will go here. And I will fill out the rest of the curving sides with High Dance, Columella, and their delightful children."

"And who's at the top," she asked, fascinated despite herself.

"Ah." He rubbed his hands and grinned, the expression changing his painted cat-face. "That I save for Night Shadow Star. You know how at the top of the sheath, just below the bone, a woman feels the most wondrous sensations? That I've saved specifically for Night Shadow Star." His eyes sharpened. "She's the erotic one, you know."

Across from her, Columella called, "You think this will work? Old-Woman-Who-Never-Dies will strike you down! What you're doing? Sacrificing your sisters and relatives? This is *perversion*! Evil. A twisting of Power that will end in disaster for the *whole world*!"

He raised a hand as two of the Tula took steps toward Columella. He barked an order in Caddo. The two Tula nodded, collected ropes from Lace's litter, and closing on Columella, muscled her into submission and began tying off her arms and legs.

High Dance just sagged in his bonds, cringing. The children whimpered and huddled in on themselves.

"Cousin," Walking Smoke told Columella, "I'm doing nothing that the laws of Power prohibit. *Hunga Ahuito* wouldn't have created the world, divided it into the three realms, or allowed souls to travel between if he hadn't anticipated, *expected* exactly this outcome. It's a fulfillment, don't you see?" He almost giggled. "I'm setting the world free."

"Your souls are going to be destroyed." Sun Wing struggled to find something, some bit of reason. She cried, "You won't know that you've succeeded, brother. Piasa will devour your souls! You'll cease to be in an instant."

A sadness filled his eyes as he walked over and studied her. "Do you think it's easy to be me? It's not. Chunkey Boy was the chosen one, the one born correctly. I'm the Wild One, Thrown Away Boy, the discarded child. At first I didn't realize it, little sister. I played my part, just like in the Beginning Times. I had to fit in. I had to live up to the responsibility. We all did. Me, my brother, and dear Night Shadow Star. Even when the voices first started whispering to me, I knew—but I didn't yet understand."

"Understand what? You had everything!"

"No matter what I did, what kind of trouble I talked the other two into committing." He laughed mockingly. "Nothing was ever *wrong*, little sister. I learned that you can rape, and kill, and steal, and defame. And *no one cares*!"

"I care," she whispered, clinging to fraying hope.

"I think that's a lie." He leaned forward, pressing his painted cougar-face close to hers. "What will you do? How will you make the pain go away? How will you keep them from mocking me behind my back? And what Chunkey Boy—or Morning Star, as he called himself—and Night Shadow Star did together? I *saw* them! How do you fix that? *I loved her!*"

He rocked back on his heels, stood, and began pacing in circles, his hands flexing and twitching in unison. "If it was good enough *for him* it had to be good enough *for me*! And Night Shadow Star! Oh yes, good enough *for her, too*!"

His smile was a delicate and fleeting thing. "The question remains . . . Were those screams of joy that burst from her lungs? Was that passion I wrung from her? Was she struggling in a fit of exploding delight?" He glanced at Sun Wing, as if desperate for the answer.

When she just blinked in confusion, he chuckled, voice lowering. "Or was she just disgusted? Ecstasy? Or disgust? She'd just lain with a God! Wasn't Thrown Away Boy good enough?"

His entire body seemed to vibrate, his eyes pressed closed, and he bellowed, "And for that they bundled me away *and banished* me?"

At the violence in his voice, she cringed back, horrified to realize that she could no longer feel her arms, and her legs had gone numb and senseless.

For long moments he stood like a wooden carving, muscles knotted, back arched, his head tilted up to expose his corded neck.

Some of the Tula had dropped to their knees, expressions of worship on their beaming faces.

"But I didn't do anything to you," Sun Wing whimpered, the hot rush of tears filling her eyes.

"Oh, yes, you did," he gritted. "You're one of them. You would betray me as quickly as you betrayed your beloved Morning Star and the *Tonka'tzi*. All I had to do was dangle a promise, and you leaped for it."

Her voice squeaked as she whimpered, "I'd never betray you."

Walking Smoke grunted his disbelief and called to one of the Tula. The man promptly jumped up, retrieved the long ritual knife and reverently handed it to Walking Smoke.

She squirmed against the ropes as her brother knelt before her and touched the knife's sharp point to the bottom of her foot. Her heart hammering against her chest, she gulped a frantic breath. Her foot had no feeling. She couldn't even pull her numb leg back.

Walking Smoke's cat face smiled into hers. "Rejoice, little sister. It's your turn."

Returning to the pot of black drink, he filled his large cup, lifted it to his lips, and gulp after gulp drained it. Again a Tula provided him with rattlesnake master.

She threw her head back and screamed as the Tula undid the ropes that fastened her to the bench.

Her thoughts shattered and fragmented, her muscles electric with fear. Whimpers broke from her throat; her bladder let go as they picked her up as easily as a snared rabbit and bore her to the center of the room.

Walking Smoke bent double as he threw up; the hot cassina tea shot from his mouth to spatter on the gore-coated matting.

A wailing squeal broke from Sun Wing's throat as one of the Tula approached with the corrugated cooking pot, its sides stained with dried blood.

Her eyes fixed on the knife he held, on the missing chip broken from the edge just back from the tip. A piece the size of the fragment Aunt Blue Heron had retrieved from a murdered woman's ruined pelvis.

Sun Wing felt something tear asunder in her souls, a ripping that gave way to a washing wave of black terror. She filled her lungs and screamed. . . .

Sixty

The muscles in Night Shadow Star's legs trembled as she climbed the steep bluff path from the canoe landing on the Father Water's western shore. Her breath came in gasps; a hunger-knot had tied itself in her empty stomach.

Perhaps she'd spent too much time traveling in the Spirit World. She shouldn't be this winded, feel this weakness, after only running for half the night.

She stopped to catch her breath, remembering old times when she, Chunkey Boy, and Walking Smoke had sprinted full-bore up this same steep bluff.

Below her, the mighty river glistened silver in the predawn light; the Cahokian floodplain beyond was but a smoke-hazed darkness accented by the gleaming curls of oxbow lakes. In the distant east, the horizon lay like a rumpled black line below the graying sky.

Thunder rumbled in the west. On the wind she could smell rain through the smoky scent of Evening Star town.

Filling her too-tense lungs, she heard Piasa's whispered urgings, saw a flicker of his movement in the corner of her eye.

"Yes, yes, I'm going."

She placed her right moccasin on the trail and forced her hot muscles to bear her onward and upward.

She'd broken a sweat by the time she climbed through the trail gap and onto the clay-capped terrace. The Four Winds guardian posts, each portraying *Hunga Ahuito,* rose on either side, mere shadows against the dark and rolling clouds scudding in from the southwest. Again she heard the rumble of thunder rolling across the land.

Piasa's Spirit presence followed her as she forced her tired legs into a trot. Clan houses lay to either side, their members subject to Evening Star House's governance. She caught the sickly stench of the charnel houses where they stood beside low, conical burial mounds.

To the side of one such mound, a knot of people stood around a crematory pit. The contents had burned down to a glowing bed of coals that consumed the last of the bones. For the mourners, the ritual had been an all-night affair, the final farewell for the soul of their relative. These had been dirt farmers, probably come from the west where cremation was considered a way of releasing the life-soul from the bones; the thought being that rising smoke would carry the newly freed soul to the Sky World and the ancestors.

The mourners barely noticed, her black-clad shape little more than a passing shadow in the predawn.

Granaries and warehouses rose to either side of the broad path. She touched her chin out of respect as she passed Evening Star town's version of the Four Winds women's house. Into its seclusion Matron Columella and her female kin would retreat every twenty-eight days to pass their bleeding in seclusion.

And when will mine come again? She'd passed two moons now without cramps or menstrual discharges. And unless some Spirit had taken her senseless body during one of her soul-flying trips, she couldn't be pregnant. No man had lain with her since her husband had led his army north nearly a year ago.

She passed between the partially completed addition to the Four Winds charnel house mound on her left and the large conical burial mound to her right. Apprehension rising, she trotted into the central plaza. Trampled grass whispered beneath her feet. She touched her forehead in respect as she passed the World Tree pole. The mighty red cedar had been felled in a distant forest, carried here by hundreds of sweating laborers. The great log had been carved and finally erected in the center of the plaza. Its sides were covered in detailed reliefs that depicted stories from the Beginning Times.

She crossed the chunkey court and approached the Evening Star House palace, little more than a dark, hatchet-roofed silhouette that rose against the stormy skies.

Three men rose from the bottom of the ramp stairs. She could see a couple of litters off to the side, and recognized Sun Wing's ornately carved one. Her porters and a figure that was probably Feather Wand were sleeping in blankets beside it. The rest of the slumbering figures, she assumed, were messengers from the various Earth clans and assorted agents, all waiting to see High Dance.

"Who comes?" the first man asked, obviously the speaker as he raised a hand palm out to stop her and brandished some sort of staff of office.

"I bring a message for High Chief High Dance of the Evening Star House."

"The High Chief and the Matron are involved in personal ceremonies and will not receive visitors for another day."

"I am sent by Lady Night Shadow Star with a personal communication for the High Chief and the Matron."

"I'm sorry."

"You will not let me pass?" She could feel the tension rising in her gut. Her stomach began to churn, a sick burning sensation.

"I would take your message in."

She shrugged, a slow smile of inevitability on her lips. "Then I'll have to wait."

Like a cold wave rolling within, the anxiety washed away, her pounding heart settled, and a crystalline certainty hardened between her souls.

She clearly remembered her question to Piasa: *"Walking Smoke's going to kill me, isn't he?"* And the Water Panther's response.

Those chosen by Power were accursed.

Dispassionately she turned to the warrior on the right, a tall muscular man with a war club in his hand. "How about you?" she asked. "Are you up for an entertaining time under the blankets? A diversion while I wait?"

"He doesn't speak our tongue, woman."

"I don't care if he can speak. Is his shaft serviceable? And if it is, what language would he praise me in?"

The man's voice filled with disgust. "He speaks Caddo, woman. But neither he, nor his companion, is free to 'entertain' themselves with a woman."

So the guards were Tula. She flipped her arm dismissively. "Thank the Spirits I've got fingers then, eh? I'll wait over to the side, maybe entertain myself with my bow."

"You do that," the man said coldly. "Or else you could return whence you came and tell Lady Night Shadow Star that if she were to come herself, I have orders to escort her immediately into the presence of the Evening Star House chief."

A cold breeze of certainty shivered her souls. He was inside, waiting for her.

She touched her chin with an insolent flick of the fingers and stepped back. The speaker chattered away in Caddo, eliciting laughter from the two Tula, one of whom pointed at his crotch and said something boastful.

Night Shadow Star slipped her bow from her shoulder, used her hip to string it, and withdrew an arrow.

The first Tula had just seated himself on the lowest step when her arrow drove through his breastbone with a snap. As the warrior stiffened and half rose, she was nocking her second shaft. The angle wasn't good, and her shot pierced the second Tula's left bicep before it thunked hollowly into his chest. From the amount of shaft remaining, it had stopped just short of his heart.

The Tula stared down at his arm where it was pinned to his side, made a half step, and turned toward her. Which allowed her to drive her third shaft through the hollow at the base of his throat.

The startled speaker had raised his hands, staring first at her, and then at the impossibility of his so-quickly-killed friends.

Her bow in her left hand, her right shucked the war club from where it hung in her belt. She advanced on him, head down, flicking the war club as if testing its balance.

The speaker glanced imploringly at the dying Tula. The first was kicking weakly, eyes wide, as he clutched the arrow shaft sticking out of his breastbone. The second was making gargling sounds as blood foamed out of his mouth and nostrils.

"No help there," Night Shadow Star told him. "And if you run, I'll shoot you right through the middle of the back."

"Who *are* you?" the man cried, imploring hands up as he dropped to his knees.

"I'm called Lady Night Shadow Star, of the Morning Star House, Four Winds Clan."

"He wants you." In growing light, she could see tears tracking down the man's face. Finding no give in her eyes, he threw himself prostrate, facedown on the packed clay.

"He'll get me. But first, you tell me. Who's in there?"

The man was groveling, his chest heaving as he sobbed. "High Dance and Columella, their children, Lady Lace and Sun Wing."

"Are High Dance and Columella working with Walking Smoke?"

"No. They, and all of their children, are captive, too. Part of the ritual."

"And you were supposed to let me pass? Who else might be on that list?"

"The Keeper and the *Tonka'tzi*."

"And if a squadron of warriors were to show up?"

"The Tula were to run inside and warn him. I was to tell the squadron commander that if he tried to approach, the hostages would be killed before he could take the palace. All Walking Smoke wanted was time. He told me he would be finished by midday."

She nodded to herself, glancing around. Her attack had come so silently, she hadn't even awakened any of the sleepers.

"Who are you?"

"River Rock. A Trader. He hired me because I speak Caddo."

"What did he Trade for your service?"

"He said I'd get a copper headpiece."

She pivoted, slamming the war club's spikes down on the back of his skull. River Rock stiffened, lungs contracting in a huffing grunt. His arms and legs jerked and quivered as he died.

"Bad Trade," she told him before she stepped over and kicked Feather Wand awake.

"Lady Night Shadow Star?" he asked as he peered up in the dim dawn.

"Get up. Find War Chief Brown Bear Fivekiller or his second. I need the Four Winds Clan squadron assembled around High Dance's palace. As soon as you alert them, contact the Earth Clans, same message. Tell them no one is to come or go without my permission."

"Yes, Lady!" he leaped to his feet.

"Where are Sun Wing's warriors? Surely she had an escort."

"She didn't bring any, Lady. She said she didn't need them."

"Pus take and rot you, sister. What were you thinking?"

But she knew: Walking Smoke would have instinctively understood—and cautiously manipulated—the spoiled youngest child; arrogant and ambitious, she'd have been ripe for conspiracy.

Night Shadow Star glanced off to the east as the first drops of rain began to spatter on the hard-packed earth around her. *Morning Star? Why did you place her, of all people, in charge of investigating the assassination attempts?*

But then things were never as they seemed with the Morning Star.

She started up the steps, replacing her war club and nocking another of the stone-tipped war arrows in her bow. She was nearly to the top when she heard the screaming from inside.

A woman didn't survive to become a Four Winds House matron if she proved even the slightest bit squeamish. The demands of the matron's position included sitting in judgment, making life and death decisions, and watching them carried out. It included participation in declarations of war, and living with the consequences of doing so. A matron's choices and judgment had the potential to ruin an entire people, to end in bloodshed, war, and fire. In case of the worst miscalculation, it could culminate in the butchering of everyone you knew, and the possibility that you and your family would die of torture while hanging in some enemy's square.

Never in her life had Columella seen a person in such absolute and abject terror as Sun Wing when Walking Smoke's Tula lifted her bound body from the floor.

Panic contorted her young face. Tears soaked her cheeks. Her mouth had gone shapeless and kept popping open only to close slightly before opening again. Snot bubbled in her nostrils each time she screamed.

But terror even silenced those, strangling her cries into a strained whimpering accented by half-formed squeals.

Sun Wing's body appeared paralyzed, seized as solid as river ice, her fear-glittering eyes having fixed on a pointless eternity. Urine dripped from her thighs and buttocks.

As the Tula carrying her lifted Sun Wing's wet rump high and lowered her head toward the bloodstained pot, an eerie wailing screech broke from her lips. Sun Wing's hair had come undone and fell in a midnight swirl across the bloody, vomit-soaked matting. She seemed to come to her wits, glancing this way and that, meeting Columella's pitying eyes. Her gaze was that of a mindless thing—some inhuman and crazed creature. Then she jerked it away to fix on the corrugated ceramic pot as one of the Tula positioned it to catch her blood.

Walking Smoke was singing, his eyes glittering with anticipation. His painted body glistened in the firelight, the man's muscles now tensed in anticipation. He tipped his head back and lifted the knife. As he did his blue-painted penis stiffened into an erection.

Columella pursed her lips in disgust.

"Where is Power?" she asked under her breath, fearful Walking

Smoke would hear. "Where is the lightning to strike such living pollution dead?"

"Gone," High Dance whispered. "Taken by Walking Smoke. Drawn into a rope. One he has twisted, looped, and pulled into such a hard knot that it's strangling on itself."

"You brought him here, brother."

"I . . ." High Dance turned his face away as Walking Smoke's singing voice filled the room.

Columella slitted her eyes, heart hammering, as Walking Smoke's incomprehensible song bellowed from his lungs. The man's blue-painted erection strained and quivered. He stepped forward and placed the blade against Sun Wing's throat.

One of the Tula holding Sun Wing upside down, uttered an agonized shriek. Then he twisted away to display an arrow jutting from his back. As he turned Sun Wing loose and pawed behind him, she fell head-long into the big corrugated pot. It shattered under her weight.

Walking Smoke's song stopped, the knife still poised. He appeared surprised and confused, blinking, as if Sun Wing's taut throat should still be beneath the keen blade. The other Tula had stumbled as Sun Wing fell. He bent down to reach for her, his hands slipping along her skin, smeared as it was with the colorful images of tadpoles and caterpillars.

The wounded Tula, eyes bugged, mouth open, tried to straighten, only to gasp in pain and disbelief.

"Hold!" a sharp voice commanded.

Columella sought the source and stared. Impossible! But there stood Night Shadow Star, wearing a black dress that fell to just above her knees. War moccasins hugged her calves. Her hair was in a braid; eyes hard she backed along the wall. An arrow was nocked, her bow drawn.

"Leave her alone!" Night Shadow Star ordered. "Tell your Tula. The next one who touches her dies."

Walking Smoke, the surprise vanishing from his features, smiled warmly, and said something in Caddo. The remaining Tula, faces lining in frowns, backed away, their attention turned to Night Shadow Star.

"You've come at last!" Walking Smoke's glee matched his smile. "I've made a place for you in the circle." He squinted one eye. "I don't think your interruption will change the Power. I can start over from the beginning again with Sun Wing. The important thing . . . what Old-Woman-Who-Never-Dies will pay attention to, is the blood. A couple of mistakes in the ritual? What's that when compared to Four Winds blood?"

Night Shadow Star seemed to have just noticed the body parts spread out in the partial circle on the floor. She fixed on them, a cold realization reflected in her face.

"I really am relieved," Walking Smoke told her warmly. "I can't tell you how much better it is this way. Power interceded, you see."

"I expect that it did," Night Shadow Star said through clamped jaws. "It's brought me here to kill you."

"Is *that* what you think? You? Here to kill me?" Walking Smoke chortled as he ran a finger along the rippled knife blade. "Had Power wanted it to play out that way, you'd have driven an arrow into my heart. No, my precious love. You're here to complete me, to join me in accomplishing the most audacious resurrection ever."

She narrowed an eye, aiming down her slim shaft as she settled on her target.

Columella silently begged her, *Kill him already!*

Walking Smoke flicked the long chert knife in his fingers, saying, "I thought if I killed you that night outside your palace, it would be proof of my worthiness. Then Power whisked you away in the darkness." He laughed as if at himself. "Silly me, I thought it was my unworthiness. But no, it was Power, saving you for here, now. Bringing you to me for the final piece."

"Of what?" she barely gestured with her bow to indicate the semi-circle of body parts. "What is that?"

"The opening from the womb, of course." Walking Smoke raised the knife in his left hand, his right seeming to dance at the end of his wrist, the fingers flicking this way and that.

Columella gaped. *Pus and rot! Don't you see what he's doing? Shoot!*

The Tula, as a whole, tensed as they watched his hand signals. Some nodded, their wolfish eyes darting back to fix on Night Shadow Star.

"Womb?" Night Shadow Star swallowed hard. "You're making a *womb* out of my sister's body parts?"

Columella caught the faint quiver of Night Shadow Star's arms, the strain of the bent bow beginning to tire her muscles.

What are you doing? Release the gods-rotted arrow!

"The sacred opening, like that wonderful sheath of yours, Sister. The passage of life through which Piasa's souls will emerge in order to consume my body."

"Choose one of your Tula, Brother. Point him out to me. I want to see you order him to pick Sun Wing up and carry her outside."

Columella could see the trembling in Night Shadow Star's bow arm now. *Kill him while you can!*

"Shoot him!" she finally shouted.

"Silence!" Walking Smoke ordered. "This is between me and my sister."

Walking Smoke grinned, pointed to the dying Tula with the arrow jutting from his back. "That one."

The warrior had sagged to his knees beside where Sun Wing flopped in the wreckage of the broken pot. Blood was welling from his mouth. He coughed, crimson dribbling down his chin in a frothy strand.

"I'll shoot!" Night Shadow Star insisted.

Walking Smoke almost giggled in delight, and quicker than a snap, dropped to his knees. At the same time, he wound his right hand in Sun Wing's hair and lifted, his muscles straining as he pulled the young woman up before him. In a blink he had the long-bladed chert knife across her throat.

Sun Wing's panicked lungs drove a whistling squeak from her stretched throat.

Columella's gut sank. "You've killed us all, you silly spoiled little sheath."

Night Shadow Star was obviously shaking now, straining to keep her hold.

"You're not the girl you once where, Sister," Walking Smoke told her. "You've gotten soft since you and I shared that magical moment. Go ahead, shoot! You might as well. If your arrow kills her, she's just as dead as if I do it with my knife."

"Let her go," Night Shadow Star insisted. "Once she's outside, it will be between us. Just the two of us. Your Power, and mine."

Some awareness in the corner of her eye made Columella glance toward the back. She almost missed it, would have returned her attention to the drama playing out before her. But the faint blue movement was smoke rising from the bottom of the high, woven-cane wall. Even as she watched, a section just above the sleeping bench began to blacken. A steady plume of blue appeared, drifting out of her personal quarters.

Fire?

"You can't win, Sister!" Walking Smoke cried, drawing Columella's attention back to the nearest threat.

Walking Smoke was chattering along happily in Caddo.

"Look out!" Columella cried, trying to rise to her feet. Her numb and bloodless legs, too long bound, betrayed her and she only flopped.

Night Shadow Star caught the closest Tula's movement, swung her arrow—now almost clattering against the bow. The shaft discharged. The Tula had anticipated it, dodged. Then he was on her.

Columella was struggling against the ropes, cursing her numb legs and arms. In desperation she tried to pitch herself from the bench, only to half hang.

Despair filled her. It took a half breath, maybe more, before she realized the ropes that held her were vibrating, as if something were sawing on them.

She glanced at the back wall, seeing the first flames as they burst through the tight lattice of woven cane.

Then her ropes parted and she fell, half paralyzed by numbness, to the floor.

When she glanced back where Night Shadow Star had been, it was to see two Tula dragging her, kicking, biting, and fighting toward the middle of the room. The rest were collecting her bow and the quiver of arrows they'd ripped from her back. Another had her copper-studded war club. He was pointing to blood on the spikes, showing it in amazement to his fellows.

"Ah-ha!" Walking Smoke screamed, dropping Sun Wing and leaping to his feet. "Come, Sister! Because I love you! You can be next! Got to hurry now. Bleed you, bleed Sun Wing, and then the rest."

To Columella's amazement, Night Shadow Star had ceased struggling, flipped her braid out of the way, and was smiling at Walking Smoke.

"Your Power and mine, Brother. I've felt your caress. Soon, you're going to feel mine."

Someone was tugging on Columella's ropes. She closed her eyes in defeat. No doubt one of the Tula had finally noticed that she'd fallen.

Her souls bitter and broken, she swiveled her head and stared into Flat Stone Pipe's frightened eyes as he hid beneath the bench and sawed at her bonds with a gray chert blade.

Sixty-one

The words spoken by Sun Wing's porter echoed in Fire Cat's souls: "She's in there!" The man had pointed up the Evening Star House palace stairway, his rain-wet shirt clinging to his shoulders, hair plastered.

"Wait!" the Keeper had called as her own porters were lowering her. "War Duck's squadrons will be here in less than a hand of time." Even as she said it, she was staring at the still-cooling bodies of two arrow-skewered Tula and a third, brain-bashed, man.

"She may not have that long," he'd growled back having already strung his bow. And as he charged up the stairs, he'd nocked an arrow.

He found the door half open, slipped sideways through it, and into confusion. A knot of three Tula stood just to his left. One held Night Shadow Star's copper-bitted war club in his hands. Another was inspecting her slim Osage-orange bow, the third, and closest, had her quiver.

Fire Cat caught just enough of a glance to see two more Tula dragging Night Shadow Star toward a naked-and-painted man in the middle of the floor. Sun Wing's nude body lay at the painted man's feet. An arch of bleeding and disarticulated body parts as strung across the floor. The wall benches on his left held panicked and crying children. Halfway down the wall a dazed-looking man appeared crestfallen, and a bound woman lay on the floor.

The place smelled of blood and death.

He had no more time. The three Tula with Night Shadow Star's weapons turned to gape at him in surprise.

Fire Cat shot the closest one, driving an arrow through the Tula's chest. Then he lashed out with the bow in a slashing strike that drove the two remaining Tula back and bought him enough time to rip out Makes Three's war club.

The man with Night Shadow Star's bow raised it to block Fire Cat's strike. The force of the club's impact snapped the thin stave like a twig.

"Sorry, Lady," Fire Cat apologized for her bow as he set his foot, pirouetted, and slammed his club past the third man's guard. He felt the solid hit, heard the ribs cracking like crushed kindling. Fire Cat skipped, the Red Wing war cry breaking past his lips in a fierce joy.

Adrenaline surged through him, charging his body, and he caved in the side of the second Tula's head. Even as the warrior dropped, Fire Cat landed on one foot, turned, and screamed his rage. Tula warriors were charging toward him from all over the room.

As he started forward he caught a glimpse of the back wall behind the dais. Flames and smoke curled up from the woven cane.

"Hoookaaiiiyaaaa!" he screamed, daring again to vent the war call he'd thought forever stilled in his breast and soul. And into the midst of them he charged, his souls singing with the thrill of combat.

Before they killed him, by the Blessed Stars, they'd know what it was to face a Red Wing war chief.

"Hoookaaaiiiyaaa!"

At the sound of carnage inside the palace, Blue Heron looked up from the rain-slicked corpses on the ground. So much for waiting. She threw her hands up in despair. Her porters stood hunched in the pounding rain, four of them vying to hold the flat rain shield above her head in an effort to keep her dry.

She glanced around distastefully as a howling war cry issued from the half-open palace door.

Staring across the morning-gray and rain-slashed plaza, she could see no sign of War Duck's squadron. They'd just begun to form as she and her party had loaded into canoes for the ferry trip across the river.

A second cry howled from behind the door.

"Pus, rot, and blood!" she bellowed. Thrusting an arm out, she ordered the gawking crowd, "You all! Yes, you! I *order* you in the name of the Morning Star. When chief War Duck's warriors arrive, tell the squadron first to get up these stairs and storm the palace. You tell them the Keeper said so!"

"Keeper?" her war second, one of the ten warriors who'd accompanied her, asked.

"We're going in there. If it's a Tula, kill it. They'll be the ones fighting us. Hard to miss."

And with that she plucked up a rain-soaked war club from the dead Tula lying at her feet and started up the stairs.

I have lost any sense I ever had.

But perhaps the Red Wing had bought them the time and opportunity they needed. Had to admire that. Even now he was probably dead, and if Walking Smoke's Tula hadn't secured the door, if they weren't nocking arrows in their bows even as she charged up the long stairs ahead of her ten warriors, maybe it would be enough.

Maybe.

To her surprise, huffing and puffing, she made it to the top, flicked a salutary finger at the guardian posts—it would have to suffice—and ran as fast as her old legs would carry her.

Hearing her warriors' feet pounding on the wet clay behind her, she panted her way into the protection of the veranda, half expecting a hissing blur of arrows to skewer her.

Even more surprised, she charged through the door unopposed, and into the palace great room.

Where she stopped short, trying to make sense of what she saw. Madness everywhere. Three Tula were moaning and dying to her left, children were screaming, the back wall was on fire, human body parts were being kicked around on the floor as the crazy Red Wing danced, and whirled his war club, in the midst of a frenzied circle of Tula. Sun Wing, thankfully alive, lay in the midst of a broken pot. A beguiling smile on her face, Night Shadow Star was tugging on a painted man whom Blue Heron assumed was Walking Smoke. She seemed to be leading him back past the dais and toward the burning wall.

"Keeper?" her war second asked.

"Go!" she ordered. "Kill Tula."

Then she charged forward, half stumbling over slippery pieces of human beings and bloody matting. The way the fire was now racing up the back wall, it wouldn't be long before the roof caught. When that happened, it didn't matter how hard it was raining outside, the tinder-dry interior would explode in flame.

With fighting all around, men screaming, shrieking, and dying, she bent down at Sun Wing's side, her fingers fumbling at the knots.

"Hey! Niece! Wake up! Help me here."

Sun Wing's glazed expression remained frozen in fear, her swollen eyes fixed on nothing. Half-strangled pants broke from her heaving lungs. Inhuman, barely audible squeals slipped past her locked jaws and compressed lips.

Blue Heron yanked at the knots, caught movement, and ducked as one of her warriors backed toward her, smashed a heel into her side, and toppled backward. As he did, a Tula war club hissed wickedly through the air where his head would have been.

Blue Heron huddled protectively over her niece's body as the Tula uttered a blood-curdling scream and leaped on the fallen warrior.

Hideous shrieks sounded and Blue Heron's body rocked as the two men fought on top of her; each time one of them kicked, she bore the brunt.

And then, peering from under her arm, she watched the Tula lift his war club, and slam it down on her warrior.

Enough of this!

Her fingers wrapped around the handle of the war club she'd taken from the Tula outside. Getting to her knees, she swung the stone-bladed ax into the back of the Tula's head. Watched his body jump under the impact, stiffen, and fall forward onto her now dead warrior.

She was panting, air tearing in and out of her lungs. Her heart was hammering at her chest. The sensation of the Tula's skull crushing, the snapping sound of the bones breaking, and the feel of it through the war club's handle, would be with her forever.

She gasped, placing her left hand to her heart. Coming to her senses, she shot a look around the room. Fire Cat still stood, his helmet now missing and blood streaming down the side of his head. Two Tula danced about trading blows with him. Another Tula was staggering as he slammed blow after blow into her war second's stumbling body. Around her lay dead Four Winds warriors intermingled with dying Tula.

As she exhaled and glanced back to Sun Wing, a hard hand knotted in her hair, lifting.

Blue Heron shrieked at the pain, struggling to get her feet under her. She'd never been lifted by her hair before. Never wanted to experience it again. Scared witless, she glanced sidelong at a bloody young Tula warrior. The man's face, so close to hers, had a desperate look. Anxiety lay in the darting of his eyes as he looked around the room. The rear wall was roaring in flames now, smoke billowing.

The way he held her, her back was toward him. If she tried to kick or strike, the agony in her scalp became unbearable.

"What do you want?" she hissed.

"Out," he barked in a guttural accent. "You save."

"Do you know who I am?"

"Out. You save."

"I'm the Four Winds Clan Keeper. I can—"

A long chipped-stone ceremonial knife was placed against her throat, the keen edge slightly angled over the still healing scar where a similar blade had once been placed.

"Out. You save."

"I can help you," she suggested, trying to control the fear in her voice.

"Out. You save."

"All right!" she gasped. "Out. I save."

He muttered some sort of agreement in Caddo, and began dragging her toward the door.

She tried to resist but the knife just pressed tighter against her throat.

On the verge of squealing in panic, she nevertheless heard a familiar chiding voice say, "Keeper, you do get yourself into the most fascinating predicaments."

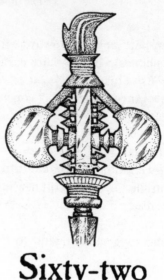

Sixty-two

Seven Skull Shield reached out from behind and fastened his hand on the Tula's right wrist where it held the knife against the Keeper's throat. At the same time his left hand clamped on the Tula's throat; he squeezed, digging his thumb and fingers deep into the man's neck, surrounding the Tula's voice box. As he did, Seven Skull Shield arched his body, pulling the Tula up and back.

"Let her go, you piece of steaming shit," he growled, and put every ounce of strength he had into crushing the man's windpipe and peeling the knife hand from the Keeper's throat.

The Tula's left hand finally turned loose of the Keeper's hair, and Blue Heron wiggled out of his grip and away from the deadly knife.

And then, like having a wildcat in a bear hug, Seven Skull Shield's life got very, very interesting.

The Tula might have been greased the way he slipped out of Seven Skull Shield's grip, and whirled, landing catlike on the balls of his feet. The long chert blade was held low, poised to strike. Like an animal's, the Tula's face contorted into a feral visage, lips up, teeth exposed, a growl bursting from his now hoarse and bruised throat.

"*You piece of stinking dog shit!*" Seven Skull Shield bellowed, rolling his shoulders. Then he screamed, balanced on his feet, and threw himself at the Tula.

"*You maggot-mouthed bit of latrine filth!*" He tried to catch the knife hand, missed it, curled away and partially blocked the darting cut. Not enough. He felt it slicing along his ribs.

"I'm gonna break you! Cook and eat your tongue! Stomp your pus-dripping shaft! Pop your maggot eyes like eggs, you piece of vomit!" He drove himself into the Tula, bulling the man into a pile of bodies. The Tula toppled backward as he tripped over a severed leg.

Now in his element, Seven Skull Shield let the fury boil up from his gut. His knee, faithful weapon of the consummate brawler, jerked up like a stone maul at the same moment the two of them slammed onto the floor. The Tula grunted as his testicles were crushed.

"Gonna beat you, stomp you, pull out your guts!" Seven Skull Shield howled, raising his head and driving it down like a rock. The Tula's nose crunched under the impact. *"You sucking scum. Fly piss, worm penis piece of slime! Gonna hammer your balls with a rock!"*

The Tula tried to jerk his arm down in an attempt to drive the knife into Seven Skull Shield's side. Sensing it, he slapped the blade sideways, hearing the brittle stone break musically, the majority of it sailing away.

"Now you worm-shit maggot-shafted shit, you're mine! Gonna stomp your stomach, beat your brain with a stick . . ." He hammered his head into the Tula's mashed nose again, rose, and drove his elbow full into the man's mouth. Teeth broke; the Tula's jaw snapped with a crack. Again and again, he jacked his knee into the Tula's crotch, and saw the man's eyes go wide and pain-dazed.

"Gonna rip your pus-dripping shaft from your body, use it like a flail and stuff it down your putrid throat, you maggot-brained filth!"

And then, to his irritation, a war club flashed from the side of his vision and drove itself into the crown of the Tula's head.

At the snapping of the skull, Seven Skull Shield felt the Tula's body stiffen, quiver, and still.

"Gonna beat you, burn you—"

"I don't know what's worse"—the Keeper sagged to the floor beside him, the bloody war club in her hand—"being held by the hair with a knife to my throat, or listening to that howling nonsense when you're fighting."

Seven Skull Shield rolled to his side, wincing at the pain in his elbow. Fire burned along his ribs, and when he looked down, his shirt had been half cut from his body, his side a sheet of blood.

"I really hate these Tula."

"Where have you been?" The Keeper stared at him through exhausted eyes.

"Slipping around unseen with that little dwarf of Columella's. There's a hidden passage into her room. Took a while to get everything soaked with hickory oil. I've been setting fire to the back of the palace."

"You did well. This place is going up like a torch. We've got to get out of here."

He glanced around, seeing Fire Cat staggering on his feet, blood running down the side of his head, a splintered war club in his hand. The Red Wing was headed toward the rear and the worst of the fire.

Little Flat Stone Pipe was tugging for all he was worth, trying to drag a crawling Columella toward the doorway. Chief High Dance sat bound, screaming for someone to help him.

The woven-cane wall was now a solid sheet of flame. Balls of fire rolled up and along the roof, bits of burning thatch falling from the thickening smoke above.

Seven Skull Shield batted at a glowing ember that landed on the Keeper's head.

"Help me." The Keeper pointed. "Sun Wing may not be worth it, but she is my niece. Help me carry her out. And then there's the children. They're Columella's and that fool High Dance's, but that doesn't mean they deserve to burn for it."

Seven Skull Shield crawled over to Sun Wing, tossed her limp form over his shoulder, and wobbled to his feet.

"Hey! You fool! It's *burning* back there!" he yelled as he watched Fire Cat staggering into the maelstrom.

"She went this way!" Fire Cat shouted back over the roar of the fire. "She and that brother of hers."

"There's a crawl hole under the bed. But it's too late! You'll cook back in that room!"

And to Seven Skull Shield's surprise, the Red Wing shot him a weak grin. "Well-done or raw, thief, don't let the dogs eat me." Then the man ducked his head, and charged blindly through the door and into the burning room.

*T*his is a mistake!

Fire Cat figured it out too late. The heat stunned him, his skin burning, his hair singeing as he cowered behind the nonexistent shelter of his arm.

Some deep-seated animal instinct made him drop to the floor, thankful to find air rushing along the matting.

He blinked, staring around. Neither Night Shadow Star nor Walking Smoke were there.

Columella's bed was a roaring pyre.

He glanced back just in time to see part of the cane wall fall, blocking the doorway he'd just dived through. No way back now.

"A crawl way," he repeated before a bout of coughing wracked him. Gritting his teeth he levered himself forward with his elbows. Heat burned the back of his head and neck; but for the soaking blood from his scalp wound, his hair would have exploded into flame. Prickling pain seared his shoulders above the armor, his buttocks, and the backs of his legs.

Nevertheless, air, fresh air, was roaring in from under the bed.

Got to hurry!

Like an ungainly worm he scuttled forward, winced in fear, and thrust his body beneath the burning bed. His mad scramble was panicked—and probably the fastest crawl a human had ever made, but he found the passage.

Panic seized him. His shoulders wouldn't fit. The armor had hung up.

I'm burning alive! The pain was like he'd never felt and a scream vented through his tight throat.

Before the last of his senses left, he managed to wiggle his shoulders through at an angle. Panting in fear and pain, he dropped down, following the narrow tunnel beneath the wall, and up. He emerged under a clever, grass-covered door on the backside of the temple mound.

Wondrous, cold, wet, glorious rain pattered down on his hot and singed hair; it beat on his blistering face. He sucked the cool wet air into his fevered lungs and gasped as he hung half out the doorway. Behind him the palace was roaring as the fire burned through the roof.

Where did they go?

And what had it meant? He'd been in a knockdown, tight-balled battle for his life with three Tula. He'd only got the slightest glimpse. Night Shadow Star had been smiling, a sensual invitation in her eyes as she took Walking Smoke's hand and coaxed him back toward Matron Columella's smoke-filled and burning room.

Why?

Neither her body nor his had been in the inferno. He had seen that much before he'd had to slit his eyes and dive for the floor.

Rain was washing the blood down from his torn scalp. If he'd ducked but a blink later, the Tula would have cracked his skull for good.

So, they got out. Probably the same way I just did.

And he could see it: the slicked down grass where two bodies had slid down the mound.

Fire Cat gulped another thankful breath of cool air and levered his body out of the opening. Like those before him, he began to slide. The wet grass was more akin to ice as he rocketed down the steep slope, hunched into a ball, and took the impact at the bottom. Still, it knocked the wind out of him, and for a moment, he lay in agony.

When his breath came back, he sucked it in, tested his limbs, and found nothing broken. Climbing to his feet, he could see the trail. Fresh tracks stippled the mud: a man's bare feet and woman's in moccasins headed east.

Fire Cat blinked and wiped at the water and blood trying to blind him, then fought through a dizzy spell as the world spun. Hammering a fist into his nauseous stomach, he staggered out onto the trail, hurrying after Night Shadow Star.

The skin on his back might have been flayed down to raw meat and exposed nerves. Where the rain had once felt so good, now it soaked his hemp-fiber shirt where it touched his blistered skin. With clumsy fingers he undid the straps and almost fell as he lifted the armor over his head.

He couldn't believe it as he tossed it to the side. The back was charred.

If that had been my skin, as agonizing as the rest was, I'd have never made it.

The armor's protection had saved his life.

He chuckled to himself, throwing a glance over his shoulder where a fountain of fire leaped high from the dying palace to do battle with the rain.

Dizzy and blinking, he studied the trail and pushed his weary feet into a stumbling trot. The way led through buildings, and right up to the edge of the steep bluff. Rain pattering on his head, he saw where they'd started down. Looking out over the edge, he could see them as they slipped and slid down onto the sandy beach below.

"All right, Lady. Service has brought me this far. Let's see just how much farther it's going to take me."

Sixty-three

After having tossed Sun Wing outside to safety, Seven Skull Shield coughed and batted at the falling embers as he went back in search of Blue Heron. The inside of the palace was filled with smoke, the heat unbearable. And most horrifying, he could smell human flesh cooking as sections of roof burned through and dropped onto the dead and dying warriors scattered around on the mat floor. Some were Tula, others Four Winds, but they all burned and screamed and smelled the same as their flesh crackled, hissed, and popped.

Columella had managed to get to her knees beside the Keeper. Together with Flat Stone Pipe they worked futilely to free the children.

Seven Skull Shield, seeing their fumbling attempts, shouted, "Go! Get out. We'll get the children."

Each child had been bound separately, making the task that much more difficult. And worse, they were hysterical, screaming, kicking, throwing themselves against the ropes. And once untied, their bloodless arms and legs wouldn't support their weight. Each one had to be carried to the door and literally pitched outside like a sack of cattail roots before going back for another.

"We're not going to get them all!" Blue Heron screamed at him where she tried picking one of the tight knots apart that held a ten-summers-old girl.

Seven Skull Shield ducked instinctively as another section of roof let loose in the back and slammed into the floor with a thump. An explosion of sparks shot upward in twisting fire.

"Aragh," he growled, "enough of this."

"We can't *leave!*" Blue Heron cried. "They're children!"

He shot her a soot-streaked grin. Positioning himself over the bench, he filled his lungs with the smoky air and gripped the outside pole that ran between the supports. Bowing his back, he bent his legs and heaved, bellowing, "*Worthless shit-infested pus-sucking wood! Give! You foul worm-riddled piece of dung-dripping. . . .*"

With a crack, the length of bench broke free, Seven Skull Shield and the children tumbling loose. Instead of trying to free them, he simply roared, threw his back into it, and dragged the whole mess backward. He could see the Keeper, doing what she could, tugging on the last child in line.

He blinked, coughing, ever more desperate for breath. Every muscle in his body might have been pulled in two; sweat was dribbling soot and blood into his face. Then he was in the cool rush of air from the door. Almost a gale, it blew in to feed the flames.

Hard hands grabbed him by the shoulders and tugged, and with the help, he was through, warriors pouring past him, grabbing hold of children, lifting.

Together they staggered out into the blessed rain, a line of men carrying the children—still bound to the pole—down the long ramp stairs.

Seven Skull Shield gasped, coughing black phlegm from his throat and using his fingers to blow soot-laden snot from his nose. In the process, he finally noticed his lacerated elbow; inspecting it, he plucked one of the Tula's broken teeth from one of the bleeding punctures.

A tug at his hunting shirt made him look down. Flat Stone Pipe, his too-round face smeared black, was looking up at him.

"He's not worth it, probably. But High Chief High Dance is still in there. I can't get him by myself."

"Come on, then." Seven Skull Shield reached down, wincing as he lifted the little man to his shoulder. On wooden legs he started up the stairs, feeling the trembling in his muscles. "I swear by big swinging breasts and fat bouncing buttocks, I'm going to sleep for a quarter moon when this is finished."

"I'll find you the bed," Flat Stone Pipe agreed. "And put the woman in it for you."

They'd made the top, finding two warriors standing just back from the door, arms up against the heat.

"You're not going back, are you?" the older one asked.

"Chief High Dance is in there!" Flat Stone Pipe pointed with his short arm, his stubby finger out.

Seven Skull Shield made it to the door, had just started to look in, when the whole of the roof came crashing down.

No matter how exhausted the rest of him was, his instincts were still quick. Even as he turned and ducked, he had Flat Stone Pipe's small body shielded.

As a gale of fire, sparks, and smoke jetted from the doorway a single terrible scream could be heard. And as quickly, it ceased.

As she made her way down the narrow cut, Night Shadow Star carefully placed each foot, testing the wet soil for purchase. For the moment she wished she were barefoot like Walking Smoke, whose toes found better grip in the slick mud.

This way! Piasa had whispered in her ear. And directed her to this slit of a gully eroded into the steep bluff. A trail of sorts existed here. People, after all, constantly scrambled up and down the bluff face from the river. Portions of this one, however, proved treacherous in the falling rain; a rivulet of muddy brown water was already rushing in the bottom.

"You did this," Walking Smoke told her angrily. "It's the same as when you stuck your finger in my eye when we were little!"

She caught a flicker of Piasa as he crept effortlessly down the slope to one side. "You did it to yourself, Brother."

"It won't stop me, you know. It's only a matter of time before I succeed." He flipped his head the way he had as a boy when it was wet. "How did you know about the escape tunnel beneath Columella's bed?"

"Piasa told me."

He shot her a measuring look from where he climbed down, one hand clutching an old root; whatever tree it had once belonged to was long gone. His naked body was a colorful mess of smudged paint and mud, all running in the rain. His eyes had become black stones in a mess of black and yellow.

"Piasa *told* you?" His voice mocked her. "He's mine. *Mine!* And I'm going to bring him to this world in the end."

"All right, fine. Why do you think I'm doing this? Pus and blood, Spud! You haven't changed. You're still a spoiled, whining little monster."

"And what are you?" He shot her a look as he slid, caught a foot on a piece of sandstone, and edged sideways in the gully to a better hold. "I heard. Moping. Soul-flying to the Spirit World. Grieving because Makes Three got himself killed up north?"

"*Don't* use his name. Ever. Or I'll—"

"Fly off to the Underworld and weep for him to return?"

She flicked the mud from her fingers. "I hate you, you know. What you did to me that night? I'd managed to lock it away, hide it down deep inside. My husband proved to me, allowed me to actually believe, that men weren't all like Morning Star . . . like you."

He paused blocking the narrow defile, water splashing over the foot he'd wedged in the drainage bottom. "That night? He was *no longer* your brother. That was just Chunkey Boy's body. Morning Star can claim any woman he wants."

"I've made my peace with Morning Star. Though not to his liking." She tossed her wet braid aside, and glared down at him. "You had no excuse, Brother. It was incest and rape. And for that, I'll never forgive you."

He gave her a mocking grin. "We're *not* like other people. The same rules don't apply to us. Call it a bond, a special celebration of Morning Star's happy return to us. Seeing you and him? I just *had* to see what it was like to follow a living god."

"He hurt me. *You betrayed and humiliated me!*"

"Forget it, Sister. The world's changed since that night. I have, you have. The voices were right when they told me to take you. They whispered in my ear that as good as it was for me, it would be just as good for you. Oh, it was good indeed! The final proof that I was the Wild One. And you know what else? I realized that night that I loved you more than I'd love any woman ever. The voices told me that you'd come to understand eventually, that though it might hurt you for the moment, it would make you stronger in the end. And they were right. That's why you came to me, why I let you lead me out of that fire."

"I just want you dead."

"You had the chance, Sister. You could have shot me down when you first walked into the palace."

"Oh, I wanted to. Believe it. He kept whispering in my ear to wait, to hold. Even as my muscles weakened."

"He? Piasa?"

"He said it was a test. I only begin to understand."

"Understand? You mean how we're going to change the world again?" He paused. "Oh yes. We unleashed a spinning series of events that night. I'd always loved you, dreamed of you. No woman could ever live up to you, Sister. I knew that as a boy . . . that I'd always try and measure other women by your standards. And then, when I sneaked in, and saw him between your legs?"

"If you really loved me, couldn't you have told him to stop?"

"It was like being hit by lightning!" he cried. "I saw how it would all work! The voices, you should have heard them! They began singing, laughing, crying, 'Yes! Yes! Yes! This is the way!'"

"Nothing exists beyond your needs, does it?" she asked sadly as the cold rain trickled down her face and dripped from her nose.

"You don't know what it was like, being in exile. I never laid with a woman when I wasn't dreaming of you, remembering . . ."

"You're possessed of twisted and polluted souls, Brother. Hurry up. The sooner we're down, the sooner we're in a canoe. The sooner you can have another chance at calling Piasa's souls."

He continued his descent. They were past the steepest part, and could now turn and walk the rest of the way. She ground her teeth, wanting to spit on his rain-streaked back.

"How long were you in contact with Sun Wing?"

"A couple of years," he told her. "She was such a simple thing. And so easy to understand. I watched a girl just like her down among the Pacaha. She became my inspiration. Funny how seeing things from the outside suddenly makes you understand. Like Sun Wing, she'd been given over to indulgence, fawned over as the youngest, but perpetually frustrated by the knowledge that she'd never be the ruler. That's when the voices told me to contact Sun Wing, to begin telling her stories, dangle the possibility before her. I only had to tempt her, and she was mine."

"Why did you take Lace first?"

"No matter what Sun Wing might have told me, giving her proof that I was clearing her way to the *tonka'tzi*'s chair could only reassure her."

"Did you feel nothing when you killed Father? Tortured Lace's husband? Slit her throat and cut the baby out of her body?"

"Did I feel it?" He threw his head back and howled in ecstasy as he shook fists at the storm-lashed skies. "You should have *felt* the Power! The rapturous joy that almost burst my chest and bones. Sister, think. No man alive has ever offered the blood of Morning Star House in sacrifice. Then, to follow it with Sun Wing's and yours? Perhaps the Keeper's, or Matron Wind's?"

They were walking side by side now, hurrying down onto the beach.

The rain-grayed sand was firm under their muddy feet as they approached a line of canoes, each marked with a family or clan emblem. This early, and given the intensity of the rain, the beach was abandoned.

"I felt like I had the sun burning inside me." His face expressed a reverential awe. "To have experienced that . . . like a blinding light searing through my heart, lungs, and gut? *Blessed gods, Star!* Not even the tingling jetting of semen can compare, and it was consuming my whole body. Pleasure, pain, joy, harmony, ecstasy . . ." He sighed. "The only other time I felt anything even close was that night when my seed exploded inside you."

"Lucky me."

She reached the closest canoe, a small dugout crafted from cedar. Given the blunt bow and thick hull, it was probably a dirt farmer's. She certainly didn't recognize the designs painted on its sides. The section of rope that tied it to a stake upslope looked old and ratty. Though firmly beached, the rope provided additional security should the river rise unexpectedly.

She untied the knot, glancing in to see three paddles.

"I can assure you, Brother, what I felt that night was nothing but pain. Every kind of pain, physical as well as soul-bruising disbelief and that shattering sense of betrayal. I know what we got away with as children. We were evil, Brother. And you have just grown worse."

He seemed to be ignoring her, pointing up at the slope. "Someone's coming."

She followed his finger, seeing a muddy, bloody, man slipping and sliding as he followed their path down the drainage-cut bluff.

Fire Cat. She bit off a hollow chuckle. "Come, let's be on the river. The sooner we're away, the sooner I can fulfill my promise to you and Power."

Together they pushed the canoe out onto the rain-stippled water. Night Shadow Star jumped into the bow and picked up a paddle. Mud was running from her moccasins to mix with the rainwater pooled in the hull.

As Walking Smoke hopped in the stern and began to paddle out into the river, she untied her calf-high moccasins.

"We're not evil," he said reasonably. "Just like in the Beginning Times, we are changing the world. First we brought back the Morning Star. In the future, when people sing of the Wild One, they're going to sing how Thrown Away Boy, who would have sacrificed his sister, brought Piasa from the Underworld to this one."

He uttered that silly little laugh that once had charmed and then infuriated her. "And yes, I would have killed you that night. But it wouldn't have been permanent. I would have brought your souls back. Given you another body. Not only did I love you that much, it would have been epic."

"You're *not* Thrown Away, or the Wild One, or any such nonsense. I'm not Corn Woman! Chunkey Boy wasn't the Morning Star, either. That came later. He was nothing more than a mean little boy, and later a violent youth, who never had to face the consequences of his actions. Not until the living god took him."

"Then who are you, if not Corn Woman?"

"I'm Night Shadow Star, Piasa's mouthpiece, accursed and alone." She barked a bitter laugh. "And here's the irony: You're the one who made me that. It was you who broke me down, rubbed my face in the muck of my own false sense of arrogance. You caused me to see the vile being I had become. You forced me to live it from the other side, the victim's side. You made me *feel*, Brother."

He snorted, his paddle trickling water as they drove for the center of the river. "And if I am not Thrown Away, who am I? Who but the Wild One could call the Power of the Underworld? I cut my father's throat! Sacrificed my sister! If I am not great, what am I?"

"A witch," she said simply. "One possessed of demented voices and polluted Power. Evil. A witch driven to sate your appetites for status and authority no matter how much misery, pain, and despair you inflict on others. You never see past yourself."

"You think it's about me?"

"Completely."

"It's about the *world*, Sister! About how I'm going to remake it. I'm surrendering *myself* to Piasa. Sacrificing *my* body. How can that be about me?"

She turned then, staring back at him, seeing the gleam of anticipation in his eyes.

"When you surprised me that night, beat me into submission and pinned my arms above my head, do you remember what you said as you were ripping my skirt off my hips? How you were weeping with joy? Do you remember your words when you drove your knee between my legs? Or the whimpered words that passed your lips as your seed spilled into my torn sheath?"

"I was taken by the Power of the moment, changing the world, changing you to—"

"You cried, 'Oh, yes. Oh, yes.' And 'How I've wanted this.' Over and over. I wasn't there, Brother. Not as your sister, not as a terrified girl, not even as a person. I was a just a hot piece of meat with a terror-dry sheath to plunge your spear into. That's when I knew you for what you were. And I've hated you ever since."

For the first time, his eyes narrowed. He flipped his head to sling the rain off. "Then why are you helping me?"

She gave him a triumphant grin. "Helping you? Piasa told me how it had to end. It took every ounce of my strength to keep from shooting that arrow into your accursed heart. I looked at the pieces of Lace's body, remembered her sweet face. Saw again how excited she was at her first pregnancy, and the fact that she actually loved her husband. She was trying so hard, studying at how to be a good Matron Wind in anticipation of the day she ascended to the Four Winds chair.

"I loved my father. As much for the license he gave us as children, as for the service he gave to Cahokia and its people as *tonka'tzi*."

"He—"

"Quiet! I *loved* them all. And you murdered them! Would have murdered Sun Wing, me, Columella, and those children! Pus and blood, I wanted with my very soul to drive that arrow through your heart the way you *drove your shaft into my sheath that night*."

"Then why didn't you?" he asked through a sneer. "It's because you know my Power, want to share it, to—"

"Piasa kept whispering for me to be patient, that I was clever enough to eventually get you here."

They were drifting on the current now, rain spattering on them, stippling the river's roiling surface. Someone had pushed a canoe out from the shore, a single figure, paddling like a madman in an attempt to catch up.

Walking Smoke arched an eyebrow, chuckling to himself. "Why would Piasa choose you? Look around. We're on the river. Headed south. In a quarter moon we'll be beyond Morning Star's reach. I don't have to conjure Piasa's souls in Cahokia. There are other places that—"

"You are *just* where we want you," she told him simply.

Walking Smoke threw his head back and laughed. "Quite the opposite, Sister. You're alone with me. On the river. And as much as I appreciate your help getting out of Evening Star town, you still *ruined* my ceremony. And for that you must be punished." He cocked his head. "But fortunately for you, I do love you so. The last time I shared my love, I didn't hear you gasp when you reached your pleasure. But you've given yourself to me now. Before Piasa takes my body, I *will* hear that explosive little cry of delight."

"Want to try now?" she asked, reaching down and peeling her moccasins off, the canoe wobbling as she did. One after the other, she tossed them into the river. "Are you desperate enough to take me in a canoe, here, in the rain?"

His chortling laugh sent shivers through her as she struggled to pull her sopping wet dress over her head. With a flourish, she sent it sailing to slap down on the waves. Carefully shifting, she turned in the canoe to face him.

His face was possessed of rapturous awe as he stared at her naked body. "You never cease to amaze me, Sister. Oh, yes. I'm up for the challenge. I will have to hurt you, you know. I can't just forgive the part you played in spoiling my ceremony."

She opened her arms in an inviting embrace, taunting him by arching her back, spreading her knees against the hull, and leaning back. "I'm yours, Brother. To do with as you wish. If it's better for you, more pleasurable if you hurt me in the process, do it."

He raised himself on the gunwales, his blue-stained shaft already rising. As he carefully clambered onto her body, she whispered, "I can't tell you how I've waited for this. Piasa finally says it's time."

And with a violent twist of her body, she capsized the canoe. Even as they spilled into the cold water, his hands reflexively clamped on her throat.

Sixty-four

Columella's palace roared like a cyclone. Flames, sparks, and smoke rose torchlike into the falling rain. The whole roof cascaded down into the walls with a cracking and banging barely drowned by the fire's howl.

Blue Heron's cowed servants had rushed up to her immediately after she and Seven Skull Shield had descended the stairs. Now they all huddled around, holding the rain shield over her head where she squatted. Beside her, Columella crouched, knees together, a stunned and devastated expression on her face as she watched the fountain of flame shooting up from inside her walls. Her children, soaked and shivering, watched the palace burn with terror-bright eyes.

The dwarf, Flat Stone Pipe, stood, his small arm over Columella's shoulders. His pug face was soot-streaked, eyes swollen from the smoke.

"Close one," Blue Heron told Columella. "From what I saw of the inside, you didn't want to live there anyway. Walking Smoke's sense of décor was somewhat limited." She paused. "Sorry about your brother."

"What possessed him? To risk everything . . . his children. My children! All of Evening Star House! I'd hang him in a square myself!"

"How long ago did Walking Smoke contact you?"

She shook her head absently, then at a nudging from Flat Stone Pipe, came to her senses. Eyes narrowed, she gave Blue Heron a hard look. "Pus and blood, but you're clever." Then she laughed humorlessly. "No, Keeper, I had no part in this. Granted, I've got my own pots in the fire, but this was High Dance's doing. And worse, the fool had no idea who he was dealing with. He only knew him as 'Bead.' Neither Flat Stone Pipe nor I had any idea who he was. I was taken by complete surprise when he walked in with his warriors yesterday afternoon." She shook her head. "Am I *that* incompetent?"

"Maybe we all are." Blue Heron shot her old adversary a measuring look.

Columella's bitter lips curled. "Oh, I think there was more than enough collusion in Morning Star House to go around. Sun Wing, for one. She bragged to Walking Smoke that she'd 'given him' the Lady Lace and fed him information on your investigation."

Blue Heron looked over where her niece, untied, some use of her limbs restored, cowered under a blanket held by warriors. The young woman looked sick to her stomach, eyes focused on some distant terror.

"I think her life is going to take a turn for the worse, Cousin. The Morning Star trusted her."

"Did he?" Flat Stone Pipe asked in his high-pitched voice. "The Morning Star plays his games like a master fisherman, with baited lines running all directions. While he sets the hook with one line, he's letting a fish run on the other to better reel him in."

On her other side, Seven Skull Shield, holding a split of cedar over his head yawned.

"Tired, thief?"

"Too long since we had any kind of sleep or food. Seems like a lifetime since we were sitting out back of your palace. And I'm cold to the bone."

She spared the palace another look as something cracked inside the walls and more sparks shot up. The rain seemed to intensify.

"I'm glad you showed up when you did, thief. It's an irritating admission, but I think once more I owe you my life."

He gave her a sidelong appraisal, grinning, most of the blood washed from his blocky face. A new bruise reddened his forehead. "You didn't do so bad yourself. I had him, you know. You really didn't need to bash his brains out."

"Yes I did." She smacked her lips distastefully. "As much screaming and howling as you were making, I'd have done anything to shut you up."

"Why are we sitting out here in the rain," he asked. "There's a perfectly good Four Winds Clan House right over there. It's got a big veranda. I'll bet the roof is rainproof, and there's a roaring fire inside."

"There's a reason I keep you around, thief." She gestured, allowed Seven Skull Shield to help her up, and ordered, "Let's go someplace dry where we . . ."

At the edge of the plaza, the clacking cadence of a marching squadron barely preceded the arrival of tight ranks of warriors as they emerged from between the Snapping Turtle Clan charnel house and its conical burial mound.

All around her, people were climbing to their feet, arms crossed on their chests, shivering in the rain. Everyone watched the squadron as it trotted across the spacious plaza, the warriors ducking their heads by the rank as they touched their foreheads and passed the World Tree pole.

Blue Heron walked out, smiling as Five Fists Mankiller—marching in the squadron first's position behind the two-headed eagle standard that denoted Morning Star's squadron—stopped short, shouting orders.

The squadron second shouted a repeat of Five Fists' commands, and moved his arms in the choreographed gestures of command.

Heedless of the rain, the formation broke, lines of warriors wheeling, trotting forward, and turning until the clustered knot of survivors was surrounded.

Blue Heron stepped up to Five Fists, two of her porters trying to keep the rain shield over her head.

"Good to see you, old friend. Your timing's a little late. Where's War Duck's squadron?"

"Disbanded at the river on the Morning Star's orders, Keeper." The tension in Five Fists' eyes indicated he was unhappy about something.

She pointed back at the burning palace. "We could have used your help about a half a hand of time ago."

He was looking around at the crowd. "I see the Lady Sun Wing. Where is Lace?"

"Walking Smoke killed her. Offered her blood to Piasa, and chopped her and her baby into pieces before spreading them on the floor." She hesitated. "Since when did Morning Star put you back in charge of a squadron? Thought that was Lightning Eagle's honor?"

His speculative eyes roamed the crowd again, then returned to hers. Rain was spattering from his wood-and-leather helmet, the feathers that normally decorated it were sodden and sagging.

"Is this everyone who was in the palace when Walking Smoke was attempting the ritual?"

"It is." She lifted a hand. "Well, everyone but Night Shadow Star, Walking Smoke, and the Red Wing."

"Where are they?" Five Fists lifted his hand, fingers flexing in the sign language of the squadrons. His war second stepped close, waiting.

"I don't know. I'm not even sure if they escaped the palace or burned in the back. The last I saw, they'd gone into Columella's personal quarters, but the wall was on fire. The smoke pretty thick. The Red Wing went in pursuit. The thief, however, tells me there was a tunnel back there. They may have escaped that way."

"Take twenty warriors. Find them," Five Fists ordered his second.

The man touched his forehead, wheeled, and charged off ordering, "You twenty. With me."

She watched the warriors race off around the edges of the mound. "What's going on here, old friend? Something about this just has the wrong feel."

"I am sent to return everyone to Cahokia under guard. Morning Star's personal orders, Keeper. Everyone."

"So, it's like that, is it?"

"I'm afraid so, Keeper."

She glanced sidelong at Columella and the dwarf. "Yes, he does play with a great many baited lines, doesn't he?"

She just never thought she'd be one of the ones he finally reeled in.

Sixty-five

No!" Fire Cat screamed as Night Shadow Star's canoe flipped over. He couldn't believe it. He was no more than a hard stone's throw from overtaking her. Close enough to have seen her undress and apparently offer herself to that soul-sick and twisted brother of hers. It hadn't made any sense.

And then she'd deliberately rolled the canoe?

Fire Cat rose to his knees, using his weight behind the paddle to drive the canoe forward. In the slashing rain, he searched the roiling river's surface. Night Shadow Star's canoe had canted back onto its side, waves breaking over the rain-dimpled curve of hull.

She had to come up soon. So did Walking Smoke.

And when he does, I'm taking this paddle and driving it through the top of the abomination's head.

Fire Cat slicked bloody water from his face and pulled his soaked hair back. Doing so made him flinch as his torn scalp protested. His burned skin stung like a thousand bees had been at him. A weary fatigue lurked in his very bones. He could feel cold eating at his core, triggering the first shivers to run down his goose-fleshed arms.

"Come on, Night Shadow Star."

Daring the slick and sloping sides of the hull, Fire Cat stood, balancing, as his canoe drifted up to the swamped dugout. The river's surface, rain-hammered, roiling and rippled by the breeze, had turned into an opaque maze of expanding rings. It reflected a leaden gray, the murky water impenetrable.

"So what, Fire Cat? Do you dive in yourself? Swim down? Try and find her?"

With a palm he wiped beaded water from his face again, raindrops still pattering on his bare head. Braced as his legs were, he locked his knees to keep them from trembling.

He pursed his lips, squinting around. She'd been under for too long. As a boy he'd spent enough time diving in the upper river to know how precarious the currents were when they ran deep. She could be anywhere within a bow shot by now.

"Come on, Piasa. She says she serves you? Give me a sign."

Even as he said it, he started. Beneath the surface the water flashed a weird blue, as if cerulean lightning had flickered. His canoe rocked as though a wave had lifted the bow, in defiance of the flat water around him.

He dropped to his knees at the last second, weaving to balance the now bobbing canoe. His heart hammered frantically against his breast.

"What in the name of . . ."

Bolts of real lightning flashed down from the heavy gray clouds. Four blinding flashes—the deafening explosions like hammer blows—wove a pattern around him as they struck the river. He had a vision of instant steam, boiling water, and a bellow of pained rage from below.

What should have been a blink of the eye seemed to stretch into an endless agony. Unimaginable energy pulsed around him, bore him up, and expanded as if to fill the world. A whirlwind of emotions tore through him: rage mixed with exaltation, defeat, and surprise, all spinning and confused.

Like a slap to the soul it ended, left him stunned and flattened, facedown in the sloshing water where it washed back and forth in the bottom of his pitching canoe.

Terrified, heart racing, he cowered against the sodden wood and blinked. Afterimages of black and white lay behind his half-blinded eyes. His ears rang with a high-pitched tone. The air carried a steamy sulfurous odor. Raising his head, he looked around. Rain now slashed down with vengeance.

Night Shadow Star's swamped canoe, its hull in splinters, was charred.

"By *Hunga Ahuito!*" It had been a direct hit.

Shaking, his teeth chattering, he pawed cold rain from his face and struggled for breath. How long did he stay? How long did he search?

No one could hold their breath for that long. She had to be down there, drowned, her body drifting along the dark bottom, her long hair spilling in a black, undulating wave as she slowly tumbled, loose limbed, her dark eyes sightless, her mouth open and filling with silt.

He saw it by chance, having the entire river to search. Just a bobbing dot—like a ball that barely popped to the surface only to recede.

Desperate, the paddle clutched in shaking hands, he drove his canoe toward the spot, orienting himself by the distant roofs of River Mounds. Tracking the progress of the current, following by instinct.

There! Once again he caught a glimpse: a head, yes. But was it Night Shadow Star's?

The ache in his blistered shoulders knotted into a cramp, his physical effort barely keeping the cold at bay. His scorched hands had started to hurt, and his belly suffered from a nauseous tickle. Exhaustion was sucking the last reserves from his souls. Try as he might, ignoring the pain of his burns was no longer possible.

Again the head bobbed up, closer this time.

With three hard strokes he pushed his canoe forward, timing it . . . and yes. He reached down as the head bobbed up, twined his numb fingers into hair, and lifted.

"Who are you?" he said through panting breath. Fatigue-clumsy as he was, he almost swamped as he lifted. Shipping his paddle, he managed to paw the long black hair out of Night Shadow Star's slack face.

Keeping a hold on her hair, he repositioned himself amidships, found his balance, and pulled.

It took two tries before he managed to get his clublike hands under her armpits. Winded, he pulled, wondering where his strength had gone, and barely managed to lift more than her breasts from the water.

"No sleep for days, Lady. Ran all night. Fought most of the morning. Haven't eaten. Got burns all over my back. You might have just found the limits of my oath."

Her mouth opened and closed, water spitting out.

"Okay, I hear you." He set himself, filled his lungs, and gave one last tug, feeling her slip up. Her rump caught on the gunwale.

It was enough. He stuffed his hand between her legs and levered her limp body into the canoe.

For a moment, he lay atop her, gasping for breath. Somehow he'd managed to tear his scalp wound open again, and rain-washed blood was streaming down the side of his head.

She wasn't breathing, but placing his hand on her breastbone he could feel the slowing beat of her heart.

"At least I'm practiced." He set himself, throwing his weight against her chest, watching water surge from her mouth.

"Come on, Lady. You wouldn't want me walking free, now would you? You and I, we've got a lot of hate left. Can't go wasting it by slipping off to the Spirit world, now can you?"

Again and again he pressed down. Almost capsizing the canoe, he got his knee under her rump and pressed again, hearing her throat gurgle as air passed.

"That's it."

He climbed on top of her, supporting her neck, pinching her nose, and placing his mouth over hers. Then, as he had in her quarters, he breathed his soul into her body.

For how long, he ceased to know or care. But her heart kept beating, and periodically she'd breathe, her cold exhalations on his cheek.

When the moment finally came, he'd just filled her lungs, then used his right hand to press it out of her. Once again he had placed his mouth to hers, blowing her lungs full of air. He raised his head, pressing on her chest, to see her eyes open and fix on his.

Then she coughed, water bubbling out of her mouth, and coughed again. As if her souls had finally returned to her body, she began to shiver, the spasms increasing until her whole body was wracked.

In relief, he dropped his head, panting as if he'd run for a hard day.

Awash in rainwater, his body atop hers, he collapsed limply and let the river carry them where it would.

Sixty-six

Bright sunlight shot a shaft of yellow through the Morning Star palace's large doorway. Its glow helped to illuminate the magnificent great room with its spanning roof. So, too, did the crackling fire in the central hearth. Light reflected from polished copper and gleamed on brightly painted and carved wood. The stunning reliefs on the walls around them almost seemed to pulse with life and Power.

Blue Heron sat appropriately on the right of the fire, or from Morning Star's perspective, on the left. Beside her were Columella and the dwarf, and then Sun Wing. Her niece, clothed now, might have been partially soul-dead. And who knew, perhaps Walking Smoke had completely scared the souls out of the young woman's body. Finally, in that first rank, *Tonka'tzi* Wind sat, her head down, expression thoughtful.

In the rear were High Dance and Columella's children, hardly at any kind of ease, and still traumatized. For all they knew, given their panicked young minds, they might have just been plucked from the stew pot and thrown headlong into the cook fire.

Still missing were Night Shadow Star, Walking Smoke, and the Red Wing. And that, Blue Heron mused, was curious indeed.

Smart man, that Red Wing. He'd been clever enough to either burn to death or vanish.

And if I'd had the sense of a head-struck duck, I'd have kept the thief in sight.

As they'd made the long march back to the Morning Star's tall mound, Seven Skull Shield had been there one minute, plodding along, looking absolutely exhausted. And the next he'd disappeared, the warriors marching along the flanks apparently having completely missed his departure.

"Go with Power, thief." She smiled grimly, delighted that cunning Seven Skull Shield had read the nature of their "escort" correctly.

"Why are we here?" Columella asked out of the corner of her mouth. "I didn't do anything wrong. More to the point, my children are innocent of absolutely everything."

"No, they're not," Blue Heron whispered back. "They were born into the Evening Star House. Taken to the palace where Walking Smoke tried to raise the Piasa's souls in his own body and destroy the world. Sometimes, Matron, as you well know, that's all it takes to be condemned."

Columella closed her eyes and took a deep breath, the kind of action someone stilling a racing heart and trying to find balance would do.

"Why are you here, Keeper?" Flat Stone Pipe asked, his pitched voice low. "Were you part of this, too?"

"I'm guilty, all right. I didn't catch him in time. Didn't stop him from committing his atrocity. My niece was sacrificed at Walking Smoke's hand."

"You use his name. You think he's still alive?"

"You heard the runner. They found no bones in Columella's burned quarters. The door to your access tunnel was found open."

Columella, voice tight, began, "Night Shadow Star—"

"Serves Piasa," Blue Heron snapped. "If she's with Walking Smoke, I'd stake my life that it's for the Water Panther's reasons and not her own."

A conch horn was blown. A line of recorders entered from outside, walking along the west wall and seating themselves. From boxes and baskets, they began withdrawing their pots of various colored and shaped beads.

Blue Heron craned her neck, looking back at the door where Five Fists, War Claw, and party of warriors stood blocking the exit.

"My children did nothing wrong," Columella insisted in a pained whisper. "Can I save them? Offer myself for the square before he has a chance to come to a decision?"

"For what?" Blue Heron felt her curiosity rise.

"Anything. Everything!" Columella gestured her hopelessness. "Yes, I plotted against you. We all do. There's no secret in that. Every

House in the Four Winds Clan wishes to supplant your House, wishes to serve the Morning Star."

"And until now I did a pretty good job of keeping the lid on all of you," Blue Heron growled.

"Quiet," Flat Stone Pipe hissed. "The Keeper is no friend of yours, Matron. No matter what you offer to save the children, she's awaiting judgment in the same row as you are."

The conch horn sounded again, and Blue Heron, like the rest, bowed her head forward until it touched the matting.

She heard the Morning Star as he walked out and took his seat on the raised clay dais.

"Rise," he called softly.

Morning Star wore a beautiful eagle-feather cape thrown back over his shoulders. The white apron suspended from his waist had been embroidered in a zig-zag lightning pattern on either side of a long-nosed Birdman image. His face was completely painted in white, the two forked-eye designs around his eyes in gleaming black. A black rectangle covered his mouth. Atop his head had been fixed a striking copper headpiece depicting the arrow-through-cloud motif; white-shell long-nosed-god maskettes covered his ears. Sturdy war moccasins clad his feet.

"Where are Night Shadow Star and Walking Smoke?" he asked softly, fixing his eyes on Blue Heron. "Tell me, Keeper."

She touched her forehead. "I do not know, Great Lord."

"What went wrong, Keeper? It is your job, is it not, to keep the clans safe, to keep them in line, to keep the plotting and violence to a minimum. Yet now I learn that my banished brother was able to return, operate freely, assassinate his father who was our *tonka'tzi*. He almost murdered me. You yourself will bear his scar upon your throat. He apparently subverted Evening Star House for his own purposes, and then murdered the *tonka'tzi*'s daughter, and colluded with the lady Sun Wing. All that, right under your nose."

Blue Heron ground her few remaining teeth, aware that her ears were burning. "As those things developed, I was prompt in my reports to Lady Sun Wing"—she swallowed hard—"as the Morning Star directed me to be."

From under her lowered brow she tried to read Morning Star's expression. She could detect no reaction other than his long pause.

"Matron Evening Star," he asked next. "When did you learn of Walking Smoke's arrival in Cahokia?"

"That it was Walking Smoke?" her voice strained. "I learned that on the day he and his Tula warriors walked into my palace and seized it and me."

"But Chief High Dance knew?"

"Not in the beginning, great Lord. I warned him. Told him that Bead was dangerous." She took a deep breath. "Great Lord, my children are innocent of everything. If you need to punish someone, I offer myself, having done nothing to accommodate Walking Smoke. Exile them if you must, but take my life in return."

"I didn't ask you for your life, Matron. Such protestations smack of guilt."

"No, Great Lord. Not guilt. But if someone has to pay, to balance the Power through sacrifice . . ." She couldn't finish, but prostrated herself facedown on the matting. Her body was trembling, fear eating her alive.

Beside her, Flat Stone Pipe had closed his eyes, head down. What Blue Heron could see of his expression looked desolate.

"Sun Wing?" Morning Star asked flatly. "How long were you working in your brother's service?"

Sun Wing, however, said nothing. She just sat; her expression as empty as last year's seed jar. The corners of her lips twitched, her hands clenching and fidgeting. She seemed oblivious of where she sat, who she faced.

"Sun Wing?" Morning Star asked so sharply that *Tonka'tzi* Wind flinched, her downcast, sidelong glance frantically willing her niece to speak, to at least acknowledge the Morning Star's presence.

"Sun Wing?" Morning Star demanded once more. "Look at me."

Blue Heron swallowed dryly, whispering, "Come on, girl. At least admit you're alive."

Though the gods alone knew for how long, given her guilt and collusion.

"Sun Wing?" Morning Star's voice softened. He tilted his head the slightest bit, as if disappointed. "Has she spoken to anyone? Given any hint that her souls remain within her?"

"Not to my knowledge, Great Lord," Blue Heron offered as the silence stretched. "She'd just seen her sister sacrificed by Walking Smoke. Was apparently on the point of having her throat cut when Night Shadow Star burst into the room. It is possible, Great Lord, that her souls were frightened completely out of her body. It might be worth employing Rides-the-Lightning to see if he can call them back."

Morning Star hadn't shifted his gaze from Sun Wing. Those tells

Seven Skull Shield had described were barely visible. The tightening of the corners of the mouth, the lifting tilt of the head.

"Squadron First."

"Yes, Morning Star?" Five Fists called from the back, touching his forehead and bowing.

"Detail some warriors to take her to the Earth Clan's soul flier. By my order he has four days to call her souls back into her body that I might question them."

"Yes, Morning Star!" Five Fists was already issuing orders. Four very nervous-looking warriors trotted forward, bent, and with wary reluctance, lifted her litter as if it were host to a nest of water moccasins.

"By the Morning Star, no," *Tonka'tzi* Wind whispered, eyes clamped shut against tears.

"Keeper," the Morning Star asked, "if there was any lesson to be drawn from this, what would it be?"

"That we can guard against everyone but those who know us best, Great Lord." She lifted her head, squinting as she dared to look him straight in the eye. "Walking Smoke changed the rules. He didn't sneak back into Cahokia seeking to ingratiate himself, or to play subtle political games. He came, knowing our strengths and weaknesses . . . knowing our hearts and habits. And he came to destroy those who once loved him."

He almost snorted in response, his nostrils flaring slightly, a hint of worry on his lips.

"And where is he now, Keeper? Sneaking up the stairs as we speak? Secreting himself to assassinate me in my sleep? Stirring the Powers of the Underworld to unleash disaster in our world?"

"I . . . don't know." She felt her heart sink as she stared into his implacable eyes. Then, seized by some insane impulse, she added, "But you're aware of that. You knew all along, didn't you? What was it? A whispering of the wind? Some voice from the Sky World that told you he'd come back? That he'd already bent Sun Wing to his will?"

She pointed, hearing gasps from around the room. "That's why you had me climb the tower out there with you that day. That's what you were trying to tell me, wasn't it? That's why you had me report to Sun Wing. You were keeping her close, watching, trying to determine who was with or against you."

She raised her hands, knotting them into fists. "By *Hunga Ahuito*'s shadow, why didn't you tell me?"

Her sister was staring at her with horrified eyes, her mouth open, fingers to her lips.

Columella, still quivering, made a whimpering sound. Flat Stone Pipe had thrown himself flat, no doubt hoping to be ignored in the coming explosion of rage.

"Do you challenge me, Keeper?" his voice was flat, emotionless. "Do you *question* me?"

Blue Heron tried to swallow, her tongue sticking. *Too far. I've gone too far.*

She saw it in his eyes, the sharpening for the kill.

Knowing she was already dead, she stated hoarsely, "I might have been able to save some lives if I'd known. Might even have caught him, stopped him before he slit Lace's throat, hung her husband up like a gutted bird. How dare I, huh?"

So this was what it felt like to condemn oneself to death? It was a hollow, gutted feeling, a draining of hope.

She chuckled humorlessly, exhausted eyes meeting his.

"Squadron First!"

"Yes, Morning Star!"

She didn't need to look back to know Five Fist was bowing and touching his forehead.

"Take the Keeper out and tie her in a square where the entire world can admire her courage. Make her a—"

"You will *not*!" a strident voice called.

Blue Heron turned to see Night Shadow Star burst through the open doorway, the Red Wing behind her and to the right. She elbowed Five Fists aside as they passed through the rank of warriors without so much as a raised hand.

She wore a black fabric war shirt with intertwined red Tie Snakes embroidered over each breast. It was belted at the waist where rested a copper-bitted war club, larger than the old one that had burned in Columella's palace. A Tula bow hung from her shoulder; the quiver strapped on her back bristled with arrows.

Behind her, the Red Wing wore battle armor; a wooden carapace and breastplate bound by fitted leather protected his vitals. It certainly fit better than what she'd seen him wear last time. He, too, carried a Tula bow, arrows packed in the quiver on his back; his war club, brandished in his right hand, looked more wicked than hers.

"Greetings from Piasa and the Powers of the Underworld," Night Shadow Star's voice rang out. "He and I hold you to our bargain." She passed Blue Heron without even a glance and strode into the sacred and inviolate space between Morning Star and the sacred fire.

The room might have been a charnel house at midnight, so thick had the silence become. Blue Heron doubted people were even breathing. The recorders appeared frozen, beads forgotten in their fingers; the warriors in the rear stood in awed amazement.

Morning Star alone seemed unfazed. "Where is your brother, Night Shadow Star? Walking Smoke's chaos has taken us far enough down the path of destruction. He has had his chance, and it failed."

Blue Heron watched Night Shadow Star cock her hip, her right hand resting on the head of the war club. "Speak his name no more, great Lord. That man is gone, the mere uttering of his name unseemly."

"He is dead?"

"He is defeated. At least for the time being. But to call him dead? That may be a matter of definitions." Her smile was a grim thing. "It took all of my resolve to keep from killing my brother when I had the chance, but Piasa kept whispering into my ear to wait, to hold, and finally, to deliver him to the river. That, I was able to do. And when the time was right, I capsized the canoe and dragged my twisted brother down to the depths."

She took a deep breath, head back, eyes closed. "And what I saw there . . . ?"

As the pause stretched, Morning Star asked, "Yes?"

She opened her eyes, meeting Morning Star's stare. "My brother believed himself to be the Wild One. Like the stories of old, he wanted to unleash chaos and remake the world by resurrecting Piasa inside himself. My task was to deliver him to the Underworld Lord for punishment. Which I did."

She hesitated, as if searching for words. "I saw the Piasa dart up from the depths. As he did his presence filled the river with a remarkable iridescent blue light. Piasa fixed on my brother as he sought to choke the life out of me. In that half a heartbeat, before Piasa could seize my brother and devour him, the Thunderbirds struck. Four bolts of lightning flashed down and boiled the water around us."

People gasped, and Blue Heron raised a hand to her throat. It made perfect sense that the great Spirit birds would have taken the opportunity to strike when their old adversary was so close to the surface and vulnerable.

"My souls were stunned. The world went away. When I could see again," Night Shadow Star continued, "he was gone."

"Piasa or your brother?"

"Both. I floated limply, tumbling, alone. Everything was black. I could hear the rain hissing on the river's surface. My lungs ached, desperate to breathe. For all I knew, I might have been dead." She shifted, as if reliving the experience. "And then a hand reached down, grabbed me by the hair, and rudely pulled me from the river and back into this world."

"But you didn't see your brother die?"

"To Piasa's disgust, the Thunderbirds struck an instant before Piasa could wreak his vengeance. Did the lightning kill my brother? Perhaps his body tumbles along the sandy river bottom disturbing only the clams and moss. He had, after all, threatened the Sky World by seeking to unleash the Powers of the Underworld. Or perhaps the Thunderbirds took him for their own reasons."

Or perhaps—Blue Heron felt a shiver run through her—*he is really the incarnation of the Thrown Away Boy, and his Power rescued him at the last moment.*

Were that the case, eventually he'd be back, perpetually in conflict with his brother. And to her horror, it meant that Walking Smoke was more than just a twisted witch, but that his Power might be even more dangerous than anyone had anticipated.

He might still be alive?

She instinctively ran her fingers over the newly formed scar on her throat. An icy chill had settled between her souls.

Morning Star sat silently for a moment. Was that a look of wistfulness that reflected from his dark eyes? Did she see the faintest quiver of his lips? Perhaps Chunkey Boy's memories of better days played somewhere between the living god's souls?

Blue Heron sighed.

Night Shadow Star stated, "The threat posed by my brother is over for the time being. Piasa ensures me that Power between the worlds has been restored to balance."

Morning Star said, "Convey our gratitude to the Piasa. He has saved us the construction of a square and the trouble of disposing of your brother's remains. You may go, Lady Night Shadow Star."

"We are not finished here, great Lord. You and I had an agreement the night I saved your life: I forgave the debt of your life; in return the perpetrator was mine to hunt."

"Did you know at the time it was Walking Smoke?"

"I did not. Piasa didn't see fit to share that bit of information until that night when I came here, to your palace. The night when I told you, the Keeper, and the *Tonka'tzi*. But you knew, didn't you? That he came so close to killing you, that I thwarted the attempt at the last instant, threw you completely off balance. The impossibility that your life was saved by Underworld Power had you reeling and confused."

He smiled—a cunning sort of expression. "I wasn't sure where the truth lay. Was your brother's alliance with you? Or with Sun Wing? Or with both of you? After we made our bargain, it came to me that you might have hired that man to cut my throat. Accompanied him here that night. It wasn't unreasonable that you waited until he placed the blade to my skin, and murdered him at the last moment to win my trust."

"You cast a wide net, Morning Star. The problem with drawing it in is that you have swept up everyone. Piasa, Horned Serpent, and Snapping Turtle could care less who you sacrifice in your plots and games. They sought only to counter the threat to Power." She stepped forward, placing one foot on the dais.

At the affront, Five Fists and his warriors came rushing forward; the Red Wing whirled and, in a war chief's voice, ordered, "Hold!" He raised his arm in emphasis and bent it in the Cahokian war signal to maintain position.

Five Fists and his warriors, trained as they were, stopped short.

"But *I* care!" Night Shadow Star told Morning Star as she peered into his eyes. "Look at me through the god's eyes, as you will, Morning Star. But we have a history, you and I. As Chunkey Boy or Morning Star, you know my words are true when I tell you my brother came very, very close to destroying our world. He didn't realize that with the slitting of Sun Wing's throat, it would have been irreversible. The boundaries and barriers between the worlds would have fallen. Piasa would have been ripped from the Underworld and thrust into ours. My foolish brother thought he needed the blood and bodies of all three of his sisters? Two would have sufficed, because I was already Piasa's."

For the first time, Blue Heron, from her angle, could see the cold uncertainty that entered the Morning Star's eyes.

Night Shadow Star straightened, stepping back. "Yes, you do understand, don't you?"

She half turned away, then glanced back at him. "You and I have an alliance. Fragile, yes, but an alliance nevertheless. Other threats are looming, great Lord. The danger is not passed. Word of my brother's actions will travel. Others will try to follow in his footsteps. When they do, we must be ready."

She gestured toward Blue Heron and her companions. "With the exception of Sun Wing, these people serve you. They serve Cahokia. They are, however, under my protection. No harm will come to them."

"And Sun Wing?"

"She is yours, Morning Star."

With that, she turned, walking smartly past Blue Heron, back straight, her long black hair flowing. The hand resting on her war club was white knuckled. Behind her, the Red Wing followed with eyes forward, his war club at the ready.

When Blue Heron looked back at the Morning Star, he was smiling, eyes almost twinkling, as if some great victory had been achieved. And that puzzled her. She thought they'd all just avoided disaster by the narrowest margin.

Or had he planned it from the very beginning? And if he had, what did that say about the depths of Morning Star's cunning and guile?

Sixty-seven

In the cord-makers' workshop in River Mounds, Seven Skull Shield threw his head back, singing, *"Such a pretty young lass, she lay back on the grass."*

He filled his lungs, booming out, *"With her eyes on the skies, I parted her pale-skinned thighs.*

"Oh please, she did beg, so I drove in my peg.

"She gasped and she cried, she moaned like she'd died."

Black Martin, in a pained voice, said, *"Enough* already! Your voice is as soothing as sandstone grating on wood."

"But there's true art to the song, don't you think? A sweet poetry of the soul. The kind of reflection on my life that—"

"I'd rather hear dogs tortured," Big Fish muttered from the back of the workshop. He was using a flyer to spin cord from separate fibers.

The way the cord and rope-spinners told it, Cahokia was literally held together by their craft. And there was truth to their claim.

Seven Skull Shield sat on a stump just inside the door and watched the cord makers as they practiced their magic. Everything from thread to string to cord to rope was made here.

Wild Hare worked at separating fibers from a skein of hemp. He was a middle-aged man, thin, with ropy muscles. His head, topped by a black mop of hair, was shaped like a wedge, thick and flat at the top and skinny at the bottom. The way his fingers played over the fibers reminded Seven Skull Shield of a spider fiddling with strands of web.

All around him lay skeins of different fibers Traded from everywhere. Hemp, basswood, and cedar bark made up the majority of the rough fibers. Combed cottonwood down for fine lace and hanging moss from the far south were some of the more exotic wares. Pounded and separated sinew had its own place as did a water jar in which lengths of intestine had been sunk. Bales of buffalo wool and human hair hung from the rear wall.

Where morning sunlight shone through the door, Black Martin sat on a tattered blanket, a length of tanned buckskin spread over his thigh. His lined brow had deepened into a pensive frown as he concentrated on slicing a narrow strip, or plait, from the hide. He followed a faint black line made from stretching a soot-covered string over the hide and snapping it. For this fine work he used a freshly struck obsidian flake.

"Obsidian is expensive stuff," Seven Skull Shield noted. "Lots of demand for it. Some of the societies insist on obsidian for their bloodletting and scarification rituals."

"I don't have much trouble getting it," Black Martin noted. "The societies, they have to offer services. Surveying, healing, telling fortunes, and casting spells." He grinned up at Seven Skull Shield, which exposed gaps in his bad teeth. "Me, all I have to do is offer a Trader one or two of my ropes. No one in the world makes better ropes than I do. I test each one for strength."

"All ropes break eventually," Seven Skull Shield noted.

"Which is why we're always making more," Big Fish replied as he carefully stretched fibers around his flyer and spun it. The rotating disk twisted another length of cord.

"Look at this." He gestured at the coils of string and cord around the room. "Can't make enough fast enough. That pile of hemp over there? A Deer Clan man brought that in. Wanted a new fish net by the new moon. If I had five more skilled men, I might keep up."

"You're not doing so bad, you still have a granary full of Traded corn left over from the winter," Seven Skull Shield noted. "Best Trade it before it molds."

"And you're not doing so poorly yourself," Wild Hare shot back. His brow raised skeptically. "We've heard all kinds of stories about you. Unbelievable things. That you're tied in tight with the Morning Star up on his mound. That you've been driving that tree trunk you call your pisser into the Four Winds Clan Keeper. Bit old, even for you, isn't she?"

"Um, that's not exactly the case."

"Figured as much," Black Martin noted, lips twitching as he kept an even pressure on his cut. "No way a woman with her kind of authority and prestige would look twice at a bit of human flotsam like you. High Chiefs are more her type. If half the rumors can be believed, she's been married to most of them at one time or another."

"Say," Wild Hare noted, "just why are you here?"

"Thought I'd come and make your lives happy with my songs."

"I'd rather hang in a square than hear you sing. The only time we see you is when some husband just missed catching you in his wife's bed. Usually you're in here with us because he and his clansmen are out there somewhere, prowling around with war clubs in their hands and blood lust in their hearts."

"Thought we were your refuge of last resort," Black Martin agreed. Then he stopped short, his careful work forgotten. "Pus and blood! The Four Winds Clan isn't after you for bouncing the Keeper up and down on that shaft of yours, are they?"

Seven Skull Shield rubbed his face wearily. "Haven't you been paying attention? The assassinations? The Morning Star's brother coming back, trying to resurrect Piasa in his own body? Palaces burned, searches for missing women?"

Wild Hare peered at him from under lowered brows. "Yes, something. Who has time for gossip? We've got orders to fill. Traders are going to be flooding in with fiber and looking for finished cord and rope. We're getting a reputation. People up and down the river value our rope and cord. And then there are the new people who will be moving in. More dirt farmers come to praise the Morning Star and play chunkey with their crummy little clay chunkey stones. That means the clans are going to need more cord and twine to bind thatch, hold rafters together, tie up latrine screens, hang doors, mend packs. Ropes to erect guardian posts, lift logs . . . a thousand things. Pus and blood, man, we have *important* things to attend to."

Seven Skull Shield threw his head back and laughed. Then he sang, *"She grabbed my hard shaft, it left me half daft . . ."*

"You worry me," Wild Hare noted. "I'd think you were here to find out if I knew you'd been in my wife's bed. Unfortunately, she's one of the only women in Cahokia who has the same high regard for you as she has for fresh dog shit when she steps on it barefoot."

"And if you want my wife, she's yours. Just don't bring her back when you're done." Black Martin had returned to the fine details of his cutting.

"I'm just here to lay low." Seven Skull Shield reached into a pack he'd stolen and removed a smoked fish that a distracted Trader hadn't been paying enough attention to. "My every inclination is to be on a canoe, headed south, even if I had to paddle for my keep."

"Then why aren't you?"

"Because, assuming the Keeper's still free to follow her instincts, the canoe landing will be well-watched."

"What about your other . . . um, friends?"

"They know about Crazy Frog, Black Swallow, and the rest. Somehow old loyalties pale in comparison to the wealth my old companions might accrue should the Morning Star offer trinkets in return for my remarkably beautiful hide." He sighed. "And with Crazy Frog, there's a chance he'd expect me to live up to a bargain I may no longer be able to fulfill."

"Just because you burned the Evening Star palace down?" Black Martin asked in mock amazement. "Don't these Four Winds rulers take affront over the most inconsequential things?"

"Apparently they've no sense of humor," Wild Hare agreed. "What's another palace here or there among the Power kissed?"

At that moment, a boy of perhaps ten appeared in the doorway, carefully stepped around Black Martin, and grinned at Seven Skull Shield.

Swallowing his mouthful of fish, Seven Skull Shield asked, "What have you got for me, tadpole?"

"You know Crazy Frog's wife, Mother Otter?" The kid's cheeks were smudged. His face seemed to be all big eyes, a button nose, and round mouth. A filthy rag had been wrapped around his skinny waist. His bare feet where caked in malodorous mud.

"Did she say anything about me?"

The boy nodded, face expressing the seriousness of the situation. "She said nobles had been there. Morning Star's warriors . . . and it scared her. She kept repeating that Crazy Frog told the nobles over and over that he didn't know for sure where you were."

"Didn't know for sure?" Seven Skull Shield mused.

"Does Wooden Doll mean anything?" the boy asked. "Mother Otter said you were probably at Wooden Doll's under the covers. Under what covers? Looks to me like you're sitting on a stump in the cord makers' workshop."

Seven Skull Shield chuckled. "Wooden Doll is a longtime friend of mine, boy. A woman of insatiable appetites and a loose . . . Well, never mind. Good. All to the better. They can sniff around every single one of my delightful lady friends for as long as—"

An authoritative voice outside the door boomed, *"Seven Skull Shield!"*

He froze, heart racing. Then, in panic, shot to his feet. Two warriors were peering in, their faces tattooed in the Four Winds Clan pattern.

"He's not here!" Seven Skull Shield insisted, trying to adopt a nonchalant look as he plucked up a piece of rope and inspected the braided strands with a critical eye. "He was. Earlier this morning. Traded that pot up there for a length of rope. Said he was going to offer it to a Pacaha Trader for passage south downriver. If you hurry, you might catch him at the landing."

"I doubt it," a familiar voice said, and the Keeper stepped between the warriors.

Black Martin had scuttled to the side, his painstaking cut having gone wildly astray, ruining two lines on his hide. Now he gaped up, looking like a trapped mouse.

"Hello, Keeper," Seven Skull Shield added mildly and took another bite of his fish. Best eat all he could. There'd be no telling when he'd get another meal.

Unless, of course, these warriors would be no more vigilant than that last bunch.

Blue Heron cocked a skeptical eyebrow as she glanced around, taking note of the interior and its occupants. "Crazy Frog was right, I'd never have found you."

"Then how did you?"

She tilted her head toward the boy. "You'd want as much warning as possible if we were hunting you. Glancing around Crazy Frog's, he made the most sense. A little boy, looking homeless, working so hard to appear like he wasn't listening. Clever, thief. Very clever."

"It would probably be a rude observance, and not at all diplomatic to bring up, but I did distract that very nasty Tula up there in the palace when he had that gorgeous, brown chert, ceremonial knife to your neck."

She chuckled to herself. "Yes, you did. Meanwhile, come. Unfortunately, there's something I've overlooked for too long, a comeuppance, if you will, for bad behavior."

"Not that I'm ungrateful, but the idea of hanging in a square . . ."

She'd half turned toward the door and the waiting warriors. "Oh, well, yes. That's indeed a possibility given your charming proclivities."

"My . . . what?"

"Your tendency toward theft, seduction, and generally bad behavior. Most likely you *will* end up in a square. But not today. I once said you liked challenges, enjoyed taking risks." Her smile turned crafty. "This comeuppance, if you're up to it. There's a personal item of mine that the Fish Clan chief, Two Throws, took with him when I divorced him years ago. It's a trifle, really, a small pot with the Thunderbirds engraved on it. He keeps it as a memento. But I'd like to have it back if you can get it."

"Is that all?"

"Of course not. We're stuck in the middle of some sort of Power struggle between Morning Star and Night Shadow Star." She paused, made a face, and slapped a hand on the door frame. "And then, to my surprise and horror, I discover that I've actually *missed* your charming company."

"Thank the Spirits," Wild Hare whispered just loud enough for the old woman to hear. "He can go sing to someone else."

"No, he can't," the Keeper told him. "If he so much as hums under his breath, I'll hang his sorry carcass in a square for a week. But pus and blood, if he starts a fight, I'll brain him myself before I listen to that racket."

"Steal a pot, huh?" Seven Skull Shield mused as he collected his things and headed for the door.

"I thought you'd be interested," the Keeper told him with a sly smile. "And I'll bet Smooth Pebble's baked acorn bread will be done by the time we get there."

"You drive a hard bargain, Keeper."

"Indeed I do."

Epilogue

The morning sun had crested the eastern bluffs and shone through Cahokia's smoke-hazed air. It cast a long shadow behind the Morning Star's high mound with its tall palaces. From the vantage of her veranda, Night Shadow Star watched the crowd that had assembled to watch the Morning Star in his daily chunkey game. As per routine, the living god had bounded down the stairs, his copper-clad lances gleaming; every bit of his stunning regalia, the colorful feathers, the head maskettes, the pure-white apron, and his copper headpiece, were perfectly fixed. The Traders and hawkers proudly displayed their wares, and runners were already trotting along the Avenue of the Sun on the way to deliver reports to the *tonka'tzi*.

To the south, laborers, in an endless line, carried basket loads of clay as they covered the old *tonka'tzi*'s mound with a new layer of earth. The engineers were already at work planning a new, larger, and more opulent palace than the old one.

From the feel of the air, Night Shadow Star knew enough to enjoy the cool morning, for midday would be hot. She seated herself on the edge of the porch and laid a cloth sack beside her. Then she stared out past Piasa and Horned Serpent's guardian posts, aware that in the passing crowd, people were stopping, pointing up at her palace, and whispering in awe.

In the great room behind her, Fire Cat's voice exploded, "I don't care. The Lady's been up for almost a hand of time. And don't tell me you're a Four Winds. That means rat droppings to me. If you can't have a satisfactory meal prepared, I'll find someone who can."

She smiled in spite of herself. In the end, she'd probably be forced to speak to the Red Wing, but until then, she rather enjoyed having her palace spotless, with fresh water and food, an ample supply of firewood, and everything neat.

I lost too much of myself when Makes Three died.

She heard Fire Cat as he stepped out onto the porch and brought her a fine ceramic plate heaped with steaming catfish seasoned with greens, squash, and a cup of mint tea.

"Thank you," she told him, fighting the urge to smile. It kept getting harder to remind herself that this man killed her husband.

"Are you all right?" He was squinting at her, his tattooed face suspicious. "Is Piasa plaguing you for some reason today?"

"Sit, Red Wing." She took the plate and cup, blowing to cool the food. "Not Piasa. Not this time."

He dropped to his haunches beside her, squinting as he fixed on the chunkey court where Morning Star played one of the Earth Clans chiefs. She read the mixture of disdain for Morning Star, and longing for the game.

"Were you good at chunkey?" she asked.

The barest flicker of a weary smile tugged at his lips and vanished. "I was very, very good." He shrugged slightly. "Another life, Lady."

With her fingers, she plopped a bit of tasty catfish into her mouth, sucking air to keep from burning her tongue. Her memory filled with the sensation of him blowing air into her lungs, driving water out, and the warmth of his body on her cold flesh. When her souls had battled back from death, and she'd opened her eyes, it was to fix on his. They'd been dark, worried, and desperate. She'd seen his souls—touched him in the most unsettling of ways.

Yet he still insists that he hates me?

More than once she'd caught herself dreaming about his muscular body, wishing he'd smile just for her. She'd already felt his strong hands as they massaged her skin, had reveled in his gentle touch. What other man would have denied himself liberties when she'd been vulnerable? Too often she had to remind herself that his touch was forbidden.

Too much pain lies between us. And the way ahead is just as dark and foreboding.

She'd never forget the glimpse of him in Columella's palace as he charged, screaming the Red Wing battle cry, into the midst of the

Tula. How his body had been so warm and reassuring against hers in the canoe. But for him, she'd have died that day in the river. Here was a man worthy of her. If only she could step into his warm arms and revel in his . . .

She stifled a chuckle, amused at her foolishness. Power had twisted their lives, left an inseparable gulf between them, and the future? Best not to contemplate that.

Unaware of her thoughts, he gestured toward the crowd that passed below her palace; most pointed or paused in their passage and stared with awe. Cahokia pulsed with the story of how she'd vanquished her brother. "You've become another of Cahokia's legends."

"At what price?" she whispered.

"You had no choice."

She nodded, images spinning through her of Walking Smoke as a young man, his smile crooked, his eyes fiery with insolence and challenge.

"I expected to die with him, down there. Probably would have if he hadn't had his hands clamped on my throat. I couldn't have sucked in water if I'd wanted."

"I saw . . ."

"Yes?"

"A flash, Lady. The most incredible blue, like underwater lightning."

She nodded, remembering. "That's the moment Piasa arrived. The sheer violence of it, the blinding light and Power . . ." She shook her head. "You can't imagine. You should have seen the look on Walking Smoke's face. I doubt he'd ever felt such sheer terror before."

"Maybe not. But I was in the canoe. An instant later I had lightning blasting the water all around me. I discovered a whole new meaning of the word."

"The Thunderbirds. It isn't often that they have such a chance to take shots at Piasa." She swallowed another mouthful. "Can you imagine the chaos and warfare if my brother had succeeded? Spirit beasts battling among us, sundering the earth, throwing lightning bolts, blasting winds, fiery skies, and the burning forests?"

"He was your brother," Fire Cat told her. "No matter what, that still has to hurt."

She glanced sidelong at him. "We have no proof that he's dead. If he survived . . ."

Fire Cat's eyes narrowed to a bitter squint. "He will be back someday."

To change the subject, she said, "Speaking of family, I hear you've somehow managed to entice the Keeper into Trading your mother and sisters away from the Morning Star."

"I'll sleep a little better because of it."

She sipped her tea, hearing the cheers that rose from the crowd as Morning Star scored the winning point. She didn't need to look to see his opponent dropping to one knee and offering his neck.

"You and I . . . We may be enemies, and our obligations to the dead remain . . ." She struggled to find just the right words. "Whether or not my brother survived, Piasa tells me something unpleasant is coming. Morning Star senses it. It will be dangerous, perhaps deadly . . ."

His chuckle was dry and humorless. "Just spit it out, Lady."

Having finished her breakfast, she licked her fingers, then asked, "Do you intend to keep your oath to serve me?"

He stiffened, offended. "I have without fail, have I not?"

"Will you continue?"

His eyes had narrowed, suspicious and angry. "I swore then, I swear now."

She laid the plate aside and gave him a wary smile. "I suspected as much." Reaching into the cloth sack beside her she produced the little pot with the serpents engraved on its side. "Do you remember this?"

His wary gaze recoiled. "The pot with my flesh and breath in it?"

"The very same." She handed it to him.

He took it reverently. "What am I supposed to do with this?"

"Rides-the-Lightning said to inhale when you open it to recapture the essence of your spirit. He recommended tossing the skin scraps into the fire so no one can use them against you."

"I . . . thank you, Lady." He frowned down at the pot. "But why?"

Her souls shivered. "Remember the time I awakened you in the night?"

"With the knife ready to plunge into my heart?"

"I was thinking of when I was seated at the side of your bed. The subject I tried so desperately to speak of, and managed so poorly, was respect. If Piasa is right about the future, you may be free of your obligation sooner than you might think."

"I see." His level brown eyes were boring into hers. "Anything else?"

She nodded, reaching into the cloth bag again and handing him Makes Three's prized black chunkey stone. "Piasa says you might want to practice, Red Wing. He says our lives may depend upon it."

She watched him heft the stone with a practiced hand. His eyebrow arched. "Did Piasa give you any hints as to what was coming?"

"Danger and death, Red Wing. It will fall upon us to stop it. You and me, the Keeper and the thief. Nor can we discount the Morning Star's calculating intrigues."

He nodded respectfully. "Then I'd best be prepared." Somehow he managed the pot, stone, and her plate, before retreating to the house and leaving her with the half-drank tea.

She closed her eyes, exhaling wearily. "I'll never have peace, will I?"

"You serve Power, Night Shadow Star. Among those who do, peace is reserved for the dead." Piasa's faint whisper stirred through her souls.

Night Shadow Star laughed bitterly, a sense of lonely desperation filling her. She opened her eyes and stood. Then, tossing the last of her tea out, she turned, fully resigned to face the coming storm.

Historical Note

Did Cahokia Have a Written Language?

Did Cahokians have a written language? The question has long plagued archaeologists. For many, it is the final criterion that would make Cahokia a "civilization" in the classical sense. We think they did, and have traveled out on the limb again. Given the complexity of Cahokia and the distances over which it had to communicate, at least a form of recorded communication would seem to be indicated. Several clues lead us to suggest how Cahokian "writing" may have worked.

The first tantalizing clue lies in Khipu, the system of knotted cords used by the Inca to record and send messages. While discussing the problem of writing, our longtime archaeological colleague, Brian O'Neil, suggested that Cahokians might have used something similar. Then we seriously considered the Iroquoisan practice of "writing" in wampum. The best synopsis can be found in Bruce Johansen and Barbara Mann's *Encyclopedia of the Haudenosaunee (Iroquois Confederacy)*, pages 326–329.

Wampum could be anything from a string of different size, color, and shape beads that communicated a simple message, to a complex two-sided, blanket-like "belt" in which entire treaties, political agreements, and all the participant's speeches were recorded. (European settlers and their governments were instrumental in the destruction of these great documents since they told a different story than the paper documents in places like Albany.)

How does wampum relate to Cahokia? We refer you to Melvin Fowler's *The Mound 72 Area: Dedication and Sacred Space in Early Cahokia*, pages 132–136. Note the description: "No evidence of stringing material was found, but the arrangement of the beads indicated a pattern of stringing in two directions as one would get in a woven shell-bead mat or blanket." This sounds very similar to two-sided "treaty" or record-keeping wampum. And it may have been a great deal more sophisticated than the Iroquoisan system, since the size and shape of the beads, as indicated on pages 134–135, would have added a great deal of complexity to the meaning of the patterns. And that's without the addition of color.

Finally, consider the bead cache under 72Sub1. Three strings of large beads. Strings I and II each have fifty-one, and String III contained fifty-seven beads. "The strings are 60 to 70 cm long, and the beads are of such weight that it is highly unlikely that these strings would have been worn as necklaces."

And finally we refer the reader to Feature 236, a cache of over 36,177 beads of all shapes and sizes. Again, "No evidence of stringing material was found within the bead pile." It had rotted away. "In some areas of the pile however, beads were aligned in such a way as to indicate that they had been strung in series. Some of the larger beads had seed beads stuck in each end, indicating that some of the larger beads were strung with seed beads, and perhaps with other kinds in between. Apparently the pile was made up of many strings of beads that had been mixed well before placement in the pit."

Our hypothesis is that Burials 13 and 14, known as the "beaded burials," are lying on a great falcon-shaped wampum belt, one that probably related either the great mythical stories of the Morning Star, or perhaps the exploits of the two individuals buried there.

Like all hypotheses, this one, too, awaits the research to prove or disprove it. Perhaps a clue can be found in some of the surviving Iroquoisan wampum, or like Linear A, it will remain indecipherable.

Bibliography

Alt, Susan.
 "The Invisible War: Structural Violence and Fear in The Cahokian
 World." Paper presented at the 77th Annual Meeting of the Society
 for American Archaeology. Memphis, Tennessee, 2012.
Beahm, Emily, and Kevin Smith.
 "Hero Twins and the Old Woman Who Never Dies: Mythic Themes
 in Middle Cumberland Iconography." Paper presented at the 77th
 Annual Meeting of the Society for American Archaeology. Memphis,
 Tennessee, 2012.
Bendon, Danielle, Robert Boszhardt, and Timothy Pauketat.
 "To 'The Mountain Whose Foot is Bathed in Water.'" Paper pre-
 sented at the 77th Annual Meeting of the Society for American Ar-
 chaeology. Memphis, Tennessee, 2012.
Benson, Larry V., Timothy Pauketat, and Edward Cook.
 "Cahokia's Boom and Bust in the Context of Climate Change." *Amer-
 ican Antiquity,* 74:3 (2009): pp. 467–484.
Byers, A. Martin.
 Cahokia: A World Renewal Cult Heterarchy. Gainesville: University
 Press of Florida, 2006.
Birmingham, Robert A., and Lynne Goldstein.
 Aztalan: Mysteries of an Ancient Indian Town. Madison: Wisconsin
 Historical Society Press, 2005.
Brown, James.
 "The Architecture of Cosmic Access at the Spiro Great Mortuary."
 Paper presented at the 77th Annual Meeting of the Society for Amer-
 ican Archaeology. Memphis, Tennessee, 2012.
Dalan, Rinita A., George R. Holley, William I. Woods, Harold W. Watters
Jr., and John Koepke.
 Envisioning Cahokia: A Landscape Perspective. DeKalb: Northern Illi-
 nois University Press, 2003.
Dye, David.

"Mississippian Warfare and Soul Capture." Paper presented at the 77th Annual Meeting of the Society for American Archaeology. Memphis, Tennessee, 2012.

Fagan, Brian.
Ancient North America: The Archaeology of a Continent. New York and London: Thames & Hudson, 2005.

Fowler, Melvin.
"The Ancient Skies and Sky Watchers of Cahokia: Woodhenges, Eclipses, and Cahokian Cosmology." *The Wisconsin Archaeologist*. Vol. 77 (1996): Nos. 3–4.

The Cahokia Atlas: A Historical Atlas of Cahokia Archaeology. Studies in Illinois Archaeology. No. 6, Springfield, Il: Illinois Historic Preservation Agency, 1989.

Fowler, Melvin L., Jerome Rose, Barbara Vander Leest, and Steven R. Ahler.
The Mound 72 Area: Dedicated and Sacred Space in Early Cahokia. Illinois State Museum Reports of Investigations, No. 54, Illinois State Museum Society; Springfield, Illinois: 1999.

Goldstein, Lynne.
"Mississippian Ritual as Viewed through the Practice of Secondary Disposal of the Dead." *Mounds, Modoc, and Mesoamerica: Papers in Honor of Melvin L. Fowler*. Illinois State Museum Scientific Papers, Vol. XXVIII; Springfield, Illinois: 2000.

Hall, Robert.
"Sacrificed Foursomes and Green Corn Ceremonialism." *Mounds, Modoc, and Mesoamerica: Papers in Honor Of Melvin L. Fowler*. Springfield, Illinois: Illinois State Museum Scientific Papers, Vol. XXVIII, 2000.

An Archaeology of the Soul. Urbana and Chicago, Illinois: University of Illinois Press, 1997.

Hally, David, John F. Chamblee, and George R. Milner.
"Macro-Regional Analysis of Mississippian Mound Site Distribution." Paper presented at the 77th Annual Meeting of the Society for American Archaeology. Memphis, Tennessee, 2012.

Heckewelder, John.
History, Manners, and Customs of the Indian Nations Who Once Inhabited Pennsylvania and the Neighboring States. The First American Frontier Series. New York: Arno Press and *The New York Times*, 1820.

Hewitt, John N. Brinton.
"Wampum." *Handbook of the American Indians North of Mexico*. Fredrick Webb Hodge, ed. New York: Rowman and Littlefield, 1965.

Holt, Julie Zimmerman.
    "Was Cahokia the Center of a Theater State?" Paper presented at the
    77th Annual Meeting of the Society for American Archaeology.
    Memphis, Tennessee, 2012.
    "Rethinking the Ramey State: Was Cahokia the Center of a Theatre
    State?" *American Antiquity*, 74(2): (2009): 231–254.
Iseminger, William.
    Cahokia Mounds: America's First City. Charleston, South Carolina:
    The History Press, 2010.
Johansen, Bruce Elliot, and Barbara Alice Mann, eds.
    "Wampum as Writing." *Encyclopedia of the Haudenosaunee (Iroquois
    Confederacy)* pp. 326–329. Westport, Connecticut: Greenfield Press,
    2000.
Kelly, John E.
    "The Grassy Lake Site: An Historical and Archaeological Over-
    view." *Mounds, Modoc, and Mesoamerica: Papers in Honor of Melvin
    L. Fowler*. Illinois State Museum Scientific Papers, (2000): Volume
    XXVIII.
Kelly, John, and James Brown.
    "Assessing the Impact of the Ramey Plaza and its Creation on the
    Cahokian Landscape." Paper presented at the 77th Annual Meeting
    of the Society for American Archaeology. Memphis, Tennessee, 2012.
Lankford, George E.
    *Native American Legends of the Southeast: Tales From the Natches, Caddo,
    Biloxi, Chickasaw, and Other Nations*. Tuscaloosa: University of Alabama
    Press, 2011.
    Looking for Lost Lore: Studies in Folklore, Ethnology, and Iconography.
    University of Alabama Press, Tuscaloosa: 2008.
Lankford, George E., F. Kent Reilly, and James Garber.
    *Visualizing the Sacred: Cosmic Visions, Regionalism, and the Art of the
    Mississippian World*. Austin: University of Texas Press, 2011.
Man, Barbara A.
    "The Fire at Onondaga: Wampum as Proto-writing." *Akwesasne
    Notes*, 26th Anniversary Issue, n.s. 1:1 (Spring 1995): 40–48.
Matthews, John Joseph.
    The Osages: Children of the Middle Waters. Norman, OK: University of
    Oklahoma Press, 1961.
Mehrer, Mark W.
    *Cahokia's Countryside: Household Archaeology, Settlement Patterns, and
    Social Power*. Northern DeKalb, Illinois: Illinois University Press,
    1995.

Millhouse, Philip.
"The Role of Apple River Culture on the Northern Mississippian Frontier." Paper presented at the 77th Annual Meeting of the Society for American Archaeology. Memphis, Tennessee, 2012.

Milner, George R.
The Cahokia Chiefdom: The Archaeology of a Mississippian Society. Gainesville: University Press of Florida, 2006.

Pauketat, Timothy R.
"Archaeologies of Religion and Powers of Cahokia." Paper presented at the 77th Annual Meeting of the Society for American Archaeology. Memphis, Tennessee, 2012.

Cahokia: Ancient America's Great City on the Mississippi. Penguin Library of American History, New York: Viking, 2009.

The Archaeology of Downtown Cahokia: The Tract 15A and Durham Tract Excavations. Studies in Archaeology No. 1, Illinois Transportation Archaeology Research Program, University of Illinois at Urbana-Champaign: 1998.

The Ascent of Chiefs: Cahokia and Mississippian Politics in Native North America. Tuscaloosa: University of Alabama Press, 1994.

Temples for Cahokian Lords: Preston Holder's 1955–1956 Excavations of Kunnemann Mound. Memoirs, Museum of Anthropology, No. 26. Ann Arbor: University of Michigan, 1993.

Pauketat, Timothy R., and Alex W. Barker.
"Mounds 65 and 66 at Cahokia: Additional Details of the 1927 Excavations." *Mounds, Modoc, and Mesoamerica: Papers in Honor of Melvin L. Fowler.* Illinois State Museum Scientific Papers (2000): Vol. XXVIII.

Pauketat, Timothy R., and Thomas E. Emerson.
Cahokia: Domination and Ideology in the Mississippian World. Lincoln, Nebraska: University of Nebraska Press, 1997.

Perttula, Timothy K.
The Caddo Nation. Austin: University of Texas Press, 1992.

Porubcan, Paula J.
"Human and Nonhuman Surplus Display at Mound 72, Cahokia." *Mounds, Modoc, and Mesoamerica: Papers In Honor of Melvin L. Fowler.* Illinois State Museum Scientific Papers (2000): Vol. XXVIII.

Price, Douglas T., James H. Burton, and James B. Stoltman.
"Place of Origin of Prehistoric Inhabitants of Aztalan, Jefferson Co., Wisconsin." *American Antiquity* 72:3 (2007): 524–538.

Radin, Paul.
The Road of Life and Death: A Ritual Drama of the American Indians.

Reprint of the 1945 Bollingen Edition. Princeton: Princeton University Press; 1973.

Reed, Nelson.
Excavations on the Third Terrace and Front Ramp of Monks Mound. Reprinted from *Illinois Archaeology,* Vol. 21 (2009):1–89.

Reilly, Frank.
"Cognitive Approaches to the Analysis of Mississippian Shell Gorgets." Paper presented at the 77th Annual Meeting of the Society for American Archaeology. Memphis, Tennessee, 2012.

Reilly, F. Kent, and James F. Garber.
Ancient Objects and Sacred Realms: Interpretation of Mississippian Iconography. Austin: University of Texas Press, 2007.

Schroeder, Sissel.
"Settlement Patterns and Cultural Ecology in the Southern American Bottom." *Mounds, Modoc, and Mesoamerica,* Illinois State Museum Scientific Papers (2000):Vol. XXVIII.

Slotkin, J. S., and Karl Schmidtt.
"Studies of Wampum." *American Anthropologist,* Vol. 51 (1949): 223–236.

Steponaitis, Vincas P., and David T. Dockery III.
"Mississippian Effigy Pipes and the Glendon Limestone." *American Antiquity,* 76:2 (2011): 345–354.

Steponaitis, Vincas P., Samuel E. Swanson, George Wheeler, and Penelope Drooker.
"The Provenience and Use of Etowa Palettes." *American Antiquity,* 76:1 (2011): 81–106.

Stoltman, James B.
"A Reconsideration of the Cultural Processes Linking Cahokia to its Northern Hinterlands During the Period A.D. 1000–1200." *Mounds, Modoc, and Mesoamerica: Papers in Honor of Melvin L. Fowler.* Illinois State Museum Scientific Papers (2000):Vol. XXVIII.

Stoltman, James B., Danelle M. Benden, and Robert F. Boszhardt.
"New Evidence in the Upper Mississippi Valley For PreMississippian Cultural Interaction." *American Antiquity,* 73:2 (2008): 317–336.

Theler, James L., and Robert F. Boszhardt.
"Collapse of Crucial Resources and Culture Change: A Model for the Woodland to Oneota Transformation in the Upper Midwest." *American Antiquity,* 71:3 (2006): 433–472.

Townsend, Richard F., ed.
Hero, Hawk, and Open Hand: American Indian Art of the Ancient Midwest and South. New Haven and London: The Art Institute of Chicago in association with Yale University Press, 2004.

Watson, Robert, J.

"Sacred Landscapes at Cahokia: Mound 72 and the Mound 72 Precinct." *Mounds, Modoc, and Mesoamerica*: Papers in Honor of Melvin L. Fowler. Illinois State Museum Scientific Papers (2000): Vol. XXVIII.

Wilson, Gregory, and Amber VanDerWarker.

"Merchants, Missionaries, or Militants? A Critical Evaluation of Cahokian Contact Scenarios in the Central Illinois River Valley." Paper presented at the 77th Annual Meeting of the Society for American Archaeology. Memphis, Tennessee, 2012.

Yerkes, Richard W.

"Bone Chemistry, Body Parts, and Growth Marks: Evaluating Ohio Hopewell and Cahokia Mississippian Seasonality, Subsistence, Ritual, and Feasting." *American Antiquity,* 70:2 (2005): 241–266.

About the Authors

A professional archaeologist for more than thirty years, W. MICHAEL GEAR is the *New York Times* bestselling author or coauthor of forty-six novels. He holds a master's degree in anthropology.

Kathleen O'Neal Gear is currently principal investigator for Wind River Archaeological Consultants. She is the former state historian for Wyoming and worked as an archaeologist for the U.S. Department of the Interior. Kathleen O'Neal Gear twice received the federal government's Special Achievement Award for "outstanding management" of our nation's cultural heritage. She was inducted into the Women Who Write the West Hall of Fame in 2005.

With close to seventeen million copies in print worldwide, the Gears' books have been translated into twenty-seven languages. In 2008 the Mountain Plains Library Association honored Michael and Kathleen with the MPLA Literary Contribution Award.

The Gears live in Thermopolis, Wyoming, where they raise champion bison.